Sellenria
The Starship and the Citadel

Chuck Boeheim

With Daniel Elswit

Lampworks Publishing

Published by Lampworks Publishing
Cover art © 2018 by Rene Aigner

For Chidori, Adrian, and Meredith,
Wife, Son, and Daughter.
"… just ourselves, not what arbitrary labels tell us to be."
-CTB

To Betsy,
My beloved fellow adventurer
on life's journey.
-DE

Contents

Chapter 1

Aquila

"I AM THE only remaining crew member of the Corvus. Jonan Gremm, commanding."

The gem was crimson, and haunted by ghosts of generations past. It held my eye, compelling me to lose my gaze in its depths. It was the size of my fist, and contained pinpoints of light within it, like stars in their glorious chaos. A sense of vertigo, of falling, of losing myself in the luminous spaces. And then came the voice. It couldn't be heard by any recording device. It never varied. It told a tale of mutiny and betrayal, and it bore the name of my ancestor.

This singular artifact had been found in a bank vault under my family name, misplaced in the banking world's bureaucracy for generations. I am an archaeologist: I don't just admire old artifacts, I dig into their history. I had uncovered records that Jonan Gremm had signed on as crew on the *Corvus* and had never returned. A mysterious voice might be a hallucination of some sort, but archived records that linked the same two names made it impossible to believe it was merely a product of my mind. I had to know the truth.

I had uncovered no record of anything like this gem in two years of searching. Ornament? Recording device? Information storage crystal? Nor could I find anything about its history. Where had it originated? How had it come to be in a bank vault on my world? I had found nothing in my research to identify or explain it in rational, scientific terms. Somehow, though, I was loathe to consult anyone else until I knew more. This was my own private mystery to solve, and now I was on my way to solve it.

I dismissed my comfortable study, leaving me with the hard, close, and very real walls of my cabin on the starship *Aquila,* one day out from my home planet of Trondhjem. My physical study was millions of kilometers behind me, leaving me with only a simspace reconstruction. I sat for a time contemplating the pleasant but bland four walls of my cabin. Bland was fine. When I was working intensely on a problem, noise, lights, colors, and conversation were almost painful assaults on my senses. A colleague of mine once told me that it was a sign of a high degree of introversion. Since introversion was only a problem to the extroverts around me, I had never made any attempt to change this. I was in that state now and faced the prospect of the departure banquet in the evening like an execution, or perhaps a thesis defense.

I was too keyed up for reading and didn't have the patience for any of the dramas in the ship's library, or the frame of mind for the comedies. Finally, I settled on a familiar standby to occupy my mind, a simspace library of archeological sites of old Earth. The shipboard cabin faded out around me, replaced by low, green hills in a place once called England, and a ring of stark and enigmatic stones. Twilight was coming on the land as I walked among the sarsen sandstones and laid my hand on their cool surface. I could have run time back to the uncertain era of their construction and populated the simspace with some scholar's conception of the builders. I preferred this snapshot of a more modern time when the monument had been recorded for this simspace, still more than two thousand years in my past, around the time of the diaspora from old Earth. Those earlier simulations were only guesses. The builders had left too few clues about the purpose of this monument, and the mysteries about how and why it had been built had never been fully solved.

As I walked among the stones, I glimpsed a hooded figure standing among them. I walked forward to a better vantage point. I saw no one there. A more thorough tour of the monument site turned up no further sign of another person. This simspace had always been empty unless I had invited someone to share it. I shrugged it off as a glitch, where the sim-makers had accidentally captured one of their recorders. Perhaps I had never turned my attention in that particular direction before while running this simulation. It was getting dusky, and I usually visited this site in broad daylight so that I could see more of the details of the construction. I took one more breath of the evening air of old England then selected another site from the library.

I was standing in the hot sun of the southwest of the North American continent. The damp of England gave way to the parched heat of the desert. The entire landscape was a monument of other-worldly colors formed into wind-carved fantasies of rock and cliff. Built into the cliffside, seemingly a part of the rock formation that had been shaped for the convenience of man, was the dwelling of a long-vanished people. The ladders that leaned against roof and wall were reconstructions from fragments that had been found. I could see from my vantage point on an adjacent pinnacle the active excavation in one area of the ruin. I often took my students to that place, to let them experience the painstaking removal of fragments of the past and the reassembly into evidence that might reveal the culture of the one-time inhabitants. For the moment, I was content to take in the entire view and think about the interplay of man and environment.

The hairs on the back of my neck prickled, a subliminal sense that I was being watched. There should be no one else here since I was running this as a private simspace. There was no sound in the air other than the wind, no scent other than the dry tang of pinyon and sagebrush. I turned and my heart skipped a beat as, just for a moment, I saw a figure in a cloak of feathers and a mask of carved wood standing in the shadow of a large rock. I shivered. Either this simspace had gotten seriously glitched when it was copied into the ship's storage, or I was imagining things that weren't there.

Spooked, I abandoned that location as well. I took refuge in a simspace of my own creation, where I knew I wouldn't be subject to accidental quirks or sly spoofs left by simspace developers. Tiers of wooden seats rose before me, dark wood worn to a comfortable glow. Brass plaques numbered the rows and chairs. Tall windows to one side let slanting sunbeams through imperfect panes, picking out motes of dust in the air. I stood at a podium, a sheaf of notes before me, hands resting on wood darkened by the hands of generations of lecturers before me. The air held the scent of oil and old polish. I had crafted my lecture hall to demonstrate archaeological research in the teaching of archaeology itself. This was the sort of classroom in which Evans or Schliemann or Sturmholt might have taught. I was at times wistful for the university environment of the past, when simspace and realspace classrooms co-existed in actual physical buildings and students and faculty might interact face to face. I was often known among my peers by an archaic term: curmudgeon. That had not always helped my advancement options.

This simspace was not immune to tampering either. At the far back of the room, in the highest row of chairs, sat a figure in a black hood and cloak. The figure stirred and appeared to look at me, though its face was just a black space under the hood. *Be careful to whom you tell your plans.* The voice echoed inside my head. I couldn't determine whether it came from my implants or whether my psychosis was beginning to write its own script.

"How did you get into my simspace?"

Some things are not as private as you thought.

"Are you real?"

As real as you are.

That was no help if one part of me was talking to another part.

"Why does anyone care about my plans?"

The Void Guild. They want you to find the Corvus.

"If they want to help me, why should I be concerned?"

I didn't say that they wanted to help you.

"Whose side are you on?"

The hooded figure gave a deep and not reassuring chuckle. *That would be telling.* The figure faded into the gloom.

I banished the simspace, filled with equal parts indignation and fear. I spent the rest of the afternoon staring at the bland walls of my cabin. Who knew about my quest? No one. I had taken a sabbatical from the University for unspecified studies and made my arrangements in private. Who cared if I found an ancestor who had been gone for four hundred years? No one that I could think of. Who could break into my encrypted simspace and tamper with its elements in this way? According to the simspace company literature, no one. Not hackers, not governments, not even the company themselves. My thoughts chased themselves in circles until the evening loomed close.

❖

A chime sounded in my cabin, signaling time for the evening banquet, which I now dreaded more than ever. There would be other people there; many other people, none of whom I had ever met before. There would be small talk, questions, and that undercurrent of status measurement and comparison as perfect strangers tried to assign you a place somewhere in their social constellations. In short, the nightmare of any introvert. I put on my role of urbane university professor like a disguise, telling myself it was no worse than a faculty dinner. I hated those too. I could have pled fatigue and requested a meal in my cabin, but that would be allowing my anxieties to dictate my actions; I wasn't going to give in to them—today. The ship provided me with directions to the grand ballroom.

I almost left the room with the gem in my hand. I pulled up short, berating myself for not locking it up. I opened the room's safe but hesitated with it halfway inside. *Wouldn't it be safer with me?* With a troubled feeling, I put the gem in a jacket pocket where it wouldn't be overly evident. I was even more rattled by the voice, which I had started thinking of as the Other, than I had thought.

This evening, the corridors of the ship were dressed stone. A soft breeze wafted down the passageway carrying a tang of salt air. I stepped into the ballroom through a grand arch formed of the trunks of two trees that stretched into the sky above, much loftier than the real ceiling that I had seen earlier during the ship's tour. The ballroom was now a patio of inlaid stone, balustraded by a low wall on three sides. Beyond the wall, green hills adorned with flowers tumbled down to a rocky coastline upon which broke the surges of a sparkling blue sea. Ragged rocks and small islets dotted the water's expanse, while in the distance a conical mountain trailed a serene plume of smoke. The scene designers were trying to outdo themselves again.

After I had survived an hour of cocktail purgatory by endeavoring to blend in with the virtual vegetation, a woman approached, glass in hand and a glow on her cheeks. She wore a shimmering suit that fooled the eye, one moment blue, the next moment green. I had seen her earlier in the company of a man in a formal white tunic accented with a wide black belt and an aristocratic air. "Dr. Gremm!" she hailed me. "The archaeologist! I've read your book 'Cultural Divergence in the Diaspora.'" Her implants would have informed her of my name and profession, but I first felt pleased and then dubious that she had actually read one of my books. Not many people read my books, even when they were assigned reading. Though the ship supplied a label with her name floating in my vision, she introduced herself as custom dictated. "I'm Anna Stepanov, Professor. You might call me a historian-in-exile," she added wryly. "I write about preserving the culture of New Petrograd, and your book had wonderful insights into the people who settled there."

"Здравствуйте Lady Stepanov. I'm pleased to make your acquaintance." She dimpled at my greeting in her language. Her reference to that world affirmed that she had read my book, and placed her for me as well. The Stepanovs were the last of the aristocracy of New Petrograd, now homeless. Their grandparents had had the good fortune to not be at home when the undetected asteroid had slammed into their planet. We spoke pleasantly for a time about the roots of her people, stretching back to the Slav and Byzantine cultures of old Earth. However, now that I was in the company of someone who moved in higher society, we began to be joined by others.

The next person to drift over was an older gentleman in conservative clothes. He had looked up from his engagement with a too-earnest young couple and caught Anna's eye. She raised her hand to him, giving him the opportunity to excuse himself. "Hello, Anna, you look lovely tonight. Thank you for the rescue; they were getting tiresome."

"You're welcome. This is Stenn Gremm of Trondhjem; Stenn, this is Che Ramellat. His company builds ships, including the lovely *Aquila* that is carrying us on our journey. Stenn was telling me he's on sabbatical from his University."

"And what are you using your sabbatical for?" asked Che.

"I have a grant to … to … to trace the migration patterns of the diaspora from Earth through unique heirlooms such as gemstones." This sounded rather lame to me. If this had been a faculty gathering, I would have been torn to shreds. I had rehearsed my story, of course, but I'm a very bad liar.

"You must have a very generous granting agency," said Che. He said it lightly, as a jibe, but I could tell that he wanted to know where I got the funding for passage on a starship. Starships were so few and so expensive that only the very wealthiest people on each planet could afford them.

"I have a private sponsor who has a personal interest in the subject, and I'm not at liberty to disclose the identity of that sponsor."

"We can have fun guessing," said Che with mischief in his eye. "I'm sure that it's someone we know."

That was unlikely, since my sponsor had been dead for four hundred years, and none of these people looked older than one hundred and fifty. Considering compound interest, the bonds in the bank vault with the gem had been worth a fortune. This research expedition was self-funded; there had been no grant process and no peer review.

Before the conversation could resume, we were joined by a florid man with flowing white hair, who was introduced to me as simply Momsen. I soon gathered that he was one of those authors who had become so famous that a single name suffices. It occurred to me that these widely traveled and well-connected people might have heard things that I had not, which suggested a convenient exit strategy for this segment of the conversation. "I wonder if I can ask whether any of you have heard—that is, there is an obscure name that I have heard in connection with my research. Perhaps it's indigenous—I mean part of the culture of—other planets?" I had let myself get flustered. I took a deep breath and tried again. "Have any of you by chance heard any stories of a planet named Sellenria?"

Che said, "There's no known planet with that name, either settled or mapped." Anna nodded her head at that assertion. Momsen said, "Sellenria …" and trailed off thoughtfully. It was a raconteur's trick to get everyone's attention, and it worked. All eyes turned to him as he tried to recall a distant memory. That lasted for a count of seven, just long enough to build up interest, but not enough to let the next conversation start. Then, "I ran across an old story or two when I was doing research for my novel, 'The Color of Air,' which, as you probably know, is set on the fictitious world of Pinwheel. I spent many years collecting material for that story, trying to find the most unusual, out-of-the-way places, the most poignant stories, the ..." Anna laid her hand on Momsen's arm. "Oh, yes, to the point. I found some old tales about a mysterious planet named Sellenria, not found on any charts, perhaps not even in a fixed location. Any starship that came across it vanished. Any exploration party that landed on its surface went silent. It didn't fit with the story I wanted to tell, so I ended up not using that material; I put it aside with the thought of devoting an entirely new novel to that old tale. The right protagonist has not come along to jell the story for me yet, and I've had other projects, so it remains locked away in my chest of ideas."

Che snorted. "And which of the two starships that we have lost vanished on your mythical world? Was it the *Scutum*? Or the *Corvus*? We only have eighty-two starships, we're likely to notice if they start going missing."

"As I said, it was only fiction ..." started Momsen.

"Surely you meant eighty-one?" put in Anna.

Che wore a pleased smile. "I'm happy to announce that I've just received word by ansible that the *Reticulum* has been commissioned and will be starting its inaugural run on the Marrakesh to New Lisbon line."

A round of congratulations, along with Momsen's *sotto voce* comment, "Reticulum? Soon you'll run out of constellations. Then what?" But the mention of the *Corvus* had grabbed my attention.

Just then, a young woman approached. She had chosen to shave her head, though her dark, expressive eyebrows looked somehow familiar. She wore wisps of cloth knotted intricately together to look like a cloak of feathers. It was modest enough at rest, but a sudden breeze could turn it unexpectedly revealing. I tried to keep my eyes in carefully neutral directions as she approached. She noticed, and her eyes twinkled at my discomfiture. She addressed Anna first, saying, "Father was looking for you, Mama. Apparently, you're the only one who can untangle his social calendar and avert an interstellar incident." The gentle sarcasm in her voice conveyed that this was a family joke.

"I suppose I must go and attend to my husband," said Anna. "Elise, this is Professor Stenn Gremm. He wrote that book I've told you about."

"Good evening, Professor. It's nice to add a new face to our circle."

We exchanged a brief handclasp. Close up and standing next to her mother, I could see where she had gotten those eyebrows. They stood out all the more beneath her shaven scalp.

"Hi Uncle Che. Hey Momsen." She obviously knew the other two well. "I was just hearing rumors that intelligent alien life may finally have been found on some new planet beyond the fringe. Is it true?"

"Alas, it is not," answered Momsen. "I've heard those rumors recently as well. In the telling, a simple animal that knows how to use a stick to get the equivalent of snails out of their shells and a basket to carry them in has grown into a tool-using society. They don't even have language and are about as intelligent as a sloth. Our first meeting with beings with whom we can converse is still in our—probably distant—future. Then we will see whether we will subjugate them, trade with them, or bow down to them."

I privately thought that I was going to be heartily tired of Momsen by the time of our next port of call, eight light years from here and a month from now. Elise distracted me from that thought by leaning closer. "Dr. Gremm, are you wearing an insect on your lapel?"

I smiled. "Yes, I am. It's a scarab, a type of beetle that was worshipped by the ancient Egyptians. They would wear amulets such as this one for protection and luck, and would be buried with them as well."

"It's lovely. Where could I find one like that?"

"You might try a museum, perhaps on Antigone. I made this one myself. I work glass as a hobby. It keeps me grounded in realspace for a few hours at a time. It's a hobby you can't do in simspace, or at least not in any satisfactory way. You wouldn't have anything to show for it afterward if you did." Elise seemed quite interested in my hobby and peppered me with questions for some time, until some friends closer to her own age came and snatched her away. At that point I decided I had absorbed a near-lethal dose of social interaction and departed the "seaside" reception, wandering back through faintly gothic virtual stone-faced halls to my cabin.

The lights came up as I walked into my cabin. I re-instated my simspace study about me, wanting the comfort of familiar surroundings. I sat in my favorite chair and held the gem up to my eye again, seeking answers. As always, the infinite spaces seemingly held within its unfaceted surface drew me in. Lights that were not stars streamed past me as I let my vision sink into its depths. After several minutes I could hear voices, first indistinctly, just above the level of noise. Then one voice came clear, starting as it always did, as faithful as a recording.

❖

It is the fourth day after landing. I am the only remaining crew member of the Corvus. The ship rests against the foot of the mountains at the edge of a desert plain on this planet called Sellenria. It will never travel between the stars again. The mutineers killed the crew, but this planet killed the ship. And now this ship, which brought me safely from space to ground, is trying to kill me. It provides me with supplies and shelter, but the radiation leak from the warp torus has made it impossible to stay inside without a protective suit.

I've carried all the supplies I can to a nearby cave. I certainly won't starve for a long time while I wait. I do feel like I'm waiting, though I can't say for what. Rescue seems unlikely, even though I sent off one message before we went down. Repair seems even less likely, with the crushed hull and half-eaten control systems. I do not think I could carry enough supplies to cross the desert, nor am I certain I would be any safer on the other side.

Sophi, I said that I would come back to you from this trip, no matter the wonders I found on other worlds. I never dreamed that I would be stranded in an alien desert, unable to keep that promise or even to tell you why I did not return. Do not think that I broke my word willingly, and if I ever find a way to return to you, I will.

CHAPTER 2

Encounters

SIX DAYS OUT, I stood in the observation dome of the Aquila, watching my homeworld, my students, colleagues, journals, and one or two friends (though that might be stretching a point), dwindle to a speck among specks on the tapestry of stars. The helpful shipboard systems projected labels over my field of view; otherwise, Trondhjem would have already been lost among the stars. We had been traveling outbound for almost a week and hadn't yet engaged the interstellar drive. My reveries were interrupted by the sound of steps entering the observation dome, not entirely unwelcome. Time passed so slowly out here that I fancied I could hear eternity's clock tick.

"Good day, Doctor Gremm. I hope I'm not intruding on your meditations."

I turned towards the speaker. "Good day, Captain. Not at all. I was just thinking about how little the view changes out there." I had met Captain Aubrey briefly during the reception the first night out. I was impressed that he remembered me. Then I remembered the warning of the simspace intruder. Why had he remembered me? Was this meeting really a chance encounter?

"It won't have changed much even by the time we arrive at our next star system. The universe is enormous beyond comprehending. Is this your first time out?"

"No … well, yes. I've been as far as the Trojans, but this is my first interstellar flight."

"You'll be experiencing it any minute now. We're far enough from the planet to turn on the Alcubierre-White drive."

"If we're about to turn on the drive, shouldn't you be on the bridge?"

"It's much less of an event than leaving orbit because we don't actually move in any normal sense of that word. We just wrinkle space a little so that it seems like we're moving. Also, it might surprise you that the ship doesn't have a realspace bridge. The crew and I join the simspace bridge from wherever we happen to be. The days of physical control devices are long over, and I'm partial to being here where I can watch the stars as we engage the drive."

The Captain swept one hand across our field of view. An overlay of the ship's systems appeared over the stars on the observation dome. With deft movements of his fingers, he flicked a small schematic of the ship to center and spread it to fill the view, crowding other subsystems off the edge. Now we could see the majestic ovoid body of the *Aquila* encircled by the torus of the drive. The view dove through the skin of the torus, revealing the plasma of exotic matter circulating within. The Captain exchanged acknowledgments with his bridge officers. On the schematic, the roiling plasma was squeezed down to a thin cylinder encircling the ship within the enclosing torus. The forward edge of the cylinder began to curl inward, like vase being shaped by a celestial potter. Superimposed lines of gravitational gradients focused in the ship's path. Space *dimpled* directly ahead of us: a stone thrown in the cosmic pond. I realized this was a real optical effect, not a simspace visualization of the unseen. Ripples spread concentrically until a ring perhaps 20 degrees in diameter was displaced. I involuntarily stepped back from the glass. Perspective flipped, and I felt we were falling into an infinite well, which might sweep me from the deck and send me tumbling ahead of the ship into the darkness of the universe. I don't like heights and wondered what had possessed me to come into the observation dome. I shut my eyes for a moment to dispel the disconcerting image.

"We're now supraluminal," announced Aubrey, appearing not to notice my sudden shakiness.

"How 'fast' are we going?" I tried to take my mind off the well we were plummeting into with some abstract numbers.

"About 10 C now. We'll bump it up to 75 C in an hour after double-checking our calibrations."

"It certainly doesn't feel like we're traveling 10 times the speed of light."

"Technically, we aren't. We're just warping space such that the effect is that of moving at that speed. But you, sir, want to see the stars shifting across the sky like in a science fiction holo show. In reality, the galaxy is just too vast to oblige you. Even at top speed, it would take us two years to cross the closest galactic spiral arm, and over a thousand years to cross the galaxy even assuming we could survive the direct path through the core. Sit here for a few hours some time; ask the ship's computer to point out a few of the nearest stars and see if you can see them move. It will take a lot of patience."

I mentally rejected the thought of wanting to see the stars moving. It would be too much like falling into a vast abyss.

The Captain turned to me. "I understand you're interested in the *Corvus.*"

The abrupt change of topic took me by surprise. How had he known? Had Anna or Che told him about our conversation? "Well … yes, I had an ancestor on that ship. I hope to find out what happened to him."

"I may have some information that can help. Perhaps you'll join me in my cabin this evening after supper? I have my own stock of something that the makers claim is a faithful reproduction of an ancient Earth drink called Scotch."

I accepted, but with misgivings. The warning that the unknown person had given me in my simspace on the first day of the voyage had me spooked about talking to the ship's officers.

So it was that a little after the evening meal I followed a sprite through the maze of the ship, which in this section appeared to be paved in brick with contemporary artwork on the walls, and came to a door like many others. As I approached, an unobtrusive label beside the door advised me that this was the Captain's private study. I knew that if I hadn't had an invitation, the label would be blank and the door anony-mous. I raised a hand to request entrance. Before I even completed the motion, the door slid open before me.

I stepped in hesitantly, put slightly off balance again by the different customs. Did the Captain's homeworld not practice the ritual exchange before entering a private space? Or was this a shipboard custom? I found I could not cross the threshold without uttering my part: "Stenn Gremm is at your door."

"Come in! Find a chair that suits you, and I'll break out a bottle."

The door closed behind me, leaving me unsettled that he hadn't offered even the abbreviated "My space is yours" that close friends would have used.

Aubrey was busy with glasses and bottle as I looked about. One wall bore images of shelves full of old books and instruments. Other walls had replicas of old paper maps, upon which the ship's course was plotted. I could see the position updating to keep pace with the ship's progress. A final wall had images of various space, air, and even ocean-going ships of the past. I stepped closer to examine the books, thinking that they looked remarkably realistic for a holo image, almost as good as retinal projection. Without thinking, I committed the gaffe of reaching out to touch the holo, but instead of passing through the surface, my fingers came to rest on solid books. I stepped back in awe. There was a fortune in rare, physical books in front of me. On all the settled worlds, books were largely a metaphor for information published in simspace, a convenient packaging for handling and browsing, as well as a link to our past. I had handled actual books on only a few occasions before. I suddenly had a new appreciation for the wealth and power of the Void Guild. I managed to stammer, "Nice collection."

Aubrey said, "Thanks," and handed me a glass. An airborne essence demanded the attention of my nose. I brought the glass cautiously closer.

"May the stars rise up to meet you," pronounced Aubrey, and raised his glass.

I raised mine in return. "Er, maybe you can tell me the right response to that one."

"And may their light shine warmly on your face," he supplied, and I echoed.

The first sip was a hot ball of smoke that rolled over the tongue and down the throat before detonating warmly in my stomach. My eyes watered and throat constricted at the assault, and I gasped for air. After that moment passed, I tried another small sip and started to appreciate this assertive liquid.

"Whew! Where does this come from? And what do they put in it?"

"It's produced on a planet named Caledonia. It's unique to that place since it involves smoking malted grains over a fire made from a particular kind of bog moss that takes centuries to establish. It's an example of the kind of trade good that is profitable over interstellar distances. It's fantastically expensive on the local markets, but there are very wealthy people on every planet who are willing to pay the price."

"So you stock up on easily transported luxury items? Is that your main staple of trade? The way that ancient sailing ships carried spices and other rare goods around the oceans of old Earth?"

"To a certain degree, but information is what pays the bills. We carry vast libraries of technical data from planet to planet, conveying the latest discoveries and inventions. Literature too. The ansible is instantaneous of course, but the bandwidth is so limited that it's more efficient to ship entire libraries by starship than to transmit a single news journal. We also carry the entangled qubits that make the ansible work. Since each world has to have a supply of qubits for each other world with which it communicates, maintaining a full mesh of entangled qubits for all the worlds takes up an important part of our cargo space."

I had had an education over the past week on the economics of interstellar travel from my dinner companions. Each ship was immensely difficult to build and costly to operate because of the quantities of exotic matter needed to scuff up space before us like a carpet runner. With over 500 worlds in human space, and eighty-two starships taking months to cross the voids between them, most worlds only saw a starship make port every few years. Passenger and cargo space were premium commodities. What he said made sense.

We talked for some time. Aubrey told me of the worlds he had visited and asked about my own work. He seemed to have a genuine interest in archaeology. He had read widely in that subject, and in many others. My usual social awkwardness didn't kick in. I don't have trouble talking about something with people; I have trouble talking about nothing. Small talk with me leads to uncomfortable silences.

Eventually, I brought the subject around to my particular interest, or obsession.

"So, Rafe, what can you tell me about the *Corvus*?" We had drifted into first names between the second and third glasses. "And how did you find out that I was interested?" In my head that had sounded like a casual question, but once uttered it sounded defensive and insecure.

Aubrey extended an invitation to enter a simspace with him. The simspace was identical to his quarters, with the old books and charts adorning the walls. In the simspace, he walked over to the bookshelf and motioned to me to follow. One of the bookshelves hinged away from the wall like a door, revealing a massive safe behind it. Aubrey spun the tumblers and began entering a combination. I could see that behind the scenes he was running some computationally heavy cipher challenges to open the records storage, but I appreciated the metaphor of the safe and tumblers to represent it. The door clicked open.

He reached into the safe and extracted a pile of folders and binders and handed the heap to me; that simspace gesture transferred a few terabytes of data to my personal document store.

"This is what we know about the *Corvus*. It's a puzzle with most of its pieces missing. As an archaeologist, that might be right up your alley."

I took the folders and filed them away, glad that the simspace metaphors didn't extend to having to carry them back to my cabin. I slipped them into my own metaphorical safe, and we returned to our scotch.

❖

I decided to forgo breakfast the next morning in favor of pharmacological treatments for the after-effects of too much of a good thing. Rafe Aubrey had volumes of stories to tell about strange people and far-away places and had kept me engaged deep into the night and deep into his supply of scotch. On arising for the second time, I spent a long time in the bathroom scrubbing and steaming the last regrets away.

When I finally sat down in my study in simspace, a cup of strong realspace coffee in hand, I had regained my resolve to find some answers. The records handed to me by the Captain were waiting for me, and I immersed myself in studying them.

The Guild records confirmed that the *Corvus* had left Rockscape as scheduled. It carried 102 crew and 1213 passengers, 300 of whom were bound for the new settlement on Istanbul. (One-quarter of the Guild's flights were allocated to the settlement of new worlds. You paid whatever you had, however much or little that was, and got a one-way ticket. The Guild's core mission was to protect humanity by spreading it as widely as possible.) The cargo was engineering equipment for terraforming Istanbul, and qubit cores for ansibles there and on Antigone. Because of the relative positions of the three systems, the *Corvus'* course was for Antigone first, then Istanbul.

The *Corvus* never arrived at Antigone. The next available starship was sent on a parallel course, looking for a gamma-ray burst that might indicate that they had slammed into a dark mass somewhere between stars. Not that there was anything that could be done in that case, but it would have been a definite answer. Nothing was found. She had vanished without a trace.

I sat back in thought. Could the message that I heard in the gem be nothing other than imagination? That voice haunted me. I heard it every time I looked into the gem, which I felt compelled to do nearly daily. I heard it at night in the darkness when my eyes wouldn't close. I even heard it when I was giving lectures, in the parts I had given so often that I put myself on autopilot. The voice was impossible to authenticate, of course. I had searched for and found no other examples of Jonan's voice for comparison. But before I heard the voice in the gem I had no prior knowledge of Jonan Gremm, or that he would have been on a starship on that date. There was no way that I could have heard them, written them down, and only later found the confirming details unless there was something to the story. However, it appeared that I had one bit of authenticated evidence that the Void Guild did not.

I spent the remainder of my day in my cabin, amid a growing frustration that the Void Guild knew little more than I had already found out. The Captain's offer had contained the exciting possibility of inside information, but I had gotten only tedious manifests and schedules that added nothing to the question of where the ship had disappeared. Eventually, I went to the gym for some exercise. Even an introvert needs human contact at times; it's just that a little bit goes a long way. But when I got back to my cabin and loaded my simspace study, which I had re-encrypted with strong ciphers, there was a note on my desk. It said: *When you hear the voice, draw this.* It ended with a circle that had a wavy tail trailing to the upper right, like a stick figure of a tadpole. I sat down hard in my chair. The Other couldn't possibly know about the voice I heard in the gem, could it? I hadn't told anyone about hearing voices, for fear of being locked up for treatment if I did. Or was the Other trying to tell me about a situation still to come, when I would hear a voice and have to draw a passcode, while an unknown person held a knife to my throat? No, that belonged to the simspace dramas. I could test the hypothesis that it was referring to the gem right now.

I retrieved the gem from my safe and sat with it in my hand. I looked deeply into it and felt the now-familiar sensation of falling into a crimson void. The murmuring began, then the cadence of the voice, as if dictating a log entry. As it spoke, I drew the figure with a finger on the surface of the gem as instructed. An image formed, suspended in front of me in the dusky light of the gem. Before me was a desert at twilight, flat and mostly barren, but growing the occasional spiky plant. I had a slightly elevated vantage point, as if atop a low rise or building. In the distance, rolling hills relieved the flatness of the plain. Stars were already plentiful-ly evident in the sky. The voice started again but on a new passage this time.

❖

The stars are beautiful tonight, Sophi. They remind me of the stars when we went out together into the Windlit Desert. They are bright and steady right down to the horizon. What we called the Unknown Sailor sits in his rigging over the western hills. The settlers here call it the Warrior. Sailor or Warrior, he has acquired a bright gem on the buckle of his belt. I have now been here 347 days. Perrhen says he must leave soon. He tells me that he will travel near an ancient ruined city. It was abandoned at about the time that the Pyramids were built on Earth if I understand his counting of dates correctly. His numbering system seems to be in base eighteen. He tells me there is an artifact of great power there, which can be used to open a doorway between worlds. If there is any way this offers a chance to get back to you, Sophi, I must take it. I will travel with Perrhen, seek out this artifact, and bring it back to study.

❖

Perrhen? A doorway between worlds? Cities older than the pyramids? I now wondered if my ancestor had started to hallucinate after nearly a year by himself in the desert. Then the familiar worry settled in again, that I was hallucinating when I heard the voice in the gem. I was unlikely to find external corroboration of this passage. But how had the Other known to tell me to activate this message? I looked for the paper on my desk, but it had vanished. I spent the night carefully recording this new passage and drawing the scene that I saw while wondering if everything, including the Other, was all in my head.

CHAPTER 3

Destination

"AND MAY THEIR light shine warmly on your face," I replied as the Captain and I touched glasses together a few days later. Aubrey gave a slight nod that I had remembered the toast. I didn't mention that I had looked it up beforehand to be sure I had it right. I had also memorized a stock of other toasts in case he had another one for this occasion. Over-preparation was one of my coping mechanisms for social situations.

We spent some time in idle conversation until I was beginning to fret about ways to bring the topic around to my list of questions. As the Captain was filling our glasses once again, he saved me. "So, Stenn, were the records of the *Corvus* helpful to you in your research?"

"Very helpful, thank you." Not really, but I wanted his assistance. "It raised the question in my mind whether my ancestor might have stayed behind at Rockscape. I only know for certain that he arrived there."

"Let me check. I have the Guild rosters in the library. What was your ancestor's name?"

"Jonan Gremm."

I could see Aubrey's eyes move back and forth as he requested searches for the information via his implants. The data must have been well-indexed, for there was barely a pause before he said, "The crew rosters of the *Corvus* show Jonan Gremm signing on at Trondhjem for a two-year hitch. Just as an aside, that was and is still a common occurrence. Two years of Void Guild wages could set a young man or woman up with a sizable stake for establishing themselves on their home planet when they return, and competition for those berths is stiff. He was still on the ship's roster when it departed Moriond bound for Rockscape, and again when it departed Rockscape bound for Antigone."

"Could *Corvus* have arrived at Antigone, but been disabled? Could it have landed somewhere in the system and never been found?"

"I think that's unlikely. As we travel, we sweep up the small amount of dust and gas that exists between the stars. When we drop the warp field, all that collected material tries to keep on traveling at our former effective velocity. However, that's faster than the speed of light, which isn't allowed, so the dust dumps all of its excess energy as bright blue radiation. It's like a great blue sword stabbing ahead of the ship, announcing its arrival. Any civilized world would have recognized that signature and sent ships to investigate if the incoming ship didn't make radio contact."

"I think the *Corvus* must have come to rest on an uncivilized world, then. I have an ansible transmission that seems to prove that the ship survived whatever befell it."

"There's no record of such a transmission."

I tendered an envelope to him in simspace. This metaphor contained the transmission and the authenticating chain of ciphers that indicated when it had been received and where it had been stored. This was the piece of evidence that he hadn't seen yet. It still had the brief text: "SOS *Corvus*. Ship disabled. Attempting to land on Sellenria. Jonan Gremm, Commanding."

Aubrey looked this message over carefully, and painstakingly verified the message's provenance and authenticity. The math was beyond me, but the keys could be compared to those known to be in use at the time. If a single bit of the message had been altered, the keys wouldn't verify. I already knew that these did.

As he finished his checks, Aubrey looked up at me. "This is authentic. It's been misfiled all of these years. It's so improbable that it's likely no one even thought to look. Where did you find this? What's Sellenria?"

"I uncovered this in a file of dead letters back home. The message had been sent from Antigone to Rockscape and dismissed as a hoax, and then much later the database had been replicated to other planets, including Trondhjem. I previously had the name Sellenria from a journal entry left to me by my ancestor. This is the only hit that I got in the planetary database. Momsen told me the other night that Sellenria was an old legend from the early days of the diaspora. I had never heard of it before, either."

Aubrey's mouth quirked. "Momsen? He's quite a character, isn't he?"

"So how did this come to be sent from Antigone back to Rockscape?"

"Do you know how the ansible works?" Aubrey inquired. I shook my head. "Obviously, radio transmissions or other communications that take place at the speed of light are nearly useless over interstellar distances. We can't wait years or centuries for messages to travel between worlds. The ansible makes use of quantum-entangled particles. When one particle changes state, the other does as well, instantly, no matter how far apart they are. The pairs of particles are called qubits. One ansible sends a message by toggling the state of its qubits; another ansible receives the message by watching its corresponding qubits change state to match. But you can't tell which direction the matching qubit is, or how far away it is. You just have to know that your qubits are entangled with counterparts that were sent to a particular place. If the *Corvus* was carrying a set of qubits created on Rockscape and destined for Antigone, and they used those qubits to send a message from wherever they ended up, the message would have appeared to come from Antigone. Each ship should have its own supply of qubits for its communication. I think this suggests that the *Corvus's* supply had been damaged and they were using their cargo to send an emergency message. Either that or someone was trying to misdirect a subsequent search."

"Speaking of searches, do you know why only a single search was done for the *Corvus*?"

"I wasn't around then, obviously, but the circumstances of today aren't much different. The nearest starship was probably several months away at a minimum. The chance of a rescue arriving in time to help a disabled ship is minuscule, and the chance of something happening to a starship at light speed that would only disable it is also minuscule. Even the product of those two probabilities is enormous compared to the chance of actually finding a ship. We must assume that if they can't signal their position via ansible that they're dead or without power. The single sweep that was done was to see if they could intersect the expanding gamma-ray burst that would mean that they hit something. Failing that, the chance of finding a small dark object in a very large dark empty space just doesn't warrant a more thorough search."

I took a breath. Could I trust this man? I weighed the situation for a moment and made my decision. "I have an image that I've found, which may show the place the ship landed, and it includes a part of the night sky. As I've been watching the constellations from the observation dome, I've begun to wonder if we could find the world on which this set of stars can be seen. I'm afraid that I wasn't able to capture the original, so I've reproduced it as accurately as I can." I slid a simspace facsimile of my drawing across the table to Aubrey.

"It's almost Orion as seen from Earth, with the addition of an extra star in the belt," said Aubrey. "Where did you get this?"

"I'd rather not say at the moment." *Because you would think I was crazy if I did.* "Would the stars have this configuration on either Rockscape or Antigone?"

"Easy enough to find out."

Aubrey loaded a simspace that reproduced the view from the dome. The stars wheeled, centering a distant sun before us. We moved toward it, fiery streaks raining off our bow as great hydrogen furnaces leaped out of our way. Entering the destination system, the sun slid out of the way and a planet swelled into view. Our viewpoint swept down onto a red sphere with a circumferential ocean girdling the planet at the equator. Forested zones were brushstroked across the interior in the rainshadows of mountain ranges. This was Rockscape.

Aubrey brought us to ground on a scrubby desert, looking skywards, then sped our subjective time through the seasons until night fell on the constellation of Orion standing astride the distant mountain range. The shape may have been subtly distorted from the drawing, but we could see at once that the bright star was far to the left of its position on the drawing.

"It's not Rockscape. How about Antigone?"

We launched again into the sky, crossing the starry gulf. The next world was more oceanic, with the landmasses seeming more like large islands in the world-ocean. There weren't many deserts on this planet, so Aubrey brought us down on the rim of a volcanic caldera twenty kilometers in diameter. As he spun the seasons through the sky, I wondered what it had been like when the slumbering giant we rested on had been awake and angry. The stars came to rest with the familiar figure on the horizon …

"That's not it either. Now the extra star is too far to the right."

"Assume that's the correct star for the gem on the belt buckle. Can you position us in space so that it lines up exactly with the drawing?"

"Certainly." Aubrey picked a control ball from the air and rotated it. The drawing adjusted size and orientation until it overlaid the constellation almost exactly. Only the stubborn white star remained unmatched by the penciled marks.

Aubrey chorded commands on the surface of the control ball. Our viewpoint left the planet's surface to hang again in the void, then sped across light years tangent to the vector towards the three stars of the belt. The white star drifted into alignment with the jewel on the belt that Jonan had drawn. When the light overlapped the dark, Aubrey stopped and examined the correspondence of the images. We rushed a little Orion-wards, then back, then drifted rimwards. The alignment tightened up, then snapped into place.

"There you go. We're within a few light years of the source of this drawing."

"Are there any habitable planets nearby?"

The viewpoint hunted, quartering the sphere around us. "Nothing within twenty light years. The nearest would have a noticeably different view of the constellation. But we're looking at the view that is used by the general public. Let me add my security override so that we can see any systems in this area that are not explored or settled. Ah, there we go."

An unmarked star system directly in front of us lit up with markers indicating habitable but unsurveyed planets. There was a double planet system orbiting a common center of gravity in a comfortable location in the habitable zone for terrestrial life. The larger was 95% of earth mass, and the secondary was Mars-sized.

Aubrey whistled a low and off-key sound. "What is it?" I asked.

"I think we found your planet. It's not far from the track the *Corvus* was following. There's no record of any landings here, but there's a security block on the planet and instructions to get permission from Guild headquarters before entering planetary space within this system. It is marked as having an inhabitable biosphere on the larger planet."

"What's the reason given?"

"None given. No warnings, no information. I've never seen a blank like this before. It's like someone has censored the entry."

"It sounds like someone might already know something about the disappearance of the *Corvus*."

"You may be right. What are you going to do now? Your passage is to Antigone, but that's based on a false lead. There's probably nothing for you on Antigone, though they do have some rather nice museums."

"I'm not giving up at this point. Do you know what archaeologists do these days, Rafe? We try to find the power source for an ancient recording device so we can read its contents. We look for the holy file specification that unlocks an archive of city plans drafted in a forgotten program before simspace was invented. We search for the lost encryption keys for the shipping records of the first settlement on a planet. Don't get me wrong; it's rewarding to reconstruct how people used to live. It's exciting to uncover an archive of art that's been lost since before the war and the dark ages, but ..." I took a deep breath. "This is the first chance I've ever had to do something truly meaningful in my field. The trail leads to this planet. I've got to get there somehow."

"I can't promise anything, but I'll ansible the Guild to find out more."

❖

I was standing in a broch on the Isle of Shetland on old Earth when the Captain signaled me. These enigmatic round structures had never been fully deciphered. Few argued about it anymore, but it was still an open question whether these were dwellings, forts, granaries, giant dehydrators, or showpieces. Some riddles were not going to be answered until science delivered a time machine to us, and so far we remained wanting. I hoped that what awaited on Sellenria would not be that variety of mystery.

Aubrey's voice drifted in through the dusty air, muffled and faint through three-meter-thick walls. "Hello! Is this the place where you hang out when you spend all your time in your cabin?"

"One of many," I called. "I hadn't expected company."

"You didn't have a do-not-disturb seal on your sim, and I thought you might want to hear what I just heard from the Guild."

"Of course! Come on in."

The captain made his way around the outside of the broch and ducked in through the door and dim passageway beyond, cut through the immense walls. Aubrey had to duck-walk for several meters to make his way inside. "Whew, were people that much shorter back on earth?"

"From what we've been able to gather, people were generally short until after the industrial revolution, when diets improved. Some pre-diaspora archaeologists remarked on how short the doors were in ages past."

Aubrey was looking around the interior of the broch. The sim had dressed him in the clothes of an early twentieth-century archaeologist. It was the first time I had seen him not wearing a Void Guild uniform. He looked rather good in the leather jacket and fedora.

"So what is this place? An ancient castle?"

"It's called a broch. People in the north part of old Scotland built them. No one quite knows why. They left no written record. We tried to decipher their lives by comparing their architecture to other known cultures, and by finding a few tools and housewares buried at the sites."

"Interesting. So that's what archaeologists do."

"Rather more than that, but that's not what you came here to talk about."

Aubrey flashed a grin at my impatience. "You're right. I have the most unusual orders from the Guild that I've ever seen. They direct me to divert the ship to the planet you located as we pass near it between our stops at Rockscape and Antigone. We're to make a one-person lander available to you so you can conduct your investigation. I'm to ensure that my ship has no contact with the planet during the flyby. They promise to send another ship to pick you up in a year. It looks like the Guild is underwriting your expedition."

"A year? Can I live there for a year?"

"I have updated biosphere data, though it is strangely classified as need-to-know. The biosphere will support terrestrial life. It has a well-developed ecosystem of native flora, keeping an oxygen/carbon dioxide balance that is very favorable for us. We will leave supplies of food for a year, and a stasis pod if you need to use it."

The Captain took his leave and ducked out through the door of the broch. I was left trying to recall the speech I had given about having an opportunity to do something truly meaningful. I suddenly had a difficult time summoning the same enthusiasm when faced with the actual opportunity. In fact, I was somewhat short of breath.

It was then that I noticed the hooded figure seated at the old, debris-scattered hearth of the broch. It put forward its hands, and there was a small fire in the hearth to warm them. It was a casual, contemptuous display of the degree of control of my simspace the Other had. "I suppose you overheard all of that," I said.

Oh, yes.

"If you are here again, that means you have advice."

Take the Void Guild's offer. As long as your interests are aligned, you are safe from them.

"Is the planet safe?"

It is both habitable and inhabited. You will find much to study.

"What if I don't go?"

The Void Guild may find it inconvenient that you have learned as much as you have. Those who want your artifact already find you inconvenient. You would be safer out of reach on the planet.

"Can I trust the Void Guild's promise to come back for me?"

The drawing waved a hand to snuff the fire. His figure became wispy and spiraled upwards with the smoke. *If you succeed, you won't have to count on that.*

CHAPTER 4

Descent

THE SHIP'S DAILY news channels ran an advisory that the *Aquila* would make a brief detour to release a planetary survey drone. A ship's officer appeared as part the announcement to explain that such events were rare but occasionally necessary to map out potential industrial or scientific bases to fuel the engine of human commerce. She assured us that the ship would make up time after the detour so that it would arrive on schedule at Antigone.

I had an interview with the ship's doctor that was rather unsettling. After a thorough but reasonably standard examination, he told me that I looked completely fit. Then he floored me with his next comment. "A heart attack at your age would be pretty unlikely, and you've been seen getting regular exercise in the gym. It could be something infectious, but that's too likely to spread panic on the ship. I think an aneurysm would be the most likely thing to strike you without warning."

"Excuse me, what are we talking about?"

"I thought the Captain discussed this with you. The other passengers are going to wonder why you disappeared in the middle of a voyage. There aren't too many ways off a starship mid-flight. We think it's best if we give out the story that you had a sudden medical emergency and were put into a stasis pod until we reach Antigone."

I nodded uncomfortably. The planet was, for some unexplained reason, classified. The Captain had made clear that part of the deal was that I couldn't tell the other passengers about my stopover. I was just now working out that if I vanished, anyone looking for me would assume I got as far as Antigone. I could disappear from the universe with as few traces left behind as the *Corvus* and Jonan.

I had been using the ship's gym regularly during the voyage to combat the sedentary shipboard life, the overabundance of food, and the long hours of a journey that was measured in months. I redoubled my regime, not knowing what conditions I would encounter. I wanted to be as fit as possible. I did long runs on the treadmill that in simspace crossed alpine vistas, pounded down jungle trails, and jogged along vast sandy beaches. The treadmill did its best to simulate each of those terrains, though it had its limitations. I also added some gymnastics routines. I had been on the University gymnastics team in my youth, though the best that could be said was that I added depth to the team. I quickly found out that decades mattered, and there had been at least six of those, anti-aging treatments notwithstanding. I eased off after tearing a ligament in my knee. The doctor put me in a robo-surgeon that fabricated a new ligament *in situ* in my knee, knitted to the tatters of the old one. After twenty-four hours of immobility, the leg was as good as new, but the doctor gave me a stern lecture about knowing my limits.

I did not socialize a great deal during this time. I was busy with my preparations, but even more, I felt awkward speaking of everyday matters with my fellow passengers when I could not share the great undertaking I would soon start. Still, I would venture out once in a while to observe that human society flowed on as before, though I only waded in the shallow waters around its edge. On one of these occasions, Elise Stepanov saw me and came over, bursting with some news. "Dr. Gremm! Stenn! Mother lent me your book and I've been listening to it. I had no idea that anthropology could be so fascinating. I'm on leave from my studies because I couldn't find anything that excited me, but now I know what I want to do. I just sent an ansible message to re-enroll when we get back later this year. I want to thank you for making it so interesting."

"I'm honored to have been an inspiration." I rarely succeeded in connecting with my students, let alone inspiring them. On impulse, I unfastened the scarab beetle pin from my lapel and pressed it into her hand. "This is to remind you to follow your heart. There's always someone to do what's important, but only you can do what you love."

"That's so sweet, Professor. Thank you. I hope I can do both."

I was buoyed by Elise's enthusiasm for days. The sense of history repeating didn't escape me, however. I had passed an artifact on to another before landing on Sellenria. Had Jonan made a similar gesture four hundred years ago? Was that how I had come into possession of the red gem?

I regretted not being able to say goodbye to the few acquaintances I had made on the journey, as I made my way to the lander. I had raised one last glass of scotch with the Captain on the previous evening, though I was careful to limit myself to a single toast. I had no desire to be fighting morning regrets at the start of my adventure. Rafe repeated his assurance that a pickup flight would return for me. He told me a specific date, one year and three weeks in the future, standard time, based on the schedule of the next starship that would pass nearby. The specificity was comforting, and I'm sure he believed it. I set a chronometer for that so that I could know when the date arrived, even on a planet that quaintly insisted on having its own days and years (about 107% and 93% of human standard, respectively).

I only got to see the blue beam of light by video pickup, as it stabbed ahead of the ship the moment we dropped our warp field. I was already aboard the capsule and had already suffered my "medical emergency" that would confine me to a stasis pod for the rest of the flight, at least as far as the passengers would know.

A ship's officer materialized next to me in the cockpit, in jarring violation of the custom that someone appearing remotely via simspace should enter the scene through a conventional entrance. "I'm going to pilot you remotely to the surface," she informed me briskly. "The autopilot can land you, but you'll be better off having us find a suitable place to set you down." She stood at the pilot's station and placed her hands on the controls. "Ready to launch in five minutes."

I looked sideways as she ran through the checklist. I had seen her once or twice on board, a tall figure of angles and planes, a face of sharp cheekbones and sharper jaw, shades of granite in the eyes. I felt both reassured by her air of competence and uneasy at her cool distance. I didn't have long to ponder the roots of this dissonance, as the pod unceremoniously launched with a hard thump of acceleration.

We had come out much closer to the planet than we would have to one that had interplanetary commerce. It already hung large in the heavens to our starboard side. We were rotating about our axis, and the apparition rose to loom above us as I felt faint changes of thrust. Our nose rose as if we were climbing towards the orb of blue and white and ocher. Our velocity and acceleration must have been considerable, buffered by the small artificial gravity system of the lander. Now we were rotating once more, until the planet was beneath us, and we were falling towards the far limb of night that was coming into view on the face below us. I had to close my eyes and choke back nausea. I really hated heights and this suddenly felt like a drop from the most extreme height imaginable.

I felt some bumps and was compelled to open my eyes again. The planet had transformed in minutes from a celestial body hanging among the stars to a landscape unfolding beneath us. "We're just entering the edges of the atmosphere," the pilot informed me. "There will be some buffeting for a few minutes." And there was. More than a little. The worst part wasn't the shaking itself, but the way that the pilot stood at the controls completely unaffected by it. Of course she was; she was a hologram. But that defied all the conventions of the eye, the inner ear, and the entertainment industry. I gripped my armrests and closed my eyes again.

Many long minutes later the ride smoothed out and I opened my eyes again. We were speeding over the dark side of the world. There was little to see below, no lights of civilization, no recognizable features. Ahead of us, though, the planet's companion was rising into the sky. Mars-like in size and color, it began to illuminate the landscape with a ruddy glow. We were passing over a continental mass, barren in much of the central portions, with what looked like a gigantic volcanic caldera on prominent display. The coastal areas were lushly colored, though it was difficult to make out detail in the strange and dim lighting. We passed over an ocean as the sun rose in the sky, then another continent came into view, this one much smaller. A pair of continents, in fact, connected by an isthmus. The one that straddled the equator seemed to be largely desert, but the northerly one looked promising. I pointed and the pilot nodded concurrence.

As the lander started to bank to circle to the north, the image of the pilot flickered. She looked surprised and started reviewing ship systems. "We're having communications difficulties," she said. A moment later she blinked out entirely and was gone for heart-stopping seconds. When she came back, she worked quickly on the controls. "I'm setting your destination in the autopilot to look for signs of settlement and land near but not in an appropriate zone. That will get you down safely if I get cut out. Wait, that's strange …" She disappeared once more.

I didn't like the sound of that last statement. I started to unbuckle, reflexively reaching for the controls. I stopped myself, knowing that I had no idea how to operate this craft and the autopilot would do its job as long as I didn't get in the way. My state had reached high anxiety when a sudden bang from the rear kicked it over the edge into panic. Half of the boards went dark, then seconds later the lander started to tumble. All I could do for long minutes was hold the arms of the chair in a death grip and wait for the end to come. The wait stretched on for so long that I began to actively wish for the ship to smash into the ground just to put an end to terror. Finally I saw the ground rise up to meet me. The tumbling slowed, then stopped. The antigravity engines roared a dreadful song of overload then failed, smashing me down into my seat. Ground met metal with a crunch as I came to rest on the surface of what I hoped was Sellenria.

CHAPTER 5

Morghaest

I STOOD UNSTEADILY, my heart still pounding wildly. Acrid smoke filled the cabin, burning my eyes and nose. All of my loose gear had fetched up in the low corner of the lander. My ears were ringing from the beating the headrest had given me. The descent had been a twenty-minute plunge through chaos, mixed with a strong dose of terror. I remembered my head snapping from side to side during the uncontrolled tumble, and the shooting pain in my neck confirmed it. I broke out the medical kits and draped a diagnostic collar over my shoulders. It told me in reassuring tones about the substances it was releasing to relax spasming muscles, prevent swelling, and heal torn tissues.

I examined the lander. Most of the systems were offline. The generator had failed and the lander was running on stored power. Remote access wasn't available; I couldn't contact the lander's systems through my implants, reducing me to manually keying in commands and receiving information displays on primitive flat panels. I managed to get a diagnostic log open. If the times that I saw in the log were correct, the failures began before landing. First they cut off the lander from control from the *Aquila*, then cascaded through the control systems. Had the lander been sabotaged? As I pondered, the display sparked and went dark. I checked other systems; they were all dead or failing. This went beyond sabotage. I remembered the line from Jonan's recording about "half-eaten control systems." Is this what had happened to him?

The medical collar's treatment had made me feel steadier. My mission hadn't changed: explore this world, study the culture and its origins, and find out what happened to my ancestor. I decided to strike out and get started. I dressed in the outerwear that I had commissioned the *Aquila's* fabbers make for me. It was designed to be lightweight, warm, and waterproof. *But was it in style?* I thought, with a touch of hysteria. I wanted to observe the culture without attracting undue notice, but I had no way in advance to tell what they wore.

I tucked the pouch with the gemstone into an inner jacket pocket and hefted the pack of portable equipment and slung it on my back. I brought a language translator linked to the implants in my ears, a vocal transcriber for my notes, and food supplies to last me until I found a settlement. I also had a small ansible with one cartridge of qubits entangled with counterparts on the Aquila. There was no point in using it yet. I needed to find out more about my situation. *And determine if you can trust them.*

I frowned. My inner voice wasn't in the habit of addressing me in the second person. It was also starting to sound a lot like the Other. I shook my head, which still caused a pain to spear up my neck. Either the drugs or the battering my head had taken, I decided.

I levered the door open and took my first breath of the planet's air. I switched on the transcriber. "This is Doctor Stenn Gremm, recording my first steps on the planet I believe to be called Sellenria. I have just opened the door and taken my first breath. It feels very moist after the sterile atmosphere of the ship. I smell forest, loam, mint-like scents from crushed vegetation, and scorched metal. The temperature is pleasant, and the oxygen level is high. The gravity is on the low side. The combination is invigorating, and I'm ready to start exploring."

I swung out of the hatch and dropped to the planet's soil. "The ship is in bad shape, but it is still shelter, and a possible base if I need it. It also has a self-contained medical unit still in working order that I can't carry with me and the remainder of my supplies. I would like to lock up the ship, but the hatch is warped. My first job is to secure it." I switched off the recording and started trying to straighten the bent metal. Finally, after using up half an hour, a local rock, and a number of curses that were probably ineffective this far from their cultures of origin, I decided to lay heavy rocks against the door to hold it mostly shut. I piled some branches and other debris around the lander so that it wouldn't stand out unless someone got close to it.

I had had a quick view of what appeared to be a road not far away as the lander had plummeted the last few thousand meters, and I started off in that direction. The forest was open, with widely spaced trees and patchy underbrush. The canopy was dense above, which probably kept the lower layers shaded and open. I continued making notes as I walked. "The forest vegetation is of many different types, of all sizes, obviously a very old and mature forest. Much of it looks suspiciously terrestrial. The *Corvus* arrived about four hundred years ago. If they were the first settlers to bring species from old Earth, there does not seem enough time for a forest this diverse to have established itself. This woodland must have been seeded much earlier from stock brought on another starship. However, the *Aquila* had no record of human contact with this world." Previously, I would have jumped to the conclusion that records had been lost in the early years of humanity's chaotic expansion into space. After my encounters with the Other, I was more inclined to conspiracy theories.

"Some of the vegetation is decidedly non-terrestrial. The local equivalent of chlorophyll seems to be a dark teal color, and the plants seemed to favor stumpy red-brown bodies covered with a teal lambswool. Some of them put out arms like the earthly saguaro that I once saw in a hothouse." One specimen of these was covered by a terrestrial vine, with the effect of a tartan gone badly awry.

I saw no wildlife, though any that had been nearby had probably cleared out during the concussion of my landing. There were no paths, and I was forced to keep my eyes to the ground to pick my way over uneven terrain that was littered with fallen branches and trees that had passed their expiration date. I began to feel a bit more relaxed and even a little euphoric. I was exploring an unknown world. At least a world unknown for centuries. The possibilities and opportunities for study were beyond imagining. I needed to remember everything, document everything.

I caught the first flicker of movement out of the corner of my eye. I stopped and looked that way. Nothing. A few steps later, I saw a flash of red on my other side. Again, nothing there. I continued, wondering if I was imagining things.

A moment later I saw the red flash ahead of me. I stopped and waited. After a moment, a dead branch spread bright red wings, flew a short distance to another tree and vanished again. I moved stealthily closer, keeping my eyes on the point where I had last seen the creature. It burst into movement once more, landing on a nearby rock, and I got a good look at it before it vanished. "I have seen my first specimen of native fauna. It is a small winged animal, long and somewhat flat, resembling a salamander. It has four legs and large articulated wings. The wings are positioned about one-third of the way between forelimb and hindlimb and may be modified midlimbs, making this the first known six-limbed species. It has adopted the color and texture of the surface it rests on, making it nearly invisible. Now it is scampering down to the forest floor and picking up a nut from a nearby tree. It is sitting up on its hindlimbs, shelling and eating the nut. In posture and behavior, it reminds me strongly of a squirrel."

I continued walking and began seeing more of the "squirrels" inhabiting the trees. When they were still, they were well-nigh invisible, but when they moved they flashed beautiful colors. I startled a flock of them into flight, and it was as if a rainbow had burst forth under the canopy of the trees.

Presently, I reached the road. It was quite wide, of packed earth with dressed stone blocks lining both sides. It was formerly well-maintained, but now showed signs of neglect. Weeds peeked between the stones and some of the blocks were cracked or askew. I stood, wondering which way to go.

A badger stuck its snout from a burrow near the road. That is, if a badger had six legs and smooth skin. The powerful digging forelegs and its low, wide stance in the mouth of the burrow were what called the image of the terrestrial badger to mind. It also seemed to share the camouflage trait with the forest squirrels. "The Inn of the Forest is a short way ahead," it said and disappeared back into its burrow.

I stood for a full minute before I slowly raised my hand and triggered the transcriber. "I am now wondering if I am trapped in a fantasy sim-space, or if I am really exploring a new planet. One of the native animals just addressed me and offered me directions. The translator identifies it as a dialect derived from archaic English, from around the time of the first exodus. The animal's enunciation was distinct and understandable, and the translator rendered it directly into Trondnorsk for me. The question now is whether the creature has language or whether it is merely repeating what it heard, like a parrot? Either way is remarkable."

I decided to take the badger's advice since I had no better information of my own. Over the course of the next hour, two more badgers accosted me with information about the inn. It seemed a rather peculiar sort of information network. It was ultimately effective, as a rambling wooden structure came into view in a clearing in the woods where another road intersected this one, leading from a direction that I had decided was south.

I approached the building while rehearsing the phrases I wanted to use, based on an assumption that the badgers had picked up the common human tongue. I needed to acquire the local language as quickly as possible so I could remove the filter of the translator in learning the indigenous culture. I came to the door and hesitated. Did one announce oneself outside the door, or enter first? Since it was a place of business and expected customers, I decided on the latter. I opened the door and announced with what I hoped was casual confidence, "Stenn Gremm is at your door."

"Yah, what of it? You want dinner, it's in about an hour. You want a room, I got one. Two Dukes for the night; four if you want a girl with it."

I stood in the door while taking in the vast room with the roaring fireplace at one end. A spit turned some unnamed creature above the fire. Wooden trestle tables filled the space, stained and carved by past occupants. A great bar filled the far wall, presided over by a man built to the same scale. A black beard tumbled over his chest, caught by a gold ring at his breastbone and braided beneath. His head was as bald as his beard was full. Against the wall behind him, a double-headed ax rested, looking both sharp and ready for use. Half the tables were occupied by men and women in travel-stained clothes.

"I require—no, want—a meal. Room later," I stuttered. "No girl." I knew I was missing something. Oh. "Kindly thank you." That could have come out better. The room assaulted me with smells of roasted meat, beer, something that had boiled over and burned in a kettle, unwashed bodies, and scents that I probably didn't want to put a name to. I hoped I would be able to get that meal past my nose.

I sat down at one of the far tables, sweating profusely. If one of my students had performed that poorly in a fieldwork sim, I would have failed him. I had been doing sims for years in hundreds of cultures, and even live telepresence work. Now, faced with the scarred, greasy wooden interior, the primitive spit over the fire, and the glowering reality of the proprietor, I had made a hash of my first sentence. My hands shook; I hid them under the table.

A presence eclipsed the dim light. The proprietor stood with an enormous flagon in hand. "Beer." It wasn't quite a question.

"Yes. Thank you." He grounded the flagon on the table with a sound like doom. More beer than I could drink in a week sloshed wetly across the table. I reached for the flagon to test the contents, then became aware that the eclipse hadn't moved on.

"Two copper princes," he said.

"I am from far away. What trade here do you?"

He rolled his eyes, and I was glad that some gestures seemed to be universal. "Coins." I didn't have any. "Metal." I started thinking about taking the cover off of one of my devices. "A joke."

"Er, what?"

"You can't pay, you entertain. Tell stories. Sing. After dinner." He left, having settled that to his satisfaction if hardly to mine. I could not even begin to comprehend the thought of standing in front of a group of strangers and singing songs. I felt anxiety begin to rise and briskly shoved that whole line of thinking into a corner of my subconscious for the present time.

I pulled the flagon towards me and tried to lift it to my lips. After straining with it, I had to settle for tipping it towards me and sipping from the rim. In the dimness across the room, I could see the proprietor laughing.

The beer was surprisingly good. It had a dark amber tint and a complex taste that hinted at several different grains. A woody hint of some herb balanced the bitterness of the grain. I drank deeply and started to think a little better of my start in this world. As it settled into my stomach, I could feel the warmth of the alcohol and wondered whether my kidneys or my liver would succumb first if I attempted to finish my flagon.

The door swung open again, and someone entered. A dusty travel cloak concealed a tall and slight figure. A wide-brimmed hat was pulled down over his eyes, shadowing his face. He walked directly to the bar and acquired a similar flagon of beer, bouncing two coins on the bar in return. He carried his flagon to a table on the far side of the room, where he could sit with his back to the wall and watch everything that went on. As I watched, he lifted the flagon with ease and drank. I started to feel that I might have gotten in over my head.

I looked back to the proprietor to see if he was still amused. Thunderclouds had gathered over his craggy eyebrows, and the glare he sent toward the newcomer should have scorched the grease from the tabletops. I heard him mutter "Cray Leth!" loudly enough for the thin man to hear, but that produced no reaction.

That was an interesting word. My translator didn't pick it up, and it certainly didn't sound like English or any other Terran tongue that I knew. I snagged the utterance from my audio recorder and committed it to my field notebook. "This appears to be the first new term I've heard," I dictated to the transcriber. "Unknown derivation could be unique to this planet."

The proprietor slammed down the tankard he was holding and seized his ax. I thought at first he was going to confront the newcomer, but then he advanced toward me like a storm front. "You! Warlock! Are you trying to curse my inn?" He swung. The ax bit deep into the table, obliterating my audio recorder, which I had placed in front of me. He raised it again, taking aim at me this time.

I held up my hands, tissue paper before a tornado. "Not am I! Who? I do not know, what?" I was going to fail this examination in a very final and bloody way.

"Stop!" The thin man had crossed the room like the shadow of a raptor. One hand had stopped the descent of the ax, while the other held a long and very sharp knife just below the golden ring on the innkeeper's beard. Despite their vast difference in size, the smaller man disarmed the innkeeper in seconds. He had lost his wide-brimmed hat in the rush, and now red-golden hair tumbled down his—no, her—shoulders.

"I wish to speak to this traveler. Go back to your work, Geistman."

"He was speaking a curse! He spoke strange words into that *thing* ... that thing of the Grimmerroth."

"I see a terrified stranger who doesn't know our language. He will not harm you, I will see to that."

"Not six months past you killed Lord Mallord under this very roof, and brought down the Daughters on me," the innkeeper said bitterly. "Now you protect a warlock who has no money, who speaks an unknown language over his uncanny tools. We'll all have the pox by morning, or worse."

"Tend to your stew, Jo Geistman. I'll keep him from tearing your inn down long enough to get a meal from you."

She sat uninvited at my table and looked curiously at me. "You are not what I was expecting," she said.

It took me a moment to realize that she had spoken in modern Galactic. "What ... How ... Why? Did you stop him, I mean? How do you speak Galactic? Cray Leth? Is that your name? Who are you?"

She appraised me evenly, as if she hadn't just stopped a giant with an ax. "You can call me Gilwyr."

"That answers one of my questions. No, it doesn't even answer that one."

"I know that when a blue sword is drawn across the sky, I should look for a traveler from far away. Two nights ago, I saw the blue sword, and this morning I heard thunder in a clear sky. One looks for a traveler at an inn, and here you are."

How does she know that? The captain had said that any civilized world would recognize the blue light of a starship arrival, but who on this world would know about it? Any interaction with supraluminal starships was centuries and many generations in the past.

"How is it that you know this language?"

"I learned it from my mother. It is not unlike Dalactyn, though it is very different from Anglich, which our innkeeper speaks."

"Where was your mother from? Did she fall from the sky?"

Gilwyr frowned. "This is not a campfire tale or a story for children. People don't fall from the sky. We lived in Cloudhaven, and she died when I was young. That is all that I know, other than she told me to watch for the blue sword."

Gilwyr's mother must have been stranded here by some previous starship. Another contact with this planet that had been lost in the Void Guild's records. I wondered again what game they were playing. Her mother had been left here and died here. I felt a chill.

"My name is Stenn Gremm," I said. "I'm a scholar. I study people, and their customs and culture and history. Is there a place where people study these things or collect books and records, a library?"

"There is a university in Misthaven. It is several days of walking from here."

"Can you give me directions to this university, and who I should ask for when I get there?"

"Do you know what you did to anger our friend Jo over there?" I admitted that I did not. "Unless you learn, you will have a very short visit. The next person you offend may not be as genial as he is. I do not believe you are even carrying weapons."

I tried with some disquiet to picture someone less genial than the innkeeper. "I don't see you carrying anything larger than that knife," I countered. "How dangerous can it be?"

With an icy stare, she reached over her shoulders and withdrew two long swords and placed them on the table. They were over a meter long, with a narrow blade of a lustrous metal joined to a simple leather-covered hilt with a minimal and elegant guard. They looked sharp enough to split hairs. Curiously, they didn't resemble any historical workmanship with which I was familiar. I captured an image with my ocular implant and sent a search daemon looking for closest matches in the compact artifact database in my backpack. If I could classify these, I might gain some clue to the ancestry of these settlers.

The great door of the inn, which I had noted on my entrance as being stoutly built from a dark, dense wood, shook to a heavy blow from outside. I nearly jumped from my seat at the thunderous sound. Gilwyr coolly picked up her swords. The innkeeper seized his ax and yelled an imprecation at the abuser of his property. The other guests arose uneasily from their seats and backed away from the door.

Another blow landed on the door, even greater than the first. The door shattered into splinters that flew across the room. A reddish-brown shape stood without, bulking taller and wider than the doorframe. It began to force its way through the opening to the sound of breaking timber. "Morghaest!" shouted the innkeeper, hurling his ax at the man-like figure. The ax embedded itself in the creature's shoulder, pinning it to the doorframe and nearly severing its arm. The morghaest, if that was its name and not just some general curse, struggled briefly at the restraint before reaching across its body with its other hand and snapping the handle from the ax. That finished severing the arm, which fell to the floor. A new arm immediately began growing from the stump, while the creature stomped on the detached arm where it wriggled on the floor and absorbed it back into its body.

Gilwyr was across the room in a blur. Her silver blades flashed, removing the creature's head. She kicked it out of the doorway and continued to slash, removing chunks of the beast with every motion. It was slippery progress that was set back every time a chunk rejoined the monster. What kind of creature could take such damage and reassemble itself?

"If I manage to clear the door, run!" Despite Gilwyr's still unflappable demeanor, I could hear that she was becoming winded. There was a general movement of the others to follow her advice, though some fled up the stairs to perceived safety. I grabbed my pack and made ready to follow her sensible suggestion. As soon as I moved, however, I was the center of the morghaest's eyeless attention.

"It wants the pack! Give it the pack!" called Gilwyr across the mayhem.

"I can't! It has all my research in it!"

Gilwyr took advantage of the creature's distraction and sliced at its legs. She severed one at the knee, though I wasn't sure if it had anything like discrete joints. It toppled forward into the inn and Gilwyr danced backward in front of it. The innkeeper rushed forward, having secured a more workman-like ax from the woodpile near the hearth. He buried the head of ax deeply into the morghaest's back. I sagged with relief that he had finished it off.

A mighty arm swept up and swatted the innkeeper across the room. I watched in disbelief as it absorbed the ax into itself and reattached its severed leg. It rose again, still headless but having regrown one arm. It had advanced into the room, leaving an opening for me to try for the door. I sidled around it, trying to hide the pack behind my body where it couldn't see it. Sight seemed to make no difference to the creature as it rounded on me and swept me aside almost casually. I lost my grip on the pack and dropped it while staggering back across the room.

Headless, it still scooped up the pack unerringly and held it to its chest. The pack blurred at the edges. It began to crumble to sand and be absorbed into the morghaest. My notes, my analyzers, my reference library, not to mention the food and medical supplies I'd carried from the lander, and perhaps most distressingly my ansible, were lost. I wailed in despair. My link to everything I knew as civilization was gone.

I don't think it could hear me, but it still turned towards me and started groping. Unlike the pack, the creature didn't quite seem to know where I was. A paw swung through the space my head had occupied before I ducked. It slammed a fist down, missing me but splitting a table in two. There didn't seem any way past its flailing reach. Gilwyr called to me, "You must have something else that it wants. Give it over! Quickly!"

"I don't have anything else! What if it wants me?"

"That's not likely."

Her tone was so dismissive that I wanted her to be wrong for an instant before my rational brain told me to hope that she was right. The morghaest swung blindly for the space I was in and I blocked with my forearm in desperation. I felt my bare skin touch the morghaest's gritty surface. I saw my hand's edges turn fuzzy as a cloud of dust boiled up. My last thought was that this had been a short field trip. Too bad I had flunked it.

I watched in amazement as the morghaest crumbled into a heap of mud on the floor. From the expressions on the faces of Gilwyr and the innkeeper, they had expected that outcome as much as I had.

"Right. We had better go." Gilwyr hustled toward the door.

"I've lost my equipment! I can't go on without it!"

"You won't get it back by staying here. It seems that I am now going to Misthaven as well. There are those who need to know that a morghaest has been seen again. Since you attracted it, you are now of interest as well."

"What was that thing? Are there more? It didn't look ... it looked like something that shouldn't exist!"

"It shouldn't but it does. They are warped creatures, created by the Grimmerroth."

"Created? But ... it's almost dark. Isn't it safer to stay here?" As the reality of the destruction of the last few minutes sunk in, I started having a bad case of shakes.

"Does it look like we're welcome to stay?" I looked at the innkeeper. We weren't. The other patrons had mostly fled and those that remained cowered in corners, apparently as afraid of me now as they had been of the morghaest a few moments previously. The innkeeper was loudly insinuating that we were somehow responsible for his door and that we should pay him for it and then clear out. Gilwyr put down two coins of impressive heft and soft yellow-red hue. They bore a seal of two crossed swords of the sort she had lately been employing. He argued some more and she added a third. Encouraged, he began to elaborate his claim. She placed her hand on the hilt of her own sword. Negotiation completed.

As we walked out into the gathering gloom, I asked her if she couldn't have been as persuasive about a bed for a night.

"I never intended to sleep there tonight. It was easier to fight off that morghaest than his bedbugs," she said.

CHAPTER 6

Gilwyr

MY SHAKES GRADUALLY gave way to bleak depression. I had no equipment, no food, no medicine, no communication. How could I do my research without my tools? What would I do if I got hurt? How would I function on this primitive world? Maybe I should return to the lander to get some of the backup supplies that I hadn't been able to carry. But this stranger was guiding me in the opposite direction, following her own agenda. She set her own pace, too, one that soon had me sweating to keep up.

Gilwyr knew precisely where to step off the main road onto a side trail. This trail led shortly to a glen enclosed by a low rock face, down which tumbled a small waterfall into a clear pool. It was a beautiful and secluded refuge, though I wasn't in much of a mood to appreciate it. It was undoubtedly on this world's list of top ten picturesque spots for sleeping in the wild—in the unlikely event that this planet had a tourist industry to make such a list.

Gilwyr took some leather from a pouch at her belt. "Here. It is too late to hunt tonight. Also, I do not think it is wise to leave you unguarded until we learn whose interest you may have attracted." She began to chew on her piece of leather while I examined mine.

"This is food?"

"Dried meat. The pressed grain cakes are even drier. If you hadn't attracted that morghaest we would have both had stew. Geistman's stew isn't as good as his ale, but I wouldn't turn it down." She took another bite of the leather as if to make a point.

I hesitantly imitated her. I thought I was going to lose a tooth on my first bite. After a few minutes of chewing, it began to seem somewhat edible.

"What was that creature back at the inn?" I finally asked. "You called it a morghaest, but I don't know what that is."

"Are you simple, or have your people forgotten their history? In the first war, the Grimmerroth released the Dust on the world to destroy the wondrous devices of the ancients. People were unable to make anything more complicated than a sword without it crumbling into ruin. Then in the last war, he formed the Dust into these mindless creatures to be his army. They were defeated, but can still arise when something attracts their attention."

"Obviously we don't have morghaests where I'm from. My people made those devices I carried, and nothing tried to eat them before I landed here." I was nettled by her accusation that I was simple.

She frowned. "I suppose that is true. I know of no place in this world that is free of them, though."

"I come from very far away. I journeyed for many months to get here." And from farther than she could possibly imagine.

"You seem very ill-prepared to have made it this far. The goddess of scholars must have been watching over you."

"I had a very sturdy ship."

"If your boat had these artifacts on board, it will be gone by now, even if you anchored it far from shore. The morghaests work quickly. People in this land know not to make mechanisms of metal." She shook a steel and flint from her pouch and began to efficiently kindle a fire as I absorbed this.

The lander was ... had been ... inoperable. Still, it had been a base where I could have waited for Aubrey if he came back in a year as promised. My last link to home was severed, and I was well and truly stranded on this planet. If these morghaest creatures took apart anything of metal that landed, it explained the lack of outside contact with this world. Once here, there was no way back. There never had been. How much had Aubrey known and not told me? Or the Other? A vast feeling of abandonment opened up before me. It was black and deep and endless, and at the bottom there was despair. I hadn't hit bottom yet because the abyss was so deep, but it was only a matter of time.

I looked up. Gilwyr was waiting for me to continue. She had removed her hat and cloak as the fire warmed up, and I could see how very young she was. I had the feeling that she was always alert, ready to fight a monster or save a stranger as the moment demanded. She radiated a confidence that pushed back my despair as the fire pushed back the evening chill. It kept me from the abyss, at least for the moment. If she saw how close to the brink I had teetered, she gave no sign.

After a moment, I was able to go on with the conversation. "These morghaests, they're just standing around waiting for things to appear so that they can stomp on them?"

"No, they assemble themselves out of whatever is nearby." She pulled her sword from its sheath and examined it. "The one today was sand. I am going to have to clean and sharpen these before I sleep."

"Like a Golem, then? Made of myths and legends. How did you stop it?"

Her eyes were wide and witch green in the firelight. "I did not. They were thought to be unstoppable. I wish to consult with Greylander de Oxendon at the university, for he has studied the old lore. I think we must eventually go to Cloudhaven to present you to the elders."

"What do you mean, you didn't stop the morghaest? I certainly didn't."

"But you did! You touched it, and it fell into dust."

"Nonsense. I thought it was going to turn me to sand too. You'd been hacking at it. It just took a while to die." I had a sudden suspicion. "How many of the things have you fought?" She looked reticent. "When's the last time anyone has fought one?"

"It has been a generation," she admitted. "The last one was before my birth. People fear to make the things that attract them."

"You see? It's been exaggerated in the telling. They're hard to kill but not impossible."

She looked doubtful. "Still, I know that you must be Cray Leth." More unfamiliar words. This seemed a positive thing for me to be; it was settled in her mind and I saw no reason to change it.

I tried another line of questioning. "Were your parents sword fighters as well? Did you learn from them?"

"My mother was not Cray Leth. She died when I was small. The Cray Leth took me in and taught me the dance of the blades. I am Cray Leth now."

"You keep using that name. What does that mean?"

"That is a long story. It takes a lifetime to tell. Go to sleep now and perhaps your pillow will whisper a part of it as you sleep."

"But I have no pillow. No blanket to sleep under, either."

"You see, you already hear the story of the Cray Leth."

I shook my head at her obscure logic and lay down by the fire. She took her blades from their scabbards and began cleaning them. As I shifted around, trying to get comfortable on the cold ground, I could hear her start to run a whetstone down the blades. Normally I would be fascinated by the primitive skills, but I was exhausted and fell asleep directly.

I awoke later. Something was missing. Some sound. I realized that the sound of whetstone on steel had stopped after what seemed like hours. I could hear Gilwyr walking around the campsite, so I knew not to be alarmed. The fire had burned down, and I had become chilled. I was shivering with the cold that had seeped into my bones from the hard ground.

I heard Gilwyr stop beside me. Then I felt her covering me with her cloak. She lay down behind me and pulled the cloak over both of us. Nestled up against my back, she put one arm over mine and fell quiet.

Listening to her breathing change to the deep rhythm of slumber, I told myself it was no more than conservation of body heat, a primitive necessity. Sleep didn't return to me, however, and my rebellious eyelids stayed open against the night. I lay still against her warmth, acutely aware of her closeness. Her scent, of fresh air and of earth and of sweat and of woman, disturbed me. Scents bypassed the disapproving veneer of civilization and awoke primal instincts that urged me to take notice. The night passed by one breath at a time, slower than the stars moving across the lightyears on the deck of the *Aquila*.

The morning was dew-soaked and cold. I pulled the cloak tighter, but drafts still poked their icy fingers underneath the edges. I reached the point of wakefulness where I abruptly realized I was alone under the cloak. I opened my eyes. The campsite was orderly and peaceful in the morning. One tendril of smoke trailed straight up from the banked fire to just below the tree canopy, where it coiled several times before spreading in a thin fan away from the rising sun. There was no sign of Gilwyr.

I stood stiffly, keeping the cloak held tightly around my shoulders. I used the latrine that Gilwyr had dug the night before (and graphically described the use of, plainly displeased that her student hadn't taken the necessary prerequisite courses). She still had not put in an appearance.

The lightening sky illuminated the glen, and I saw her at the edge of the meadow. I started towards her but stopped when I saw that she was naked. I began to turn back, thinking she was doing her morning ablutions. I stopped when I saw that she was facing a startling apparition in the sky. I knew that this planet had a smaller companion, but that knowledge did not prepare me for the enormous ghostly red face looming across a full degree of the morning sky. It was three-quarters illuminated, sinking into the west opposite the rising sun, streaked with Rorschach blackness and brilliant white clouds hanging in wispy minor accent. It was this mesmerizing countenance that Gilwyr was facing.

She was standing square to the companion planet, a sword in either hand, arms held away from her sides. After moments of stillness I could see that she was moving very slowly and deliberately, now sideways to the planet, one sword held out point upwards towards the red face, and other drawing back, held high, hand level with jaw. In profile, I could see the long graceful muscles that had stopped an ax standing taut on her arms. She was lean and superbly balanced, long-limbed and small-breasted. Her hair was igniting in the gathering dawn as it cascaded down her back.

She was moving faster now, forward sword coming down in a sweep to the right, the rear sword coming down in a slash cross-body. Faster she moved, always in perfect control, silver blades slashing molten channels through the air. She advanced and retreated, dancing feet across the trampled grass. As she reached a crescendo, she suddenly threw one of her blades in the air. Spinning, hand met hilt as it descended at exactly eye height. She flowed from the spin into a lunge at the instant that the sunlight finally spilled over the horizon. She held that pose for a long moment, a glowing statue of flesh and steel and golden curls, and the most beautiful sight I had ever seen.

She stood and held her hand out to me. "A gentleman would be offering me my cloak about now."

I hadn't known she had seen me. I felt my cheeks flame as I pulled the cloak from my shoulders, tangling up the fastenings embarrassingly. Her laughter pealed across the field. "Keep it for now! You need it more than I do. And now that we've established that you're a gentleman, just remember," she closed the distance between us as I frantically prioritized what I should and shouldn't look at. Her blade came up to stop in front of my nose. The number one priority for my eyes was suddenly settled. "Remember," she continued, "that I'm no lady!"

She breezed past me, a force of nature that was at once lovely, deadly, and unpredictable. I followed along to the campsite, where she stirred the fire to life before casually donning her clothes.

"What was that?" I inquired. The anthropologist in me was late to awaken this morning but was finally engaging. "Was that a ritual, or a dance performance, or your morning calisthenics?"

"That was the dance to Rhea as she rides off on her falcon hunt, seven days before her bonding to Sellen. She is at the height of her power and not yet aware of the treachery in her court. She is at her most confident as she is attacked by a wild *Tumboor* and finishes it with the fabled flying hidden blade. You would know this if you were Cray Leth, and I would have to kill you if had witnessed my kata and were not Cray Leth."

It seemed I had been adopted into her tribe. "Er, I didn't mean to spy on you. I was just wondering where you went."

"You are safe. You know the story now, so you are Cray Leth."

I decided that my companion was inscrutable as hell. Then her description sank in. "That was a dance to Rhea? Where is Rhea?"

Gilwyr gestured impatiently to the west. "Her red face hangs from our sky this morning. She is at peace, with no signs of white storms, or red storms, or the dreaded black veil on her countenance. Our travels to Misthaven should be swift and easy."

"And Sellen?"

She gave me a puzzled look. "Do you know them by other names? We stand on his face, though that's difficult to see except from the highest mountains. He lights Rhea's face when she turns to the darkness and is consumed by the treachery in her court. The tellers of tales believe that they can see the far future from the shades of colors he casts on her darkness. I think they are fanciful dreamers, all of them."

"Sellen and Rhea? Sellen-Rhea? Sellenria?"

"Yes, that is what we call their alliance."

If I had any doubt that this was the planet where Jonan Gremm had landed, that dispelled them. I had heard that name in his voice within the gem countless times, pondering its meaning. That name was the link between the gem and the confirming ansible message. It was a name that even Momsen had heard, calling it a legend. A puzzle piece had fallen solidly in place.

CHAPTER 7

Myths

GILWYR BUILT UP the fire before going down to the stream. She waded out into the water while I watched from the bank. I started to ask what she was doing, but she motioned me to silence. She leaned over to peer into the water and waited with one hand upraised.

She appeared to have endless patience. Not a muscle moved as she waited, not even when a fly landed on her nose. I frantically rubbed my own nose in sympathy. The fly flew on, and still she waited. My attention started to wander as matched red and green insect analogs cruised over the water. As a consequence, I missed it when her hand suddenly moved. My first warning was an incoming silvery missile and her call of "Catch it!"

I made a grab; her throw was so accurate that I could hardly do anything else. I found myself holding a fat fish that wore an old man's face with a large nose and fleshy jowls. I howled and yanked my hand away from the revolting image. The fish met the ground, flopped twice, and threw itself back in the water. "What was that?" I spluttered.

"That *was* breakfast," she said severely. She wore her disappointed look again, but I was catching on that she was teasing me when she did that, and behind that facade, she was laughing at my reaction.

"Give a guy some warning," I said. "Where I come from, breakfast doesn't look like a theater critic with indigestion. What are those things?"

"They're called the Grimmerroth's Children. They're plentiful because no one will eat them. They're really very good to eat if you don't look at them."

"All right, I'll hang on to the next one you throw this way."

It didn't take very long for four of the ugly fish to end up on the bank. Apparently, they were slow and rather stupid, relying on their appearance to avoid capture. I was puzzling over this as Gilwyr prepared them for the coals. This defense mechanism seemed to indicate the humans were their primary predators, as it seemed unlikely that a bear—or the local equivalent—would be deterred by this ruse.

They were, in fact, delicious. I asked Gilwyr how they came by that name.

"I do not know, and my teachers told me I asked too many questions, which means that they did not know, either." It seemed there were some universal traits of teachers. "We know that the only thing the Grimmerroth ever truly created were the morghaests, and those were only a pale imitation of Polnedra's creations. I think the Grimmerroth was jealous of Polnedra and tried to twist her creations into something hideous, like these fish. He could only change their outward form, however. Their substance still remains nutritious and life-giving."

I filed this under a local form of animism, perhaps tied in with a creation myth. It was most likely a forced evolution, where people refused to eat fish that sported vaguely human features. In a relatively short time, only the most human-looking would survive. It looked as if local society had not developed scientific principles to the point of explaining natural phenomena, and still relied on myths to explain the world to themselves. My finger repeatedly twitched with the reflex to trigger my transcriber, but of course that device was now no more than a pile of sand in the inn. How was I going to keep my field notes without it? I would be reduced to actually making marks on paper, assuming that these people were even at that level of development.

It occurred to me that their medical knowledge was probably at a similar level. I had better not get sick or injured here. But for how long? I was reminded that I was likely exiled on this world, and no one was going to read my anthropological treatises on these people. I fell under a cloud again and was deeply gloomy.

Gilwyr didn't seem capable of being other than unflappably self-reliant and went about getting us ready for the road without noticing my funk. Shortly thereafter, she led the way back to the road and set off for Misthaven, trailing me and my dark cloud behind her.

We hadn't gone very far before we were accosted by another talking (six-legged, chameleon-skinned) badger. "The Inn of the Forest is not far ahead!" it said cheerfully. They apparently weren't terribly observant about the direction you were traveling.

"What's with those things?" I asked.

"Oh, the innkeeper feeds them if they say that to travelers. They're harmless."

"I mean, where I come from, animals don't talk."

"Quite a few animals here can talk. Talking and thinking are two different matters, aren't they?"

It was around an hour later that it occurred to me to wonder if that was a subtle jab.

The forest was thick, and the road sometimes further gone in ruins than it had been near the Inn. Gilwyr wore only her normal alertness, which I took to mean that there was little that concerned her in the forest. After a while, the sameness of the road started to get to me, and I asked Gilwyr to tell me more about Polnedra and the Grimmerroth.

"Before them came Milhadron, before whom there was nothing." Gilwyr was clearly reciting a well-known legend. "Milhadron wished for a place to abide, so he swept out the Ocean of Light with his hands. On the edge of the Ocean of Light, on the thin shore against the Mountains of Darkness, he built a small house, and there he abided.

"Milhadron desired a child so that he could watch the delight of young eyes seeing everything for the first time. He created Polnedra to be eternally a child who could play by the shore of the Ocean of Light. He watched, with the indulgence that became the trademark of any father who came after, as his daughter built castles in the sand, tossed stones across the waters, and made shapes to float over the waves. And the sandcastles stood as the great towers of stars in our heavens, and the skipping stones became the planets and the comets crossing the skies, and the vessels that floated in the Ocean of Light became our worlds.

"And because Polnedra was created to always delight in new things, she kept creating, ever smaller and more detailed creations. She pushed up mountains on her worlds in imitation of the Mountains of Darkness. She poured water where she had scooped out the mountains and filled the oceans, in imitation of the Ocean of Light. She made trees to cover the hillsides. She created smaller creatures to hide among the trees, and larger creatures to roam the plains. She experimented; some creatures she made to eat the plants, and some creatures she made to eat each other. Being both a god and a child, she did not yet know of cruelty or kindness.

"She gave to some animals the power of color-shifting because it made more interesting the game between hunter and prey. And from others she withheld it, to see how they would counter that disadvantage. She gave to some creatures, like that *ongar* that told us about the inn, the power of speech so that she could listen to their chatter. But this came to little more than boasts and threats, and Polnedra quickly bored of it.

"So Polnedra made the first people. She gave to them the gift of speech, as well as something new: the power of thought. These were fine and interesting things, but something was lacking. So Polnedra struck sparks from her hands and let these settle among the people. Each spark contained the tiniest fraction of Polnedra's creativity. Because she left the distribution to chance, the people received greater or lesser sparks, or sometimes none at all. And she watched, and listened, and was amused."

Gilwyr paused, rummaged in her pack for a moment and pulled out what appeared to be a hard, flat biscuit. She broke it in half, handed me a piece, and started moving again.

"Where does the Grimmerroth come in?" I asked, eager to keep her talking. It's not every millennium that a field archaeologist gets to hear a brand new creation myth. I ached for the loss of my recording equipment. The poetry of the tale of this child god was beautiful. I felt as I had the first time I watched the old glassblower in the museum fashion something wonderful with flame and glowing glass. It had felt like a glittering droplet of truth.

"As she listened to the people she had created, Polnedra became aware of an agony building up in her creation. She did not understand this, but it did not please her, so she asked her father for advice. Milhadron had been watching, but saying nothing, because he believed in letting his child make her own mistakes. But now, when she asked, the mountains rumbled with his voice. 'Child, these creatures are thrice removed from godhood. I see all, and it is. You see all and are delighted. These lesser creatures see all and are crushed by it. You let them contemplate eternity, but cannot give them the minds to encompass it.'

"Polnedra asked her father to fix what she had done. At first he declined, telling her she was responsible for her playthings. She persisted, and he relented. But he did what was wise; instead of raising her playthings to godhood, he instead helped them bear their creation. He took the cosmos from its footings in the Mountains of Darkness and set it spinning. With the spinning came night and day, light and darkness, and so he created Time.

"And he gave to Polnedra's creations the gift of mortality so that they would have no more of eternity than they could bear.

"Polnedra was glad that her creations no longer suffered, but it was not quite the answer she had been hoping for. She withdrew for a while. First, she sulked and threw stones. One hit Rhea and scorched its surface and ended many of her creations. She was sincerely penitent and sought to undo this, but Milhadron had made Time to turn in only one direction.

"She pondered how she could have done better than her father. After a while, she decided that she would impart a larger portion of eternity to her creation. But she didn't want to make a mistake as large as her first, so she made a single creature, and dropped an extraordinary amount of creativity into him. And she called him Glimmer.

"At first this was splendid. Glimmer took up the tools of the smith and hammered fine instruments of iron and copper. He took up the brush of the artist and made creations to elicit joy and love and fear, and any other emotion he cared to essay in any who viewed them. He took up the pen and wrote stories and poems to move the mind and soul of any who read them. He was handsome, and admired, and influential. Polnedra was pleased and manifested in his garden to spend an afternoon in conversation. In this, she made a grave error.

"After the conversation, Glimmer saw what he could have been. Polnedra was young, eternal, beautiful, and could create with the touch of a finger. Flowers dropped from her fingertips as she walked around his garden. For an age after her visit, that garden had flowers found nowhere else in the worlds.

"Glimmer threw himself into creation with a fever, trying to equal his creator. He became stern and uncompromising, striving for ever greater perfection. Yet everything he made he saw only as a shadow of Polnedra's originals. His art became darker, his work at the forge became twisted. His words drove others away. He released demons on the world that killed many. It was then that he became known as Grimmer, first in jest and then in fear.

"His words inspired those who leaned to the darkness themselves. He took delight in whispering in their ears, first in one ear and then another, so that Polnedra's children would first argue, then fight. He made weapons for them to use and invented reasons for them to be used.

"Finally, Polnedra could stand the strife in her creation no longer. She lured Grimmer to a cave in the deepest mountains. She could not reverse Time, but she could stop it in a small area. She touched Grimmer and froze Time in that cavern, turning him into a twisted statue. After he became frozen in his twisted form, he was known thereafter as the Grimmerroth. But Grimmer had suspected her motives and had fashioned a blade that he plunged into her breast and held. As she touched him and froze Time, she froze herself in Time as well.

"To this day, they stand in the darkness, frozen in Time. A few have found this cavern upon occasion. If someone touches them and warms them with a little of their own Time, they are released on the world for a while. The Grimmerroth creates twisted things and twisted people to sow war and destruction on the world. Polnedra tries to rally people to defeat him. Because she is locked in Time and without her powers, each time she faces him she must choose a hero to fight for her against the Grimmerroth."

Throughout this remarkable recitation, I desperately wished for my field recorder to get a reliable transcript of Gilwyr's tale. Failing that, I was going to have to find whatever passed for paper and pen on this planet and start keeping a journal. The ease with which she recited the tale spoke of a strong oral tradition, which would be fascinating to study, but also suggested that they might not be much in the habit of writing. I concentrated on remembering as much of the tale as possible, making notes to myself as she talked.

As a myth it had all of the classic elements: How did the cosmos begin? Why is there good and evil in the world? Is there knowledge that is too great or too terrible to bear? Even if I couldn't identify the roots of this tale in any known mythology, humans still asked the same questions of themselves. Beyond my professional excitement in this material, something about the mythology appealed to me. The universe was made as a plaything by a child god? Strife and conflict were because she didn't understand what she was creating? I wished it were true; it was as good as any explanation I had heard. It even explained the existence of time and mortality.

Glimmer had seen something beyond what he could ever be, something he could never attain. We tell ourselves these stories not to keep that feeling at bay, but in the hope that we may handle it better, and with more dignity than he had.

CHAPTER 8

Road

THE FOREST ENDED abruptly, giving way to rolling prairie. Low vegetation was at war for possession of the landscape. Terran grasses of green and gold contended against the native teal in broad patches while the occasional tree stood in tall command over its forces. The road assailed the plain, dividing it into north and south, conducting travelers to a place that was neither.

Gilwyr surveyed the hills and skies before leaving the cover of the forest and setting foot on the road. I asked whether she was checking for any particular hazards out in the open. She only replied that she always felt exposed on this part of the road where there was no concealment, leaving me to wonder what she might want concealment from.

At close range, the native plants looked like knee-high feather dusters. Evolution seemed to have settled on the lambswool-like fuzz that Gilwyr called *wen withe* instead of leaves; all the local flora sported some variation of this covering. As the road descended again, Terran grasses abruptly took over once more. I guessed that any differences in soil composition that gave aid and succor to one side over the other determined the deployment of the two armies. The hilltops tended to be teal besieged by an ocean of gold around their lower ramparts. I twitched my finger and said, "The line dividing native and Terran foliage is sharp. Perhaps the native foliage thrives on better drainage while the Terran grasses prefer somewhat moister conditions."

"Who are you talking to?"

I pulled up short in embarrassment. "I'm sorry, it's a habit. It's the way that I record my notes for my research."

"Record? Do you have a memory stone?"

"You might say that. It was made of metal, and it was eaten by an impossible creature." I conjectured that she was talking about some sort of mnemonic device—a system for committing facts to memory and recalling them later. A pre-technological society would have need of tricks like those.

The day grew hot under the unshaded sun. Gilwyr set out with a brisk stride that soon had me dripping sweat. It was quiet on the prairie; no insect buzz or birdcall that I might have expected in this place. My calves and thighs began to protest at the pace, and I suspected that I was going to have a few impressive blisters by evening. I glanced at Gilwyr, who had the grace to at least have a light sheen of sweat across the bridge of her nose but was otherwise unaffected by the heat or the exertion. I had thought myself in reasonable shape before the journey with my daily workouts on the *Aquila*. I knew to expect field work but also expected to be able to hire vehicles and equipment to travel to my destinations. I had been utterly unprepared to hike overland for days in primitive pre-industrial age conditions.

I was wrapped up in measuring my physical discomfort: was the rate of increase linear or did the first derivative also have a positive slope? I missed Gilwyr's first hissed "Get down!" and seconds later was sprawled face-down on the road, her weight thrown atop me. My head was spinning with dust and impact and sweat and woman-scent when a sudden shadow occurred overhead. I got a brief look upward before being pushed firmly down again. Something flapped overhead like a detached piece of the sky, invisibly blue against blue, a ripple in the air.

"Stay flat," she said into my ear before rolling off to the side. I turned my head enough to watch as she shook a sling out of her sleeve and picked up a fist-sized rock. She rolled into a quick crouch, swung the rock around her head several times and let fly. I was disappointed at first that it didn't connect with something in the sky; I had come to believe that she would be infallible with any weapon she picked up. However, as the rock fell to earth in the tall grass, the prairie erupted into motion.

What had appeared to be open prairie was filled with gazelle-sized, six-limbed beasts that had hunkered down in the grass all around us. They had the camouflage trait of all the land animals I had seen on this planet, blending invisibly with the color and texture of the grass. Thousands of the creatures suddenly bolted. Over the grass, they were still invisible, and it appeared that a great wind stirred the land while earthquakes shook the pebbles in the road. Where they crossed the road, they were briefly visible as fleet bright shadows. Where they incautiously ran into the native vegetation, they were blazing beacons for the half-dozen paces that it took them to take on the teal color.

A half dozen paces were their undoing. Bits of the sky wheeled and plummeted to earth. I thought at first that I had hit my head when Gilwyr tackled me, then the sky shards rained down on the gazelles, resolving at the last second into blue Pteranodon-like creatures. Their strategy appeared to be to fall upon their prey so heavily that a broken back rendered the gazelle an easy meal. At least a score of the flying lizard things came down among the herd and fell to squabbling about the choicer bits. On the ground, I could see that they stretched their flying membranes between midlimb and hindlimb, leaving forelimbs free for grasping their prey.

Gilwyr stood, looking unconcerned now, so I levered myself up to sitting. "What were those things?" I asked.

"*Cray zen*," she replied. "Winged warriors. They hunt in packs where the *tir chin* congregate."

"Were they hunting us?"

"Not really. We don't taste good to them. But the *cray zen* don't learn that until after they've broken your neck and taken the first bite. It's better not to be part of their education."

"Oh, well. Too bad you missed your first shot at them."

"I did *not* miss my shot," she said coldly. "I wouldn't harm one of them unless I had no choice. I helped them by pointing them to their real prey."

I felt like I was declining in her estimation and immediately compounded it by wincing as I attempted to regain my feet. She saw and pushed me back to sitting and pulled off my boots. I cringed and she shook her head at the angry red blisters on my feet. "You have soft feet even for a scholar, Stenn Gremm. This will not do, we have far to go. Wait here."

She walked up the road to the nearest teal zone and started searching among the vegetation. Shortly I saw the flash of one of her blades and then saw her trotting back up the road with what looked like the top of a cactus in her hands. She put it down next to me, inverted like a bowl, and stirred the pulp inside into a paste. She took my socks and pressed them into the paste, working it into the fabric, and handing the sad gloppy mess back to me. "Put these on."

I grimaced fastidiously at the feel of the coating, like a thick cream. I pulled one on and felt an immediate relief. "What is this stuff?"

"This plant produces a poison." I froze in the act of pulling on the second sock. "It's not harmful in this concentration," she continued, "but it does produce a numbness that should help you get through the day." I had to admit that my feet felt much better, so I finished pulling on socks and boots and succeeded in regaining my feet this time. I walked experimentally, grimacing at the unpleasant squishiness in my boots. After a bit, though, I came to realize that the plant pulp was acting as a salve to lubricate and cushion the places where my boots had been rubbing me.

The adrenaline from the attack and the salve on my feet kept me going for much of the afternoon. After we stopped for water at a clear stream that wandered conveniently near the road at one point, however, my legs refused to bear my weight any further that day. Gilwyr took pity on me and made camp for the night.

There were some creatures nearby that seemed like rabbits at first. The rear limbs were long and muscled like a rabbit's, and it used its mid-limbs in the manner of a rabbit's fore-limbs. It sat upright and used its fore-limbs to hold and pluck the lambswool from the teal flora and cram it into its little mouth. Topped with moderately long ears, the effect was that of a rabbit-headed centaur. They didn't run when Gilwyr approached, and she killed two of them quickly, leading me to dub them slowhares. They made a passable, if somewhat gamey, stew.

I had an excessive number of questions about the native wildlife, and the origins of the strange terms that she had for them. I found myself unable to voice them, with my head drooping immediately after our meal. She made me wash my socks in the stream, then sent me back to do it better, before laying them before the fire to dry and allowing me to finally go to sleep. She again spread her cloak over both of us and lay close along my back where her heat burned against my skin. I wondered if this was an invitation to intimacy, and whether I would fail in her estimation if I did not take the initiative. It could as easily have been simply custom out of necessity for shared warmth, and I could offend her by misconstruing it. I tentatively placed my hand over hers as we lay together. She squeezed it once and said, "Sleep." I was unable to gainsay her.

In the shivery pre-dawn, I awoke as she slid from beneath the cloak. I watched through slitted eyes as she walked barefoot to the edge of the smoldering fire, there to drop her clothing in a careful heap and remove her blades from their scabbards. Naked, she took her pose with her swords and held it while the light slowly pushed the night westward. Her initial movements flowed too slowly to see; blades rose and fell without any feeling that she had moved. The first motion was too fast to follow, a blocking motion, defensive. A blur of parry and riposte followed attackers in all directions. A brief surge turning the offensive, but not enough. At the end, crouching crossed blades overhead, capitulation, blades lowered. I sensed it was over, but she remained, withdrawn in herself. I rose then and laid the cloak around her shoulders.

She made an angry movement, then clutched the cloak around her. After a moment she said, "This kata always makes me sad. The treachery in Rhea's court is finally revealed, intrigue turns to struggle, daggers are turned aside only to become swords. She finally lays down her weapons to end the strife."

"If it makes you sad, why do you perform it?"

She indicated Rhea hanging, ruddy, in the sky. "It is the day for it. Rhea is waning, the story must run its course. It is a reminder that not all battles can be won with swords. There are times to lay them down so that alliances can be remade. One cannot redress wrongs if one is dead. Besides," she smiled. "Without this chapter, one cannot have the next one, where Rhea returns victorious."

We built up the fire and broke our fast. I was extremely stiff and hobbled around for a good while, but gradually got my muscles warmed up. Gilwyr found another teal cactus and coated my socks with fresh salve. We started on the road again before the sun was two hands above the horizon. (I was briefly pleased I had remembered the old way of measuring time, with a hand held at arm's length against the sky. But I still ached for the missing simspace overlays that my implants had provided, supplying time, temperature, weather forecasts and other modern measures of the world.)

That day saw the prairie changing into gradually more settled lands, and the first humans we had seen since the Inn, at whom I peered with unbridled interest. Fields were cleared and planted with earthly grains and other crops, and Terran goats and cows grazed in the pastures. We stayed that night with a homesteader who seemed to have a prior acquaintance with Gilwyr and had crusty bread, cheese, and a vegetable stew for dinner. They showed us to a room with a single bed, and we slept much as we had slept while on the road. I supposed that it was just the way things were done here.

In the morning Gilwyr was once more up before dawn. I don't know where she practiced her katas that morning, but I missed seeing the redemption of Rhea. I hoped that I would have another chance. I said as much as we set out on the road again. She arched an eyebrow at me. "Indeed? Is that because you wish to experience the telling of Rhea's tale or because you are a man who likes watching an unclothed woman?" She let me fumble the answer repeatedly as I assured her that I was purely interested in how the story progressed, but that she was very beautiful to watch, but I didn't mean that the way it sounded. I ended up flustered and very red-faced as she laughed heartily.

At mid-morning we reached the sea and turned north. The sea cliffs were nearly a hundred feet high, and the waves crashed far below us. Near noon we came to a high rocky headland. The sheer drop to the ocean on our right forced us to ascend several hundred feet before rounding the shoulder to see what lay beyond. What lay beyond was Misthaven.

Misthaven was a remarkable sight. A placid river issued from the plains, passing the city where the wooden docks knelt down to drink the waters. Sailing ships were tied along the docks, universally fitted out with huge banks of oars, the need for which would shortly become clear. Downstream from the port, the river picked up steam, finally flinging itself from sixty-foot cliffs that crashed upon sawtoothed rocks that guarded the sea.

"How do the ships ever put out to sea? Do they use the oars as gliders to launch themselves over the rocks?" I asked.

"Let's make camp here," replied Gilwyr. "The falls are called the Tears of Rhea, and tomorrow is Rhea's final crescent. I would very much like to perform Rhea's Triumph tomorrow morning in this place."

She said no more, so we set up camp, and she disappeared into the brush for an hour, returning with a brace of the long-eared slowhares for our evening meal. As I worked as her assistant in preparing the dinner (I'm sure that I still was a net loss in time and efficiency, but she insisted), I became aware that the world-shaking roar of the surf had redoubled. Looking back at the cliffs, I saw that the waterfall had become half its former height, and the sharp rocks were entirely covered. Some ships had appeared from around the headland and were standing out to sea, waiting.

"That has to be the most amazing tide I've ever seen," I said slowly.

"The tides are moderate in these latitudes. You should see them in the Great Bay, where they're twice this."

I paid closer attention for the rest of the afternoon, though the smell of roasted slowhare filling the air competed with the magnificent view. As the shadows grew long, the rising sea finally met the river level and pushed back into the river basin. The tide was almost spent, however, and only raised the boats at the dock a modest level. That was the signal for pandemonium.

Fully half the ships at the dock had been ready to launch and raced towards the mouth of the river under full oar. Simultaneously, the ships standing offshore made a mad dash for the docks. Now I could see the reason for the combination of sail and galley. The ships all needed to sprint to get past the danger zone before the tide began to ebb again. For several minutes I thought that there was going to be an enormous pileup in the mouth of the river, but the sailors were apparently all well-practiced in this ritual and passed each other at safe distances.

It seemed that high tide was over in moments. All the boats had cleared the river mouth when the top of the waterfall re-appeared. Those heading for dock were straining against the quickening current but looked like they would all make port. Those heading out to sea were skimming over the waves away from the sucking undertow that was forming along the cliffs.

A hiss shook the twilight as if a dragon had awoken. I found out later that the high tide every day poured cold water down a long, winding volcanic vent that cracked the mountainside. Steam billowed out of the vent to fill the river valley. The gathering shore breeze of evening started plaiting the fog into layers and braids and tucking the docks under their evening blanket of fog. Gilwyr finally spoke, "Not the gods, nor man. It was the river that gave Misthaven its name."

CHAPTER 9

Misthaven

WE SPENT THE night high up in a sheltered cove near the headlands. The thunder of the falls kept me from losing myself too deeply in slumber. I awoke at intervals to hear the pounding waters swell in volume with the passing of the tide until it became one with my heartbeat and the rush of blood in my ears. Finally, it reached a crescendo at low tide as the rocks at the base of the falls was exposed, and gradually receded again. I slept at last with the gentling voice of the water and the heat of Gilwyr at my back.

I was galvanized into wakefulness by the quenching hiss that signaled high tide reaching the thermal vent. I do not know if I had been struggling in the grip of the nightmare before awakening, or whether it was something that my dreaming brain synthesized on the spot to match realspace sounds to dreamspace logic. No doubt my subconscious had a backlog of new input to process after the sensory assault of the past several days.

In my dream, I had returned to my lander in the forest glade, which was still as I had left it. Somehow Gilwyr had come to be inside it, and I had to get her out. I had to fight my way through a pack of Cray Zen that tore blue from the sky to hurl at me on near-invisible wings armed with razor-sharp pteranodon beaks. I had a branch or staff with which I laid about left and right to drive them off until I succeeded in reaching the relative shelter of the capsule. The hatch was locked. I tried to bash it open with the same rock that I had used to hammer it shut. Gilwyr came to peer out through the thick glass window set in the door to see what the noise was.

Morghaests clawed their way from the ground, undead groundskeepers with a hatred of things of metal that fell from the sky. They surrounded me in the red light of Rhea, arms outstretched. I hurled staff and stone at them, which only dissolved into the Golems as they hit. I ducked under their reach; they let me go, uninterested.

The morghaests turned their eyeless attention to the capsule. They plunged fingers through the outer shell and peeled great strips from the skin of the ship. One brute seized the hatch in both hands and tore it from the frame. The hatch began to fuzz and crumble and melt into the morghaest, making it ever larger. Gilwyr lashed out with her blade from inside but could not get a clean stroke, confined as she was by the width of the empty hatchway. I screamed within the hollows of my head for her to get away, but no sound would come.

I lurched forward, and I saw my hand reach out without volition and fall upon the shoulder of the morghaest. My hand blurred, as it had at the Inn, and the morghaest began to crumble and slump. I thrust it aside and reached for Gilwyr to draw her out. She came into my arms and embraced me, but then cried out wordlessly. I watched in horror as she began to crack and crumble as the morghaest had, until all I held was a form of sand that slipped through my arms and was gone. My wail of anguish merged with the dragon hiss of the volcanic steam, and I awoke.

I bolted upright, fighting with the entangling cloak that seemed a dreamspace morghaest dragged back to realspace with me. My heart was pounding, my chest heaving, the night still dark, and the noisy, restive air was cold. Gilwyr had sprung to a crouch, hand upon blade, but collected herself quickly. She gathered me into the cloak, saying, "It's only a night terror. The Grimmerroth sows them among your dreams to leave little bits of doubt and fear among your waking thoughts. Shake them off now, before they take root."

I held tight to her until my breathing slowed. "I was trying to save you from a morghaest. You were cornered. I failed, and you crumbled away, and I lost you." I didn't add that it had been my hand that had made her crumble.

She laughed, gently. "You were trying to save me? Ah, you have strange dreams Stenn Gremm. I am Cray Leth."

I think we both became aware that we were holding each other tightly at about the same time; face to face, not spooned as we had slept. Gilwyr's scent filled my nostrils, and I could feel her breath against my neck. I felt a sudden desire for my guide. She stiffened and pushed away a bit and frowned. "What is this hard thing between us, Stenn Gremm?" she asked.

I turned my face from hers in mortification. I had offended her. I recalled my dream where I had held her and she had crumbled. My subconscious had painted the symbolism with a heavy brush, but I could miss the obvious when people were concerned, especially attractive alien swords-women of unknown cultural background.

But her hands were moving, confusing me. She drew down the zipper of my jacket and slid her hands within. My breath caught as she explored, sliding her hands down my chest …

Her hands fell upon the pouch holding the gemstone in the inner pocket of my jacket, and she drew it out. "This is what I felt!" she proclaimed, sitting up to examine it.

"Please don't open that," I said quickly. "I'll show it to you when it's light if you like."

"This unsettles me." She was still holding the leather bag with the gemstone in it.

"Wait for light, when you can see it," I started, but she was already loosening the drawstrings and sliding it out onto her palm. The living gemstone that emerged struck us both silent. The channels that traversed the blood red interior of the stone carried tiny pips of light that rushed about with all the orderly chaos of an ant colony. An entire universe was within its fractal branching, infinite in depth yet contained within the palm of her hand. From every angle, it opened up vistas that receded as far into the distance as the stars above. In all the time I had it, it had been vast, but static. Now it pulsed like a thing alive.

"Where did you obtain this stone?" Gilwyr asked.

"It has been in my family for hundreds of years, as far as I know." I didn't wish to disclose anything more at the moment. I felt somewhat invaded by the way she had taken it, shaken by the preceding dream, disturbed by my lapse in controlling my feelings, and wary of the degree of interest she was showing.

"I saw a mention of a thing like this in a book of lore. But if you brought it with you it cannot be the same thing, can it?" I hastily agreed that it was unlikely, and quickly put the stone away. She stared at me for a moment more, then stood to make ready for the morning.

It was the time when the first notes of dawn appeared in the sky, largo con dolcezza. Rhea was a single oboe voiced in the eastern sky, thin and reedy. Gilwyr made ready for her entrance. When the river mist drew a ghostly bassoon counterpoint across the land, she let her clothes fall to the ground and took her place facing Rhea.

It was in my mind not to watch her this morning. I did not want to feed this desire I had found. She was young enough to be my daughter—if any of my previous life had led me into activities conducive to producing one, which it had not. Nor had she encouraged me in that. She had fallen to teasing me a bit as we had traveled, but in all respects took her role as my protector very seriously. That she performed her morning katas naked was evidently a deeply spiritual thing to her; she approached it as natural and right. Yet she did not mind that I watched. She even seemed to take pleasure in it. My mind was ambivalent, but my eyes would not turn away.

Her movements this morning were powerful, controlled, restrained. The exuberance of the first day had given way to subtlety and precision. I watched the play of her muscles and the grace of her limbs, the sheen of the gathering light on her flank and the flash of her blades. In that moment she was Rhea, and by the child god who made this world, she was beautiful.

Afterward, we were both contemplative. Few words were exchanged during the morning activities. We ate lightly and set out with Gilwyr promising a hot noonday meal once we got to the city.

We had to cross the river at some point to get to the city on the opposite bank. The south bank was lined with high bluffs with little access to the river. The road followed the tops of the bluffs past the city to where they finally gave way enough to cross the river. This gave a good vantage of the city as we walked by, just above the fog line.

The city was arrayed in tiers on a steep land. The lower city was on a brief alluvial plain. I had seen the docks yesterday, but today they were still hidden under a thick white blanket of fog. The fog seemed almost liquid in quality, being slowly stirred by eddies and stretched into striations by the movement of the water. Above that the buildings marched up the hillside, first showing only their roofs, then their walls, and finally their doors as the city grew towards the sun. A great cleft rent the land, dividing the city in half. Gilwyr informed me that the city was divided into the upriver and downriver sections, and into upper and lower quarters. The lower city was rough and tumble, full of sailors and adventurers, brothels and bars. The upper city held the homes of the elite and the places of power and finance, while the slopes between held a spectrum of artisans, merchants, and markets. The upriver city was dominated by the palace of the mayor and ranks of government functionaries. The downriver city was the home of the University, holding the libraries and archives, halls of arts and of sciences, and the quarters of scholars and students.

Upriver from the city, we came to a place where the banks drew closer. Two large rafts were plying the river between the shores. They were propelled by massive bargemen whose muscles stood out like granite outcroppings as they vigorously polled against the current. Stout cables were strung across the river, and the rafts were anchored to the cables to prevent the rafts from being swept downriver and over the falls. We crossed in the company of two farm carts loaded with produce along with their farmers and oxen, a dozen goats, and a peddler with a depleted cart returning to the city for more wares to sell.

The barge landed just upstream of the edge of the fog bank. From this close, it wasn't quite a sharp edge. As the road entered the precinct of the mists, the first tendrils appeared like hurrying wraiths crossing the paving stones. Their touch was cold and clammy after the warm sun, which was dissolving the wraiths even as we walked. Further along, the wraiths locked arms and closed in, still holding their territory against this invader that would desiccate them with a touch.

The first buildings loomed out of the mist, warehouses and dockside taverns. The docks themselves must have been close, but we couldn't see even as far as the far end of the warehouse we were passing. From the texture of the sounds, I guessed that the docks were just beyond. Draymen hauled loads between the warehouses and the docks. A certain quality of man hung around on corners and in alleyways, regretting last night's drinking and looking forward to tonight's. A certain quality of woman could be seen in upstairs windows, very likely not looking forward to the evening's work. On several occasions I started to dictate notes, only to attract stares from those nearby and amusement from Gilwyr.

We left the lower town and began climbing the streets towards the downriver half of the city and the University. We passed the shops of bakers, butchers, and greengrocers, the studio workshops of glassblowers, and the din of smithies and woodworkers. At the last of these, I heard a whine as of a turbine, which seemed out of place in this pre-industrial town. Looking inside I saw steam escaping from a housing that seemed to be the source of the sound. A vertical wooden shaft spun at high speeds, driving an elaborate set of worm gears, transverse shafts, and belts and pulleys. Around the shop floor stood lathes and drill presses and shapers, all tapping into the overhead distribution system. I marveled at how the entire system was designed to transfer the power of a single engine to every other mechanism in the shop. Gilwyr informed me that most of the shops here tapped into the natural steam vents of the area, which was the reason the town had grown up around the volcanic crevice. I tried to trigger my implants to search my databases for similar machines in other cultures, only to recall that my pack had been eaten by the impossible servants of the twisted warlock created by the child god who made the world.

That was the moment my worldview crashed on the sheer mundane reality of my surroundings. My sojourn in the wilds of Sellenria had been strange in the extreme, but one that had no human context to it. It was by definition without the comforts of human ingenuity. But now that I had entered a town, I found that I was reaching for simspace access and not finding it after a lifetime when city and simspace had been synonymous. I could not look up a fact that I couldn't recall, or call upon pattern recognition to identify sights and sounds and smells. I could not record my observations or consult with colleagues on interpretations. I felt half-blind and half-deaf, and the sudden understanding that all these people spent all their lives in that state left me shaking and disoriented. Gilwyr had to steer me to a tavern and put a bowl of stew and a flagon of ale in front of me to allow me to collect myself.

And that was my introduction to Misthaven.

CHAPTER 10

Greylander

I CONCENTRATED ON the spoon before me. Soup waves broke on the shores of the spoon, escaped back into the soup ocean below. (Where was the list of ingredients? The nutritional analysis? My simspace display was blank.) Tastes of salt and umami. Chunks of some meat. (Terran? Native?) Bowl of heavy earthenware, handmade, salt glazed. (Where's my artifact catalog?) My hand was shaking, tunnel vision contracted to just my plate. To look up was to risk reality overload. I felt I was in a broken simspace where the controls refused to respond, and the data overlays had gone blank. Some people did that deliberately; set a timer or a trigger word to end the simspace; called it immersive, called it a game. I didn't want to play a game right now. Reality should have a heads-up display.

Gilwyr, naturally, didn't understand my affliction. She pulled a dense, dark air of detachment around her and wrapped it in her cloak and hat. It told any onlooker that she wasn't looking for trouble but would finish any trouble that introduced itself. It appeared to be her tavern persona since she had worn it when I first met her in the forest. She sat against the wall, surveying the room and drinking her ale while I struggled with displacement anxiety.

Most of the tavern patrons were dressed as tradesmen and tradeswomen. Clothes were mostly handwoven, with some of soft leather such as those Gilwyr wore. (Where was my library of fabric weave images, to identify their heritage?) I inspected the barmaid's blouse when she came near; it appeared to be of cotton or flax. Gilwyr cleared her throat menacingly at either the barmaid or me; the barmaid and her blouse quickly retreated. My spoon was pewter; around the room, I also saw wooden implements. (I reached for information on forging and casting; it wasn't there.) Everything was as it should be in a pre-industrial society.

I had been born into a society that lived augmented lives. We had implants in our eyes and ears shortly after birth. Our early training taught us to extend our memories and perceptions with these tools. Any fact could be retrieved by thinking of it. Anything we saw or heard could be pattern matched and analyzed. I had prepared for field work by bringing a unit with me that had exabytes of relevant libraries. A monster had eaten it, and with it, a significant portion of my ability to make sense of the world. Everything around me was unfiltered and unanalyzed, and seemed surreal; colors were oversaturated, smells were almost palpable, noises were nearly intolerable, nothing was labeled or cataloged. On our trek to Misthaven, it had been a dull ache of something not right. Faced with the raw input overload of the city, I was suffering a meltdown. I reached up to my temple and felt for the tiny dimple that I had never touched, but knew was there. After a moment's hesitation, I pressed the switch, deep under the skin, the emergency shut off for my implants.

I gained 20 degrees of vision on either side, an area that was normally filled with simspace displays. The overstimulation eased to a degree. My implants, deprived of their pathways, must have been generating feedback. I felt even more cut off from the familiar. I was on my own on this planet, with no more senses than neolithic man had possessed. Everyone in the room had the same lack of augmentation (where were their floating name tiles?), but I was the only one who knew what I was lacking.

My spoon dredged the bottom of the bowl of stew. It had been quite good, and I was feeling steadier now. Gilwyr wasn't about to give me time to relax, however. "Let's go," she said. "Everyone's looking at you." To my eye, it was she that everyone was watching—I was merely incidental. I was dressed somewhat outlandishly, but she looked both beautiful and deadly; she attracted the notice of most of the men and many of the women. Many seemed to be wondering what their chances were with her. Some might also be perceptive enough to wonder if they would survive the attempt. The entirety likely wondered why I accompanied her.

We left without any interactions with the clientele. The proprietor thanked her by name, and I understood that she had already established her reputation here.

She took me next to a shop that sold men's clothes. She selected soft leather breeches, a shirt that felt like rough flannel, a vest, a belt, boots. She added a cloak like her own, close-woven, waterproof, warm. I thought the effect looked rather dashing, though there was no mirror in the shop to look myself over. I made sure there was an inner pocket for the gem. The shopkeeper wanted to burn my strange off-world clothes, but I insisted on bundling them up and keeping them.

After that, we walked up steadily steepening streets. Doorways into buildings were on the first floor downhill, and on the third floor uphill. On the sides, the doorways were of odd shapes. Stone appeared to be the most plentiful building material, with wooden framing for the doors and windows. The windows were glazed, though the panes of glass were small and unevenly cast; impurities rendered many of them with a greenish cast. Heavy shutters, steep roofs, and deep gutters led me to deduce that heavy storms were not infrequent. Lamps with wicks and sooty chimneys were prepared for nighttime illumination.

The buildings ended, but the hill continued to climb. Above this, the hillside was rock-strewn and rough. The path cut to the right across the hillside, switched back to the left, and once more to the right immediately before ending at a brooding stone building that covered the entire top of the hill. "The University," said Gilwyr, setting foot to the path. The way had been leveled with a low curb of stone on its outer side. It appeared well-trod and well maintained, though at one point a section had partially washed out and not yet been repaired. We edged around the subsidence and continued upwards.

The path rose to a spur at the level of the outer wall. From there a suspended plank bridge crossed the gap to meet a stout wooden door set into the wall. The path, bridge, and door were probably wide enough to allow a narrow cart to pass but little more than that. The University looked built for defense. I wondered what they were defending against.

The door stood open, though, and unguarded. We passed within. The way was long and dark, crossing entirely through a building and emerging in a central courtyard. Grass grew abundantly between gravel paths. Several trees provided spots of shade; sheltered benches encouraged those passing by to linger there. A statue stood near the center of the courtyard, a stoic man with one arm raised as if in declamation, and the other arm cradling a book. Buildings lined the sides of the courtyard, some having the look of dormitories, refectories, and craft shops. The building directly across the courtyard was an eminence of dark stone. Windows deep and narrow were scattered sparingly across its face. Whoever resided there either liked the dimness or had very high bills for lamp oil.

Gilwyr steered me onto the path that led into the maw of that building. The path had no branches. It ran straight into the darkness of the building, brooking no deviation. A feeling of doom built up at the base of my neck, a feeling that the doorway ahead was a dividing point in time, when *before* became *after*. I recalled facing the doors of a University for the first time, the day I enrolled as a student. Immensely far away in both time and space, that had been a light and airy place, but the sense of a boundary in life had been the same.

We passed through the archway, which repeated the motif of great wooden doors that could withstand waves of invaders if only they were closed. It might have made the inhabitants feel secure about repelling the next invaders that happened along, but none had come by recently. I could tell from the brass arcs inscribed on the floor where a supporting wheel under the door would roll. The brass was covered in a heavy patina of dust and oxidation. The doors hadn't been closed in many years. I wondered if they still could, should the need arise.

The inside opened up into a great hall. Stairways rose to the left and right to connect with balconies running the length of the hall. In the upper reaches, skylights that had not been visible from outside admitted more light than expected to the interior. A few people could be seen crossing the hall, emerging from the many corridors around both levels of the hall, and disappearing into others. Gilwyr lead me up the stairs to the left and down the third corridor. Here were doors, some closed, some half-open on spaces tidy or not depending on the occupant. At the far end, she pushed open the final door onto what might have been a large room but which was stuffed so full as to be almost impenetrable. Books were stacked on every surface, shelved floor to ceiling, and encroaching on the floor as well. I couldn't be sure, but some of the shelves may have concealed deeper shelves yet. A desk was placed in front of a small window, which was held in the grip of a smothering vine on the outside. To the side of the window, an easel held a half-finished woodland scene. Line drawings, some rough sketches, some intricately detailed, were tacked to the window frame and a number of other available surfaces. In the center of the room, an immense figure stood at a reading table, looking up as we entered.

"Gilwyr. And what have you brought for me this time? A problem or an opportunity? Or both?" His voice was a deep rumble, but he did not seem displeased to see her. His eyes were deep set beneath shaggy brows. His nose canted somewhat to the left as if it had been broken at some point. His cheeks were ruddy above a black beard. Both beard and hair were worn neatly trimmed and had liberal amounts of gray sprinkled through them. He was clothed a deep green tunic, brown breeches, and a saffron-colored shirt with a plain collar. On his feet were boots of soft leather that looked well worn. His right hand bore a ring with a deep red, unfaceted gem, which reminded me of the much larger one that had been left to me and that now rode securely in an inside pocket of my coat.

She presented me. "Stenn Gremm, Professor. I met him at the Inn of the Forest on the old South Road. We were attacked there by a morghaest.

After that was settled, Stenn asked me to conduct him to a University. I think you and he may have similar interests." She turned to me. "This is Professor Greylander de Oxendon. He brought me to the University and has supervised my studies."

I made a slight bow and offered my hand in greeting. De Oxendon looked at my outstretched hand for a moment, then slowly reached out and enfolded it in one of his own. This world seemed to have more than its share of massive people, but Gilwyr's mentor loomed mountainous over lesser men. I was starting to be conscious of my somewhat slight stature by this world's standards.

"I am pleased to make your acquaintance, Stenn Gremm. You are interested in the University then. If you are a scholar, then you're certainly welcome here." His gaze shifted to Gilwyr. "But I think you leave much out of your brief tale, my dear. No one else I know would say calmly that they 'settled' a morghaest. What could have attracted its attention? None have been seen for many years. What awakened one now? Did you outrun its pursuit? They are relentless, you know. If one has awakened, it is only a matter of time before it arrives here. We must make the city ready if this is so."

"We had no choice but to engage in battle with it. I wounded it with my swords, and then when it touched Stenn, it crumbled back into dust. It may have gotten what it wanted, and had no need to pursue us."

"Morghaests are drawn to what they desire most. This thing it wanted, was it yours?" De Oxendon was looking back at me.

"Err ... Yes, I believe it was after some instruments I had with me."

"Hmm. I see." The mountain brooded for a moment. Then, "Gilwyr, go tell the Steward to prepare a chamber for our guest. Then ask the kitchens for a midday meal for the three of us."

"We already ate in town before coming up here," she replied.

"Indeed? Then I would be grateful if you would bring me some bread and cheese. From the angle of the sun, I seem to have missed lunch again."

Gilwyr departed, appearing somewhat miffed at being sent on errands, but de Oxendon was clearly not someone she argued with. I couldn't imagine anyone arguing with him.

De Oxendon regarded me for a bit. "You come from far away?" he rumbled at me eventually.

"Yes, it took me months to get here." I started to feel uneasy. I didn't know how well these people had mapped their world. If I made up a name would he accept it or tell me that there was no such place? I recognized that I could not bluff this man. The city may have been pre-industrial and the University still pre-technological, but it would be an error to believe the minds within were not as sharp as my own.

"You came by ship?"

"Yes, by ship …"

"Yet you were in the middle of a forest."

"My ship was wrecked. I walked from there, looking for settlements." That much at least was literal truth.

He watched me for a few moments and then said, "I know of no one who has sailed past the Outer Islands; they are always pushed back by the trade winds. There are tales of another great land far beyond the Outer Islands, but I have assumed that it is either fictitious or uninhabited. What is the name of your homeland?"

"Uh, Trondhjem."

"A strange name. It has an uncouth sound if you'll forgive my saying so. Yet you speak the language of the Dalactyn court, albeit with an odd accent. You offered to clasp hands in an archaic form of greeting, while a Dalactyn noble would have raised his fist to heart in salute. The Anglich commoners touch their fingers to their foreheads in greeting. In no other part of this land is the ancient hand clasp a common greeting, as far as I am aware. And you tell me that you come from so far away that it might almost be easier to fly to Rhea."

Should I admit to coming from Rhea? He might believe it at this stage in this culture's development. I am a poor liar, probably because I despise any distortion of the truth. I didn't want to fail this interview the way I had nearly failed my first encounter at the Inn of the Forest. *The best lies tell the truth and leave out the important part,* counseled an inner voice. Again, I seemed to hear it as the voice of the Other. So I said only, "All that is true. My land has some skill in building ships that can make long journeys. I am a wandering scholar who traveled here on such a ship. I came because my life's study is how societies change and evolve and we know little of your land. If I could stay here a while to learn of your arts, and customs, and languages, I would be very grateful."

De Oxendon ruminated within his beard for a few moments. Then, "I have some affinity to wandering scholars. You are welcome to remain here as long as you abide by the laws and customs of this University. I would caution you to say nothing of your origin for now; perhaps explain your accent by saying you came from Okko Island, which is a perilous journey in itself. Ah, Gilwyr is returning."

De Oxendon must have had acute hearing. To my ears, Gilwyr didn't make a sound, even as she entered the room. She was carrying a basket that held a loaf of bread, a wedge of cheese, a sausage, and a flagon of ale. De Oxendon raised his eyebrows. "I thought you said that you two have already eaten?"

"We have, this is all for you. You are so absent-minded that I wouldn't want to come back next time and find less of you. I know I have seen you eat three times this much at a single sitting."

"I seem to manage well enough when you are not here to fuss over me," he grumbled. He took the basket and stacked some books higher to clear a bit of space for his repast. He rummaged through artifacts on a side table, moving aside various carvings, pottery, glassware, and the skull of a creature that had three eye sockets. He finally uncovered a large dagger, with which he proceeded to saw a hunk from the loaf and carve slices of cheese and sausage.

Gilwyr sniffed. "That's a fine use for a *cray-jon*. That was a gift from the Blade of the Cray Leth to you."

"I'm hardly going to kill anyone with it, now am I? Is it better to put it on a shelf to gather dust, or put it to use?" he replied.

I couldn't tell whether Gilwyr was genuinely indignant, or whether they were just bantering. I was mainly trying not to think about how encrusted with old food it had been before he had employed it. That would lead into even more disquieting thoughts about how my previous meals had been prepared.

"Did you see to a chamber for our guest?"

"Yes, I asked the Steward for a room for a visiting scholar, he has one for twelve coppers per night."

De Oxendon drank noisily from his flagon. Wiping his mouth, he commented, "That's higher than I remember." To me, "What do you usually charge for your services?"

"I beg your pardon? I don't follow you."

"At your own University, what services do you render, and what do you charge for them? Do you do translations? Replicas? Political consultations?"

"I simply teach and publish papers."

"That's all? How do you support your University?"

"I don't. The University supports me to teach and publish papers."

De Oxendon laughed. "More than anything that says you are from a distant land! What an outlandish idea! Here everyone provides some service for hire and pays the University for room and board and materials. So what service can you provide that someone would pay you for?"

I thought furiously. I couldn't think of any skills that anyone on this world would pay for. Translation services for any languages that I knew other than Galactic would be non-existent. My political advice would be worth nothing until I learned the local politics. Analysis of ancient cultures was not likely to be a paying proposition. I wouldn't be able to do bookkeeping or finance without my simspace avatars to support me. I shook my head. "I'll have to think on that. I can't think of anything I can do that would be of value here."

De Oxendon looked grave. "That presents a problem. The University is quite strict on this. It does not even allow one scholar to support another; all income must be from outside the University. Even students must pay to study here, even if they begin by washing dishes, which pays barely enough for a student's cot in the dormitories."

Gilwyr spoke up suddenly. "There is one exception that you are forgetting. A full guild member can take on and support an apprentice who is learning the craft. That apprentice can engage in studies for as long as his apprenticeship lasts."

"True, but I don't know who would be willing to take on an apprentice at this time ..."

"I will take Stenn as my apprentice. I am a full member of my guild and can claim this privilege. My guild income is easily enough to support an apprentice if I wish. As my apprentice, he can sleep on a pallet in my chamber and eat at my table. Will this be satisfactory?"

De Oxendon nodded gravely. "It will work if Stenn is agreeable." He turned to me. "Stenn, it will not be a station you are accustomed to, but no one will pay an apprentice any attention. It might work for the best for you. All things considered."

This was moving too fast. I was befuddled by the upended funding model, but grateful for Gilwyr's apparent generosity. "I believe that would be satisfactory," I managed.

"Good. Go and show your new apprentice around, Gilwyr. I will see you later."

As we retraced our steps to the main hall, I asked Gilwyr, "You never mentioned that you were a guild member. What trade are you master of?"

"You agreed without knowing that? I will have to knock some of that trust out of you if I am not to have a dead apprentice. I am an assassin."

CHAPTER 11

Apprentice

FOR THE REST of the afternoon, Gilwyr introduced me to the University. The libraries were vast caverns of books. Treadle-operated printing presses laboriously made new ones, one page at a time. Leatherworks and binderies made them whole. Scholars in their chambers wrote with quill pens in longhand, making sure that the printers always had a backlog. Students carried books about or sat reading them wherever there was sufficient light. The activities that I saw all around made scholarship palpable in a way I had never felt before. I wanted to handle these leather-bound volumes and savor the reading of text that stood on its own, not covered with annotations and cross-references and marks of what others thought important. If I ever made it back to Trondhjem, I resolved to create a new simspace for my lectures to capture the atmosphere of this University. It wasn't until days later that the absurdity of that idea penetrated.

Supper came early, but sundown came earlier. The planet had an axial tilt of fewer than five degrees, leading to little seasonal variation in climate; days and nights were of nearly equal length. The dining hall was already illuminated by a pair of chandeliers when we arrived, each with a score of candles lit and flickering. Additional sconces around the room threw angled light across the tables. Darkness ebbed and flowed unquietly in the corners. Multiple shadows attached to every person and object, shifting and following, the ghosts of scholars long past still coming to dine with the living.

For all the dimness, the corridors were blacker yet. From these tunnels, the inhabitants emerged. Students and apprentices carried candles before their masters so that each appeared to arrive in a bubble of light, like an eldritch carriage. Gilwyr lit no candle but walked steadily in the dark, an unobtrusive touch upon my elbow to keep me from tripping and embarrassing us. We moved to a place at one of the tables and remained standing.

When everyone had gathered, four figures emerged from four corridors, each carrying his or her own candle. Greylander de Oxendon was one of them. Another was a cadaverous figure in deep black robes with a white belt. The third was a tall woman, face still beautiful despite the years that she had undeniably seen. The fourth was short, as ugly as a bulldog, with a military air about him.

These four moved to their places among the tables and seated themselves. Immediately, the masters moved to take their seats as well, and their students placed the candles they had carried on the tables in front of their masters. The students then proceeded to their own seats, obeying some order of precedence that I couldn't immediately discern. Gilwyr had seated herself ambiguously, somewhere between the last of the masters and the first of the students. I stood behind her seat until she unobtrusively raised a finger to signal me to seat myself at the foot of the table. I was the last to sit down. Of course, this drew attention to me.

I received frank appraisals from the other denizens of the lower table. I was not only new, I was unusual. The others were young, many probably teenagers. People of my age sat further up the table. Despite my new set of clothes, I still felt out of place, an artist's conception of a dweller in this time and place, realistic and patently false at the same time. My clothes were too new, the cut of my hair too unfamiliar, my skin too pale. There were probably dozens of signs, mannerisms, and expressions, some too small to notice on their own, but adding up on the whole to: foreigner, outsider. Then the conversation started, and it was no longer appearance alone that was going to get me singled out.

"Saw, yer hail fer the coast aways, aye? Live in ter fog, ye do?"

My inquisitor was a friendly-faced young man across the table. He spoke the dialect I had heard in town, derived from ancient English, but with pronunciation drift rendering over half the words unintelligible to me. Gilwyr had called it Anglich. If I had my simspace adjuncts, I could estimate the age of this colony by the amount of linguistic drift that had accumulated. As it was, simple communication was going to be a challenge.

"Yes, aye, I from very far have come. I speak not much this speech yet. Do you know this language?" The last I spoke in Galactic.

"You are Dalactyn?" The others nearby looked surprised, suddenly guarded.

"No, Okko Island to the north. We split from Dalactus over a hundred and fifty years ago, but our language remains similar." Gilwyr had agreed that was a good story to explain my strange accent, and she had filled in some additional detail. She told me that it also avoided any hint that I had allegiance to Dalactus. It appeared that they weren't on good terms with the people of Misthaven.

"I am Elias, a student of alchemy under Dame Whyte. Fortunately, we have to learn Dalactyn because many of our texts are written in that language. What is your name?"

"I am Stenn. I am a student of languages and cultures. Gilwyr took me as an apprentice so that I could study here for a time."

"Gilwyr? Well, strange begets stranger, they say. She was barely human when Ox brought her here. Grew up among faery folk, she did. Some say she learned the sword and the knife from them, and I can believe it. She didn't have to train any time at all to best all the weapons masters in the University. She even keeps a fey name, doesn't care to take a real name." He stopped to translate to the others who were listening. An uproar immediately broke forth, mostly in Anglich.

"Prentiss w' Gilwyr? Dead man!"

"Can ah hae yer nice shirt when yer not need'n it?"

"Nae, twill be full o holes!"

"She want to teach ye th' knife, or she want yer sword in her bed? Either way, ye'll be losin' yer balls soon!"

That last was met with gales of bawdy laughter. I glanced over to where Gilwyr sat, but she was paying no attention. She was reading a folded note while a messenger stood waiting by her chair. She frowned, then tucked the note away and dismissed the messenger with a word. She seemed preoccupied and directed no attention at the commotion surrounding me.

I was growing nettled by the insinuations by the students, both about Gilwyr and my chances of surviving being her apprentice. I pretended I was an actor in a simspace drama. It was time for a roguish remark to let them know I wouldn't be ruffled. "My first day in your land I killed a morghaest. I think I can handle Gilwyr."

Silence fell, abrupt and aghast. Several made signs that were evidently wards against evil. Some muttered ritual responses; I made out the names of Polnedra and Rhea in them, and then, quite clearly: *Grimmerroth.*

Elias was looking at me in astonishment. "You saw a morghaest?"

"Yes, I did."

"And you *lived?*"

"The evidence favors it."

"You *killed* it?"

Perhaps that had not been the most strategic thing to say if I were to be an invisible student, unseen and unheard. "Well, that's where I met Gilwyr. She helped."

"Hah. Helped a *lot,* I wager. If anyone alive could kill a morghaest, my money would be on her."

I protested weakly that I had done my share in the encounter, which helped cement the certainty in their minds that I had cowered behind a table while Gilwyr did the morghaest slaying. I felt smugly pleased in my skill in deflecting their interest. Nothing to see here, just an empty braggart.

A brawny boy was moving down the table with an iron pot that might have doubled as ordnance in the days of castle sieges. A slighter shadow followed him with a ladle, dipping a portion from the pot for each person in turn. I could see that I was going to be low man in this respect as well; I hoped there would be something left when they got to me.

It was then that I noticed the wave working its way up the table. A group of people would lean in to listen, expressions of disquiet would cross their faces, then they would turn to the next people upstream, who had been straining to overhear. Then they universally turned to stare at me, though with expressions varying from disbelief through fear. The thought that I had not deflected interest sufficiently began to occur.

The bearers of the food ordnance arrived. They were scraping the bottom, but there was still a ladle for me. Something resembling stew landed in the worn and scarred wooden trencher in front of me. I had not paid attention to my place setting before the food was lobbed in; I hoped it was reasonably clean, and I was not sorry that the light was too dim for me to verify my suspicion that it was otherwise. The aroma was enticing; my stomach rumbled that it had been too long since the midday meal.

"Stenn! Attend me!"

Gilwyr was standing behind my chair. She had frequently looked deadly in our short acquaintance, but never angry. Not until now. I knew I never wanted her angry at me again if I survived this.

"Stand when your Guild master addresses you!"

I stood.

"We're leaving. Come."

I wanted to protest that I hadn't eaten yet, but I wanted more to keep on living. I followed along behind her. We walked the dark corridors in silence, crossed the torchlit great hall, and down another length of inky darkness to a chamber. There she finally struck a light and touched it to candlewick. Flickering light filled the space, dazzling after the dark.

"Are you some kind of *dun-moir*?" Gilwyr demanded. So much for my hope that her anger was an act. "Where in the nine tombs of Dalactus did you get the idea to brag about seeing a morghaest, let alone slaying one? The first lesson of the apprentice assassin is never be seen, never be noticed. You just linked your name with failing that lesson for all time! Don't be like Stenn, teachers will tell the students. Be stealthy, they will say, don't fail your master like Stenn. When an apprentice fails to return from an assignment, they will say that he went with Stenn. If your own disgrace isn't enough to disgrace me as well, you dragged my name into the morghaest killing! That will attract attention that I don't need and which could endanger me! Those in power will wonder how to use a morghaest-killer as a tool, no matter whether I can do it or not. They will think they can build something forbidden if they but have someone who can defend it. Your loose talk puts us both at risk."

"I'm sorry, I didn't think ..."

"That's very clear to me."

"When it comes down to it, I'm not sure you appreciate how much of a reputation you already have ..."

"Silence!"

I had felt shame as she elaborated my failure, followed by anger in her treatment. This was carrying the role-playing too far. I had been a tenured professor for twice as many years as she had lived. I started to retort until I looked into her eyes. My anger was doused by cold fear as I understood that she could quite possibly kill me if I didn't measure up. It was in her code of conduct. It was apparently permitted by this society; there was a Guild for it, after all. It might even be demanded by her honor if my failure reflected on her. I had never before looked into another human's eyes and seen a promise of death. I hung my head in silence, chilled to the bone.

Her eyes held me like a needle holds a bug in a display case. After a moment, she gestured. "This is my chamber; that is your pallet. I have to go out on some business this evening. Stay here, don't leave this chamber, and don't speak to anyone. I will be back much later." She turned, pulled a package from a chest, and left.

I sat down at the table, that along with its two chairs, a simple bed, a rough pallet, a washbasin on a stand, and a broad chest were the entire furnishings of the chamber. I had much to think about. I watched the flame slowly consume the candle and emit useless curls of reverie into the air. Most were circular, downward spirals into themselves. Some waved indecision back and forth in passing air currents. All led back to their origin in the bright flame that was Gilwyr. All vanished in the dark air without conclusion. Hours passed with only the candle's march towards the end of its life to mark their passing. Occasional footfalls passed the door, the glow of their own dying candles briefly illuminating the crack under the door.

I didn't hear footfalls, or the latch, or the hinges, before a breeze from the open door guttered the candle. A woman stood in the doorway, dressed in a blue jacket with long, blue iridescent skirts, divided for movement. Her blouse had lace at the wrists and throat, and a plunging neckline that bared the inner half-moons of her corseted breasts to each other. Low, black lace-up boots completed her outfit.

"I ... I'm sorry, madam, you must have the wrong chamber," I stammered, hoping that she understood Galactic/Dalactyn.

"You would bar me from my own chamber now? I'm not sure if you have the wits to survive this apprenticeship."

That voice, I knew it. I had heard it in anger a few hours ago, though now it sounded more amused. I had to look twice to see that it was Gilwyr under the coiffed hair and makeup. While I was far from unaware that she was female, it had escaped me that she could undergo such a feminine transformation.

"Um, is this connected with your guild business?"

"Yes, there was a ball tonight, and a minor landholder to deal with. He was blocking the Council's plans to expand trade with the northern towns that are traditionally more aligned with Dalactus. It was felt that his son would be more receptive to signing the new agreements. I thought it would be a few more days before the Guild found out I was back in town."

"And?"

"And what?"

"Did you slip a knife in his ribs on the dance floor? Arrange an assassination in the arbor with a garrote? Arrange an accident on a high balcony?"

"All of those methods would have delivered messages. A knife would have been a political killing. A garrote would have signaled disfavor in high places, which wasn't the intent. A broken neck from a fall would have intimated a hidden enemy bent on sowing doubt and discord. In this case, it was a matter of orchestrating the timing of a succession that would have happened sooner or later. A few extra herbs in his cup of mulled wine and his heart will just stop sometime tonight. It will appear to be natural causes. No questions will be asked. And the gentlemen in question will spend his last few hours in happy anticipation of the tryst he thinks he has arranged two days hence."

Gilwyr was removing her clothes as she spoke, folding them neatly in a bundle. "I'll have to take these into town to sell them tomorrow, and buy a new set for the next formal occasion. Never show up in the same dress twice. The women remember, even if the men don't. It's good that you asked about methods, Stenn. You might have an aptitude for the Guild after all."

She was now dressed in a simple shift and was scrubbing the make-up from her face at a washbasin. She had missed my sarcasm completely. As an anthropologist, I studied cultures in their context: if assassinations were allowed by law and custom and were an integral part of the functioning of the society, then I was expected to study the belief systems that gave rise to that practice. In writing about my research, I would be required to compare and contrast that social system to similar ones that outlawed the practice. As a product of my own culture, I was horrified that this young woman could so coolly say she had just poisoned a man.

Could I carry on this charade of apprenticeship to Gilwyr? My hours of introspection in the candlesmoke whorls had yielded only soot. She had been right that I had spoken incautiously in the dining hall, with consequences I couldn't know. I knew nothing about morghaests, or the legends and prophesies that might surround them. If they destroyed technology, anyone who had a way to neutralize them would gain an edge over their neighbors. Perhaps a military edge. I would have to keep my mouth shut.

Gilwyr handed me a blanket and a flannel nightshirt. "For sleeping," she said.

I changed into the nightshirt, feeling self-conscious about being naked in front of her. There was no privacy here, and none was expected. I could hardly cavil after her casual nudity. I wrapped myself in the blanket and lay down on my pallet, which was hard and thinly stuffed with straw. Gilwyr blew out the candle, and the sounds of her climbing into bed seemed amplified by the darkness.

After a few moments of darkness, her voice came to me. "Stenn?"

"Yes?"

"I seem to have become accustomed to sleeping next to you."

"Yes?"

"Come here."

I got up in the darkness and settled down in her narrow bed with the blankets over us. I kept my back to her so she wouldn't feel my involuntary reaction that her close presence elicited. I fell asleep feeling oddly safe in the embrace of an assassin.

CHAPTER 12

Training

RAIN FELL IN the darkness. Fat drops, liquid ice. The air was biting cold as well. I tried to pull my blanket closer, but it was trying to crawl away. Didn't I sleep indoors last night? Where was I? Where was Gilwyr? She had been warming my back all night …

At that thought, the previous evening rushed back. I opened my eyes, just in time to get the entire basin of water in my face. I leaped up, only to smash back down from the blanket that malevolently entangled my feet. The sky outside had just begun to lighten, and I could see a figure standing over me against the narrow window. I shook off the stars still exploding in my head and lashed out with my feet, trying to knock the other off balance. I missed, then I felt a knife against my throat. I froze.

"An assassin sleeps lightly, or he is a dead assassin," said Gilwyr. "That is today's first lesson. Now we begin training."

"You were *serious* about this? I thought it was just a cover story."

"You cannot afford to be less than serious about it," she replied. "There is no such thing as a pretend assassin, even an apprentice. You are either serious or quickly dead."

I could have refused, but the knife at my throat convinced me otherwise. The knife also convinced me that I needed to learn some self-defense. A culture that had a guild for assassins played by different rules than mine. The nearest equivalent that I knew was a faculty committee, and their assassination methods weren't as direct. I got up and pulled off the clammy nightshirt.

"Wear just trousers and shirt. We will get more suitable clothing later."

I dressed as instructed, but hesitated at the pouch containing the gem. I stuffed it under the pillow to conceal it for now. I would find a better hiding place later.

We made our way to a door in the rear of the University. Gilwyr made it clear that we were to be silent, and that my best efforts at stealth were far short of her expectations. Once we were outside, we started out at a brisk jog and soon escalated to a steady cross-country pace. The trails descended the rear of the University precipice then ascended to the high farmland away from the river. The sky was deep blue in the east, the light just driving the last few stars from the sky.

The trail was hard-packed, the footing sure. The land began to rise, but Gilwyr didn't slacken her pace. I started to breathe heavily. The trek to Misthaven had toughened me some; I think that I would have lasted less than ten minutes at this pace before that time. I might have lasted twenty before I started flagging, though I had no timepiece to measure my torment. Still we kept going, and going, and going. I thought my lungs were going to burst.

"Gilwyr … I have to rest."

"You must have had a soft life." She wasn't even breathing heavily.

"Compared to you … I'm sure … I did … I'm also … three times your age."

She stopped so abruptly that I collided with her on the trail. "Are you saying you think me but nine years old?"

It took me a few moments to catch my breath enough to answer. "No, I think you're in your mid-twenties."

"Are you jesting again? You would have one foot in the grave if you were that old. Perhaps both feet."

"I assure you I am not. Where I come from, we have medicines that slow aging. My people routinely live to be two hundred years old."

"And now that you are here?"

"Without those treatments … I'll age as quickly as you do." That hadn't occurred to me yet. If this planet didn't kill me outright, I could look forward to a short, cold old age full of chamber pots and ever-dimming candlelight.

"Make no excuses. You look like a man of twenty and eight, you will train like one. Today we will turn back here. Tomorrow we will go half again as far. You have more left in you than you think."

She turned to go back downhill. I had at least regained my breath with the brief pause. As I stood straight again, the rocks seemed to swirl in front of me. I wiped the sweat from my eyes and looked again. Nothing. Perhaps a wave of dizziness. I got my feet into motion once more, following Gilwyr. She was right; I did have more in me.

The eastern sky was brightening. The sun would rise in moments. I could see that the valley below the University was fog-filled, covering most of the town. The University was an outcropping on one of the twin hills rising above the town; the other was higher and was capped by an even more massive structure. The castle of the Lord Mayor and his Council, Gilwyr had told me. Was that where she had gone to the ball last night? Had she spoken with her victim, the landowner, before she had poisoned him? Had she flirted, to get close to him? Had she danced with him? Shared a glass of wine? And had anyone discovered his now cold body this morning? Were any mourning him yet? Was the young heir being awakened to be told of his new responsibilities? Was it just business as usual for this world?

We arrived at the back gates of the University just as the sun was turning the edges of the fog to molten silver. We entered a small courtyard, which a central sparring post and various straw targets declared as a place to practice the arts martial. My legs were rubbery from the extended run, and I suspected I was going to have an additional hurdle of stiffness to surmount on my second morning of training.

A wooden sword came flying through the air towards me. I managed to catch it, though I jammed the index finger of my left hand in doing so. Gilwyr demonstrated the stance I was to take, and I commenced hacking on the post. She didn't show too much concern with accuracy or form, leading me to assume that she just wanted my arms as sore and rubbery as my legs. That made a kind of sense; I wouldn't have the strength to achieve any accuracy until I had built up some muscles that simspace anthropologists have little need for.

As I hacked, the sweat poured into my eyes, burning despite repeated attempts to wipe it away on my sleeve between slashes. The courtyard wavered and blurred, and I again thought that I saw ripples in the stone. I did see an enormous form emerge from a doorway to converse with Gilwyr. From the size, I guessed that it was Greylander de Oxendon. Gilwyr allowed no slacking, however, waving me to continue my attack on the defenseless post.

I had entered a zone of exhaustion where everything was happening in slow motion when I heard a commotion approaching. The first sound was a dull thud, as of a distant underground detonation, coming from the direction of the rear gate. Gilwyr and de Oxendon broke off their conversation and looked around, confirming that the sound was as unusual as it seemed. There were a series of loud clanks as if an angry blacksmith were starting his forge. When a rising scream sliced the air and was as suddenly cut off, we moved as one towards the courtyard door.

A cannonball punched through the door, splintering it far and wide. I threw my arm in front of my face and felt the sting of a dozen flying daggers of wood. The cannonball hit the ground ten meters from us, growing a dozen legs as it did so, and ran-rolled towards us. I was the first to engage it, not for reasons of speed or courage, but because it headed directly for me. The creature launched itself into the air, lengthening into a gnomelike figure. I took a half step back to get my stance and swung my practice sword as I had swung at the post, a marionette programmed to hack. I connected with a blow that numbed my arm to the shoulder. I deflected the nightmare thing and sliced off some of its legs.

Gilwyr reversed her practice sword and drove it two-handed down through the center of the creature. It quivered for a moment with the wooden sword protruding from its body, then it convulsed, shattering the sword into splinters. Gilwyr was still standing over the creature as it spun and struck upwards. Gilwyr was knocked through the air, landing on her shoulder a dozen paces away.

De Oxendon was a few steps behind, having stopped to snatch a cudgel from the weapons racks. He struck the creature with a force that sent it skidding across the practice yard, snapping the shaft of the cudgel in two. The thing regained its feet and launched itself at me again with a singleness of purpose, extending taloned hands that reached for my face.

In slow motion, we collided. I could feel gritty-sandy claws reaching for my eyes. Then time skipped, and I was on the ground with a white-hot poker through my left eye. Suddenly my assailant was gone. I clasped my hands over the agony that had been my left eye. Seemingly a thousand years later, bits of conversation drifted through my anguish.

"What *was* that?" Gilwyr.

"A watchbreaker. A small morghaest; attacks small mechanisms." De Oxendon's rumble.

"Rhea help him, look at his eye!" Was that anguish in her voice?

"There's something still in it. Quickly, take him to your quarters."

I felt her attempt to lift me and fail. "I can't," she said.

"Your shoulder?"

"I landed on it."

"What is wrong … ah. You have dislocated it. I must straighten it for you. Be strong."

I heard Gilwyr cry out, a short, sharp sound driven by pain and cut off by force of will.

Now I am lifted and borne through the corridors. The journey is the journey to hell, an eternity in itself. Time no longer passes; there is no past and no future, only an unending present. Each step drives pain farther into my eye socket; I have the awful feeling that something is crawling inside, searching. De Oxendon has me slung across his shoulders, in a position that is pulling my right shoulder painfully. Eternity ends, and I am deposited into the bed I had left just a short time before.

I felt a wet cloth against my face, a drop of cool water for a raging inferno. I thrashed. I heard the door open again, and de Oxendon's voice. "I have tools. We must try to remove it."

Gilwyr swept the pillow aside. The pouch I had hidden underneath rolled free, the gem spilling out onto the bed. The gem was a blaze of red light in the dim room. I seized it and found it cold, pulsing, and somehow comforting. I clung to it. The thought that the cold might soothe the fire in my eye came to me out of the chaos. I held the icy cold gem to my eye, against the intruder I could feel lodged there.

A red supernova occurred in my eye socket, and pain hammered me down into unconsciousness.

The River Lethe flows into the River Styx; I was borne on a bobbing cockle poled by a morghaest who called himself Charon, who demanded a coin for the passage. I asked how long the crossing would take. Charon laughed and said that there was no time in the underworld. He poled the dark waters, and we sailed the dark ruin of my eye. Each time he dipped his pole it stabbed my eye afresh and left whorls of agony behind. Time indeed did not seem to be passing, since the darkness was without end. It came to me that I was sailing in a cockle in my own eye, which introduced an infinite regression of eyes within cockles within eyes, and this was why time was not passing. It was dream logic, but it was my first purchase on rationality to claw my way back to waking.

I opened my right eye to see Gilwyr sitting beside my bed, and the bulk of de Oxendon pacing behind her. Gilwyr was holding her left arm cradled by her right. I heard the exclamation, "He's awake!" and the sounds of de Oxendon crossing the room.

"What happened?" I attempted but only croaked. Water was held to my mouth, which I sipped and dribbled and choked on before I got tongue and throat to function again. I succeeded in my utterance the second time.

"A watchbreaker," said de Oxendon. "Do you have any small machines that they would have attacked?"

"Implants. Tiny machines in my eyes and ears. They don't work here. Unnngh!" Charon stuck his pole in my eye again, deeper.

"By the child god, you were lucky the watchbreaker didn't kill you. Where did you get this red gem?" He was holding the gem in one hand, inspecting it carefully.

Anxiety jolted me, seeing it in another's hands. I started to reach for it but pain and weakness hammered me back down. "Ancestor left it for me ... very old. Think it came from here ... this world. Do you know it?"

"As far as what it is, I wish to consult some old lore before I venture a guess. In the end, you may have to go ask the ... Gilwyr's people ... for an answer."

"There is something still in my eye. Can you get it out?"

"A small remnant of the watchbreaker was embedded there. When you touched it with the gem, the remnant was ... changed. It's not as it was, and I cannot remove it."

"It still hurts like hell. What is it?"

Gilwyr handed me a small mirror, as large as the palm of my hand. It was large enough to see that my left eye was entirely gone, and the socket was filled by a faceted crystal the same deep crimson as the gem itself.

The River Lethe took me once again and pulled me under.

CHAPTER 13

A blind eye

WHEN I OPENED my eyes … Opened my eyes. The phrase came so naturally. Only one opened, only one would ever open now. How long until I schooled myself to the singular? Both eyes open: a phrase denoting clear-sightedness. Turn a blind eye: overlook some detail that should be noticed. On a civilized world, I could have a new eye grown, but here, this had a leaden permanence.

My vision was blurred as if my right eye didn't know how to focus without its companion. The bridge of my nose was a prominent obstacle blocking my view of everything on my left. Figures moved, indistinct as though seen through gauze. One was slender, one massive. Voices discussed me, one contralto feminine, one rumbly masculine. Words were said about my waking. I croaked an affirmation. Memories flew out of the darkness like an issuance of bats: dim light, hushed voices, and a bitter medicine that made the world go away. Hands helped me to hold my head up enough to sip some thin wine. That set off a round of coughing but cleared my throat sufficiently to form a few words.

"Can I skip training today?"

I heard an unfamiliar sound. After a few seconds, I identified it as Gilwyr, laughing. "You have already missed three days, you want to miss another? Never have I seen an apprentice so unmotivated."

"Three days?"

"Yes, we have been giving you *yarnow* root to keep you asleep, until you healed enough to bear the pain."

"It seems to have worked. Now it's only a sharp knife being driven into my eye." And *yarnow* root was probably why I was feeling punchy about the whole thing. I was nearly euphoric that I was still alive.

"We were prepared to give you more *yarnow* root if you awoke screaming again."

"I did that, did I?"

"Oh, yes. Several times."

"Humph. The boatman on the River Styx seems to have taken a holiday." Their blank faces at my attempted flippancy said I was probably still semi-delirious. "Let me see that mirror again."

They produced the mirror, which I now saw was of polished metal, somewhat tarnished around the edges. I held it up to my left eye, which yielded less than useful results, then fumbled to find an angle where my right eye could get a good view of the left. The eye socket had suffered some damage, but the bones didn't appear to have fractured. A red crystal entirely replaced my eyeball. The red was the same as the large gem that Jonan Gremm had left me, but while that was smoothly round and filled with interior channels, this was faceted on the surface and had no features visible in the interior. My eyelid could not close over the gem; even if it could, it would probably be painful without the lubrication of a natural eyeball. Whether my eyeball had been squished out by this intruder or had somehow been turned into crystal, I didn't really want to know.

"That doesn't look like it will be easy to remove," I said.

"It is not," said de Oxendon. "I have some skill as a field surgeon. On the first day, I tried to remove it, but it has taken root quite solidly. I did not want to cause you any additional trauma, and it seems completely inert; I thought it better to leave it. Here, we have made this for you." He proffered a leather eye patch with a pair of straps, one at the top and one at the bottom. I accepted it and held it in place with one hand while awkwardly failing to tie the strap with the other. Gilwyr reached behind me and tied both straps snuggly. With the straps fastened, the patch fit closely over my eye with no danger of flipping up or slipping off. I checked the mirror.

"I look like some kind of brigand now."

"An eye patch will get you noticed," acknowledged de Oxendon.

"Not a good thing for an assassin," put in Gilwyr.

"But not noticed as much as a gem for an eye would be," he continued. "That would incite talk of you being a warlock or a creature of the Grimmerroth. People would either fear you or try to use you. If you want to remain free, do not let anyone know what is beneath the patch. And for Rhea's sake, do not let anyone know that a morghaest attacked you within these walls. If that were to be known, you would be exiled to protect the city."

"What can you tell me of these morghaests?" I asked de Oxendon. "Gilwyr told me that they were made out of dust and sand, but that seems impossible. I've never heard of anything like them. Are they alive?"

"They are said to be the Grimmerroth's attempts to shape creatures from the earth and breathe life into them, as it is said that the child god, Polnedra, created the creatures of the earth, including the Grimmerroth himself. His imitations are without mind or speech, capable only of destruction."

"Gilwyr told me the story of Polnedra and the Grimmerroth as we traveled. That was a legend, but these morghaests are real."

"Ah, you've heard the story; that makes the explanations a bit easier. Throughout history, evil people have been said to be touched by the Grimmerroth. Especially evil people have been called the re-incarnation of the Grimmerroth. Four hundred years ago, a wizard appeared in the Moaning Hills, in the southern desert. He built a citadel from stone, seemingly overnight, and a sickness lay upon that place so that any who approached withered and died. He was a grotesque figure, garbed in black, with only a mirrored blackness in place of his face. This wizard created the morghaests as his soldiers. Before him, they were a legend but never seen. They may have existed in the distant past before records were kept and the wizard only revived them. In the minds of everyone, the Grimmerroth had returned. It fit too well with the ancient legends to be otherwise."

"You still haven't told me what a morghaest *is*. I don't believe in evil spirits or undead soldiers, or magic in general. There must be some rational explanation for them."

"Rational explanations, meaning ones that fit with your knowledge of the world? This is a different land than yours, Stenn, and you may need different knowledge to understand how it works. It is an article of faith among many that morghaests are the grotesque creations of an ancient creature in imitation of the child-god who created him. Be circumspect in challenging that faith."

"But what are they? Has anyone tried to figure out what they're composed of and how they move?"

Gilwyr answered. "Morghaests are made out of sand, rock, soil, clay, or whatever is available. The spirit of the Grimmerroth animates them when Polnedra's creations overreach and create things they should not have. The morghaests remove creations that the gods have forbidden to men. When their work is complete, they disappear back into the earth."

"That's not how the world works," I said, frustrated at the gulf that separated our thinking. Animist religions often replaced science during dark ages between civilizations. I had studied these systems of thought as an anthropologist; I never expected to find myself immersed in one. To these people, the answer "because the gods willed it" was sufficient answer to both "why?" and "how?"

"You may tell that to the next morghaest that rises up against you. I'll wait to hear your story of how you made it give up and crumble back to earth with your cry of 'You're impossible!' I fear I may wait a long time for that story."

"I'll get you a story, but probably not that one. I'm ready to get out of bed now. I think I have some training to catch up on."

Gilwyr exchanged glances with de Oxendon. Was that concern on her face? It wasn't an expression that visited her very often. "I don't know if you're ready to get up yet," she said. "You were injured quite seriously. Perhaps you should rest more."

"No, the sooner I stand, the sooner I can start training, and start studying. If I'm going to be stuck here in Middle Earth, I'm going to meet it on my terms. I'm going to learn how to defend myself, and I'm going to rip the answers I need from the dusty scrolls of this old library. If the answers aren't there, then I'm going to pin a morghaest down and teach it how to sing."

This may have been a sudden burst of bravado, but I felt ready to take on the world. A small voice told me that I was definitely on a drug-induced high. At that moment, though, I saw in narcotic clarity that I had only felt fully alive when I had seized the day. When I had passed through the (virtual) gates of Trondhjem University for the first time as a student. When I had bucked my advisory committee and defended a contrarian thesis to win my teaching post. When I threw over that post to set out on this voyage to find an ancestor and find something that no one had before. There was a mystery here, a life-threatening mystery, and I was ready to tackle it—if only someone would help me to my feet first.

Gilwyr had a mixture of respect and puzzlement on her face. "I approve of your resolve, if not your wisdom. But what is Middle Earth?"

I laughed. "A land from a very old story. I will tell it to you sometime, as much of it as I remember. Now help me up."

My body was weaker than my resolve. I barely had the strength to stand, then eventually to walk around the room. I washed the worst of the stench off and used the chamber pot. I didn't want to think about what these people had gone through to take care of those matters while I was senseless. Stubbornness got me that far, but then my legs gave out and I was helped back into bed.

"Some food might help restore his strength," said de Oxendon. "I can sit with him, if you would be so kind as to get something from the kitchen, Gilwyr. It's well past the evening meal, but they should still have something laid out."

"I suppose you wouldn't take it amiss if I brought back something for you as well?" said Gilwyr archly.

"I wouldn't, at that," he beamed. Gilwyr went obediently on her errand, seeming somewhat subdued.

Once she was gone, de Oxendon turned to me. "Gilwyr is hiding it, but she is taking your injury very personally."

"Is it some code of honor, Professor?"

"Please, I left titles behind when I left Dalactus. My students call me Greylander. We fought side by side in the courtyard, and you struck the first blow. You may call me Ox, as Gilwyr does."

"I am honored, Ox. What of Gilwyr?"

"She had already assumed the role of your protector when you met her at the Inn. It is doubly so now that you are her apprentice. She is sworn to protect you, and she was unable to do so. Among those who raised her, that is a sacred trust."

"She said she is Cray Leth. Are those the people who raised her?" And the students had said she was raised by faery folks, which made no sense.

"She told you that, did she? Well, that's ..." he trailed off, absently twisting the ring on his finger. After a moment, he shook himself and seemed to continue, but it was a different thought. "You know she was injured, don't you?"

"I don't follow you. She was injured by the Cray Leth?" Ox had veered off

"What? No! Three days ago, when the morghaest attacked, she tried to defend you. She dislocated her shoulder, and I had to set it for her. I only found out later that she also broke her collarbone. I wanted you to know that she did all she could for you."

The memory of the fight came back, seeing her thrown through the air to land on her shoulder. I winced. "She seemed normal just now."

"It still pains her, but she won't let you see it. Please keep an eye on her. She is unused to failure and may need some good counsel to help her believe in herself again."

"I don't consider it failure to get knocked around by something much stronger than we are. We're all still alive, aren't we?"

"You will find that she has a higher ideal."

I had to smile at that. "I can well imagine that she does."

"Before I go, can you tell me what you did to stop the morghaest?"

"What I did? I was under the impression that you beat it off."

"I assure you that we did not. We heard you call out a word, and your attacker crumbled back to dust."

"I did? What did I say?"

"I cannot tell you. It was not in a language that I know."

I shook my head. "I haven't a clue. I don't remember anything but the pain. Perhaps it had gotten what it came for?"

"According to the lore, they never stop. Once awakened they keep coming until no one is left standing."

We heard the sound of Gilwyr returning, and by silent mutual agreement, we let the topic lapse. Gilwyr was accompanied by a kitchen boy bearing a platter with some cold cooked potatoes, a rind of cheese, and a pot of pickles. Ox took his leave after partaking fairly lightly in the repast, considering his size. I ate hesitantly at first, then ravenously after my body recognized how long it had been without sustenance. Gilwyr toyed with a few pieces of food, picking them up and then putting them down again without ever quite getting around to putting one in her mouth. I wondered how to broach the topic that Ox had burdened me with. As I so often did, I tried out different conversational openings in my mind and played out how she might react to each one. As I so often did, I ended up never managing to say any of them.

Gilwyr ended up breaking the awkward silence. "Stenn ..."

"Yes?"

"I cannot continue your apprenticeship."

"What? Why?" This was not one of the conversations I had rehearsed.

"I failed to protect you. You were injured on your first day of training because I was careless. I was not ready to take on an apprentice. I must return to my people, ask their forgiveness, and submit to more training if they judge me fit."

"Do you know anyone who could have done a better job?"

"That is beside the point. It was my job to do, and I did not."

"Under Guild rules, can an apprenticeship agreement be broken?"

"An apprentice can be dismissed if found to be unsuitable by the master."

"Did you find my performance unsuitable?"

"No ... you did as well as any apprentice would have done."

"Can I break the agreement?"

"No, the agreement is binding on both parties."

"Then is what you are proposing honorable?"

She lowered her eyes. "No, it is not. But failing you is less honorable."

"How long do you think I will last without you? Do you think I would have made it this far on my own? I thought I could when I first came to your land, but it's stranger and more dangerous than I knew. You didn't fail me when something stronger and faster than you got past you. I escaped with my life because we all worked together. But you would fail me if you abandoned me now. I know you won't because you'll see that I'm right once you have time to think about it."

I put my hands on her shoulders for emphasis as I said this. She turned her face from me to cover up her wince, but not before I saw it. "You're injured."

"It's nothing."

"It isn't nothing if you did it helping me."

I unlaced her shirt and pulled the collar aside. Her entire left shoulder was an angry bruise, and the line of her collarbone had a little jag on that side. "Do you have a long strip of cloth?" I asked her.

She found some linen in her trunk. I helped her get her shirt over her head. She wasn't able to raise her left arm above shoulder level, so this took some maneuvering. I bound the linen in a loop over the shoulder and around her body under the armpits. After a little experimentation, I found an arrangement that kept pressure on the shoulder to encourage the bones to stay aligned. She moved her arm experimentally and was now able to lift it above her head.

"That's much better. Thank you, Stenn."

"Why didn't Ox do that for you?"

"He wanted to, but I wouldn't let him."

I had arisen from the bed to bind her shoulder, but now felt a wave of fatigue wash over me. I sat down heavily. Gilwyr pushed me down and told me to sleep. She slid in beside me, still shirtless. We had to shift positions several times before finding one that she could tolerate on her shoulder. Her warmth and her scent close to me made me feel safe, and sleep swiftly closed around me. As it did, I heard her say from the darkness, "I won't fail you."

CHAPTER 14

Library

THE FOLLOWING MORNING my strength was returning, and my resolve was ... pretty good. The narcotic high had worn off, but I still felt the same way about my training and my studies. I awoke when Gilwyr stirred, which was a good while before the sun itself had arisen. We did some light exercise in the courtyard while the sky began to flood with the deep blue that was not yet quite dawn. Gilwyr favored and protected her injured shoulder, while I relearned balance and navigation with only a single eye. As we finished, I could tell that she was stiffening up. I suggested that she put some ice on her shoulder to reduce the swelling. Her expression said that it was the most outlandish suggestion that she had ever heard. I supposed that they had no ready way of making ice at the level of technology that they had.

After we dressed, Ox took me to the library. The librarian had lived among his books so long that the leather had seeped into his skin until it was as dark and wizened as an old binding. His thinning hair hung long and lank from the fringes of a polished dome. He hugged the books he was carrying to his chest protectively, guarding them from the touch of those who might read them and in so doing, smudge or wrinkle them. He was introduced to me as Andr Auclerc. I thought there couldn't have been a more clichéd match to the job of medieval librarian.

"I am pleased to make your acquaintance," said Auclerc in a cultured baritone, touching two fingers to his forehead in the Misthaven style of greeting.

"Pleased I am to make as well," I got out. The word order of Anglich was still tripping me up. Did I manage to leave the object out of that sentence?

"Are you Dalactyn, then?" Auclerc asked, switching smoothly into that language.

"No, I'm not, but that is the language we speak as well," I replied.

"I'll be happy to give you some tutoring in Anglich while you're here. You'll need more fluency to read the source materials you're looking for, and some of them are in quite ancient dialects."

"I might have more facility with ancient Anglich than I do with modern. I've studied it extensively over many years."

Auclerc snorted. "Did your nanny read Old Anglich stories to you in your crib?" Oops, I had forgotten that I didn't look that old by their standards. He disappeared into a small room behind his writing table and returned with an ancient volume that he put in front of me. The pages were brittle with age, and I cringed at his handling of the volume. "Read this," he commanded.

It was handwritten, but fortunately in a clear, neat hand. I translated into Galactic/Dalactyn as I read. "On the sixty-seventh sun ... hmm, sixty-seventh day that would be ... of our walk ... travel ... probably journey is closest, we came at last to a place of shelter ... a sheltered place ... with clear water coming from subterranean ... underground springs. We hope the water will be not spoiled ... not ... ah, uncontaminated, as all of the surface streams that we have come upon are hopelessly ... er, I'm not sure how to translate that word ..." I skidded to a halt as I realized what this text contained.

"Stop!"

I looked up. Auclerc was highly agitated, mouth gaping like a beached carp. Ox wore an expression of intense interest, though he did not seem as upset as the librarian.

Auclerc gasped a few times until I began to fear that he would expire if someone didn't throw him back in the pond. "But ... no one ... No one has been able to read this," he finally got out. "Half the characters are no longer used, and we can only guess at their intended sound, and a number of the words are ones we cannot translate."

Ox intervened smoothly. "Stenn comes from a small settlement north of Okko Island in the Eastern Sea. They have been isolated for centuries, and have kept alive some knowledge of the older languages."

"That would explain the strong accent in your Dalactyn as well. For how many centuries have your people been cut off from the mainland? It may shed some light on the mystery of the origin of the Dalactyn language. Is Stenn your family name?"

"No, my family name is Gremm."

"Rhem?"

"It is spelled G R E M M, but the G has become nearly silent over the years. Now it only causes the R to assume a fricative sound." Some waving and gesturing were required to get this across as the letter shapes, and names had diverged in the centuries since the settling of this planet. On Sellenria the J and G had merged, and a K with a descender was now used to denote the voicing of that consonant (the "hard G" of earlier years). Nor was there any orthography in their usage that would represent the initial sound of my name. Some of my linguistics colleagues would have given their right arms to study the linguistic drift in this isolated culture. (I always thought that sounded like a light sacrifice until I landed on a planet where the penalty was likely permanent.)

Ox began backing towards the doorway. "I see two people who have much to talk about. I would like a summary of what you find out, Stenn, but I have no desire to be present throughout the discovery. Please come and fill me in later."

Auclerc looked me over appraisingly. "A one-eyed scholar from an unknown island who knows more than his youth would suggest. What more would appearances deceive?"

I tried to sort that out. It had the sound of a line from a play or a story. Cultural references were going to trip me up; I was glad that Ox had given me a reasonable explanation for ignorance in that area. "I'm just what I appear to be, no more, no less."

Auclerc laughed, "That must be your version of Duke Anthony's reply. And look what he turned out to be in the end."

I was definitely going to have find that story or play and read it, to find out what swamp of allegory I had just waded into.

"You have full access to the archives, courtesy of the head of the school of Literature and History. A full translation of this book alone would earn your berth at the University for ten years or more. Just remember that the Archives get ten percent of your earnings from that, on top of the University fees."

"That sounds like a profitable place to start, then. Do you know where I can get a pair of white, non-staining gloves?"

"Whatever for?"

"The oils from our skin will yellow and degrade the paper in the book. This book is so old and valuable that I don't want to damage it any further."

"Are you telling the head of the Library and Archives that he doesn't know his craft?"

"Ah, well, it's a practice I learned from my own master on … my island." I belatedly realized I needed more details for my backstory, and that I needed to commit the name of my new "homeland" more solidly to memory.

"I don't have any such thing around here. You might be able to find some in one of the shops in town that sell finery to the nobility, but it will cost you a handsome coin."

I compromised by finding a cloth that appeared clean and tearing it into strips. I found it very difficult to grip the pages with a flat length of fabric, and I was concerned about damaging the edges of the page. I finally hit upon a method of winding strips around both thumb and forefinger so I could grip the pages between them. With these preliminaries, I began to translate.

On the sixty-seventh day of our journey, we came at last to a sheltered place with clear water coming from underground springs. We hope the water will be uncontaminated, as all of the surface streams that we have come upon are hopelessly radioactive. Of the one hundred and seventy-three souls who crowded aboard the remaining lander, only ninety-seven have made it this far. The skies are still dark, as they have been since the ship ruptured its warp torus as it fell from orbit on the far continent. Alton forecasts that we may have two to five years of winter before the atmosphere clears again; I hope we will have enough supplies to see us through until we can bring in a crop. The other continent where the ship crashed must be entirely uninhabitable now.

Day 68: The climate is growing steadily colder without sunshine, and we must prepare for an extended winter. Our first priority is shelter, our second, food. I suppose it is a tie; without both of these we will die. Both trees and stone are available here. One team will construct a shelter from the local trees; a second team will construct one from stone. We will see which can be completed fastest, and which will serve us the best. From that, we will determine which type we build for the colony. We have concentrated food sufficient for the three hundred planned colonists to last the first year until the crops come in. It is bittersweet news that we can survive three years. We have a chance of making it because we have lost two-thirds of our number.

Day 83: The scouting party returned with the news that they have located the pod with the livestock. The pod's systems have failed as all our systems have. Many of the animals have escaped and have been living on the native vegetation, which lends weight to the arguments of some that we can consume it as well. It is likely to not contain all of the nutrients that we might need but should help meet our caloric requirements. A combination of native and Terran foods may sustain us.

Day 87: We have rounded up or rescued more livestock than we had hoped, and therein lies a problem. We cannot afford the food to keep that many animals alive. I have ordered that we keep four goats, four sheep, a dozen chickens, and two pigs alive. I wish we could spare the cows, but they will consume too much feed that is needed for people. Some are advocating that we set the rest free to survive or not. There is much debate over whether that is more humane than killing them now, but there is a more practical consideration. If we kill and eat the excess animals now, we will increase our odds of survival through the unknown winter ahead.

Day 88: After a long and gruesome day, we have butchered and preserved the excess animals. A team is trying to recreate methods of making candles and soaps from their rendered fats, and others are resurrecting techniques of tanning leather. By a vote of the colony, we have preserved two cows, after some laborious calculations that seem to show we can stretch the food supplies with the meats that we are now preserving sufficiently to allow us to keep the cows. If the winter lasts more than three years, we will have to sacrifice them, but by then it will look pretty bleak for us as well.

There was much detail that was left out—this was a log, not a narrative after all—but a picture was starting to emerge about the beginning of human life on this planet. The writer, who remained unnamed, but whom I guessed to be the leader of the party, implied that their ship had suffered catastrophic failure. It had crashed on the far continent, causing a nuclear winter and probably sterilizing the entire continent. It spoke volumes about the tenacity and resolve—and sheer luck—of those colonists to survive with no modern equipment. Two of the other worlds that humans had settled had suffered asteroid strikes. Angstrom's settlers had barely survived with emergency supplies brought in by the Void Guild. The world of New Petrograd hadn't been so fortunate; the entire biosphere had been ripped away by the impact and every human on the planet, nearly ten million people, had perished. The impact of a starship was nearly as devastating as an asteroid due to the quantity of exotic matter in the warp drive.

I started to construct a possible history of human occupation of this planet. The ancient starship from this account had been the first arrival. Something native to this planet had caused massive failures, and the ship had crashed, resulting in an ecological disaster, date unknown. An upper bound was the beginning of the diaspora from Earth, nearly two thousand years ago. In the intervening centuries, the survivors of that ship had built a civilization here. Then, four hundred years ago, the *Corvus* was commandeered by parties unknown, and met a similar fate, though apparently minus the extinction-level impact. Who had those people been, and where had they disappeared on the planet? Had they assimilated into the general population? The presence of a second language was likely their legacy.

I heard a scuff of feet in the dimness. I covered my notes, not ready to share them if someone became curious. A tall figure shuffled out from a narrow space between shelves. I had seen no one go in and wondered if there were back ways into this place. The figure stopped at the edge of the light thrown by the candles by which I was reading. It wore a cloak, even inside, with the hood pulled forward to cast the face into darkness. This apparition looked at me for a long moment.

"Your pardon," said an oddly sonorous voice. "I find not often anyone looking through these materials." He also had an accent I had not yet heard in this city.

"I am Stenn Gremm. I arrived only recently; I am interested in how cultures develop, so I'm often found in the company of old manuscripts and artifacts."

"I am Dan'l, a scholar of the road. Hmm, 'itinerant,' I think you say. Please forgive my cloak. People find my appearance disturbing."

"An accident?" I unconsciously touched my eye patch, then dropped my hand in embarrassment.

"It may be said. You are Gilwyr's new apprentice, not so?"

"I am. Other students have already offered their opinions on the wisdom of my career choices."

Dan'l made a faint sound of amusement. "The road with Gilwyr will always be interesting. However, I know of no one who could give you a greater chance of surviving it."

Dan'l started to turn to depart but paused. "My own study is of what you may call alchemy. If you encounter any mention of the subject, would you pass word to the Librarian? I have a particular interest in gemstones." Then he was gone before I had time to react. Could he know of the stone I had brought with me? To my knowledge, only Gilwyr and Ox had seen it. I arose and paced for a while, which was good for my circulation but yielded nothing new in the way of insights.

I returned to my reading, puzzling over some of the words that might have been anachronistic formations, or might have been words the colonists made up to fit their new conditions. The next two years of logs were primarily a journal of struggle against a wintery darkness, where the jobs of ensuring shelter, water, and food were paramount. Another twelve colonists died during that time. At last, a log entry noted:

Year 2, day 247: After a month of steadily increasing temperatures, it finally rose above the freezing point of water, and some pools of snowmelt were located. The sun came out from the clouds for a few hours yesterday and for nearly a half day today. We believe we are in a location in the southern equatorial zone, so we hope the climate will be temperate once it stabilizes, but the climate may be many years away from a new equilibrium.

Year 2, day 311: We have started some seedlings today. The ground has thawed to a depth of a half meter, and the average daily sunshine should support plant life. Shoots of the native vegetation are pushing through the ground, where it has lain dormant for two and half years. We do not know how much of the ecosystem has survived, but we are hopeful that we can establish our Terran species alongside whatever has survived. We plan to start breeding the livestock soon to increase their numbers.

Year 3, day 13: The resiliency of the native ecosystem is amazing. Not only are a large variety of plant species re-establishing themselves, but also many species of small- and medium-sized fauna are appearing. We speculate that they have some way to remain dormant for long periods to survive such a global winter. While we rejoice to see such a rapidly recovering planet, there are those who wonder uneasily what evolutionary pressures led to these adaptations.

It had taken me most of the day to read this far in the log. I had realized as I translated that I had a dilemma on my hands. This account was of great historical importance, but the people of this world were unprepared to hear it. Perhaps I could recast the story as the survival of a tremendous natural disaster, an extinction-level event. On the one hand, my academic integrity was vastly uneasy with even considering editing the story. On the other hand, scientists had ended up jailed or buried too often in human history for the sin of presenting truth too soon. As I mulled it over, I convinced myself that it was no less than the truth to say that it was the story of an extinction-level event. It was equally true that it was the story of the few people who had survived it and re-established civilization. There was an epic in that story all by itself. I simply had to withhold for the moment the facts that the survivors' own starship caused the disaster, and that they had come from a far distant world. I could live with that, I decided, and I could gradually "discover" evidence that lead people to the deeper story behind it.

Gilwyr arrived to inform me that the evening meal would begin soon. I put my materials away, placing my notes in my pouch to keep them private for now. I had written them in Trondnorsk from habit, and was now glad that I had, for no one here would be able to read them.

Auclerc emerged from the depths of the library, and I thanked him for his assistance.

"Did you make good progress today, young scholar?"

"I managed a few pages. I became bogged down in some unfamiliar words. If you have any other texts from this period or slightly later that I can cross-reference, it might provide me with additional context for understanding this text."

Auclerc stared owlishly at me. Perhaps that wasn't how scholarship was done in this society. I tried to remember how pre-technological discourse had been conducted. Some examples came to mind of times when presentation had mattered a great deal more than evidence. I began to feel displaced in time rather than space.

Auclerc indicated the back room where he had retrieved the book. The hand he raised in that direction was much steadier than I would have guessed from his age. "There are more in there. That's the room for all the material that no one asks for. The master before me put it in there to make it easier to get to the volumes that people wanted."

"Thank you. How are the items organized?"

"I expect that they're in the order that he carried them in there."

"But how do you find anything again?"

"That's why there's a librarian."

He turned to Gilwyr. "It's a pleasure to see you again, Mistress Gilwyr. You don't come down here often enough these days. What brings you today?"

"I have come to retrieve my apprentice from his *wen-withe* gathering down here. He probably has no clue that it is nearly time for the evening meal."

"Your apprentice, is he? And de Oxendon's student as well? This is all very interesting. A one-eyed scholar who reads ancient Anglich but not modern, with unusual ideas of methodology. You know that it is said that libraries are for that which you want to keep out of sight, but which you are not yet ready to discard."

"Is that why we keep you down here, old man?"

Auclerc's chuckle was a deep, rich sound. "Just so, mistress. Oh, and one more thing, Stenn 'Rhem. The printer has offered to print your first translation in exchange for a tenth part of the sales. Normally you have to bear the printing costs yourself. Moreover, I've made some inquiries, and several individuals would bid on the opportunity to see your handwritten manuscript prior to publication. Think on it. If you decide aye, I can make discrete introductions."

Bemused, I thanked him and departed with Gilwyr. Once out of the library, I asked, "Is that the way that academic society works here?"

She replied, "He has named figures several times his usual rates and waits to see how sharp your blade is, how experienced your response.

Will you block and parry? Will you feint and draw your opponent out? Who are your allies and what are their weaknesses? It is the first steps of the dance when you take the other's measure, show your strengths yet conceal your reserves."

"Are we talking about scholarship or swordsmanship here?"

"Is there a difference?"

If she was speaking metaphors, it was much deeper than I wanted to go.

CHAPTER 15

Commission

AS WE ENTERED the dining hall, I was still preoccupied with the day in the library. My head was full of ancient manuscripts, starship survivors, and shady librarians. Also, the self-styled 'scholar of the road,' Dan'l. Gilwyr had denied knowing anyone by that name, though he had quite clearly known her. I hadn't quite forgotten my missing eye, but I had forgotten that the others at my table had not yet beheld my eyepatch. As I stood behind Gilwyr's chair waiting for the heads of the schools to take their seats, I could feel that those nearby were pointedly looking elsewhere. The masters sat, allowing me to move down the table, away from Gilwyr's protective sphere. People stared more and more frankly as I walked to my place, and a wave of sudden silence preceded me, with a breaking crest of chatter behind.

I took my seat across from Elias, feeling his direct stare on the blankness where I had no vision. I had to hold my head turned to the left to survey the table with my remaining eye. He had no hesitation in voicing the question in everyone's faces: "She tried to kill you, then?"

"Certainly not. If she had tried to kill me, I would without question be dead." Might as well hold up her reputation. I couldn't blame her even for accidentally injuring me in training without affecting her reputation, and I had learned not to mention morghaests. So: "I … fell on a knife while practicing."

As Elias translated for those nearby, merriment at my misfortune—Galactic should have a word for that—erupted around me. "Lost half yae brains, nae hae ye?" "Aye, told ye he wouldnae last the week. Pay up." "Dinnae count, he did it hisself." "Ah wantta see the pit!" A large boy named Cam, who had a crooked nose and a torn ear, reached for my face, meaning to pull down my eye patch. I reacted without conscious thought, intercepting his wrist with my left hand and twisting it down on the table. My right hand drew my knife and had it poised across his wrist before he knew what was happening. Everyone froze. Into the sudden silence, I said, "That sight would cost you a hand."

I fixed my one eye on Cam and slowly lifted my hand from his. He cast his face down and mumbled that he hadn't meant harm. He sat, and I sat, and I hoped the lights were low enough to cover my shakes. This planet had changed me. It had felt like the will of another moved my hand, lending it speed and skill I didn't know I had. My training had only just begun, and already I was reacting with the threat of violence. *You're a dangerous person now. They'll respect that. It will give you power, and safety.* I told the inner voice to shut up.

After the ice thawed from the altercation and conversation resumed, I practiced my Anglich for the rest of the dinner. When I made a hash of a sentence, I could see the other apprentices remembering my knife and deciding that it would be safer to forego laughing. By the end of the meal, I felt I was making progress. I knew a significant amount of the vocabulary; it was mostly a matter of assimilating the pronunciation changes and getting the word order straight. Galactic was a more heavily inflected language in which word forms counted for more than word order; not so with Anglich.

Dinner was ending, and the first masters were excusing themselves and standing. Apprentices watched their masters, ready to depart when they did. Good apprentices anticipated their master's needs, inattentive apprentices had their ears boxed by their masters. Across from me, Cam started to slide his chair back, then paused. He glanced around the table and very deliberately inverted his mug, thumped it on the table and said "Stenn." Elias followed suit immediately. One by one each of other students thumped their mugs and intoned my name. Was I supposed to follow this ritual as well? Should I say my own name? I felt a light cuff land on the left side of my head. Gilwyr had appeared like a ghost at my side.

"Not fair sneaking up on my blind side."

"Your opponents will not play fair. Let's go."

As we left the dining hall, Gilwyr said, "I see you are now head of your table."

"I am?"

"Did you not see everyone else invert their mug on the table?"

"Is that what that meant?"

"That was their acclamation of the honor. Starting tomorrow, your place will be at the head of the table. Still the lowest table, but you've moved up."

"This was just for pulling a knife on a bully?"

"By the reports that reached me, you acted decisively, but with restraint. You peers admired that."

"When I attended University, it was cutthroat, but never literally."

We reached Gilwyr's quarters. She checked in both directions in the corridor before entering. Even after the door was shut, Gilwyr listened for footsteps in the hallway and then silently checked outside the windows. I couldn't imagine who could be hanging outside above the ten-meter drop.

"Two weeks hence there will be a reception at the Palace for a Dalactyn prince who has intellectual pretensions. I couldn't get an invitation from my usual discreet agents, so I let it be known that we have among us a learned scholar of history. The prince is extremely eager to hear about his work with ancient manuscripts. The Palace has sent an invitation to this scholar to attend the reception. I was sure to intercept the invitation and send the reply in Ox's name."

"Sounds like we have some interests in common. I'd like to meet him as well."

Gilwyr held the polished mirror up to my face. I was dense. I didn't tumble to her meaning until she started to register annoyance. "Me? I'm not ready. I don't know the customs yet! I can't speak the language! I can barely manage a credible apprentice!"

"You did fine with Master Auclerc today. You'll do fine at the Palace. You just have to make small talk—and they all speak Dalactyn—while your wife mingles with the other guests."

"So that's your purpose. Who is your target?"

"Someone who is attending the reception, who will be identified when we arrive."

"And the weapon?"

"You're learning the right questions to ask. It will be a knife: it appears that this has to do with political succession."

"If you get caught, do you get punished, or the person who hired you?"

"Stupid question."

"Well …"

"I would never get caught."

"Assume that someone less skilled than you got the commission?"

"First, the code of the Guild prescribes that we would die before dishonoring the Guild by disclosing the identity of our employer. Second, this is not an academic exercise where we start sentences with 'assume that.' The Guild chooses the best person for the commission, who completes that commission or dies with honor."

"And have you chosen the right person to help you?"

She looked at me steadily. "I have. Now go to bed. The morning will start early and the day will be long."

It was sinking in that I was going to help kill someone. She had already killed one person (that I knew of) since I had known her. I thought I had come to terms with it. Within their cultural context, this was an established institution. Now that I was to be part of it, the morality of my world kicked me in the teeth. How could I square my moral convictions with the world I found myself in? Gilwyr had been kind (if also demanding and uncompromising), generous, and protective towards me since I met her. But she didn't think it was wrong to kill people.

I turned from her gaze and pointedly went to my small pallet on the floor. I wrapped myself in the thin blanket and lay with my back to the room. I was acutely aware of the silence that stretched out for several long minutes before she moved to snuff out the last candle and lie down in her bed. She didn't ask me for an explanation, and I wasn't sure how to explain the gulf between our world views. If I told her that I couldn't play the role she wanted, would that violate my agreement with her? I might lose my place in the University and be on my own in this world once more. Or worse. I had insisted it was an unbreakable agreement when she believed she had failed me. If I refused, her guild code might demand that she kill me. My hands were shaking. I thrust them into my armpits to warm them and tried to hold the blanket closer. I tried not to think about how much I missed Gilwyr's warmth next to me.

Morning came early, as promised. I awoke with a clearer mind. If I were not here, Gilwyr would still be accepting commissions and performing them. My goals were still to observe this culture, discover the fate of my ancestor if I could, and find my way home. My mission was not to change the culture, even those parts I found abhorrent. I knew I would face a crisis if I were confronted with a need to kill someone myself, but I hoped to avoid that. I tried to tell myself that I was not simply rationalizing.

The training was intense. At the end of an hour of running, climbing, crawling, jumping, and scrambling, I was rubbery in the legs and the arms; unready to be armed with a blunt iron sword and knife to face Gilwyr. She had paced me the entire way and still seemed as fresh as when she started. Her shoulder must still have pained her. She gave no sign.

We faced off in a closed courtyard. I had the wit to try to imitate her stance: left foot forward, sword held at guard, knife in the left hand. I must have had a thousand details wrong, but she only corrected a few, raising my sword tip higher, demonstrating a more secure grip, adjusting my stance to present a smaller target. Then she landed a blow with the flat of her blade on my upper arm.

"Hey!" I protested.

"Your enemy will neither correct your posture nor give you warning." She let fly another stroke. I barely got my sword up, taking the blow on my knuckles rather than the blade. The weapon dropped from my nerveless fingers. I stumbled backward out of range. I tried to transfer my knife to my right hand, but the fingers wouldn't close. She took a step in, and I could see her coil for a lunge. I could picture her blade sliding between my ribs, though I knew that the blunt blade would only bruise me. I swung desperately with my knife, catching and deflecting her blade. She was momentarily open, surprised by my block, but then I felt her knife beneath my sternum, and I realized that surprise hadn't slowed her reactions.

She tapped me lightly with the tip of the knife to underscore that I was dead, then stepped back. "You lost your posture as soon as we engaged. You were fighting square on to me, giving me a large number of targets. You were thinking about each move, which made you too slow; you have to react, not think. If it hadn't been for your lucky block with the knife, the fight would have been over before it started." She bent to retrieve my sword and tossed it to me. "Again."

I clumsily caught the sword and would have mortally injured myself had it been sharp steel. I worked my right hand until the fingers could close around the hilt again, and resumed my guard. I thought that my knife block hadn't been entirely luck. I had seen where she would aim and where my knife could meet her blade. I almost felt like I had visualized it as ghostly red images of the two blades meeting just before they actually had.

This time she thrust first, aiming for my throat. I swept her sword away with my own, then blocked the knife thrust that followed it. This time I saw the phantom blades clearly an instant before the real ones. She spun, bringing her blade down on my shoulder. I couldn't block, so I stepped away, still taking a glancing, but not disabling, blow. Gilwyr stepped up her attack. I blocked furiously, always on the defensive. Sometimes she got through, not because I didn't anticipate her, but because she was much faster and I was unable to block in time. Finally, she feinted, stepped inside of my guard, and knocked me off balance with her hip. As I teetered, she grabbed the front of my shirt and pulled me close. I could feel the knife blade touch my ribs. I was dead again.

"You've fought before," she said in my ear. "Are you feigning clumsiness to put everyone off guard?"

"Never before," I panted, nearly out on my feet. "All of my fights to the death have been waged with words."

"Then your instincts are uncanny. You are slow, but you often anticipated my moves."

I had, in fact, done better than I had expected. She must have telegraphed her moves by subtle changes of balance and eye direction, which my subconscious presented to me as the phantom blades. First the voice of the Other, and now what was almost a simspace overlay. Did I have a fragment of my implants remaining or was I losing my grip on reality?

Gilwyr called the training to an end. We went to wash, and to get breakfast at the refectory. We were handed a hard roll and a slab of cheese there, which we carried outside to eat. I distracted myself from matters of swords and morality with mundane speculations of the anthropological variety. I had once done a paper mapping the spread of humankind throughout the stars by the strains of yeast that they had carried with them to make their bread, which seemed one of the most ubiquitous of human foods. It would have been fascinating to sequence the genome of this yeast, to see where it might have branched off that great tree. Sadly, I lacked the equipment to do that analysis. Cheese was not quite as widely consumed since the gene to digest dairy had gone missing from a large section of humanity sometime in the fifth century of the Diaspora. However, its presence here seemed to indicate that the cows had indeed survived that first winter, along with the appropriate bacteria to culture their milk. Through such small things, we trace the progress of humans through the cosmos.

Our next task was securing clothing for the reception. We made our way down the hill to the commerce district, and into a small shop. Clothes were piled everywhere, on shelves and tables, and hung from racks. Other than in Misthaven, the only clothing stores I had been in were virtual. When I entered the simspace of such a store, it exclusively had clothes for a man of my height and build, and would quickly bring to the front those that closely matched my desires, removing all other clutter. Anyone else entering the same store would have had a completely different experience, aligned with their selected gender, orientation, and profession. Here, clothes for workmen elbowed clothes for bankers, and the garments for ladies flirted with those for gentlemen. A twinge of the cultural overload that had overtaken me on the first day threatened to reassert itself, but I forced it down. I still missed my simspace augments, but I was learning to cope.

A petite woman came from the rear of the store and greeted Gilwyr warmly. "Lady Marrethe, how nice to see you again. That lovely gown you commissioned me to sell has fetched a handsome price. I've kept it in your account until you returned."

"It's good to see you again Abby, and I told you that you could keep those proceeds. I'm grateful that you were able to procure it for me on such short notice."

"Oh, I couldn't, it's far too much for a commission!"

"Abby, I insist. You can help us by getting us something unusual for a party to which we've been invited. This is my cousin Arkady, just arrived in town from his father's estates, and we're to attend a costume affair in two weeks. We've been assigned to be a scholar from Okko and his sister. Can you come up with something by then?"

"That's a bit of a tough one, milady. Not many Okko make their way here. I have an old-style academic robe in the back. It's no longer in fashion and has the right look. I can change the cut of it a bit and make it look Okko. For you, I would think something high-necked with a half jacket. I have one that I can remove the lace trim from; they're not big on lace there."

"That sounds perfect. Thank you so much, Abby. You can send it around to my house this afternoon?"

"Of course, milady."

Gilwyr handed Abby a golden coin.

"Oh, that's far too much, milady!" Abby protested.

"Nonsense, it's a rush job, and I trust your discretion."

Gilwyr ushered me out of the store, fending off more protests from Abby over her generosity. Outside, I raised an eyebrow. "Lady Marrethe?"

"Yes, in case anyone traces me here, Abby knows only that I'm an idle and eccentric minor noblewoman who has odd requests for clothes from time to time. She'll deliver our order to a house where I supposedly live, and a servant in that house who is in our employ will deliver it to the university. This is as much for Abby's protection as it is to break the trail back to me."

I fell silent and said little on the way back to the university, having been reminded that I was going to be a decoy while Gilwyr assassinated someone. No matter how I rationalized it, I would soon be party to cold-blooded murder.

Chapter 16

Doubt

SEVERAL DAYS AFTER receiving this commission, I was in the library once more. I had completed a translation of the logs of the first settlers into Trondnorsk, and was working on a version in Dalactyn that omitted the interstellar references. The tale would be one of a small band of humans surviving a global catastrophe to re-establish civilization. As far as it went, that was completely accurate, and would let me live with my conscience. Later on, when I thought society was ready (or when a rescue ship came and needed explanation), I could discover some 'lost pages' that filled in that part of the story.

I had turned my attention to my original goal: to find hints about the arrival of the *Corvus*. The time of its loss coincided with a great war; all of the contemporaneous writings I could find were about that war. Most of this was written in the style of a heroic epic rather than an accurate history. I would have thought the morghaests were metaphors for troops with better armor if I hadn't seen them for myself. But of the *Corvus*, not a word. No mention of blue lights in the sky, no tales of flying ships. The entire roster of passengers and crew appeared to have been swallowed up by the planet.

I was working my way through memoirs written by a merchant from Misthaven. By his own account, he had spent the war years avoiding any places where there were hostilities. However, he had filled four volumes with stories related to him by refugees, deserters, and innkeepers who retold stories that they had probably heard third hand. I assumed he had filled four volumes, but the library only had volumes one and four. My careful sifting of the books in the storage room had not yet revealed the missing volumes. Since the author had made a point of collecting stories of strange happenings, I thought there was a good chance that he had recorded events that I might recognize as the landing party of the *Corvus*.

I heard a footfall behind me. This world had already changed me to the extent that I placed my hand on my knife as I turned. I saw a cloaked figure in the shadow of a doorway and heard Dan'l's soft chuckle.

"A wary scholar, most odd. Are you *cray* or *kir* I wonder? Gilwyr, definitely *cray*. Grey'land'er is *kir* on his skin, but it is hard to say what is in the depths."

There was that word *cray* that Gilwyr used. "Do you know Gilwyr's people?" I asked. "When I told her of meeting you, and she said that she didn't know anyone named Dan'l."

"She may not know Dan'l, but I think she knows me." This guy was frustratingly enigmatic. He turned to go but paused. "The book you hold has companions."

"I know. It's missing volumes two and three."

"I have seen them in the chamber of Grey'land'er. Also books five and six." With that, he was gone.

These books appeared to be the best source I had found so far, so I made the trek from the subterranean library to Ox's chamber on the second floor. The door was open and I could see Ox across the room, eclipsing the easel that stood by the ivy-enveloped window, a bear in his den. I hesitated, fighting down my inbred impulse to announce myself in the formal way of my home. What was the custom here? I was looking around for a bell or a knocker when Ox said without turning, "Come in, Stenn. Please allow me to finish this one detail while it's fresh in my mind."

I entered and stood diffidently in the middle of the floor. How had he known it was me? Perhaps he had superb hearing. I recalled he had heard Gilwyr coming before I had. I shrugged it off and looked around. The clutter remained as before: ink pots and pens, books with sheets of notes stacked atop of them. (The handwriting of the notes was firm and even, uncluttered in contrast to the room he inhabited.) Here were some lenses mounted in a frame (a tubeless telescope or microscope perhaps), there was a leather helmet for someone who might have been half Ox's size. A set of tiles with glazes of glorious yellows and purples teetered haphazardly on a shelf. The melange suggested someone who had curiosity about everything and the time to indulge it. Then, since he was currently involved in applying paint to canvas, I looked more closely at the prior productions that hung variously with more attention to space availability than to arrangement.

One was a castle wall section in which stood a statue or a relief of an armored soldier. This was done in the black and gray shading of a charcoal sketch. Another was a massive and ornamented bier with the name "Aylward the Wise" inscribed on the side. The drawings were detailed and precise, with proper attention to light sources and perspective. Those techniques seemed more advanced than the general level of this culture would suggest.

I moved on to some finely-drafted architectural-style drawings. Among them was one that depicted a flying machine along the lines of a hot-air balloon. The balloon was ovoid and tethered to a canoe-shaped gondola beneath it. It wasn't clear what would propel it forward. However, its intent was conveyed by the two armored soldiers it carried. I wondered if Ox was the da Vinci of his era, imagining devices that his world wouldn't be capable of building for centuries. But, he had struck me as a historian rather than an inventor. Perhaps he was a polymath who dabbled in many fields.

I heard him put down his brushes and turned to see what he had been working on. On his canvas stood a stately but eldritch tree, tall with concentric puffs of teal fuzz hugging the trunk at intervals. It must have been a native species, but this one had developed branches, unlike the ones I had seen. These branches were likewise ringed with teal puffs, stretching out to the edges of the frame. At two levels the tree supported large platforms, apparently for habitation, for ladders ran from the ground to their level, and a golden glow of light radiated from unseen sources on the upper surfaces of the platforms.

"That's a beautiful scene. Where is it?"

Ox frowned. He hesitated for a long minute before saying in a distant rumble, "I am not sure. I *believe* I have seen it. It may be a dream."

I thought I would remember if I had seen a place that vivid. I said only, "Your artwork would be in demand in the galleries of my home city. It's refreshingly realistic." The truth was it might not sell back home, though I certainly would have purchased it. The art world of Trondhjem was currently in the grip of a trend that its adherents called anti-representationism and its detractors called impenetrable.

"Hrrm. It's really only for myself. Some things defy words and must come out another way. That is why I paint."

As I watched, he put down his brush and dipped a stylus in some black paint. He drew several symbols on the corner of the canvas. I stared. One of them was an exact duplicate of the one the Other had shown me to coax a different view out of my red crystal. Could that be a coincidence?

"Was there something you wanted to ask of me?" inquired Ox, derailing me from asking about the symbol.

"Oh, yes. I was looking for some missing volumes of 'Marle's Memoirs,' and Dan'l said that he had seen them in your chamber."

"Who?"

"Dan'l. I've seen him twice in the library. He calls himself a 'scholar of the road.' I don't know what he looks like because he always wears a cloak."

Ox waved his hand absently. "There's no student or scholar by that name." He seemed distracted, not as focused as he had been on previous occasions. I thought it odd that Dan'l could have seen the volumes in these chambers when Ox didn't know him. I didn't press it.

"So do you have those volumes here somewhere?"

Ox moved a few piles around. "Let me think. Marle ... He had a story about the island of Misty Hallow. That was when I was collecting Anglich folk tales to study their changes through the years. That means it is with ... these books. Gribbon ... Keltei ... Groat ... ah, here they are." He handed me the missing books.

I hesitated then. There was another reason that I had come to Ox's chambers. There were questions I wanted to ask, questions about Gilwyr. The commission still weighed heavily on my mind. I didn't want to betray Guild confidences on the grounds that it might not be good for my health, but I did want to find out where Ox stood on the moral and ethical quandaries I faced. I fingered the books, not really looking at them as I tried to decide what I could ask. I looked up to find Ox peering down at me, like a schoolteacher waiting patiently for a slow student. I might be nearly twice his age, but he had a gravitas that made me feel like a beginner again. I knew I had seldom been as patient with my own students or even my colleagues. If this world was changing me, here was a change I could make for the better.

"There's something else?" He knew that there was, but gave me room to get to it in my own time.

"Gilwyr ... she ... I ..." I took a breath, started with an indirect approach. "The students say that she was raised by faery people. I haven't been here long, and I can already see she's not like others. She's from someplace different, isn't she?"

"From beyond the edge of the map," murmured Ox. He didn't meet my eye. The question seemed to draw him back to the canvas with the eldritch trees. I wondered if they were connected.

"Can you tell me more about her people?"

"They ..." He stopped and shook his head. "No, it's not my story to tell. You may find it advisable to travel to her land to learn about your artifact and your eye, as well as your strange attraction for morghaests."

"My first concern is about what I may have gotten myself into right here in Misthaven. You are aware what she does for her Guild, are you not?"

"She settles rivalries, eases successions, at times makes political change possible, at other times ensures political stability. Her Guild often prevents conflicts from turning into wars that end up killing people who had no part in the disagreement."

"What keeps them from being a tool for chaos? Taking a commission on the one person who can stop a war, for instance?"

"The Guild's province is the stability of the realm. They maintain the balance among the rulers and the commanders and landowners to keep any of them from abusing their power. The Guild will not take any commission that they deem to be unjust. Their reputation for justice is so great that they're often called on to adjudicate disputes before the parties ever reach the stage of requesting a concluding commission."

A "concluding" commission. I shivered.

"Do I take it that you don't have this Guild in your own land?"

"You are correct in that."

"And you seem not to approve."

"We don't consider it right to kill another person."

"Withhold your judgment and learn how our system works. You may come to commend it to your people."

I inclined my head to him, still troubled. Like it or not, this was the society I had to live within.

Two weeks passed in a blur of intensive training—which increased to twice daily as I grew stronger—research in the library and practicing Anglich with my dinner companions. I had indeed been accorded the head chair at the apprentice's table. I came to enjoy the verbal jousting that honed my language skills and simultaneously taught me something of the culture of these people. In particular, I started picking up a distinct antipathy towards Dalactus and Dalactyns. Elias revealed that they had initially regarded me with some suspicion because I spoke 'Dalactyn,' though that had waned when they discovered that I knew nothing about that city. Ox was tolerantly considered to be 'almost Anglich' by most. I started to understand that the Anglich who lived in Dalactus were denied many opportunities, forced to serve in the army but not allowed be officers, and were in general regarded as an underclass.

❖

On the day of the reception in the late afternoon, Gilwyr sent a page to the library to summon me to her chamber. I was glad to leave off my research. Not only had I not been able to find anything, including the Librarian, but my mind kept jumping to the evening affair no matter what else I put before it.

"Gilwyr, I ..." I started, then backed out of the room, convinced that I had entered the wrong chamber. It was only when I heard her low laugh that I recognized the dress that the shopkeeper had described. Gilwyr had darkened her skin and her normally long, bright hair was midnight dark and worn shoulder length. "That's quite a transformation," I remarked.

"Let's do the same for you." She helped me into the dark gown. It was simple but voluminous. I would have to be mindful of dangling my sleeves in the food and drink all evening. Then she added a cap, a sort of lopsided tam that rode low over my left eye. It was built with a pull-down band to cover my eye patch. "Isn't that a little obvious?" I asked.

"This is a customary cap worn by gentlemen who have lost an eye," she replied. "Or at least it was. It's a little out of fashion now, but that would be expected of someone from Okko."

"Are one-eyed gentlemen common?"

"Between duels, infections, and bickle birds, there are always some around."

"Bickle birds? You have a bird that attacks eyes? I only have one eye left!"

"We usually wear goggles when entering forests where they nest. You're safe around here. Now take that costume off again. You're too pale for an Okkoan. We need to fix that."

She applied pigment to my face and hands, darkening my exposed skin to a shade similar to hers. Then I donned robe and cap again. The result, viewed in the mirror, looked suitably scholarly and sufficiently unlike my previous appearance. Gilwyr checked that I had my dagger in my belt, and added another in my boot. We both donned cloaks against the evening chill. We were ready, or nearly so.

Gilwyr retrieved one more item from her chest. "I think you're ready to wear this." She handed me a short sword, unadorned, but light and serviceable. I pulled it a few inches from its sheath and saw by the wavy lines in the metal that it was of steel that was folded and reforged for strength. (This meant that the local artisans could not yet refine steel of sufficient purity. I almost sent a search daemon looking for comparison artifacts before recalling, again, that I had lost my daemons.) I belted it underneath my robes so that it was concealed yet easily reachable, though I worried about it snagging on the fabric if I needed to draw it.

What if I needed to draw it? This was no longer practice. This was no longer a cover story for my presence at the University so I could do my research. This was now a real and deadly game. I was about to become a participant in this society's political process, no longer a detached observer. What if I refused? Dismissal? Or death? And which would hurt more?

That all begged the more central question. Could I stand by while a living person was killed? Could I kill that person myself if needed?

You have it in you. You will find it when you need it.

It was the voice in my head again. If I hadn't known that my implants were destroyed, I would have thought they were hacked, and whispering to me. The Other had seemingly been able to come and go at will in my shipboard simspaces. Could he/she/it have extended into my personal implants? But the presence had been even stronger since the watchbreaker attack, and I didn't think I had any implants left after that. I covered my consternation and looked to see if Gilwyr had noticed. She was looking me over critically, and said as if she were confirming my inner voice, "You're ready." With that approval, I followed her out the door.

CHAPTER 17

Reception

WE TOOK THE rocky path down from the University to the edge of the town. The light of the sun was fading from the sky, while Rhea echoed a lesser reddish light, three quarters illuminated high overhead. The narrow path, treacherous by daylight, was now an invitation for a turned ankle or a plunge from the sheer height. At one point, I heard a rock tumble in the shadows and was instantly alert, remembering the morghaest attacks. Nothing threatened, and we continued to the bottom, then set off walking towards the second, higher hill in the town, and the castle that dominated it.

Overhead, Rhea's expansive face cast eerie illumination on the streets and shop fronts. Daytime colors were washed out, unsaturated. In the harbor, the tide was rising, as it had when we first approached the city a few weeks ago. Ships were making ready for the mad dash for the open sea at the moment of high tide. We could hear the calls of sailors rising through the still air. A sudden massive hissing rent the air as the waters poured into the thermal vent, absorbing and covering all other sounds. White mist boiled from the vent tinged bloody on top by Rhea. It settled over the lower town, spreading its namesake covering.

"It's a time to be alert," said Gilwyr. "The mist conceals forms, and footfalls are lost under the commotion. There may be footpads and assassins hidden where they can approach closely without being discovered."

"But we *are* assassins."

"I am an assassin, you are an apprentice. An apprentice who forgets that there may be other assassins will not live very long."

The castle was looming over us by now. It was of the same age and construction as the University, but on a larger scale. Unlike the University with its single winding path up the hill, the castle had a broad avenue leading to the gates. It was no less defensible, however. The buildings on either side were high and solidly made, with defensive emplacements on their tops. The entire avenue was a killing box, inviting invaders to assault the front gates while bottling them up and allowing the defenders to slaughter them with crossfire. Tonight though, it was open and brightly lit and showed every sign of long prosperity. Unless the practice had been to drop flowerpots on invaders, the walls were unready for defense.

Liveried footmen conducted us to the main hall, ablaze in light and resplendent with lords and ladies. Other footmen took our cloaks, and heralds announced Arkady and Marrethe Kingspike of Okko Isle. No one paid the slightest attention.

Clumps of people stood around the hall, engaged in conversation or in eating and drinking. Tables along one side of the hall were laden with food; servants circulated with trays of drinks. On a stage at the end of the hall, several minstrels played stringed instruments that might have owed their ancestry to handheld harps that had married into a family of miniature pianos. Attire for the gentlemen ran to waistcoats with tails, breeches tucked into low boots, ruffled shirts, and high collars. The waistcoats were colorful, bordering on garish, with purples and reds being favored. Some, whom Gilwyr indicated as estate owners from the surrounding countryside, wore leather breeches and higher boots, and omitted the tails from their jackets. The ladies wore gowns of ankle length in pastel colors, generally low cut, some to the point where every curtsy brought the chance of unexpected events. The fabric had a silk-like look to it, which intrigued me since Terran silkworms had proven very difficult to establish on new worlds, and only a handful of the settled worlds were known to have a viable silk trade.

We drifted towards the food tables, trying to look like the rural bumpkins that we were supposed to be. It wasn't much of a stretch since I already felt out of place. I was uncomfortably aware that my gown and Gilwyr's dress stuck out as very much out of style in this crowd. I could see people appraising us and whispering after we had almost passed by. I noted that there were a number of soldiers in uniform posted around the room, attempting to look discrete and stiffly formal at the same time. There were also a few soldiers in a different garb: a white tunic, crossed with a leather harness, sandaled footwear laced up to mid-calf, and prominently displayed short swords. These soldiers were uniformly female. Gilwyr saw my inspection of them and told me they were members of the Daughters of Rowena, the Dalactyn Prince's personal guard. "The Daughters are all Dalactyn; Anglich are not allowed to serve. The regular soldiers are entirely Anglich and there is little love lost between them." After she pointed it out, I could see the frost between the two sets of guards.

Gilwyr kept her eyes downcast demurely and followed a step behind me as we moved through the room. I was confident that no one in the hall escaped her scrutiny. No one sought to engage us in conversation as we filled our plates from the buffet. "What are these things?" I inquired as I tried to select the items that seemed least likely to injure me.

"Those are dried sea spines. Very crunchy and slightly venomous. They'll leave a tingle on your tongue. Those are vark fins, another sea creature, which is prized more for its texture than its taste." This latter item was pale blue in color and had the appearance of a long triangle of cartilage. "As an Okkoan, you would be expected to primarily eat seafood."

I tried to follow her example in filling my plate. I only took one of the oyster-like shells filled with green curd, almost dropping the whole plate when it stretched out a tiny arm and tried to pull the vark fin over its shell. At that point, I decided to be an adventurous Okkoan and added some braised ribs to my selections. I took a step back from the table and bumped into someone standing behind me. I turned to find a florid man with stringy yellow hair, who was wearing a coat of bright red, held with a wide black belt over his ample middle. Both the belt buckle and the sash over his shoulder were gold in color. The white shirt under the jacket was excessively ruffled. From his outfit, I would have guessed that he was either the court jester or someone of formidable importance. From his disapproving stare, I leaned toward the latter.

"Your pardon, sir," I said politely in Anglich.

"And who might you be?"

Gilwyr had turned upon hearing me speak. She curtsied low and said, "We beg your pardon, Lord Mayor. This is my husband, Arkady Kingspike of Okko, a noted scholar visiting the wonderful University here. I am Marrethe."

The Lord Mayor's face creased in puzzlement. "Did I invite you?"

Gilwyr produced a rolled paper with an official seal and handed it to the Lord Mayor. He peered nearsightedly at the ornate writing. "Oh, I see," he said. "My secretary did, at the request of the Dalactyn prince. Very good, glad you're here. The Prince isn't here yet; I'll let him know you're here when I see him."

I bowed. "Very good, your Grace. I have been admiring your palace. A most imposing edifice set in a most dramatic setting atop this hill."

"Thank you for your kind words, my dear Arkady. But I am not your Grace, I am the elected head of the town. Lord Mayor is all the title I need, and this is my home, at most a mansion, not a palace."

"An impressive mansion, then. Were you to call it a woodsman's hut, it would still look as magnificent. The town is obviously prospering under your leadership."

The Lord Mayor nodded and moved on. Gilwyr said in a low voice, "You were most unstinting with your praise, dear husband."

"I've survived enough faculty fundraising dinners to know when to praise a potential benefactor."

I sampled the vark fin. It was somewhere between gelatinous and cartilaginous, with a taste of salty ocean to it. The flavor was not entirely disagreeable and the crunchy texture was interesting, but I would just as soon leave the vark with his fins.

Others were coming to talk to us now that we had been seen to have the approval of the Lord Mayor. An older man approached first and touched his fingers to his forehead in the Misthaven greeting. "Welcome to our city. I am Bartoldus, purveyor of fine wines and ciders. It's a pleasure to have someone visit from such a distant place."

"It seems like another world," I agreed. The irony had the flavor of vark fin.

"The ruins in Okko, they're quite old, aren't they?" Bartoldus had a peculiarly intense expression. I had seen it before and had a sense of what was coming.

"Well, we have no way of telling exactly how old they are, of course," I temporized.

"Older than the human race, perhaps?" he persisted.

"Well, I don't know ..."

"And they're beyond anything we could build now, aren't they?"

Oh no, not an 'Ancient Astronauts' cult. "I suppose they are ..."

"I knew it! Beings from another planet! Visitors from Rhea came thousands of years ago and built advanced cities, and then left again! Will you join the effort to build a great signal fire to attract their attention?"

Others had come up during this conversation. "Bartoldus, are you on about that again? You know that the Kir Leth built those structures." It appeared Bartoldus was only one of the local crackpots, and the rest were gathering to ridicule him.

"Have you ever seen a Kir Leth? No one has. They're mythical creatures. Catch a Kir Leth, and he'll grant you three wishes!"

Kir Leth? Was this a local term for elven folk? I wanted to make a journal entry ...

A willowy and unfocused-looking woman explained earnestly: "No, when Polnedra created the world six hundred and twelve years ago, she filled it with old-looking ruins for us to wonder over. She told legends of the Kir Leth so that we would have stories to tell. She made up histories and created books with those histories in them so that we would remember them. Look no further than the child god."

"I thought this was the seat of learning," rumbled a deep voice behind me. "And all I hear is pudding-headed drivel fit for villagers."

I turned and thought at first that Greylander de Oxendon had come. But this man wore a sleeveless white tunic over leather breeches, belted with a wide black belt that held a short sword and knife. He wore a short purple cape over his shoulders. His beard was trimmed close and was absent of any gray hairs. The resemblance was strong, but this was a younger version of Ox. "Prince Gerard," murmured Gilwyr, and curtsied. I followed suit and bowed.

The others bowed and took their leave until we were alone with the Prince. Gerard looked us over in silence for a moment, until I ventured, "I daresay you have mistaken this hill for the other in Misthaven if you were looking for an informed discussion."

Gerard threw his head back and bellowed a laugh. "True words! This is the house of politicians and sycophants. They are all trained to believe whatever suits them, facts be damned. And there's none of that at the University, I warrant?"

"Last I checked it was still inhabited by humans, so I doubt it's free from politics and agendas, but reason has a hope of prevailing there."

"You are a refreshing cynic. You are the scholar from Okko I have heard about?"

"I am. Stenn… er, Arkady Kingspike at your service, my Lord. And this is my wife, the Lady Marrethe."

"You should come with me to Dalactus," said Gerard. "We have the authoritative archives on the War of the Grimmerroth. You might find those instructive."

"Thank you for the invitation. That is a topic I'd like to know more about, but I would like to finish my researches here first. I think that could take me a number of months."

"Of course. I will have to leave soon, for the King is unwell and will likely not live to see the end of the year, and I will need to be there for the succession convocation. Perhaps by the time you visit, I will be King in Dalactus."

"Ah, you are next in line for the throne?"

Gerard's face clouded. "It is unclear. It must be settled soon." He brushed it aside. "Tell me about these ruins on Okko."

"Still a mystery." Gilwyr had told me enough to allow me to bluff, but my knowledge was very thin. I hoped I would find a way out of this conversation before he dug through my veneer. "We don't know who built them or when."

"Indeed. There is no record in Dalactus or Misthaven or any of the coastal towns of any significant trade with a community there, or of any major migration to Okko or away from Okko. So who settled that ancient city?"

"We do not know. We have been unable to determine how long it has been abandoned."

"I know of this problem. When I am King, I will bring all possible pressure to bear on the priests on the temple of Rhea to agree to allow access. How would you determine the age of the ruins once you have free access?"

"We would determine the rate at which new soil accumulates in that area, and excavate sections near the outer walls to determine how far they have sunk, and hence estimate their age. If any timbers were used in the construction, we could match their ring patterns with other known samples. There's also evidence of a global freeze about two thousand years ago, and we can look for the line of sediment that marks that boundary in the layers of soil around the walls."

"That's very exciting, to know that there are such definite researches that can be undertaken. That leaves me with a puzzle, then."

"What puzzle is that?"

"You're not Okkoan, despite your attempt to play the part. Your accent is not Dalactyn, but it is not Okkoan either. And your skin has been darkened for this part. Very skillfully, I might add. Most people would not see it. Yet you are definitely a scholar. So why are you here? I think it is so that an assassin might pass right under our nose in your shadow."

Gilwyr had frozen to utter stillness. I could sense that she was evaluating this sudden discovery, ready to fight or vanish depending on Gerard's next move. I tensed. If she planted a knife in Gerard's eye socket in the next few seconds, I wanted to be ready to run. Fast. And far.

Gerard leaned close to both of us. "It was a good disguise. I just want you to know that when someone sends you after me someday, it will not be good enough. For tonight, do not worry. I will say nothing. Ah, you want to know why I will say nothing? Ask our scholar here, he is good at deductions." I thought furiously. He must not think that he is the target.

Does he think he will benefit from the death of whoever is Gilwyr's target? Or does he want leverage to hold over someone later?

Gerard started to turn away, then caught sight of someone making his way through the crowd to us. "Ah, this should be interesting," he said.

Ox stopped before us, in presence and poise so much like the Prince that the resemblance was magnified. He was wearing blue trousers tucked into low boots, a white shirt, and a nearly floor-length cape that swept dramatically behind him. He had the *cray jon* dagger in his belt, and a single red rose adorning his right breast.

"Gerard." He nodded to the Prince. "How is Father?"

"On his bed, and I do not expect him to arise again. He asks about you."

"I wish that I could attend him without that becoming a political statement."

"I will convey that to him. Will you attend the succession convocation?"

"You know I have no interest in the throne."

"Yet you have not renounced your claim to it."

"It gives me leverage. You know what I would have first before I sign that document."

"I do know, and it is not in the best interest of Dalactus."

"No, but it is in my best interest."

They stared at each other, unyielding. Gerard broke away first, saying, "Perhaps you will take counsel from your young scholar from Okko here. He has an insightful mind."

"Does he now?" Ox frowned at me, then glanced at Marrethe/Gilwyr and frowned more deeply. He evidently thought we resembled someone he knew.

"I have only recently arrived," I said. "We hadn't been introduced yet." I had been trying to unobtrusively sidle away.

"Ah, yes, I have heard about you. We must talk soon." I saw recognition in his eyes as soon as he heard my voice. He knew me, and by association, Gilwyr. He knew why Gilwyr would be attending such a function in disguise and was refraining from interfering. Gilwyr was still frozen in place from when Gerard had seen through her, but something of the quality of her stillness had changed. She was staring at Ox's rose as if she had never before seen a flower.

"As must we," said Gerard to Ox, "but not here and not now. Until then." He nodded stiffly at Ox, then at us, and took his leave.

"Not here and not now," Ox echoed. It was uncertain if he was speaking to himself, to the receding Prince, or to us. He turned away as well.

We put down the plates we were holding, no longer interested in food. The green mollusk on my plate decided that it was time for an escape; it heaved itself off the plate and started inching away. There were times when seafood could be too fresh.

Gilwyr was angry, but not breaking character. We strolled, nodding and exchanged a few words with others while looking involved enough to not be drawn into conversation. When we were away from others she said, low and intense, "This couldn't be more fouled up if a *tan houfa* made a nest in the middle of it."

"The Prince is a sharp character and he is planning something, that much is clear."

"But I didn't know he was a Prince."

"Gerard? He was introduced as a Prince."

"No, Ox! I knew he was Dalactyn. I thought he was a minor noble in the house of de Oxendon. A younger son who became a scholar. Not the Prince's brother!"

"Older brother, too, I'd judge. That would mean ... he's standing between Gerard and the throne."

Gilwyr's voice was brittle with emotion. "And my commission tonight was to kill the person wearing a red rose."

CHAPTER 18

Assassination

"MAYBE HE JUST picked a red flower to wear tonight by accident. We should see if anyone else is wearing a red flower tonight."

"Do you believe that?"

I thought about what I had just heard. The succession of a kingdom at stake. Concessions demanded. Impasse reached. Expediency chosen over negotiation.

"No."

"They are testing me."

"They?"

"The Guild. They gave me this commission, knowing that Ox is my mentor. If I am worthy of the Guild, I will carry out my commission. If I refuse, I will have broken my Guild oath, and will be expelled and killed."

I thought about how many times that tactic had been used throughout human history to bind a person's allegiance to a group or cause. It had always been an abstract to me, a thing that happened to other people. Now it was real, and I felt the stirrings of anger.

"Can we slip a note to Ox to give his flower to someone else?"

Gilwyr shot me a withering look. "The Guild will have other people here. They will know I have seen the flower. Now I must do the deed."

"Could you really kill Ox?"

"I am Cray Leth."

"Is that your answer to everything? You aren't just Cray Leth, whatever that means; you aren't just an assassin. You aren't a label. You are a unique human being who is more than the sum of your labels. Look beyond the labels and find the right path! Ox is like a father to you, isn't he? I've seen you fuss over him like an indulgent daughter. Doesn't that mean more than the politics of another kingdom?"

For a moment, I thought I had swayed her. Then she snapped her role closed around her like a shell.

"We haven't seen the gardens yet, my husband," she said brightly. She took my arm, and we strolled through the hall towards the archway framing the gardens. Few people were outside since the night had grown chill as the mist had risen. Here the walls and paths were softened and washed out. Torches were lit at intervals throughout the garden, casting light and enough heat to burn away the questing wisps of fog. The wisps were strengthening, though, and seemed likely to prevail in the end. The plantings were rectilinear and orderly. Shrubs and flowers framed larger plantings where native and Terran species were intermingled to artistic effect.

Gilwyr was wrapped in introspection as we walked. Finally, she said, "The Kir Leth say that time is a road. You travel a road of the earth or a road of time with various companions, who may start or stop at different places. If a companion stops and you go on, the companion does not know that you have gone on, only you do. Thus, when you kill someone, you only injure yourself. The other person is no longer with you to be injured. Assassins take this injury on themselves to resolve difficulties and to bring about outcomes. This is difficult to say in Dalactyn or Anglich. When said in Kir Leth, it becomes self-evident."

Kir Leth. Cray Leth. Were these the people who raised her, who were said to be faeries? Religious sects of some sort? No time to ask now, a life was at stake. We were interrupted by the crunch of gravel behind us. We turned to see who had followed us. Ox was striding toward us, his gaze intent. This was not an accidental meeting. I saw Gilwyr put her hand to her throwing dagger. I was a step to her left. Could I reach her in time to stop her? Should I warn Ox instead? I knew that I would be dead either way.

"Gilwyr, if you are here, you have a commission," Ox said as he came near. "You must stay your hand tonight. If you tip the balance in Dalactus, both Dalactus and Misthaven will suffer."

"Where did you get the red rose, Ox?" she asked tightly. At least I had planted enough doubt in her to make her ask that.

"One of the Daughters of Rowena gave it to me. It's my house flower." His eyes widened. "This was your mark?"

I knew the path Gilwyr's dagger would take. I saw in my mind a red-limned blade flying through the air to bury itself in Ox's heart. The real dagger, the one of silvery steel, remained in Gilwyr's hand, indecisive. I put my hand through the opening in my robe and grasped the hilt of my short sword. I could see my sword sweeping free of my robe in an attempt to deflect her dagger. I was too far away, and I could see the stroke falling short.

"I am bound by Guild oath, Ox. I accepted the commission."

"Not if it was falsely given. Do you know who bought that commission?"

"Prince Gerard …"

"Not Gerard. He has honor. We may not agree on policy, but ..."

"I'm glad you have such a high opinion of me, Brother." Gerard was approaching along the path. "Is that why you sent word for me to meet you out here in the damp?" As he passed a torch, I saw that he, too, was wearing a red rose. Gilwyr lowered her dagger in confusion.

Ox saw it as well. "We are being played, Brother, and the game is deadly."

An insubstantial red knife flew from behind me to pierce Gilwyr, imbedding itself deeply between her shoulder blades before vanishing. I jerked my short sword free of my gown, reacting as I had been drilled, often painfully, for weeks. I saw the knife again, and this time the outline of my sword leaping to block its flight. This is simspace, I told myself as I swung, this is a combat simulation to guide me. I took the guidance and slashed; my steel sword met the steel dagger in mid-air. The all too real dagger flew into the plantings, deflected.

Gilwyr whirled at the sound. "We're under attack," I called, but she grasped the situation before I had the words out. She threw her dagger and produced a second one from her boot in the same movement. I turned to see her dagger protruding from the eye socket of one of the Daughters of Rowena. Gilwyr flowed over the ground to take the Daughter's sword from her hand before she started to fall.

I saw a red sword outline suddenly protrude from my sternum then fade from sight. I turned and beat aside the sword of another Daughter intent on ending my life. Surprised, she was open, but it took me too long to recover to take advantage of it. She tucked her left shoulder and rammed me with it, sending me off balance. I fell heavily. She brought her sword to front in a two-handed reverse grip, ready to pin me like a beetle to the ground. I rolled just before it descended and swept her legs from under her. She fell and lost her grip on her blade. I saw her reaching for it, and lashed out with my blade. Her hand bounced free and blood spurted from her severed arm. I regained my footing and finished her with a straight thrust below the sternum, just as Gilwyr had taught me. Gilwyr hadn't prepared me for the shower of blood, terribly real in its crimson, viscous, metallic-smelling, life-ending flow. Fear, revulsion, shame, and outrage were demons shrieking in the darkness beyond the fight. I knew they would be tearing at my guts when this was over—if I still had any.

I straightened up to survey the battle. Another Daughter was engaging Gilwyr, while a fourth was closing on Gerard, and a fifth threw a dagger with deadly accuracy at Ox. I saw a red outline of it slamming into his throat, cutting off life and breath. They were out of reach. There was nothing I could do. Then Ox raised his forearm in the dagger's path, and the dagger thunked home into his arm instead of his throat. So the simulation couldn't predict everything. The Daughter took four steps to close with Ox and took him with her sword in his ribs. Ox fell.

I saw in ghostly red the cut that would end this and knew what I had to do. I leaped forward, and the shock of slicing human bones and tendons nearly tore my grip from my sword. I saw, as if in a simspace drama, her head landing several paces away on the path, and her body fountaining blood from the neck until it slowly toppled over.

Gilwyr had finished her assailant. She dashed past me and dispatched Gerard's attacker in a single stroke. We looked at each other in the sudden quiet, then as one rushed to where Ox lay.

He was moving weakly in the underbrush. We pulled him out, hoping we could save him. Miraculously, there was no blood, and with a groan, he reached across and plucked the dagger from his forearm. As the sleeve fell back, we could see that he was wearing arm shields of heavy leather underneath. Gilwyr was feeling for the wound in his side and uncovered a vest of fine metallic links shining through the rent in his outer clothes. He was laboring to catch his breath, but he was alive. After a moment he managed, "I am bruised, maybe a broken rib, but only that. See to Gerard."

That was a less happy story. He had a deep wound in his side that bled and bubbled, and his breath was frothy with red. "My brother?" he asked us.

"He lives," answer Gilwyr. "Who did this?"

"Terrell. He has… ambitions. For … crown. For land … For power."

We heard the heavy crunch of gravel as Ox came up to us. "Terrell? He had only his circle of disaffected lordlings." Ox's voice sounded pained but controlled.

"He has more… now. I fear … he has support … of the Daughters now. He wants conquest … they want battle."

"We must get you to a doctor," said Ox.

"No. My lungs are filling. I have only… a moment left. Go. Claim the throne, Brother. Keep it from Terrell. Do not … tarry here."

Gilwyr spoke up. "He's right, about getting out of here at least. We're likely to be executed for the murder of Gerard if we're found here. Quickly, there's a gate behind that hedge." Cold, calculating, and undoubtedly correct.

Ox knelt and took Gerard's hand. He leaned close, and they exchanged final words, too quiet to hear. Ox placed his hand on his brother's brow, and said in a low voice, "I will avenge this, Brother."

He arose, and we hastened away, down to the end of the garden. Scenes from the fight reenacted themselves in my head while the demons of civilization that I had held at bay began to tear chunks from my intestines. I had ended two lives and watched Gilwyr end three more. I wanted time to absorb that, to reconcile and rationalize. Yet we were not out of danger, and I willed myself to continue moving.

We let ourselves out of a gardener's gate, which opened into the back of the serving quarters. We found our way through the dark yard to the gate where supplies were brought in. Security was lax, but there was still a guard, nearly asleep on his feet, though I doubted we could escape his notice if we went past.

Gilwyr and Ox were studying the gate. "How do we get out?" I asked. "We're covered in blood. Even if we get past, the guard will connect us to Gerard as soon as the alarm is raised."

"I will take him out," said Gilwyr. "Stay here a moment."

"But, he has done nothing," I protested.

Ox laid his hand on Gilwyr. "I concur. There has been enough killing tonight."

"That will be more difficult. It would be best if he did not see us."

"It would be best if we didn't leave a body indicating we left by this gate," I countered. Gilwyr glared at me.

A cry went up in the main wing. It appeared that Gerard had been discovered. The guard startled to wakefulness, and after casting about in confusion, dashed towards the source of the noise. Sometimes if you procrastinate, your problems solve themselves.

We slipped out the side gate, Gilwyr complaining about the lax discipline of the guard. "He should have stayed at his post," she said.

"Be glad that he didn't," rumbled Ox. Once outside we were enveloped in dense fog, thicker than I had seen it since arriving in the city. We walked downhill along the lane toward the town below, holding left hands outstretched to touch the wall. The opposite wall was lost in the mist, even though the lane was narrow. The fog deadened the sounds and laid clammy fingers of dread on the backs of our necks.

We came to a cross street. It was too foggy to see the other side. Gilwyr had me stop and raise the hem of my robe. She started cutting strips of cloth from the bottom of my robe and tying them together until we had a long cord and I had a draft around my calves.

Gilwyr set out holding one end of the cord while Ox and I held the other end taut. After a moment, we felt two tugs on the cord and walked out into the fog reeling up the line as we went. We came upon Gilwyr on the other side of the street and resumed feeling our way down the hill away from the castle. After we had crossed two more streets in this manner, we reached a bridge across the chasm that divided the town. Where we had crossed before, buildings had been extended across the chasm, so that we had not seen its depths. At this location though, only a narrow span crossed the gorge, bare and exposed, with but a low railing between us and the abyss. It seemed ideal for an ambush, but after a whispered conference we felt we were ahead of any alarm, and not following the path that our assailants might have expected.

We started across. It was impossible to see more than the railing of the bridge itself, and the depths were lost in mists entirely. However, the quality of the sounds changed. There were no longer hard surfaces to reflect sound. Our footfalls dropped into the depths and never hit bottom. There was a vast and sourceless hissing in the darkness, and the smell of sulfur hung in the air.

I was trying not to think of the depths below when a sudden vertigo assailed me somewhere near the middle of the span. I fell to my knees clutching the railing while the world spun around me, then rocked unevenly as if I were being carried. An eye came at me out of the darkness and looked into my depths. I think I cried out. Then a blackness enveloped me.

I opened my eyes to the worried faces of my companions. "Were you injured in the fight?" inquired Ox.

"No. I'm fine. Just a sudden dizziness." A strange dizziness, swaying, almost … seasick? I had felt that I was moving, being carried, examined. Suddenly I knew. "Someone has taken the gem!" I looked in alarm at Gilwyr. "They took it from the chest in your room and placed it in a sack. They're carrying it away."

"How do you know this?"

"I could feel the gem being picked up and carried. I saw the eye of someone looking into it."

Gilwyr and Ox looked at each other. At first, I thought they were doubting my sanity as much as I was, but then Ox said, "They sent people to the University, even while we were at the reception. The

Daughters always prepare multiple layers of attack and defense. It's no longer safe to return there."

"We must leave Misthaven then," said Gilwyr. "We can take sanctuary in the mountains, or make our way to Cloudhaven."

"I think we must make our way to Dalactus, and find who stands with Terrell."

"We must first send scouts."

"No time. I fear that Father's time may be even shorter than we thought if Terrell helps him along."

We all looked at each other. After a moment, Gilwyr nodded. I added my assent. Where Gilwyr went, I went, and the depth of that feeling surprised me. We stood, and crossed the bridge without further incident, and went down into the mists of Misthaven.

CHAPTER 19

Night Skirmishes

WE MADE OUR way through a town in which we could see only a pace before and after us. The light of Rhea perfused the fog with an anxious red glow. After a while, I asked who this Terrell was and what his plans might be.

"Terrell is our youngest brother," replied de Oxendon. "Third in line for the throne, and a superb example of why inheritance is a poor method of choosing a monarch. He has always been self-centered and petty, far too acquisitive, and a shallow student of past military campaigns. He would see Dalactus expand its borders to what they once were, and has advocated annexing Misthaven to Dalactus. Misthaven has always been a free city, and the kings of Dalactus have found it useful to let it flourish as a seat of learning and innovation, trade, and a refuge for malcontents such as I."

"You're first in line for the throne? Why don't you just take the throne and institute reform?"

"It would not be so easy. There would be few who would support my radical notions, just as there have been few who supported Terrell's reactionary ones. Gerard would have made a good middle ground. I only wanted him to foreswear any concession to Terrell's crowd that would have lessened Misthaven's independence. Gerard felt that he needed their support too much to do so." Ox paused for a moment. "The other answer to your question is that after my stay with the ... with Gilwyr's people, I felt that I had a different road to walk."

Gilwyr waved us to silence, and we made our way thereafter with only the minimum of speech needed to stay together and moving in the correct direction. No one was abroad in the heavy mist. Dark building walls loomed on either side, and a few candles and lanterns lit windows, but apparently, most townspeople went to bed soon after nightfall and didn't stir out until dawn. In this part of the city there were few street lamps, and if it hadn't been for Rhea's ruddy glow, it would have been nearly pitch black.

At length, we came to an intersection with a broader road, though the only indication of that was the change in the sounds of our footfalls reflected from the building faces. I knew our location when we passed the ornate door of the jewelry maker. We were on the high street below the University; the rocky path to its gate was a little farther on.

"You two can stay at the safe house I have on this street." Gilwyr's voice was barely above a whisper. "I must go to my chamber to retrieve my swords."

"No," said Ox. "We should stay together."

"It's too dangerous for you to go up there. We know that Terrell's people have been there."

"And you believe your safe house is safe? Your masters in the Guild know of it, do they not?"

"I do not like what you are suggesting."

"It's almost certain that your Guild was a participant in this setup tonight. This was meant to look like an assassination attempt of one of us upon the other—of me upon Gerard unless I miss my guess—where the Daughters intervened just too late, leaving both brothers tragically dead, probably along with one assassin who might have had sympathies with one of them. I've long suspected Auclerc of having Dalactyn sympathies."

"What does the librarian have to do with it?" I asked.

"He is the guild master of the assassins," said Ox. I gaped and looked to Gilwyr for confirmation.

"He was my master in the trade," she acknowledged. "But that is not known outside of the guild. How do you come to know it?"

"If you watch the web, see when a strand is laid, feel when it vibrates, you can deduce where the spider must hide."

"Speaking of deductions," I said, "Auclerc may have deduced that I had an artifact of value from some of the old manuscripts that I searched for. He has made sure that items of interest can only be found in that library by asking him for them. That's a good arrangement for a spider, wouldn't you say?"

"Indeed. Well Gilwyr, it is all together or not at all."

We ascended the hill on the road faced with shuttered merchant storefronts. The mist began to tear into rags and streams, pushed into a tatterdemalion shawl by the light winds higher on the hill. Another few hundred paces and we finally rose above it, and turning, could see the Rhea-lit expanse blanketing the lower town. The river could be seen only as a slow subsurface churning that pulled the mist along with it as it plunged towards the falls. The volcanic vent was a fantastic fountaining of fog as the rising warm air lifted streamers high above the surrounding blanket, only to splash down again as it cooled. The mist moved like a liquid body, a sea in which people drifted like fish, at least the few brave enough to be about.

We passed the final shops and started on the path up the naked rock to the University. Even in the angry light of the moon, the way was dark, narrow, and treacherous. There was a supply of torches in a barrel at the start of the path for those who might need light to ascend. We forewent the torches in favor of stealth. Torchlight is for those who are not hunted or hunting, and we were both.

Gilwyr was in the lead, Ox bringing up the rear. Ox was surprisingly light on his feet for his size, leaving me to be the noisy, graceless member of our troop. I concentrated on placing my feet carefully, to not dislodge any needless stones. About halfway up the ascent, a weathered archway straddled the path flanked by waist-high remnants of stone walls that might have been a guardhouse at one time. At about fifty paces distant, I could see the red outlines of drawn blades behind the walls. I reached out and placed my hand on Gilwyr's shoulder. She stopped, questioning. I leaned close to her ear and said quietly, "Two men, behind the wall, blades drawn."

She nodded, drawing her dagger. The sword she had liberated from the Daughter of Rowena she had held the entire way, lacking a scabbard in which to sheath it. She hefted it in distaste, not liking the weight.

"Would you prefer this one?" I asked, holding up the lighter blade she had given me.

She nodded her thanks, and we exchanged. "I will return this shortly. You have earned it."

She took a few swings experimentally. "Rhea take this dress," she breathed. She quickly slit the buttons from the front and peeled the dress away. She kicked off the boots to stand barefoot, clothed only in breeches. "Count to twenty and then proceed up the path," she whispered. Then she was gone, floating across the steep rocks like an errant scrap of fog.

I counted to twenty, and we started to move forward. I tried to be stealthy, but Ox began conversing in a normal voice. "She's quite a woman, isn't she, lad?"

I started to shush him before I realized that we were intended to be the distraction. "I can truthfully say I've never met anyone like her," I replied as we walked towards the archway. The swords came to the alert beyond the wall. *Through* the wall. Why hadn't I noticed before that I could see the swords while the men were hidden? I couldn't see through the wall; I could see the swords despite the wall. If that sounds confusing, it is because everyday words were unprepared to describe how I saw and what I saw.

"Treat her gently. She is somewhat like a wild animal."

I did not want to be having this conversation at this moment. My instincts were telling me to pay attention to the people who wanted to kill us. I recognized his gambit: we weren't particularly alarmed and were talking about Gilwyr as if she was not present. "I've noticed that she's extraordinarily deadly."

"Quite so, in that she is competent. And in much else. Yet she is altogether taken with you and doesn't even recognize it yet. Do not injure the wild thing accidentally."

"What? You can't be serious." I almost lost track of the hidden assailants. They were close by the archway, waiting to swing as we passed. Cowards. I saw the short sword and dagger of Gilwyr glinting redly in the darkness, moving to intercept them just as we arrived at the arch. I also saw more swords in the dark behind her. The Daughters, I remembered, always planned multiple layers of attack. I thought to call out, then bit my tongue. If I warned the two at the arch, then Gilwyr would face four foes. I hoped she could take out one or both before the reinforcements arrived.

A few more steps and I knew it would be too close for comfort. I hefted the short sword in my hand. It was broad and substantial, not as finely balanced as the one I had fought with earlier. I would be unable to swing it until I was through the archway, by which time I would have been sliced into sections by my opponents. Gilwyr was only a few steps away and the rear guard almost atop her. I had to act.

Gilwyr was approaching from our left. I vaulted over the wall to the right, landing behind that enemy. This was a male Dalactyn guard in a white tunic with a bronze breastplate. I swung before he could turn, and the raised hand with sword attached sailed into the darkness. His howl filled the night. His companion fell back at the blood that pulsed from the severed arm, right into Gilwyr's blade as it slid through his ribs and into his heart. "Behind you!" I called.

She was too close to pull her blade out in time. She took the sword from the slackening hand of the guard and held it high to deflect the blow that was aimed at her neck. She followed through to shove the body against the legs of the Daughter who appeared from the darkness, pulling her own blade loose in the same motion. Now with two blades in her hands, she parried an off-balance cut with her right and drove home with her left to finish the fight. I advanced on the remaining Daughter and immediately found myself in trouble. She was fast and very strong. I anticipated her overhead cut and blocked it, but the impact numbed my fingers. I almost dropped my weapon. I shifted to a two-handed grip in time to parry the backhanded return blow, but only barely. That brought her close, stepping inside my guard. She slammed me with her hip, throwing me to the ground. I saw a red blade come down with deadly force across my neck.

That vision dissolved to be replaced by another phantom blade slicing through the Daughter's own neck. Then Gilwyr's real sword sliced and the Daughter's head fell in confusion to the ground.

In the sudden silence, Gilwyr stood over me with a hand extended. She was spattered with blood and lit by the ruddy light of Rhea, a lovely and terrible goddess of war. I clasped her hand and pulled myself upright. Ox was coming up the path between the arches. Our fight had only lasted seconds. "Are you hurt?" she asked.

"No, I am not. Is any of that blood yours?" Her right arm was covered in sticky red, and she was everywhere covered by droplets that trickled downwards over her bare skin.

"Not a bit of it." She pulled the cape from one of the bodies and used it to wipe the worst of the gore off. "If none of the blood that you are wearing is yours, Rhea was watching over fools. Your stance was off-balance, your center was too high, and the last time you dropped your guard, you should have been dead. Especially considering your foolhardy confrontation with one wearing the sash of Demetria."

"Now you tell me. I thought she was a bit more difficult than the others."

"A bit? Demetria's Ten are the most elite fighters of the King's guard."

Ox came up to us. "I am glad you are both unhurt. Stenn, how in the name of the child god did you see that ambush? I could see nothing."

"I can see …" As I spoke, I saw one final blade, behind me and to my left. I turned, to find the guard whom I had relieved of a hand rushing towards us, with a dagger raised in his left hand. He died on the point of my sword before he took another step.

I resumed my sentence without a missed beat. When did killing become so routine? "I can see their weapons, like red phantoms in the air. I can see them behind me, and even behind stone walls. I can see where they will swing seconds before they move and I can see how my sword must swing to block or attack. I cannot explain this, but it has been growing on me. It was only tonight that I learned that I was not just making mental images of moves in a fight, but seeing things that I could not know. I just saw that guard's dagger, even behind me, before I heard him or saw him. I saw the guard's swords as they waited behind the wall, even though I could not see the guards themselves."

"I have heard of nothing like it, have you Gilwyr?" said Ox. She shook her head, saying only that I needed an extra drubbing at practice for having turned my back on a still-living opponent.

"That's a matter to be researched when we have time and ability. We have neither out here on this rock." He noticed Gilwyr standing largely unclothed in the wind. "You must be cold, child. Take my cloak. No? Well, it will give you better concealment in the dark than your mist-pale skin. Go ahead, we don't have far to go, and I won't feel the cold." Gilwyr reluctantly took the oversized cloak and secured it over her shoulders.

"Why did you take off your dress back there?" I asked. "To distract them?"

"No, I would never stoop that low. I could not move freely and without noise in that outfit, and that fabric offered no protection against weapons. If I had been wearing stout leather, I would likely have made a different choice. In a fight, control as many facets as you can: your clothes, your footing, your weapons, your terrain, your lighting, and use them to your advantage."

"I admire your singleness of purpose."

Gilwyr looked puzzled but had no rejoinder. I saw Ox covering up a small smile as we turned to resume our ascent to the University.

No one further impeded our progress, and we passed through the gate of the University. The massive outer doors stood open, as they apparently had for many a year. The lighter inner doors were closed, and the night watchman let us in through the inset wicket gate. He was taken aback by our blood-spattered clothing. "Hae a'bt a' trouble out thar? Want ye the Surgeon?"

"Nae, we fared better n' t'others," said Ox. I seldom heard him speaking Anglich. "Any strangers come nigh this night?"

"Nae, ha'nt seen any. Been quiet since we closed th' gate."

"I hope it stay quiet. G'night ser."

Ox said quietly as we entered the corridors, "They must have been inside earlier, then."

Gilwyr replied, "I can come and go at night without any seeing me. It is not difficult."

"I suppose you are right. Careful now, they may be waiting."

We swept Ox's chambers first. He had locked his door, and it did not appear to be disturbed. "I must change and gather a few papers. I will be ready to go in a candlemark," he said.

"Lock the door behind us. We will return for you by then," said Gilwyr.

We went further down the corridor to Gilwyr's chamber. That door stood ajar, which was not as we had left it. I held my hand up and after a moment whispered, "There are two swords, vertical and unmoving to the left of the door. That should be your long swords in their rack in the tall chest. There is a dagger under your pillow. I don't see anything else in the room."

We entered cautiously, but no one was waiting for us inside. I wasn't sure how far to trust my visions, so I was glad to have no unpleasant surprises. Gilwyr lit a candle and barred the door, and we inspected the room.

The low chest had been broken open and the contents scattered. The only thing that seemed to be missing was the gem. Gilwyr's possessions were disarranged but untaken. Whoever had been there had a very specific desire.

"We must dress for the road. Waste no time." Gilwyr tossed aside Ox's cloak, poured water from an ewer into a basin, and efficiently began sponging the blood from her skin. She also scrubbed most of the pigment from her face and hands that had darkened them for her disguise as an Okkoan, murmuring that she wished she had time to remove the color from her hair as well. I also scrubbed myself quickly, and dressed in leathers for the road and donned my traveling cloak. Gilwyr returned my sword to me and strapped her two long swords to her back where she could draw them over her shoulders. Armed and ready, we returned to collect Ox, and to depart the University by the upper gate, taking the precipitous trail down the back side of the rock, away from Misthaven.

CHAPTER 20

Road to Dalactus

"TELL ME ABOUT these Daughters of Rowena. Are they the King's guard?" We had finally made camp, hours later, after Rhea had descended too low in the sky to provide illumination for travel. Camp was dark and cold since Gilwyr, our de-facto leader in matters of stealth, didn't want to risk a campfire this close to the city and possible pursuit. She had found, or already knew of, a hidden spot in a rocky cleft near the path we had been following. Here we bedded down, wrapped in our cloaks. If Ox raised an eyebrow when Gilwyr snuggled close against my back, it was hidden in the dark. Despite my exhaustion, the images of people dying by my hand flashed at intervals, gruesome statues illuminated by lightning flashes in the darkness of my mind. I asked the question to give my rational mind other matters to dwell on than the sharpness of swords, the shortness of life, and how much I had changed.

"The Sons and Daughters of Rowena are the elite corps of the Dalactyn military." From the darkness, the surrounding rocks lectured us in de Oxendon's voice. "They take only the best trained and most skillful fighters and tacticians for their ranks."

Gilwyr growled something about the tactics of sleeping before the sun rose again. Ox said, "I will be brief. Rowena ad Aulam was renowned for her cool head, meticulous planning, intricate strategies, and her ultimate sacrifice in winning the War of the Grimmerroth. After her passing in the final struggle with the Grimmerroth, a militia sprang up led by those who had served her. They began to attract the many young soldiers who were inspired by her example, calling themselves the Sons and Daughters of Rowena. They based their code of honor on Rowena's exemplary conduct and schooled themselves in the military arts. As a Prince of Dalactus, I served in their ranks for five years.

"While the cadre was known as the Sons and Daughters of Rowena, the Daughters felt a special bond with Rowena ad Aulam. They supported the legends that cast Rowena as the incarnation of Polnedra and claimed a sacred duty to guard the kingdom against the Grimmerroth and all his works. King Edmund, son of Roland, gave the Daughters the official title of 'King's Guard and Protectors of the Realm.' The Sons of Rowena tend to begrudge them the title, considering them zealots."

"The King's Guard, but the King is dying. Where do their loyalties lie now?"

"At least some of the Daughters appear to support Terrell. I fear that the number of them involved in the assassination means that their support runs deep and high, likely to General Bercarius herself. I hope to find that at least some of the Daughters, and hopefully the majority of the Sons, supported Gerard, and will transfer their support to me. There is no way to tell until we reach Dalactus. Sleep now, for we will be up with the sunrise."

I closed my right eye and covered my left. The dead who haunted me had been lulled into drowsiness by Ox's dry classroom voice. I soon followed them. I was visited by a species of sleep that was quick and heavy, a dark shroud under which the nightmares moved uneasy.

It was full light when I awoke. Gilwyr was already up, performing her customary katas. Ox was arising, a troubled look on his face. His dreams could not have been pleasant either. He stood and stretched. With his size and his nickname, it was tempting to say that he lumbered, but that would have been deceiving. He was immensely strong and surprisingly light on his feet. He had kept up the pace last night and had scrambled and vaulted over rocks and obstacles as well as any of us. If he had spent five years in the Sons of Rowena, I had to assume that he was well-trained in the combat arts as well.

I arose and went to join Gilwyr in practice. After the previous day, I had a grim enthusiasm for improving my fighting skills. Soon Ox joined us with his short sword and confirmed my suspicions that he was a competent and formidable fighter. His size and strength were overwhelming, and he was a good deal faster than he looked. I only kept up with them by the advantage of what I was beginning to call my second sight. Ox and Gilwyr exchanged glances and then came at me together. I met Ox's cut, but it was like an unstoppable force. My sword went skittering across the rocks, and I scrambled to retrieve it. They came at me again. In my second sight, I saw Ox's sword feint to my left in a repeat of his previous move and then return for a backhanded stroke. Second sight told me where to meet his blade in time to beat it down. I stepped within his guard ready to tap him with my dagger. As I moved in, however, I saw the red harbinger of Gilwyr's blade swooping in. Without even looking, I parried her stroke to the rear, tapped Ox on the sternum with the flat of my dagger, and turned to engage Gilwyr. Ox disengaged, as befitted a man with an imaginary dagger in his heart, and watched as I had a brief and ultimately fatal encounter with Gilwyr. Second sight or no, she was blindingly fast and unpredictable.

"Extraordinary," said Ox. "You say you can actually see where the sword will strike before it does so?"

"Yes, I see a ghostly red image of the sword where it will be a second before it is. I also see the ghost of my blade where it must be to defend or attack."

"Even behind you?"

"Even so."

"Would you consent to an experiment?"

Moments later I found myself tightly blindfolded and facing two opponents. I could see their swords dancing redly behind my eyes. Their ghosts moved to engage me, and I let my ghost be my guide in defense. They pressed me smartly so it was all I could do to hold them off. Attack was not an option. While I could see the swords, I could not see the terrain—I had to feel my way cautiously with my feet, nearly losing my balance on several occasions. I thought I was doing rather well, considering I was blindfolded, when I suddenly felt my sword arm grasped from behind and my weapon plucked from my hand.

I tore the blindfold from my eyes to find that Ox had handed his sword to Gilwyr and circled behind me. I could only follow the swords, and so had lost track of him. "An impressive skill," said Ox. "But now we know its limitation."

"You can only see weapons?" asked Gilwyr.

"Only metal. I don't believe I can see a club or a rock."

"Interesting," said Ox. "But we should be on the move. Let us break our fast and be on the road."

Over a portion of bread, meat, and cheese that we had packed from the University, Gilwyr remarked, "I have never heard of a magic crystal like this one. Have you, Ox?"

Ox shook his head. "I have not. In the legend of Rhea, people inhabited the City of Glass in the sky, and it was said that there were powerful wizards who made many wonderful and terrible things. That was thousands of years ago, if it ever was more than an evening's tale of fancy. Nothing of the like has been seen since the War of the Grimmerroth. Even the Grimmerroth, dark wizard that he was, had nothing like this. Are such things known to you, Stenn?"

"Yes and no. No, there are no magic crystals where I come from. No magic, either. But people have understood the laws of physics, chemistry, and biology that are the cause and catalyst of all things, and use those laws to create tools to do work for them. In my land, I would say those images are a simspace construct, a type of virtual or augmented reality."

"Those words make no sense to me."

"We have machines that can create images of things real or imagined, and make them appear to come to life. Other machines can project those images on the nerves in our eyes, and make us believe that we are seeing them." Once I started down this path of thinking, I saw a curious correspondence to what I was experiencing. "Such a machine can know your stance, and those of your opponents, and calculate the most likely way for them to attack you. And knowing your size and strength, and skill perhaps, it can calculate the best way for you to counter the attack. Then it projects those images into your eye, overlaying the reality that you see, as a guide to action. So yes, in my land we could make something akin to this. But here, where I don't see even the simplest mechanical devices, it seems impossible."

"And this isn't magic?"

"No, it is a simulation, created by machines made by people."

"What is a simulation?" Ox was packing the last items into his pack.

"It's …" I grasped for words to explain it that didn't unleash avalanches of new words that needed their own explanation. "It's when you make a model of something, to predict how it would work in reality, to see how well you understand it."

"As when I predict that if you talk about these calculating machines and simulations to anyone else, you will be hastily executed for being a warlock?"

"Very much like that. You know how people in your city think, and you judge the likelihood of the outcome in that hypothetical situation. Now if you had accurate numbers, say that ninety percent of the people felt this way, and a model of mob dynamics, you could calculate how the probability increases with each person that I talk to of a sequence of events leading to … um, do they really think that way?"

"They do. And your simulations would show you in pictures how this would end?"

"My imagination is doing a fine job of that right now."

"This is magic, Stenn. Magic is feared by people who have been assured that it is all too real."

"But these are machines, built by people."

"Do you know how to build a calculating machine? Or an image machine?"

"I know in general how they work, but, no, I can't craft one."

"There you are, Stenn. An unnatural power created by special practitioners using knowledge unknown to the average person. What else is magic?" Ox cinched his pack as if it were sealing his argument.

"To me the difference is clear, but I cannot immediately refute your argument. I will have to think on it."

"Think on your feet, then. It's time to be moving."

As we packed, Gilwyr was looking speculatively at me. "I have traveled much of this land, and never has anyone spoken of a place such as you describe. Just where are you from, Stenn Gremm?"

Perhaps I had said too much. But I trusted Ox and Gilwyr, and it was hard not to confide in them. "I am from another world, in the sky. Not Rhea, but another too far away to see." I stopped with that to see how she would take it.

"If you do not wish to answer, just say as much."

"That is my answer, and it is truthful."

She looked at me steadily. "Then I must conclude that you have your own reasons for believing these things, and have imagined a world where they are so. You admit you do not know how these things are done, and you cannot create them yourself, but you cannot bring yourself to call them magic." She set her pack on her shoulders and turned her feet to the path, ending the conversation.

I looked to Ox to see his reaction. He looked back thoughtfully but wasn't ready to comment. We both followed Gilwyr.

We departed the cleft and rejoined the road. By daylight, I could see that we had been traveling through some low hills, which soon opened up into a broad valley. Farms dotted the valley floor and climbed the hillsides. Low fences of piled stone marked off the various farmsteads. The valley floor had green leafy crops alternating with ripening grains. Upon the hillsides were scattered orchards, and what appeared to be vineyards. Surrounding the Terran green were some plots of native teal. Here and there in pastures goats went about their business of turning grass into milk.

Ox and Gilwyr debated our route. Ox felt that there was a chance of ambush in the valley, with the many vantages on the hillsides and the scant cover on the valley floor. Gilwyr was of the opinion that we wouldn't be opposed until we reached the city of Dalactus. There was apparently only one way into that city, and it would easy to set a watch on that entrance.

"I agree with you," said Ox. "The best place to stop us would be the bridge into the city. However, the Daughters of Rowena always plan in depth. They will try to stop us at multiple strategic points along our route. They always plan for the failure of some of their strategies."

"Then let us turn aside here. I know another way, no longer used."

We left the road and made our way into an orchard, walking among trees bearing yellow, red, and green fruits. The farmers here were letting the trees cross-breed and combine at will, not practicing the more advanced husbandry of starting their stock from cuttings. Apples do not breed true, and the only way to have a consistent variety is to continuously clone, by cutting, the original stock. Apple stocks are another way that those in my field can sometimes trace human migrations if the lines are maintained.

"What did Rowena ad Aulam do that earned her such a reputation of preparing for every contingency?" I asked.

"It was in the second year of King Roland, who founded the de Oxendon line on the throne of Dalactus, that a dark warlock appeared in the southern desert. He cast a wasting spell on the first party to encounter his stronghold. Only one of this party made it back to Dalactus to report to the King. He was terribly afflicted by the warlock's curse, with his skin sloughing from his body, and died soon after. King Roland sent a force to investigate this threat. They reported a great stone edifice had grown up in the desert, a citadel surmounted by a massive arch of burnished metal. A figure appeared to them from within, telling them that their lives would be forfeit if they trespassed. This figure was dressed all in black, and only a shining darkness where his face should have been. The party returned to Dalactus, though they lost many to the wasting sickness as well on their return. They reported that the Grimmerroth had returned.

"King Roland next sent an army under the command of his top general, Haward Baldewar, to besiege the citadel. They surrounded the structure, but any that they sent inside to challenge the Grimmerroth never returned or staggered back outside with their flesh sloughing from their bodies. All that General Baldewar could do was to set up a siege line. This angered the Grimmerroth, who raised an army of shambling creatures made of rock and sand, and sent them against the besiegers. To the common troops, these recalled the legends of Polnedra and the Grimmerroth, in which the Grimmerroth tried to imitate Polnedra's creation of living beings, only to find that his creations had no soul or intelligence. These new creations became known as morghaests, and are called that to this day.

"The morghaests broke the siege and routed the army. General Baldewar retreated northward, pursued by the horde of morghaests. They fell back and tried to hold the city of Coygne, a large and populous trading center on the edge of the desert. The morghaests overran the city, razing it and snuffing out nearly a hundred thousand lives. The General and his forces split, a small force retreating to Castle Horn to try to hold the south, and the main force retreating all the way to Dalactus. The morghaests were fortunately not able to cross the chasm surrounding the city, and the defenders held the bridge. The creatures didn't have the intelligence for a siege of their own, so they broke up and ravaged the countryside. Half the kingdom lost their lives in this catastrophe, and many smaller villages have never recovered.

"Roland exiled Baldewar for this defeat. Roland's temper was legendary, and none of the other generals was willing to venture a plan. Fortunately, a captain in Baldewar's army, Rowena ad Aulam, had studied the morghaests as they had retreated. She took a small force and went into the countryside where the morghaests still roamed. She spent months honing methods of combat that exploited their weaknesses. When she was ready, she returned to Dalactus to present her plan to Roland.

"Roland approved, and elevated Rowena to General, placing her in command of the entire remaining army. After months of additional preparation, Rowena set out. They marched south, overwhelming any individual morghaests they encountered and establishing garrisons to protect the towns. Finally, on the edge of the southern desert, they encamped. Scouts reported that there was no visible activity around the citadel, so Rowena began to make her preparations. She sent in diggers under cover of night. Each night they dug trenches and pits and concealed them. Each day they hid, and the desert appeared empty.

"A party of sappers was sent in to start a tunnel from behind a sheltering rock outcropping. The tunnel extended, over the course of many nights of digging, under the desert floor and under the wall of the citadel. Once there, they packed the end of the tunnel with blocks of fertilizer and laid fuses back to the entranceways, which they concealed with sand and brush again.

"The army marched on the Citadel. As they approached, morghaests began to manifest from the earth to oppose them. War carts that had appeared to be siege engines now revealed their purpose. Weights and lever arms wound back and hurled boulders with tremendous force—horizontally. The boulders smashed into the morghaests, blasting them into sand. Once dispersed, it took them hours to reassemble. The remaining morghaests milled around, unsure what to attack.

"The Grimmerroth appeared on the citadel battlements to direct his forces. Morghaests erupted from the ground beneath the siege engines, where they could not be fired upon, and ripped the wagons into pieces. The morghaests heaved boulders from the earth and hurled them against the attackers. The lines broke and swirled in confusion; the men seemed ready to break and run.

"Now from the rear, great balloons came forth. They were driven by wooden-shafted propellers, turned by dozens of men. Coming over the battle lines, they dropped stones on the morghaests on the ground, while staying above the range of stones they could fire in return. The tide of battle turned again, and General ad Aulam pressed on. She drove the vanguard so hard that no few of them fell to fire from their own airships.

"As they grew nearer, some enterprising engineer on one of the airships attempted to drop a bomb on the morghaests. It went off prematurely, and the entire airship exploded in flames. The Grimmerroth must have realized that the balloons were filled with an explosive gas. Beams of light flashed out from the Citadel, igniting the remaining airships. Destruction rained upon the troops in the field. The forces of the Citadel regained the momentum.

"The attackers had come within range of the castle. Rowena brought forward troops with broad leather and wood shields. They charged and battered the morghaests, knocking them into the concealed pits which kept them confined for long enough for the army to sweep past them.

"Finally they were at the wall. At Rowena's signal, the fuses were lit, and the charges under the footings of the wall were detonated. The outer stone walls crumbled, opening the way for the final assault on the citadel within. Rowena and two of her lieutenants won through the breach. There, within, they saw the black-cloaked figure of the Grimmerroth. He offered no fight, but turned and fled into the inner structure.

"Rowena followed with her lieutenants. Near some monstrous machine in the heart of his citadel, they caught up with the Grimmerroth. Rowena engaged with him, and they fought. The lieutenants were never quite clear on what happened next, but they reported seeing a bright light and a glowing darkness that streamed into a hole in the air. They did agree on seeing the figures of Rowena and the Grimmerroth seemingly falling into the distance, into nothingness, still locked in combat, frozen in time. To them, it was a re-enactment of the final struggle of Polnedra and the Grimmerroth, which is why Rowena is such a revered figure to this day."

Ox finished his narrative as we were coming to the head of the valley. I was digesting the points of this story, wishing for my recording devices to take it down for later playback. "I see. Any single strategy would have failed, but Rowena won the day by having multiple waves of attack to follow up each setback. You expect her Daughters to follow her example?"

"Count on it. Is this the road you propose to take, Gilwyr?"

We had come to the head of the valley, and before us lay the remains of a road, hidden in underbrush and drifted with leaves.

Gilwyr gestured, "This is a way that they will not expect us to take. The Silent Road."

Ox was pensive. "I have heard of this road, and I mislike its reputation. How certain are you that we will all come through this to the other end?"

"I am Cray Leth. You bear a cray-jon, a dagger from the Blade himself. Stenn is an apprentice to a Cray Leth and a morghaest slayer. We will emerge again. Perhaps not unchanged, but we will emerge."

CHAPTER 21

Silent Road

THE SILENT ROAD. It was forgotten. It was overgrown. It was washed away in places. It was anything but silent. An arboreal species swung through the forest in howling hordes. Like the other species I had met thus far, these creatures changed colors, but with the opposite intent. These flashed reds, greens, blues, and most of the non-primary colors as well. They weren't using their chromatic abilities for camouflage but seemed to be using the evolutionary gambit of advertising that they were too mean, nasty, or poisonous to eat, so please leave them alone.

One of the creatures swung down from the trees to look at us with evident curiosity. I signaled my implants to capture images of the encounter and swore when I predictably got no response from my absent assistants. It could take me years to stop reaching for that which was no longer there.

The creature repeated my curse back to me, verbatim and in my voice. I stared. It looked like a small monkey, with long upper arms for brachiating through the trees, shorter mid and lower limbs built for clasping tree trunks, and a diminutive wizened face with huge eyes, framed by large pointed ears. The body was hairless and was covered with a tumult of colors. As I watched, the face assumed a human flesh tone, the top of the head became brown, and the body adopted a grey color, with a wedge of lighter color pointed upwards toward the neck with darker banding around the neck. It was imitating me! It had my skin and hair color matched perfectly and was figuring out the linear patterns of the cloak I had fastened at my neck, and the lighter color shirt visible beneath it.

"Back away slowly," said Ox. "Do not alarm its mother."

"This is a juvenile?" I asked, turning my head a fraction. I heard the animal repeat, "This is a juvenile?" At the same moment, I saw motion from the corner of my eye. Then I was lying on the other side of the trail with my ears ringing, a headache banging behind my eyes and a feeling of a missing interval of time. "Oh, my head," I moaned. "What did that thing do?" Ox and Gilwyr were already at my side, confirming that I had blanked out for a few seconds at least.

"That was a juvenile *Stith*, which the Dalactyns call Howlers," said Gilwyr as they helped me to my feet. "The mother warned you three times to back away, then when you didn't listen, she showed you why everything in the forest gives a troop of *Stith* a wide berth."

"I still don't know what she did."

"She shouted at you."

"Sorry, my ears are still buzzing. Did you say shouted?"

"Yes, they can shout loudly enough to stun most attackers. You're lucky that she wasn't closer, or she could have broken your eardrums. A troop of *Stith* can surround you, and render you unconscious with their concentrated sound. They can break blood vessels in your eyes and nose. It can be fatal if they keep up the attack too long."

I shuddered. "I'll stay out of their way. But ... it was mimicking me."

"Yes, they learn quickly. Since no one travels this road any longer, these mostly speak Kir Leth. They've been chattering about how rare it is to see a party of the Mute traveling this way."

"Wait, they have their own language? You said the mother warned me? I didn't hear anything."

"They speak Kir Leth. The warning was said in skin-words only, which is why you must always keep your eyes on them."

"How intelligent are they? How large is their vocabulary?"

"How do you measure these things? They talk quite a lot and tell elaborate stories, but they don't make things or build villages. Their words are sounds and colors and patterns all at once. Since we cannot speak skin-words, we cannot master the fullness of their language and they call us the Mute. Let us move on now, and travel quietly, so we don't attract their attention. I want to listen to their chatter to see what they can tell me of what lies ahead."

My thoughts were jangling, and not just because of what felt like the worst hangover of my adult life. I suspected that the *Stith* had given me a slight concussion. But the import of this revelation was enormous. Humanity had visited many hundreds of worlds, occasionally finding higher life forms, but most often nothing more than lichens and molds. Nowhere had intelligent life been found. Of course, the great hope was always to find technological civilizations or at least their remains, but this was the first instance ever seen of a species that had even gotten as far as language development. It would be a tremendous academic achievement to be the first to study the differences in cultures of the first non-human intelligence encountered, even if they were still pre-tool-using primitives. I felt a renewed urge to find a way to return home so I could tell the human sphere about this discovery.

This put so many things I had heard from Gilwyr in a different light. I had assumed that when she spoke of Kir Leth, she was talking about an offshoot group of colonists, or perhaps a cult of some sort. Now she had named that as the language these Stith spoke. Many of the words that she had used for native species seemed to come from that language. It now dawned on me that she must have spent time among them, learning their language and their customs. I remembered the Kir Leth philosophy that she had quoted on a few occasions, which had sounded nuanced and sophisticated. There was a rich lode here, and by good fortune, I had become companion and apprentice to an experienced guide.

We traveled for some time without conversation. Gilwyr was listening to the *Stith* news broadcasting service, and from time to time she would point out other denizens of the forest. The "squirrels" and "badgers" I had seen earlier were abundant and were *botbots* and *ongars*, respectively. The forest grew denser, and all Terran species were crowded out. The native tree-analog species was ten to twenty meters in height, with a straight bole and a canopy of teal lambswool, resembling enormous mushrooms in outline. The underbrush resembled ferns interspersed with the rounded barrel-like plants similar to those I had seen on the plains, all in the Sellenrian teal color scheme.

We traveled until nightfall, then camped in a grove. Gilwyr disappeared for a time into the underbrush with her sling and stones, while Ox proved adept at lighting a campfire with flint and tinder. About the time the fire was going well, Gilwyr returned with a number of *botbots* and some tubers. She efficiently skinned the *botbots*, skewered them, and placed them around the fire. While these roasted, she nestled the tubers around the edge of the fire. I felt rather useless, possessing no woodland skills.

Soon we were eating roasted *botbot* from their skewers, and peeling the blackened skin from the tubers to eat the steaming pulp inside. *Botbot* had a mild flavor, somewhat nutty, but was similar to other roasted types of meat that I had eaten. The tubers had a flavor like apples with a combination of sweetness and tartness that was quite appealing. It might have been the appetite that I had worked up by walking all day, but I greatly preferred this meal to the "delicacies" that I had sampled at the reception.

"That was a delicious meal," I said while nibbling the last bits of meat from the *botbot*. "People can eat the wild species without harm?"

"Most of the animals in this forest are edible," said Ox. "One has to be careful with some of the blue-green plants because some of them are poisonous, but as long as you learn what to leave alone, you can get by. If we eat only from the blue-green kingdoms for many months, then we become sick."

"What do you mean by blue-green kingdoms?" I thought I knew but wanted to see how they interpreted the world.

"Our natural historians divide the world into five great kingdoms of life." Ox drew a circle on the ground with a stick and divided into quadrants, then drew an oval beneath it. "On the lower part of the circle are the plants, the blue-green plants on the left, and the green plants on the right. On the upper part of the circle are the animals, the six-limbed animals on the left, and the four-limbed animals on the right. The animals on the left live in harmony with the plants on the left. The animals on the right live in harmony with the plants on the right." Pointing to the oval, he continued, "On the bottom are the animals of the sea, which most put into their own separate kingdom. However, since the plants in the sea are all blue-green, some argue that both the animals and plants of the sea belong in the left side of the circle, and there are only four kingdoms. The animals on each side can eat some of the plants and animals on the other side, but if that's all they eat they eventually waste and die."

This seemed like the perfect opportunity to broach the origin manuscripts that I had found in the library. I had an audience of two, with whom I had built up some trust. They were unlikely to denounce and lynch me out here in the forest if I upset their worldview. "That is because the green kingdoms came from another world. The blue-green kingdoms are native, but the green kingdoms are not. I don't know how it's possible for them to be similar enough that we can eat them without being poisoned. But members of each kingdom must require some different nutrients and vitamins that the other does not supply. The sugars and starches of the plants must be similar, and probably at least some of the amino acids in the animals, but there are some complex molecules that animal bodies need that must be unique to each heritage."

"This is not part of our lore. What is your source for this outlandish claim?" asked Ox, his brow knitted. He wasn't going to accept my claim readily, but he was at least willing to hear me.

"The manuscript I found on the first day in the library was written by the colonists who came here in a ship that crossed between worlds. They crashed here; the manuscript described their struggle to survive the winter. It tells how they carefully preserved their seeds and stock until conditions let them replant them. All of the green kingdoms came from that stock." I hoped this wasn't too radical for them to accept.

"A great ship that contains every plant and animal in the world? I think you have uncovered a work of fiction."

Gilwyr looked incredulous. "It would have required a ship as vast as Rhea!"

"The colonists came in a large ship, it is true, but it was as big as the main building of the University, not as big as Rhea. They carried the seeds of the green kingdom plants and the embryos of the animals. When they arrived, they meant to plant the seeds and raise the animals. But their ship crashed, creating an explosion so great that it blotted the sun from the sky. It caused a winter that lasted for two years. They lost most of their people and a large part of their seeds and embryos. When the winter ended, they established Misthaven and started developing the land to support themselves and thrive. The native blue-green vegetation and six-limbed animals were also decimated, which gave the Terran species time to establish themselves."

"The Long Winter is a legend, a fable of long ago," said Gilwyr. "It is told that the world fell into strife between the opposing kingdoms. The Grimmerroth whispered to the green and the blue-green that they should covet each other's territory. Polnedra saw this and sang songs of harmony and cooperation to calm them. Yet they still warred, seizing land, depleting the fertility of the soil, and poisoning the waters. Polnedra wept to see that all that she had created was in conflict. The Grimmerroth saw the tears fall, and he turned the land cold so that they fell as snowflakes, for the tears of Polnedra bring peace and healing. The Grimmerroth thought that Polnedra would relent, to save her land, but she did not, for Polnedra saw how she might restore balance. She continued to weep, and the Grimmerroth continued to blast the land with cold, for if he stopped now, the land would be awash with Polnedra's tears and all his evil works would be undone. And so the world was covered with snow for years on end, and all life came to a standstill. Then Polnedra breathed warmth upon the world again and spring came once more. Life burst forth anew from seeds and spores, and from creatures hibernating deep in the ground. But they emerged without their memories of the previous conflicts. Now that there were fewer of Polnedra's subjects, she bade them separate into different territories so they would not come into conflict again. Even today, the kingdoms keep individual fastnesses, only mingling along their edges, and harmony was restored."

Gilwyr added, "I have heard much the same tale told in Kir Leth. Is this not more believable than half the species on this world coming from another? It also explains the skeletons of animals that no longer live that have been found buried in rocks or mud. They would not give up their animosity, and Polnedra did not awaken them from their hibernation after the winter was over. There have always been five kingdoms in this land since the world was created. You must be mistaken about this."

"I'm fairly certain that your mother came from another world as well. Otherwise, she would not have told you to watch for the blue line in the sky that is the wake of a ship that travels between the stars. What about your father? Do you know where he was from?"

"I only have a mother," she said coldly.

"Everyone has two parents," I persisted.

"I am Cray Leth, I only have a mother!" She stood, angry, and reached for her swords. I had only known her for a month, and that familiarity had just foundered on religion and beliefs. After glaring at me for a tense minute, she strapped on her swords and stalked off into the night.

After an awkward silence, Ox said, "That's an odd, sensitive subject with her, lad. She knew her father, Bear, and was fond of him, but she refuses to believe that he was her father. I have never gotten to the bottom of this. It has never seemed important enough to upset her so by discussing it."

A short while later we turned in. As I closed my eyes, I felt that I saw faint ghostly flashes of red. I focused my attention on this other sense of mine and located Gilwyr by her swords, some distance away. I watched them move for a time and came to understand that she was standing on a hillside, practicing her katas under the ruddy light of Rhea. They were angry-seeming movements, violent and blindingly quick. I watched as they became gradually more controlled, more meditative. Eventually, they stopped, and I saw her returning. She came into the camp and stood over me in silence. I made no movement and feigned sleep. Eventually, she went to the other side of the fire to lie down. It was the first night on the road I had spent sleeping alone, though sleep was long in coming that night.

The morning was as bleak as our moods. Gilwyr was not ready for any apologies. Part of this was undoubtedly my inability to phrase them in ways that she didn't find condescending. I was soundly thrashed during practice and shouldered my gear for the trail with a number of new bruises and two shallow slashes.

The next three days on the Silent Road were much the same. I mused that the road could have been named for the amount of conversation we had over that interval. A series of thunderstorms broke overhead, drenching us thoroughly and creating a real hazard from falling branches underneath the great teal trees. By the time we made camp in the pouring rain on the third day, I was bemoaning that I had ever found the idea of fieldwork romantic.

Gilwyr found a cave where we could shelter for the night. It was so well hidden from view that I was surer than ever that she had come this way before. However, there was no dry wood to burn, and both Ox and Gilwyr failed to ignite the soggy materials at hand. Night was falling quickly in the gloom. Sleeping in a cave without light was hardly more appealing than sleeping outside under our cloaks in the downpour, which we had done the previous two nights. I was standing at the entrance, staring out into the dismal night when a sudden dizziness assailed me. Bright candles blossomed before my eyes and a half-seen room spun about me. A face appeared, distorted as if through a lens.

"Someone is examining the stone!" I cried out, staggering in the darkness. Visual cues clashed violently with my inner ear, and I dropped to the floor before I completely lost my balance and bashed my head on a rock wall. Gilwyr and Ox were at my side quickly. "There was a face. Thin, pasty, face, scraggly beard, eyebrows you could cut yourself on. Dark hair. Intense eyes. The room was dark, just a few candles. There was a tapestry in the background, two swords crossed on the right. Stone on the left, probably a hearth."

"You describe Terrell and a room in the Castle Dalactus," said Ox. "They must have reached there."

"Is there any way he can use this magic crystal as a weapon?" asked Gilwyr.

"I have no idea what the crystal can do," I said. "I thought it was just a stone full of spooky lights until it gave me this red monocle. He probably knows less than I did. They'll probably put it somewhere as decoration."

"I hope you are right. Terrell would exploit anything that gave him an advantage, natural or supernatural. The peoples of both Dalactus and Misthaven would not fare well under his rule. For now, I am going to try to warm myself with the thought that I'm not outside getting drenched, and get some sleep."

I could hear the sounds of Ox wrapping himself in his cloak and settling in. Gilwyr was still by my side and made no immediate move away. I whispered, "I did not mean to say anything painful or offensive."

She pushed me down and snuggled next to my back for warmth. "I know." I somehow knew that this was all the apology that she would offer. The cave suddenly seemed much less threatening. Sleep came easily.

The next morning the rain had abated, to be replaced by dense fog. We regained the road and resumed our march, now through a tunnel of spun cotton stretching endlessly before us, revealed one step at a time. The hooting, howling, chirping, whirring, mewling wildlife was doing none of those things this morning, holding their breath as if afraid to inhale the fog. We walked in muffled quiet. It was the first time in our journey that the Silent Road fulfilled the promise of its name.

About midday, the road began to decline, or the land on either side to rise. Soon we were in a narrow valley that the fog did not penetrate, but persisted in forming a roof close overhead. The walls closed in, becoming a narrow canyon. A stream began to our right, taking the braggart's share of the right of way, leaving a narrow path for us to walk single file. The walls became sheer, towering above our heads, and I wondered how we would climb to safety if another cloudburst were to swell the stream. For that matter, it seemed as though there should have been more runoff from the previous night's storm than was evident. Was something diverting the excess water?

We passed the first doorway before I recognized it for what it was. Overgrown with vines, there was still something of the straight lines, the right angles that catch the part of the eye that discriminates the made from the natural.

I stopped to inspect what lay under the vines. I tried to peer within, but the vines were too thick. It looked like the door had been cut directly back into the rock. Looking backward along our path, I saw that I had already passed several doors without recognizing them. "What is this place?"

"The Silent City," answered Gilwyr.

"How old is it?" I asked.

"It was abandoned long before the fall of the Long Winter."

That date seemed impossible if it predated the arrival of humans on the planet. I wondered if these were the caves in which the original colonists had weathered that winter. "Who built it?"

Gilwyr said only, "Come along."

She set off on the path, deeper into the cleft. I looked at Ox, who shrugged, saying, "I have never heard of this place. I'm as curious as you are about the answer to that question."

Soon doorways were opening on every side, not only at ground level but all the way up the wall of the canyon. Were they reachable from within, or had there at one time been ladders to ascend to them? Finally, openings occurred that were not obscured by vines, and I ducked inside. It was an empty chamber, improbably regular in outline, without internal connections to any others. It seemed that access to the higher levels would have been through ladders or ropes and pulleys or some other means. Was this a defensive arrangement? And if so, against what?

Gilwyr hurried us on. I had a growing feeling as I counted the doors that this could not have been the camp of the first colonists. There were too many chambers for the few survivors to have excavated. I also could not imagine what they had used to carve so regularly into the sheer rock. The thought did occur to me that there was something odd about the arrangement, but recalled pyramids, and cliff dwellings, and Incan cities from old Earth and assured myself that people were capable of a wide range of inscrutable behavior.

Around a further bend, five statues guarded the path. I slowed as I absorbed the strange visages. They were statues of *Stith*, or at any rate, much larger, *Stith*-like creatures in poses that appeared tormented. Patterns of colored stones were inlaid on their bodies in what I guessed might be the visual portions of their language. I had walked through a simspace of a temple atop a mountain on old Earth that was populated with human figures in various stages of anguish and horror. Were these of a kind with those?

"These are the companions of the Grimmerroth," said Gilwyr. "He twisted their minds so that they could not hear Polnedra's song. This is Ermt, who would not hear the words of her mouth." The first statue had its upper hands clasped over its pointed ears. "And this is Lor, who would not see the words of her skin." The second had covered its eyes. "This is Izn, who would not speak words that he knew to be true." The third had both upper hands across its mouth. "This is Ans, who refused *verthine*." This one had all four upper limbs clapped down against its sides in an oddly ambiguous gesture. "And this is Bek, who covered his skin to conceal his dark thoughts." The final one pulled a cloak tight around its body. "They are here to warn travelers to leave their ignorance behind at this point, if they have carried it this far, and to proceed with an open mind."

As she spoke, she was removing her clothes and storing them in her bag, then rolling her cloak and lashing it on top. Ox began to do the same. He appeared as if he wanted to say something but was at a loss for words, which seemed unusual for him.

"What's going on? Do we need to do this?"

"You would not want to look like Bek as we approach Polnedra's temple. We are Mute, but we must still show that we have nothing to hide."

I might have objected had it only been Gilwyr, but Ox's quiet acceptance left me little choice. I followed their example and slung my now-heavier bag across my back. I felt uncomfortably exposed and vulnerable. The air was damp and chill without clothes. Aimless breezes strayed across my nether regions disconcertingly, and every thorn threatened damage. We followed Gilwyr down the canyon.

Only a few hundred meters later, the canyon came to an end. What continued was more like a crevice, or the very tall and narrow opening to a cave. Light poured from the entrance, making the interior something that eluded the eye in the polychromic glare. The light seemed to pass through some unknown and apparently invisible material, giving the impression inside of windows of stained glass, or curtains of rainbows. "The Temple of Polnedra," said Gilwyr. "Our way lies through it, and out the other side."

I suppose by this point I should have been prepared to find people within, but I wasn't. However, given the long history of finding ourselves alone in the cosmos, I might be forgiven for my surprise in discovering that these people were not remotely human.

CHAPTER 22

Silent City

THERE WERE THREE beings—people—within. They were slightly smaller than humans, I think. They seemed to have two knees so they might have been taller if they straightened their legs. They had long, double-jointed upper arms that ended in too many fingers, and shorter mid-arms that they kept crossed over their bodies, about where a human ribcage would have ended. Their faces were long, with large eyes, and somewhat bat-like large ears. They had no discernible nose. Their bodies were hairless and unclothed and covered with shifting patterns and colors. I could see no external evidence of gender that I recognized as such.

One of them was sitting on a bench, holding a staff. The other two stood flanking the bench. These two wore belts, from which hung several tools, including finely worked knives that were along the same designs as the one Ox carried. They were intelligent, tool-using beings, the first that humans had ever met. How advanced were they? On the one hand, the setting was primitive, and the lack of clothing tripped biases in me that suggested pre-civilization. On the other hand, the knives and other objects had implications of mining, and metal-working, and other, more-developed skills. Any inferences from human culture were likely to lead me astray.

Gilwyr addressed the three. She interspersed her words with hand motions, in which she formed shapes or drew patterns on her skin. I caught a few words that I had heard before, such as "Kir Leth," and "morghaest," while she held one hand in a crescent shape under her left collarbone and drew a straight line down her sternum with the other hand. The next phrase was accompanied by a complex steeple of fingers held over her right breast, followed by a wavy motion across her rib cage. I began to wonder if this was a type of pantomime, a trade language of sorts. I had heard of such languages arising on old Earth when traders arrived at new ports. Or it might be akin to the sign language employed in the distant past when deafness wasn't a curable condition.

Now one of the standing aliens replied. Its voice was sonorous, as if it had a sounding board within its chest to amplify the sound. Patterns of color formed and re-formed across its torso as it spoke, but it wasn't until I saw an image resembling steepled fingers on its upper right chest that it came to me that these color displays were part of its speech. Gilwyr's reference to skin-words, and that we were called the Mute, suddenly shifted into context. The language of this people was partly, perhaps even primarily, visual. Did they have to see one another to communicate? How complex was this language? As complex as our own? Did they have as many words? Did they even think in terms of words and sentences as we did? Did they conjugate their verbs through color, red for present tense and yellow for past? A thousand other crazy questions assailed me as I watched this exchange.

"Thank you for your courtesy in addressing us in Kir Leth." The seated one spoke, in such a natural voice that I nearly missed the transition. "I know that our language is difficult for the Mute. You employ the sign language most gracefully, Gilwyr. I am pleased that you have not forgotten." Gilwyr bowed her head at the compliment. "We thank you also for your courtesy in not approaching us cloaked, as so many of your kind would. We would give you such assistance as we can offer."

While he had been speaking to us, forms had continued to flicker across his body. The other two had turned their heads to watch him. My suspicion that he was translating seemed to be confirmed when the one who had not yet spoken said first a preliminary audible word, and then a lengthier sequence of skin-words once the other two had turned their eyes that way. The seated one said, "Erinwen says rightly that any may claim sanctuary here as long as they abide by the covenant of peace that governs us."

"We are not seeking sanctuary," replied Gilwyr. "We are seeking passage through the city. We must make our way to Dalactus unobserved, and enter the city. This is Greylander de Oxendon, Prince of Dalactus, who is known to you. His younger brother Terrell is attempting to usurp the rule of Dalactus and has already killed the third prince who has a claim to the throne. We fear that Terrell will seek to extend Dalactyn rule to Misthaven."

"Human ways are frequently inscrutable to us, and we have no interest in your affairs. The notion that an accident of birth makes one fit to rule seems especially peculiar. A leader persuades the opposition to follow or removes it through assassination. Terrell has adopted the second tactic. Which do you choose, Greylander de Oxendon?"

Ox was silent for several moments. Then, "By preference and belief, I would choose persuasion. After spending a year in meditation and study in Cloudhaven, or *Wys Talayan* as you name it," adding a sign over the left-center of his chest to complete the name. (He accented the third syllable of the name, saying "wise ta LAY an".) "I have carried the name and the word of Venn within me since that time, though I cannot display it on my skin as you do. I would rather spend my life in contemplation in the University than take the throne. I would rather gain the throne through the acclamation of the people than take it by force. I would much rather that Terrell had not taken the life of Gerard, who would have made a better ruler than I. Still, this is where the road has brought me, and I must walk it to its end. My people will suffer under Terrell, and he may well destroy the community in Misthaven I value so greatly, so I must oppose him."

"Will you kill your brother?"

"If I must."

"If?"

"You are forcing me to be honest with myself, as you always have, Perrhen. I will kill Terrell."

Their eyes turned to me. "This one is not known to us. What do you seek, in the company of a Prince and an Assassin?"

My heart thumped in my chest. I was being addressed by an alien being, speaking Galactic. My head swam with a sense of the unreal. "I am a scholar from a distant land. Gilwyr befriended me when I arrived and has taught me much. Ox sponsored my studies at the University. They nursed me back to health when I was injured. I was present when Gerard was killed and helped fight Terrell's men. They are my friends; I go where they go."

"And what do you conceal beneath that eye covering?"

My hand went to my eyepatch. "I was injured, as I said. I lost my eye."

"Yet it is not sunken and empty. We see shades of red that your eyes do not. We can see that there is something underneath that covering."

I slowly untied the cord holding the eye patch securely in place. As the gem glittering in my eye socket came into view, the aliens froze. Had they been human, I would have called them shocked. A moment to absorb something new, something unexpected, must be fundamental, a space to recognize the sudden change and the need to react. They broke into excited speech, the sound-words more sharply spoken, the skin-words flashing fast and vivid. They broke off, and the seated one asked, "How did this happen to you?"

"I was attacked by a morghaest. Twice. The first time, the morghaest consumed my backpack, destroyed an inn, and turned back to dust. The second one stabbed me in the eye, and left a fragment of its claw in the socket after Gilwyr beat it down."

"That is not a morghaest fragment."

"I don't know what happened next. I had a gem: round, as large as my fist, the same red as this crystal. Somehow when I touched that gem, my eye and the morghaest fragment were turned into this crystal."

"Where is this gem now? Do you have it with you?"

I glanced at Ox and Gilwyr. Ox nodded a quick affirmative. "Terrell stole it from Gilwyr's chamber. And I'm still linked to it in some way. I can sometimes see Terrell and see his surroundings when he takes it out to examine it. I hope to recover it when we reach Dalactus."

The three conferred once again. "This situation may be very unfortunate. It may be in our interest to help you recover this … gem. If it is the relic we think it might be, it belongs in our possession and under our protection, either here or in Cloudhaven."

"How can that be? I found it far from here." I didn't want to get into interstellar travel with a primitive people before I knew where their superstitions might lie. I also didn't want to be mistaken as a god or a demon by them. Demons generally aren't treated very well, nor are presumed gods when found to have mortal limitations.

"Our distant ancestors used *aelo tai* such as the one you describe to travel to other stars. One *aelo tai* anchored each end of a passageway to another world. But it was believed that all the off-world *aelo tai* had been destroyed in a conflict long ago. All the passageways to the other worlds were lost. Do you know of this? Your face suddenly speaks a deep red glow."

"No, your people are not known to mine, nor have any of your settlements on other worlds been found. I am reminding myself of the folly of judging another people by the path our culture has taken."

He emanated a somewhat disturbing sound: a perfect imitation of a human male voice making a short laugh at a witty comment, a chuckle. However, there was no accompanying facial expression, no feeling in the sound to convey that it was genuine. It was as if he had recorded the human sound that signaled amusement, and used it when it seemed appropriate.

"Very wise," he said. "We have been observing humans since we found them here after awakening from the Long Winter. It is an understatement to say that we still do not understand you."

"How did you learn our language?"

"Some few humans have come among us, including your two companions. I spent several years in the company of one human in travels around the land. We have other contacts, but we are … shall we say … well suited, that most humans seem to think we are—what is your word for an entertaining lie? A story? A myth?"

"They do seem to," I replied. "I've heard several people refer to you as a mythical people, akin to stories of Elves and Faeries that were told on Old Earth long ago. It seems to fit our racial makeup to tell stories of wise elder races living in seclusion."

"Indeed. Perhaps our peoples have met, in the distant past," Perrhen said obliquely.

"So this is true?" said Ox. "We did not believe Stenn when he said that he had come from a far-away star."

"It is a possible truth," said Perrhen. "We once were able to make that trip. I did not know that any portal had been used, however."

"He said that he came in a great sailing ship," said Gilwyr.

"Is that so? That was a way that we never mastered," said Perrhen. "Come now and be our guests until tomorrow. You can set off on your road rested and fed."

He rose, and led us through a doorway in the back of the chamber, deeper into the hillside. The interior was illuminated uniformly by a glowing carpet that clung to the ceiling. I reached up to touch the surface of the carpet and found it silky smooth and yielding, and somewhat warm. Was this a life form, equivalent to a cave-dwelling lichen? We walked from chamber to chamber, some oval, some rectangular, every one furnished with the glowing ceiling. Artifacts appeared in some chambers: storage shelves and cubby holes, recognizable furniture such as benches and tables, unrecognizable furniture that might have been trellises, or pillars and railings where no human would have placed them. They enjoyed flowers, it appeared, and had many flowering plants in a variety of holders. Vases appeared to be something that had evolved here as well, seeming to be one of those things that everyone is driven to invent to fill a common need.

We came to a chamber that had tables laden with food and drink. Perrhen motioned to us to seat ourselves. We had our choice of soft carpets on the floor or low benches. The benches were soft enough but too low to sit on comfortably, and little support for doing other than lying down, which seemed indecorous. I joined Gilwyr where she sat cross-legged on the carpet. Ox settled himself on a bench, using his pack as a backrest. Perrhen climbed a tree-like branching structure and established himself in the fork of two branches. The other two arranged foods on plates and offered them to us.

I looked somewhat dubiously at the food, and Perrhen assured us that they had selected only the items that we could eat without harm, and he hoped, with some enjoyment. I sampled one of them, disks of melon-like fruit covered with a spicy relish reminiscent of chutney. "This is delicious," I declared.

"We are glad that you find it pleasing. We will try to remember which ones you enjoy. We have discovered that we cannot perceive the taste you describe as bitter, so please sample small bits to be sure we haven't inadvertently given you something that you consider unpleasant."

"That's fascinating. Do you know how similar we are in other tastes, like sweetness?"

"We seem to taste sugars and salts much as you do. We can taste the sourness of acid fruits, perhaps more acutely than you do. There is a fermented taste that we enjoy, called *kreen,* that humans say is quite foul. We often like the same spicy and savory foods that you do, though there is one spice, named *astin* that is highly prized among the Kir Leth, but which humans cannot taste at all."

"Your name for yourselves is Kir Leth, then?"

"Yes, it is. Your companions did not tell you of us before you arrived?"

"I believe they assumed I knew more than I did, and I misinterpreted what little they did say." Gilwyr was oblique at the best of times, but Ox … he had become lost in thought whenever the conversation had touched on Gilwyr's people. He had either said nothing or began talking about something entirely different. It had not occurred to me until now to consider that his behavior was strange.

Gilwyr and I were sharing a plate. She picked out items for me to try and warned me away from several others. There was a hard-shelled pod that, when broken open, contained an interior the texture of fresh bread. Long slender fruits like bananas were full of red seeds that popped between the teeth like caviar. Bright yellow flowers had a pleasant buttery taste. Medium-sized berries had a jam-like interior that could be squeezed onto the bread-pods. The food was excellent, cunningly prepared and extremely fresh. I thought it was the best meal I had had since arriving on this planet. There was no meat, and I refrained from asking whether they ate it. It might seem a savage practice if they were evolved from herbivores.

As we ate, Perrhen told us that this city had been abandoned long ago, before the Long Winter. Now only a few pilgrims came to tend the shrine in the center of the city, to read some of the old texts, and to meditate. They were followers of Venn, a teacher of philosophy remarkably similar to the Terran Buddha. They revered him as having restored purpose to their race after the war that ended their star-faring era. I wanted to know more about this war, and the epoch that preceded it, but the Kir Leth seemed reluctant to talk about it.

Some hours later, the three humans were yawning. We could not see outside, but it must have been nighttime. Perrhen noticed this. "That is the signal that your kind uses to each other when you must sleep, yes? Forgive us if we have not been sensitive to your need for this state, for we do not share it."

"You don't sleep?"

"By habit, we spend the hours of darkness in quiet contemplation or study, but we do not need to become unconscious for part of every day. That seems to be a trait of the four-limbed only."

They led us to some nearby chambers that had thick carpets on the floor. "These should be suitable for your sleep. You may rest on the floor, so you do not fall when you release your consciousness. Our own rooms for resting have vertical structures where we can perch as we meditate, like the trees that were our ancestral home. There are two chambers here so the two females can have one and the male can have the other if that is your wish."

I looked at him curiously. "Only Gilwyr is female. Ox and I are males."

"Oh, please pardon my error. It is so confusing to keep your two species straight. Is not the male species generally much larger than the female? You two are similar in size and Ox is much larger. I thought I had figured it out correctly this time."

I felt a flush of embarrassment. I was unprepared to discuss reproductive biology with an alien and was mindful of Gilwyr's strange reaction to the topic of her parentage. I confined my answer to features, not function. "We are all a single species, but we take two forms. Males have these external organs and more body hair, while females have wider hips and distinctively larger breasts."

"To our way of categorizing life, those differences in form would be enough to classify you as similar but different creatures, along the same radiant from the center, or origin of life, but occupying slightly different points in the spectrum. Perhaps I am not translating the word 'species' correctly?"

"I think we may not have a common understanding of the term," I agreed. "And it could be quite an extended discussion to come to one. I think I'm too tired this evening to make the attempt."

Our hosts bowed to us and took their leave. (Had they evolved that gesture independently or learned it from humans and performed it solely for our benefit? It could even be accidentally similar in form and have a different meaning. Assumptions could lead us into serious misunderstandings.)

Ox said, "Just as well you deflected that topic, Stenn. I'll take this room, so you don't have to listen to my snoring. You two can have your privacy."

I groaned inwardly. Even Ox was making assumptions.

Gilwyr led the way into one of the chambers. Ox disappeared into the other. I stopped just inside the door, feeling as if I were sinking into soft mud. It wasn't mud, but a very thick layer of the warm, gel-like matting that had covered other surfaces. The skin was tough, so we didn't actually sink in, but … skin. That was exactly what it felt like: soft, pliable skin. Gilwyr pushed me playfully, and I fell into the yielding surface. It was warm and indecently sensuous; my body responded involuntarily. I had no clothes to conceal me. I felt exposed and tried to think of other things.

Gilwyr fell atop me, still feeling playful. "Don't the Kir Leth grow the most comfortable beds, Stenn?"

"Grow? You mean this is alive?"

"Of course it is. All of their homes are living. Stenn? Are you well? Your man-thing is all swollen. Is it something we ate?"

I felt color rising in my face. "No, it … that's … normal. It will go back down in a few minutes." I was putting together that Ox had said that Gilwyr was raised by the Kir Leth after her parents died and that the Kir Leth didn't seem to have a clue about gender. She was hardly naive about human society, but her reaction when I had brought up the topic of her father suggested that she might have a very selective blind spot. If she didn't know what my response meant, I had to assume she didn't know about sex, or some other parts of that messy, complicated human story. Now was not the time to educate her, even if I felt able to do so. In truth, I had little experience of any kind with relationships, let alone the intimate variety. If I did venture into that unknown territory, I did not want my intentions misconstrued, especially by a deeply scary assassin raised by aliens. At the moment, I could not have even told you what those intentions were.

"Oh, that is good. I was afraid that something might … have caused …" her voice trailed off as sleep claimed her.

"Something did, but not what you think," I murmured, stroking her hair. Tonight, I didn't see the deadly assassin in her face. I saw the girl-child, just barely a woman by the standards of most civilized worlds, innocent of her human heritage. She would have to learn before it hurt her. I drifted off to sleep with her in my arms, feeling that, just for a while, our roles had reversed.

CHAPTER 23

Blight

THE NATURAL LIGHTING in the cave dimmed during the night. I expected to have trouble sleeping, between the turmoil of meeting the first other sentient species known to humans, all the puzzles of their nature, and the complexities embodied in the naked woman snuggled against me on this living bed. Like so many of my expectations, insomnia eluded me this night. I slept deeply, awakening only when the ceiling brightened again. I felt rested, my mind composed. My dreams must have done a better job of sorting my experiences into manageable heaps than my waking mind. I began making lists of questions to answer and issues to solve.

Gilwyr stretched against me, threatening to upset some of my tidy heaps of issues. She lifted her head from where it had lain on my chest and smiled at me. Her face was relaxed; that wary look that was so much a part of her was gone. It made her look her age, years younger than she had in Misthaven when she was responsible for keeping us alive.

"It's so peaceful in the dwellings of the Kir Leth," she said. "Time seems to pass more slowly here."

So I was not the only one who felt that way. I thought of stories from old Earth of the lands of elves and faeries. They had been described in much the same way. There surely could be no connection, but it intensified the feeling I had of displacement, of crossing the gulfs of stars in ships that could wrinkle space, only to land in a folk tale. I had lost all of my modern augmentations, fought both demons and evil princes using swords alone, and had dinner with elves. I wondered if dragons would be next.

She showed me the cubby where we could take care of our morning eliminations. The living floor in this room absorbed all liquids and enfolded all solids, sending the nutrients, so Gilwyr said, to feed the other living furnishings. It was certainly a far more pleasant place than the smelly hole that we had used in the University.

Perrhen was conferring with Ox as we returned to our sleeping chamber. "You will want to be getting an early start," Perrhen said. "We have been conferring among ourselves all night. It is our opinion that this *aelo tai* is a grave threat in the hands of one such as Terrell. We do not know what it is capable of. We could not have told you that it would transform your eye in that way. The art of making such things was put aside long ago and with it much of the knowledge of what they can do. Please recover it from Terrell, and convey it to Cloudhaven. There are those there who may know more of this than we do. Our time here on our pilgrimage is nearly finished, and we will be returning to Cloudhaven ourselves. We will look for you there."

"We will try," Gilwyr replied.

"Here are some provisions that should see you to Dalactus. It should be about five day's journey from here. Here too are some cloaks that we have made for you. They are made from a living fabric that will color-change to blend into the background. They need sunlight and water to remain healthy, though they can go several days without. They may aid you in entering the palace. You should put on your clothing now. We thank you for your courtesy in going uncloaked among us, but you are now free to resume your own customs."

"What is the best path to Dalactus from here?" asked Ox.

Perrhen pointed to some designs on the wall that I had taken for decorative scrollwork. "Follow the signs directing you to the north gate and the road to *Mir Talayan*. *Mir Talayan* is the ancient Kir Leth city upon which present-day Dalactus is built. Before you reach the north gate, you must find your way through the Blight. The Blight is a place of darkness both outer and inner, and through it, one glimpses the end of Polnedra's dreams. It will try you, but I believe you will win through."

I opened my mouth to ask more, but Perrhen had already turned away and took his leave of us. We opened our packs and dressed. It felt a familiar relief to be wearing clothes again. A little of the Kir Leth attitude remained with me, however, telling me that clothes kept secrets within them. It was true in a way, even for us. Our postures, flushes, goosebumps, and even sexual signals communicated as well as words, though not always what we wanted to communicate. I knew there were some things I was not yet ready to say.

We took that doorway and began our walk towards the north gate. This ancient city was vast, a series of interlocking chambers like a honeycomb. The Kir Leth did not appear to have ever invented corridors or else shunned them for some esthetic or cultural reason. Rooms opened directly into other rooms, even if the function of the room seemed merely connective. We passed rooms that might have been storage, or perhaps retail shops, with walls covered with niches and cubbyholes for storage or display, all empty now. Other rooms might have been living quarters, or meeting rooms. Some of these still had the branching structures that they had used as furniture, but smaller artifacts were entirely missing. Despite the feeling that we must be deep within the earth by now, the lighted ceilings were still bright, and fresh air still moved around us. The living systems that the Kir Leth had built had endured the ages much better than most human cities.

"Were you aware of this city?" I asked Ox at one stop for rest.

"I was not. Even though I spent time among the Kir Leth in … Cloud-haven, they did not tell me of this. Nor did I know that there was a Kir Leth city underlying Dalactus. I explored that city extensively as a youth, and never came upon anything like this."

We moved on. Gilwyr knew enough of the Kir Leth writing system that she was able to pick out the glyphs for *Mir Talayan* at the junctions where there were inscriptions on the walls. I began to imagine what this city would have been like when it was teeming with Kir Leth. We moved past families who were eating, working, or meditating. Here a teacher led a class in study, and there a market sold (bartered? distributed?) food for their tables. Workers pursued inscrutable tasks in shops and offices or worked on the maintenance of the living city systems. I admitted that I was probably wildly wrong in my imagery, but the weight of history was so palpable in these ancient honeycombs that I kept expecting to turn a corner into a part of the city that was still inhabited, finding the people going about their daily lives.

It was impossible to tell the time of day inside the city, nor how far we had come. Exhaustion was setting in when finally the lights began to dim, signaling that night had come in the world above. Just then the way opened up before us. I thought at first that we had come into the open but it was an enormous hall. It was several hundred meters long and half that in width. Galleries ran around the entire hall. I counted ten levels of galleries towering above me until the topmost levels were lost in a ceiling of luminous mist. Branching structures ran up the sides of the galleries, suggesting that the Kir Leth had used them to gain access to those galleries. It seemed that they had not abandoned their arboreal ancestry. Some branches arched far over the open area. Did these provide pathways? Seating?

"What is this place? A cathedral? A park? A meeting hall? A sporting arena?" I asked.

Ox said softly, "I have no idea." Gilwyr shook her head.

We sat on a group of low, backless benches near where we entered the hall. I wondered briefly why the Kir Leth hadn't invented chair backs

—different spines, perhaps? It was a little thing to distract from the hall full of questions that stretched before us. Gilwyr read some of the signs that seemed to indicate sections of the hall. "*Lind Leth*—Tree People. *Lyr Leth*—Star People. *Tam Leth*—Stone People. *Kir Leth*—Quiet People. *Cray Leth*—Bold People. *Sar Leth*—Leaders. *Mir Leth*—Mystics."

"Perhaps this was a debate hall," suggested Ox.

We discussed the possible history of this place as we ate our evening meal. Our hosts had wrapped a dense bread in some leaves. The bread was fragrant and fresh when broken and had tastes of herbs within it. I could not tell whether it was prepared and baked as in earth breads, or whether it was the flesh of some plant, like the lighter melon-like pod I had broken open the night before. As we ate, the great vault above us darkened and reddened, simulating the sunset outside. Cool winds flowed down from above, reinforcing the illusion that we were outdoors. We sought nearby chambers with the soft floors. Though their original purpose was still unknown since the Kir Leth didn't sleep and seemed to rest in tree-like structures, they suited us very well for sleeping, which we did deeply and at length.

In the morning, we continued our journey. We traversed the length of the great hall and faced a branching of ways at the end. In the first failure of preservation that we had seen, the center passage was dark, the walls covered with unhealthy-looking moss. Gilwyr studied the signs on the walls then pointed to the darkened tunnel. "That is our way."

"Of course. Why would I have expected anything different?" I complained. "Is there no way around?"

"If there had been, Perrhen would have told us to take it." She led us to a side chamber. "Lift me up. I need to reach the ceiling."

Ox and I cupped hands and boosted her up. She couldn't quite reach, so she stepped up onto Ox's shoulders, where she balanced as if his shoulders were level ground. Using her knife, she cut three strips from the luminous ceiling covering, then jumped to the ground in a single fluid motion. She handed us each a strip and demonstrated rolling it into a tube that we could use to light our way. Thus equipped, we returned to the dark passage.

The city continued in its previous honeycomb pattern in this direction. Here, however, the luminous ceiling covering was dead, shriveled and peeling away in strips from the rock above. An odor of decay filled the air. In the side chambers, the floor coverings had dissolved into putrid green pools. Water dripped down the formerly clean walls, feeding the puddles of slime. The local equivalents of lichens crusted the walls. The floors became slippery in places, nearly causing nasty falls for Ox and me. On the other hand, Gilwyr appeared incapable of losing her balance and led on deeper into the darkness.

We traveled much as we had the day before, trying to cover as much ground as possible. We ate while on the move, as none of us relished the thought of sitting on any of the surfaces we encountered. The air became oppressive as we left the regions in which it was continuously renewed and recirculated.

"What happened to this part of the city?" I asked as we walked.

"I have heard the Kir Leth speak of a war," said Ox. "I believe it killed many of them and ended their desire to make war ever again. They refuse to discuss the details or the weapons that were used, but I suspect that this area was one of the casualties. Before the war, the City of Glass may have really existed, perhaps on Rhea. Many beautiful and powerful things came to an end in that conflict."

I thought about long-lived radiation areas or biological weapons dumps, then tried not to think of those things. I hoped that the Kir Leth would not have sent us on this path just to get fried by radiation or stricken by disease.

"Why didn't the Kir Leth tell us more about this area? They could have warned us to bring a lantern or at least torches. They must have known the light would fail."

Ox said, "I don't think they see as we do. They can find their way easily in the dark. It probably didn't occur to them." I recalled how Perrhen had seen my changes in skin temperature yesterday. Their vision might extend into the infrared. What Ox said was plausible.

We pushed on through the dreary darkness. I wished I had counted rooms to judge distance. It seemed that we had come at least as far as the previous day, but with no change in the light, we could walk all night and not know it. We found no place that we wanted to rest, so we kept going. At length, my light wand dimmed and wilted, drooping from my hand like a damp cloth. It flickered and died a handful of rooms later. The other two wands were in sad shape as well.

Gilwyr had a length of rope in her pack. We strung it between us to use as a guide, expecting the worst. We tried to pick up the pace for a time, to get the most distance out of our remaining light. It wasn't long, though, before we were down to one wand, and then even that guttered and died. We were left in the miasma of the Blight without light or direction.

"Now what?" I asked.

"The way to the north gate should be straight from here," replied Gilwyr. "We have to avoid traveling in circles. I'm going to pay out more line. I'll go first across the room. You stay here in the doorway until I tell you to follow."

We listened to Gilwyr's footsteps receding in the darkness. How many paces across were most of the chambers? I thought that there were around thirty. I tried to count, but the sounds of the steps became indistinct after a dozen or so. It seemed much longer until she stopped and called back. "I'm at the other side. Stenn, come across now. Ox, hold the line until Stenn is across."

I crossed the darkness. The space felt simultaneously vast, as I took step after step without encountering the far wall, and claustrophobically close. I could feel the weight of mountains pressing down on me from above, compressing the darkness into tar that dragged at my limbs and slowed my feet. I was shocked when I touched something soft and yielding in front of me and actually recoiled before realizing it was Gilwyr. I clutched for her and hung on, a rock on the shore of a sea of darkness. Her grip on me was just as tight.

Gilwyr called to Ox to come across, and we reeled him in. Even his normally imperturbable manner was shaken. His grasp on my shoulder was firmer than it needed to be. We regrouped and started across the next room.

Our progress became a nightmare of inches. One room at a time, one rope length at a time, one advance after another, always with the hope that the next room would bring some glimmer of light, some indication that we were nearing our goal, or even traveling in the right direction. What we wouldn't have given for a candle! At length, we slumped against a wall to take a few hours of sleep, making sure that we would not lose our orientation as we slept.

We awoke and began our trek again. We might have been going for days. There was nothing that would measure the passing of time. We could have counted footsteps, or rooms, or heartbeats, but they all ran away in the dark and would not be counted.

We were crossing a space like all the ones that had gone before it when I put my foot on something slimy and fell hard. My head bounced off the rocky floor, and I saw stars. When they cleared, I heard Gilwyr calling my name.

"I'm here. I slipped. Where are you?"

"I'm at the door. Keep coming."

I groped in the darkness. "I've lost the rope."

Ox's voice boomed behind me. "I've lost it too. It jerked from my hands when Stenn fell."

Gilwyr called, "One at a time. Stenn, follow my voice. Come towards me."

I had lost track of my direction when I fell. I got to my feet and started forward. "I'm coming."

"Keep walking towards me. Don't get turned around."

Her voice seemed to shift around me, reflected from the walls.

"Keep talking."

"You sound farther away. Come back towards me."

"I am walking towards you. Are you moving?"

"No, I'm staying in one place."

I came to a wall. There was no doorway and no Gilwyr. "Where are you?"

"I'm here. Keep following my voice."

She sounded as if she were behind me. I must have walked in a curve. I turned back and groped along the wall. I came to a doorway, but she wasn't in it. "I'm at the doorway, did you leave it?"

"No, I'm still here. Where are you?"

Her voice came to me through the doorway. "I must have wandered into another room in the dark." I entered the new room. "Gilwyr?"

I heard her say something indistinctly. It sounded like it was ahead and to my left. I went that way. "Can you hear me?" I kept groping forward until I reached a wall. "Gilwyr! Ox! Are you there?" I didn't hear anyone now. I kept groping forward until I found another door.

I heard faint voices ahead through the doorway. "I've lost Stenn!" cried Gilwyr.

"I'm here," I called back.

Now I heard Ox. "He's near me. I'll go around the room to my right and try to locate him."

I moved into the new room, calling, "Ox, stay where you are. The echoes are confusing us."

"Ox, can you hear me?" Gilwyr sounded anxious.

"I must have entered another room." Ox's voice came from several directions. "I'll try to come back."

I heard Gilwyr's reply from a different direction than before. "Keep talking. I'll try to find you."

"Now you're on the other side of me. Do these rooms go in circles?" Ox's voice was growing fainter.

"Ox, can you hear me? Keep talking." Gilwyr was diminishing as well.

Ox once more, even more faintly: "Gilwyr, I can't hear you anymore. Are you still there?"

I called in panic, "Ox, Gilwyr, I think you're going in opposite directions!"

One last voice echoed plaintively through the dark. "Stenn, Ox? Can you hear me?"

Silence.

I called until my voice was hoarse. Only echoes came back. I tried walking with my left hand always on a wall, trying to circle back to where I thought I had lost them. The walls stopped having left turns. I halted and listened for the smallest whisper. I thought I heard a faint drumming and tried to follow it. It grew louder and louder until I recognized it as my own heartbeat. The darkness became a wall of unalloyed despair that I could no longer penetrate. I surrendered to it and sank in a pool of misery on the putrid moss.

CHAPTER 24

Black Crystal

I HEARD MOANING in the darkness. After an extended period of irritation at the sound, I recognized it as my own voice. *Gilwyr would be disgusted with me.* That thought was enough to haul myself to my feet and take stock. I still had my pack, my clothes, some rations, some water, my sword and knife, and my wits. I couldn't see anything in the blackness, and I had moved away from the walls so I could not orient myself. Vision was useless, so what did that leave me?

I strained to feel the slightest movement of air that might indicate an exit. The atmosphere was absolutely still, stagnant and clammy. The temperature was uniform. Sounds reflected off flat surfaces. I experimentally clapped my hands and listened for echoes. Two echoes came back, the one ahead of me taking slightly longer than the one from behind. I moved tentatively in that direction and clapped again. The echoes equalized. A few more paces and the echo ahead came quicker than the one behind. A few more claps and I arrived at the end of the room and a door leading onward. I hoped I had not gotten completely turned around in my wanderings. I rewarded myself with a meal of Kir Leth bread and a ration of water.

I traversed a few more rooms in this manner, gaining confidence that I could navigate with a kind of primitive sonar. I diverted myself from dark thoughts by wishing that humans had descended from bats rather than primates. Much later I dismissed the first few glimmers of red to cross my vision as stray cosmic rays or an input-starved optic nerve. They continued and nagged me with their familiarity. That familiarity continued to nudge until it clicked that I was seeing with my second sight, courtesy of my crystal eye. There was a source of radiance that I could perceive some distance off through layers of stone, and it was growing in intensity as I approached. I pressed forward, hoping that it meant the end of the Blight.

I entered a chamber that echoed distantly, a sign that I was in a large space. The source of the radiation was just ahead, probably within the large chamber, but I could see it only in second sight. Of visible light, there was still none. I approached and began to perceive that what seemed to be a radiant sun at just above waist height was another *aelo tai* like the one that had come into my possession on Trondhjem. By second sight it had glowed in the crimson of that vision. Now that my right eye beheld it, however, it glowed with a black radiance. It was rather the reverse of radiance, pulling the light into itself in tortured streamers. It was held on a pedestal that was visible in outline against the anti-glare. I reached for it, with the thought that I could use it to illuminate my way out of this maze. I found that it was warm to the touch. It resisted leaving the oval indentation in which it rested, coming away slowly as if attached with many invisible strands of glue.

As soon as it was in my grasp, I knew the thing was evil. I wasn't a believer in abstract evil, preferring to think in terms of motivations, gain versus loss, and selfishness in zero-sum games. I felt that those explained ninety-nine percent of what was called evil in the world, generally by the side who had something to lose. This was evil. It was the cause of the Blight, corrupting and rotting the beauty of the old Kir Leth city. I knew things about it: it was a weapon from an ancient war. From the final war. It subverted communication between the Kir Leth to sow discord. It was a cousin to the red *aelo tai* but had been subverted to destroy the city. How did it tell me these things? I couldn't say, other than to guess that my connection with the red *aelo tai* made me receptive to some information transfer.

Light struck me with physical force. I threw up one hand to shield my dark-adapted eye from the glaring brightness. I had the impression of a circular space, with raised seats surrounding it: an arena. I heard a noise behind me. I whirled, forcing my hand down from my eye and squinting to see. Ox and Gilwyr had come up behind me. I should have been overjoyed to see them, but I started guiltily and pressed the stone against my ribs to conceal it.

"What have you found, Stenn?" asked Ox.

"A light switch, it would seem," I said, shading my eyes. "I touched the pedestal, and the lights came on."

"Was there anything on the pedestal when you found it?"

"No, it was empty."

It's not like you to lie so easily. That sounded like the voice of the Other again.

If they know you have the black stone, they will take it from you. This voice was lower-pitched, authoritative, a voice you wanted to believe. It was not a voice I had heard before. It was getting crowded inside my head, but I would have to worry about that later.

"An empty pedestal, here in the one place where there is light? I find that hard to believe. Show me what you took."

I kept my hand behind my back. The guilt was burning my hand, but still, I had to hide the stone, or risk losing it. The burning became a searing pain, and I realized it was more than guilt burning. I had to look. I had to drop it. No, I couldn't! I hung on grimly.

Gilwyr circled to my left, into my blind spot. "What are you holding, Stenn?" I turned to keep her in view, but Ox took a step toward my other side. When I looked back towards him, Gilwyr seized my hand and forced it upwards. To all of our surprise, it was empty. There was an angry red circle on my palm, and the burning pain was now moving up my forearm.

"What have you done with it, Stenn?"

"What makes you think I had anything?"

"You have the look of someone who is hiding something. You have been holding back since the day we met," said Gilwyr.

Ox continued, "You concealed dangerous machines. You concealed the red gem. You've never explained your reasons for coming here, or why the morghaests pursued you. You say you are inexperienced at fighting, yet you have an uncanny ability to anticipate your opponent. I think only one explanation makes sense. You are a wizard who has come to this land to find the tools of the Grimmerroth so that you can be the next to bear his name.

"Give us what you found," said Gilwyr.

"If it's as evil as you say, won't it just corrupt you instead?" I addressed this to Ox. He had uncertainties that I could play on. I needed to sow doubt.

"I will only use it to defeat the usurper. With it, I can overthrow Terrell and take the throne. I can weed out the oppressors from the Court of Dalactus, and establish a new rule of justice and equality."

"History is littered with the regimes of tyrants who were convinced they were making their countries great again. It never ends well." An appeal to his better sense might work.

Ox's eyes flickered briefly to one side. Gilwyr would be angry with him later, for having telegraphed her move. I whirled quickly in the other direction and pulled my blade from its scabbard. She moved in a blur, and I managed to parry in time. Second sight hadn't warned me of her attack. I backed away from Ox so that he wouldn't have a chance to take me from behind, though he seemed satisfied to let Gilwyr finish me off. They have changed, I thought. They're not the people I knew.

The Blight changes everyone, said one of the voices in my head.

Gilwyr reversed and slashed backhanded. I beat it aside, recovered, and essayed an attack of my own. She stepped back and let my momentum carry me out of position, then came back with an overhand attack. I dove and rolled out of the way as the tip of her blade whistled past my left shoulder. I felt a line of fire cross my skin. There was no doubt this time. I had lost the power of second sight entirely. It was my one advantage over her, and I had a sinking feeling that I had depended on it too much.

We squared off again. Think of this as a practice bout using wooden swords, I told myself. You can't see wooden swords. I had been forced to watch my opponent rather than using second sight to watch the swords.

Those were blunt, and you received many bruises, the darker voice said.

If I don't try, it will be worse than bruises, I shot back.

I told myself to shut up and watched Gilwyr's eyes, her placement of her feet, her grip on her sword, her adjustments of balance. As she came in for an attack, I saw the shifting of her weight that signaled that this was a feint. I stepped inside to execute a solid block of the stroke that followed, jarring both of our arms. I straight-armed her, sending her staggering back across the packed ground. I followed up, pressing my attack. I had an opening when I could have nicked her in the side, or worse. I didn't take it. *Every act of kindness, each thought from the goodness of your heart, weakens the darkness,* said the Other.

How was I going to win if I couldn't bring myself to injure her? We weren't fighting with the usual leather protections. Any stroke was going to bite flesh. What would it take to end this fight? Would I have to surrender to avoid harming or killing her? I was certain that she would never surrender. I wasn't certain that she would even accept my surrender.

Her next move would be a double-feint straight-on attack to keep me off balance. She rushed me, starting a feint to my right, then starting a reversal, watching for me to commit to the block, and then switching back to the original attack. I saw the ruse and knocked her sword wide. The spot between her breasts that would end this was open. I couldn't take it. She whirled away and the moment was lost.

How had I known what her attack was going to be before she made it? It was familiar somehow. We had done this before. When? Then it came to me: a practice in the forest when she was angry with me. She had thrashed me thoroughly. This was a replay of that fight. I knew what she was going to do next.

She circled to my left, into my blind spot. I turned to keep her in view. I watched for the cut that would come from the right when I placed my weight on my left foot to follow her circling. I swung, cross-body, knocking the sword from her hand, then reversing and driving my hilt into her jaw. She dropped to the ground before me.

As she lay sprawled in the dirt, I remembered when we first slept in the uncursed part of this cursed city. She had sprawled like that on the bed, unclothed, unaware of the effect she had on me. That feeling of lust washed over me again, and I put my hands on my belt.

Take her. Dominate her. Break her. She will follow you then. Otherwise you'll have to kill her.

The voice had miscalculated. A wave of icy shame washed over me. I lost my will to fight, I lost my desire. I bent over on the dirt and lost my last meal. The revulsion I felt at what the voice had urged me to do was so great that it took me out of the illusion. The arena, Gilwyr, and Ox faded like a simspace show. The darkness returned, and the floor felt slimy again. Had that been a hallucination? A hologram? A vision of some old religion's purgatory? Unsteadily, I regained my feet.

The bruises and the gash on my arm had felt so real. It had the quality of a nightmare, with events that had their own internal logic but which broke down on awakening. Ox and Gilwyr would not have acted like that. But if it was my nightmare, did that mean that I might be capable of a deed that vile? I wished that Polnedra was real so that I could pray to her that I wasn't. More than ever, I wanted to escape from this *avskyelig* noisome black cave and see the sunlight once more.

Where was that black stone? It no longer illuminated the chamber in black radiance. I had hoped to carry it with me to guide me out. Perhaps by doing so, I could even cure the Blight. I could become a hero to the Kir Leth, restoring their city to them. I had a vision of this city come back to life, reopened for commerce to the stars. I would be renowned through-out human space as the person who opened up the first non-human world to commerce, president of the first university for the study of xeno-anthropology, and ambassador to the Kir Leth. But where was the stone?

I remembered the burning pain in my hand that had traveled up my arm. I now felt something like leaden indigestion nestled right beneath my breastbone. I prodded the area and felt a hard, oval object lodged there beneath my sternum. The *jævla* stone had hitched a ride on me like a *faen* parasite. There had been other pains in shoulder and chest as it had migrated, but I had ignored those as I had fought. What had it done to me? I had to get out of this place.

I looked around. The darkness wasn't so dark now. I could see faint glimmers, and second sight was working for me again. I could even see the path I needed to take to get to the north gate, not far from here. Second sight seemed different now. The glimmers were black rather than red and outlined the tunnels and chambers rather than metallic objects. It showed me the way out, so I would take the gift and worry about it later. As I walked, the ceiling began to give off a wan and sickly light. It was nothing compared to the illumination in the healthy part of the city, but I could begin to make out my surroundings. It might even help Ox and Gilwyr find their way to the exit.

Soon I was climbing from a cleft in the side of a rock face. It was overgrown with bushes so anyone coming upon it wouldn't see the access to the city. No wonder the *jævla* four-arms had managed to keep the place hidden all this time. I was cursing in my native tongue, which I rarely did, even in my own head. Somehow I felt justified after my experience. I found a stream nearby where I drank and refilled my bottles, then washed off the mud and slime as much as I could. I washed my clothes and hung them out to dry, and decided to catch some sleep. If my pathetic companions emerged by the time I was ready to move on, they could still prove useful. If not, well, I didn't really need those people anymore. I wrapped myself in my cloak, lay down, and slept.

In my dream, I returned to the arena and faced Gilwyr once more. The fight played out as it had before, and ended in the same way. This time, I gave in to the voice that urged me on. As I arose from an act that I cannot bring myself to recall now, though it was only a dream, I saw myself as in a reflection. I was a twisted monster, fitting heir to the Grimmerroth.

As dreams sometimes do, the sequence repeated. We fought. I took control of the sequence, struggling to remember who I was, and who I aspired to be. Gilwyr was gloriously skillful, a joy to watch. I remembered watching her practice, watching her perform her katas. I saw strength and innocence and grace. I saw Ox standing watchful, and remembered how he had cared for his people. I defeated Gilwyr as before, but walked away, silencing the dark voice.

The battle repeated. We fought again. I remembered my training: she was merciless while a lesson was in progress, but afterward, she had tended all my bruises. I remembered how she fought the morghaests with me. I remembered how I fought the Daughters of Rowena with her.

I remembered how she and Ox cared for me after I had lost my eye. This time, I ended the fight by lowering my sword and taking her hand. Together we told Ox that our only strength was in unity, and we left the arena together.

When I awoke, I was more in control. I had built a buffer against the black crystal. It had overwhelmed me with emotion, temptation, and suspicion. The arena was a metaphor for my fight against it. I could feel it still whispering and influencing, but I had pushed it off to arm's length. I had enough distance to recognize that my bitter thoughts had not been my own. The voice of the Other had helped me, though I no longer knew whether that was an avatar that had hacked my implants to act as a sometime guide, or whether it was a fragment of my personality that I had embodied with a voice. I felt that I had been assaulted enough times since landing on this planet to qualify for some degree of mental trauma.

I chose my friends to confront me in the arena. Perhaps I already had suspicions about them?

I almost let that thought slip into my head as my own before I recognized that it had been planted. I was going to have to watch myself. How could I trust that I was thinking for myself? I had only known Gilwyr and Ox for a short time. It was only sensible to keep in mind that their self-interest might not always be in my best interest. Was that right, or had that thought be planted as well? My grip on sanity felt tenuous.

I heard a cry, and Gilwyr came stumbling out of the cleft. "Stenn! I was afraid I had left you behind in there. We looked for you when the light returned, but we couldn't find you. We hoped you had gotten ahead of us!" Then she was embracing me, getting me covered with slime and cave dirt again. I didn't mind.

"After we were separated, I wandered alone for hours," she was telling me. "Just before the lights returned, I encountered a phantom that took your form." She paused. "I think it was a phantom. You did unspeakable things. And so did I. But you disappeared in the mist when it was over, so I think it wasn't really you. Was it?"

I had a sudden chill. What if hadn't been a hallucination?

"I also fought your phantom, but they were creations of a black *aelo tai* that caused the Blight. I found it after I fought you, and took it from its pedestal. The lights began to return after I pulled it from its socket, so I hope that the Blight will begin to heal now."

"What did you do with the *aelo tai*?"

"I … threw it down into a crevice in the rock, into the darkness."

Shame. Be ashamed of me. Hide me from your friends. They will covet me.

"We should try to find and destroy it."

No. It will give you strength to do what is needed.

"We would never be able to find it again." I knew that I should tell her the truth, that I still carried it, but somehow I couldn't do it. This passive omission was somehow easier to rationalize. I could tell her later.

Gilwyr gave me another squeeze, and I winced as she put pressure on my upper arm. She lifted the cloak from my arm to see what pained me. When she saw the slice across my upper arm, her face went pale. She looked me in the eye for a long moment, then turned away. I felt my own blood draining from my face, leaving me feeling unsteady. If the fight had been a hallucination, how had I received that cut?

Gilwyr went to bathe. She didn't bother with a cloak afterward but lay in the sun to dry off. I kept busy, trying to not look in that direction, while the voice urged me to take what I wanted. I doubted my self-control now.

An hour later, Ox appeared from the cave, and explanations were made all over again. He was even more disturbed by the black *aelo tai* than Gilwyr, but there was nothing immediately to be done about it. His eyes were haunted by his experience in the cave. He had had one of the twisted hallucinations as well, but he wouldn't speak of it.

Ox climbed to an overlook above us on the rock wall and told us that we were less than a day's march from Dalactus. We decided to camp for the night and to make that trek by daylight. Gilwyr and I slept apart by mutual consent, but I lay awake wondering what I had been capable of in her hallucination. And what depths of her own soul had she learned about?

CHAPTER 25

Dalactus

"SO THAT'S DALACTUS," I murmured, peering across the chasm. I don't know what geological forge had wrought this country that had been folded over on itself, creased and torn on a bias to form some of the most impassible territory I had ever seen. We had left the road some time ago, as the incidence of Dalactyn patrols had increased. We were several hundred meters to one side of the point where the road launched itself across a chasm on a narrow bridge. The bridge was of dressed stone, with graceful supporting arches meeting above the chasm in a keystone span that would have made the Romans proud. On the other side, the outer walls of the city were a sheer extension of the cliff face. The only entrance was across the bridge and through the gates. On the city walls above the gates, massive boulders were poised to destroy the bridge if the city should be besieged from that direction.

With rugged mountains at its back, the city held the place of a natural fortress. In front of it was a sheer drop to the ravine below, crossed only by the single bridge. Forbidding walls guarded the entire length of the plateau that fronted the ravine. The plateau held the city and outlying farms that fed it, and ample supplies of water flowed from the mountains. It could be held indefinitely against a siege, Ox told us.

"Who is there to besiege this place? Misthaven didn't look very militaristic. Are there other kingdoms? Did you have to defend yourself against the Kir Leth?"

"The Kir Leth are so reclusive that the majority of the population believes that they are mythical or extinct. They foreswore their warlike passions long ago after …" His voice drifted off and he was silent for a moment before continuing, "There were a number of other kingdoms in the land before the War of the Grimmerroth. Those that were not devastated in that war were gradually abandoned in the years afterward. No one knows the cause of this decline, but population numbers fell, and large areas that were previously settled and cultivated have been given back over to the blue-green and six-legged kingdoms. It was as if humankind lost the desire to live outside our enclaves in Dalactus, Misthaven, and Coygne. Refugees from those failed kingdoms streamed into the cities, slowly, over a hundred years or more. Dalactus has maintained its practice of the military arts and has a vocal minority of the nobility who advocate aggressively resettling abandoned kingdoms. Terrell is among this number. Misthaven, in contrast, has focused on the advancement of learning, culture, arts, and trade. There are some smaller settlements still, such as the one on Okko island, but none with populations that could threaten Dalactus."

"And yet the city maintains a guard on the wall and a checkpoint on the bridge."

"Tradition. The checkpoint is not usually so well manned. Terrell must be expecting me to return, now that his assassination attempt has failed."

"We can't go in that way," said Gilwyr.

"Not even with our Kir Leth cloaks?"

"Not for this purpose. The cloaks won't keep you from making sounds or casting shadows. There's no way to stay far enough away from the guards to stay undetected. The illusion is not good enough at close quarters."

"How do we get into the city then?"

Ox considered. At length, he said, "When I was a boy, exploring far more of the city than my elders would have approved of, I found an opening from the crypts into the lower valley. I used it when I wanted to spend a day beyond the city walls without the knowledge of the headmaster. I've never seen any signs than anyone else knows about it, and I've told no one."

"That is our way in, then," said Gilwyr.

"We have to descend through this defile, and should then cross after dark so that we're not seen from above."

I looked over the edge. "Down there?"

"There will be some rope descents required."

"Did I ever tell you that I'm not good with heights?"

My companions were thoroughly acquainted with that fact by the time we reached bottom. After I had frozen several times, once on a ledge when I couldn't bring myself to trust the rope, and twice when faced with chimney descents where I doubted my strength, Gilwyr threatened to leave me stranded halfway down the cliff face to find my own way down. Even Ox was beginning to lose patience with me. I finally stopped looking down and concentrated on the square meter of cliff face directly under my fingers and toes. I was grateful when at last I reached down with my foot and touched solid ground.

"Whew, I told you I wasn't good with heights."

"You have been complaining a good deal more since we emerged from the Blight," observed Gilwyr with some asperity.

"Sure, needle the apprentice."

"I have noticed a good deal more whinging myself," agreed Ox.

I saved your miserable lives in the Blight.

The dark voice had been insinuating itself into my thoughts whenever fatigue or irritation gave it a crack to pry its way in. On a few occasions when my guard was down, I had said something I regretted. I tried to reframe my response. "Sorry. It seems like we all have been out of sorts since then." It still came out as irritable.

"We have time for a round of practice before it's dark enough to cross the valley." Gilwyr laid her hand on her sword.

Ox was more understanding. "Stenn is right. We have all been on edge since our walk through that dark place. We all had experiences that tested us, tested our moral compass. We'll never leave the memories behind, nor should we, but we should use them as reminders that we always have a choice, and those choices define us. Let us continue now with no more cross words among us."

Ox's words lifted my spirits. He was going to make a fine king, I thought.

"I think Stenn was the most affected," he continued. "He actually touched the black crystal. He deserves our thanks for getting us out of the Blight."

Thanks for giving me an excuse, old man.

I told the voice to shut up.

From here we could look up at the walls of the city. I could see that great stone soldiers stood in niches on the outer wall. Each one must have been ten meters tall. I could see six from where we hid in the shadows. If there were an equal number on the other side of the gate, there were an even dozen.

"Those are unusual decorations for a defensive wall," I said. "Don't they create weak spots in the wall where attackers can climb?"

Ox replied, "It is said that in the War of the Grimmerroth, they left their stations and strode across the land to engage with the morghaests. I don't give those stories much credit. They seem to be embellishments by story-tellers to coax more coin from the pockets of their listeners. Even if any in Dalactus possessed the knowledge to motivate those giants, it would be like using the Grimmerroth's own tools. As Venn has said, if you use your enemy's tools, you become your enemy." I recalled being told about Venn in the Silent City. That seemed like it was ages ago, before the Blight.

At dusk, we crossed the valley floor to the Dalactyn side. During the closing hours of daylight, Ox had surveyed the opposing cliff face closely until he had identified landmarks that he remembered from years before. We made directly for the shadow shaped like an upwards-pointing dagger and found that the hilt was a crevice, deeper than it looked, that led back into the blackness. Several paces inside the mouth of the crevice, as the light was failing us, Ox reached behind a fallen boulder and pulled out several old torches. "I left these here thirty years ago and more," he said. "More evidence that no one has used this way in all that time." We lit the torches with flint and steel and used them to continue deeper into the darkness.

We came to a boulder that seemed to block further progress. Instead of finding a way around the boulder, however, Ox began a crab-like ascent of some toe- and hand-holds along one wall, working backward towards the way we had come. As he passed over our heads, he squeezed himself into a crack that could not be seen from the ground. "Oof. I was smaller the last time I tried this passage," came floating back to us from the gloom. "Come ahead now. I'm through the tight spot."

I climbed the circuitous path next. When I reached the level where Ox had disappeared, I saw his torchlight shining through a narrow passageway. I stood in the mouth to light Gilwyr's way on the climb. She stepped lightly up the treacherous way as easily as if it had been a staircase. Together we entered the passage.

Inside was a honeycomb of rooms that was by now familiar to us. None of the rooms had their organic systems anymore, but the shape of Kir Leth construction was unmistakable. Ox was shaking his head. "I thought the Silent City looked familiar to me," he said. "But I couldn't place where I had seen that architecture before. This was where. It had been so long that I had forgotten all the details."

"This must be *Mir Talayan*," said Gilwyr. "How far does it extend?"

"I've only seen a few rooms. The rest may be sealed off, or blocked by rockfalls. There are earthquakes in this area from time to time. You'll see evidence of one shortly. Our way lies upward, however."

A sense of wonder filled me as I stared around at the ancient remains of another Kir Leth community. How old was this place? Had it been occupied when Earth's pyramids were new? How many such cities existed on this world? What was the history of their people? A lifetime of study awaited if only I could come and go from this world as with other worlds.

We followed a ramp that led upwards at the end of the room. After we had climbed above the level of the roof of the room we had just departed, another room opened. The ramp switched back and ascended to another room, and another, in a zigzag course. After we had reached the fifth level, the way upward became a narrow, tightly spiraling ramp that ended in a blank wall. Ox pushed outward on this wall, which opened smoothly and noiselessly into the room beyond. I felt the rush of cold night air as we entered.

We were in a chamber that was enclosed on three sides, with the fourth entirely open to the elements, a wide portal in the cliff face. The walls were covered in stone boxes stacked nearly to the ceiling. Looking backward, the door had vanished into the wall behind us. The stone boxes had been cleared from that area, some of them pushed aside, a few broken open. Human skeletons spilled from them across the floor like fossilized creatures born from eldritch eggs. A cold spider of unease walked up my neck. I had visited plenty of crypts before, but always in simspace. These were the actual remains of people who had walked this planet centuries before. Simspace had not prepared me for this.

A chill wind blew in through the opening from the night outside and whispered around us. "I think no one has been here since I opened the door thirty years ago," said Ox. "This is the lowest and oldest level of the crypts. The remains interred here predate the time when Roland founded the line of de Oxendon on the throne. I found this chamber when I was exploring the crypts, and saw that a draft pulled my torch's smoke through a crevice behind these coffins. I found that door, and the hidden latch. I kept it my secret while it was useful to me as a youth, and forgot about it later."

I went to look over the edge, where darkness rushed past, borne on a twenty-knot breeze. There was nothing below us but night, endlessly falling. My knees trembled, and I had to hang on to the nearest coffin for support. I looked up and saw there were more openings like this one, the upper ones bleeding light out into the void. By that light, I could see that the upper cliff face curved out into a massive overhang, and above that, the cold, bright, and ever so inaccessible stars. This was not an invasion route into the city; no army could get past that curling lip. The inner passages, I was sure, would be very narrow and easily closed or defended. I was gaining an appreciation for the mindset of the builders and inhabitants.

We climbed through the crypts of Dalactus. The chambers were connected by more of the steep spiral ramps that had led us into the lowest level crypt. Despite all of my training of the past months, I was lifting feet of lead by the time we reached the upper levels. Here, the rooms were lit with thick candles that looked like they would burn for days, and Ox confirmed that it was a weekly ritual for the priests to renew and relight them all. The chambers were thankfully empty of such caretakers now.

Ox informed us that family rank determined the level at which your coffin would be placed—nor was that a static assignment. As the fortunes of prominent families rose and fell over the years, their ancestor's remains might be elevated higher in recognition of great deeds or shuffled downwards to make way for newer or more favored tenants. The seals of houses were hung rather than carved so that such reordering might occur more readily. In the topmost chamber, Ox paused before a large and ornate sarcophagus and bowed his head in respect. "King Roland rests here," he said. "Among all of them, this one is never moved."

The final ascent was a lengthy spiral that must have been piercing the overhang that I had seen from below. We finally emerged through an archway into a narrow, dark area. Moving to one side into the open, I saw that exit from the crypts was behind and underneath an altar-like table. The top of the altar was a greenish glass that was over a handspan in thickness, regular in shape and without defect. My heart skipped a beat as I realized that it wasn't simply a primitive piece of glass, but rather, it was a precisely shaped window. In fact, it was the viewing port from a starship. A surviving piece from the *Corvus?* Or perhaps even from that earlier ship that had brought the original colonists? No, that had been destroyed. Their shuttle perhaps? I wondered if anyone now alive knew the origin of this slab of glass.

The altar was in an alcove in a building that might have been either a temple or a museum. Statues stood in niches around the perimeter of a great hall, lit by candles. A domed roof was lost in the shadows. I dearly wanted to linger, to study the architecture, to catalog the sculptures, to understand what had grown up on this world nearly from scratch. Ox hurried us along, however, telling us in a hushed voice that there might be attendants around.

Outside the temple, we were immediately in a maze of narrow streets. They were clean, well-paved, and had what appeared to be oil lamps at intervals. I wondered what they were burning in them. We had only gone a short distance before Ox pulled us back into an alleyway while a patrol of three guards walked down the street, checking doors and windows. We waited until they had passed.

"Let us put our cloaks on now," said Ox. "There will be other patrols." We pulled out the cloaks that Perrhen had given us and pulled them close around. "Remember not to stand where you cast a shadow, or stand in front of a light. Cover your hands and faces if they might be seen. Trust to stealth first, and the cloaks last." My companions seemed to disappear in the shadows. I had a moment of panic that they were leaving me in the city as they had abandoned me in the Blight, then Gilwyr pulled her cloak aside, making her face and hand appear to float before me. "Stay close," she whispered.

We went back out into the street. I was able to follow Ox if I concentrated on his outline. While he moved, there was an Ox-shaped ripple against the backgrounds ahead of me. When he stopped, he blended in almost perfectly. I looked down and saw what he had meant about casting a shadow. An elongated specter followed him on the ground, pivoting through arcs as he passed each street lamp. When he stepped between me and one of the lamps, the illusion was broken. The living cloak attempted to blend in, but it couldn't glow as the lamp glowed, and so it appeared as if Ox was wearing a painting of a street scene at night. If you knew that an enemy was using such cloaks, you could arrange lighting that would make them very difficult to use effectively. I hoped that the Dalactyns weren't aware of their existence.

We made our way through the town street by street. At each corner, we checked for patrols before proceeding. Twice we waited for guards to disappear into side streets. At each lamp, our shadows dogged our feet, reminding me of the whispering shadow within me. Had I really thought a few moments ago that Ox and Gilwyr had abandoned me in the Blight? That had been an accident. Or had it? Could I trust my own memories? I had fallen, right? The rope had jerked from my hands ... was that before or after I fell? Had someone jerked it to make me fall? I couldn't be sure. I resolved to be more watchful of these people who pretended to be my friends. They had their own shadows inside. Everyone did.

We cut through an alley where darkness ran like dark water between lighted streets. As we neared the farther street, I saw the distinctive red shapes of swords in the street beyond in my second sight. Three swords: three guards. I hissed a warning to Ox, who was still in the lead.

We peered around the corner. The guards were banging on the door of a shop across the way, their backs to us. It was one of the few shops that had a gleam of light spilling into the street, and as the guards raised a commotion, the other lights winked out. The light that had caught the patrol's attention did not, perhaps realizing that it was too late. The door cracked open, reluctantly I thought, and a face peered out.

"It is past time for lights to be out," I heard the guard saying. "Why are you still squandering lamp oil?"

"We have an order from the palace that we must fill by tomorrow." The voice from within was definitely frightened. "Working by lamplight is the only way we will finish in time."

"Then you won't mind if we inspect your work." The guard started pushing the door open.

Ox bent down and found a brick in the alleyway. I thought he was going to attack the guard, but with a mighty heave, he threw it far over their heads so that it clattered loudly in the street near the next intersection. The guards jerked their heads around at the sound. "Have your light off by the time we make our next round," warned the guard. They trotted off to investigate the noise.

The light in the shop winked off. Two figures slipped out onto the street and hurried in the opposite direction from the guards. Another departed after an interval, then two more, then a final one headed towards our alleyway.

Ox placed his hand on the figure as it entered our hiding place and slid his cloak back to reveal his face and hands. "Friend," he said. "My hand is ungloved." Gilwyr and I kept very still, hidden by shadows and cloaks.

The person started but kept quiet, and peered up at him. "But my knife is sharp," he replied. "You know the password."

"I am just this night returned. I seek the Hidden Hand. I had not expected to find it quite so poorly hidden."

The man was trying to see Ox's face. His breath hissed. "Prince Gerard?"

"Gerard is dead. I am Greylander, returned from Misthaven."

"My Prince! We are most glad to see you. If Gerard is dead, then we are indeed in dire straits. Have you come to oppose the tyrant Terrell?"

"I have. I was coming to Hoge's shop, but I see he is too well-known now. I would endanger him, and myself, if I appeared there."

"Go to Norrice's lampworks in old Harwood district. Tell her Budge sent you."

"Thank you, Budge. Tell no one for now. What no one knows, no one can give away."

"I will. Rhea guide you, Prince."

Our destination was many streets away, in a part of town with fewer sellers of wares and more places of manufacturing them. We made certain that no patrols were nearby before going up to the door beneath the sign with a lamp on it. Ox knocked on the door in a specific rhythm: three, one, two. After several minutes, the door opened a crack. The password was exchanged, and we entered the house of the Hidden Hand.

CHAPTER 26

The Hidden Hand

THE WOMAN WHO admitted us had a plain, lined face and short grey hair. She had worn a worried expression for so long that it was permanently etched into the creases in her brow and around her mouth. "Who is it that's calling at this hour after curfew?" she asked.

"Are you Norrice? Budge sent us here when the patrols were sniffing around Hoge's meeting. I distracted the guards long enough to disband the meeting, but his shop is not safe."

The woman sniffed. "Hoge is careless, and Budge is a fool. Thank you for what you did. I am Marta Norrice, as you guessed. And by what name are you known?"

"Greylander de Oxendon."

Norrice had weapons in a cabinet by the wall, and in a desk in the center of the room. Her eyes flicked to these two places then back to us. She calculated the odds of reaching them in time and of further using them against three of us. I'm quite sure that she underestimated the danger that Gilwyr posed, but it was still a clear answer. She made no move.

"And what is a de Oxendon doing in this part of town, using those names and those words at the door?"

"I've been sympathetic to your cause since I was a youth. I went to meetings at Hoge's before I left to travel the land then eventually to teach in Misthaven. Most did not know my family name, but Hoge did."

"Our cause, as you call it, is the removal of your family from the throne you usurped. It's the restoration of this city to the Anglich who built it before the Dalactyns arrived to rename it. How are you sympathetic to that?"

"Injustice cannot be addressed by turning back the clock. The river has flowed on and reshaped the land. The people who live today are not the people who were displaced. Who now could say where they would be if my ancestors had not come? They might have all been slaves of the Grimmerroth if not for Roland and Rowena. We must deal with today."

Norrice looked Ox over carefully and spared a glance for the other two of us as well. "Do you oppose Terrell?"

"I do."

"It seems that we both want this one thing, at least. But we differ on what will happen after we accomplish that change. How can we work together knowing that?"

"I pledge to include the Hidden Hand in ruling the city, and to allow Anglich peoples to serve in the guard, and in the ministry."

"Any outcome that has a de Oxendon, or any Dalactyn, on the throne is not acceptable to us."

"Are things so absolute? You would not support me even if it were the only way to rid yourselves of Terrell?"

"We might aid you only to find that you were worse than Terrell, only after we had exposed to you our plans, our leaders, and our numbers. It would then be a straightforward matter to consolidate your rule and remove your opposition."

"I respect your candor, Norrice. It would have been easy to simply help me long enough to remove Terrell and then betray me when my guard was down. I'll be as forthright with you as you are with me. Terrell is the least of your problems or mine. The landowners and the palace guard who support him are the ones who are invested in the status quo. They are the ones who assassinated Gerard and who attempted to assassinate me."

"Gerard is dead?" Norrice appeared genuinely dismayed.

"Yes. Terrell set us up to appear to assassinate each other, or failing that, to have the Daughters who accompanied Gerard make it look as if we had."

"Gerard's own guard turned on him?" Norrice shook her head. "The rot goes deeper than I had thought. You talk of reform when what is needed is revolution."

"There are many good and decent Dalactyns who had no part in making this society. Their ancestors may have, but that is long in the past. I am committed to justice for all who live in this city, with a minimum of bloodshed. A past injustice cannot be undone with an opposite injustice today."

Norrice considered. "You are naive, but you seem to have a good heart. I will allow you to stay here as long as it doesn't endanger my people. I will not hinder your attempt to unseat Terrell. I will not give you any other aid unless it furthers our cause. And I will not forget that our cause will eventually put us in conflict."

"That is fair. I only ask what you would willingly give. I hope we can talk more. You are passionate and intelligent, and I would like to hear more of your opinions. I would like to find a future for our city where we are not enemies."

Norrice smiled slightly. "You are a reasonable man, Greylander de Oxendon, and reasonable men are dangerous. Let me show you to a room where you can sleep."

This turned out to be a storeroom that had a few rude pallets for sleeping along one wall. Whether this was for workers who sometimes had long shifts, or whether this was a hiding place for conspirators was never said. The beds were hard, but we had slept on worse.

"How did she mean that reasonable men are dangerous?" asked Gilwyr.

Ox replied, "Reforms and reconciliation will keep people from revolting—and keep Norrice from her goal of self-rule. Oppression serves her aims better than progress. She is the dangerous one. She would go beyond removing the rot and burn down the town to cleanse it."

"Were the Anglich here before the Dalactyns, then?" asked Gilwyr. "Does she have a cause?"

"Our oldest records say that the Dalactyns traveled from the south, just before the War of the Grimmerroth. They were a small group, only a few hundred. They found a thriving city here, and being well-educated and wealthy quickly found places in the city's elite. Roland de Oxendon became a friend and advisor to the old king, Pandulf. Pandulf had no heirs, so he named Roland to be his heir and successor. He passed away just as the threat of the Grimmerroth began to rise. Many of the Dalactyns were skilled in the military arts and began the strengthening of the city's defenses. They raised and trained an army to oppose the Grimmerroth, and it was the Dalactyn general Rowena ad Aulam who defeated him. In those days, the Dalactyns were acclaimed as the saviors of the city. It was only much later that the cause of Anglich rule gained any currency."

I had been silent up until then. "So, it was a peaceful takeover?"

"Not so much a takeover as a mingling of two peoples."

"I have studied many migrations. Some end with a true melding of cultures, others remain stratified. And of course, there are many instances where the stronger culture completely eradicated the weaker. It would be interesting to collect the data to compute the Hendricks Integration Coefficient for this city. That could be used in Sturmholt's equations to predict the degree of class struggle and the likelihood of the society destabilizing in conflict."

My companions were staring at me as if I had claimed to speak fluent Kir Leth, skin words and all. "You are talking mathematics, no?" asked Ox. "You have mathematics that reduce people to equations?"

"Not individual people. Only large populations. The equations are very complex and can't be solved by unaided humans. I have to do the calculations in simspace, where I can see the fields of symbols floating in my head, and run my fingers over input sliders and matrix solvers. There isn't any way to make use of the population theories I know with the technology that exists on this planet."

"I begin to glimpse how different our University must have been from yours, and why you didn't fit in," said Ox. Gilwyr said nothing but looked troubled.

Several days later, we were no closer to our goals. A few other Anglich leaders had come to hear Ox for themselves. They were at least as skeptical as Norrice, and one old firebrand advocated ridding the city of one prince right away. He was dissuaded by others pointing out that if that was what Terrell wanted, they should hardly be eager to do his work for him. Those who thought of ransoming us to the Dalactyns were likewise dissuaded by their comrades. None were eager to help us.

One visitor was an old cabinet maker named Birch, hands stained with wood and lacquer, and a face that might have been rough-hewn from his own stock. He listened calmly as Ox talked about including Anglich in the city council and the palace guard, both of which currently barred their participation. When Birch had heard enough, he interlaced his gnarled fingers and inverted his palms. Knuckles cracked like small-arms fire in the quiet room, stopping Ox mid-oration.

"Ye seem to have a good soul, for a prince," he said. "I'll give ye credit that ye speak Anglich to us rather than Dalactyn. But ye haven't lived our life, ye haven't worked with naught to eat, ye haven't watched the children ..." He choked up for a moment. "Do ye know that one out of every three cabinets I make are coffins? Aye, and because there's no one else to do it, I lay out the bodies, and cart them out to the Anglich grounds. Three hundred and fifty-seven last year, between me and the other four cabinet makers. Children that starved, good people who died in the mines, and no few who died because a Dalactyn was bored and wanted amusement."

Ox was silent for a long moment. Birch waited with the patience of a man who could spend the entire day sanding a piece of wood until it took the shape he wanted. Ox took a deep breath that had a catch in it. "You are right. I do not ... cannot ... understand the life of the Anglich. But I thank you for giving me that glimpse. It redoubles my conviction that this division of our people cannot continue to stand."

"Ye can describe the fanciest spindle leg for yer table that ye want. 'Till ye can turn that out on your lathe, yer not going to get anyone to pay ye for it."

When not quietly listening to Ox's conversations with the Anglich, I spent the time fascinated by the lampworks. The business assembled new lamps with bodies of glass or hammered metal, or cleaned and refurbished old lamps with new parts. Lamp oil was sold by the small keg to larger households or dispensed into smaller vessels brought by the customers. I learned that the lamp oil was tapped from a particular tree that produced high-quality liquid oil. A related tree had layers of wax just under the bark, which could be harvested in sheets, much the way that natural cork had once been harvested. From these could be made fine candles that burned brightly with little smoke. After seeing the living support systems in the Kir Leth city, I suspected that these represented ancient genetic engineering, though the locals accepted them without thought as the bounty of the land.

The black *aelo tai* was an always-felt presence. At times, it weighed as much as the hot, dense matter in a starship's core. It should have dropped through my bowels, the floors beneath me, and through the crust of the planet like a stone through fog. It was a mental weight as much as a physical weight, though it dragged at my limbs as if someone had dialed up the local gravity field. The dark thoughts and moods that orbited its event horizon were powerful. I had moments when I loathed myself, my companions, this world, and all the little inconveniences that beset me. Fortunately, for most of the day, I could function normally. It was only occasionally when I was tired or off guard that the darkness would loom large and near, and I would have to struggle not to be drawn entirely into its black maelstrom.

The red *aelo tai* at least conveyed the second sight to me. I could see no benefit to this dark burden; I wished I could be rid of it. And yet as much as I loathed the black *aelo tai*, every time I thought to tell my companions about it, the voice would whisper a doubt about their motives, or my safety, or opportunities lost. By the time rational thought overcame those doubts, the opportunity had passed. It reminded me of the times when the Kir Leth had come up in conversation and Ox's thoughts had seemed to wander off to a different topic.

On the fourth night, after curfew, the soft coded tap on the door sounded once more. Norrice opened the door cautiously then stepped aside to let a figure enter. Gilwyr and I leaped to our feet with swords at the ready, and even the imperturbable Ox startled and reached for his blade. The woman was slightly shorter than Gilwyr, with an oval, open face, and dark hair that was trimmed short on her right side but hung in a braid to mid-chest on her left. She wore the white tunic with the leather and sandals we had seen before, with an additional sash of rank. She carried herself with confidence, though a slight tightness around her eyes made me think she didn't feel as sure of herself as the image she tried to convey. Our immediate thought was that we had been betrayed, as Norrice admitted one of the Daughters of Rowena. In her turn, the Daughter took in our drawn blades and reached for her own. "Stay your hands!" barked Norrice. "If you spill each other's blood, you won't find that you might have common cause."

"What cause would that be?" asked Ox. "The Daughters of Rowena orchestrated the attack in Misthaven on my brother and me."

The Daughter looked in confusion at Ox. "Prince Gerard? The word from the palace has been that you were killed by Misthaven assassins."

"Gerard was killed, and I was nearly as well, and by those who wore your sash. It was an assassin and her apprentice who saved me."

"Prince Greylander?" her eyes widened. "We have not had word of you in a score of years."

"After the events in Misthaven, I felt compelled to return, to see what had become of the city I had left."

The Daughter drew her sword. Both Gilwyr and I tensed, but she reversed it and extended it hilt-first towards Ox, going down on her knees before us. "I am Bridocke, Captain of the Order of the Sons and Daughters of Rowena. I swear my fealty to your person and your cause, Prince Greylander de Oxendon. I support your claim to the throne of Dalactus."

"I accept your fealty, Captain Bridocke. Please rise." Ox returned her sword to her, which she sheathed.

"Now tell me," he continued. "Why are you visiting a lamp maker's shop in this part of town after curfew?"

She looked uneasy. "I … The Hidden Hand …" She looked at Norrice, who gave a slight nod. "I … I am a member of the Hidden Hand. They were suspicious of me at first, of course, but my father vouched for me. I give them what aid I can, warning them of patrols and raids."

"Ah," said Ox. "Your father was Anglich, was he not? Your real father, I would imagine, not the husband of your mother. The Daughters would not likely admit a half-Anglich, or promote you to Captain if they knew."

Bridocke nodded in chagrin. "My lord is very perceptive."

"Are there divisions within the Order?"

"There is an inner circle around Lord General Bercarius who support Prince Terrell. Terrell has won them over with talk of the glory days of Dalactyn military power, of bringing more provinces and even Misthaven under Dalactyn hegemony, and sending expeditions to resettle the western lands."

"And outside of that circle?"

"Most will go along with the leadership. A fair number talk about adventure or staking out new dukedoms for themselves from the old abandoned cities. A few think it's not what the old king would have wanted and that all those plans will be carried on the backs of the Anglich. I don't know how many because wise soldiers watch their tongues. I know there are a few others who help the Hand when the lords and their snitches aren't looking."

"Can you get me a meeting with any in the Guard who supported Gerard, or who seem uneasy with Terrell?"

"I fear that's a rather small circle, my lord. There are few whom I would trust to not turn you over to Terrell to gain his favor."

"I should start with those, at least. I cannot leave Dalactus in Terrell's hands. Any benefit to a few nobles and officers will come at the cost of the Anglich who make up the citizens of the city, and most of the soldiers in the army. That is not what a just ruler would want."

"I will feel out a few of the officers," promised Bridocke. "There are possibly a half dozen whom I would trust. I will return in two nights to tell you if I can arrange a meeting."

"I would be grateful, Captain Bridocke. Please be discreet. You could come to a swift end if you confide in the wrong person. I would not put you in unnecessary danger."

"I put myself in danger the moment I pledged my fealty to you," she replied. "There is no turning back." She clasped her fist to her chest and bowed stiffly.

Ox returned her salute. "That's a two-way obligation, Captain. Your welfare is now my responsibility. I take that very seriously."

Bridocke bowed deeper, then departed.

Norrice had been listening. "Did you mean all that? De Oxendons are not known in this town for being good for their word on much. Your brother Gerard was better than your father, and a far sight better than Terrell. Gerard spoke fair, but seldom followed those words with actions, at least in this part of the city."

Ox sighed. "As when we were boys together. And Terrell also grew as he started."

Norrice hesitated for a moment. "I will speak to the leaders of the Hand again. You … may be our best hope." She disappeared into her quarters and closed the door. That last had cost her. She didn't change convictions easily.

"You'll make a good king, Ox," said Gilwyr.

"He will," I agreed. "Compassion makes a good king. It's not a good qualification for *becoming* king, though. That job tends to go to the ruthless."

"I fear you may be right," said Ox.

CHAPTER 27

Terrell

A DAY CAME and went without word back from Captain Bridocke. Gilwyr lit a candle and sat cross-legged in deep contemplation of the small flame. I knew her well enough by now to know that she was wound nearly to the breaking point by inaction. Her meditation was a form of discipline to keep her from fretting and pacing. I didn't have her degree of concentration; I paced enough for both of us.

Ox seemed outwardly calm. When customers came to the store, if Norrice gave a nod, Ox would engage them in conversation about the city, the working conditions, the taxes, the curfew, or conditions in general. Almost always the views were that life was better in the old days and that change was needed. There were stories of Anglich men being taken as conscripts for work on the estates of Dalactyn nobles. There were stories of previously middle-class merchants being driven into poverty by Dalactyn control of the market prices. Class distinctions were being deepened, Anglich were being excluded from civil service and military positions, other than foot soldier, of course. We could see that all this news distressed him deeply.

When there were no customers, Ox read quietly. He read the few books that Norrice had, plus all of the news pamphlets and flyers that he could get. From their content, it was clear that we would have been arrested and imprisoned for possessing many of them. When he started reading the shipping manifests and accounting ledgers, we concluded that he was brooding over his enforced idleness and trying to hide it from us.

In the days since we had arrived, a stream of raggedy children had come through the shop. Sometimes Norrice gave them small deliveries to make, other times they brought in orders for lamps on crumpled scabs of paper that Norrice laid out on her workbench in a neat row. I gradually became aware that not every scrap of paper ended up on the bench. The occasional paper ended up in the pocket of her apron, to be tossed casually into the fire as she passed by. I contrived to look at the orders on the bench at one point, under the guise of genuine interest in the operation of such a low-tech establishment. They were unintelligible to me, being some sort of shorthand marks rather than proper writing. After a while, I did notice that many of the messengers took the time to scan the other slips as they passed by. I wondered why they had such an interest in who else was ordering lamps.

"Because they're not just orders," said Gilwyr when I told her of my observations. "Each one has a code on it that tells the current positions of Dalactyn patrols and checkpoints in each neighborhood. The runners bring in their reports along with the actual orders for lamps, and memorize the other reports that they see." Gilwyr was still staring into the candle flame, which was now guttering low in its holder. It had been a three-hour candle when she started.

"How did you know that?" I asked in amazement.

"Yes, how did you?" asked Ox, looking up. "I have been looking for possible contacts in the ledgers, but Norrice seems to do business with everyone."

"The Guild uses the same system in Misthaven, but at bakeries rather than lampworks. I don't know the local code, though." The candle finally expired with a flicker and a thin spiral of smoke that rose through the air. Gilwyr stood and stretched, seemingly not stiff at all after hours of sitting.

"Then the notes that she pockets must be other kinds of reports from her network."

"Quite likely," said Ox, "but don't let Norrice know that you've noticed. She's still highly suspicious of us, and she might take it badly if she thinks we're spying on her."

Our break came shortly afterward in the grimy pocket of a ragamuffin messenger. Norrice came to the back room where we were lurking, fingering a scrap of paper that may have had all the biological requirements for the evolution of a new life form. "There is an informal reception at Duke Islip's mansion tonight. You can go as cousins of Lord Dearing who are visiting from their country estate. They seldom come to Dalactus, so it's unlikely that anyone will recognize that you aren't them. Lord Dearing is away this month and his townhouse is empty. You can go there this afternoon; the housekeeper is one of us. She will outfit you with clothes suitable for the evening."

"Who will be in attendance?" asked Ox.

"The invitations used wording that indicates that the members of Dalactus Primus will be gathering. It seems they may be making a bid for the succession without even the grace of waiting until the old king is dead." The group she named consisted of the most reactionary elements, who advocated a return to a more militaristic past. They also blamed their gradual decline on interbreeding with the Anglich, the dilution of the Dalactyn language with borrowings from Anglich and in general scapegoated the people they ruled.

"Why would we want to attend their gathering?" I asked. "We're not likely to find anyone to help us in that crowd."

"Because if there is a plot to install Terrell on the throne, our best chance of uncovering it is by listening to their rhetoric," said Ox.

"Exactly," said Norrice. "But you can't go. You're instantly recognizable, if not for yourself, then for your strong resemblance to Gerard. We couldn't smuggle you into that gathering, and if we did you would never come out again. Everyone thinks you are dead, so none of them would think twice about ensuring that it was true." By the same logic, the Hand could have disposed of him quietly as well, I thought. They must have felt they had more to gain by keeping him alive.

"Then who ..."

"Your friends will go. A master of the Assassin's Guild should have no trouble with that situation." She saw the look that I shot Gilwyr. We hadn't divulged that information. "We have people in the Guilds as well. It's useful to know who has issued commissions on whom. It didn't take long to find one who had heard of you, Master Gilwyr. Your companion, though, no one seems to know about him."

"My apprentice," said Gilwyr shortly.

"So? An opportunity for training, then?"

So it was that evening that Warin and Atheley de Vaux pulled up to Duke Islip's mansion in the city, by way of Lord Dearing's more modest townhouse. We were attired as a country squire and lady, which tended to the more practical than some of the gaudy outfits that we saw alighting from other carriages. We waited our turn at the entrance behind a couple who would have put peacocks to shame. She wore a gown of azure that tapered from broad shoulders to narrow waist before blooming again into long skirts, where the azure was slashed by two panels of white. Her sleeves went to the elbow where they divided to flow in long filmy waves that reached to her knees. She enjoyed exaggerated gestures that stirred those sleeves into dramatic arcs to punctuate her exclamations. Her companion wore a waistcoat of severe cut that only underscored the flamboyance of its crimson color. Against the drab and utilitarian garb of the townspeople, the opulence underscored the gulf in the status and privilege of this nobility. We were announced by the attendants at the door and commenced our mingling with the crowd.

My first impression of the crowd was that these were people who thought that life was going well for them. I could see it in the confident postures, the bright eyes, the hearty laughter. On a closer look, I picked out signs of tension: the narrowed eyes after one person turned his back, the cold smile on a steely-haired woman as the man before her fidgeted. Politics shared the room with celebration, the look of people expecting a good future and wondering who to stab to get there.

Our first encounter was with a small and sharp-faced man who looked less like a weasel and more like something that hunted weasels. I saw his eyes turn towards the door at our announcement; over the next few minutes he made a meandering way towards us through the crowd and eventually appeared at our elbows. "Lord and Lady de Vaux! How pleasant to make your acquaintance at last. Ailred has often told me fondly of his stays at your country estate. It sounds like the hunting is superb. I am Lord Easton, but please call me Henry. How is old Ailred these days?"

Ailred was of course our purported cousin, Lord Dearing. Gilwyr had had the presence of mind to press the housekeeper for enough information to allow us to keep up the ruse at a casual level of conversation. "He is doing well, hardly any limp from that hunting accident earlier this year. He left for his trip to the coast the day after we arrived in town, so we didn't have much time to inquire after his more recent exploits."

This one would put his arm around your shoulder and a knife in your back. With a smile. The black *aelo tai* stirred under my breastbone. This environment interested it, or at least stimulated it. I didn't need the distraction and told it to keep quiet.

"You arrive at a time of some political … uncertainty. I'm sure that news travels rather slowly out in the provinces, and possibly not accurately. Have you had an opportunity to assess the situation?"

"I'm sure our picture of politics in the capital is woefully incomplete," I said. "But we had heard with interest the proposals to reduce the land taxes and make the merchants and shopkeepers pay their fair share. That is welcome news to us. It has become almost impossible to keep a middling landholding afloat, and many of the smaller ones have already been forced to sell out to the larger holdings or to the crown."

Lord Easton smiled as a fox might smile. "You'll find like-minded people here tonight. I'll make sure you are introduced to those who have influence in such areas."

It had taken all of my acting ability to say that much, knowing that the economic model was entirely backward and the proposed taxes were shifting the blame without fixing the problem. However, this was the line that would get us closer to the primary conspirators.

Lord Easton handed us off to Lord Oakley and Sir Myerscough, who in turn introduced us to Lady Leighton. Before long we had talked to the houses of Hackney, Gresham, Denholm, Breeden, and Trollope. At every stage we heard bigotry, scapegoating, and the simplistic invocation of a return to better times that had probably never existed. These were the hallmarks of reactionary movements throughout human history on all of our many worlds.

"We haven't found the ringleaders yet," I said to Gilwyr when we had a moment to ourselves while a rather bear-like man regaled most of the crowd with an improbable story of hunting in the mountains.

"No, we might have made some contacts who can introduce us, but it could take days to work our way in."

"We may not have days if the old king is in as poor health as they are saying."

"It may be time to make a direct request, then …"

"… and *then* the bloody stag turned and ran straight into our camp!" the voice roared over the crowd. "Only my wife and her maids in its path. And my wife, my wife! stands up as calm as you please, takes a bow from the rack, and puts an arrow right in the beast's eye!" There was a general roar of approval from the crowd, while the young, blond-haired woman at his side blushed in embarrassment. *This one entertains, but he does not Persuade.* The stone under my breastbone felt like a bad case of heartburn, and it grumbled like one too.

A sudden silence fell, in which the sound of one person clapping, very slowly, punctuated the hush. "Bravo, Sir Riley! Perhaps we should give your wife a turn at managing your estates. She sounds to have a sharper aim than you do. That's the second time you missed."

The company turned as one to face the new arrival. At once I knew it was Prince Terrell, dressed in an opulent burgundy waistcoat trimmed in gold, and black breeches. The family resemblance was apparent, though he was not nearly the close match to Ox that Gerard had been, and was clearly younger than his brothers. He had a pleasant enough face but his eyes told a different story. They flickered across the crowd like those of a hawk selecting prey, and the crease lines around them said that a smirk was a more frequent expression than a smile. He must have quietly slipped in, as he had not been announced. Several men who had been present for Riley's story but who had seemed to find it unamusing now appeared around the suddenly pale minor lord. They escorted Riley from the room, where it seemed that he abruptly had no friends. Everyone studiously looked elsewhere and resumed their conversations. Riley's wife faded away through the servant's entrance.

"It seems that Prince Terrell has learned who 'accidentally' put an arrow into his favorite horse, while he was riding it." Lord Easton had appeared at our elbows during the great realignment of the conversational cliques following the addition of Terrell and the subtraction of Riley.

"What did Riley have against the Prince's horse?"

"It wasn't the horse he was aiming at."

Easton wandered away to work the centers of conversation in the room. We attached ourselves to various groups in Terrell's vicinity to pick up the gossip. I was glad that my experience at faculty receptions had given me ample practice in engaging in a conversation with half my attention so that I could listen to the much more interesting conversation nearby.

Terrell did not have the gravitas of his elder brothers, but he had a quick and cutting wit. He greeted the host, Lord Dearing, with warm compliments on his house, his art collection that graced the halls, and his extensive wine cellars. Terrell winked at his host and said, "You're a man of great depths, Dearing. Couldn't reach bottom with a twenty-foot pole, eh?" He moved on to the next group while Dearing was still working out whether this was a compliment.

As Terrell circulated around the room, we heard snatches of his conversations. It wasn't that he had a loud voice, not like the booming of Lord Dearing or some of the others for whom bluster was a mark of office. Terrell's voice was that pitch that cut through other conversations, whether or not one wanted to listen to it.

Across the room, Terrell had launched into the topic of expanding Dalactyn settlements. "... our prosperity depends on opening up new lands, new forests to hunt and fields to farm. We have been stagnant too long. It is our duty, it is our right, to feed our people and to provide new estates for our sons and daughters to increase in number." There was a murmur from the circle around him. Terrell replied, "Those lands belong to no man! There's no one to oppose us." Murmur. "The Kir Leth? A myth! Have any of you seen one? Where do you hear of them? Misthaven, that's where! Misthaven says there are Kir Leth in the forests, so we shouldn't settle there. Whose interest does that serve? Misthaven, of course! We're not afraid to settle there. There are no Kir Leth, and even if there were, our garrisons will be there as well. The Sons and Daughters are on guard against brigands, they are on guard against slavers, and they are on guard against foreign raiders. A few mythical Kir Leth will be no match for them!"

He has great Persuasion. He knows how to divide people to make himself stronger. I had been ignoring the black *aelo tai's* observations about the other guests, but this one seemed spot-on.

"On guard against non-payment of taxes, too, I'll wager," I muttered. "Are they really buying that?"

"He seems to be saying what they want to hear," said Gilwyr.

"He is telling their part of the story, true," said a new voice. A woman had come up behind us. She was of medium height, but with a presence that was twice her size. She had iron grey hair and wore a military uniform with a broad sash. "They need to hear their reasons for support-ing the new estates, just as the merchants need to hear about their new markets, the mine owners about new surveys, the farmsteads about new fields and pastures, and the malcontents about new settlements. The story is different for each of them and they need to see how they benefit."

"I see," I said. "And which story is yours?" Out of the corner of my eye, I saw Gilwyr make a hand sign. I had learned it during assassin training. It meant "caution."

"My story is that Dalactus formerly controlled all the land from the Tamesas down to Coygne. My story is to see the return to that shining, thriving kingdom. I'm sorry, but we haven't been introduced. I am General Bercarius, of the Daughters of Rowena."

I bowed, though I wasn't sure if nobles bowed to officers or vice versa. "I am Warin of Vaux Manor, and this is my wife, Lady Atheley."

"Welcome to Dalactus, Lord and Lady de Vaux. Your estate is a long way from here, up bordering on the freeholders of the Crumbling Hills. You might be looking to Dalactus for a greater presence in your district to deter raiders."

"We've had very little problem with raiders," said Gilwyr smoothly. "In fact, we do a great deal of trade with the freeholders. Taxes are already high enough without supporting additional troops and paying for settlements far from our holdings."

"Ah, then you'll like the way this unfolds," said a familiar voice behind us. Terrell had arrived in our presence. I suspected that Gilwyr and I weren't the only people in the room with discreet hand signals. "The Royal Treasury will invest in this expansion. Other families can contribute, and will receive commensurate 'opportunities' to establish their claims early. With more land under taxation, you may even see your taxes fall. Everyone will benefit, but those who risk the most will gain the most."

Gilwyr curtsied to the prince and I hurriedly bowed as well, trying to remember the etiquette drills that hadn't yet been sanded into smooth natural reactions by practice. General Bercarius said, "Prince Terrell, may I present the Lord and Lady de Vaux? They have recently arrived from their manor bordering the Crumbling Hills."

"Yes, yes, I know where Vaux is. Had a quite exciting hunting expedition there, some years ago. Your father was an excellent host, de Vaux. How is the old man?"

I thought fast. That hadn't been included in the hurried briefings we had received from the housekeeper. If I was the current Lord, then the previous one had to be dead, didn't he? "I am sorry to say that the years caught up with him and he passed away, sire."

"I heard that it was a mountain screamer that he was hunting that caught up with him, but I'm sure you were just being poetic. He was a fine man, very impassioned about the conditions of the underclasses. I've never seen as prosperous a village as yours."

"Does that affect your thinking about the Anglich in Dalactus, sire?"

"It may. When I am king, I will convene a council on the matter. There are those who say prosperous peasants make for a larger tax base, much as a fertile field makes for more productive sheep. But there are also those who say that may give the sheep ambitions of being shepherds."

"Forgive me, sire, for we are just arrived in town and news travels slowly across the mountains. I thought I understood that you were third in line for the throne?"

I heard a slight indrawn breath from the general at this audacity, but Terrell didn't mind explaining what he clearly thought was a marvelous development. "Until recently, that was true. But then my dear brothers had a falling out. My eldest brother's assassin killed our middle brother, and he in turn was either killed by the guards, or escaped and is now an outlaw. In either case, I have moved to the front of the line, and my father is frail after a life of hard living. I anticipate a time of change will be upon us soon."

"We await that time with anticipation," Gilwyr said deferentially while bowing. I hastily bowed as well. Terrell nodded his dismissal and turned away to converse with the general. We drifted away into the crowd.

"He knows!" I whispered urgently when we weren't in earshot of anyone. "We've got to get out of here!"

"Calm," said Gilwyr. "If he knew, we would already be in prison. He told us he knew we were pretenders when he corrected you on the manner of the old Lord's death. He wants to see what we will do. If we leave hastily we will appear to have something to hide. We will remain relaxed and confident until other guests begin to leave."

The next hour was far worse than any faculty reception had ever been. It was even worse than the first evening's reception on board the *Aquila*. At those times, the fear of being a fraud, of being found out, of saying the wrong thing to the wrong person was groundless, a product of my introverted insecurity. Tonight it was real. *It was always real. Tonight, though, the stakes are worth playing for,* said the voice within.

However, the time passed; Gilwyr charmed those we spoke with and avoided any further controversial topics. I knew now that she understood Kir Leth better than humans, but she could act. I saw her miss a few double entendres, which people put down either to naivety or sophistication, depending on their own perceptions. I tried to emulate her confidence.

Finally, other guests began to leave. As with any function I had ever attended, once the first few guests made their move to don their cloaks, there was a general flurry of departures. We melted into the middle of these, taking our leave of Duke Islip at the door and finding our carriage in the courtyard. I started to speak once we were in the conveyance, but Gilwyr held her finger to her lips. We rode in silence to the Dearing mansion.

Inside, we hastily changed. Gilwyr said, "I wish we had brought the Kir Leth cloaks. We must not be seen leaving." At my questioning look, she shook her head in disgust. "Did you not notice that we had a different driver on the return trip? We have to assume he was in the employ of Terrell or the general."

We slipped through the garden gate and made our way through shadowed alleyways. I watched in second sight for weapons or armor moving around us. I saw a few patrols in nearby streets, but none followed or took any notice of us. Still, we took a circuitous route and exercised great care the last few blocks to check for watchers. Finally, we arrived at the back door of the lamp works, tapped the coded knock, and slipped inside. Gilwyr stayed by the door for several moments, listening. At last she shook her head. "That was too easy."

CHAPTER 28

The King

THE NEXT DAY, Norrice's assistant fired up a coal-burning furnace. I was only moderately interested in the proceeding until he poured sand into a vessel in the furnace, and I realized that he was preparing to make glass. At that point, I parked myself by his elbow and watched avidly. The process was recognizable, even allowing for centuries of divergent evolution, and that was assuming that knowledge of glass-making had survived the long winter. It was entirely possible that it had been forgotten and then rediscovered.

The glassworker, whose name was Gent, was heavy-set, methodical, and sparing with words. He had massive scarring on his forearm that I had noticed earlier in the day. I now had a guess where he had gotten his scars, which he confirmed when he saw me looking. "When I learned not to hurry," he said, flicking his eyes from the rubbery white flesh to the glowing mouth of the furnace.

After a while, Gent dipped a hollow metal tube into the glowing mass of glass. When he had accumulated a suitable glob on the end, he withdrew it and spent some time spinning the rod and shaping the material with a tool. When it met his satisfaction, he lowered the rod vertically into a mold on the floor and blew through the tube. Moments later he unlatched and opened the mold to withdraw the shape within. He now had a rough lamp chimney. He quickly trimmed it to size and broke it away from the rod, then placed it in a lower-temperature kiln attached to the furnace where it would gradually cool to prevent thermal stress from shattering it. He repeated the process, and more quickly than I would have thought possible, his primitive, manual process filled the kiln with eleven chimneys.

Gent wordlessly handed the rod to me and quirked his eyes towards the furnace. Excited and apprehensive, I stepped up to the mouth's hell-glow. I inserted the end of the rod into the molten glass and withdrew a lambent blob. I twirled the rod as I had seen him do until it seemed even and rounded. Gent ran a paddle over the surface to shape the glass into a smooth ovoid. He had me place the end back in the oven for a moment to reheat it and then pushed the mold toward me. I lowered the glass-covered rod into the mold and blew into the pipe. I was incautious and got a whiff of superheated air back up the pipe and bent over coughing. When Gent kicked the mold open, I found a deformed blob that didn't fill the space. "Need more glass," he said. On my second attempt, I gathered a generous portion of glass and repeated the steps (except for the coughing). This time I ended up with a thick-sided bell that looked like a child's clay sculpture. I persisted through a third and fourth attempt, struggling with the crude equipment. My prior experience had been with a furnace that I had considered antique at the time, but the electric heat source had been much more even. Nor did I have the simspace overlays to guide my hands and monitor the glass temperature. On my fifth effort, I stopped wishing for what I didn't have. I let myself become one with the glass, feeling the wash of the heat over the mass, the flow of material as it reached the right temperature. When I knew it was right, I puffed into the mold once more. Gent opened the mold to reveal a very creditable globe, which he conveyed ceremonially to the kiln for curing. "Faster than most," he said with approval.

"I've made small glass items before, though the methods were quite ... different," I told him. I felt exhilarated with this accomplishment of non-augmented craftsmanship. I extracted some more glass from the furnace, then used a smaller tool to harvest a workable ball from that. I rolled it into a body, attached a smaller ball at one end, pricked two ears up from that ball, and added a rope of glass for a tail. After a few moments, I had the figure of a sleeping cat to show off. Before I knocked off, I turned out several more figures, including my favorite, a scarab. As I placed them in the kiln to gradually cool, I reflected that I hadn't been tormented by the voice of the black *aelo tai* in all that time. Something about the activity, or my concentration on it, had blocked its effect for a time.

❖

The series of taps came at the door an hour after dark. Norrice looked up with concern from the account ledgers she was working on. "Go into the back room," she said. "That pattern was almost right but not quite."

Gilwyr put her hand on her sword. "I can back you."

"No. If they're not of the Hand, I'll try to send them away. If there is a fight, I might lose the entire lamp works. Quickly now."

In the back room, we doused the light so we weren't betrayed by the glow. Gilwyr muttered, "If we have to fight, the light will blind us for a moment."

Ox was listening near the door. "One person, adult, sandals, light weight."

"Captain Bridocke?" whispered Gilwyr.

"No, the Captain was heavier."

"How can you tell?" I asked. Did they have their own second sight?

"There is a floorboard that creaks near the door. You can tell a lot by listening."

"You heard me coming in your chambers in Misthaven," I recalled.

"There was a loose stone in the corridor."

"Deliberately loosened," added Gilwyr.

"Ah, you knew."

"Of course I knew, you old *tan barg*. I stepped on it just to make you happy."

"Shhh."

Footsteps crossed the room, then a rap came, but on the door to the candlemaking room, not the storeroom in which we waited.

"Norrice thinks we should come out but has some doubt, so she is misdirecting the caller and letting us choose." Ox interpreted the situation for us. "We should take the risk."

There was a hooded brightness as Gilwyr rekindled a lamp. "Let your eyes adjust for a moment," she said.

"The visitor only has a belt knife," I said, looking in second sight.

Gilwyr opened the door and we reentered the front office. It was occupied by a young man in the dress of guard, but not an officer. He was quite young and exceedingly nervous.

"The Captain …" He had to stop and swallow. "The Captain told me to come here after dark to deliver a message."

"What message? Who did the Captain tell you to deliver it to?" demanded Ox.

"Didn't say who, just where. Said that the King sends for you. Said to hurry, he might not last long."

"Wait here. We will prepare."

We went back into the storeroom. Gilwyr turned immediately to Ox. "It's a trap. I will kill him now and we will find a new refuge."

"It may be a trap or it may be our opportunity. I cannot afford to chance if my father is willing to see me on his deathbed. My mind is made up. Get your cloaks."

I had been silent through this exchange, watching the transformation of Ox from thoughtful schoolteacher to tactician. I wasn't certain of his wisdom, but I could understand his calculations.

We put on our cloaks and arms, ready to depart. When the messenger saw us, however, he put up his hands. I saw that they were trembling.

"You won't be able to take swords into the palace. You should leave them here where they're safe." He looked around at Norrice scowling at him. "Er, I assume they're safe here, aren't they?"

"I told you ..." Gilwyr started, but Ox held up his hand. He unbuckled his sword and handed it to Norrice. Reluctantly, we did the same. As we moved out into the streets, Ox said to us in a low voice, "If this is a trap, we will be so outnumbered that a sword will make little difference."

We traveled through streets dark and echoing, the clear air so different from Misthaven at night. Cold breezes rolled down the mountainside to prowl the streets and assault travelers at intersections. We met no patrols, though twice we heard them in the distance.

We came to the castle at a side gate within a walled yard. This wasn't an entrance for high-ranking guests; it was narrow and dank, with a switchback within to slow down the momentum of any attackers.

Our escort produced a rope and cut it into the sections. He knotted each into loose loops and demonstrated placing his hands through them. "Slide these on behind your back so it looks like you're prisoners," he whispered. "We have to get past the guards." He withdrew his sword and had us precede him. There was, in fact, only one guard, who waved us through with boredom. It seemed that prisoners escorted into the castle at night was not unusual.

We were led through servant's passageways that seemed as unfamiliar to our guide as to us. Several times he stopped to consult a map on a crumpled paper to find the correct turning. I wondered if Ox had never encroached on the servants' territory as a child, or if he didn't want to reveal his familiarity with the castle to the guide. We slipped our ropes off to use our hands to feel our way in the dimness.

We ascended a stair to an upper level, then a short additional curved passage that ended in a wall, with a door to our left. "I'm to leave you here," said our guide. "This is the King's chamber."

"What is your name, lad?" rumbled Ox quietly.

"Grahm."

"Thank you, Grahm. I will remember." Ox's voice promised reward to the true and retribution to the false, all in three words. Grahm turned away. "And thank Captain Bridocke for sending you."

Grahm looked back, puzzled. "Captain Bridocke? It was Captain Burgesse what told me where to find you." He scuttled back down the passage.

We looked at each other. Gilwyr mouthed, "Trap." Ox hesitated, then replied, "We've come too far to turn back."

Ox took a deep breath and pushed the door open. Gilwyr crowded through ahead of him, convinced that assassins lurked in the bedroom. Ox looked only to the gaunt form on the bed. The coverlet was arranged so neatly that it could already have been the funeral shroud. The King's white beard flowed over the cover and his long hair fanned out over the pillow. His arms were emaciated and lined with blue veins that showed through the translucent skin. Ox laid a hand on one bony shoulder. "Godric? Father?"

The King took a deep breath that ended in a horrible rattle and opened his eyes. "Gerard? They told me you were dead."

"Gerard is dead. I'm Greylander. Terrell had Gerard killed in Misthaven."

"I remember now. Said you did it. Knew better than to believe Terrell, though." The King coughed. "You must take the throne, now that Gerard is dead. You're too soft. Too much scholar, too little ruler. But Terrell would be a disaster. Civil war in a year I would say. Take it."

"I am willing, now," said Ox in a voice of distant thunder. "It is my duty."

"Take my scepter to show the people I've given you my blessing. It is within the vault behind the tapestry in the alcove across from the window. It contains the history that all Dalactyns swore to forget and that the kings swore to remember." King Godric was racked by a cough that left him panting and weak. "Should have died a month ago. Was waiting for Gerard to come back. News … four days ago … almost killed me. Now I can finally close my eyes." He did that for several minutes, then awoke with a twitch.

"Greylander. We haven't always seen eye to eye."

"No, we have not."

"It doesn't matter now. I won't weaken you by telling you how to rule. Find that for yourself."

"Thank you, Father."

"Who are your companions? Are they trustworthy?"

"This is Gilwyr, a master assassin. This is Stenn Gremm, a traveler from far, far away. I trust them completely. They saved me from the trap that took Gerard's life."

"Good, good. A few trustworthy people are the best coin a king can have." He attempted to chuckle but it came out in a ghastly rattle. His eyes closed again. I thought he had gone, but then his eyes flew open once more. "They have come for me. The ancestors." He smiled then. "Your mother has come for me. You are king now." His eyes didn't close, but his breathing ceased. His face retained the peace that had come across it at the end. I saw a single tear slide down Ox's cheek to lose itself in his beard. I inclined my head and stepped away to give him some time. Death is a less frequent visitor on my own world, usually arriving in secluded hospices, out of sight of passers-by. Though I had already seen death on this world — even caused death — remaining in its presence was unsettling. Gilwyr remained at the bedside and I wondered if she had seen enough death that it no longer affected her.

After a long silence Ox left the bedside. "And now you've seen the only tear that I've ever shed for my father. I agreed with few of the choices he made in life, and he agreed with none that I made in mine. Now I must put aside my choices in order to put his to right. It's somewhat galling."

"You're not doing it for him. You're doing it for your people." That sounded trite as I said it, but Ox nodded heavily.

Ox approached the tapestry across the room. He spared no more glances for the still figure in the bed. Pulling the tapestry aside, we could see the faint outline of a rectangle on the wall. If Godric hadn't said there was a vault here, we would have dismissed it as a chance alignment of stones. We tried pushing on the rectangle, but it didn't move. There was no purchase to pull on it, either. No latches, no finger holes, no grips. It was only by chance that I found the round hole in the wall nearby, filled with a plug of stone, which might have been drilled to hold a support for a bar to hang another tapestry. Or it might be something more.

I pried the plug out with the tip of my belt knife; cold air blew through the now-open hole. "Look around," I said. "I think there is something that fits this hole."

We searched the room but found nothing. I returned to the tapestry to look behind it, though it seemed too obvious a place. As I did so, I noticed that the ornate end of the pole supporting the tapestry was somewhat stained and worn. I reached up, grasped it, and turned. It moved, and I withdrew a meter-long rod that was concealed within the hollowed-out pole.

The rod slid smoothly into the hole for three-quarters of its length, then stopped. Nothing else happened. I pushed, slightly, probing the bottom of the hole. There was the slightest springiness there. I took a firm grip and shoved the rod down as hard as I could, feeling an unseen lever move. There was a *thunk* deep within the wall. "Now push the door," I told the others.

Ox and Gilwyr put their shoulders to the formerly immovable wall and almost fell into the space beyond. As we stepped through, we could see that the slab was set on wheels to allow it to move, and had been held by a bar that the rod had pushed aside. "Remarkable mechanism," said Ox. "How did you figure it out so quickly?"

"It … reminded me of a game I once played." The hours I had spent playing simspace games were a guilty pleasure I wouldn't have admitted to my contemporaries at home.

The doorway revealed a new room, filled with artifacts and scrolls. Not just scrolls, I saw as my eyes adjusted. There were books, printed and bound in covers that had never been stamped in a press on this world. Instruments, cracked screens, and even a few weapons were arranged on shelves. This was clearly a cache that had been scrounged from the the wreckage of the *Corvus*. But what had happened to the people? Had my ancestor brought these bits with him to trade? The thought that he might have stood in this very room tingled. The ghosts of the missing passengers clustered around me in the glooming, clamoring for their stories to be set free.

Prominent in the room was a low table, almost an altar. On this was a peculiar scepter, with a shaft that looked like machined stainless steel, and a large knob on one end that was tightly wound with cloth. The shaft had certainly come from the wreckage of a starship or a lander. Ox lifted the scepter from its resting place and contemplated it in silence.

I looked further into the clutter. I picked up a slim leather volume and ran my fingers over the stiff binding. A steel table knife, still improbably bright, had the letter "C" engraved in the handle. I put this down and tucked the leather book into a pocket at the sight of a document, written in ink on a large sheet of the coarse yellow paper of this world, that was displayed on a free-standing podium.

We, who named ourselves the Order of Dalactus, set out to find a new home.

We sought self-rule, a society of equals, founded on the principles of nobility and chivalry.

Our path to this home did not honor those ideals.

We resolve to start fresh, setting aside the past, choosing to forget.

To the Kings who succeed me alone, I entrust this knowledge.

Preserve it against the day when it once again may be needed.

We sailed a great ship across the sea of stars and burned it so we may never return.

— *Roland de Oxendon, First King of Dalactus*

My knees threatened to give out underneath me. The passengers of the *Corvus* hadn't disappeared. They had installed themselves as the ruling class. The man standing next to me, who I now called a friend, was descended from the mutineers who had killed the ship's crew and stranded my ancestor here with them. Their language should have been a giveaway. But I had assumed that when and if I found the descendants of those mutineers, they would have preserved their heritage, at least in the form of legends. Instead, they had deliberately covered it up and forgotten it.

Gilwyr exclaimed from behind me while I was still getting my bearings. "Ox, take a look at this."

Ox and Gilwyr huddled over whatever she had found. I idly fingered some of the artifacts, my mind on the strange fate that had thrown me together with these people. After a time I realized that I was holding a leather-bound book in my hand, turning it over and over. I had barely started to open the volume when a shadow fell across the doorway. The shadow belonged to two guards, backed by many more, but the voice belonged to Terrell, somewhere in the rear. "Thank you for obtaining the scepter for me, brother. Our dear father was holding out on me. He may never have told me about this wonderful room if you hadn't opened it for me."

He motioned to the guards. "Take them away." Rough hands fell upon us. Gilwyr disarmed the first guard, but the next one put his sword at Ox's neck until Gilwyr surrendered. I tried to elbow the one holding my arms behind my back. I felt my eyepatch ripped away in the scuffle, and the cry of "Warlock!" raised among the guards. I saw the shadow of something raised over my head for a brief moment before it crashed down on me and I remembered no more.

CHAPTER 29

Captive

A BEAM OF light was stabbing me in the eye. Sharp ends were pricking my face ... and my back ... why? Oh, I was shirtless. I was cold too, shivering in the damp dark that covered me. I focused on the light, discovering that it was quite a dim shaft of light, made to seem bright only relative to the darkness and the throbbing headache. The pricking was from the coarse straw that made up the pallet that I lay on. A groan was cliche at this point, but my condition seemed to require it. I sat up and almost passed out again at the savage stabbing headache. I explored with my fingertips. A lump on the back of my head, oozing wetly, took credit for the headache. My eyepatch was missing; my red *aelo tai* was still in place in my eye socket. Presumably, whoever carried me here had seen it. My breeches seemed to be my own and were the only article of clothing that I wore.

I lurched painfully to my feet then staggered, barely catching myself on the wall. I heard the sound of four-legged bedmates evacuating the straw pallet, disturbed by the movement. The light came from a small barred window in a stout wooden door. There were no other openings in the walls of my cell. After a few false tries, I made it to the door, only to find the vista outside was what one would expect from a dungeon cell.

I extended my second sight. The bars glowed crimson in front of me. I could see a massive bolt and padlock on the outside of the door. Through the stone, I could see padlocks and bars marking three other doors nearby. There was no other metal within range of my second sight.

How had I gotten here? Had Norrice betrayed us? Or that half-Anglich guard? Or ... there had been another guard, hadn't there? He had taken us to the Palace. There had been a fight. Now I was in a dungeon. Pieces were missing from the sequence.

Someone betrayed you.

I paced the cell. It was four paces wide and eight paces long. My pallet was in the left rear corner, and I discovered a chamber pot in the right rear corner. Fortunately, it was empty. I marked it carefully in my memory so I could find it when I needed it, and so I wouldn't step in it again as I paced. The cell was an unvarying four paces by eight paces by four paces by eight paces. I tried making a list of reasons why this cell was better than being lost in the Blight but gave it up when I couldn't think of even one. Four by eight by four by eight. I lost count after fifty-seven circuits of the cell. I started to count all over again when I heard sounds outside. I saw some bits of metal approaching in my second sight; keys or the like, no sword.

I looked out the barred window. A guard was approaching. He was dressed in the tunic of the guards, but without the sash that designated the Sons and Daughters of Rowena. I tried calling out to him. "Where am I? Why am I being held? What's going on?"

The guard didn't answer but came to a halt in front of my door. "Back up," he said and rapped the bars with a truncheon. I took a step back. He opened a slot at the bottom of the door and slid a bowl and a cup in. "Hey!" I called. "Tell me what you want. I'm sure we can work something out." The jailer didn't answer, but turned his back and walked away.

I felt for the bowl in the dark. It had a slab of hard bread in it. My cellmates had found it first, though, and sank sharp teeth into my thumb. I swore and kicked, forgetting that I didn't have boots on. Fortunately, I connected solidly and felt a rat-sized body sail across the cell. I swooped down and seized the bread before the creature could return and also rescued the cup of tepid water. I used some of the water to wash the bite on my hand, hoping it wouldn't get infected, then set to gnawing the bread.

What had happened then? I couldn't remember. I paced the cell again. Four, eight, four, eight. Don't kick the chamber pot. Four, eight, four, eight. Look out into the passageway. Was the light growing dimmer? Was it late in the day? What day was it? Where were my companions? My thoughts tramped in the same circle as my feet, always returning to their starting point. In stories, prisoners left in the dungeon for years would eventually go mad. I thought that it would take me days, not years, to reach that point.

You'll be here for years, forgotten.

Finally, weary, I returned to my pallet. I started to lie down but remembered the vermin that shared my cell. I stomped and kicked the straw thoroughly to clear any inhabitants out, or at least serve notice that I was not to be trifled with. I hit an object in the straw, rectangular, with leather covers. I swooped down and picked it up and carried it near the small window in the door to examine in the little light that I had left. It was a book, old, handwritten, with some bites recently taken out of the edges of the leather covers.

I went back to the pallet, turning it over in my hands. I had flashes of a chamber with ancient books and artifacts. Ox was there, and Gilwyr. It felt like something that had happened, but where did it fit in?

All this straining at memories was causing my headache to worsen. Not only did lying down make my head feel like it was going to explode, I quickly remembered how uncomfortable the straw was. I propped myself up against the wall and fell asleep with the book cradled protectively in my arms.

My dreams were uneasy. I found myself programming an archaeology simspace for a class. When started, the program wouldn't stay within the scripted parameters. I was swept into a high, cold desert, where the lifeless winds stirred the sand covering the eroded foundations of a citadel. Somewhere in the ruins, I would find something that I had lost. I started searching, knowing that I should have a map, but someone had taken it. I walked through the fine sand, feeling a curious slowness and lightness. Gravity was less than Earth-normal here. For a moment, my simspace overlaid the numbers on my vision: 6m/sec, or about six-tenths of Earth's. And the atmosphere was unbreathably thin. How was I living? Now I was wearing a light pressure suit that I was sure I hadn't been wearing a moment before. This simspace wasn't ready yet, with this number of glitches in it.

How would I find what I was looking for? Did I still have my second sight? I found that I did, and with it, I could see the outlines of buildings and tunnels under the sand. I continued to walk. Puffs of dust rose where I placed my feet and were snatched away by the thin wind. I became aware of a curious glow in the sky and soon beheld a wondrous blue globe rising above the horizon. At this point I understood that I was on Rhea, looking at Sellenria rising in the sky. No, I reminded myself, the planet was Sellen. There was no Sellenria without Rhea.

I came upon an archway buried under the sand, with broad stairs leading down into the city beyond it. These were visible only in second sight. To my normal eye appeared only sand. I wanted to enter this ancient city, but I had no tools with which to excavate. If I had control of the simspace, I could override the programming and move the sand without tools. So far, it had been acting not at all like the simulation I had been programming and had not responded to my will. In dream-logic I decided that if this were a Sellenrian simulation, then it would respond to Sellenrian rules: I willed the *aelo tai* to move the sand.

The sand parted like the sea in old Earth fables. Waves of sand split left and right, flowing uphill and away. The sand swirled in rivulets around stones and eroded walls as the land sank before me. For several moments, the desiccated landscape appeared liquid, draining upwards away from the arch. Finally all was still, and the way to the lower city was before me. I felt a profound disquiet that it had not been the red *aelo tai* that had responded to my will—I had felt the power radiate from the black *aelo tai* beneath my breastbone.

I descended the slope of sand, which met stairs that took me to the level of the arch. This had always been an underground entrance it seemed. I passed through the arch and into the city below.

This had been a Kir Leth city. I recognized the architecture on all sides as being very like that in the Silent City. It was abandoned as well, with all artifacts removed. The living systems that had given the Silent City light and air were likewise gone, probably unable to survive in the almost non-existent atmosphere. Either this world had possessed an atmosphere in the past, or it had been sealed and self-sufficient. I saw only what was revealed by my suit lights—long, wide hallways (or were they streets?) extending into darkness before me, with blank doorways at intervals along each side. Sometimes I would come to a crossroads, and looking down the alternate ways, more of the same. Once, at one of the crossings, I came upon a statue of a Kir-Leth, with all details smoothed away as if by eons of wind-blown sand. In the way of dreams, I skipped ahead, knowing that I had walked for hours, but not feeling that hours had passed.

I came into a chamber, larger than most, which had at its center a pedestal that I recognized from the Blight. This pedestal also had an *aelo tai* on it, this one white, glowing with a pearly light. The black *aelo tai* tugged at me, telling me that this one was a danger to me. Whether or not it was, I gave it a wide berth. I had already adopted two wayward *aelo tai* and didn't feel that I could handle another one. I departed, musing whether the perception that white and black are opposites was culturally or perceptually based. The Kir Leth may not have considered them as mutually antagonistic as human cultures often do.

In the next chamber, I found a book. The binding looked human-made, even ordinary. I opened it to find not writing, but a simspace control panel. However, it was in a language I had never seen before, with trailing, vaguely runic letters. While this was a fascinating archeological simulation, it wasn't the one I had programmed, and I wanted to regain control. I tried moving some sliders that looked like interface controls, but nothing happened. Something started trying to tug the book out of my hand, and I saw that a six-legged, rat-like creature had sunk its teeth into the book and was tugging at it. I felt another tugging at the leg of my pressure suit and looked down to find a number of the creatures starting to tear at the suit fabric. More came scurrying across the floor in a dark tide and began climbing my leg. I punched at the simspace controls in panic. If anything, the creatures came faster.

A simulation should always have a safe word, an emergency shutdown if the programming was faulty and the situation became intolerable or inescapable. I tried a few that I had used in the past: "Nile! Tigris! Euphrates!" Nothing happened. What could the safe word be for this simulation? I felt teeth penetrate the pressure suit and graze the skin underneath. Terrified that I was going to be eaten alive, abandoned by my companions, alone on the airless moon of a forgotten planet, I cried out, "Gilwyr!"

Simulation and dream ended with a start. I was back in my cell, and the rat-creature was trying to eat the leather cover of the book in my hands, tugging it from my grasp. Another had nipped me in the leg. Awakening in a frightened rage, I backhanded the creature across the cell. I kicked the other one (or more) away from my leg and staggered to my feet. I heard scurrying and chittering sounds in the back of the cell. The wan light that had entered the cell earlier was gone, and the wavering illumination of torches filtered through the barred window.

I was still filled with the terror I had felt at the tide of sharp-toothed vermin that had attacked me in the simulation inside my dream. Rage welled up to fill my breast, rage at my helplessness, rage at my captivity, rage at my dream, and rage at the dirty, scuttling creatures that tried to feed on me while I slept. The black *aelo tai* channeled my rage and blasted it outwards. I heard a half dozen shrill cries from the back of the cell; then all was still.

Breathing heavily, I paced, my mind a turmoil. I had been in a simulation inside a dream. Was this still a dream? Was I in simspace now? Had this entire adventure on Sellenria been a simulation? How could I tell? Usually in a simspace one had a heads-up display in peripheral vision with virtual controls for stopping or pausing or altering the experience. For total immersion, most often for games or training, some people turned off their heads-up displays. Reportedly it was nearly impossible to tell virtual reality from physical unless there were some flaws in the programming. I had never participated in such games, but what if I was in one now? I was in a primitive dungeon in a backward culture that still had kings and guilds (and chamberpots, my nose reminded me). The world was populated with strange creatures out of a fantasy story, and some things I had seen could only be explained as magic. Either these things were real, or I was trapped in a simspace, or I was losing my sanity.

The book. Where had I gotten the book, and what was it? I opened it, but unlike the book in my dream, it was an ordinary book, written in longhand in ink on thick paper. Even holding it up to the torchlight that filtered into my cell, I could make out little. Where had I gotten it? Holding it close to my eye in the dim light, I could smell the old leather and heavy paper of the binding.

The smell of the book brought back a memory. I had been in a chamber of manuscripts and artifacts. It was a hidden chamber, a chamber filled with the smells of old leather, old candles. We had gained access somehow. It had contained the records of the founding of the de Oxendon line, and the renaming of the city. Other manuscripts chronicled the War of the Grimmerroth. I had opened the room, I recalled now. Ox and Gilwyr were still with me, and we had been enthralled by the trove of history. Enthralled and … disturbed? What had we found? How had we found it?

A vision flashed back to an ornate bedroom. An old man, bedridden, white-bearded. The King. We had been conducted via servant's passages to this bedroom. The old king had given Ox his blessing and named him the new king. We had found the artifacts, and I had just found an interesting book. Guards had rushed in, and I had stuffed the book into my pants to have my hands free. Pain had crashed into my head and I had woken up here. My captors must not have noticed the book in the darkness and had let it fall in the straw when they threw me in here.

Your companions decided they didn't need you anymore.

Yes, that was what happened. There had been no one else in the secret room. Ox must have decided that the strange scholar from another world was a liability in his new role as king. I wondered if Gilwyr had survived. Gilwyr was intensely loyal to Ox and would be an asset to him as an assassin.

Now that I recalled what had happened, the black rage rose again. I had saved Ox's life on several occasions and supported him in his fight for the kingship. What if it had all been arranged by Ox? He could have staged the fight that caused Gerard's death, to cast himself as the sympathetic figure. He knew about the red *aelo tai* and had sent his men to steal it. He knew we would return to the university, and could set guards along the path to abduct us. I could see now that he had planned the whole thing.

I was tired of the part I was assigned in the medieval drama. I was the one that bad things happened to. I didn't rescue anyone and become the hero, I wasn't a warrior or even a very good assassin. I had no chance of becoming king. I wanted to write my own script from now on.

Take control. Embrace who you've become.

Finally, the voice was making sense. I called on the rage, the darkness, the *aelo tai*. If the rules of this world used magic, then I would become a warlock. I could feel glimmers in the dust, in the stones, in the air, all of which could answer my call. I used the black *aelo tai* and called to them. I felt a great stirring in the world around me, a sense that I could summon forces to do my bidding. Almost, they came together, then as suddenly all was quiet. I sagged against the wall, drained and despairing. I couldn't even be an evil wizard in this world. I was destined to rot in this cell at the pleasure of the lords of this world.

It was then that the morghaest broke down the door to my cell.

CHAPTER 30

Fugitive

THE MORGHAEST WAS over two meters tall and wider than the door. It didn't bother to stoop or squeeze to get through the opening. It gripped the stone doorway and waited while the stone turned to powder and sloughed away. I cowered into the back corner of the cell, panic rising. I had come away from two encounters with its kind, but I had had Gilwyr and weapons to back me up. This time, I was unarmed. I could throw a book, a chamberpot, and a couple of dead rats, and then I was done. I anticipated a short encounter and a bloody end.

The morghaest took one step inside my cell. I led with my best shot: the chamberpot. It lodged in the creature's chest and began to crumble, becoming part of my attacker. That seemed to be a particularly gruesome way to die. I inched to one side, hoping it wouldn't see me. Indeed, I didn't know how it could see at all. The face was featureless, without eyes or ears, but it turned its head as if tracking me. As I moved, the light from the corridor fell upon me. It dazzled my good eye and reflected crimson from the *aelo tai* embedded in the other.

The morghaest froze. I waited, but it remained a motionless statue, a terrible golem come to terrorize me in my cell. After minutes passed and I continued to be not yet dead, I slowly clambered to my feet. The creature stirred and my heart leaped into my throat, but it just shuffled backward. Was it afraid of my red *aelo tai*? I remembered that the *aelo tai* had reacted against the watchbreaker fragment in my eye. I took a step towards the morghaest, and it took a step back. I felt a tugging at my breastbone as I did so, and again had the sense of glimmers in the air around me, glimmers that were somehow as aware of me as I was of them. A great gathering of glimmers towered in front of me, taking up the same space in which the morghaest stood. The creature had come together from those motes, and I had summoned it. While I could see it with my crimson second sight, I could *feel* it within the black *aelo tai*, and its analog of perception, blacksight.

Very well, magic worked, and I had just performed magic, ergo I was a warlock. I was either mad, or locked in a simspace, or on a world that had some seriously crazy things in it. I could embrace the madness and rule the world, or stay here and rot in this cell. I raised my hand to indicate a direction and formed a desire in the pit of my stomach where these feelings seemed to live. The morghaest turned around and began bashing and crumbling a hole in the wall. As I emerged from the cell, I saw that it had already broken down an outer door. If it had used the same means of egress, it would have saved itself the trouble of demolishing a stone wall. It wasn't very intelligent if indeed it had any autonomy whatsoever. It might be purely a thing of my desire, crafted with the power of the *aelo tai*.

We passed the crumpled form of a guard. A leather helmet had been no match for a blow that could punch through stone. I did not pity anyone who had held me captive. I did not pity anyone in this city. I sent my morghaest against the outer door. There were still-living guards outside of this door, guards who had time to raise their weapons briefly before they and their weapons were battered aside. We emerged into a more spacious hallway, not nearly as noisome as the dungeon, but still utilitarian. I scanned the vicinity and was drawn to a brilliant red glow that I could perceive on the floor above me, a bright star in second sight. Stairs were at the end the corridor to my right. I directed the morghaest that way and followed in its wake.

We were evidently near the kitchen, as servants now emerged bearing trays of food. They dropped the trays and fled, though one had the bravery or foolishness to heave his tray at the morghaest. The morghaest swatted tray and servant aside almost without noticing. I stepped over the broken body and grabbed a loaf of bread from the tray. It was much better bread than they fed their prisoners. *I should be anguished by the death of innocent people.* Was that the Other? *No, that is who you were.* For a moment, I saw the body of an innocent young man at my feet, likely with a family at home, dead for no other reason than he was in my way. Grief almost overcame me, grief and remorse. My knees shook and my vision blurred with tears. *Remorse will not get you out of here,* said the black *aelo lui*. The feeling faded. There were no longer any innocents.

Several more broken guards came tumbling down the stairs. I picked up a serviceable sword, then remembered I was rather poorly dressed. I picked boots, shirt, and coat from a man who wouldn't be needing them any longer and dressed myself. I recovered my loaf of bread and followed the path of destruction upwards. Emerging in a great hall, I stopped to munch on the bread and survey the scene. The morghaest had scattered bits of guard liberally around. I thought the one draped over the statue of some king or other was particularly pleasingly arranged. The bread was quite good as well.

The crimson star still shone in second sight, behind closed doors at the end of the hall. I could see a good number of swords and other bits of metal within as well. The noise must have not penetrated the heavy doors to alarm them. I looked forward to their expressions of surprise.

The morghaest charged the doors, shattering them before its bulk. Timbers flew across the room to mow down bystanders like ripened grain. I had the creature halt for effect inside the door as I stepped into the stunned room. I took in the massed people arranged by social rank. I grinned. I had interrupted a coronation.

The man in the seat of honor was not Ox. Terrell sat on the high throne with a crown on his head and a scepter in his right hand. To his left sat Ox, draped in lesser finery. *So Ox sold out to Terrell.* He had had me tossed into the dungeon in the bargain, an inconvenient outsider. I wondered what had happened to Gilwyr. Ox had probably realized that even with the blessing of the old king he didn't have the political backing to take and hold the throne, and had traded his support for a lesser measure of influence in the court. It was probably a better deal than total defeat and no influence. *The odds of him having an accident in the near future are high.*

I saw Gilwyr then, standing behind Ox, heavily bound and surrounded by spears. Some of the spears were pointed at Ox, presumably as an assurance of her good behavior. Ox raised his hands from his lap, and I saw the manacles binding his wrists. Then it came back: *Terrell did this.* As this last piece fell into place, it was like a top-heavy iceberg starting to tip. Dazed, confused, and imprisoned, I had listened to the whispering of the *aelo tai.* I had believed that my friends would betray me and that my actions were justified. As the iceberg rolled, the layers of compassion and empathy that had been submerged were returned to the surface. I was nearly overwhelmed by what I had just done and the faces of broken people swam before my eyes. I was still in danger; my *friends* were still in danger. I had to keep myself together until we were free. I had to continue to act the part of the warlock.

Now all eyes were on me, and on the glittering red *aelo tai* in my eye socket, and on the shambling creation that was so obviously doing my bidding. I heard a swelling whisper of "Warlock" from the masses of people who were trying to edge away from the center of the room that I held. That was also giving the spearmen a better view to skewer me. I had to break the standoff.

I started pacing down the center aisle. I had to sustain my character if I was going to win free of this castle. I called for the best acting that I was capable of. I took a final bite of bread to indicate unconcern, then tossed the remainder away. The morghaest fell in behind me. Second sight showed me a single spear arcing through the air towards me. It was a simple task to meet it with my own blade and slice it in midair. The Grimmerroth may have been an old myth on this planet, but he was real to them. If that gave me the leverage to get out of this city alive, I would play the part for all I was worth.

A guard stepped forward to block my way, sword at the ready. Second sight showed me that he would step to his right and cut at my left side. As he began his step, I shifted to a two-handed grip on the some-what heavy sword I had appropriated, and swung in a low arc, cutting upwards, separating him from his sword at his elbow. As the crowd gasped, I felt again the dancing particles that surrounded me and saw through black sight how to call them to assemble. I touched the tips of my fingers to his breastplate and called. The guard cried out, briefly, as his skin boiled, absorbing clothing and armor, bones, internal organs, and some chunk of the stone floor on which he stood. In moments I had a second, lesser morghaest to flank me. I struggled not to let my revulsion show on my face. *He was dead anyway. He would have bled to death from that wound.*

A wail of terror went up from the assembled court, and the larger part of them stampeded for the door. A double row of guards arrayed themselves between me and the dais where Terrell still sat, along with Ox and Gilwyr. I paced deliberately towards them as if I feared nothing, though that was as far from the truth as it was possible to get. I advanced to within two paces of the line of guards. None moved to attack me. I had proved my invulnerability in their minds. I had the psychological advantage. Time to press it home. I raised my hand again in the gesture I had used when I had made their comrade into a shambling golem. "Who shall join my army next?" I grated. "Step forward and receive my touch. Give me absolute obedience, and I will make you an invulnerable soldier." I had no idea how this worked or whether I could do as I said, but impressing them with the idea that I had mindless, invulnerable creatures to do my bidding was foremost in my thoughts.

I had believed that voiding one's bowels in abject terror was just an expression, but my nose told me that several of the guards facing me did just that. I took one step forward. It only took one guard to break forma-tion to send them all fleeing for their lives. There was nothing between me and the dais now. I mounted the steps.

Terrell held his seat, though I saw that his knuckles were white where they gripped the arms of the throne, and his eyes were wide and darting furtively from side to side. General Bercarius stood behind him, holding her hand on his shoulder and a short sword at his ribs. *So Terrell would flee, but his General is forcing him to stand his ground and not lose face? Interesting.* The red *aelo tai* rested on a cushion beside the throne. Now that I was close, I didn't see the brilliant light in second sight any longer, but I was too busy keeping track of all the weapons around me to worry about it.

I drew up to Ox's level. I directed the smaller morghaest to put forth a hand. Ox flinched, but with an effort of will that broke out sweat all over my body, I caused the morghaest to grasp just the chain of Ox's manacles. The chain and the iron bands dissolved into powder and fell away. Ox snatched his hands away and felt them carefully as if fearing he was going to crumble himself.

I turned to Terrell. "Your father declared that Greylander is the rightful king. Step down and give the throne to him and I'll let you live."

Terrell gave a short laugh. "A king backed by the Grimmerroth? That would never stand. Dalactus has always guarded the realms of men against the Grimmerroth and his creatures. Unless my brother is prepared to engage in a reign of terror to keep the population in line, he would soon have an open revolt on his hands. Dear brother has never had an appetite for ruling, much less a rule of that sort."

Ox spoke. "He is right, Stenn. You just ended the legitimacy of my claim by supporting me. All we can do now is flee." I heard the bitterness in his words, though a moment delayed as if my emotional reception was disconnected. The expression on his face … it wasn't gratitude, it was revulsion. What had I done? My anger still raged and needed to strike out at someone.

I growled. "Then give me one good reason why I should not kill him now for imprisoning me."

"Think on the alternatives."

I looked at the General, steely-eyed behind her King. Would she step in if Terrell fell? Or would it be one of the lordlings that we had encountered at the party? It was more likely that civil war would ensue with many claimants and none qualified to lead. The Anglich would seize the moment as well. The city would probably tear itself to pieces.

I needed to channel my anger. I pointed to Gilwyr without taking my eyes off of Terrell and the General. "Release her."

Gilwyr was guarded by two Daughters and one Son of Rowena. Terrell gave a curt nod in their direction, but I caught a discreet hand signal from the General. In second sight I saw one of the Daughters plunging a spear into Gilwyr's belly. I put forth my will. The smaller morghaest moved with inhuman speed and smashed that guard into pulp before she could act. The General's eyes widened. Still, without looking in Gilwyr's direction, I said calmly, "Now, use the small dagger in your belt to cut her bonds. If you intend to so much as nick her as you do, you'll be dead two seconds before you even think of it."

The other Daughter moved with exaggerated care to withdraw her dagger. Holding it in plain view at all times, she started sawing the ropes holding Gilwyr's wrists. Then she knelt, and I tensed, but then understood that they had bound Gilwyr's ankles as well, and the guard was only following my orders.

"Now lay aside your weapons and give Gilwyr any of them that she wishes." I could see in second sight the swords and spears being put aside and then lifted up again as Gilwyr examined them. She chose two swords and a dagger and tossed the rest of them out of reach.

"We're leaving now," I said. "I will know if you come after us, and it will go very badly for you if you do. Send anyone after us, and I'll come back and tear your palace down. Oh, and this is mine." I snatched the red *aelo tai* from its cushion. I was glad that Terrell hadn't thought to hide it in the commotion because I still couldn't see it in second sight. I motioned my companions to my side; they joined me with enough reluctance to set my paranoia tingling again. We left the throne room, and I detected no motion behind us as we departed.

"Which way?" I asked Ox as we came back out into the main hall.

"The front entrance is that way. There is also a side entrance for the servants in that direction. I am not convinced I should go with you, however." I couldn't bear the way he looked at me.

"I feel just as sickened as you look. I had no choice if we are to get out of here."

"That may well be, though ... never mind, we will discuss this later. Go this way."

As we approached the main gates, Gilwyr drew us to one side, then took a quick look through a slotted opening set in the door. "As I thought, they are going to test us," she said. "There are two squadrons of Rowena's best out there. I don't think they've had a chance to bring up cannon yet, but we must act quickly before they do."

"Cannon?"

"Cannon are known to at least temporarily stop morghaests, blowing them to bits, from which it takes them some time to reassemble."

"Can you control the morghaests at a distance or make them follow directions?" asked Ox.

"I only just discovered that I can control them. I haven't had time to experiment with them to find out what they can do. I think if I point them in a direction they'll keep going."

"Then we'll send the morghaests out the front entrance to engage the guard. We'll divert to the servant's entrance. With any luck, they'll think we're just hanging back." Ox shook his head. "I can't believe I'm sending morghaests against my own people."

"Your own people did put you in chains," I pointed out.

"That, on the other hand, is all too easy to believe if you know my family."

"All right, let's go." I sent my will to the morghaests, which immediately charged through the door. They didn't bother opening the doors first but simply burst through them, sending shards of wood flying outward as deadly missiles. Ox looked sadly after them. "Those doors have stood for hundreds of years," he said. "How terrible to be the one to destroy them."

"We can afford the luxury of regret if we make it out of the city alive," said Gilwyr. "Let's go."

We ran for the kitchens, where Ox said there were gates through which the servants brought food and supplies. I looked ahead for the images of weapons in second sight that would indicate an ambush. I saw only pots and grates, spoons and knives. We burst into and through the kitchens, scattering chaos in our wake. None of the cooks or scullery help had any thought of obstructing us. One kind (or terrified) soul had the courtesy to open the outward door for us, though probably with the thought of getting rid of us as quickly as possible.

Outside we met the first resistance. There were two guards outside, but they did not appear to be on alert. Word of the events inside must not have reached them yet. "Do you think we can just walk out?" I asked.

"I think they'll challenge us," replied Ox. "We're rather conspicuous, and you don't have your eyepatch on."

I'd forgotten all about that. I cast about something to disguise myself. An old woman cowering nearby had a floppy felt hat. I snatched it from her head, ignoring her indignant squawk, and jammed it on my own.

Pulled down far enough, it should shade me from casual inspection. "That should do," said Gilwyr.

"Apologies, old one," said Ox to the woman, "but you have helped your kingdom today." We moved on out through the gate.

The guards didn't pay much attention at first. Then they noticed that we were not the sort of people that usually exited through this gate. I was in grubby breeches and a guard's coat and boots. Gilwyr was in her normal breeches and jerkin attire, while Ox was dressed for the coronation in a court robe. Ox addressed them sternly, "Thank the child god that not all the guards have left their posts. These two have been causing trouble inside. Please see that they're ejected from the palace grounds." I almost missed his gambit and turned on him, thinking betrayal once again, but Gilwyr bowed her head and stumbled past the guards. Once I joined her, and the guards had turned their backs on Ox to hustle us out, he reached out with two enormous hands and knocked their heads together, dropping them like sacks of potatoes. "Better a headache than a sword in the gut," he said. "There have been enough deaths today."

We exited through the kitchen gardens and down a path. At the outer wall were two more guards, and these were more alert than the previous two. Gilwyr and I were forced to engage them, but they were not a match for us, and we struck them down quickly. Then we were out in the town, traversing the narrow streets.

"What's the best way out of the city?" asked Gilwyr.

"We should go towards the mountain," said Ox. "Few know the mountain passes, and they won't expect us to go that way. They'll watch the bridge and chasm the closest. We have the best chance of making it if we can get the Kir Leth cloaks and weapons that we left at Norrice's lamp works. Head south first, and we can lay low near the old monument. Then at dusk, we can work our way into the mercantile district and circle back, so we run the least chance of leading the guard to her."

"Norrice is compromised, Ox," said Gilwyr. "Terrell didn't just wait for you to show up, he sent that guard to give you a message you wouldn't ignore to make you walk right into that trap. We could be walking into another one if you go back there."

"I know, Gilwyr. I wouldn't go there if I didn't think Norrice had already been found out. I wouldn't put her in danger she wasn't already in. This way I can warn her, and at the same time get back the articles that we need. We will just have to take care that there aren't any hazards that we can't deal with inside."

We left the palace precincts and entered the late afternoon bustle of the town. We didn't precisely blend in, but no one seemed to pay us much heed. We had a murmured exchange about obtaining less conspicuous clothes, but none of us had come away from the palace with any money, and Ox opined that a theft would be a greater risk than continuing in these clothes. And so we made our way down to a grassy park, in the center of which was a small tomb, both of which seemed to be shunned by the local residents. Inside the tomb, we waited for darkness to fall.

CHAPTER 31

Tomb of Pandulf

THE TOMB HAD a shabby air of majesty: grandeur covered with dust and stately arches choked with debris. Words had been scratched into the stone with uneven hand and less than decorous intent. Someone had thought enough of the occupant to build this monument, but subsequent generations did not share that sentiment.

"Whose tomb is this?" I asked.

"Pandulf. The last Anglich king," rumbled Ox. "Roland built this monument to him in gratitude for being named the first Dalactyn king, and generations of Anglich have cursed Pandulf's name for that same deed. He is also remembered for failing to confront the Grimmerroth before he became too powerful … the last time. And does history now repeat itself?"

"What do you mean? Gilwyr, why have you drawn your blade?" She was behind me and had made no noise, but I could see the blade in second sight. I felt through blacksight for the dancing motes around us, ready to call them to my aid again if I should need them. Suspicion overtook me like a wave as I did so, making cold calculations.

Look out for yourself. No one else will.

"When we were in the King's Archives, we found some old manuscripts …"

"When were we in the King's Archives?" I remembered, but I was fishing. I felt there was something I didn't recall yet.

"Directly after Father passed away. You opened the hidden door behind the tapestry after Father told us to find it there, don't you recall?"

"Between leaving the lampworks and waking up with a headache in the dungeon, I have only fragments of memory." *Give them room to trap themselves.*

"There was a fight in the Archives when Terrell's men overpowered us. Were you injured then?"

"I suppose that would explain the large lump I have on the back of my head."

"Then, in brief, Father was indeed dying." Ox summarized the events of the night accurately, stopping when we gained access to the Archives. I turned from him, appearing heedless of Gilwyr's still-drawn sword, but in fact watching it closely in second sight. "I awoke in that miserable cell thinking you had betrayed me. What made me think that?"

"We will talk of that in a moment. In the Archives, there are documents that would be very inflammatory to the Anglich were they to come to light. I suppose each king has been tempted to destroy them for that reason, but they also contain our heritage as Dalactyns. There is a treatise written by Roland's mentor setting out the ideals on which we were founded, and the inspiration to carve out a place where we could live those ideals. They were noble ideals of chivalry and self-governance and strength but tainted by the methods by which they were achieved. Roland's party commandeered a ship to bring them here, committing piracy and murder. Then, when they arrived in this land and found it inhabited, they departed from their intended path of creating a new kingdom in the wilderness to remake this one in their mold instead."

"I can see why your family wouldn't want this to be well-known. You have not yet explained the drawn sword."

"Moments before Terrell's men rushed in, I found some diary pages, written by Roland himself. Members of his cadre had prepared well for their piracy. They kept only a single member of the ship's crew alive and coerced him into working for them while killing the rest. Upon arriving in this land, they left him behind on the ship, or he escaped, and he returned to wreak vengeance upon them. This was the cause of the war, for he became the Grimmerroth, and his name before that was Jonan Gremm. You said that you received your red *aelo tai* from a distant ancestor. When we found that you share a family name with the Grimmerroth, we were forced to ponder the connection."

I sat down abruptly. Darkness closed in and blood roared in my ears. I lost both second sight and blacksight. I am *not* going to faint, I told myself. That only happens in fiction. I clenched my guts and fought back. I heard Gilwyr step closer. A vagrant bit of the training I had received from her told me I should be on my guard. I felt her hand on my shoulder and tensed.

"Stenn? Are you injured?"

My voice didn't want to cooperate. I forced out, "No. I just learned the fate of my lost ancestor, that he was kidnapped and enslaved by pirates, and then he became an evil sorcerer." I turned to Ox. "And it was *your* ancestor who killed his crew and stranded him here. I'm fine. Just leave me alone."

"We feared you would be dismayed."

"Dismayed? It feels like you just jammed a training stave into my breastbone."

I groped for second sight, recovered it. Gilwyr's sword stayed ready, but not threatening.

"What did you mean by history repeating?" I asked Ox. "Do you think because our ancestors were enemies that we are now enemies?"

"It is not that. I know you by your actions and you know me by mine. I do not think we are enemies."

"Then what?"

"Morghaests began appearing as soon as you arrived. Now you seem to be able to summon and control them. You broke out of the dungeon and held off the king's guard. You have a strange vision that shows you hidden weapons and allows you to anticipate them. It may be that the Grimmerroth has some ancient affinity for those of your blood. I fear that fate might walk you down that same road of destruction."

Gilwyr still had her hand on my shoulder. "You haven't been the same person since the Blight. The Blight changes those who emerge from it. You have been brooding as if dark thoughts tormented you. When you do speak, you often throw words like daggers, not caring whom you cut. And today I saw you do acts of cruelty that I did not think you capable of."

I thought back on the day. Perhaps I had changed. No, I *knew* I had changed. My conscience quailed at the memory of what I had done. The wash of paranoia that had covered me when I felt threatened receded now. My companions deserved to know.

"I must tell you this. I am ashamed that I waited until now to do so. When we were in the Blight, I did take the black *aelo tai* from the pedestal. But I wasn't able to throw it away. It wouldn't let me. It burned through my skin and became part of me. After seeing all the biological engineering that the Kir Leth have done, I think these *aelo tai* are some kind of semi-living symbiont. They find a host to carry them around, and in return, they grant that host extra abilities. The red *aelo tai* gives me augmented vision and predicts a few seconds into the future. The black *aelo tai* lets me see and command … this is hard to explain … something in the soil and stone and sometimes in the air. Something that can remake those materials into morghaests. It also feels like I'm carrying the Blight with me. That feeling of evil, of paranoia, of hopelessness. I've been trying to fight it, but every time I let my guard down it gets stronger. When I reached rock bottom in the dungeon, thinking that I had been abandoned there, it broke loose. It controlled me until the rage subsided. It frightens me, how powerful I felt."

"The same scene by Rhea-light or Sun-light is vastly different and both are true," said Ox. It sounded like a quotation. "That explains much."

"You said the Blight changes everyone. How has it changed you?"

Both seemed reluctant to answer, but Ox went first. "I came away with a desire to rule that I did not have before. I had previously thought that I might be forced into ruling for the good of the people but I did not desire it. After my experience in the Blight … I felt a certainty that it was my right to seize the throne. Who could be more just than me? I would punish the usurpers and the sycophants, then move on to the corrupt and greedy, the slothful and lazy, those who stinted their duties or shorted their taxes. By the time I was done, it would be a perfect kingdom, and I would be a just king, the justest who ever ruled. And the worst tyrant, worse by far than Terrell. In waking moments, I fear to take the throne more than ever, for what I might do if it were to come to pass. In my dreams … I'm too ashamed to tell you of those. I must fight them every night."

I thought Gilwyr was not going to answer, but then she said, "I was raised by the Kir Leth. I learned their ways and thought I was one of them. But I was restless and risked the rebukes of my pod-mates to seek out and become one of the Cray Leth. I learned from them and became one of the best. But still I was restless, and I journeyed to the human lands and learned how to live in that society from Ox, with his boundless patience. I joined my guild and became one of the best. Until we became lost in the Blight, I thought that I could change my skin at will and be Kir Leth or human, Cray Leth or Assassin. The Blight showed me how other people saw me, how deluded I was. I was always restless because I did not fit in. I am not truly Kir Leth because I am mute. Neither am I truly human. Both sides shun and exclude me, neither side understands me, and I see now that I don't understand them." In second sight, I could see her sword tremble in her hand, just a little.

A brief time passed in which only the wind spoke among the dead leaves on the ground. We each had our thoughts and our reasons for not giving voice to them. I think that we were all, as I was, realizing that our thoughts were not our own. Gilwyr put away her sword.

"What will you do now?" I finally asked Ox. "Try to rally the Hidden Hand against Terrell?"

"That is no longer an option. Once word is out, as it surely is now, that I was allied with a warlock, if not the Grimmerroth himself, there are none in this town who would deal with me."

""But if I could use the black *aelo tai* to defeat the palace guard and put you in power, allowing you to fulfill your promises to the Anglich, wouldn't they come around to supporting you?"

"Put that notion out of your head. No good has ever come of employing this power. It warps and twists. Good intentions are its foothold on your mind. You would start out intending justice and end up with ruin. We must take that *aelo tai* far from here."

"How do you know that's not the Blight speaking?"

"Because I very much want to do what you suggest, which means I must resist it."

I felt the hard bundle I had wrapped in cloth, the red *aelo tai* that I had carried from Trondhjem. "I made a promise to recover the red *aelo tai* and to deliver it to Perrhen. I made that promise before the Blight, so it should still be pure. I've accomplished half of that promise. I should finish the other half. Both the red and the black are of their making, and they may be able to tell me how to be free of them."

"I think that is right. We will set off for Cloudhaven after nightfall."

"You don't need to go with me. The influence of the black *aelo tai* may wane if you're away from it."

"It wouldn't matter if it did. The townspeople—Dalactyn and Anglich alike—won't be swayed. They won't see any outward change, and I'm still associated with a warlock who summons morghaests. I must leave for a time, perhaps a long time. It would be a good opportunity for me to seek the council of the Kir Leth again. And since we share a common burden from the Blight, I think it would be best if we stay together to watch each other's backs."

"You'll be traveling with that same warlock who cost you your chance to claim the throne. Will that weigh on your mind?"

"You saved my life in Misthaven and led the way out of the Blight. I walked into Terrell's trap on my own against your counsel, and if you hadn't broken up his coronation, I probably wouldn't have lived much longer. I can forgive you for casting a shadow on a future I wouldn't have had if not for you."

"Doesn't the Blight whisper otherwise to you?"

"Of course it does," he replied, and I could see in his eyes that was a battle fought by inches and won by moments.

We waited until nightfall, past curfew, and until after the first round of patrols of the city guards should have finished. Then we slipped through the darkened streets towards the lampworks. We stopped outside while I probed inside with second sight. "Norrice's weapons are stored in their cabinet. There is one sword that is carried by someone who is pacing back and forth in the outer room. Just one."

"I can take care of one," said Gilwyr. She nimbly climbed the rough stone wall of the building to the roof and disappeared.

"What if it's a trap for us?" I fretted.

"Gilwyr can handle it."

"What if they know I can see metal and brought wooden staves?"

"You, Gilwyr, and I are the only ones who know of that ability. If you haven't told them, then they don't know."

"I think I can turn that sword into dust …"

"No! Use the black *aelo tai* only in dire need. The more you use it, the harder it will be to turn away from it."

"How do you know?"

"It whispers to me too, remember."

I saw the sword inside stop pacing abruptly. From the angle, I could imagine Gilwyr having an arm lock on the person carrying it, who hadn't even drawn it. The sword stayed like that for a moment, then resumed moving in a purposeful pattern through the room.

"It seems that the person inside is not a foe," I said. "They're coming out together. They're heading for the rear alleyway." Still, Ox and I stood ready until both figures emerged into the alley. A person appeared who was shorter than Gilwyr, the one who carried the sword. Gilwyr followed, and I could see that both of them bore burdens. As they came into the light, both Ox and I recognized the face, and especially the single braid on her left.

"Captain Bridocke!" exclaimed Ox. "How do you come to be here?"

"Captain no longer. I've resigned my commission. Hurry, come away before we're spotted."

We hurried in silence through several streets, holding to the shadows as much as possible. Gilwyr was looking behind us as we walked, motioning us to keep the noise down. As we turned a corner, she grabbed Bridocke's arm and slammed her up against the wall. "Are you playing us false?" she snarled under her breath.

"What? No! I sent a runner to report that you had been seen near the bridge and pulled the ambush away from the lampworks and sent them down there to help cordon the streets."

"Well, you were followed. Go on ahead. Keep an eye on her. I will find you shortly," that last addressed to Ox and me. Gilwyr faded into the darkness.

We put a few more blocks behind us, frequently turning to break up the line of sight. Gilwyr rejoined us at an intersection, wiping her sword on a piece of someone else's coat. "There were two. Not the best, but probably told to follow you as a surety." She looked at Bridocke. "You weren't trusted."

Bridocke was dismayed. "No surprise that I wasn't trusted, but I thought I'd shaken anyone who might have followed."

"Now that we have shaken them, double back this way." Gilwyr turned down a narrow, cobbled street leading steeply uphill, the houses here seeming stair-stepped, with each rising above the one before it as they marched upwards.

"You aren't going through the catacombs?"

"No, that's too predictable. You'll forgive me if I don't say more just yet." Gilwyr led us further away from the business district, now through a warren of pinched, steep streets with ramshackle dwellings, climbing ever higher. Dalactus was built with its back to the sheer slopes of the mountains to the northwest. A narrow stone bridge gave access across a deep ravine that split the plateau on which the city was built. We crossed without incident and moved in the direction of the mountains, watching as property values declined precipitously. Soon we were among huts and lean-tos, with animals penned around the sides, or in many cases sharing the dwellings with the people. We saw eyes within, following our progress, but we encountered no one along the way.

At last, we came to the edge of the town, where only a narrow path cut up the steep shoulder of the mountain ahead of us. "I thank you, Bridocke, for your help this night," said Ox. "We must be gone over the first summit before daylight, or we'll risk being spotted."

"My liege, I would accompany you. I swore fealty to you, and I will not give up that service, short of death. I have crossed these mountains with my kin many times before joining the Daughters. I know the paths that will get you through them. Please don't dismiss me here."

Gilwyr looked like she was going to object, but Ox didn't hesitate. "I accepted your service. However, this is a perilous journey and a destination from which many do not return. Is it still your wish to accompany us?"

"It is."

"Then let us be on our way. I see you have brought provisions for us, which shows foresight. Divide the burden up four ways, and take the lead. We want to be at the Waterbreak by daylight."

"Yes, my lord."

Our party, now four, departed Dalactus and began our ascent of the mountain.

Chapter 32

The Mountain

A GOAT MIGHT have called this a path but I was no goat. I was in better shape than I had been in my life, yet I was winded in the first thousand paces. My ankles and knees were battered by the rocks, and I scraped my hand raw on a sharp outcropping. Ox marched tirelessly ahead of me, and Bridocke kept pace. I at least had the slight satisfaction of hearing Ox curse and rub his ankle once or twice. Gilwyr, on the other hand, was bounding ahead of all of us to scout the path, and returning to report that the way was clear, then dropping behind only to catch up with us shortly to say that there were no signs of pursuit. After one of these times, I heard Bridocke mutter to Ox, "Was she born to goats in the mountains that she can race about in the dark like it was a level highway at midday?" I was not the only one grudging Gilwyr her agility.

Ox said only, "She did have an unusual upbringing. She rose to the top of her guild before her twentieth year."

"What guild is that?"

"The Assassins."

Bridocke fell silent, perhaps reassessing her own standing in this company.

Twice more Gilwyr came back to report, and to urge us onward. Twice more I felt rest snatched away from me as we kept climbing past the point where she had waited for us. Rationally I knew she was expending more energy than I was, but it seemed as if she simply flitted to each new resting spot while we labored over boulders. We would no sooner reach her perch before she would be off to the next.

The third time this happened, I kicked a rock in frustration. I was willing to go all night if needed, but I wanted a breather from time to time, especially on this mountainside. The rock was indifferent and my toe protested my stupidity. Gilwyr should slow down; even she could twist an ankle on a trail like this in the middle of the night. She wasn't stupid enough to kick a rock but one could be unseen in the shadows, or even roll unexpectedly into her way. All it would take would be a slight nudge and any one of these rocks could topple into the trail …

"Gilwyr!" Ox's voice floated back to me. I tried to see around him, but his bulk was blocking my view. I finally closed up with him to see Gilwyr hopping towards us on one foot. "What happened?"

"A rock shifted just as I stepped on it and I twisted my ankle. It's not too serious. We should wait here until Rhea rises, in about a candlemark. I should be ready to go on by then. There doesn't seem to be any pursuit. They may not realize we've left the city and are even less likely to think we've gone this way."

"Probably because they're sane," I muttered. In truth, I was frightened. I had been thinking of a rock shifting in just that way, causing Gilwyr to twist her ankle, and it had come to pass. It was enough to believe it was an aspect of the second sight that gave me glimpses of the future, but the thought that chilled me was that I had caused the stone to shift by thinking about it. I had called rock and debris together to form a golem, setting it in motion. It was no leap at all to think I could have done this, merely because I wished to take a break. I turned away, fearing that Gilwyr could read the shame on my face even by the faint starlight.

I walked a score of paces up the trail to where the vista opened up towards the east. The city of Dalactus was below us, with its faint gleams of lantern light. The chasm that protected the city was an inky pool of darkness outlining the far edge. Beyond that, a painter with a silvery brush suggested the ridges and defiles of the broken land under which we had passed in the hallways of the Silent City. The far horizon was limned by the ruddy glow of Rhea, not yet ready to show herself, but throwing her veil into the sky to prepare it for her entrance.

I heard footsteps behind me on the path. Second sight informed me that it was Bridocke by the way she wore her weapons and that she was not currently a threat to me. Why was I thinking like this?

She came to stand beside me for a few moments, surveying the city that she had left—possibly forever, I reminded myself. "This is the best vantage on the mountain road," she said after a while. "We're about to cross over to the back side of this shoulder. By the time we climb high enough to see over it again, the city will be just a far-away smudge."

"Thanks for letting me know. I've been lacking a tour guide to show me the highlights so far." I meant that as a light comment, but it came out bitter, acerbic.

I could feel her gaze in the night. I knew when one of her thumbs brushed the hilt of her knife. I couldn't tell the thought behind it.

"You're a puzzle, Stenn," she said. "Where do you come from, with that accent? What's your guild? Why do you follow Prince Greylander? For that matter, what sort of a name is Stenn? Family, given, or earned?"

"The easy answer is my name. Stenn Gremm, Professor of Anthropology at a university so far off you've never heard of it."

"So you have students, as I've heard Prince Greylander does in Misthaven? It is strange to think of a prince as a mere teacher."

"Yes, though my own teaching days seem a different lifetime than this one."

"Did you come to learn from the Prince?"

"Ah, well, I came to learn about this land, though I ended up as Gilwyr's student, not Ox's."

"You? In the assassin's guild?"

"I seem to have shown an unexpected aptitude for killing people. My students back home probably suspected it all along, but it was a surprise to me."

"Is it true that a morghaest freed you from the dungeon?

"Yes."

"Did … was it an accident? Did you just take advantage of the destruction it caused to escape?"

"No. I called it. I didn't know I could do that. I won't do it again. It was a terrible thing." Unless someone throws me into a dungeon again, I qualified to myself. There might be circumstances when terrible things were required.

"How are you able to do such a thing? Are you a warlock?" She attempted a cool demand but I heard a tremor in the words.

"I don't know. It may be a thing that I carry, which I was charged to bring to Cloudhaven. It may be my heritage. It may be both."

"Things have taken strange turns of late," she said. "A blue sword appeared in the sky several months ago. Now morghaests and warlocks are appearing. Next, you'll tell me that Kir Leth are real and you've met them."

I started at her mention that she had seen the blue glow of the *Aquila's* arrival. It must have appeared like a portent to them, even less explicable than a comet. I decided not to tell her just yet that our destination was a Kir Leth city. I said only, "Things are likely to get stranger if you travel with us, Captain."

"Don't call me that any longer. I renounced the Order and the rank with it when Terrell used the Order to stage his coup."

"Do you have a given name then?"

"I've never much liked my given name, Margr. My mother-sister had that name, and she had every bit of meanness that my mother did not. Just call me Bridocke. It was the only name my father ever used, and that's good enough for me."

"Then that's what we'll use."

"I want you to know, sir warlock, that my first duty is to protect the Prince. You may talk fair, but so did the Grimmerroth. I hope we will not find ourselves at odds over this."

"I've been protecting Ox since the attack at Misthaven. So far I've dispatched five—or was it six? I lose count—of your former order who were trying to take the Prince's life. And that was without using any warlock-craft." Was that a word?

It was at that moment that Rhea rose over the horizon, illuminating the peaks with ruddy light. Bridocke was looking me in the face, and I saw her eyes snap to the *aelo tai* in my left eye socket. I had not recovered my eyepatch after my stay in the dungeon. She drew a sharp gasp, then fled back down the mountain towards Ox and Gilwyr.

As I watched her go, I could hear Gilwyr in my mind, berating me. "Never boast. Your opponent underestimates you? Encourage it! It will make your job easier in the end. Your friends underestimate you? They could be your enemies by nightfall." I waited with my thoughts until I heard my companions ascending the trail towards my position.

As they drew near, Ox called ahead. "You gave Bridocke quite a fright with your eye. We told her how you lost it in a fight and replaced it with one of red glass to frighten your enemies." So that was to be our story. As good as any, I supposed.

We continued climbing. Gilwyr kept to a more reasonable pace now, favoring her ankle slightly. I wondered if it would handicap her in a sword fight. I imagined myself in a training bout with her, attempting to take advantage of the change in her balance and speed. She would want to keep me guessing. She might fight normally, bearing the pain. She might exaggerate the injury to lull me into stepping too close. She did not fight by a complicated moral code; she fought to win by any means necessary. I would close on her opposite side to force her weight back onto that ankle. She might pivot and backhand, or might even switch hands; that would pose no disadvantage to her. I would maneuver her towards some broken ground, where her weakened ankle might betray her. She would take the bait, pretend to stumble, fall to a crouch. I would close. She would uncoil from her crouch into a lightning uppercut. I beat it aside barely in time. She hip-checks to knock me off balance …

"Who are you dueling, lad?"

I hadn't noticed Ox dropping back to walk alongside me as the trail had widened. I lowered my hands to my sides. At least I hadn't drawn my sword, but I had been blocking and parrying as I walked. I was glad that the light of Rhea wasn't enough to illuminate my embarrassment.

"Just one of the fights that we fought getting out of Misthaven. I keep replaying them in my head. I know I could have done better, and perhaps saved your brother. I know I could have done worse and easily taken a fatal cut myself." That last was especially true, and many of my dreams since that time had ended that way.

"Who among us hasn't thought that we could have done better, in the clear light of morning? Or worse, on a dark night like this one, as guesses and regrets crowd close like prowling wolves? I have made my share of mistakes as well."

"And Gilwyr ..."

"What of her? She has acquitted herself impeccably in every encounter. She has less to reproach herself over than any of us."

"Do you understand how she thinks? She had a commission to assassinate the wearer of the red rose at the dinner party. She had to choose between her loyalty to you and her guild oath. That can't be sitting easy on her mind. She feels she has failed us on several occasions: when the morghaest injured my eye, when your brother was killed, and just now when she failed to prevent our capture by Terrell. And you heard her confession earlier today, of not knowing where she belonged. How would she side if she had to choose between you and the Kir Leth? I couldn't tell you."

Ox said no more and seemed preoccupied as we continued our march.

Rhea disappeared into gathering clouds as it rose. The night grew darker, and fat drops of rain started falling on us as we walked. We closed our cloaks around us and tried to press on, but the rain increased in intensity until it was driving against us in sheets. Rivulets, then rivers, then torrents sluiced across the path. We were driven to hang on to each other or be lost in the storm. Ox bellowed, "We must find shelter! If we don't get washed away, a rock slide will do the job instead!"

Gilwyr shouted back, "We have to get down from the mountain. There's no shelter here, and there still may be pursuit."

"No one would pursue us in this storm!"

Bridocke spoke up. "There is a cave, not far from here. It's small but it will keep us safe."

"Lead on," said Ox.

Bridocke moved to the front of the line. I held on to her cloak, Gilwyr held mine, and Ox brought up the rear. I could hear Gilwyr say in a low voice to Ox, "Do you trust her?" and his reply "I have little choice at the moment." Bridocke gave no sign of having heard.

I had no idea how Bridocke was going to find anything in this howling darkness, but after a miserable eternity punctuated twice by the sound of boulders hurtling past us, once behind us and once just ahead, we came to a rock face.

"The cave mouth is just below us," said Bridocke, pointing down a ravine. "There used to be a rope here, but it must have rotted away." I instantly felt a flash of suspicion. Paranoia again? How could I ever trust my feelings now?

"Are you sure this is the right place?" asked Gilwyr. "You said you hadn't been this way in years."

"I am sure. I know this mountain. One does not take its storms lightly. This has been my refuge more than once."

"If we go down, we may not be able to get back up without a rope," said Ox.

"If we continue and a rock slide sweeps us from the mountain, we're not getting back up even with a rope," countered Bridocke. A clattering of rocks from somewhere in the darkness lent urgency to her words.

"It seems we have little choice," said Gilwyr. "I will go first to find a safe path."

"You do not need to prove your mettle yet again, Assassin. I know the path already. Stay close and we'll all reach the cave together." Bridocke sidled over the edge, then reached back to offer Gilwyr her hand. Gilwyr hesitated a moment, then clasped Bridocke's forearm, and Bridocke clasped hers in return. Gilwyr reached back to link hands with me, and I grasped Ox's arm in turn. I realized that this forearm grip was stronger than merely holding hands, though perforce we had to face in alternating directions. Since we were sidling downwards, it didn't matter, and Ox made an admirable anchor for our chain.

I felt a remarkable connection form with my companions through the touch of those cold hands, emanating from the black *aelo tai* inside me. I could feel a rivalry growing between Gilwyr and Bridocke, Bridocke's fear of me and my eye and odd powers, Bridocke's desperate hope that she had chosen wisely in throwing in with Ox and fear that she hadn't, Ox's worm of doubt about both of them and deep distrust of the enigma that I brought to the succession question. Even though human technology had long ago developed mechanisms for controlling machinery by thought, the transmission of thoughts and emotions from person to person had remained elusive. Despite my belief that I was seeing technology and not magic at work on this planet, it was becoming difficult to tell the difference.

We crab-walked down to a ledge, about six meters down from the trail. There indeed was a deeper blackness in the night, opening into the side of the mountain. We crowded inside, glad to be out of the torrents that fell from the sky. Gilwyr and Bridocke immediately fell into a competition to be the first to produce a light. As I shivered, I wondered if I was enough of a warlock to cast a fire-lighting spell.

Gilwyr produced the first light, emerging as the dominant woodsman in our small tribe. Bridocke produced dry wood from the rear of the cave, stocked long ago for travelers such as we. She managed to reinforce the feeling that this was her cave and us her guests, and in doing so claimed the role of householder, offsetting Gilwyr's provider/protector role.

I realized I was thinking again in anthropologist's terms, which only served to remind me of how little I had done professionally since arriving on this planet. I had plunged so much into the business of survival here that I had nearly forgotten my life before my arrival. The worlds were so different that immersion in one made the other one seem like a fantasy.

We had a fire going but were still soaking. Gilwyr stripped down to her trousers and spread her clothes on rocks near the fire, then began going through her pack to see what had gotten wet. I saw the wisdom in this and followed suit, as did Ox. Bridocke hesitated, but when she saw the unconcern evidenced by the three of us, chose conformity over discomfort. Another point to Gilwyr in their little game, it seemed. Other than Gilwyr's complete lack of body modesty, which I now attributed to her upbringing among the clothing-averse Kir Leth, I had seen little nudity in either Misthaven or Dalactus. I wondered whether practices varied and whether it rose to the level of an actual taboo, or was more on the order of a custom. In either case, group conformity won out in our little cave household.

Ox broke out some bread and cheese from the packs, saying that we should eat first the supplies that would spoil the fastest. We sat around the fire, finally getting warm again. Bridocke drew up her legs to at least partially obscure her breasts, while Gilwyr lounged at ease, smirking at her discomfort. Ox took no notice, but I was strangely torn between a studied unconcern to defuse the situation, and in a strong desire to take an interest to try to provoke further tensions between the two. After struggling with this internal battle for some time, it came into my mind that the peacemaker was my natural personality and that the provocateur lived in the vicinity of the black *aelo tai* that beat like a second, dark heart within me. All of the divisiveness and doubt in our little party was flowing from that *aelo tai*, through me. Whether this expedition held together and succeeded or fell into squabbling and disbanded was up to me. I had to counteract the effects of the *aelo tai* in our midst.

"This cave looks like it might once have been a Kir Leth dwelling." This remark from Gilwyr brought me back to a conversation earlier in the day that had been mostly idle chatter. I recalled Bridocke's earlier dismissal of Kir Leth as legends and looked towards her for her reaction. The comment had caught her attention, but she hadn't reacted yet.

"It could have been," acknowledged Ox. "There's been some rockfall, but there are signs of the arches they liked to build. Bridocke, are there any more chambers behind this one, or blocked passages?"

"No, just what you see here."

"It could have been just an outpost then, or a wayfarer's shelter as we're now using it."

"But, you're talking as if the Kir Leth are real!" Bridocke looked like she was trying to decide whether Ox and Gilwyr were pulling her leg or whether they had taken leave of their senses.

"They are real," Ox said gently. "I've spent time among them, and Gilwyr was raised by them. In fact, we met three Kir Leth just before arriving in Dalactus and traveled through their underground city. They keep to themselves and rarely contact humans. But they're very real, and our destination is their realm of Cloudhaven in the west."

"What?" Bridocke jumped to her feet at that, realized that she was still uncovered and after a flustered moment grabbed her damp cloak to hold around herself like a shield against insanity. "If they're real, then the stories … how they trick people, make them lose their way … or make them fall asleep while decades pass in a single night … or tempt them with knowledge that makes them fall mute, or age horribly. Are those all true too?"

"No, those are just stories told to scare children. They are gentle people …"

"Except for the Cray Leth, who are the finest assassins and warriors in the world," put in Gilwyr.

"My liege, must you go there? I know I said that I would follow you, but I thought you were going to fight for your throne and the rights of the Anglich. I'm not sure I can follow where you are going."

"I would not have anyone follow me who didn't go willingly. But sleep on it now, and we can tell you more as we travel, and I hope to put your mind at ease. If my path does lead back to the throne, I know it leads first to Cloudhaven."

CHAPTER 33

Overland

I WOKE DURING the night to the sense of being watched. The fire had burned low, and only embers remained. The wind had abated; the night was quiet. Ox snored intermittently on the opposite side of the fire. I saw no eyes in the darkness, but even if they were eyes that reflected light as most Terran species did, there were no light sources to reflect.

I should not have been surprised that Gilwyr had come alert. Either she had the same feeling or had sensed my tension. "What is it?" she breathed in my ear.

"I feel like we're being watched," I breathed back. Long moments went by as we both strained our senses for movement, sound, reflections, or disturbances in the air. I reached out with blacksight for any morghaests or their ilk and found nothing. I started to reach out with second sight and felt a sudden intensification of interest. I stopped and waited. After more long moments, the feeling faded and was gone. I released the breath I hadn't realized I was holding.

"What was it?" whispered Gilwyr.

"Something was looking for us. Something that knows when I use second sight. I stopped myself before I used it, and it went away after awhile."

"Any idea what it was?"

"None."

"Go back to sleep then. Wake me if it returns."

With that, her breathing deepened, and she was apparently asleep again. Either she was able to convince herself there was no further threat, or she was supremely confident of her ability to awaken at the slightest disturbance. Probably both. I took a great deal longer to drift off.

When I awoke, light was filtering in the cave entrance. Outside was a spectacular view of a rugged, mountainous country with mists lying heavy in the valleys, wisps beginning to curl languidly upwards towards the sun. In the foreground was the equally breathtaking view of Gilwyr practicing her katas on the ledge outside. Just inside, Bridocke stood frozen, her expression equal parts admiration and scandal. Ox still snored peacefully under his cloak.

The sense of a watcher broke upon me again, this time more forcefully. Someone was searching for us, or for me. I could see the eye in second sight, shining redly in my vision. I forced it back, and it withdrew enough for me to see a face: Terrell. As he had accidentally contacted me earlier during our travels, before either of us knew much about the *aelo tai*, he was now deliberately searching for me. But how? I fell to my knees, covering my eyes, trying to prevent him from seeing my surroundings. I withdrew second sight, through which I had been watching Gilwyr's katas without even being aware of it. I made my world small and dark and waited.

"Stenn! What's wrong?" That was Bridocke's voice, nearest. I heard Gilwyr's steps sprinting closer, and the grunt of Ox arising from his sleep. I hoped the red *aelo tai* wouldn't relay sounds. I had no evidence that it would but didn't want to find out otherwise now. I huddled away from them, trying to present a dead dark void to Terrell's searching.

I felt hands on my back, then someone tried to gently pry my hands away from my eyes, perhaps thinking I had injured them somehow. "Stop!" I whispered urgently. "Terrell is searching for us. Be quiet until he gives up." They desisted from trying to help me and waited, voicing little murmurs of puzzlement.

After many minutes, Terrell's presence departed. I sighed and looked up. "He's gone. Where's my backpack? Where's the red *aelo tai*? How is he doing this without the *aelo tai*?"

Gilwyr got my pack and pulled out the leather bag that held the *aelo tai*. I gingerly withdrew it and held it up to the light. "This is a fake!" I cried in dismay. "This is only a piece of red glass. There's no internal structure to this at all. It's just an inert bauble."

"Terrell must not have wanted to risk displaying the real one," speculated Ox. "He is shrewd, and paranoid, with good reason, given all the enemies he has made. If he thought it was powerful, he would have both wanted to flaunt that he had it and to protect it from falling into the wrong hands. A duplicate would be just the sort of thing he'd come up with." I remembered with a sick feeling that I hadn't been able to see this fake in second sight when I snatched it. I should have realized the deception then.

"What powers does that give him?" asked Gilwyr.

"I have no idea. I don't think it can give him second sight unless it's connected to his eye, and I don't know whether you need to have your eye gouged out by a morghaest first to properly cast the spell. For that matter, I think the implants I already had in my eye played a role as well, and I'm the only one on this world with those. The main danger is that by gazing into the gem he can apparently see what we see, which might allow him to locate us and send pursuit."

"Can you attack him through the *aelo tai* when he makes contact?" Gilwyr pressed.

"If I have time to prepare and am in a safe place when he returns, I might try."

"Why wait for him to take the initiative? Take the fight to him."

"He can just put the *aelo tai* down and walk away," I pointed out, "while I can't. I can't contact him unless he's holding it. But speaking of taking the fight to him, shouldn't we be thinking of sneaking back into the city and attempting to take back the *aelo tai*? We promised to take it to Cloudhaven, and now we don't have it. We also don't know how much we risk by letting him keep it."

"I don't think that is wise," said Ox. "There are too few of us to take it by force, and it's too risky to attempt to take it by stealth. If he captured you and forced you to aid him, we would be giving him an even greater weapon."

"I would tear his castle down if he did that."

"Even if he held a hostage against your good behavior?"

I didn't have an answer to that one.

"You still carry two *aelo tai*. I think our purpose continues to be true. We should carry those to Cloudhaven and ask if the Kir Leth can help us."

I nodded acquiescence, and we started to pull our belongings together in preparation for resuming our journey. Ox had carried the supplies we had eaten last night and offered to carry a share to replace them. I handed him a small pouch of dried fruit. Gilwyr shouldered her pack with a stubborn look. Ox hefted his load experimentally, and said, "I've still got room for more. Bridocke, let me carry one of those water bottles."

"I'm merely a guard, my Liege," she said formally. "It's not my place to give you more weight to carry. If my Liege wishes, I will carry his pack as well."

"Is something bothering you, Bridocke?"

"It's not my place to say, my Liege."

"Confound it! You asked to join this party, and you'll join it as an equal. I don't want to hear My Liege all the way to Cloudhaven!" Ox could bellow like his namesake when he wanted to, and we were all startled at his outburst. Bridocke, however, plowed ahead determinedly.

"An' I were not the one who decided that were the destination, equal or no." She had switched to Anglich as her color rose. "I were not the one to decide whether we sat around half-clothed like Dalactyn nobles with no morals in their bathhouses. I was certainly not the one to decide to tell th' poor Anglich girl that our warlock here had a simple glass eye an' don't worry about it. I thought you were different from the other Dalactyns, but you still think you have the right to only tell the commoners what you think they need to know."

That must have stung Ox, for his response was uncharacteristically peevish. "I didn't want to spook you before I knew how you'd handle it, that's all."

"So you get to decide what I can handle and what I can't? That's 'equals' to you?"

"Well, then, go back to Dalactus!" Ox was out of patience.

"Oh no, I'm going to Cloudhaven with you. Either you order me to go back and admit that you think I'm not as equal as you say, or you acknowledge that I can accompany you as an equal and you won't be withholding information that I need to know."

"Do as you please, then!" Ox shouldered his pack and marched out of the cave, beginning the steep ascent to the trail without looking back. Gilwyr followed but stopped to clasp Bridocke on the shoulder, seemingly in approval. My final lashing cord snapped as I was tying it, and Bridocke waited as I re-laced it. When we ascended to the main trail, we found that the other two had gone ahead. Bridocke and I struck out after them, hoping they would wait for us somewhere. I worried about missing a turning and becoming hopelessly separated from Ox and Gilwyr, but though the trail wound across the mountainside, there were no branches or intersections with other paths.

After a time, I became aware that we were gradually descending. I thought we had crossed the summit of the mountain in the night during the storm, but the vista that opened up showed me how wrong I had been. We rounded a corner from the westward-facing slope that we had crossing, turning onto a north-facing slope. The true mountain revealed itself to us, ruling over the lesser hills of this broken land. We had climbed one of her vassals, kneeling at her feet. She reached up to touch the dome of the sky, wearing a crown of jagged white from which her pennants streamed. Lacy snow-fed waterfalls adorned her teal skirts. Farther down these streams joined forces into a glittering torrent that raced down the valley. I could see a plume of mist rising near the head of the valley that I thought might mark the presence of a larger waterfall. I glimpsed the figures of Gilwyr and Ox for a moment, perhaps a kilometer ahead of us until the trail took them into some wooded land and I lost them again.

As we surveyed the vista, Bridocke brought up the morning's conflict. "Was I dreaming, or drunk? Did I really talk like that to the Prince? I don't know what came over me to say those things. It's not my place to question him." She tugged at her braid as I had seen her do when she was uneasy.

Guilt nagged me as I recognized the working of the black *aelo tai*. That was how it worked, wasn't it? It was very subtle; it could twist even good motives into conflict. I said only, "I'm glad you stood up for yourself." Was I encouraging conflict by telling her this?

"Do you think he'll forgive me?"

"I don't think it's his place to forgive you. You were entirely right. I think that once he cools down, he'll apologize to you." As I thought about it, Ox hadn't reacted in character either. I had come to expect him to consider matters thoughtfully and to be very principled in his responses. He had been influenced as well.

"Do you think so?"

"He will. He sees himself as the one who will right the wrongs his family has done. You accused him of being the thing he hates. He'll apologize to prove to you that he's not like the rest of them."

Bridocke frowned. "That sounds like the appearance of an apology more than the deed itself."

Had the black *aelo tai* twisted my words to sow more doubt or was that no more than inept phrasing on my part? I decided I shouldn't say more. "You can decide for yourself when you hear him."

"What about you, sir Warlock? Can I trust you?"

No, you should not, I wanted to shout. I heard myself saying, "Warlocks have professional secrets, of course. But I'll always advise you as honestly as I can." It was even true, damn it all, if "as honestly as I can" were understood to include "while under the influence of an alien mind-control device."

"Where is your home, sir Warlock?"

"Far, far away."

"The outer islands?"

"Farther."

"The far continent? No one lives there."

"Farther than that, even."

"Oh, so you come from Rhea, then? I suppose if the Kir Leth are real, and morghaests are real, and warlocks are real, so must be the city on Rhea and the great sky bridge that they used to travel here and back."

"That's probably as close to the truth as I can get."

Bridocke rolled her eyes. "I'm not sure if an outlandish half-truth is better than a believable untruth. Let's hurry. I think they'll wait for us above the Waterbreak."

They were indeed waiting for us in a little meadow that bordered the rushing snowmelt river. A deep thunder came from up ahead, screened from us by the forest that closed in downstream. It was still possible to converse here, but any closer to the falls and we would be shouting at each other.

Ox got right to the matter of the morning's conflict. "You were entirely right to take me to task for withholding information, Bridocke. It's the way Dalactyns have treated the Anglich for centuries, and the time to stop it is now ..." He spoke eloquently, but I could see in Bridocke's narrowed eyes that she was weighing whether it was sincerely meant. I had raised that doubt, and there was no way to erase it again. People were so easily manipulated. If you argued against their beliefs, they would counter with their own arguments. But if you planted a doubt, the smallest insinuation, you could turn them against their own best interests. This was a power I could use to get people to follow me, turn them against my enemies, give to me that which I could not take. I could ...

A wave of nausea passed through me. For a moment the mountains orbited around me, and then a yawning pit opened in my stomach. What was I thinking? Where had that come from? Could the black *aelo tai* plant thoughts like that in my head, or was it something I had always been capable of? So far it had just magnified conflict or planted missteps, but now I was taking pleasure in the discord. I had a foreboding of the direction I was taking, and it terrified me.

I noticed that Gilwyr had wandered away, seemingly uninterested. Ox was wrapping up his apology. "I want to make a break with the past. If I can regain the throne ..."

"Then there would still be a king on the throne, above the Anglich. That doesn't sound equal to me."

Ox was taken aback. It had been a handsome apology, and that hadn't been the result he expected.

"If I don't have the throne, I don't have the power to make changes."

"Mayhap it's not such a change, then. Words are fine for saying what you might do. I'm more interested in watching what you *actually* do."

Ox was looking cross again. "You were talking yesterday about service to me. Today you sound like you are challenging me. Why did you come along if you felt that way?"

Bridocke looked troubled. "I did. Something has come over me today. I feel there's truth in my words, though, and I don't regret saying them."

Ox swallowed his annoyance and nodded. "I need to hear your words. I will try not to be so cross when you say them. Let us continue; the Waterbreak is just ahead."

We hefted our packs again and moved on. I mused about this exchange. Did some people have the resiliency to resist the pull of the black *aelo tai*? Was it easier in the open sunlight than in a dark cave? I resolved to be more alert to its effects.

As we neared the trees, something vast and yellow rose above the foliage, blocking out the sun. I yelped and backpedaled, catching my heel on a rock and sitting down abruptly. I had visions of aircraft searching for us before I remembered that those didn't exist on this world. I became aware of the others laughing at my reaction. "I guess they don't have *oomlies* on Rhea, sir Warlock?" said Bridocke.

"No, whatever that is. Is it alive?" Little fins were turning the creature towards me. A large head with floppy ears, sad eyes, and disproportionally wide nostrils came into view. The mouth was full of vegetation that the creature was slowly chewing with large, flat teeth. It was about three meters wide and slightly longer, with six vestigial limbs that ended in ropy fingers that were much longer than the limbs themselves.

"Yes, they're tree grazers," said Ox. "They float among the trees and eat the top leaves from them. Instead of using their colors as camouflage, they are brightly colored to warn predators away from them."

"They don't look that dangerous. Are they full of gas?"

"Yes. In fact, if you were so unwise as to puncture one of them, it would explode in a ball of flame. They can ignite small jets of fire to warn off their enemies."

"They're full of hydrogen? That's insane."

"It must have amused Polnedra to design them so," said Gilwyr.

"Oh, right. I didn't mean to imply that your goddess was insane. Why is it holding that stone under its belly?"

"If they need to go up quickly to get away from something, they simply drop the stone. They can also sink by letting off gas, though it takes them some hours to make enough to rise again if they do."

I shook my head. I had seen the Terran hippopotamus before, since they had been re-established on my world among many others from the genetic banks exported from Old Earth. These filled the same ecological niche, only aerially. They rather resembled them in shape and facial features as well. The *oomlie* crawled off across the treetops using its long fingers as mooring lines. It joined a larger family group that were grazing farther down the valley.

"What do they do in a storm?" I asked.

"They'll deflate themselves completely and wrap themselves around tree trunks. It takes them about a day to re-inflate themselves enough to float again."

We continued downriver, finally coming to the falls about an hour later. I should have known that nothing on this world would be less than fantastical. The falls were no exception. The Waterbreak got its name from the sharp rock that divided the stream like the prow of a boat. The stream was cloven into two parts, each of which went over a waterfall that tumbled over cliff faces into twin pools hundreds of meters below. These two streams then went their separate ways, one southerly into the plains, and the other northwesterly through a country of low hills, following a valley that wended among them. I wasn't a student of geology or geography, but this seemed contrived to me. I was aware that most rivers combined tributaries into larger rivers. I had never heard of one that split into two. It seemed to me that it wouldn't be a stable configuration; one branch would erode faster than the other and eventually all of the water would go down only one fork.

This was the clearest sign yet that the Kir Leth had extensively engineered their planet, though in ways that humans wouldn't readily recognize. Whether this was for water distribution or solely for its artistic merit, I couldn't say, but it seemed highly unlikely to be natural. For that matter, I had thought that the candle trees had to be biologically engineered, and I suspected the hydrogen hippos were as well. Were they formerly raised by the Kir Leth as living chemical factories, or fuel supplies, or some other inscrutable reasons? I began to have a strong feeling that this planet had more mysteries than I had bargained for.

CHAPTER 34

Down the Tamesas

"WHICH WAY DO we go?" I asked.

"I have not been this way before," said Ox. "Always in the past, I left Dalactus by the main gate, traveling to the south and then west to skirt the mountains. The southward-flowing branch is the Ises, and I have crossed it at a ford far downstream from here. There were formerly some settlements along the Ises. They are mostly abandoned, but the path along it may be easier. The northwest branch I have only heard about, but never seen before now. It is the Tamesas, and it has a reputation for crossing fell and treacherous lands. From the maps that I recall, the Tamesas is our most direct path to Cloudhaven. The Ises is not such a wild and dangerous path, but following the southerly way to a place where we can ford it would add a week or more to our journey."

Bridocke looked troubled. "My kin have long held that the route along the Tamesas was haunted. They told tales of abandoned castles where lights still moved at night. They said people who pass that way were forever changed, and many were never seen again. I do not know how much credence to give such tales, but the people on the southern route give more sympathy to the Anglich than the Dalactyns. I think there is less risk in the southern route."

Gilwyr sniffed, "We should not be deterred by campfire tales. I have not followed the Tamesas before, but I think it should serve us. There is less chance of meeting patrols on that road than on the southern road, where people still live, and Dalactyns still rule."

"If the northwest route has abandoned castles, then that would be my vote," I said. "I would never pass up a chance to survey a new site, however briefly. But how are we going to cross over the Ises to follow the Tamesas? I don't see any ferries here waiting to get people to the other side."

"Another reason to go south," said Bridocke, nettled at being outvoted. "By the time we reach a fordable place in the river, we'll be nearly to the southern road, and it will be faster to continue on that than to hike all the way back to the Tamesas."

"I'll arrange the ferry," said Gilwyr, and disappeared back into the forest.

Bridocke turned to Ox. "My liege, I do not know if this is wise ..."

"Bridocke, if you are an equal in this party, you can call me Ox like everyone else."

"Yes, m... Ox."

"I could not overturn a majority decision and stay true to my principles, as you yourself pointed out earlier. You would not want to undermine your position by appealing that decision, would you?"

"No ..."

"Then I think we should regard that as settled."

Bridocke turned away, bottling up her response. I privately thought that Ox was being rather autocratic about being democratic.

Silence stretched awkwardly for minutes, a silence smothered by the roar of the falls. After nearly an hour, Gilwyr emerged from the forest with a rope over her shoulder, as if she were towing something. Like improbable blimps, three *oomlies* appeared one after another behind her. The rope she was holding was the finger or mooring line of the lead *oomlie*. The second and third *oomlies* were joined by their mooring lines to the first and were noticeably smaller than that one. "Here are our ferries!" she called cheerfully as she came closer. The lead *oomlie* started displaying shades of red on one side. "Come downstream. They are nervous about the falls."

Understandably, I thought. The air was turbulent near the rushing water. Gilwyr led her strange flotilla downstream. We picked up our packs to follow. I reached for Gilwyr's pack, but Bridocke coolly reached in front of me, swung it over a free shoulder, and set off without a backward glance at either of us. Ox and I exchanged raised eyebrows and followed.

We caught up with Gilwyr as she was arranging the *oomlies* on the edge of the cliff. She was encouraging them to anchor themselves to the ground as we walked up. "Ox, you take the mother *oomlie* in the front. She should be strong enough to lift you. Bridocke, take the smallest one. Stenn and I will share the larger child. We should move promptly before they become restless and try to wander off."

"How do we hang on?" I asked.

Gilwyr demonstrated, winding one ankle in one of the *oomlie's* ropy fingers, and tucking it under her armpit. It looked secure enough, and the *oomlie* obliged by wrapping other fingers around her. Ox moved to the lead *oomlie*, looking uneasily at the ground on the far side of the rushing river, at least one hundred meters lower and across fifty meters of foaming whitewater. He secured himself in the nest of trailing fingers.

Bridocke had the face of one not willing to admit that she was terrified. She refused to look over the edge as she took her place. I copied Gilwyr's technique of hooking the creature's ropes around my ankle and under my arm. It felt secure enough, as long as I was only six inches above the ground. If they could do it, I could do it. My bravado overrode my fear of heights for a moment. Long enough to get to the ground, I hoped.

"Now what?" bellowed Ox. "How do you get them to move?"

"I'll figure something out," said Gilwyr. She dismounted and walked forward until she was just behind the mother *oomlie*. She gave it a shove, but with less than spectacular results. The skin of the creature just indented like the balloon that it was, then sprang back. The *oomlie* trumpeted a mournful note and hung on tighter with its mooring lines. It didn't seem any more thrilled about taking the leap than we did.

Gilwyr laid her hand on the hilt of her sword, then seemed to think better of it. I agreed that poking a creature filled with hydrogen didn't seem wise. Instead, she picked up a dead branch laying nearby and swatted the *oomlie* in the rear.

With a deafening honk, the mother *oomlie* leaped from the cliff. Her two children followed along, still keeping tethered to the mother. Gilwyr sprinted back to our steed and caught a trailing mooring line as it passed by. She swung up to dangle next to me as we cleared the edge of the chasm. This all seemed entirely too improvised to me. I cupped my mouth with my hands and shouted against the wind to her, "You've done this before, right?"

Her eyes were alight. "Never! I hope it works!"

I closed my eyes and prayed that I hadn't heard her correctly.

I opened them again as the bottom dropped out of my stomach. The *oomlies* were unable to stay aloft. We were too heavy for them. We were plummeting towards the sharp rocks that were slicing the river into long plumes far below us.

Then mother *oomlie* trumpeted. Simultaneously, all three creatures dropped their ballast rocks and bobbed upwards again. They caught an updraft and soared skywards, honking in alarm. We didn't weigh them down equally; Bridocke's mount shot upwards faster than the other two, breaking their grip on each other. Our *oomlie* spun end-for-end through the sky, while I saw Bridocke's flip over entirely. Mother *oomlie* was left far below, but at least seemed stable. I could hear her honking instructions to her two children, and also flashing red and yellow colors across her skin as a beacon or warning.

With world-shaking flatulence, our *oomlie* vented hydrogen. Perhaps it had built up a static charge on its skin, for the hydrogen ignited, ascending in a terrible flower of yellow flame. I waited for a fiery end that never came. The flame burned out as the creature reached neutral buoyancy, and floated serenely in the sky. The flatulence continued, however, and I realized it was inhaling gulps of air and releasing them as a primitive form of propulsion. We sailed lower and took up formation with Bridocke's mount. I was relieved to see that she was still hanging on, though looking like she was scrambling back over the edge of panic. Mother *oomlie* had made it safely to the meadow on the far side of the river and was signaling its children to join it. We sailed in to an anticlimactic landing.

I flopped in the grass, relieved to be on solid ground again. Gilwyr stood jauntily, stroking the flank of the *oomlie*. Bridocke staggered from her beast and rounded on Gilwyr. "You could have warned us about that drop!" she grated.

"I didn't know," Gilwyr replied. "I've never done it before!"

Bridocke gaped. "Never done it before?"

"The older Cray Leth told stories about riding *oomlies*, and I have always wanted to try."

"You risked our lives on *that*? And you didn't even know if it could be done? We could have all been killed!" Bridocke swung a surprise punch that connected with Gilwyr's jaw. Gilwyr sat down abruptly. I started forward, hoping to intervene before Gilwyr killed Bridocke, but I realized that Gilwyr was laughing. She stood again, and Bridocke charged her. This time, she caught Bridocke's swing and stepped inside. They clinched and tried to wrestle each other to the ground. Gilwyr was still laughing. "Just think!" she said into Bridocke's ear. "Just think of the tale you'll be able to tell your children now!"

I could see that idea stealing over Bridocke's face. She slowed her attempts to take Gilwyr down as her shoulders started shaking. Soon the two women were supporting each other as they howled with laughter. On the far side, I could see Ox looking on paternally. When the laughter finally subsided, it was he who said, "We should get moving while we're in good spirits. There's a long road ahead of us, and that's the last ride we're likely to get."

That evening we made camp by the Tamesas in a broad meadow. The competition between Gilwyr and Bridocke in hunting and woodcraft was for the most part good-natured. Bridocke had a fire going strongly, giving us a chance to thoroughly dry that which had gotten soaked in the mountain storm. Gilwyr brought in a brace of slowhares, which I learned were called *kemina*. Soon the scent of stew filled the air.

I noticed some of the badger-like *ongar* milling around in one area of the field. A number of them had prominent lumps on their backs. I pointed these out to the others, who informed me that those were pregnant *ongar*, who would soon give birth. I wondered about the evolutionary advantages of carrying developing young on the back rather than in the belly. Would it be more or less protected that way? Then I noticed the activities that the *ongar* were engaged in. They were digging in the soil in a very badger-like way, and I assumed at first that they were looking for grubs or worms or whatever they ate. On a closer look, they were tending some young plants. They were weeding the areas around them, loosening the soil, and adding in moistened leaves to enrich it. I shook my head in wonder. Agriculture was one of the defining traits of civilization, and here were some badgers practicing it.

I wandered back to the fire and turned my jacket inside out to ensure that it dried completely. There was something hard in the pocket. This was the jacket I had appropriated from a dead guard in the palace, killed by the morghaest I had conjured. It seemed like a dream now, or a simspace drama in which I had participated. What if it had been only that? If you can no longer distinguish dreams and reality, either the dreams are real, or the dreamer is lost in madness. I supposed that I wouldn't have a coat now if I were mad.

The object in the pocket was the book I had with me in the dungeon. I must have stuffed it in the pocket when I appropriated the coat and forgotten about it until now. I turned it over to examine the cover, which was soft leather. The cover bore the script *The War of the Grimmerroth*. The first page was stained by the leather and time. It bore a repeat of the title, with the subscript *A Recounting of the Tactics* in smaller letters. Leafing through the pages, I saw narrative in Old Galactic interspersed with diagrams of the engagements that had occurred.

Ox looked up from sorting his pack. "What's that you have there, Stenn?"

"It's an old book. I found it with me in the dungeon. I probably picked it up in the hidden library, and they missed it during the scuffle. I must have shoved it in my pocket."

Ox looked over my shoulder as I turned the pages. I wasn't reading yet; the old language and the old handwriting would make for slow going. I was trying to get a sense of the contents and also looking to see if there were any mention of our present-day puzzle, the *aelo tai*. Most of the volume seemed to be a dry chronicle of the war, listing troop movements, strategic points held, camp logistics, and supply lines.

I turned a page, and the handwriting changed. It was in my native language: *La meg være i fred*. Leave me in peace. Had these pages been written by Jonan Gremm? I didn't know of anyone else on this planet who would have written in Trondnorsk. Was this a letter? Pages from his journal? I started to read more …

"What is this language?" demanded Ox. "It looks like nothing I have seen."

"It's the language of my home. It could have been written by my ancestor." I could have said more but was not sure where it would lead.

"I am not certain it would be wise for you to read this," he said. "There might be words that draw your thoughts in unhealthy ways, or give you knowledge it would be better not to have."

"Knowledge is not good or evil, it simply is. It's how one uses it that is the test."

"Is this so? You know you can summon a morghaest. Is that knowledge ever far from your thoughts now? Is it not always there, a way out of difficulty if all else fails?"

He had me there. I couldn't unknow that knowledge, and if driven to extremity, I would be tempted to use it. "On the other hand, if I don't learn from him, I may fall into the same pitfalls as he did. With foreknowledge, I might be able to avoid walking the same path to conflict that he did."

"We should read it together then so that another knows what you know. I will keep it in my custody, and you can study it with me in the evenings when we make camp."

"Why should you keep it? I found it, I defended it from the rats, I smuggled it out of the castle, and I'm the only one who can read it."

"It's a de Oxendon heirloom. It is rightly my property, though you have my thanks for preserving it. And the fact that only you can read it is good reason for someone other than you to carry it. I would learn enough of this uncouth language to read some of it for myself."

I began to get angry, especially with his characterization of my homeworld language. Gilwyr interjected at this point, "You need a third person, as did the merchant and the farmer in that old tale. Bridocke can carry the book for you, and ensure that both of you are present when it's opened. That should satisfy you. Now eat your stew; we sleep early tonight and arise early tomorrow so we can put as much road behind our feet as we may."

Later, as Gilwyr banked the fire and settled down against my back in the darkness, I asked quietly. "What is the tale of the merchant and the farmer? I do not know that one."

"It is a long one, and for another night. Sleep now."

Despite my exhaustion, sleep didn't come immediately. I lay listening to Gilwyr's breathing as it deepened, and the sounds from across the fire where Ox and Bridocke lay, and the sounds beyond the fire in the night. My awareness sank into the earth, to feel the dance of the motes, like flights of stars reflected in a deep black pool. They almost made sense, forming letters on a page that might have been old Trondnorsk if I could make them line up a little better. I had just time to recognize the dream logic stealing over me before it covered me in dark folds of sleep. I remembered no more until morning.

CHAPTER 35

Morghaest Bridge

WHILE THE RIVER flowed downhill, as rivers do on any sensible planet, the road took a more varying route. Where the river was broad and placid, it ran along the bank through open country. Where the river ran narrow through chasms, the road detoured up through the hills to find passable terrain. And it was a true road. Old, unpaved, but cut and leveled for cart traffic or troop movements. I wondered if they had been built for the same reason as the old Roman roads—so that armies could travel swiftly and so that their all-important supply trains could reach them. I enquired whether Dalactyns had built the roads, and Ox said only that this road had been abandoned before the beginning of Dalactyn rule.

As we walked, I explored the senses that the *aelo tai* gave me. The red one showed me metal objects, nothing else. I watched with second sight as Gilwyr ran ahead to scout the path. This sense appeared to have no definite range limit, but her swords grew smaller and smaller as she carried them away from me, until I lost them if I took my attention away. By diligent searching, I could find them again. It reminded me how my eye could not pick up the dwindling light of Trondhjem as the ship receded from it until I asked the ship to point it out. Once done, I could see it again easily until I looked away and it was lost again in the other points of light.

What was Gilwyr's sword lost against as it receded? If I blanked out normal vision, I began to see points of faint red beneath me. They could have easily been mistaken for the faint visual noise that the human eye generates in total darkness. The points were spread unevenly, and there were none above me, only below. Perhaps these were the metallic minerals in the planet's crust. Within a hill that we passed, I saw a thing like a diffuse nebula, which must have been a deposit of iron ore. At the bottom of a placid lake that we passed lay a hard knot of red fire, which puzzled me until I realized I was looking at an ancient iron meteorite.

Blacksight was different. I could see points of blackness sprinkled unevenly through the land. They occurred in soil, in stone, and in very small quantities in some growing plants. I hypothesized that the plants took them in with the minerals they drew from the soil. Running water and moving air sometimes carried them as well, and I associated them with the sediment in the streams and the dust carried by the air. Blacksight didn't give me any particular ability to sense objects, the points being too diffuse to convey any shapes.

But with blacksight, I could exert my will on those scattered points. I focused on a rock near the path. It was thick with the bright-dark points. I thought of the points moving all together to one side. They did and carried the rock with them. It jerked and toppled from its resting point, bouncing across the trail and startling Bridocke. I amused myself for the rest of the day upsetting rocks at random intervals. I enjoyed the way that Gilwyr and Bridocke jumped at every noise until they fell to fighting about whether we were somehow being followed.

❖

"How do we cross this?" Bridocke asked.

We had reached a tributary river that blocked our path with a gorge both deep and wide. At one time there had been a bridge crossing the chasm but only the abutments on either side remained. The gorge walls were too steep to climb down and the river too swollen to cross. The Tamesas was too turbulent and rocky in this section to consider rafting. Any conceivable detour would likely be days long and through very rough country. There weren't even any *oomlies* at hand; we hadn't seen one since crossing the Ises below the Waterbreak.

Darkness wasn't far, off so we made camp with the intention of starting the detour in the morning. Bridocke lost the fire-starting competition and nicked her thumb deeply in the process and was consequently in a bad mood. When Gilwyr brought in a catch of several creatures resembling footballs with snouts like pigs along with a sackful of purple roots, Bridocke insisted that the roots were poisonous. After the fight escalated beyond questionable woodcraft skills and started calling into question parentage and personal hygiene, I escaped to examine the remains of the bridge. I could hear them trying to drag Ox into the fight as arbitrator; he soon joined me in my inspection.

The blocks of the bridge had been cut and dressed skillfully. What remained still fit cunningly together in an interlocking pattern that must have been quite strong when it was whole. I had seen less well-made bridges that had stood for centuries. Earthquake?

Near the broken edge of the stone was a line of perfectly round holes bored vertically into the stone. The stone was fractured around several of the holes, and there were traces of blackening inside. I cautiously inched out to the edge on my hands and knees to peer over. There were crater-like hollows beneath each of the boreholes that confirmed my hypothesis. I wiggled my way back to safety.

"This bridge was deliberately sabotaged. Do you know if there was a battle waged here?"

"None of which I am aware. Did you use your warlock powers to see this?"

"Observation and deduction. It's what I teach."

Now that Ox had asked that question, it occurred to me that second sight could be a useful tool in my research. I looked around, seeing the bits and scraps of metal that you might expect people to lose near a traveled road. Near my feet, I could see a coin about a handspan beneath the soil. I dug the point of my sword into the ground and freed it from the earth. Ox and I inspected it.

"This is Anglich," said Ox. "None have been made since the founding of my house."

Nearby was the outline of a knife. Unearthed, it was severely eaten by rust, and little could be told about its construction. I started casting outwards and soon found a constellation of artifacts glowing in a cluster around the road about a hundred paces from the bridge. "This seems an unlikely place for a camp ..." I said.

"No, the place where we stopped is the natural place for that. It is more sheltered, has a stream for water, and access to firewood. This would be a tactically sound defense point for the road. I suspect that this was the site of a forgotten battle."

Looking beneath the surface, I could see numerous swords, helms, shields, and knives. We unearthed a few of these and laid them out on the ground. We found a number of human bones scattered in the trenches we dug. "These are Anglich as well," said Ox. "The King's Guard, I would guess from the inscription on this blade. These are four centuries old, at least."

"That might be consistent given the depth of the soil that has covered them," I said. "I don't think they were buried in graves. They are haphazard as if they lay where they fell. The skeletons are scattered as if they were picked over by scavengers before the soil covered them. This looks more like a massacre than a battle."

"I wonder who their opponent was?" said Ox. "Were they holding the bridge or attacking it?"

"If we excavate more of the sites around here, we may find some of the opposing group, and possibly identify them by their weapons."

"We must leave that for another time. I feel we should press on to Cloudhaven. There is much that hinges on what the Kir Leth can tell us and whether they will aid us."

I straightened with a sigh, knowing he was right, but still feeling the call to uncover the secrets of this ancient site. I scanned the area in second sight again. Perhaps fifty had fallen here, scattered around haphazardly as if it had been a running battle. Well, they had waited four centuries, they could wait a little longer.

I then switched to blacksight, not expecting it to be useful in detecting artifacts. Two manlike shapes glowed with the peculiar non-light of blacksight. I gasped and stepped back, thinking that something had crept up on us unawares. Then I saw that the shapes were buried in the earth at the same depth as the men. "Morghaests," I breathed. "They fought morghaests here. Killed two of them if I read the signs right."

"That puts it in a different light. This is likely a minor skirmish from the War of the Grimmerroth. I did not know of any this far to the west."

I looked around the peaceful scene where fifty had fallen. One day in the past it had been churned into blood-soaked mud. "It wasn't minor to those who were here that day." I had an unquiet feeling about this place and welcomed Ox's suggestion that we get back to camp.

After we had eaten our evening meal of the pig-faced beast (which tasted like mutton) and the purple root vegetables (which failed to kill us, to Bridocke's chagrin), I asked Ox, "Is it likely that the skirmish over this bridge is written in the chronicle that Bridocke is carrying?"

"Hmm, I wouldn't think so, or it would be better known. Let us look, though."

Searching through even that slim, though densely-written, volume took time. How had the human race made any progress before text was indexed and immediately searched and annotated by simspace agents? I had nearly given up when Ox turned a page to reveal a diagram of a familiar place. "Look, there's the bridge and the Tamesas. Here is the camp, and here the battleground. The text is brief: 'While the Grimmerroth's main force engaged the garrison of Colonel Wickelathe to the south, a band of morghaests that accounts say numbered between five and seven flanked them and headed for the bridge at Broken Gorge. With the strategic importance of Castle Tykenkote, Major Rede led all able-bodied soldiers held in reserve, some sixty-five in number, to deny them the bridge. They slew several of the creatures, but at the cost of nearly their entire force. The final six of them gave their lives in the center of the bridge to hold the morghaests there, while Private Bridocke, who had been injured, lit the fuse to detonate the charges that had been laid under the bridge. While the promise of Castle Tykenkote never came to fruition, it could have become a last resort had General ad Aulem not been successful.'"

A moment of stunned silence fell about us. We each had a facet of this to absorb. I exulted at the contemporaneously written account that documented this archeological site. This was as much as mana falling from the sky to a scholar. Gilwyr was working on the military puzzle: "But I want to know how they killed the first two morghaests. A force of sixty-five should not have been equal to the task."

Ox had his own train of thought: "I have never heard of this castle before. The writer assumes we know its strategic importance, but what was it?"

Bridocke was repeating to herself: "I have an ancestor who fought in the war. I have an ancestor who killed morghaests."

I broke in, "This castle might be important. How do we find it?" It might have clues to where my ancestor had been and how he had controlled this power. Within, I was at war between wanting this knowledge to excise my own darkness, and wanting to make sure that no one could use this knowledge against me.

None of us knew. A quick search of the maps in the book did not yield its location. "We can only hope that it lies on this road," said Ox, "or that the road will lead us to someone who knows."

❖

In the morning, I was restless. Even the deadly poetry of Gilwyr's katas didn't hold my attention for long. Bridocke was readying the fire while looking askance in Gilwyr's direction. She still harbored a combination of awe and disapproval around the morning ritual. Ox was studying the maps in the book, looking for clues to this mysterious castle. I still wanted to read Jonan Gremm's pages but could wait my turn. I knew no one else here could read them.

I wandered from camp, coming to stand at the edge of the broken bridge. I could imagine the bridge as it had stood before the battle, a graceful arch of fitted stone, built using principles that had been known since Roman times on Earth. Now, because of that battle, I had only the broken ends to frame the picture. I had claimed to my classes that it was only what endured that defined a civilization. What endured was what I studied, using that to reconstruct what was lost. I started to revise my lecture in my head; the next time I taught, I would phrase that a little differently.

I turned to look down the road to where the battle for the bridge had taken place. If I had my simspace tools, I could identify the locations of the bodies and reconstruct how they had fought and how they had fallen. I could load that into a simulation, outfitting the soldiers with period accuracy, and run it forwards and backward to test the fit of simulation to reality. I could almost see how the simulation would look, superimposed on the silent road that ran before me in the morning mist. My imagined simulation wouldn't play true, though. I didn't have accurate parameters on the morghaests. How strong were they? How intelligent? I couldn't simulate what I couldn't measure.

In my mind, the morghaests emerged from the earth. The hard ground split asunder, the man-like figures arose. I remembered how the ones I had encountered had sloughed and re-formed themselves as they had moved. These would re-assemble themselves from the ground, absorbing clods as they rose. Had they been two meters tall? Three? Closer to two, I decided, and I could imagine them erupting from the battlefield where they had lain dormant for centuries.

The Grimmerroth—Jonan—would have seen them in blacksight as pillars of radiant non-light, streaming blackness into their centers. They weren't swift. They didn't need to be; they were implacable, moving steadily forward. It had been folly for that small force to oppose them. But they had been experienced soldiers and had done so anyway. Ah, they needed to delay them, give their comrades time to finish setting the explosives and readying the fuses. This would be a compelling study to present to my classes. It would bring ancient history to life with danger and heroism. Of course, I would have to come back and carefully excavate the area, so that my reconstruction was documented and supported ...

"Stenn! Morghaests! Run this direction! We'll try to hold them off!"

With a shock, I realized I wasn't in a simspace reconstruction of the battle. This was real, and there were two morghaests plodding towards me. I had called them from the ground and set them in motion. I had unconsciously directed them as I would players in a simspace. That fit with my earlier thought that the *aelo tai* had co-opted the circuits from my simspace augment to communicate with me. Experimentally I directed them to stop, to start again, to stop and raise their right hands. The monsters did all these things.

Gilwyr was running towards me with both swords drawn. Ox and Bridocke were coming as well but were nowhere as fleet as she was. I called to her, "You don't have to be afraid of them. They're tools. I have them under control."

Gilwyr came to a stop between me and the morghaests, ready to defend me. "What do you mean, tools?" she said over her shoulder.

"They're not any more evil than a sword is evil, or a hammer is evil. They do what the wielder wills them to do."

"But they destroy everything they encounter."

"Because that was their last command from the last person who knew how to control them. I can give them a new task."

I raised my hand and pointed to the bridge. The morghaests didn't care; that was for the benefit of my companions, so they knew what I intended. My real command I gave as if I still had my implants, controlling a simspace in which I was immersed. The morghaests began moving towards the bridge. Gilwyr sidled to the right to allow them to pass, ready to start hacking if they made the slightest wrong move. I directed them to the edge of the broken bridge. I swept my hand in an arc, visualizing the graceful arch that must have spanned this gorge. The morghaests went to work reassembling the old structure, using the remains that still littered the ground, and wresting new blocks from the cliffside as needed. A feeling of strength flowed through me as if I had just discovered I could lift ten times my weight. More swiftly than seemed possible from the morghaest's deliberate movements, a new bridge took shape. They seemed to use bits of themselves to anchor the stones until they were finally used up and sank from sight into the stone as the bridge grounded itself against the abutments on the far side.

I turned to my dumbfounded companions. "There we go, two problems solved. We have no more morghaests, and we have no more detour."

Bridocke began shaking her head and backing away. "No. No. No. No. No," she repeated.

"You should be far more cautious about using your powers," said Ox. "I know you have good intentions, but legends say that Grimmerroth corrupts by giving the fairest of gifts. You do not know what the cost of those gifts might be!"

"Would you rather have hauled your royal butt four or five days upstream through broken country? You should be grateful that I've saved us at least a week of travel time. Let's pack and get moving. I'd like to find this Tykenkote. It was important in the last war, and it could still be important today."

"One cost of your powers is evident. They warp your personality and make you arrogant and rude. I fear they can warp your judgment as well."

Gilwyr added, "I have noticed this as well. What is warped can be pounded straight, however. Look forward to our practice this evening, Stenn."

I brushed past them, and past Bridocke, who was standing behind them. She shrank away from me. "You really are a warlock," she said. There was honest fear in her voice. "You raised the dead and made them do your bidding. Those are evil things, even for good intent."

I waved dismissively, but their words troubled me. I felt they were being superstitious. I had used a tool to speed us on our way; that was a good thing, wasn't it? But the tool had an affect on me; when they called my attention to it, I knew I had sounded arrogant. I was learning that meant that I had let the black *aelo tai* influence me again. It was a hard thing to admit that I couldn't trust my own judgment.

We used few words to pack, fewer to strike out on the road. As we neared the bridge, Bridocke began noticeably hanging back. I lead the way onto the bridge, flanked by Gilwyr, with Ox just behind. After a dozen paces, we realized that Bridocke was not with us. She had stopped before setting foot on the first paving stone of the bridge. She called to us, "I can't. Morghaests made this. It is made *of* morghaests. We can't trust it any longer. It's not just a stone bridge, it's an instrument of the Grimmerroth's will."

Gilwyr replied, "We will cross it. I believe that Greylander's quest for the crown leads to this castle, and after that to Cloudhaven. You said you would support him as the rightful king."

"But one of my ancestors fought here, maybe even died here, to keep this evil contained. Now you would walk over evil's bridge, in evil's company, for the sake of your throne?"

Perhaps we would do better without her.

I was appalled at the thought as soon as it occurred to me. I tried to force it out of my mind.

"I will cross it, and leave it behind. Stenn is not evil, though he carries an evil burden. We must get him to Cloudhaven where they can help him. He is also our best chance at uncovering what happened centuries ago, which may help us win today's battles."

I turned. She would follow if she saw that it was safe. Ox stood and waited, looking expectantly at Bridocke. Jerkily she put one foot in front of the other as if she had to will each step to occur. I felt her steps on the bridge; it quivered with each footfall. I frowned. Why was it doing that?

I moved steadily forward, Gilwyr by my side. The gap across the chasm seemed much less when there was a solid bridge spanning it. In moments we were stepping onto the far side, where the road continued. Ox was just behind us. Bridocke was still only halfway, arms extended as if she were walking a narrow balance beam and not a broad stone bridge. She made the mistake of looking over the side and froze, unable to move.

"Come on, Bridocke, we all made it," called Ox.

"The bridge doesn't like me!"

She was right. She took another two steps, and I could feel the bridge twist slightly with each one. Was my subconscious sabotaging the bridge because she had accused me of being evil? Gilwyr started back across to conduct her the remaining way. Expressions flitted across Bridocke's face: fear, shame, anger. "Gilwyr, no!"

Bridocke broke and ran to Gilwyr. The bridge rippled and bucked behind her, throwing her to her knees momentarily. She regained her feet, and closed with Gilwyr, reaching out her hands. The bridge cracked at her heels, opening up a crevasse to the sharp rocks and rushing water below. She threw herself forward, catching Gilwyr's hands just as the stone crumbled away beneath her feet. She dropped through the hole. Gilwyr threw herself flat, head and shoulders over the edge, still hanging on to Bridocke with both hands. I started to run back onto the bridge to help them to safety.

The edge of the bridge started crumbling away under Gilwyr. She didn't have any purchase to stand up or to pull Bridocke to safety. She could save herself by letting go and rolling away, but she hung on doggedly. She scooted back by arching her body like an inchworm, but almost lost Bridocke when one of the crumbling stones hit Bridocke on the way down. Each of these moments passed in slow motion as each of my footfalls seemed to take minutes, even though I was running at top speed. If I was on the bridge, I wouldn't sabotage myself, would I?

A great slab broke away under Gilwyr's chest, and she started to go over just as I landed on her legs. I grabbed Gilwyr's belt and hung on, though I could feel the hungry pull of gravity dragging us towards the edge. Gilwyr was bent at the waist, half over the edge, with only her legs beneath me.

The bridge stopped crumbling. Perhaps my presence stabilized it, but it was too late. We had no purchase and were still sliding over the edge. I heard footsteps behind me and felt Ox throw himself on my legs, stopping our slide. He called out, "Bridocke, climb up! We're holding on."

I couldn't see Bridocke over the edge, but I could feel Gilwyr being pulled from side to side as Bridocke worked her grip higher. Finally, Bridocke's hand groped over the edge, looking for a handhold. I transferred one hand from Gilwyr's belt and grasped Bridocke's wrist. A few more handholds and her head and shoulders appeared. From there she was able to climb the chain of bodies to safety.

With her hands free, Gilwyr was able to twist and catch my free hand and pull herself back over. I was glad for her limber strength because I probably couldn't have managed it. We regained our feet and hastened for the safety of solid ground, where we collapsed. I had the rubber-legged shakes. Ox was breathing heavily and even Gilwyr, who was always so competent and unflappable in the face of danger, sprawled with the rest of us. Bridocke was trapped in a loop between shame of her fear and fear of further shame. It was some time before we had breath to spare for words. Had I caused the bridge to crumble, just because Bridocke was afraid of me? I couldn't be sure. I hadn't overtly wished for it to fall, but had my subconscious turned a stray thought into a deed?

Bridocke staggered to her feet. "You put the Prince in danger! You're a warlock, and you can't even control your powers. You're taking him farther from the city where he's needed, and as I see it, this is much more for your benefit than his." She turned to Ox. "Why, Prince Greylander? Why do we follow him? Does he have you under his influence? Say the word, and I'll release you." She put her hand on her sword hilt.

Gilwyr had a knife at Bridocke's throat in an instant. I recognized that as contempt, that she had only drawn her knife and not her sword. She didn't think Bridocke was a match for her. "Both Stenn and Ox are under my protection. Make a move towards either of them, and it will be your last."

"Gilwyr!" said Ox sharply.

That tableau held for a few heartbeats, then Bridocke dropped her hands and cast down her eyes. "I would not harm him. I am angry, and it troubles me to disagree with my liege, but I joined you willingly, and I will stay willingly."

Gilwyr dropped her knife, and the two women looked appraisingly at each other. "Let's go then," said Gilwyr. We picked up our packs and put our feet on the road again.

Keep them at odds with each other, said the black voice.

You're doing a fine job of that already, I replied.

CHAPTER 36

Tykenkote Castle

THE TAMESAS MEANDERED, the road meandered, and we had little choice but to follow them. It meant more footsteps than a ruler-straight line but we made better time than we would have overland. As the days passed, we progressed from a moderate climate with stands of open forest mingled with open meadows into a warmer and more humid climate. It rained most afternoons for an hour or so; getting campfires started at night grew more and more difficult. The forest became lush and tangled. The "trees" were taller and spread their teal lambswool (*wen withe*) in a vast canopy. The understory was a battleground of vine-like creepers and pallid plants that shunned the sun. These latter must have lacked the chlorophyll-analog for making their own food and were saprophytic on the deep organic layer that littered the ground.

The road here was long abandoned; the forest now encroached on the sides. Its builders had built to last, with a thick stone roadbed to discourage the larger plants from taking root and destroying it. The road seemed to be a human construct, but what was its history? Had it originally been a Kir Leth road? On human worlds, highways followed earlier wagon roads, which followed even earlier footpaths, which often followed animal tracks. If the Kir Leth had built roads, people would have naturally followed their course in building their own.

The dynamics of our little group were as tangled and spiky as the vines that surrounded us. The black *aelo tai* had an agenda of discord, which it furthered whenever our guard was lowered. In those times, Bridocke wavered between heartfelt allegiance to Ox and her conviction that his family was usurpers who should all be deposed. Bridocke and Gilwyr often felt they were in competition, but in an instant could unite against Ox or me, either individually or collectively. Gilwyr was mercurial and often snappish; all of us tasted her sharp tongue at one time or another. At such times, one tried to decline a sparring match with her at all costs. Ox was probably the most even-tempered of all of us but could become autocratic and overbearing when we squabbled, though he usually apologized later. As for me, let us just say that I'm surprised my companions continued to tolerate me. The nightly sword practice became a ritual known as 'straightening the blades' after Gilwyr's comment about correcting what the *aelo tai* warped.

Thus it was that our dysfunctional company came into the first of the river ruins.

The first one we nearly passed before recognizing it. A shape that might have been a rock outcropping was overgrown with creepers and covered with soft teal moss-grass. Something about the lines made me stop and look back. The shape was a little too regular, with hints of straight lines under the vegetation; as we looked closer, we saw what might have been an arch. I pulled the creepers away from the arch to uncover a doorway. Inside was a small bare room with only a few timbers decaying in a corner that might have been a bed or a table at one time. There wasn't enough left now to tell.

"This may have been a traveler's shelter or a guard post," said Ox. "I can think of no other reason for such a structure to be stationed on a road such as this. It is too small for an inn or shop, and the hut of a farmer or herder would be close by the things they tend."

There was little more to discover, so we went on. Now we started to see Terran species intermingled with Sellenrian. Some trees—oak, I think, though I'm no expert—seemed have been planted along the road. At one point, I was shocked to witness an honest Earth rabbit hopping from our path. Further on, I'm sure I glimpsed a fox fading into the underbrush. We passed more eroded buildings and worn-down markers that told few tales. All the while the ecosystem was becoming increasingly, then entirely, Terran. Finally, we reached a settlement that seemed to be the center of the Terran enclave. A cluster of low buildings was spaced in a rectangular layout. At one time they had probably been arranged around a work yard of packed soil, but in the intervening centuries, the forest had reclaimed it. At the rear of the rectangle, a larger edifice rose from the trees, three stories tall and stoutly built of stone and timber. We stood among the crumbling buildings and wondered who had built them, for what purpose, and why they had abandoned them.

The first few buildings were for storage. One contained the remains of a wheeled cart with rusting metal wheels. Another housed a collection of tools. Digging seemed to be a preoccupation of the inhabitants, since shovels and picks predominated. The next building had a partly crumbled stone enclosure at one side. A few metal tools lay around, mostly missing handles that had probably been of wood. I picked up one that was particularly hefty. "This looks like a hammer." A broken stone vessel was on the floor to one side, and a large slab of metal was in the center of the room at waist height. "I think this was a smithy. That was the forge, and this was the anvil, and here's one of his hammers."

The presence of metal prompted me to scan for hidden artifacts with second sight. No red images appeared. It wasn't that there was nothing to see; I couldn't see the anvil, or the hammerhead, the few tools that were lying in plain sight, or even our own swords, which I knew well by now. I strained harder to see anything and failed. I held my own dagger in front of my missing eye. Nothing. I tried blacksight and met with the same failure. Disturbed, I said nothing but lead the way back outside into the light.

Out here I could again see our swords in second sight. However, it was still diffuse, as if being viewed through a veil of fog. At first I saw nothing in blacksight, but then caught a glimpse of the dancing motes at some distance away. Perhaps the problem wasn't with blacksight; perhaps there weren't any motes here to see. Still puzzling about this, I followed the others towards the largest building.

This building was of stone, an unadorned rectangle without towers or moats or defensive constructions, covered in a thick layer of green moss. The main door was large enough for sizable loads to have been brought in and out. It was rather large for a mere shelter, too plain for a manor house, too open to be a fortress against attack. It looked more like a storehouse or factory than anything else. It seemed quite anomalous as the center of this compound in the woods. What purpose had it served?

We stood before the main doors, which were decayed and fallen in but still barring our way. As Ox and Gilwyr pushed experimentally on one door, I looked up to get an idea of the construction techniques that had been used. The lintel over the doorway was a plain slab of stone that supported the weight of the wall above it. This must have been quarried locally, dressed, and hoisted into place with great effort. It was simpler than the stone arch construction that I had seen in Dalactus, which could mean that this place predated the city, or it might have merely been a more utilitarian design. It was covered heavily in the same green moss that softened the outlines of all the buildings in the compound. The moss and the other Terran plants must have been established by the settlers to create a biome that would support them, indicating that they had intended a long-term settlement. My companions had told me that humans could live on the Sellenrian biome for some time before symptoms set in that they called "wasting," but which I suspected to be vitamin deficiencies. If they had gone to all this trouble to create a settlement, why had they left?

I was so intently studying the moss that I almost missed the carved line that extended beyond the edge of the moss at one point. I unsheathed my sword and was barely able to reach the area with its tip. I scraped away the moss near the line, uncovering the letter Y chiseled into the stone beneath it. "Look!" I called. "There's something engraved on the lintel."

After a few tries with sword tips (which made Gilwyr steam about the abuse of edged weapons), Ox lifted Gilwyr above his head. She again demonstrated her remarkable balance as she stood on his shoulders and scraped the moss from the lintel. Letters appeared, first a T, and then a K, and then …

"Tykenkote! This must be the castle."

"It looks like no castle I have ever seen," said Ox as he formed a step with his hands for Gilwyr to jump down.

"Words change meaning over time," I said. "The root word for castle at various times could mean a fortification, or a manor house or an outpost. Or this place could have had another function entirely for which they had no word, and castle was the closest term to describe it. Or it could have been mistranslated from Anglich to Dalactyn when the account was written years later."

Bridocke looked at me. "When you are not a frightening warlock, you put me in mind of my childhood teacher."

"Oh, thank you …"

"He was quite boring."

"Oh."

Gilwyr looked torn between mirth and outrage. After all, I was her apprentice to abuse, not Bridocke's. After that crack, I wanted to summon a morghaest to wrest the doors open for us, but blacksight had cut out again. I was starting to worry that something was wrong with the *aelo tai* or that I was becoming sick. We ended up prying the doors open with a pole that we found back in the smithy.

As the doors fell apart, more broken than opened, I noted again that they were relatively thin, not built for defense. We stepped into the dim interior, lit by the sunlight filtering through the front door and through some relatively small window openings, largely covered with vegetation. As my eyes adjusted, I started picking out details around the room. A block and tackle hung from a rail on the ceiling, which could pick up heavy items and convey them from the center of the room to a side room or vice versa. As I looked down, I could see grooves worn in the dirt floor from the main door to the point under the end of the rail. They must have brought carts in the front door to load or unload.

The side room was a workroom of some kind. Sturdy benches lined the walls. Old tools were left where they had fallen. Some looked like they had once been grinders or drills, others were likely saws that had succumbed to rust. We all made some guesses about what they had made in this shop, but there was little evidence left to confirm any of them.

The next room had a different look to it. The benches were lighter in construction. There were some glassware vessels on them. One arrangement with a vessel and the remains of a wick was obviously a burner for heating substances in containers placed above it. I identified a pair of tongs nearby. This place had the look of a laboratory.

"What is this strange thing?" asked Gilwyr.

It was a pile of metal sheets with black crud between them, which had green leads attached to it. I scraped the green with a fingernail and confirmed from the reddish gleam that it was oxidized copper. I had a suspicion; I pried the top sheet of metal from the pile and found it dense and pliable. "This is a primitive battery," I said, hardly believing my own words. "They were producing electricity." Of course, this pronouncement didn't enlighten anyone other than me; electricity was completely unknown to my companions. Bridocke made a sign against warlocks towards me.

I tried to fit this into what I knew of this world. How had they made the leap to experiments with electricity? How had they prevented the Dust and the morghaests from immediately destroying their work?

At the other end of the same table was a large glass vessel with more of the oxidized copper leads. There were stoppered bottles nearby, one of which held a trace of liquid still. I unstoppered it and caught a distinct whiff of ethanol. I now recognized another piece of glass as a still, where they must have refined and purified the ethanol. Inside the large glass vessel was a bit of stone. When I reached in and picked it up, it was unusually dense, weighing much more than I would have expected.

"I found something," said Gilwyr. She had lifted a sheet of metal that had rested on one of the benches and found it weighing down a sheet of paper, brittle and stained but still somewhat legible. Gilwyr reached for it, but I quickly intervened and held back her hand. There was an excellent chance that the paper would crumble to dust if picked up. Instead, we stared down at an old drawing that depicted a large glass vessel, with a stone in the center, and leads running to the battery, with arrows presumably marking the current flow. Around the stone in the vessel were drawn lines, several straight, several spiraling, two forking, and that walked randomly from place to place. I suddenly felt cold, and the hair on the back of my neck stood on end. I tried to remember an undergraduate physical science course that I had taken to fulfill requirements at least six decades previously. I set the heavy stone down on the bench.

"I think this is a rudimentary cloud chamber. It detects radioactive emissions, which means this sample is probably radioactive ore. If they were mining this stuff, this entire compound is probably contaminated with radiation. Don't touch anything in here."

"What is this 'radiation'?" asked Gilwyr.

"Is it black magic?" asked Bridocke. "Were these people warlocks like you?"

"No, I think they were inventors of some kind. They were trying to make something, which was probably more dangerous than they realized."

"How are they different from you, then?"

I didn't know how to answer that, so I herded them out of the laboratory. The final door from the main room led to an ascending staircase. We took those to explore the upstairs, though I was becoming more uneasy by the moment. I wondered what the half-life of this radioactive ore might be. The thought that we should leave warred with the desire for more information about this place. Just a few moments more, I told myself. The staircase opened on the second floor to a common room with tables and a kitchen to one side. This appeared to be their living quarters. In other circumstances, I would have been eager to look for clues to how they had lived, but a proper study would take time we didn't have. There was another stairway from there to the top floor.

At the top of the staircase was a small library with a reading desk. By some miracle, there were still well-preserved books on the shelf. I very carefully pulled a few from the shelf, expecting binding and pages to be brittle after this length of time. I scanned the titles and let out a small exclamation. "These were printed pre-settlement! These are some of the handbooks colonists would bring with them to a new world. 'Metallurgy.' 'Mining and Refining.' And, oh, 'Handbook of Radiation.' This is where they got the diagram for the cloud chamber."

"These do not look like any printed books I have ever seen," acknowledged Ox. "There are stories that people had attained a high culture before the long winter, but that all of that was lost. Adventurers have looked for remains of their cities for many years. Some say that their land sank under the waves."

"Just like Atlantis," I muttered. It seemed that Ox didn't fully accept humanity's off-world origin yet.

The library connected into another, larger room. We filed through, first Ox and Bridocke, then Gilwyr, then me. Bridocke gave a small shriek and backed up into a stand of spears, which toppled backward onto Gilwyr. Gilwyr staggered, then grabbed the stand along with the spears and hurled them angrily across the room. "Oaf!" she cursed Bridocke. A thin line of red trickled down Gilwyr's upper arm. I registered concern at the small cut, but she waved me away. I stepped into the room to see what had spooked Bridocke.

There was a gruesome corpse on the bed. The skin was tattered and dried over the skull's rictus. It was blackened as if it had hemorrhaged before the person had died. The bed was stained below the skeleton, also pointing to massive blood loss. The skeleton held a sword in one hand beside it, and the sword was weighing down a heavy parchment that still showed faint writing on it. "Don't touch the sword," I warned. I lifted the old blade with the tip of my own sword and extracted the parchment from it. It appeared to be written in old Anglich.

After a moment of study, I began to make out the words and started translating. "The new ore that we found is a success and a disaster. Forged with iron in a sword or arrowhead or spearhead, it kills morghaests. In doing so, it draws the life from he or she who wields it. Those who carry these weapons vomit and flux, begin to bleed, and eventually die. It appears to be the metal itself because all our smiths succumbed first to the sickness. I have buried them all, and my soldiers and guards, and my family as well. I will lay here with this warning for those who will find me one day. These weapons must be used only as a final resort, and those who use them will pay the ultimate price. Lord Tykenkote"

It took a moment for these words to sink in. This was much worse than I had feared downstairs in the laboratory. "We must leave immediately. This entire place must be contaminated. Quickly! Outside! Touch nothing."

"But with these weapons, we might be able to arm enough people to defeat Terrell," said Bridocke.

"And they'll all die in the process. Get moving. This is … call it black magic. You don't want to touch it."

I got them out of the building and back on the road. As soon as we could get to the banks of the river, I had everyone stop. "Get out of your clothes and wash every bit of dust off. Scrub your hair and fingernails. Then wash your clothes and tools. We'll have to discard all of our food and get fresh. Be sure that you don't have a single speck of dust from that place."

They caught the urgency in my voice and did as I said. Everyone washed, and then we put on the wet clothes and put more distance between Tykenkote and us. I started to relax when my second sight returned to normal. Now I knew that radiation interfered with the *aelo tai*, which must be why the weapons forged from radioactive ore were effective against morghaests. Finally, near dark, with the castle hours behind us, we stopped and caught some fish for dinner. The smell of roasting fish made all of us ravenous, with the exception of Gilwyr, who was seeming a little listless. Finally, the fish was ready, and we started pulling apart the tender fish with our fingers and eating the morsels. After a few bites, however, Gilwyr turned pale.

"What's the matter?" I asked.

"I ..." she started. Then she clapped her hand to her mouth, turned away from the fire, and vomited.

CHAPTER 37

Moving Mountains

GILWYR WAS MISERABLY sick all night. I was awake for most of the night giving her dribbles of water to keep her from dehydration, holding her as she heaved even that up, cleaning her up when it progressed to diarrhea towards morning. When daylight finally broke, we were both exhausted.

"Is she well enough to travel?" asked Ox. Gilwyr was finally sleeping fitfully. I was trying to wash the stench of vomit out of my clothes at the riverside.

"I don't know. I'll have to see if she can stand when she wakes up. How far are we from a town?"

"There are no more towns in this direction. Cloudhaven is still one to two weeks of travel."

"Can they help her in Cloudhaven? Frankly, a town isn't much help, because no doctors on this world know how to treat this sickness."

"It is quite possible. The Kir Leth are very skilled in medicine. Do you know how to treat it?"

"I think there are some salts of iodine that can help, but I couldn't tell you which ones or how much. There are more advanced medicines that can treat the bone marrow damage. If she lives through this, even years from now she might suffer from cancer from this damage. None of that can be treated with what we have available to us."

"If she lives … You are saying this sickness is life-threatening. Then we shall continue our journey with even more resolve. We will carry her, if necessary."

"Do you know the way to Cloudhaven from here?"

"In the main, yes. The landscape changes as one gets closer and it becomes easy to lose one's way. It may take some searching before we find it."

"Do you mean a seasonal change to the landscape, such as autumn and winter?"

"No, I mean that the mountain is not always in the same place, and the surrounding hills can drift from one visit to the next. No few people have tried to find their way there, and concluded it was a myth when their maps proved to be wrong."

"I find that hard to credit."

"There are no small number of things that you say are true that I find hard to credit as well."

I didn't press it. It was probably local folklore engendered by inaccurate maps. Without the help of surveying tools and satellite imagery, mapmaking must be more art than science here.

I put my wet shirt back on, shivering in the cool morning air. I would have given a lot for a set of clean clothes about then. As we walked back to the campsite, Ox asked, "Why has only Gilwyr contracted this sickness?"

"It must be the cut she received. I don't know if the blade was radioactive itself, or whether it was covered with radioactive dust. Either way, it entered her bloodstream and poisons her from within."

Bridocke was supporting Gilwyr to sip some broth she had prepared. Gilwyr was holding it down and looking a little stronger. Bridocke had heard our conversation as we approached the camp, and looked up with a stricken expression. "Do you mean I brought this curse on Gilwyr?"

"Curse?" I asked.

"Yes, it is obvious. Tykenkote and his people stole volumes of lore from the Grimmerroth and were trying to cast his spells of destruction against him. The Grimmerroth cursed them and all of their workings so that none could use them. We have brought that curse upon us now, and through my clumsiness, Gilwyr is the first of us to fall."

"Nonsense. This is science, not a curse. If you understood the principles in those books, it would be clear to you …"

"I would then be on the same path as you, sir Warlock, and ultimately doomed."

"Not if we can make it to Cloudhaven and ask the Kir Leth for help," said Ox. "Gilwyr, can you travel?"

"Soon," she said. "Let me try standing."

Gilwyr tried to shake off Bridocke's assistance but was too weak to do so. She did stand and took several steps with Bridocke at her arm. "The nausea is passing. I will be back to normal in a few hours." I knew the remission would only be temporary, but if she could travel under her own power, we could get farther before progressive radiation damage weakened her system.

Bridocke was beginning to look distressed and managed to lower Gilwyr to the ground before she turned away to vomit in her turn. Nearly simultaneously, a subterranean disturbance that I hadn't yet acknowledged broke loose, and my stomach emptied itself as well. As I bent over the ground heaving, I heard Bridocke moan, "We're all doomed."

We were three days regaining strength to leave. Ox had been the least affected, probably because he had a much larger body mass in relation to the radiation dose we had taken. He caught fish and made broth to sustain us as we went through the initial stages. I wished I had brought the *Handbook of Radiation* from the castle library, but I was also confident that it had been as contaminated as everything else at Tykenkote. The option of trading further radiation poisoning for knowledge about our condition was one that I was glad was out of our reach to consider. I was certain that none of us would willingly return to the castle to retrieve it and I didn't even bring it up.

On the fourth day we resumed our journey. We no longer followed the road; Tykenkote had been its destination. Our progress was much slower, both because of the terrain and because of our weakened state. We soon passed out of the Terran biome and resumed traveling among the teal vegetation and its six-legged denizens. Several more times we passed *ongars* tending orderly patches of growing things. When I suggested that we could raid them for some supplementary food, Gilwyr told me coldly that they were not for eating. I presumed that they were poisonous to earth metabolisms, tasted foul, or caused stomach aches, and left it at that.

Gilwyr had the worst symptoms, probably because she had gotten a dose directly through the cut on her arm. She began having episodes of confusion where she thought we were in training for our guild, or on some courier mission. There were moments when she didn't recognize us, though she covered it up each time. She also had frequent nosebleeds, and once when I used the latrine after she had, I saw bright blood on the ground.

By the evening of the fifth day, she was doing poorly. She didn't complain, but her movements were slowing, her hair was dull and limp, and she had dark circles under her eyes. She sat listlessly while a meager meal was prepared: cold rations, since none of us had the energy for hunting. We were all suffering from the radiation exposure, with sores, nosebleeds, and lethargy. Gilwyr was the worst off, but we were all in bad shape. Bridocke continually muttered about curses and looked at me as if I should do something to counter the curse.

Gilwyr suddenly said, "Stenn!" in a rising tone that spoke of panic. She was still sitting but was now staring in confusion at a handful of her once-beautiful hair. She ran her hand through her tresses, and more handfuls came away. "What's happening to me?"

I explained gently that it was the next stage of the sickness and that all she had to do was get through this and it would grow back. So far, she had faced it with a wan stoicism. Now she was shaken, and I saw something on her face I had never seen before: mortal fear. I hoped I was not lying to her. I had no idea what the mortality rate was for her level of exposure, nor ours for that matter, especially on a world where medical treatment was effectively unavailable. That night, instead of sleeping spooned together, I held her in my arms as she shivered with fever.

In the morning she had trouble rousing, but we finally got her to sip some broth. When it came time to resume our journey, she pushed herself upright on shaky legs, fueled entirely by pride and determination. She took one step before her legs collapsed under her. I transferred my pack to Bridocke and hoisted Gilwyr on my back. She felt hot against my skin, and too light. I felt a few tears of frustration fall on my shoulder, but she said nothing.

Only an hour down the trail we reached a large side stream joining the main valley of the Tamesas. Ox looked up this wide, new watercourse and pointed. "Look! Fortune seems to be with us for a change. There is Cloudhaven!"

Beyond the end of the valley rose some low hills, and beyond those was a massif that I would describe as a plateau. A dense forest of teal covered the slopes and the top of the plateau, and a fringe of white clouds clung to the edges like the halo of hair on a wizened old man. The valley lay before us like a highway, promising swift travel. There were few trees here, little plant life at all in fact. It seemed that lush Cloudhaven was surrounded by largely barren hills.

Ox took a turn carrying Gilwyr. I was glad of the relief, for I was nearly done in already and it was still early in the day. He lasted for almost twice as long as I had before stumbling and admitting that he was feeling woozy. Without the curse—even I had begun calling it that—he could probably have carried her all day. After that, Bridocke took a turn and lasted about as long as I had, though at the last she was putting one foot in front of the other only through pure pig-headed stubbornness not to be shown to be weaker than a warlock. After that we rotated, with each shift becoming shorter and shorter until we finally collapsed in mid-afternoon, unable to make further progress.

Gilwyr would not respond to pleas to wake up, but when some water was dribbled into her mouth, she was able to swallow. Even Ox no longer had the strength to pick her up. We were considering stopping early to regain some strength for the following day, but I was becoming frantic with worry about her condition and couldn't bear any delay. I stood in the valley, staring at the plateau in the distance aching with the need to carry her just a little further.

The black *aelo tai* spoke to me. *You have the means if you pay the price.* As it spoke, I felt my consciousness expanding outwards to sense the vibrations in the ground, the dancing points of non-light scattered around me. They were more plentiful here, and more intense. I could move them and shape them. I could make many things from them, but the most familiar and the most versatile was a man-form. I saw, as if in simspace, a golem take shape from the gravel of the stream bed, rising up and standing ready. From Ox's grunt and Bridocke's cry, I knew that I was doing it again, manipulating realspace as if it were simspace. A golem of gravel was too rough for my purpose, so I caused it to walk through some loamy soil near the stream and accrete an outer shell of earth and moss. I summoned it to where we stood and it came, green and faceless, a forest spirit from a story older than history. Enough energy flowed back into me that I could lift Gilwyr and place her in its arms.

"No!" Bridocke drew her sword. "You cannot sacrifice her, sir War-lock!"

I laughed. "I'm not sacrificing her, I'm saving her."

Bridocke blocked the way with her sword pointed at my chest. "Tell me how."

"I'll have my servant carry her, no more than that."

Ox came to stand with Bridocke but laid his hand on her sword arm. "I cannot think he means her harm. You have seen how he looks at her. I could tell he was in love with her from the first time she brought him to my chamber, though I think it took him longer to discover it."

In love? With this prickly, scary, assassin who was more than half Cray Leth?

"I'll grant you that, when he's being Stenn," said Bridocke. "But when he's the warlock, he changes. He's not the same person right now."

"A fair point, Bridocke. Stenn, how say you? Is there any sophistry in your words? Do you mean to bring her to the Kir Leth and restore her to health?"

"Without hesitation," I said.

"Then let us make what time we can before the sun sets."

We turned back towards the mountain. I had the morghaest stride ahead of us on the belief that we all felt better having it where we could keep our eyes on it. I could hear Bridocke and Ox talking behind me. "Do you think she feels the same way about him?" Bridocke asked. They appeared to think I couldn't hear them. Come to think of it, my senses did seem sharper when I was using the *aelo tai*.

"I don't doubt it," Ox replied. "But she couldn't put a name to it. That's not in the Kir Leth vocabulary she learned as a child."

How could they tell us what we were feeling? My vocabulary included love, and though I'd never been in love, I knew what it was. That wasn't what I felt ... was it? *If you've never been in love, how would you know?*

That gave me much to think about as we walked, which we did until light and legs failed us and we collapsed. We stopped where the stream originated in a waterfall that came from the wall of the valley. The valley itself continued, green and broad, towards Cloudhaven, which finally seemed to have grown closer. We made a broth from bits of fish we had dried and sipped it. None of us had an appetite, which seemed a bad sign to me. My sleep was disturbed by the feeling that the mountains were restless, watching us, talking about us in grating granite voices that were felt through the ground.

When we woke, we cried out nearly simultaneously. The valley through the barren hills that had seemed a highway to our destination now veered away to the south, taking us further away from the plateau. Between us and the plateau rose an unscalable cliff several hundred meters high, blocking our way forward.

Ox broke the silence. "It is said that the Kir Leth can move mountains. I had believed that to be a feat of misdirection and illusion, not the literal truth."

"Can this yet be illusion?" asked Bridocke. "We see the cliffs, but have not touched them. Are they trying to make us turn away?"

I looked at the cliff in blacksight. It was a veritable glow of anti-light, still restless from recent disturbance. "They're real enough. Maybe it's a 'No Solicitors' sign, or maybe it's a test to see how powerful we are, or how badly we want to meet them. I, for one, am not inclined to go the long way around."

We reached the base of the cliff that hadn't been there the evening before. It was a realistically rocky cliff face, but I noticed that it didn't have any plants colonizing the crevices as other rocky expanses nearby did. The line where the low scrub on the ground left off was sharp and clear. In its own way, this wall was as fake as a hologram. I sighted along the wall in both directions, trying to sense the manner in which it had been constructed. Even with the stirring that we had felt during the night, it didn't seem possible that enough material had shifted to fill the entire valley. After a moment, I grinned, causing Bridocke to make her sign against warlocks again. Even Ox looked uneasy.

I pointed my morghaest at the cliff face. "Dig!" I commanded it. The creature laid Gilwyr on the grass (I had included that detail in my non-verbal desire), stepped up to the wall and began tossing boulders and clods behind it. The tunnel deepened more rapidly than its steady excavation would account for, and I saw that the substance of the wall was dissolving into sand and flowing out of the opening. I recalled Gilwyr's story that the morghaests had been formed from something she called the Dust. I had an abrupt intuitive leap that the Dust might have been an ancient terraforming technology that had been subverted into a weapon. The Kir Leth could control the Dust sufficiently to confound our path into their fastness.

After about a half hour of digging, there was open air and light visible through the tunnel. My servant cleared the last debris from the far end of a passageway that was only about a dozen strides long. I lifted Gilwyr and made my own way to the other side. The valley was still present and had merely been screened by a thin wall. I turned to see Ox and Bridocke inspecting the tunnel with awe and trepidation, reluctant to walk beneath that mass of rock. I laid Gilwyr in the arms of the morghaest, ready to continue. "Let's get moving," I called to the other two. "Gilwyr needs immediate attention, and the only help we know of is at the top of this plateau. Shall I call morghaests to carry you as well?"

They shook off their dazed looks and shouldered the few possessions we had remaining. We had little food, though we had filled our water bottles from the stream. There was no game in the valley, nor was there much in this entire area, so we had to hope that we could hold out until we got to the upper plateau. We were all weakening. Working with the *aelo tai* had given me a burst of energy, but I recognized that I was ignoring my fatigue and would pay the price later. Our process was so slow that I wished I *had* summoned morghaests to carry us all.

Presently we exited the valley and began climbing the shoulder of the plateau. The air grew cooler but more humid, and the vegetation grew increasingly lush as we climbed. I saw native fauna that were new to me.

A winged creature like a six-legged bat glided beneath the canopy and sought clumps of fig-like fruit that grew from the trees. Another creature slithered like a snake until we approached, then it splayed six legs out radially in a star pattern, tilted up on its edge and wheeled away at high speed. Several species had evolved the ability to spin silk-like strands. Some of these laid traps for prey to slide into, others built webs across paths to tangle passing creatures. Ox warned us to stay away from them, saying that even though they were the size of small cats, they could immobilize prey larger than we were.

We stopped to nibble some fruits that Bridocke recognized as edible and sip some water. Gilwyr remained unresponsive but we managed to get her to swallow some water. Bridocke said as we rested, "I have the feeling we're being followed."

Ox said, "I have thought a couple of times that someone was watching from the side, but when I turned my head, no one was there."

I reached out with my senses but found nothing.

Shortly after our rest stop, we entered a maze of dry washes. They appeared to have been made by erosion as rainfall on top of the plateau drained towards the edges. I hoped there were no cloudbursts on top until we were clear of the area. I doubted we could scramble up the steep sides in time if a flash flood came rushing towards us. But then again, some of these washes ran sideways or doubled back on themselves. The third time we saw the same intersection with a rock formation that I thought resembled Doric columns (at least ones that had weathered considerably), I realized we were being led.

"We need to go this way." I pointed.

"We have already been that way," Bridocke protested. So the others had noticed as well. I didn't doubt that their woodcraft far exceeded my own.

"It will be different this time."

They didn't say anything but lurched into motion. Either they were too tired to argue or they trusted me. I thought it was the former. As we moved up the wash, I used blacksight to see the landscape. Yes, this area was thick with the black motes, and ... 'twitchy' was the best word I could think of to describe it. As if it had recently been manipulated and had not yet settled down. There was a bend up ahead, which had formerly led us to the left. I formed a picture in which it curved back to the right instead. When we reached the bend, I was pleased to see the right-trending bend.

"Keep me oriented towards the center of the plateau," I told Bridocke. I was sure she was less likely to lose her direction than I was. She obliged by indicating the general direction that we should go, and I made sure that the next turn we encountered led in that direction. At first I felt resistance, as if another will was trying to divert us, but that soon dropped away, and we made better progress towards our goal.

At last, we emerged from the maze into a clearing surrounded by a lush rainforest. We stopped for a rest and asked Ox if he knew the way from this spot.

Before he answered, I became certain that we weren't alone. I hadn't been employing second sight, and I called myself stupid for that neglect. With that vision, I could now see a dozen or more bright, curved Kir Leth swords positioned near the trees. I could see nothing else; the holders must have been blending into the foliage with color-shifting skin.

I held up my hands and called out, "I know you are there. We come seeking assistance. Gilwyr is gravely ill. She was raised here among you. Can you help her?"

A ring of armed Kir Leth came into view around us as they dropped their camouflage. They spoke to each other using spoken words, hand words, and skin words flickering across their bodies.

I turned to my companions. "Anyone here understand Kir Leth?"

CHAPTER 38

Cloudhaven

I AWOKE IN a luminous cloud. It was warm in the cloud and peaceful. I felt at ease, without pain, content. I drifted for a long time, not needing to think, simply existing. It crossed my mind that I had a task, but that thought wandered away again. I had left tasks and purpose behind. It was sufficient just to be.

Much later, it occurred to me that I was dead. Death wasn't what I expected it to be. In truth, I had expected not to notice it. Belief in an afterlife had largely been left behind in the wreckage of old Earth. Death to me was the singularity where human language encountered a divide-by-zero exception. Words couldn't express the state of non-being except indirectly, because words were all about being: thinking, experiencing, remembering. It was no use talking about things you could no longer do because you no longer existed to not do them.

That was the first worm of critical thinking that crawled into my consciousness to spoil the perfect peace. Now I needed to think, to observe, and to measure. I noticed that I could hear a heartbeat. I counted the beats, which made time pass once more. I noticed that I was breath-ing, though shallowly. I noticed that I could feel faint currents against my skin. I was suspended. In what?

I noticed that when I breathed, it wasn't the quick flow of air. It was slow and stately, a liquid. It sustained me, so it contained oxygen. I had breathed air at one time, I remembered. That was my first thought of a time before this one, which lead to the next one: How did I get here?

I had been in a simspace drama on a strange planet, playing the role of a warlock. I had been in the company of a prince, a soldier, and an assassin. We had traveled across the planet looking for something. We had reached our goal and were surrounded by swords. The assassin was dying, and I commanded the golem that was carrying her to lay her gently down and then dissolve back into the ground. I had gestured that she needed help … and that I loved her. Then I had pitched forward on my face.

As the memories came back, I knew that it had not been a simspace. It had been real. That meant I had made it to Cloudhaven. What had happened to Gilwyr?

That thought finally galvanized me into motion. I sat up abruptly, breaking the surface of the fluid. My lungs expelled the last breath of liquid and took their first breath of air. It gurgled and bubbled in my airways and lungs, which still had a great deal of fluid in them, sending me into a paroxysm of coughing. I desperately wanted to see where I was, but my fluid-filled eyes—no, eye—were clenched with the coughing. All I could see was sheets of brightness. Finally the coughing subsided and I was able to wipe the fluid from my right eye—and confirm that the *aelo tai* was still in the left. Now I could see that I was sitting in a tank in a Kir Leth-style room. A single Kir Leth was perched on one of their branched furnishings. I should find out their name for that item of furniture since it had no equivalent in human culture. (Cultural anthropologist training intact: check.)

The Kir Leth bowed and said something with words and skin, then departed. Was it "I'm glad you have awakened and will prepare breakfast," or "You are our prisoner, don't leave this room?"

I heaved myself out of the tank and onto the floor, which dutifully absorbed the fluid that I sloshed from the tank and that which sluiced from my body. Looking down, I saw that my skin glowed pink and healthy, and even my scars had faded. I was completely hairless. I touched my scalp and then my face. No hair, not even eyebrows. I scraped the viscous liquid off my body with my hands and watched the remainder quickly dry and vanish, or perhaps absorb into my skin. I decided that I didn't feel like a prisoner and ventured from the room.

The next room that I entered was the hub of four rooms such as the one I had just left. The tanks in two of them were empty, and in the remaining one floated a naked and hairless Bridocke. I almost didn't recognize her without hair; despite having traveled with her for weeks, I couldn't have described the shape of her face or chin or nose. The mind could be lazy at times, only recording the minimum number of distinguishing features that the situation called for. Her distinctive braid on the left and counterpoint clipped hair on the right had been so much a part of her persona. She looked more naked without her braid than without her clothes.

I decided that if she wasn't awake yet she needed more time in the vat, so I continued exploring. I shortly saw daylight and emerged from a doorway in the side of the hill. It seemed that Kir Leth preferred to dig rather than to build. Just outside the door, I found Ox sitting cross-legged like a great pink hairless buddha. He looked much younger without his greying hair and beard. He indicated a mat nearby similar to the one that he was sitting on, making this seem even more like a place of meditation.

I looked around at the place where we found ourselves. Outside of a brief clearing around the doorway into the cave, we were in the middle of a dense rainforest, though the climate was cool and damp, not the hot and humid I had expected. Paths branched off in a number of directions from where we sat.

"I'm glad to see you have arisen," he said. "I emerged this morning and have been waiting for the rest of you."

"This is quite a spa they run here," I replied. "They could do a fine business if they advertised."

"I don't know what a spa is, but I don't think the Kir Leth are interested in business, especially with humans. I am fairly certain you are jesting, however."

"How long have we been here?"

"I do not know exactly, but from the phase of Rhea as it was setting a few hours ago, I would say that it has been a week."

"Do you know where Gilwyr is? Her tank is empty, she must be around somewhere."

"She was not here when I awoke. This was her home; she could have gone off to speak with old friends and teachers."

"You spent some time here as well?"

"I stayed here for about a year, learning from their teachers. I only mastered the most basic parts of their language, though, so much remains a mystery to me."

We fell silent after that, simply feeling the peace of this place. A small worry nagged me that I should be concerned about Gilwyr, who had been the sickest of us all. It didn't make sense that she would have arisen first. However, I couldn't hold onto that worry. The after-effect of the healing bath was a surging feeling of life and well-being that washed away concern and doubt as a spring rain washed away the dust, leaving rich soil in which the seeds of new possibilities could take root. Even the dark *aelo tai* had been silenced. For now, I amended, as the thought prompted a restless response from within. For now, I felt a burgeoning hope, exuberantly full of life …

A hair-raising (in a figurative sense only) wail came from inside. We rushed in to find Bridocke choking out the last of the fluid and splashing and slipping comically in her panic to get out of the tank. Ox and I helped her out onto the floor. Bridocke's hands fluttered about trying to decide what to cover but also darting up to touch her gleaming head. I couldn't tell if she was more concerned about her loss of clothes or her loss of hair.

We explained what little we knew to her, how we had climbed the mountain, how we had been greeted at the top ...

"Kir Leth! Actual Kir Leth were standing there! With four arms! You kept talking about them, but I thought they were people, people who did magic, but only people. And Ox, you talked to them in their language, and they started to *flicker*, shapes and colors everywhere on their skin. They had swords, and then they blew dust on us and we all fell down."

"I asked them for sanctuary, and to heal Gilwyr ..."

"*How* did you talk to them? How did you know ..." Bridocke trailed off, looking past us towards the door.

The Kir Leth who had been present when I awoke stood at the entrance. I assume it was the same one; I couldn't be sure. He uttered a few words audibly, and spoke at length in skin words, finishing with an unambiguous gesture with an upper arm towards the exit. Ox told us, "I didn't get all of that, but the gist is that a meal has been prepared for us, and then the council would like to meet with us." To Bridocke he said, "I have spent some time here, long ago. I learned some of their language and philosophy. It was then that I knew I could not be the king that my father wanted me to be." I sensed a great deal of history behind that statement, but Ox kept his face impassive.

We followed the Kir Leth outside and down the path into the forest. Bridocke was just catching up with Ox's previous statement. "Wait a while, you said that we're going to eat, and then meet the council? We don't have any clothes!"

"If you've noticed, the Kir Leth speak with their skins," said Ox. "They consider it rude to wear clothes. To them, it means that you have something to hide."

Bridocke looked down at herself and said, "I do," in such a plaintive tone of voice that Ox chuckled. I didn't react, preoccupied with wondering when Gilwyr would rejoin us.

We were walking through the temperate rainforest. Many of the trees grew in graceful spirals or natural lattices. Knowing the little I did about the Kir Leth, I suspected that these were not natural at all, but engineered. Looking upwards, I could start to perceive platforms high in the trees, blending with the canopy of the forest. What looked like a rainforest was an organic, arboreal city. Our guide stopped at one of these trees and began to ascend the lattice, with an agility that made me want to evolve another two limbs. We followed, not quite as easily, but learning the rhythm of climbing rapidly. On a mid-level platform, we found a substantial meal laid out for us, much of which was familiar from our stay in the Silent City.

A figure approached us along a horizontal walkway. I couldn't tell one Kir Leth from another yet, not having picked up on the variations that distinguished them. However, I was quite certain that I recognized the staff that this one carried. "Perrhen?" I asked as I turned toward the newcomer.

"I am pleased that you remember me, Stenn Gremm. And my old friend Ox, of course."

Ox was delighted to see Perrhen and pushed Bridocke forward. "Bridocke, this is Perrhen, who taught me much when I stayed here previously. Perrhen, *siathen allo Bridocke,*" this last accompanied by a hand gesture against his left brow.

Perrhen bowed. "I am pleased to make an acquaintance with a member of your company," he said. "Now that you are here, please have some sustenance, and then the council would like to meet with you. Please bear with our customs for a few hours, and then we'll supply you with some robes to wear. Once you have shown your willingness to go among us uncloaked, my people will accept your custom of wearing clothes. Most who live here have never met a human, and need to see first hand that you are indeed skin-mute, as the stories tell it."

I had many questions to ask, the foremost of which was when we would reunite with Gilwyr, but at the mention of food, my body informed me of its ravenous appetite. Perrhen encouraged us to eat, saying that we needed to keep our energy up to allow the healing process to complete. After the meal, we were conducted to a higher level platform where we met with six Kir Leth arranged on seven of their perches, with one left empty. We were shown to three mats that were arranged before them so we could sit cross-legged. This placed them in a higher position, but I didn't know if that had the same cultural meaning that it would to a human. Perrhen introduced them to us: "*Lind, Lyr, Tam, Kir, Cray, Sar, Mir.* We are the *Leth*, the peoples of our race." These had been the names in the great assembly hall in the Silent City. I noticed that the seat indicated by *Lyr* was empty. Had I incorrectly been calling them all Kir Leth when in fact there were other groups or factions among them? I recognized that Gilwyr had always identified herself as Cray Leth; the individual so named who faced us was the only one who was armed, with two long swords and two short ones similar to the ones Gilwyr had carried. Each thought of Gilwyr carried the anxious knowledge that she wasn't here yet.

The council inquired after our health via Perrhen's translation and asked us of our journey. Ox told the narrative, frequently pausing to let Perrhen catch up. I watched the members of the council talk among themselves as they listened. They employed few spoken words but flashed a continuous dialog of skin words to each other. I noticed a new thing as well: in the sunlight of the upper platform I could see them emitting occasional puffs of ocher into the air. I wondered what the purpose of this might be if indeed it had a purpose. Perhaps they were inhaling some ritual intoxicant while they listened to us. The story-telling interlaced with translations and questions was slow enough that I fell to thinking about Gilwyr growing up here. I could imagine her scampering up and down the trees as a child, which would explain her marvelous agility. And had she learned swordsmanship from the fearsome-looking Cray Leth who faced us or one of his kin? And who, I wondered, were the missing Lyr Leth?

"Stenn?" said Ox, nudging me.

"I'm sorry, what?"

"He asked you how you summoned the morghaests." It had been the Sar Leth who had asked, and who was now looking at me with what seemed like impatience.

"I ... What have you told them?"

"I told them how you liberated the Silent City from the Blight by bravely conquering the black gem."

I thought about the best way to answer. At least Ox had brought up the subject of the *aelo tai*; otherwise, I might have been unable to talk about it. It inhibited me from telling others about its effects, somehow diverting my thoughts, so I never said what I meant to ...

"Stenn?"

"Sorry." Best to just blurt it out. "When I touched the *aelo tai*, it made itself part of me. I carried it out of the Blight that way. It's ... still with me. It allows me to see and control dark motes in the earth. I can summon a morghaest this way."

When Perrhen had translated this, the council erupted into furious discussion. The air became thick with the ocher puffs they seemed to breathe out. I could see ocher dust settling from the air now. I had the uncomfortable thought that this might be their mechanism for disposal of solid waste. After several minutes, they put a question to Perrhen who put it to me. "Is that how you were able to force your way through the shield wall and the maze to arrive here?"

"Yes, it was."

After several more minutes of increasingly heated discussion, Perrhen stood up. "This is a very concerning development. The council wishes to discuss this among themselves, and so postpones the remainder of this session to another time. I am to take you back to your quarters for now."

As we reached ground level once again, I finally had the opportunity to ask the question that had been on my mind throughout. "Perrhen, where is Gilwyr? Why wasn't she at the council meeting? When will she be rejoining us?"

Perrhen stopped to regard me. "She is elsewhere. She was much sicker than you were, and died before we could put her in the vats."

Chapter 39

Life

MY KNEES BETRAYED me and dumped me on the ground. Perrhen's statement echoed in my head as I tried to make sense of his words, spoken plainly and unemotionally. I forgot how to breathe for a moment, and my vision contracted to a small circle focused on Perrhen's feet. I drew a ragged breath and felt my heart pound as I fought to not pass out entirely. It took me back to the moment when I saw the ruin of my eye in the mirror, a pivot point when life changed irrevocably. At this moment, the loss of an eye seemed trivial.

Ox and Bridocke looked nearly as shocked as I was, though their legs didn't give way as mine had done. Gilwyr had been like a daughter to Ox, and Bridocke had grown to respect her, no matter the times they had clashed while traveling together. But the look of sympathy and pity they gave me was almost more than I could bear. I could feel the tears that I had been too shocked to shed come to the surface and start down my cheeks. Ox put a hand on my shoulder. Bridocke turned away and I heard her sob. She whirled back and gave us both an unexpected embrace—an awkwardly brief one as she was reminded that we were still all unclothed.

Ox turned us towards the path. "We must keep on. We still have more of our journey ahead of us."

As we walked, Perrhen remarked to us, "These water-words that you speak with your eyes are very expressive, are they not? They are more like our skin words than I had known. I must learn more about this part of human language. We may have been missing an important part."

"We don't just make tears on demand," I said bitterly. "They mean something to us." Still, I recognized something familiar in his question. He sounded like an academic. Did I sound like that to others?

We spent the night in a tree. To be more precise, a spacious platform about twenty meters off the ground, high enough to trigger my fear of heights but still well below the crown. I worried about wandering off the edge in the night, but our hosts brought some creatures that glowed softly in the darkness. The silent Kir Leth who brought them placed globs of sticky food that kept the contented bugs grazing where they were needed. I had read about fireflies in Earth literature, but they had not been successfully transplanted to Trondhjem. I didn't think they had been the size of dinner plates.

Perrhen took me aside before he left. "I am sorry that this seems to distress you. You knew she was nearly at the end of her road when you arrived, did you not? Do not feel sad that your road goes on. You will always have the road you shared with her before now."

Gilwyr had said something similar. This must be Kir Leth philosophy that she had learned. "I ... She ... Her road was too short," I managed. "And our roads came together only recently."

"If you meditate on this, you will see that time is an illusion. Everything that has happened is recorded in everything that is. It is easier to say in our language. It may help you to learn it so that you can hear and see and breathe the words of those of our teachers who think deep thoughts and say them clearly."

"I have my doubts."

"*Vi har alle tvil.*"

"What did you say?"

"It is something that the first human with whom I was friends said often. He had different words to speak than others; you may not know those words. In your words they mean ..."

"'We all have doubts.' But I *do* know them. That is the language of my world. Was this man named Jonan Gremm?"

"Yes, it was. Do you know him?"

Amazement pierced the despair ... for a moment. "He was my ancestor. He left me the red *aelo tai*. That's why I came here."

"I am sorry to cause you distress again so soon, but he died also."

"I would expect so. That was four hundred years ago."

"As I said, time is an illusion. We shared a long road together and he is still with me."

"Ox believes I may be repeating his story. I must hear more, but not now. I can't think right now."

"He had a grand story, but hard. I will tell you during your stay."

Perrhen left us there, saying politely that we should stay on the platform and not wander off by ourselves. He made it sound as if his only thought was for our safety, but I felt that we were confined there. There were no evident barriers or guards, but I suspected that any attempt to depart would be futile. We talked for a time before wrapping ourselves in the blankets they had provided. It was then that the misery started. Alone with my thoughts, I had nothing to divert my attention from the new void in my life. I had only been on this world a few months (I thought—though I had lost track of how long it had been), and all but a few of those nights had been spent with Gilwyr's warmth against my back. I had never lost anyone close to me. If pressed, I would admit that I had never before had anyone close enough to mourn. Now that I had, the ache was all the worse.

Finally, I fell asleep to a dream that I was once again trudging through the changing valleys on the path to Cloudhaven. I carried Gilwyr in my arms, knowing that I had to reach our destination before it was too late. If I could get there in time, there was a chance that the Kir Leth could save her. I stumbled. I struggled to regain my feet, but I could not keep my grip on Gilwyr. Her skin was slippery, and I saw that it was red with blood. I tightened my grip, but strips of her skin came off in my hands. It started to rain. Rain and blood mixed on my hands until I could no longer keep my grip on her. She opened her eyes one last time and whispered to me, "Let me go." I could neither let her go nor hold on to her. I knelt in the rain with her until little by little the rain washed her away and I was left holding only rags.

I awakened to find the rain was real, and cold, and the rag I was holding was my blanket. I draped it over my head like a tent and sat, miserable and shivering, until dawn.

With the first light, Perrhen appeared from the mists. The rain had tapered to a drizzle, but the leaves above still unleashed showerlets of water at intervals. It was a kind of torture, knowing that another cascade would come, but never knowing just when. "Good morning, my friends," Perrhen greeted us. "The rain was very refreshing, was it not? I hope you slept well?" He paused. "Do I have that right? That is a morning greeting in your language, is it not?"

"Only if you're sincere about it," I rasped. My throat was raw. Being cured of radiation poisoning only to die of pneumonia would be the ultimate irony.

Perrhen spread four hands wide in a gesture that seemed to indicate surprise. "Were you not comfortable here?"

"To me, comfort means a roof over my head when it's raining."

"I am distressed. We enjoy standing in the rain very much. I did not consider you would want to shelter from it on such a mild night."

"We did find it rather too chilly last night," came Ox's voice from under another blanket. Bridocke was struggling to sit up while still keeping the sodden blanket wrapped around herself.

"I had the wrong color on this," said Perrhen, which I guessed was their term for a misunderstanding. "It is so hard to know how another truly feels. We must perceive temperature and precipitation very differ-ently. I have brought you some robes to wear that we grew during the night. I hope we have not misjudged these as well."

I gratefully accepted the one-piece ankle-length garment from Per-rhen and pulled it on. It was loose and flowing, rather like something you might don after a bath, not what I was accustomed to walking around in. However, it was dry and warm, which made up for a lot. On closer inspection, I could see that the robe had neither seam nor hem, even where the arms were joined to the body. He had said that they had grown them, and I revised my initial opinion that he had mistranslated. All three robes fit remarkably well, especially given the considerable variation in our sizes and shapes. I wondered how they had sized them so well for us.

Breakfast had been set out on a lower platform. There were tart fruits, a sort of steamed grain rolled up in minty leaves, a melon with a pasty, banana-like flesh, and a variety of the bread plant that we had tasted before. This last surprised me by spontaneously growing warm when it was broken open, smelling and tasting like it had just come out of a baker's oven. I soon felt warm again, and the black cloud of Gilwyr's death lightened somewhat. I wasn't ready for that burden to ease yet, which made me wonder if we had been given mood-altering foods. *And why not?* asked my anthropology training. Humans had been using intoxicants and soporifics and other substances since the dawn of time. It's not ethical to give it to us without consent, I countered. *Those are our ethics*, said the anthropologist, *we don't know what their ethics are yet. They may not even know they have any effect on us.* Not likely, I argued in return, given their knowledge of biology. It was only later that day that I thought back and recognized the divisive voice of the *aelo tai* driving my inner argument.

"These are delicious," Ox was saying. "I don't believe I had this when I was here before." He indicated the banana-melon.

"Those are seasonal," said Perrhen. "They are only available for one half of a cycle of Rhea each year. They ripen when the cool rains start as the days shorten. They are all the better for the short time we are allowed to savor them."

"Are all of these foods created by your people?" I asked.

"We simply grow what Polnedra has created for us," he replied.

Now I knew where Gilwyr had gotten the creation myth she had related to me. These people seemed too advanced to still believe in deities creating the universe from whole cloth. It might be no more than a traditional sentiment, but it sounded to my ears like a declaration of belief. On the other hand, Dalactyn wasn't his native language.

"You don't engineer them, change them to be more useful, create different varieties?"

"There is little need. Polnedra provided both abundance and diversity, and we are but the caretakers of her creations. It leaves us free to pursue less material enterprises."

"I find it hard to believe that some of the plants and creatures that I have seen could have arisen in that way."

"We have until the mists of evening fall again before the Council convenes once more. We can walk through some of *Wys Talayan* while the day passes. You may find answers to some of your questions."

We agreed, and Perrhen led the way, not downwards as I had expected but upwards into the canopy. As we climbed, the exertion helped clear my head. Engaging my curiosity, even briefly, had pushed away the oppressive cloud of loss. It was not entirely welcome; survivor's guilt was a blanket of ash that tried to smother the seedlings of renewed life as they tried to come forth. In time, the seedlings would win out unless the ash compacted into an impermeable shell before they gained a solid foothold.

In the upper reaches of the rainforest, walkways bridged the gaps between branches, shaded by a criss-cross of vines that networked the space above them. From the vines depended an assortment of fruits of many shapes and sizes. As my eye started sorting out the tangle, I saw that there were actually many types of vines, covered in different bark and bearing differently shaped fronds of the teal lambswool that served them as leaves. Some were smooth and some were thorny, some grew straight and strong and others gnarled and twisted.

"They're all jumbled together," I said wonderingly. Was this a crop?

"Aye," said Bridocke. "It's like they're growing wild."

"They would grow wild here in *Wys Talayan*," said Perrhen, "but this is a place where they are tended and harvested. I have seen your custom of planting large areas with a single species and wondered at it. I have not made much study of this area in my lifetime, but those who have tell me that in our way the plants support and nourish each other, defend each other from pests, and prevent diseases from wiping out entire species."

We crossed to the next platform by way of a vine bridge, one that looped gracefully across the void. The deck was a mat of woven vines that flexed as we walked, but seemed as strong as cables. Additional vines rose in graceful arcs on either side to form a type of railing. In my opinion, only a truly arboreal species would have found it comfortable.

"I hope the workers who wove this bridge knew what they were doing," I said.

"The vines naturally form bridges. There are Lind Leth who guide them to grow in the needed direction, and who take pride in making them into artistic creations. The vine and the guide have a conversation that spans many years; the vine asserts its imperatives, and the guide uses sun and water and gentle nudges to shape those imperatives into the form that he holds in his mind."

As we neared the far end of the bridge, a sudden wave of spider-like creatures skittered across the pathway, heading in the opposite direction. They split around our feet and used the arching railings as highways to bypass the obstacles that we posed. I peered closely at the nearest ones. They had six legs, a single long body, triangular head, and a variety of colors. The colors were changing in blocky patterns, but when I put a finger near the creatures, they abruptly faded from view. I pulled my hand back and they reappeared. I shook my head: both signaling and protective coloration even in the smallest of creatures.

"Come along," said Perrhen. "The *elt* are being released by the *elthorn*. It's worth watching; it only happens once each season."

The next tree had only a small platform. The branches of the tree were laden with fruiting bodies that resembled six-fingered gloves that had been filled with gelatin. They looked familiar, then I recalled that we had eaten them for breakfast not long ago. They had been filled with little red seeds that popped like caviar when crunched between the teeth. Ox and I had thought them delicious, though Bridocke had made a face after her first taste and left them untouched. I mentioned my recognition to Perrhen.

"Exactly so. Some of these have been allowed to ripen so that we can ensure the propagation of future generations. Here, one is splitting open even now."

The skin of some of the fruits had darkened from yellow to dull red. One of the reddest was developing cracks that curled at the edges as if the skin was drying out. I could see the red of the seeds within. I wondered if they were going to drop out, or hang waiting for whatever filled the bird niche to come along and eat them, thereby spreading them wherever they fell, mixed with ur-bird poop. I began to see motion stirring within the seeds, and I uncomfortably remembered that there were some varieties of plants that scattered their seeds explosively. I was just considering taking a step back when a seed unfurled six thin legs and heaved itself out of the fruit. As if on signal, a host of legs writhed within. A line of the spider-like *elt* issued from the crack, dropping to the deck and scampering down the trunk of the tree or off across the vines to other nearby trees.

"Was ... was the fruit infested with parasites?" My stomach turned over at the thought of what I had eaten for breakfast.

"No, those are the seeds of the *elthorn*. Though I think they do not match your word *seed* exactly. These must seek out *elt* from another *elthorn* that is not their parent, and exchange fragments of life-code with them. Only then do they roam the forest looking for the right conditions for an *elthorn* to grow. Then they will dig themselves into the forest floor and begin the cycle over again."

Was this a commensal relationship? The plant incubated the spiders, which carried the seeds of the plants to new locations? "Do other plant species have similar dispersal strategies?"

"This is a fairly primitive species. In the more highly evolved species, the motile forms have quite long and independent lives, and can cultivate many generations of their sessile forms."

Motile forms? Sessile forms? What was he implying?

Bridocke blurted out, "The *ongar* ..."

"Ah, it would be the season for *ongar* to be cultivating the *ongarborn*. You probably saw some near the river, did you not?"

I went back to that time in my mind. Before Tykenkote Castle and its deadly contents. Before the morghaest bridge even. It seemed another life. I had thought that the *ongar* were engaged in agriculture, but in reality, they were tending their children. This inverted the social paradigm completely. A thousand questions started bubbling up inside me, jostling for position. A dozen of them tried to get out all at once. "How many ... how long ... does every ... is gender ... dynamics ... territory ... w-w-when ..." I stopped as it degenerated into stuttering.

"Meditate on the asking of your questions. When you have the asking of them, I will make stillness to consider them thoughtfully and answer those that I can. I can show you more now."

The next platform had an even stranger sight. The tree that grew through the center of the platform sprouted great branches above this level. The branches started off typically enough, having an opaque woody appearance. However, they grew translucent and then transparent farther away from the trunk, carrying a luminous blue liquid within them. The movement of the liquid could be perceived by small yellow spheres that were carried along at a steady rate. From the transparent branches depended a number of large pods. I couldn't be sure, but it looked as if the pods were independent entities that were dipping their roots into the nutrients carried within the transparent tubes. It looked more like a laboratory than a garden.

"This is amazing," I said, shaking my head. "It's hard to believe that these are not engineered systems."

"They have bred true since Polnedra created them," said Perrhen.

I had heard that one too many times. "How can you believe that a child god created all of these life forms? How can you still believe in divine intervention?" The anthropologist within wailed that I should be observing this culture, not challenging it. Whether I had said that because of the *aelo tai*, or just because of my natively poor judgment, I couldn't tell.

"That is a lie to communicate a deeper truth," said Perrhen. "A story of symbols to lead a listener to understanding."

"A metaphor? A fable?"

"Polnedra was the greatest scientist among us. She shaped countless species into beautiful and useful forms. She was a master of the sciences of life, but no more than a mortal. The story illustrates how deeply she touched our world. Though we have but occasional contact with your people, the story seems to have taken root among them. I think the symbolism has been lost to them, alas."

"The Grimmerroth was also part of that story, at least as Gilwyr told it to me."

"Gleomere was Polnedra's progeny, and as much a master of the physical sciences as Polnedra was of life sciences. At first, the competition between Polnedra and Gleomere was good-natured, but it gradually became darker. They came to represent the rift between two factions of our people. Polnedra stood for those who wanted a harmonious, sustainable balance, though in truth she was not bounded by their world view. Gleomere was the champion of those who saw stagnation rather than balance in Polnedra's philosophy and opened the way to the stars. This eventually led to the conflict in which we lost the stars and much that we had achieved, and returned to this planet, greatly diminished."

"Was Gleomere the one that Gilwyr called Glimmer when she told me the story?"

"Just so. The name changed slightly when it was translated into your language, to make a kind of word-play possible. Just as the epithet *Gleomere Roth* in our language—Gleomere the Destroyer—became Grimmerroth in yours."

"Did they trap each other in a cave, the way the story says?"

"Only symbolically. They used each other's creations against themselves, rendering them useless. In neutralizing each other, they effectively stopped time. As a people, we have been leading a contemplative existence on our world, neither growing nor declining, for thousands of years since the end of their war. Until the long winter occurred, and we awoke to find your people suddenly living among us."

"Is the Blight a remnant of one of those weapons they used against each other? And the morghaests?"

"The *aelo tai* were the one great creation that Polnedra and Gleomere cooperated on. Living gems that could store and act upon information and control other systems. Polnedra's faction used them to shape the planet, acting through uncountable tiny living machines that they sowed throughout the rock and dirt. Gleomere's faction used them to open doorways onto other worlds and begin settling them as new homes for the offspring of this world. Both were corrupted and turned into weapons. The *aelo tai* were infected with a disease that spread from one to another causing them to malfunction, and to cause madness in those who worked with them. They spread dissension and conflict throughout society and eventually forced us to abandon our cities. The tiny living machines were subverted with instructions to disassemble any machine more complex than simple tools. It became known as the Dust, and it spread through all of our worlds, destroying all that Gleomere had created until all of the settlements on other worlds were abandoned and all our people retreated to our home world before the doorways between the worlds collapsed."

"And the morghaests?"

"Those came much later. Your own Jonan Gremm created them. He found several functioning *aelo tai* and was trying to open a doorway to return to his home. When others tried to take those *aelo tai* for themselves, he found a way to change the Dust, to give it instructions to take a humanlike form, and fashioned it into an army to defend himself from his attackers."

"Did he have a black *aelo tai*?"

"I do not believe so. He had recovered two of them, one red and one yellow, the two which would anchor each end of a doorway."

"A red one? Was that the one I brought with me?"

"It is possible, but that one might have been one that was left on another world as well. If it is the same one, then he succeeded in opening a doorway."

Questions were crowding faster than I could voice them, but we were interrupted by a sharp sound. One of the pods had cracked open. A half dozen small creatures dropped out to sit dazed for a moment before scampering off. They resembled the *stith* that we had seen in the forest, but they also resembled miniature versions of our host. I had a sudden chill. "Are all of the animals on this planet like the *elt* and the *ongar*? Do they … Are they?"

"Yes, if by animal you mean the motile forms. They ensure that new generations of sessile forms are planted to continue the species. Those vines are *lethorn* that just released immature *leth*. They'll forage and mature for a number of years, and those that survive will take their place among us as Kir Leth, or Cray Leth or another of the People. I may have understood the words wrongly, but I have always equated your word plant with sessile, and your word animal with motile. Are they not so for you? In truth, we have long wondered what your sessile form is, for we've never seen you emerging, and you plant and raise so many sessile forms that we could not tell which were your offspring."

I was boggling at this. The Kir Leth were intelligent plants? No, intelligent seed pods. Evolution had taken a very different road on this planet. The motile forms, as Perrhen called them, had diversified into all the niches filled by Earth's animal kingdom. Our urge was to go forth, mate, and raise children. Their urge was to go forth and plant. That would have shaped their culture very differently. No wonder Gilwyr had had an identity problem. As I thought this, my loss washed back over me, tinged with guilt that I had forgotten it, even for a moment.

"What is wrong?" asked Perrhen. "Your skin words are faint, but still visible. You just felt the thing you call sadness, didn't you?"

"I am missing Gilwyr," I said. Ox and Bridocke looked downcast at the reminder.

"She lies nearby, would you like to see her?"

"Yes, I would." I wasn't sure whether that was entirely true, but I couldn't say no. Perrhen lead us on a winding path down the tree until we were standing on the ground again.

We entered one of the few ground-level dwellings that I had seen. This one was made by a tree-like plant that stood high above the ground on twisted roots. The roots twined around the base counter-clockwise to make a dense plait of interlocking strands that formed a tight and strong enclosure. The roots divided only enough to make a single entrance to the interior. If this was a house, it was one that was grown and not built.

Within was a tank with transparent sides, which was filled with a glowing liquid. This had some similarities to the tanks in which we had awoken, but had a more crystalline quality to the fluid inside as if it were internally divided into facets that reflected and refracted the sourceless light. Suspended in this illumination was Gilwyr, naked and hairless as we had been. Her face was peaceful and the sores that had marked her were gone. I wondered if this were some sort of preservative solution, where they had repaired or covered her imperfections so she could be presented for funerary visits by her friends. Gathering tears made her image swim and blur before my eyes. I fell to my knees with warring feelings of being able to see her one last time like this, and the cruelty of seeing her floating so perfectly before us as if she could just resume breathing at any instant. I couldn't believe that she was gone …

Then I realized that her green eyes had opened and were looking into mine across the barrier that separated us. I placed my hand against the side of the crystalline tank. After a moment, Gilwyr moved her hand to touch the opposite side. She had a look of wonder on her face. The look of someone who hadn't expected to wake up again.

"Perrhen," I croaked.

"Yes?"

"You told me that she died."

"She did. Her heart had stopped and she was growing cold by the time we got her in the tank. Oh … Oh my. Did you think it was permanent?"

I couldn't answer. Ox supplied, "In our experience, it generally is."

"I must have caused you great distress. I am so sorry for that. However, some of the distress is not misplaced."

"What do you mean?"

"We have repaired her damaged cells and organs. We cannot, however, do the same for her *wythe*, her thoughts and memories. Some may have fallen beyond recall, others may be jumbled. She may not be the same person you remember.

Gilwyr raised her hand out of the crystalline solution. I grasped it in mine. "I don't care," I said. "I'll take it."

CHAPTER 40

Recovering Memories

WE HELPED GILWYR out of the tank. She clung to me, soaking the front of my robe with the viscous fluid. I didn't care. It helped me confirm that this wasn't another dream, that she wasn't about to dissolve away in a pile of goo, or gore, or sand or whatever my cruel imagination might conjure. She felt the same as before, hard and wiry, deadly muscle overlaid with a thin layer of female softness. She smelled the same, though the scent of her hair was missing. (Dreams didn't have scents, did they? I couldn't recall ever smelling something in a dream.) A faint organic smell from the drying fluid from the tank overlaid hers.

She twisted, looking around at the three human faces. Her brow furrowed as she studied each of us. She looked back at me, running fingertips over the contours of my cheek and nose, and brushing one hand over the left eye, with its baleful red crystal gaze. Then she caught sight of Perrhen and pushed away from me so that she could make Kir Leth signs on her skin. Perrhen "listened" for a moment, then translated, "She says that you look familiar to her, but she doesn't know who you are. She doesn't remember your names. She doesn't remember how to speak your language. Some of this will come back to her, some of it she will have to re-learn."

I pointed to her and said, "Gilwyr."

"G-il-wyr. Gil-wyr. Gilwyr." Something came back to her as she rolled the name around.

I pointed to myself and said, "Stenn."

"Stenn?" Just a hint of question. A flicker of something almost remembered.

I repeated the drill for Ox and Bridocke. "Ox?" She smiled warmly. "Brid-ocke?" She sounded uncertain. It seemed that her memory was most ragged for the more recent acquaintances.

Perrhen flashed some skin words at her along with a few spoken words. She signed a vigorous response. "I asked if she was hungry. She said she is ravenous, as I would expect. Let us go and replenish her body; it will feed her *wythe* as well."

A robe was waiting for her. She looked at it with puzzlement, looking at how we were attired and at Perrhen, who was not. She set the robe aside and ignored it. I picked it up and carried it for her. We ascended to another platform where we found more food set out for us. I wondered what unseen network provided food whenever it was desired. Gilwyr ate voraciously, while the rest of us nibbled at our favorite bits. I avoided the fruit with the seeds like caviar, as much as I liked the taste. The thought of the little spiders hatching from the fruit was still turning my stomach. After a moment, it occurred to me that each of these foods could have a motile form that was equally repulsive. I put my food down.

A juvenile leth scampered up onto the table and seized a bit of fruit. Perrhen shooed it away casually.

"Don't you take care of your juveniles?" I asked.

"No, they need the winnowing to select the fit and the cunning among them. If we fed them, too many would survive, and we would be out of balance. Our civilization collapsed several times before we learned that lesson."

"But you tend the pods that produce them, don't you?"

"Of course. That is the phase of Selection. We plant many seedlings, then cull all but the strongest. After the juveniles are released, that is the phase of Chance. There is both philosophy and pragmatism in this way."

"When I studied here," said Ox, "I remember the teachings said there were four phases. I didn't know then that it reflected your cycle of life so closely. What were the other two phases? I can no longer remember them."

"Before Selection comes Persuasion, and after Chance comes Determination. Determination is when the juvenile becomes an adult and is able to make judgments of reason. Persuasion is when we exchange the code of life to start new sprouts that will be selected and tended for growth."

"Why do you call it Persuasion?"

"Is it not so for you? When we accept the code of life, it brings with it the worldview of the donor. It changes us as an individual. Generally, the changes are small and mixed from many donors, but from time to time a strong-willed individual can sway many Leth to their way of seeing. Polnedra and Gleomere were two such ones, as was Venn, who ended their conflict and healed our people."

This recalled an image to my mind. "The five statues at the entrance to the Silent City!"

"Yes, they are the statement of Venn's philosophy. You must see the truth, hear the truth, breath the truth, speak the truth, and reveal the truth."

I remembered what I had seen yesterday. "The puffs of smoke, or powder, in the air around the council yesterday, reddish-brown in color ..."

"Two conversations were going on. In skin words, they were discussing what it meant to have another visitor from the stars, what the change of rule in Dalactus might mean to our people and the reactions to your use of the *aelo tai*. In their breath, they were playing notes on the level below words: desires and fears, opportunities and dangers. Mostly these are age-old positions; they are always seeking to tip the consensus a few degrees in one direction or another. With your tidings, however, a full-scale struggle broke out among them. The Kir Leth, who are by far the most numerous of us, and I count myself as among their number, were concerned with maintaining balance in the face of these disruptive influences. The Tam Leth see the possibility of reclaiming the Silent City now that the Blight has been removed. The Cray Leth wish to reassert their influence on the world. The Lyr Leth believe we should open commerce with your people."

"But the Lyr Leth seat was empty yesterday."

"They are the heirs of Gleomere, as the Kir Leth are the heirs of Polnedra. They forfeited their council seat after the war, but some still live among us. To continue, there has been a storm of Persuasion among the people that hasn't been seen within living memory. The memory crystals confirm that there has not been this much dissent since the end of the wars. That dissent was finally ended by Venn, the greatest Persuader. I do not know who would be his equal today."

"How does one become Lyr Leth, or Cray, or Kir?" I asked. "Is it a caste you are born into? Or is it like joining a political party or a club?"

"There are several of those words I don't know," said Perrhen, "but I can still answer. The Persuasion in the air is assimilated into your code of life when it is first assembled. If there isn't one that is entirely dominant, you may later choose the People with whom you feel the greatest affinity. Philosophers still debate how much free will one has in this choice, and I was fascinated to find that your language had the same nebulous concept of free will in it. One tends to stay with the same People for life unless a great Persuader comes along who can change the allegiances of others. More than allegiances, changing People changes your very identity."

Gilwyr suddenly spoke. "I am Cray Leth." She simultaneously signed the words against her skin.

"You did become Cray Leth," Perrhen acknowledged. "Even though your heritage is human." Patterns flashed across his skin at the same time, very likely the same thought expressed in skin language.

"I am Cray Leth," she repeated.

"As I said, it's a very strong identity," said Perrhen.

"Do you not remember coming to Misthaven with me to learn how to be human?" asked Ox.

Gilwyr wrinkled her brow. "No."

"Even this is more than I had hoped for," said Perrhen. "It is a good sign that she remembers language and a least one of the people she chose."

"What can we do for her?" asked Bridocke.

"Tell her of places, people, events, experiences. Help her recall them before they fade further."

"We'll do that. We should start right away."

Perrhen bowed, which I took for acquiescence. We cut short the tour of Cloudhaven and were conducted to rooms carved into a cliff. Perrhen told us that these would be our quarters now and that he hoped we would find them more suitable than the platform we had occupied the previous night.

We spent the rest of the afternoon talking with Gilwyr. We sat, while Gilwyr moved slowly around the room examining the few objects that were about. Ox started in recalling the first time he had seen her. "Do you remember when I first came to Cloudhaven? You were probably twelve or thirteen years old. You scampered around the trees like a *stith*. At first, you wouldn't speak to me, though you were so curious to see someone else with only two hands. You thought you were the only one in the world." Gilwyr was looking at her hands now as if she had never seen them before. "After a while, you would come near and draw skin words for me. I didn't understand them then; I didn't even know they were language. I spoke to you about human cities and human families. I told you of my travels. I asked you where you came from and whether you remembered your parents. You listened but didn't answer.

"I asked the Kir Leth how you came to be there. They told me that your parents were given conduct into Cloudhaven, to *Wys Talayan*," Gilwyr's fingers traced the sign of *Wys Talayan* on her skin as he said this, "and given sanctuary here. I believe their names were Locke and Bear. Do you remember them? Do you remember your parents?"

Gilwyr became agitated. "I am Cray Leth," she said again.

"Perrhen showed me a picture of them," Ox continued. "Your mother had long yellow hair and was quite beautiful. Do you remember her?"

"*Sintria ...*" said Gilwyr wistfully.

"And Bear was probably about my size, with shaggy reddish hair and a full beard. Do you remember your father?"

"I am Cray Leth! I have only mother!" Now she was angry, and I was glad that she didn't have a sword at hand. I recalled that she had gotten upset once before when I had enquired about her father. Something suddenly dawned on me. "Ox, I don't think the Kir Leth have fathers," I said. "They're born from pods." Gilwyr must identify with her adopted people so strongly that she rejected what didn't fit. She couldn't deny that she had only two hands, but she could deny that she had a father.

Ox went on talking, steering the topics toward subjects that wouldn't upset Gilwyr. He spoke about how he stayed nearly a year, studying the Kir Leth language and philosophy. He also taught Gilwyr Dalactyn and Anglich and told her of the human world. At the end of his stay, he attempted to persuade Gilwyr to return to Dalactus with him. She refused, saying that she needed to complete her training to be accepted as Cray Leth, her chosen people. Ox returned when she was in her sixteenth year. She had completed her trials and was free to go if she wished. This time when Ox set out from *Wys Talayan*, Gilwyr accompanied him.

Ox told some tales of her years at the University. She had misinterpreted Ox's explanation of the customs of wearing clothes and had appeared at the first dinner without them. Ox had hustled her away, but not before two other students had suffered broken arms for putting their hands where they didn't belong. Neither she nor Ox told the others of her upbringing, so it was widely assumed that she was a feral child, the orphan of a failed homestead on a distant frontier. Those students who attempted to harass her found that she was a match for any ten of them, so they left her alone.

In classes, she found delight in the written word and devoured literature and history. In mathematics, she was thought to be slow, until she worked out the conversion from the Kir Leth base eighteen system to base ten. After that, she realized that the math teachers had nothing they could teach her, so she moved on. She did well in the sciences, though her views on biology were unorthodox (which meant incorrect, from the professor's perspective). It was politics that she found fascinating, however, and she spent many hours deciphering the forces of desire and power that drove the human system. Ox related that she often came to him to ask for explanations of human motivations. She just memorized these without understanding, as she did for chemical reactions. Despite that, or perhaps because of that, she became astute at political intrigue.

It was no surprise that the Assassin's Guild recruited her. Her Cray Leth philosophy fit theirs perfectly, she was a skilled fighter, and by her second year at the University she could navigate the courts of power and the merchant guilds with ease. Here Ox could say little more since she had not been able to confide her guild training or missions to him.

Ox paused to pour a drink from a pitcher of nectar that our hosts had left for us. "Thirsty work, all that talking," he observed. "Too bad the Kir Leth have never learned the making of wine. I would wager that this would ferment nicely if barreled properly with some good yeast. I got the impression that alcohol is poisonous to them, though, so they go to great lengths to ensure that it doesn't. Stenn, why don't you take over for a while? Tell her of how she trained you."

"Well, yes. I guess I can." I felt self-conscious talking about it. It felt personal, but I didn't think I could ask Ox and Bridocke to leave. "Do you remember when I was your apprentice, Gilwyr? I had never held a sword before you handed me the training blade."

"I train you?" she interrupted. It was the first reaction she had had since the mention of her parents.

"Yes, you did. Do you remember, back in Misthaven?"

"No." A flat denial. She didn't remember. But, "I am Cray Leth. I train you, you Cray Leth also." Her intonation turned this halfway into a question.

I thought back to that first morning, watching her perform her katas in the dawn mist. "You told me that I was Cray Leth even before you trained me."

She looked around. "Where is my sword?" She reached over her shoulder to the place she most often wore it. Not finding it there, she became agitated. "Where?" She made a sharp sign across her skin: a demand? She threw the small pile of blankets aside, looking underneath. "Where?" She pushed frantically through the food and drink on the table, knocking much of it to the ground. "Where!"

"Peace, Gilwyr," said Ox. "I'll ask for it."

Ox strode out the door. A Kir Leth had been standing there unbeknownst to us, completely camouflaged against the background. He smoothly intercepted Ox, bowing as if asking how he might serve. Words flashed across his skin punctuated with a few spoken words. Ox replied in kind, signing and speaking a request. The first response was fairly clear: "We regret that your swords are not available right now." Ox persisted in his request, speaking more at length. Finally, the guard cordially invited Ox to wait inside while he went to find out what could be done. Ox stepped back inside, saying, "I explained that we needed swords to use in the healing process for Gilwyr. I don't think he understood why, but he promised to try."

"That establishes one thing at least," I remarked drily. "The Kir Leth have no sense of the absurd."

Ox chuckled. "Indeed. I have never seen the slightest bit of humor from them. You see it as absurd to ask for a weapon to use for healing, but they see it only as contradictory. Don't try either irony or sarcasm with them. They'll simply misunderstand."

"Are they holding us prisoners?" asked Bridocke. "He seemed more like a guard than a servant."

"I don't know," said Ox uneasily. "They might not want us wandering off and getting lost, but I feel much more closely watched than I did on my previous visits."

"There's one thing I've been wondering, Ox," I said. "You've been referring to them all as Kir Leth, but that's only one of their names for themselves."

"They do refer to themselves collectively as Kir Leth in spoken words. The skin words for the two usages have different shades of color. In the skin-signing language that we have to use, it is represented like this." He drew an ovoid with pointy ends on the table with a finger, then a second one where he traced the bottom line twice. "That first symbol is the word for their clan, the second is for their entire race. In skin words, the first word is a lighter ochre than the second."

"And the word Leth by itself?"

"They use Kir Leth," he drew the double-lined symbol, "where we would say human or Humanity. They use Leth where we would say people or person."

I noticed that Gilwyr was drawing the pointed oval repeatedly on the skin below her left collarbone, and topping it with a mark like an acute diacritic. Ox followed my gaze and remarked, "And that is the skin word for Cray Leth."

"You said clan …"

"I've never gotten a clear grasp of what they mean, other than that they are very important to them. Sometimes when they use the terms, they sound something like a clan. Sometimes they sound like trades or professions. Sometimes they sound like competing philosophies or religions."

"From what we have just learned of their biology, perhaps the word 'clade,' meaning 'branch,' is more fitting."

Ox nodded. "That does seem appropriate."

Second sight informed me that two swords were approaching us. I could tell that they weren't the ones we had brought with us. A moment later, a tall Leth walked through the door holding two training swords. Even through the sheaths, second sight told me that they were blunted. The Leth was wearing crossed leather baldrics, currently without sheath or sword but obviously meant for that purpose. I took that to mean this individual was Cray Leth.

He bowed, clasping the practice swords to his chest in one hand, then holding them out to Ox. He flashed skin words but also spoke in halting Dalactyn. "Here are swords for practice. Sir Grey-land-er, you hold honor for these others?"

"Yes, I will vouch for the honor of Stenn and Bridocke. You trained Gilwyr yourself, Aymer, and she has always conducted herself as you taught her."

Aymer looked Gilwyr in the eye. "Gilwyr not the same person." He turned brusquely and left.

I looked at her. "Do you remember him?"

"No," she whispered. But a tear gleamed in the corner of her eye.

CHAPTER 41

Sword Therapy

I ACCEPTED THE training swords from Ox and offered one to Gilwyr. "Do you remember how to use this?" I asked.

Gilwyr grasped the sword by the hilt, feeling the weight and balance of the weapon. She looked at it curiously, running a finger down the blade. I felt a creeping disappointment that even this didn't trigger memories. Suddenly she whirled, slicing viciously toward my neck, stopping a hairsbreadth short of contact. Second sight warned me, so I didn't flinch or react but held her eyes steadily with mine. "Yes," she hissed. Behind me, I heard belated gasps from Ox and Bridocke.

"Good. Let us go outside and practice," I said.

Gilwyr dropped her sword. "Yes."

I led the way out and remembered not to be startled when the guard outside materialized from the background. I wondered how many others might be nearby but unseen. Unless they carried some metal, I would be unable to detect them.

We faced off on open ground outside. Gilwyr settled into absolute stillness. From many drills, I knew what she was saying inside. *Clear your mind. Let your thoughts be quiet. They only distract. Do not focus on your opponent. Fill yourself with everything around you, the terrain, the light, the wind, opponents, and allies. Know everything that can help or hinder you so you can use them.* I did the same.

She blurred into motion, crossing the ground between us in three strides. She started with a forehand cut which I beat down, a backhand return which I blocked, then a pivot and an uppercut, which I deflected. Second sight kept me easily anticipating her moves. I played a purely defensive game, both trying to let her remember herself and taking a measure of her condition. She was less subtle in her moves than she had been, and a good deal weaker in the force of her attacks. I hoped that training and exercise would restore her.

We circled and sparred for perhaps ten minutes, working up a sweat. I could tell that I had not regained my strength after my sickness, and Gilwyr was flagging badly. My robe was far from ideal for such fencing. It allowed freedom of movement, but it billowed annoyingly around me as I moved. Gilwyr was unencumbered by clothes, which in itself could be a distraction. I had learned early in my career as an apprentice that if I allowed myself even one second to contemplate her beauty, the next second I would be contemplating the dust on the ground at close range.

Gilwyr was becoming frustrated that she hadn't been able to land a blade on me in all of her attempts. With second sight I was able to parry every attack before she even launched it. She could not miss that I had had a number of openings that I had failed to take advantage of. I didn't want to embarrass her by winning too easily, nor by throwing the match. I started hoping that Ox would notice and call a halt on some pretext.

Gilwyr launched a ferocious assault that forced me to draw my guard close. I saw each one of her strokes and deftly blocked them. I didn't see her ankle wind itself in the fabric of my robe as she stepped close, not until she suddenly yanked backward with her leg, throwing me on my back on the ground. She landed atop me, driving the breath from my lungs, and I found her inches from my face with her blade across my throat. "Do not toy with me, warlock!" she snarled.

"I am not," I got out past a constricted windpipe. "You need to regain your strength."

"You took my strength."

"Gilwyr, you were dead a few hours ago. It takes time to recover from that."

"Dead?"

"Yes, I carried you here, up the mountain. Don't you remember?"

"No."

She rolled off me and sat up. "I could not strike you. My blade moved as you wished. A warlock's trick."

"No, I could *see* your blade. I can see where you will strike before you do."

"Can you teach me to do that?"

"I don't know how. Even if I could, would you give up your eye for that ability?"

She looked at the *aelo tai* in my eye, then looked away. She did not answer.

I got to my feet and held out my hand. She did not take it but got back to her feet on her own. It was not quite a snub, it was not quite a refusal of help; it was a statement that she would do this her way. She didn't have the grace and balance that she had before. I hoped that she would regain those.

Bridocke complimented Gilwyr on her swordsmanship. Bridocke meant well, but Gilwyr threw the practice sword in the dirt and stalked away.

"Don't mind her," I told Bridocke. "I was going easy on her, and she caught me at it. My mistake."

"Yet she threw you in the end."

"Because she didn't use her sword. She couldn't touch me with her sword, and that angered her."

"How could a trained assassin not be able to touch you? You did block every stroke, though sometimes only barely, and with no great finesse or style."

In the weeks of travel, I had not explained second sight to Bridocke. At first, I wasn't sure whether to trust her and later because it just hadn't come up. We hadn't engaged with any enemies on the road, and I had refrained from using it when we had engaged in practice bouts. Now, I was stung by her remark about finesse.

I ripped a strip of cloth from the bottom of my robe. The length was a vulnerability that I wanted to avoid anyway. I made a note to ask for proper trousers from our hosts. Surely they could "grow" those too. I tied the cloth around my eyes, picked up Gilwyr's discarded sword, and extended it to Bridocke.

"I'm over here."

I pivoted a quarter turn and extended the sword toward the sound of her voice. I could see the sword on the ground, but had lost track of Bridocke. Once she took the sword, I could track her.

I felt her hesitantly take the sword from my hand. "What are you doing?"

"You won't be able to touch me either."

"You can't be serious," she said. I heard Ox chuckle; he had seen this demonstration before.

I raised my sword and tapped it against hers. "I'm entirely serious. How many bruises would you like to prove it?"

She dropped into a defensive pose, hesitant to attack a blindfolded person. Using second sight alone I pressed an attack. Lunge, forehand, recover, backhand, uppercut. Each time I could see that she would block me, each time our blades met with a clang. It was harder to press an attack by second sight than it was to defend. I had to guess where her body was from the position of her sword. I let my imagination fill it in as if it were a simulation. I knew what stance she should take, so her arm should be here, her body in line, her feet just so … I stepped inside her guard and landed a blow on her forearm.

Bridocke yelped and stepped back. She clearly hadn't expected that.

One bruise was enough, however, and she stepped back in with greater vigor. Now we had full engagement. I blocked and parried her attacks, and pressed back on the openings afterward. She was unable to land a single blow, while I got through her guard several times. I sidestepped one backhand attack instead of blocking and delivered a light slap on her upper arm. It could have been harder and she knew it. A minute later I landed another on her thigh. She redoubled her efforts for several minutes, showering me with blows. Gilwyr had previously been able to get through my guard even with second sight simply because of her blinding speed. I could see her blows coming and still be unable to block in time. Bridocke was not as fast; nothing got through.

A moment later, it was over. Bridocke over-extended, leaving me an opening. I brought my blade to rest against her exposed neck, a fatal stroke had we fought in earnest with edged weapons. She froze, then dropped her sword. "I yield, sir Warlock."

I pulled off the blindfold, blinking at the return of the light. "You see …" I started, but then my vision rippled. I saw an eye before me, peering into me, looking out through my own eye. "Terrell," I gasped, swaying on my feet. I had forgotten why I had forgone second sight in our practice bouts: I had not wanted to give away our position or intentions to the usurper. Now he and I made full contact. He looked out hungrily through my eye, seeing what I saw; I was looking directly at Bridocke at that instant. I was filled with sudden rage. "Faithless Daughter!" I screamed and raised my sword again, catching Bridocke flatfooted. She nonetheless got her sword up in time as I swung an overhead two-handed blow that would have smashed her skull. She took the full force on her blade, driving her to the ground. My fingers went numb from the impact, though it mattered not at all to my possessor. I raised my sword again ready to plunge it down through Bridocke's heart, Terrell apparently not realizing that it was a blunt practice weapon.

I was tackled from my blind side and went down in a heap. My blade flew from my hands, arcing through second sight like a crimson dragonfly. I could tell from the touch of bare skin that Gilwyr had returned just in time. I turned my face to the dirt so that Terrell could see no more of my surroundings. I especially didn't want him to see Ox, or get a clue about where we were. I fought to regain control of my limbs. A puppet master was trying to pull on invisible strings, but this puppet still had muscles and will to resist. Fixing that metaphor in my mind, I pulled each string until it snapped, letting one limb at a time go limp and stop resisting Gilwyr. I gave the eye peering into my mind a final boot, imagining that it was a rough, hob-nailed boot for good measure.

I tried to speak, spit out some dust and tried again. "I'm ok, you can let me up now." Now that I was able to pay attention once more, it felt like more than one person was holding me down.

"Not likely," came Bridocke's voice.

"I think it would be wise to restrain you for the moment," said Ox more temperately. "We should ask the Kir Leth if they have any knowledge of this strange linkage."

"I can't argue that it wouldn't be wise, even if it's the last thing I want. Put my blindfold back on as well."

I felt the blindfold being tied back on first. They seemed at a loss for something to use to bind my hands until they found what felt like a supple vine. I heard a few clinks as the practice swords were gathered up, but I refrained from reaching for second sight. I didn't want to unleash Terrell's demon on myself again.

At length, I was helped up and walked back into the cave. I existed in the tentative limbo to which the insane and infirm are relegated. Conversation occurred around me but didn't include me. "Was he normal when he sparred with you?" I heard Ox ask. "What is normal?" asked Gilwyr, a reasonable question from the recently dead. Nothing had been normal for some time. "He suddenly changed at the end of our bout," said Bridocke. "I was fighting him, then I saw the face of your brother, the usurper, in his place. That's when he tried to kill me."

I drifted with the conversation, not offering any commentary. I felt a loss of self after Terrell's attempted takeover of my body, which was exacerbated by the isolation of my blindfolded quarantine. Did I really have any free will? The Other had manipulated me into this voyage, the Void Guild had dropped me onto this planet, the morghaests had eaten my equipment, stranding me in this backward culture. I had bobbed along in the wake of the storm named Gilwyr, been thrust into the trade of assassin and the role of warlock, had my body colonized by alien gemstones, and found myself in the retinue of a prince in exile, while his evil brother tried to invade my mind. Where had I signed up for any of this?

I heard a new voice. It was the sonorous voice of Perrhen saying that he had a report of fighting amongst us. Ox gave a summary of events, then I felt them pulling off my blindfold. I turned my head away from them so that neither Ox nor Perrhen were in my field of view. If my mind were invaded again, I didn't want to compromise my friends or the Kir Leth. Perrhen came near and asked me what had happened.

"I told you in the Silent City about the red *aelo tai* that Terrell stole from me. We tried to take it back from him in Dalactus, but he had made a fake one, and we got that one instead. He still has the real one."

"I see. We wondered about the red stone in your luggage. We had concluded that there was no real *aelo tai* and that you had only had a forgery of one. We were mistaken, it seems."

"He has been trying to determine the use of the *aelo tai*. He stares obsessively into it, and from time to time makes contact with the fragment in my eye. I have shut him out every time before so that he couldn't see who I was with or where I was, but this time he caught me off guard. He saw Bridocke through my eye and flew into a rage, for she betrayed him by siding with Ox. His desire to kill her was so strong that he was able to take control of me. I almost did kill her before Gilwyr saved her by knocking me down."

After asking some more questions, Perrhen disappeared for a time then came back with another Leth, whom he introduced as Rhadmner, a member of the Mir Leth. Rhadmner didn't seem to speak our language but gestured that he wanted to examine my left eye. I gave him leave to look all he wished. He studied it carefully for a time, using a small and ordinary looking lens. Then he produced a flat oval stone of translucent turquoise. He passed this in front of my eye several times, then held it up to his own eye. I could see symbols floating inside, which made it appear to be a sort of diagnostic device.

"I thought that you said that Mir Leth were mystics?" I asked Perrhen.

"I believe that is the right word in your language. They think deep thoughts of tapestries of numbers and symbols that fold through space and time. They tell us that our shallow world is but a solitary strand in that tapestry, a set of equations that have been solved for only a single set of values. They may sit for days at a time staring into these inner spaces in search of truth."

"That sounds more like a mathematician to me."

"Yes, that's another word for them."

Rhadmner spoke to Perrhen in their language. Perrhen translated to me, "Rhadmner says that your gem is very unusual. He's never seen one quite like it. It's not entirely an *aelo tai* of the sort we make, but it has some points of similarity."

"I think the *aelo tai* merged with some machines that I already had implanted in my eye. Those implants allowed me to record and store information and to communicate with our information systems."

"I'm not sure of all of those words, but it may be that the gem in your eye is a hybrid of your *implants* and our *aelo tai*. The *aelo tai* perform similar functions."

"I see."

"Rhadmner is going to show you some words. You should memorize these."

Rhadmner displayed on his skin a hollow sky blue circle with a vertical yellow line that bore spikes resembling horns at the top. "This word should block the communication with other *aelo tai*. You can use it if Terrell contacts you again."

Another word appeared, a folded moth, the color of butter. "This word does the opposite, it unblocks communication."

"I just think of these, and they work?"

"You must hold them in your mind and verbally speak the word *aeleonshii*."

"Good, a failsafe. Let me try turning this off." I tried to recall the first image, deciding it looked like the Greek letter *phi* with horns. When I thought I had it right, I said, "*aeleonshii*."

I couldn't feel any change. "How can I tell if it worked?"

Perrhen consulted with Rhadmner. "You should feel a pulse in response."

"I didn't. Please show me the first symbol again." I studied it carefully. "How accurate do I have to be with the colors?"

"Reasonably accurate. If the blue is a little lighter, you will merely be speaking with an accent, but if it is the blue of twilight, it is a different word."

Noticing the resemblance to *phi* probably distorted my recall to look more like the Greek letter than it did. I tried to let *phi* go and memorize the proportions and colors of this symbol. Then I closed my eyes and said "*aeleonshii*."

This time I felt a distinct pulse, a blip of red pressure that emanated from the gem in my eye socket and echoed inside my skull. I practiced a few more times; then once I was sure that I could turn it off, I practiced the word to turn it on. When Perrhen and Rhadmner were confident that I had learned to control my gem, Perrhen turned to my companions and said, "I believe you can unbind him now. Terrell should no longer be able to get to you through him."

"I'm not sure we should trust him," said Bridocke. "He has acted erratically before this. He has summoned morghaests and moved mountains, and when he has done these things, he becomes a different person for a time. I think he poses a danger to you, Ox."

"And yet he saved my life in Misthaven and Dalactus, got us all out of the Silent City, and saw the danger in Tykenkote Castle before it killed us all. I think he deserves our assistance in bearing his burden."

Gilwyr, silent until now, spoke unexpectedly. "I trust. I will watch … Stenn."

Perrhen and Rhadmner took their leave, Perrhen saying that the Council seemed to have some urgent business and could not meet with us yet. That left us little to do but sit outside our cave as the day waned, engaging in desultory conversation. I was pleased that Gilwyr spoke up a few times and seemed to remember a few more words than she had in the morning. Ox and I related the story of the treachery in the garden of the Mayor's palace in Misthaven that had resulted in Gerard's death. Bridocke had not heard the full story and was newly incensed at Terrell's machinations. Gilwyr listened closely as if straining after memories, but shook her head when asked if she recalled the fight.

Eventually, Ox and Bridocke yawned and said they would turn in. I said I would sit out a little longer, wanting a bit of time that contained only Gilwyr and me. Gilwyr moved to sit next to me, and we watched Rhea rise above the treetops in silence, immense and nearly full. A storm was beginning to gather, however, and shreds of cloud began to stretch across Rhea's ruddy face. Gilwyr leaned into me and shivered. I put my arm around her, thinking she was cold. She stayed like that for so long that I thought she had gone to sleep.

Fat drops of rain began spattering around us. I stood up, lifting her in my arms. She was still much lighter than she had been, though not as wasted away as during the trek up the mountainside. She hung on to my neck as I carried her inside and laid her on the bed. I dropped my robe and lay down behind her, pulling the blanket over both of us.

She wasn't quite asleep. "I remember … this," she said. She squirmed around and clung tightly to me. "I feel empty. All I have left are shreds."

"You've remembered a lot already today. We'll help you fill in the rest."

"Is it the same if I remember … or you tell me? Is what I remember real? Or a story?"

"I don't think any of us really knows that."

CHAPTER 42

Darkness

I WOKE WITH the first light of dawn and the sudden draft of Gilwyr leaving the bed. I saw her make her way to the door, picking up one of the practice swords that stood nearby. I arose to follow her, picking up the second sword as I left.

Outside, I saw Gilwyr silhouetted against the disk of Rhea, which had crossed the sky while we slept. It was setting into the trees in the west as the sky lightened in the east with the coming of the sun. The rain had stopped and the sky had cleared, though the moss on the ground was sodden, squelching under every footstep.

As I approached Gilwyr, she was in a position of stillness, standing erect, one foot slightly advanced before the other, sword held straight out towards Rhea in a two-handed grip. I stopped twenty paces behind her and waited. The minutes dragged on, while Rhea settled perceptibly into the trees. I began to become concerned that this was a much longer meditation than she customarily held before starting her katas.

After a few more minutes of this pose, Gilwyr lowered her sword until the tip touched the ground. She hung her head, her shoulders slumped, and I heard a sob. I strode quickly to her side and grasped her shoulders. "Gilwyr, what is it?"

"I know I am supposed to do something, but I do not remember how to do it."

"At least you remembered to do your practice. How to do it will come back to you. Every morning you get up, and you practice a set of movements with your sword. 'Dances to Rhea' you call them. There's a different one for each day. I'm sorry, but I've never learned them, so I can't help you remember the steps."

She raised her sword again, then lowered it. "The steps are no longer in me."

I stepped out of my robe, emulated her stance and tried to remember at least how she started. "Try moving a few steps with me. Maybe your muscles will remember even if your head does not." I held my sword out towards Rhea and tried to remember the last time I had seen her perform. I raised my sword slowly towards vertical and advanced my right foot, sinking into a lunge. Out of the corner of my eye, as well as in second sight, I could see her follow me. "Very good, keep going, what's the next step?"

Her sword trembled and then dropped again. "I don't remember!"

I was stuck because I didn't know the next step either. "Let's start again, maybe it will come to you with repetition."

We resumed the starting pose. I could see her sword in second sight, held straight and steady. At least she was trying. Just then, I saw a ghostly red sword in second sight, off in the trees at the top of a nearby rise. For a moment, I was puzzled. The sword and its bearer kept their position, so they did not seem to be a threat. The sword was held in the same ready pose as we held, starting to rise to the vertical. I realized that someone else was doing the morning sword ritual. I could copy the movements of the other practitioner and help Gilwyr through the steps. I timed my motions to follow it, and Gilwyr followed mine. After the lunge was assumed, the third blade tracked to the right, and I followed.

This was working, as far as it went, but I could not see the other's body position, only the sword. I remembered imagining Bridocke's form as a simulation that tracked her sword yesterday. I had a sudden inspiration. If the *aelo tai* were analogous to our simspace implants, perhaps it could visualize those movements for me. I fixed in my mind the symbol for Kir Leth that Ox had drawn yesterday, which he said was the color of the ocher that they puffed into the air. Under my breath, I said "*aeleonshii.*"

It worked! Now I could see the form of the distant sword-holder as well as the sword. I moved to adopt the same pose, and Gilwyr followed me. The form in my mind became my guide as movement flowed into movement. Sword extends to the right, then sweeps in a slow arc back to the left. Come out of the lunge and pivot to the left, bring sword in close in a two-handed grip. Lunge again, left foot forward this time, sword extended straight. I followed the unknown practitioner, and Gilwyr followed me. Together we stepped through the motions of the kata, which thankfully didn't have any movements beyond my abilities, as a few that I had seen Gilwyr practice would have. We ended on one knee with swords at salute, then lowered them and stood to face each other.

"I remember, I think. Or maybe I have re-learned?" Gilwyr said. "Perhaps I could do it on my own tomorrow."

"There are forty different katas," I said. "One for each day of Rhea's phases. You go through the cycle nine full times over the course of a year."

She sagged for a moment, then straightened. "Thirty-nine more."

"That's the Gilwyr spirit. You also remember how to subtract."

She came suddenly alert at the approach of the other kata practitioner. I had seen him approaching in second sight and had waited to see when Gilwyr detected him. He had gotten closer than he would have before her death, but her senses were still reasonably sharp, and I could hope for improvement. As the figure came closer, I could see that it was Aymer. Gilwyr bowed deeply to him, and, warned by second sight, I bowed in unison with her. He returned the bow, though not as deeply, which I took as his perception of our relative stations.

"You make new Gilwyr," he said in his fragmented Dalactyn.

"I am training to be strong again, as a Cray Leth trains every day."

"Cray Leth Gilwyr died. You lost Cray Leth."

Gilwyr looked as if he had slapped her in the face. In a way, he had. "But ..." she said.

"You not remember *rhea mellianor* any longer. You followed the moves of this one," he indicated me with a mid-hand, "who followed me." Interesting. I wondered how he knew I was watching.

"I remember it now."

"You learned it again. Not same."

"I will learn them all again."

"Good. Build new Gilwyr. New Gilwyr can take trials, become Cray Leth."

Aymer turned and walked towards the entrance to our cave. I gathered up my robe from the ground, grimacing that it was now sodden as well, and we followed him.

Aymer entered the cave just before we got there. I was going to call out that we had a visitor, but Aymer announced himself by drawing his two long swords and bringing them together in a great crash. Bridocke leaped out of bed and landed in the middle of the floor, stance wide and low. Unarmed and unclothed, she was still ready to grapple with an attacker. Ox sat up in bed, blinking, but not overly alarmed. "So you still take joy in waking slumbering humans, Aymer? Haven't changed a bit."

"I do not know 'joy.'"

"Your loss." Ox climbed out of bed and started putting his robe on.

"The Council summons you. Do not go cloaked before the Council."

"As you wish. As we don't need to get dressed and I don't see breakfast offered, I dare say we are ready to go. We don't even have hair to put in order." He ran his hand over his bald head. "Ah, but that may be remedied soon, I feel stubble already."

"You look less savage without it," observed Aymer. "It is like you allow fungus to take root on your heads."

"Aymer, you are the soul of tact and diplomacy. Lead on."

We followed Aymer down the pathway among the trees where we had met with the Council previously. I ran my hand over my own head and felt the first hairs poking through. More interestingly, I also felt stubble on my face. On Trondhjem it was common to use a modified virus to switch off unwanted hair follicles. I had not shaved since I was a youth, but it looked like a beard was in my future now.

We reached the Council tree and ascended to their platform. Five Council members were already seated in their perches. Aymer indicated that we were to be seated on the mats again as he took his place in the Cray Leth seat among the Council. I had thought that I had faced him on my previous audience with the Council, but I didn't have all of the finer points of telling one Leth from another yet.

The Council did not waste time on ceremony. The Kir Leth member started speaking in skin words. Perrhen translated for us. "We are pleased to see that Gilwyr has rejoined you. We welcome Gilwyr back to her home and wish her to regain wholeness in body and *wythe* after the trial she has endured.

"However, we now have a more urgent matter to speak of. While we welcomed the news that the Blight had been removed from the Silent City by Stenn, we were very concerned that he might have borne the contagion here within him. Yet it appeared that we might have been fortunate that it was insulated by having chosen a host who was only slightly affected by it. Had one of us touched it, it would have completely overwhelmed us, for that is how it is designed. We kept all of you in isolation after that for safety. There were those who advocated destroying Stenn immediately to rid ourselves of the black *aelo tai* forever. However, the records are unclear on whether the *aelo tai* can be destroyed in this fashion or whether we would have unleashed it upon ourselves by the attempt."

I sat, stunned, as I listened to this. Were they really talking dispassionately about deciding whether or not to kill me? Disbelief gave way to anger, an anger that I was certain was wholly my own, and not imparted by the black gem. I wasn't going to go without a fight. I reached through blacksight into the world nearby to assess how quickly I could summon a morghaest.

"However, that question is now moot," continued Perrhen. "The Blight has taken root in Cloudhaven. It entered through the healing tanks in which you recovered from your sickness. We immediately destroyed those tanks and the entire hillside in which they were housed. This was too little and too late; it had already spread into the roots of the system. We are fighting it everywhere it turns up, but we do not know how to eradicate it. Cloudhaven is beginning to die."

My anger was extinguished by that pronouncement. In the silence that followed, Ox said, "This is a tragedy and a disaster for your city. However, now that the Blight has been removed from the Silent City, could you not reclaim it once more?"

"We could not move our parent pods that quickly. The Kir Leth could disperse, but it would be many years before we can re-establish a viable breeding population of pods again. We would be severely diminished before we could bring forth a new crop of juveniles. Moreover, Cloudhaven is the last remaining repository of our knowledge and culture. If our libraries fall to the corruption of the Blight, our entire civilization will be lost. The Kir Leth are contemplating the ending of their time on this world."

You can only know a culture by its ruins. Suddenly my thesis was laid bare as the hollow declaration that it was. Here was a living culture, diminished perhaps from the star-spanning empire that it had once been, but far from laying in ruins. They were Pompeii facing Vesuvius, Rome facing the Goths, New Petrograd facing the unnamed asteroid that had wiped it clean of life. You could make a name for yourself writing papers about what was left afterward, but those were such little embers against the brightly burning fire of a living culture. I was the one who had carried the contagion into their midst. I had condemned this ancient alien race, who had left the cradle of their world before the pyramids were built on old Earth, to death. I owed them everything I had in me; I had to make this right.

"Is there no defense against the Blight?" I asked. "How have you stopped it from infecting Cloudhaven so far?"

"Only by isolation," replied Perrhen, simultaneously speaking skin words to the Council members, presumably translating. "Cloudhaven cut itself off when the rest of our cities fell. We had already sacrificed our gateways to other worlds and pulled back those who had settled there. But the Blight was relentless; when the last city was infected, our people fled here to Cloudhaven. Our ancestors destroyed all of the communication and transportation systems that linked us to the rest of the world. That had been sufficient to stop the spread until an event occurred that we had not anticipated, and a black *aelo tai* was carried here."

"It sounds very much like a malicious simspace program. Our people have almost destroyed our civilization with these on several occasions in the past until we built an immune system into the fabric of simspace."

"Do you know how to create such 'immune systems'?"

"No, I only use them as a tool. I study ... dead cultures."

"You will soon have a chance to study one here."

"Do you not have any among yourselves who know the making of the *aelo tai*? Who might be able to make a cure?"

"No, those studies were abandoned long ago."

"We discovered at Tykenkote Castle that radioactivity blocks *aelo tai* from functioning. Could you use that to sterilize the affected areas of Cloudhaven?"

"I do not know how to translate that word."

"Radioactivity is the energy released when certain heavy elements split into lighter elements."

Perrhen translated this, and a discussion ensued. "And this is what made you sick, is it not?"

I had to acknowledge that.

"It would be a desperate measure. We would likely poison the very things we are trying to save."

"Is there a way to signal my people on other worlds? They may be able to find a cure, or to help you evacuate."

"We have not had such technology since the stars were lost to us. However, the remains of your ancestor's metal ship still lie in the southern desert. There may be equipment there that is serviceable."

I pricked up my ears. "Is that so?"

"I do not know that it would do any good. Even if there is working equipment, and even if the Council allows the contact, we have foresworn this path since the days of Venn. And even if your people were contacted and wished to send help, the Dust would destroy their ships and their equipment, and the morghaests would rise up against them."

The Council continued for some time after that, but no more viable solutions were forthcoming. They released us, and we reminded Perrhen that we had missed breakfast and were ravenous. He assigned a silent Kir Leth to guide us to our quarters and said that there should already be food there. He had another urgent matter to attend to and would join us later.

As we walked back through the forest, Bridocke said, "I understood little, other than this tree city is in mortal danger. It sounded like a hobnob of wizards talking, and our warlock was as incomprehensible as any of them."

Ox was pensive. "How long does it take to fly to a star? Is it like sailing to the far side of the world?"

"Messages can be sent instantly, but only if you have already carried something here from there. It is millions of times farther than sailing around the world, but our ships can sail the distance in a few months."

"I cannot picture how a living person can travel so fast and still survive."

I started to answer, but Gilwyr said, "Look!"

The trees ahead were drooping, their lambswool covering turning brown and brittle on the edges. Spots of slimy rot seemed to be taking hold on their trunks, and a smell of decay hung in the air. It was a discrete patch of forest that was affected, but the trees towards the center were much more decayed than at the edges. I interpreted this to mean that it was spreading. I looked to our Kir Leth guide (or guard) for reaction, but he gave no sign.

"But," Ox continued, "even if our brethren on other worlds can sail that quickly, I fear that it would not be fast enough. It will take us a month to travel from here to the Grimmerroth's Citadel if I remember my maps. If we found devices that still worked after all these years, and if we sent a message that was received immediately, and if they sailed for here immediately, and if they had a cure ready for a disease they have never heard of, then it might not be soon enough. I saw two of the Council exchanging skin words that Perrhen did not translate, and they said that Cloudhaven may have only three or four months until it is consumed by the Blight."

We made our way back to our quarters in silence. There was food there as Perrhen had promised, but we were somehow no longer hungry. We dressed in our robes again, mine only slightly damp now, thankfully. Gilwyr still declined to wear hers, but this seemed entirely natural by now. We ate a small meal and sat around despondently. Our guard had melted into the background after we had arrived. I suspected that he or another were still standing watch, invisible against the background.

I pounded my fists together. "We have to try," I said. The others looked at me in puzzlement. "We can't cure the blight by staying here. We aren't going to be any help in an evacuation. Trying to find Jonan's ship and calling for help may be a slim chance, but it's the only one we have. I think it's our only option."

"Is this about digging up ruins again, sir Warlock?" asked Bridocke. "That was not the best idea at the Morghaest Bridge, and it almost killed us at Tykenkote Castle."

"No, it's about saving Cloudhaven. I can't deny that there is history to be uncovered at the old ship. After all, it is the ship that also brought Ox's direct ancestors to this world. But those can wait; calling for help for Cloudhaven cannot."

"The Dalactyns came from another world? All of the kings from Roland on down?" Bridocke was incredulous. We had discussed this ... no, that was before she joined us. This was a shock to her.

"So it appears," nodded Ox. "I have only learned this recently myself."

"So ... so ... none of you are legitimate rulers! You took the throne from Pandulf and displaced all of the Anglich lords! You are all usurpers, not just your brother!"

"Now, the chronicles say that Pandulf had no heirs and willingly named Roland his successor," said Ox defensively.

"And who wrote the chronicles? Pandulf's descendants? Or Roland's? I'm sure they wrote it in favor of their family."

"Even if you question the first king, the line of descent ever since has been legitimate, and there have been many wise and good kings."

"If the first one isn't legitimate then none of them are."

Gilwyr forestalled the gathering rift between Ox and Bridocke. "We have visitors," she announced, looking out the door.

Perrhen ducked through the door, accompanied by another, who was taller and lankier, as close to "gangly" as I had seen any of their number.

"This is Danallion, a Lyr Leth who has studied among humans for a time. He is one of the few here who can speak your language."

"My road has crossed Gilwyr's a few times before," he said. "If those are memories you left on the far side of death, I am not hurt."

That voice ... that accent ...

"I fear that they are," replied Gilwyr. "I will learn to remember you again."

"And Stenn I have met before as well."

"You're Dan'l! From the library in Misthaven!"

"I think you'll have much to talk about," said Perrhen. "Danallion believes that he has found a possible cure for the Blight."

CHAPTER 43

Quest

"WHAT WERE YOU doing in the library in Misthaven?" I asked.

"Studying human alchemy, as I said to you then. It is a fascinating study; they have many different ways of looking at the processes of nature than we do. Some of the ideas they taught were rather obstinately wrong, though."

"They're struggling to re-learn the knowledge that was lost after they were cut off here and their libraries destroyed."

"I had thought that might be so."

"I only saw you there a few times."

"Shortly before we met, another student encountered me in the library. She started coming back, asking for things that she knew the Librarian would take a long time to find. She wanted to talk with me while he searched. I tried to avoid her, but she would leave a flower on my workbench where I would find it. Then one night she came to the library after hours and found me there. She started taking off her clothes. I'm sure I offended her with my reaction because she started speaking those water words from her eyes as she was leaving. I'll never understand why humans insist on wearing clothes, and then get into such a hurry to take them off again. I decided it was time to come back to Cloudhaven after that."

If Danallion didn't know what the intentions of that student were, I wasn't going to tell him. "Tell us your ideas about fighting the Blight."

"The *aelo tai* have long held fascination for me, but when Perrhen returned with news that you had brought one with you, I sought to learn more. I wished to discover what you had brought and whether it was for good or ill. Much information has been lost over time, sometimes deliberately, but I was able to locate some references that had been hidden. There are few of the greater *aelo tai* in existence anymore, but there are more of the minor ones. Ox had one such on a ring on his finger when last I saw him."

Ox looked in astonishment at Danallion. "That was an *aelo tai*? Like the gem that Stenn found? Like the black one that caused the Blight?"

"Not nearly as complex as those. Some of the minor ones still function, but many of them were created for purposes that no longer exist and are little more than ornaments. That one granted you passage back to Cloudhaven, but also exercised a Persuasion that you not talk about it to other humans."

"But I lost that in Dalactus when we were captured!"

"And still you managed to find *Wys Talayan*? You must have been very persistent."

"It wasn't easy," I muttered. If we had had the ring, would we have reached Cloudhaven in time to save Gilwyr from dying? I tried to put recriminations aside. They wouldn't help now.

"This ring prevented me from talking about this place?" Ox looked distinctly unhappy.

"It was part of your agreement, was it not?"

"I agreed to keep the confidence of my hosts. I kept that agreement out of good faith. I'm disturbed that wasn't deemed sufficient."

"My apologies that you feel that way. I will convey that to those who gave you the ring. I believe that words were not seen in the same color by both sides in that agreement."

I was thinking back on the puzzling behaviors I had seen. Ox's thoughts had strayed every time the conversation had touched on the Kir Leth. Yet after Dalactus, he had been free to tell Bridocke of our destination. And his paintings—they had been his expression of the words he could not speak.

Danallion was continuing, "But the major *aelo tai* were wonderfully sophisticated, and there are some suggestions that, at the peak of their development, they were able to think and talk like a living being."

"Ah," I said. "We call that artificial intelligence. So these crystals are like simspace nodes? Computer systems?"

"A system that computes? As in calculations with numbers? What does that have to do with thinking?"

"I couldn't tell you. Other people studied these things, and I always found it rather tedious when one of them wanted to talk to me after a colloquium."

"In the old archive I found from near the end of our final war, I happened upon an account by one of my own Leth. He believed that the combination of two *aelo tai*, one red and one—what is this color in your language?"

It was a rich yellow-red hue that he displayed on his skin. "I would call it saffron."

"A red one and a saffron one together had properties that could remove the Blight from a black *aelo tai*. The problem was that the Blight defends itself and prevents other *aelo tai* from communicating with the infected one. It would only communicate outwards, to infect others."

"How did he surmount that problem?"

"He did not. But I think we have a unique opportunity now. You have the black *aelo tai* within you and it is connected to your consciousness. You present a path to attack the Blight that it does not have a defense against."

"You're going to use *me* as a back door?"

Danallion looked around. "I'm not sure what this means. We don't build doors. I only learned about them in human settlements."

"It means another way in. An undefended or lightly-defended entrance. It means the same in simspace as it does in a castle."

"I do believe that is a usable analogy."

"Are the colors of the *aelo tai* significant?"

"Yes, they have different configurations corresponding to their functions. Red and saffron were used as the two ends of a portal connecting distant worlds."

"That's why Jonan had a red one! He was trying to create a portal to his home."

"If you found that *aelo tai* on your world, then he must have succeeded, at least briefly."

Perrhen spoke up, after having been silent through the discussion thus far. "Jonan did have one of each. I accompanied him on his search across this land to find them."

"So the saffron *aelo tai* must be …"

"In his citadel in the southern desert!" Ox exclaimed.

"It looks like we still have need of an expedition to go there, but now with a different purpose." I was turning this new development over in my mind.

"But we don't have the red one, either. We only have Terrell's fake," Ox said.

"We'll have to go back to Dalactus to get it. If I have to raise an army of morghaests to tear down the castle to get it, then I'll do just that."

"I would caution you not to do that," said Perrhen. "That is walking on the edge of a crumbling precipice. The likes of Gleomere, Sellen, and Jonan all did so, to their ultimate downfall."

Ox was pensive. I could almost see him weighing the costs of the measures he might employ to regain his throne. "This is why your people choose assassination over war, isn't it?" I asked Perrhen.

"Persuasion and negotiation first, of course, but yes, war is the equivalent of tearing down an entire castle to obtain a single stone."

"When do we leave?" asked Bridocke.

"Right away," I said.

"In about ten days," said Ox simultaneously.

"Why the delay?" asked Bridocke.

"I do not think Gilwyr would willingly stay behind, and she needs time to heal, and to retrain her body and mind. We all need that to some degree. We need to obtain supplies for the trip. And maps. You have been there, Perrhen, do you remember the way?"

"I do, but I will not be making this trip. I am too old to make that journey another time. I think my young friend Danallion will accompany you in my stead. I was a youth of only fifty years, like he is now, when I first met your ancestor while satisfying my wanderlust. Now I'm nearly ten times his age."

"What was Jonan like?" I asked. Did I want to know? I had chased Jonan's tale across the void to this world, only to find that history had recorded him as an evil warlock.

"I can tell that you and he are of the same Leth. He walked his own road, as do you, which sometimes ran through shadowed places. He took few companions with him on those roads but chose wisely. He was more Lyr than you, with more affinity for making things from metal and glass, and less for looking for meaning in legends and histories. But he had your same ability to, as we say, make the leap from the seed to the plant, what you call intuition. Should you ever meet, I think you will find much in common."

"Meet? How would I meet him? He died four hundred years ago."

"That is just time. Time is an illusion, as I've told you."

I decided that we had crossed the boundary from reality into philosophy or metaphysics, and let it drop.

For the next several days we recovered our strength, trained, made lists of supplies, and studied maps. Perrhen told the Council of our plan, and we seemed to have their blessing, or at very least their permission. Perhaps they just wanted us out of their way while they dealt with the disaster that was unfolding. The Blight continued to spread, despite their efforts to contain it.

Aymer took an interest in our training, especially when he found out about my second sight. Apparently, that was an ability unique to the fusion of *aelo tai* and offworld implants. He was able to give me some practice in how best to use that ability to guide a sword fight rather than merely react to my opponent. By the time we were ready to leave, I could avoid getting thrashed by him for several minutes and even occasionally land a glancing blow on him. Something about the way their joints were hinged gave the Kir Leth much greater speed and strength than humans, but with an economy of motion that was breathtaking. That was quite beside having four arms to my two.

I also studied the Kir Leth skin words with Perrhen. I not only had an academic interest in the language, but Ox had demonstrated how useful it was to be able to 'overhear' what they were saying. In private I practiced visualizing the words that I learned, one at a time, and speaking the trigger word *aeleonshii*. Most words did nothing, a few words produced a tentative pulse as if the *aelo tai* almost recognized the word but not quite, and a few had interesting results. I found that I could tune second sight to see more than just metal; I could see wood, or rock, or living things such as people or animals. I could also adjust the amount of time in the future I could see, from present time to a few minutes. I was still convinced that this was a simulation and not real precognition, but it was scarily accurate.

During one of these sessions, I asked Perrhen about a comment he had made earlier about our races having met before.

"We opened portals onto many worlds as we explored," he told me. "Many of these were hostile worlds, not suited for life. Some had the beginnings of life, not very far along the road yet. This has caused some to speculate that the reason we find so little other life in the universe is that we have emerged at the very beginning of the prime conditions for life to develop. It may be that if we can hang on for long enough, eventually we will see a galaxy in which life flowers, and spreads, and eventually lifts up even the galaxy itself to self-awareness."

He pulled out a crystal of light amber color and set it on the table between us. "I was curious about this as well after we talked, and I searched the archives for records to substantiate my suspicion. I found this."

He passed his finger across the crystal, and an image appeared in the air above it. In the image was a forest of trees that looked Earth-like, with brown bark and green leaves. It was night, with light the quality of a full moon illuminating the scene. A bright light flared in the center of the image, blotting all else out with the glare of a sun's heart, leaving blue afterimages in my eye long after it faded away. Standing where the glare had been was a party of Kir Leth, about twenty in number, along with some packs and equipment. They began establishing a camp, hanging a perimeter of lights around, surveying the area, performing unknown tasks with unidentifiable mechanisms. The image skipped ahead to a scene where the camp looked more established, the activity less bustling. The Kir Leth stood in groups, conversing, or perched on tree branches. There was a sudden noise from outside of the circle of the camp. In an instant, the lights were doused, and all of the Kir Leth faded into the background with their camouflage. Two figures came into the clearing, staring around in wonderment. As they came into the moonlight, I could see that they were human, not fully grown, and dressed in simple clothes. One had a bow slung over his shoulder; the other had a knife of medium length in his belt. They quite obviously had seen something, but couldn't detect the Kir Leth standing in silence and completely blended with their backgrounds. After a while, they moved on, and the scene faded out.

"Those looked like bronze-age humans," I said. "Was that Earth?"

"I don't know the name of the planet or the coordinates. The portals take no account of distance or direction so it could have been a bright star in our sky or a dim one. Those do look like your people, though."

"Did the Kir Leth stay very long?"

"Once the exploring party reported that there were tool-using people on that world who had a spoken language, even if they were skin-mute, it was placed off-limits for settlement. The records show that small surveys were sent through the portal from time to time, to check on the development of your people. This stopped at the time of our last war, of course, when we lost the portals. That would have been about four thousand years ago."

"Let's see, the Sellenrian year is about the same as Earth's, so that would have been about the five hundredth year of our Common Era. Earth was still pre-technological at that time. This is amazing, Perrhen. Do you know that we had legends of elder people who lived in the deep woods, who could not be seen unless they wished it? They held court on moonlit nights in rings of lights but would vanish if anyone blundered into their circle, very much like that scene just now. I think your folks started a legend that has lasted until the present. Why, when I was studying in Misthaven, I was told that Gilwyr was raised by faeries."

"It suits our purposes that people think that we're composed only of shadows and myth, and we help it along when necessary. It's easier than hiding completely. When humans think they see something, a pre-conceived explanation helps keep them from seeing what is really there."

"But there is some interaction between Kir Leth and humanity. They know the names of Polnedra and Grimmerroth, and you both call the moon Rhea and have similar legends about the name."

"When we first found humans here after the long winter, a few Kir Leth had some contact with them. We taught them lore about this world to help them survive and guided them to certain areas where they could develop their own biological systems. After that, we withdrew, feeling it was better that we develop separately. They gradually forgot about us, and we faded into the same legends that we told them."

"Yet you still have contact with some of them, like Ox."

"We sometimes invite a few select humans into our community to increase our understanding of them, and we often learn something of ourselves as well in doing so. We enjoin them from communicating information about us to others. I met Ox during my travels and conducted him to Cloudhaven for a visit. Other than yourself, no one has found their way into Cloudhaven or the Silent City who was not invited."

"How about Gilwyr?"

"I met her mother while on another journey. Her mother had become captive of some people who had the idea that she could be sold as property. Her companion was an unusually large male who had rescued her from her captors. They were fleeing when I met them, and I gave them safe passage to Cloudhaven. They stayed for many years, and Gilwyr became the first human child born here and raised to adulthood among us. I think Gilwyr is more one of us than she is human. As such, she can come and go as she pleases."

"I fear that she feels that she is neither, but is trying to find her way."

Another day passed, and our party was studying maps. "I have been as far south as Coygne," said Ox. "While I was serving in the Sons and Daughters of Rowena, my company rotated though garrison duty at that castle." He placed his finger on a seaside settlement far to the south of Misthaven, at the point where the land narrowed to an isthmus before widening out again.

"Where is the Inn where I first met Gilwyr?" I asked.

Ox's finger moved much closer to Misthaven.

"If that took us three days to walk, then we're about fifteen days from Coygne."

"More like twenty, I would judge. There are no roads for most of the way that we must travel; we must make our way overland. Bridocke?"

"I have never traveled much to the south of Dalactus. Most of my journeys were to the north."

"Gilwyr, have you been that far south?"

Gilwyr's brow creased. "I don't remember." She sounded distressed.

"I'm sorry, I had to ask. From there, we have to cross the desert. I would guess that to be another eight, maybe ten days. Perrhen, I think you're the only one who has been there. What can you tell us about the way?"

"The terrain is flat, the ground is hard, the winds are ceaseless. It seldom rains there; you cannot expect to find much drinkable water south of the isthmus. On the back side of the hill behind the Citadel, there is a system of caves and a spring. Jonan's home was actually there, not in the Citadel itself. Once you get there, you should be able to get water and replenish your supplies. Your estimate for travel time is probably sound."

Ox considered. "So it's around thirty days to get there, thirty days back to Dalactus, and we took nearly twenty days to get from Dalactus to Cloudhaven. Assuming that it takes no appreciable time to retrieve the *aelo tai* at each of those places, Cloudhaven will likely be nearly out of time when we return. If there is any delay in finding or obtaining either one, I fear Cloudhaven will perish."

"Would it be faster to go by sea?" I asked.

"No, the time to travel to a port, obtain passage, and then travel inland from the nearest place a ship could put ashore near the Citadel would be no less than the overland route, probably more."

"Could we ride *oomlies*?" Bridocke turned pale.

"No, they cannot make such an extended journey."

"How long do you think it would take to get the red *aelo tai* from Terrell?" I asked.

"There is no way of telling. If he stays inside his castle, we have almost no way to dig him out. Even if we had the force for a siege, he could last for months inside."

We need Terrell to come to us.

That made a great deal of sense. If Terrell came south, it would save us weeks of travel time to Dalactus and back to Cloudhaven. He would be outside of his castle, which would make him more vulnerable. He would almost certainly bring the *aelo tai* with him, not wanting to risk anything happening to such a valuable object while he was away. This was our best chance of success. I fixed the image of the folded-moth symbol in my mind and said, "*aeleonshii.*"

Terrell must have been wearing the *aelo tai* or continually holding it. I had his attention almost immediately after lifting the block. I looked at the map on the table before us. Our destination was clearly marked and labeled, though our route was not, as it had not yet been decided. I didn't react to his presence, trying to make it look like I had accidentally made a connection. I looked up at Ox and said, "If we take the Citadel, would the Grimmerroth's weapons still be there and usable after all this time?"

Ox frowned at the unexpected question. "Rowena's army was unable to enter, and the place has an evil reputation. I do not think any adventurers have raided the artifacts there in all this time. We would have heard rumor if anything had been brought out of there. And I expect anything that was left would be well-preserved in the dry desert."

"With what I believe we will find there, we should have no trouble taking Dalactus back from Terrell." I spoke the trigger word again, severing the link and chopping off the last word to make Terrell believe he had just overheard a conversation.

My friends were eyeing me suspiciously. "What are you talking about?" demanded Ox. "How will the yellow *aelo tai* help us to take the castle?"

"With the trap I just set, we won't have to take the castle. Terrell will bring the red *aelo tai* to us. We kill two birds with one stone, and save two months of travel time." I explained what I had just done. For some reason, my companions did not look as overjoyed as I had expected.

"He may come, but he'll bring an army with him," said Bridocke. "Not only will we still be outnumbered, but you've just thrown away our advantage of surprise."

"Aye, and now he'll be watching Coygne," said Ox. "He'll send an advance garrison to seal the town. We won't be able to get supplies and water enough to cross the desert."

They were right, of course. How had this seemed a brilliant plan? I thought back and realized that the thought had been planted by the black *aelo tai*. I resolved that this had to be the last time that I endangered my friends with the burden I carried.

CHAPTER 44

Rhea Be With You

IT WAS RAINING when I left. The leaden clouds obscured the light of Rhea in the sky. The rain and mist obscured all that was earthbound and more than a few paces distant. I formed the skin word for human in my mind and whispered "*aeleonshii*." Second sight obediently showed me all of my companions asleep in the cave. Thinking the skin word for Kir Leth showed me the guard who was standing among the trees opposite the cave entrance. I didn't know why the *aelo tai* wouldn't show me both of the species at the same time. Perhaps I had to learn the skin word for a more general class selection, such as bipedal sentient being.

I left the cave doorway, keeping close to the rock face. I tried to move quietly, in which I was abetted by the rush of the rain. I was soaked instantly. I had only my robe and practice sword, the map and the little bit of food that was left from the evening meal. I would have to forage along the way.

I had to make this journey alone. My judgment was distorted by the black *aelo tai*; I could not allow that to endanger my friends. I would make my way to the citadel of my ancestor, retrieve the *aelo tai* there, and use whatever weapons he had used to defeat the armies of Roland four centuries ago to wrest the other *aelo tai* from his descendant Terrell. If I had to, I would summon a legion of morghaests to smash through his lines of soldiers. It was almost poetic, the descendants of two ancient antagonists meeting to re-enact the battle of their ancestors. It could have come from one of the ancient story cycles of old Earth.

I slipped into the trees opposite the guard, apparently unnoticed. I set off through the forest, following the route that I had memorized from the map. I kept watch for Kir Leth who might be about since they didn't sleep. I only saw a few in the distance, making me wonder how many inhabitants there were in this forest city. I had never seen very many at one time.

Something moved quickly through the trees above me, but second sight didn't identify it as Kir Leth. I had a sudden worry about predators but dismissed it on the basis that the Kir Leth wouldn't let dangerous animals roam freely in the heart of their homeland. An inner voice asked if I could be sure that principle applied to such a different species. I hefted my practice sword and wondered where I could get a better weapon.

A pale blur descended with the rain from above, landing squarely in my path. I imagined that I saw teeth and claws confronting me in the darkness, and I swung with all my might. Gilwyr easily ducked my swing and landed a short chop on my wrist. My practice sword flew from suddenly nerveless fingers to fall in the mud.

"This is a poor night to be traveling. You have no supplies, no weapon, little food, and no companions. What are you thinking, Stenn?" Much of her language skill had returned over the past ten days.

"I need to do this alone. I brought the Blight here, and I put Terrell on the road to where we're going. If I find the *aelo tai*, my body is the reaction chamber in which the Blight will be cured ... or not. I don't want to put any of you at risk on my behalf."

"Do not try to talk like a hero, Stenn. You are not very good at it. You are a scholar, an assassin, and a warlock, not a hero. Your road does not diverge from ours, not yet. Come back to bed, and we will all leave together."

"My mind is made up."

"That is unfortunate. It will be much less comfortable for you to travel with a broken arm."

"What do you mean?" I barely got the words out before she had my left arm in a lock behind my back, and I could feel her poised to snap my forearm. Would she really break it? I shifted my weight to try to hook her ankle with mine, to throw her off balance. Her grip tightened; I didn't need second sight to see how this would end. "All right! I yield!"

"Do I have your word that you will not attempt to leave without us again?"

"Yes."

"Do I have your word that you will stay in our company all the way to the citadel?"

Damn. "Yes."

She marched me back to the cave, where we found Ox and Bridocke awake and in conference with Danallion.

"Where did you go?" asked Ox. "Danallion woke us to tell us he had seen you leaving."

"Stenn decided to leave without us," said Gilwyr. "I went to bring him back."

"Stenn? Why would you do this?" Ox looked like a kindly school teacher faced with a model student's perplexing truancy.

"This is my task to complete. I feel responsible for everything that has happened. I brought the red *aelo tai* from my world, and I brought the black one from the Silent City to here. I sickened us all by exploring Tykenkote Castle, sickened Cloudhaven by bringing the Blight here, and allowed Gilwyr to die. I have to set it all right again."

Ox tilted his head to one side, as if to say his pupil was missing the point. "On the other hand, if you hadn't been here, Terrell's plot against me likely would have succeeded. You freed us from captivity and you used your magic and your own back to carry Gilwyr to Cloudhaven in time to save her. Your intentional deeds more than make up for your unintentional ones."

"I should still go alone. You and Bridocke should go back to Dalactus while Terrell thinks we have all gone south. The city should be undefended while he and the army are gone. I've set up the perfect feint for you. You can go back now, raise an army from the Hidden Hand, and take the throne back from him."

"Sir Warlock makes a very good point," said Bridocke. "We should not pass up this opportunity."

"And Gilwyr?"

"Gilwyr belongs here, helping to evacuate Cloudhaven," I said.

"Yet you did not argue this with us before tonight before you tried to leave. There is something more that you are not telling us, Stenn."

I paced, agitated and wishing I could conceal it better. "I … I think the black *aelo tai* is warping my judgment. I made a bad decision to reveal our plans to Terrell, and that puts us all in danger. I can't put you at risk from that decision, and any others that I might make."

Danallion spoke up. "There may be truth in his words. The agent of the Blight may know that we intend to remove it from the *aelo tai*, and may try to make us fail. The impulse to reveal our plans to Ox's brother may have been one such attempt, and the impulse to strike out on his own may be another. Both of these may be attempted sabotage on the part of the agent."

"All the more reason for our party to stick together as planned," said Ox. "An attempt to retake Dalactus in Terrell's absence would fail, I fear. We need to confront Terrell where he will be, which is at the citadel, and we need Stenn's help to do so. We need to help Stenn recover the *aelo tai*, both of which will be at the citadel soon. Cloudhaven depends on us for that. Stenn needs our help to check his decisions for sense and sanity. Only collectively will we see this to a successful conclusion. Now let us finish our night's sleep so we can set out in the morning rested."

We all went to our respective beds, and Danallion settled himself in repose in the forks of one of the Kir Leth chairs. I shed my sodden robe, which had been adding its own physical element to the bleak shame I felt. I lay down a little apart from Gilwyr, but she was having none of it. She moved next to me and pulled a blanket over both of us. My skin must have felt like ice to her. She had been out in the rain as I had but hadn't had the saturated clothing to keep her chilled. She was deliciously warm, and I didn't deserve that.

"I failed you," I said.

"When Sellen was falling under the Grimmerroth's sway, he enticed Rhea away from her court under the guise of a hunting party, knowing that the weather was likely to change and strand them in a remote outpost. He did not know that this was part of a larger plot to assassinate and replace her top three ministers. Rhea denounced him for treason when it had only been poor judgment. Had she believed in him, she might have turned him from the Grimmerroth's influence. As it was, she drove him from the court, and with his aid the plotters drove Rhea into exile. I will not make the same mistake."

"Thank you," I murmured into the darkness. Then I twisted to face her. "You remembered a story!"

"You said Sellen's words from the story, and the rest of the words came like a line of *faelings* following their leader."

"We'll have the find the triggers that bring more of you back."

She said no more, though it was long before her breathing fell into the rhythm of sleep.

In the morning Perrhen appeared with bundles of clothes. "I am glad that these grew to completion in time," he said as he spread them on a bench for us. "They were complex to coax into the correct shapes, not to mention four different sizes."

The bundles contained breeches, shirts, vests, and cloaks. All of these were seamless, made as single pieces. They were tailored, if that was the right word, to within a millimeter of the correct size for each of us, including Ox's broad chest and Gilwyr and Bridocke's different hip and bust sizes. Bridocke was looking at hers in puzzlement. "What's wrong with whole cloth and a little needlework?" she said. "Wouldn't that have been faster?"

"Sometimes having one tool blinds you to other ways of thinking about the problem," I said.

Something you should take to heart said my inner voice, leaving me pondering what tools I might be missing.

We dressed in our new travel clothes, marveling at how well they fit. Gilwyr hesitated for a bit, examining the clothes, then began donning her set, though she omitted the shirt and elected to wear only the sleeveless vest. "I can see this will be practical," she said, "but I don't wish to give up my freedom of movement." After going unclothed since leaving the vat, she now looked out of place. Neither did she look like the old Gilwyr, with her hair grown out only into a short red cap.

We hefted the packs of food that other Kir Leth had brought and took our leave. Perrhen said that he would walk to the edge of the plateau with us. Danallion also carried a pack but spurned clothing other than a cloak against foul weather. "I'd enow o' clinging, smelly stitches when I had to hide amongst ye," he said in Anglich. "Felt deaf 'n mute 'n frozen all t' time."

Perrhen had supplied a new eyepatch for me, which I donned. Boots had apparently been more than the Kir Leth could grow in the amount of time they had, but they had done a decent job of refurbishing the ones we had arrived in. We pulled those on and left our cave.

Aymer was waiting outside. He had a shining blade for each of us. He presented a double-edged broadsword to Ox, along with the *cray jon* that Ox had carried here. He had a long, elegantly curved blade for Bridocke, and from her expression she had never held a weapon that fit her hand so perfectly. For me he had a tapered weapon, light and quick. And for Gilwyr he had a pair of assassin's blades, short, slender and straight, along with a baldric to sling them at shoulder or waist as she pleased. He turned to Danallion and held out a wrapped bundle. Danallion said in skin words: *I am Lyr Leth, not Cray Leth. I do not carry such weapons.* My practice with their language was paying off.

Aymer unwrapped the bundle and held out a quarterstaff. Danallion received it with the wry statement (meaning the skin words were tinged with light green): *That seems acceptable.*

We took our leave of Aymer and continued on the path. Only a short distance later, the remaining members of the Council awaited. "We have given you supplies, we have given you weapons, we have given you a guide," said the Mir Leth. I didn't think he knew Dalactyn; he must have memorized the speech. "Now we must charge you to use these to aid us if you can."

The Kir Leth took over. "Hope fades that we will be able to contain the Blight. Travel swiftly, find that which you seek. May it aid both you and us. Danallion, our hopes are with you. Redeem the Lyr Leth and restore them to our Council."

"We will do our utmost," said Ox, assuming the role of spokesman, and signing his reply in skin words as well.

It was only a few steps farther before another group of Kir Leth faded into view. These only held their hands to their chests and bowed. We returned both gestures. It occurred to me that I didn't know if they kept their hearts in their chest or their brains, or if that was simply where they formed the majority of their skin words. I hoped our gesture was analogous to theirs.

Beyond the next bend, around twenty Kir Leth stood on the low branches of a tree, again bowing and clasping hands to chests. This scene was repeated every few steps, sometimes with a single individual, often a group, occasionally a throng. It took several hours to reach the edge of the plateau that contained Cloudhaven, and in that time we saw many thousands of Kir Leth. I had thought the place lightly populated, but either we had been kept away from the population, or they blended into the scenery when we passed near. Their salutes, and their plea, was heartfelt and moving.

We started down the path that would drop into the canyon that led in a southerly direction. There would be no impediment to our leaving; it was only when those who did not bear a talisman such as Ox's ring attempted to enter that the canyons would twist on themselves to confuse, redirect, or trap those who entered uninvited. And even then, they might find themselves turned away as we had.

We had gone a little way down this path when Gilwyr looked back and called out to us to look up.

Legions of Kir Leth lined the edge of the plateau, gazing down on us. As I looked, I could discern more and more of them, stretching in either direction into the distance. Then I saw that they were also in the trees above, raising by tenfold my estimate of their number. I could see them all place a hand on their chest, and then in a remarkable display of coordination, a gigantic skin word flashed across the gathered host. Each individual was only a single colored chip in an ocean of language. I knew the noun, but the verb was in a funny almost-subjunctive mood that I hadn't quite figured out yet ...

"They say: *Rhea be with you*," translated Gilwyr.

CHAPTER 45

Castle Horn

TWO WEEKS LATER we departed the course of the river that we had been following. Neither Ox nor Bridocke had had a name for it, and the Kir Leth didn't name rivers. In one of those cultural blind spots, they named destinations rather than boundaries, so this was "the river that flows into the sea at the settlement of Ednull," a settlement that hadn't existed for four millennia. Two weeks into the journey, it was simply called the Damn River.

"According to the map, we should strike out to the south-southeast at the bend in the river. The next week of travel should be through the forest," said Bridocke.

"Is this the bend?" I asked. "We can't see very far. What if the river curves back towards us? We could be at this point instead." I put my finger on a kink in the river north of the bend that did just that.

"We passed that a day ago."

"Are we sure? We didn't see it."

"That's because we had to detour around the bluffs."

"The map doesn't show any bluffs. If we leave the river too early, we run into the swamps."

"I don't recall any swamps in this part of the land," said Ox.

"They have filled in and turned to forest in the time since this map was made," said Danallion.

"What? How old is this map?"

"I believe it was made about four eighteens of eighteens of years ago."

"Which would be?"

"That's 1296 years," interjected Gilwyr.

"You haven't given any thought to updating it in all that time?"

"It never seemed important."

"How can we trust it, then?"

"The major features don't change that quickly. The river is where the map says, is it not?"

"Rivers change their course all the time. Erosion, a flood, an earthquake. Swamps form or fill in. Volcanoes erupt. We can't afford the time to detour around something major."

"I am confident that there are no volcanoes between here and Coygne," said Danallion.

"So we should head that way," said Bridocke, pointing towards the heart of a profoundly intimidating forest.

"I concur," said Ox.

"Gilwyr? Do you remember this route?"

"I do not." Reminders of her missing memories still distressed her, and every day brought numerous opportunities for distress. She hung back from expressing an opinion or setting our direction in most of our discussions. That distressed me. The only good to come of it was that it reduced the personality clash between the two women.

"Wouldn't it be faster to go around?" I asked hopefully.

"It is slower going in the forest, true," said Ox. "But it should still be faster than following the Damn River all the way down to the coast and then heading southward. The coast is mountainous and there would be many detours around deep inlets and canyons."

I gave in reluctantly and we struck off into the forest. There were no roads to follow, no paths. At least initially, the understory of the exclusively native vegetation was relatively open, allowing us to make good time. Still, I fretted. "How can we tell we're still going in the right direction? Hasn't anyone invented a compass yet?"

"What is a compass?" inquired Danallion.

"It's a magnetic needle floating in a case that will tell you which direction is north."

"And how does a magnet tell you the direction of north? It will only point to the left and right hands of Sellen. These circle the world every hundred years. Far better to use the stars for navigation."

I looked blankly at him. "Hands?"

"It is ancient terminology. Any magnet has two hands, and we know that there is a giant magnet within the planet. It turns with the turning of the planet, but somewhat slower, so that the hands move across the surface of the world."

Understanding dawned. "On most planets, the magnetic field is closely aligned with the rotation of the world, so that one hand, as you call them, is always at the north pole and the other at the south pole. The association is so strong that we call the ends of all magnets the north and south poles."

"I see that would be useful, but alas, it is not the way of Sellen."

"How do we stay on course, then?"

"We watch the light on the tops of the trees; we look at the stars at night. If needed, we climb to the treetops to take a look around. And the creatures of the forest usually know the directions of the setting and rising sun if we stop and ask them."

So we traveled deeper into the woods, without a compass, while I mused on a land that seemed taken from a children's book, where one could ask a passing squirrel for directions.

Two days later, we came upon an opening in the forest. From our vantage point high on a bluff, we looked out across a north-south running valley, broad and steep-sided, that had been cleared. The trees again closed in and covered the opposite hill in an unbroken shroud. Our intended path sliced diagonally across the valley and continued to the southeast. Towards the north the valley narrowed, ending in a deep gorge, through which rushed a small stream. Structures dotted the valley, stone fences marked the boundaries of fields, and a high stone wall defended the source of the stream and enclosed a castle-like structure that appeared to be nearly part of the valley walls. It wasn't long before it became apparent that these were all long-abandoned, with crumbling walls and invading vegetation.

"What was this place?" I asked.

"I believe," said Ox slowly, "that this must have been Castle Horn. The stories tell that half of Baledewar's surviving army fell back to this castle pursued by the morghaests. They tried to mount a defense here, but were wiped out." He stopped at Bridocke's sharp intake of breath, but I could see there was more.

"What else do you know?" I prompted. "Bridocke, you recognized that name, didn't you?"

"Only that the few who have been here and returned to tell of it have come away gibbering of dark magic. None in the kingdoms would come here deliberately."

I looked across the valley at the fortification in second sight. There were few weapons in evidence, a cannon or two at most. If there had once been more, they had rusted away. Then I looked in blacksight. Darkly glowing pillars dotted the castle grounds in clusters. Some were arrayed as if they were the attacking pieces on a chess board. Others clustered in places of shelter as if they were the defenders or merely the innocents caught between the two sides. I saw no evidence of radiation.

"We must go to the castle," I said.

"You are drawn to ruins like a moth to light!" exploded Bridocke. "Why must you go poking around the resting places of people long dead? What has it ever benefited the people living now?"

I didn't have a good answer for that. "It's what I do. It's what I've spent my life doing. You're a soldier, a guard. I am an archaeologist. I study how people lived long ago. There is a mystery here and I want to learn about it."

"Again, why? And before I was a guard, I was a guide and a hunter. I left my post as guard and will be something else again. I would ask you what else you would become, but I know the answer already, Sir Warlock."

Uncomfortable questions. I put them aside. "If this was the site of one of the great battles, there may be things we can learn here that will help us later. Anything that we can find out about weapons, tactics, or capabilities is knowledge that we can put to good use."

Gilwyr spoke up. "Stenn's reasoning is sound. Simply knowing more than your adversary is an advantage. We have found this place, we should see what it offers us."

"The last ruin that we explored was deadly," Bridocke countered.

"I can't deny that. But there are risks everywhere. We must be vigilant, both to avoid the risks and to seize the opportunities that are presented to us. I do not believe the same danger awaits us here as at Tykenkote, though what else might be down there I can't say."

"Well said," approved Ox. "I believe we should take the opportunity that has presented itself to us, though we should be outside this valley and on our way again before the setting of the sun."

We set course for the castle, moving cautiously, bypassing the outlying farmhouses. A ring of low open buildings clustered around the outer walls of the fortification. These appeared to have had roofs at one time, but no longer. In the main, they were open to the packed dirt of the roadway. The others confirmed my guess that these would have been markets and shops, places of trading for the villagers and estate holders.

Beneath the walls, the ramparts looked even more imposing than they had from afar. The walls began thirty feet up the face of the cliff; only a narrow ramp led upwards to the gate in the wall. Assault from this direction looked impossible. But new channels had been made at intervals along the base of the foundation, where the rock had turned to powder and sloughed away until it undermined the wall itself and surfaced on the inner side. We looked askance at these easy ways in at first, and marched up to try the gate. Finding it still securely barricaded, we ended up tackling one of the troughs.

Whoever had entered that way had not been human, though we all knew that by now. We could not walk up the slope; it was too slick and steep to get a purchase on. Finally, Gilwyr took the end of a rope, removed her boots, and scampered up the narrowest of the channels where she could exert pressure on both sides. With her belaying from the top, we were all able to walk up the channel by working hand over hand up the rope. We emerged in the outer yard, between the walls and the castle itself.

"Why all of these fortifications?" I asked. "What was there to defend against before the morghaests?"

"There were a number of cities and minor kingdoms throughout the land in the time before the War of the Grimmerroth," said Ox. "Wars happened from time to time, over land, trade routes, or politics. There were bands of marauders as well, who would raid when they could. There were ample reasons to build walls, as you also saw at Dalactus and Misthaven."

"Where are all those people now?"

"Many were killed in the War of the Grimmerroth, and many fled back to the major cities of Dalactus, Misthaven, and Coygne. The remaining populations weren't able to sustain themselves, and fell either to the Wasting or the Barrens."

"Barrens?"

"They stopped being able to bear children. Within a generation after the war, most of the forest settlements dried up and disappeared."

"This was the great Balancing," said Danallion.

"What?" We all looked at him in confusion.

"The green and four-limbed kingdoms had grown out of balance since there were no natural checks on them. The Lind Leth brought them back into balance."

"The Lind Leth were responsible for the Wasting?" asked Bridocke angrily.

"Oh no. That would be cruel. That was a symptom of the imbalance when there were not enough nutrients needed by your species."

"The Barrens? You just stopped people from having children?"

"I emphasize that it was the Lind Leth, not the Lyr Leth, and it was not me personally, in any event, since it was considerably before my awakening."

"We were talking about the collective 'you,'" said Ox. "This is appalling! Who gave the Kir Leth the right to meddle with human reproduction? A whole generation of people was unable to have children. I can't begin to imagine the anguish that caused. I don't have to, because there are records of it from that time, stories and letters, plays that re-enact it. It's remembered as a tragedy, but if it had been known that the Kir Leth caused it, they would have gone to war with you."

Danallion seemed upset, fluttering all four of his hands and flaring uncoordinated colors across his skin. "I did not know that this had been withheld from you. It seems that I have, as they say so expressively in Anglich, put my foot in it. My sorrow to tell you this story. And still, I do not understand your reaction. The Kir Leth cull their own numbers to maintain balance. We keep all of the kingdoms in balance. I know that you humans manage and conserve the numbers of your plants and animals. Why then is it repugnant to manage your own numbers?"

I felt I had the training and objectivity to answer this. "I would say that the difference is that you have many offspring, and you do not feel attached to them as individuals until they are grown. Humans have relatively few offspring and become very attached to them from the day that they are born. Even before that. It's an experience that they desper-ately want to have for themselves, and they feel bereft when they cannot."

"Oh," said Danallion. "There is much to meditate on."

"Yes, there is," said Ox, biting his words off. His perception of the Kir Leth had changed drastically in the last few seconds, and he looked nearly ready to explode. He had studied with them, embraced their philosophy, and had come to respect them deeply. He had just realized how little he knew them. I had never seen him angry before, even after the attempt on his life. Now I had. It was terrifying.

"We have a castle still to investigate," said Gilwyr. "Let us explore so that we can be on our way before nightfall. This story is hundreds of years old, and will still be the same tonight when we sit around the campfire." She seemed largely unaffected by this revelation, more likely because of her upbringing steeped in Kir Leth philosophy than any prior knowledge of it. I looked over at Bridocke, who was still struggling to understand what had just been said but appeared to be rapidly coming around to Ox's view of it. I had participated in enough debates about cultural relativism that I was trying to see it through both Kir Leth and human eyes. If I ever got off this planet, I had fuel for a score of scholarly papers on the subject.

We moved forward into the castle yard, with a new tension that hadn't been there moments before. Perhaps that is why I neglected to scan for the sources of dark light that I had seen from the valley rim. I was as unprepared as the others for the tableau that greeted us in the inner yard.

The first thing that we noticed was that the gates had been wrenched aside. The stone on either side had been pulverized, and the iron bars of the gates themselves had great gaps in them as if the material had been dissolved away.

Past the gates, in the inner courtyard of the castle, a grouping of statues stood. With a shock, I recognized the hulking golem shapes of morghaests. For a bad moment, I thought we had stumbled into an ambush. However, they remained statues, menacing the statues of humans who were cowering against the wall. We walked over to examine these. I was secretly relieved to see that I wasn't the only one who kept glancing jumpily at the morghaests. Even Danallion seemed wary of them, and I reminded myself that he was the only one of the company who had never seen one before.

I had brought blacksight into play and was discovering that each of the human statues was a pillar of dark light, packed with the dancing motes. They glowed in the way that the morghaests I had animated had glowed. I didn't stumble into the truth until Ox said, "These look far too realistic to have been carved."

"They weren't carved," I replied. "They are ... they were people. Turned to stone. They were murdered."

"But how?" exclaimed Ox. "The story is that the morghaests slaughtered everyone here. But this wasn't what I expected to find. This isn't the work of morghaests. They are frozen alongside their intended victims."

"Dark sorcery," hissed Bridocke, backing away.

I walked over to one of the human statues, a man with the expression of one who is astonished by his own death. He wore long robes with a shaven head and carried a staff, though whether for aid in walking or for defense could not be said. "There was a monastery here," said Ox. "Though I do not know what they believed. They all perished." I could see that a number of the others were similarly attired.

I placed my hand on the statue's shoulder and looked into his eyes, wondering what he could tell me about his last moments. What could I learn from him?

What I learned was that a warlock with an alien stone in his belly and another in his eye shouldn't make idle wishes. The dark light flared even more darkly (reaching the limits of my ability to describe things not seen with normal senses). The statue stirred and spoke with a dusty voice.

"Grimmerroth! You have killed me. Have you come back to torment me?"

My first impulse at being addressed by a statue was to run like hell. I stayed to play the part. I stayed to learn the answer to my question. I stayed because that was who I wanted to be in the eyes of my companions. I heard a gasp behind me, and the footsteps that told me that my companions were increasing the space between themselves and this apparition.

"It wasn't I. It was another warlock. Can you tell me what happened?"

The statue turned its head to look at me. It moved like a jointed stone, rigid, with cracks forming where it moved. Dust puffed from its mouth when it formed a word.

"The soldiers came first, terrified. They told stories that none would credit. Then came the men of clay and gravel, tearing down our gates to find the soldiers. They could not tell soldiers from monks, or perhaps they didn't care, so they killed us all. They touched my brothers there," he pointed to the morghaests surrounding them, "and turned them into clay and gravel as well. My brothers turned on us and killed again. Their numbers swelled as we turned into them. We were the last. Then the Grimmerroth strode among them and raised a hand that burned like a red sun, and we all turned to stone. Now I beg of you, release me. Stone eyes cannot shed tears, and a stone heart cannot break, and they need to, oh they need to so very much."

"Did the Grimmerroth say anything?"

"He asked us to forgive him. Release me!"

I didn't know how, but I hoped the *aelo tai* would take care of the details. "I release you," I said, and willed it so. The man crumbled under my hand, becoming a pile of sand that started slipping away in the thin wind. I leaped back.

The faces of my companions registered shock. Bridocke wept openly. Gilwyr looked stricken as if she were recalling her own journey to death and back. Ox asked, "And the others? Are they aware?"

I scanned them, but unless I re-animated another one I had no way to know. I didn't think anything could make me do that. "I don't know. Possibly."

"Can you release them all? They've stood here for 400 years ... This is just too much to bear."

I moved to the center of the grouping and willed them all to crumble. Nothing happened. Perhaps I had to make my intentions clearer. "I release you all," I said. The results were disappointing.

Perhaps it called for drama, some showmanship. I must play the part of the Grimmerroth, as much as I loathed it at this moment. "From dust you all came, and to dust you shall return. Your road ends here this day!" I struck my staff on the ground. The *aelo tai* got the idea. All around me the morghaests and the humans slumped to the ground and dissolved into piles of sand.

"Do you feel the need to do any more exploring? The afternoon is waning and I for one want to be far from here before we make camp," said Ox, still shaken.

I had lost all enthusiasm for digging up the past. For once, it had spoken to me more eloquently than I could endure. "No, let us go."

Behind us, the sands drifted over the packed earth, mingling man and monster until we could not tell one from another. Perhaps in some sense, there had never been much of a distinction.

CHAPTER 46

Understandings

THE CAMPFIRE CLAWED a small and uncertain circle out of the darkness. The darkness fought back; a fitful wind snatched bits of fire from the pit and extinguished them. Our conversation was as fitful as the wind. None of us had spoken of Castle Horn since leaving that seemingly peaceful valley. Bridocke was the first to break the silence.

"How horrible that those people were locked in stone for centuries," said Bridocke. "Were they aware of every passing hour?"

"It certainly seemed that way," said Ox. Conversation lapsed again as we struggled according to our backgrounds to make sense of what we had seen. Ox and I wanted clues to our respective ancestor's deeds (or crimes). Bridocke was still coming to terms with myths that turned out to be more substantial than mere stories, some of which sat around the campfire with her. Danallion probably had the "Time is an illusion" perspective of his people. Gilwyr was still on her journey back to being either Cray Leth or Human, uncertain of the destination. She might echo Danallion or Ox or me depending on her mood of the moment.

"The one who spoke told only of events on the day of the battle," pointed out Gilwyr after several minutes.

"Is there anything in the lore that you studied that would tell us?" Ox asked Danallion.

"No, this is outside of our experience. I think that the Dust took an impression of their memories at the moment of their deaths, much like soft mud will retain an image of someone who falls into it. That is only an opinion, though."

"What do you think he meant when he said that the Grimmerroth asked them to forgive him?"

"In most of the histories, the Grimmerroth sent his morghaests on a rampage to terrorize the populace," said Ox. "But there is one little-regarded history that claims that after he repelled the forces of Baldewar from their attempted siege of his citadel, he lost control of his creations. In this account, he emerged from his citadel in disguise to track down and banish the roaming morghaests. It's not given much credence since it is inconsistent with his dark image, but it is even said that he wept over what his creations wrought, especially at Coygne."

"The stories are written by the victors," I said. It sounded trite and bitter as I said it.

"That is so," agreed Danallion, "in our experience as well. The Lyr Leth feel that the balance of blame and virtue in our last war was not as one-sided as the Kir Leth tell the story."

It seemed that some things transcended species.

"You would prefer to believe the version of the story that exonerates your ancestor?" Bridocke asked me.

"No," blurted Gilwyr. "He fears what the burden he carries will do to him. He voices hope that he is not bound by old stories that may or may not be true and that he may choose his own path."

That gave us all pause. Although Gilwyr had regained most of her vocabulary since her death, she still confined herself to speaking about the physical world. This was the first time she had shown herself in touch with human feelings. She had said what I felt before I was even aware of it myself.

Bridocke looked at her feet. "Forgive me, Stenn. My father did tell me I too often spoke without thought. I did not try overly hard to change this, thinking I was being forthright. Gilwyr looked more deeply than I did, and I think she speaks the truth."

"I hope she's right," I told her.

There was another period of silence. I could tell that something was bothering Ox. He was quieter than usual, but his thoughts seemed anything but quiet. He took his knife from his belt to pare a fingernail back, then kept it in his hands to fiddle with for a while. Some train of thought ran through dark territory, accompanied by an increasingly angry scowl. Finally, he spoke.

"Danallion, I must find out more about this Balancing of which you spoke. I am outraged that people who I had counted as friends and teachers did this to my people. Yet, I know that you did not do the deed. Just as I am not angry with the cooks and smiths in the castle where Terrell lives, even though he seized the crown that should have been mine or my brother's first, I am not angry with you. But I heard you say earlier that you did not understand that anger, which means there is still a divide between us. What can you tell me of what your Lind Leth did?"

"I have been thinking on this as well," Danallion said. "I was surprised at your anger even though this was not a thing done to your city. In our terms, this is similar to when it is desired to grow a plant into a specific form and size, so that it does not shade another plant, or take all the water or nutrients for itself. One controls the water, nutrients, and sunlight the plant gets to signal it to grow in the desired direction and to stop at the desired place. We have seen that humans will cut a plant to size, what you call 'pruning,' and that seems very primitive to us. This would be a last resort to us, only if things had gone very wrong."

"A plant is different than a civilized people."

"I beg you to remember that what you call plants are our parents or the parents of some other species."

Ox's eyes widened in the firelight. "So that is it. You don't have children yourself. You don't feel attached to the hatchlings from the pods. You just turn them loose in the world."

"I do not think this is a correct understanding. We care for the hatchlings as we care for the tree. If there are not enough hatchlings, we will decline as a people and vanish. If there are too many, we will starve ourselves. In nature there are balances, and one species will eat another, or out-compete another for food, or shade it from the sun. But it is a chaotic equilibrium, with cycles of bounty and starvation. Once Kir Leth grew capable of out-competing all other species with our knowledge and our tools, we upset that balance. We caused starvation and wars before the lesson of balance was learned. Now we follow the path of greater wisdom."

"I see your argument in the abstract ..."

"It's not abstract," I interjected. "Humans ruined their original world in this way, and have gone on to do nearly the same to several more planets. Twenty billion people lived elbow to elbow in enormous cities before we left our home planet. The seas were nearly dead, and eighty percent of native species had been crowded out. We're not very good with balance. This is part of what I study."

"Twenty billion? This is a hard number to fathom," said Ox.

"If every individual has but two children, you'll reach that in the seventeenth generation," said Gilwyr. "Unless enough people die to balance that, there would soon not be enough food for everyone." I gaped. Had she just solved an exponential series in her head?

"Gilwyr has the right of it," said Danallion. "Is it more cruel to carefully regulate the number of new individuals, or to let them suffer from lack of food if you do not?"

"I must think on this," rumbled Ox.

When Gilwyr lay beside me that evening, she asked me, "Is Ox concerned about children? He makes no *verthine* to exercise Persuasion on any others."

I didn't understand her question at first, then I remembered that *verthine* was the Kir Leth word for the ocher spores they puffed into the air. "Uh, people, humans that is, do it differently." I did not know how to have this conversation. I wasn't a virgin, but the (very) few women I had been with had known how things worked, probably better than I had. I explained the mechanics, briefly.

Gilwyr moved away from me. "Ew. Maybe we shouldn't lie together. I don't want that to happen to me."

"Don't worry. Just sleeping together isn't enough. It hasn't happened yet, has it?"

"What more is required?"

"Uh, why don't you ask Bridocke? Some things are easier to talk about with another woman."

"I don't want to make a child with her, either."

"Take my word for it, you have nothing to worry about there."

❖

A few nights later, in an increasingly scrubby forest in a land that narrowed towards the isthmus between the northern and southern parts of this continent, we were again bedding down for the night. Nestled against my back, though there wasn't the same need for warmth as we continued south, Gilwyr waited until I was nearly asleep before saying, "I asked Bridocke some questions today."

"And?" I wanted to hang on to the sleep that was closing in on me.

"She knows a lot more about these things than you do. Are you sure you are a teacher at a university?"

"Yes. But my subject is dead people."

"That explains much."

"What did she tell you?"

"She told me that humans are messy."

"One might say that." In more ways than one.

"It's not something I was ready to learn about."

"Take your time."

She was silent for a few minutes. I started drifting off to sleep again. Then she said, "Stenn, do you want a child?"

"It has never been high on my list of life goals."

"We are in agreement on that."

Silence. Then she added, "But if I ever do, I will choose you."

Her breathing deepened into slumber soon after that, leaving me watching the stars slowly wheeling above us while the sleep I had almost found slipped away into the darkness.

❖

"Terrell got here with his army faster than I would credit."

Ox was looking over the crest of a rocky outcropping at the distant city of Coygne. Those rocks were the last concealment on the dusty plain that stretched before us, ending with the shimmering sea and the brown smudge of the city. Just as there was no hope of us walking into the city unobserved, there was no hiding the legions encamped around the city walls, adding the dust raised by thousands of feet to the already choking air.

"I had hoped that we could get supplies, perhaps even some pack animals for crossing the desert," Ox continued. "Now we'll have to bypass the city. We may have sufficient food, but water could become a dire problem."

"Are there no further settlements to the south?" I asked.

"Beyond here the climate becomes too hot and dry to support the raising of any crops, nor is there any game to hunt. There is nothing else to draw people there: no minerals, very little water. We have about ten days of walking to get to the citadel."

"We have water for only about half of that," said Bridocke.

"If we wait for nightfall, two of us can enter the city unseen and fill our water containers. We can rendezvous with the rest of you south of the city and continue into the desert before the army gets underway," said Gilwyr.

"It is risky, perhaps we should all stay together," said Ox.

"A large group would be more easily noticed, and there are not enough of us to be a numerical advantage," Gilwyr countered.

"I presume you would be going yourself since you suggest it," said Ox. "Who were you thinking of taking with you?"

"I will take Stenn. He is trained with blades, is reasonably stealthy, and his second sight will help us to evade patrols."

"I should go," said Bridocke. "I served in the guard; I can impersonate one of them if we can obtain a uniform. We could walk right in and take what we need."

"And if any of the guards you served with are here, they'll recognize you. We'd be spending our time rescuing you from them."

"They might recognize Stenn as well."

I replied, "My formerly dark hair is now silver, and I've got a respectable beard. A few clothing adjustments and they shouldn't connect me with the incident at the palace, as long as I keep my eye covered and my hood up."

"As long as you don't cause another incident if you get cornered," said Bridocke waspishly.

That was, in fact, a worry that I had privately. During my time in Cloudhaven I had gained better control of it, but if I were imprisoned again, or if Gilwyr were endangered, the black aelo tai would urge me to use the power I had against my enemies. It might be the right thing to do, but how I could I trust my judgment? I turned to Gilwyr.

"Gilwyr, I want you to be my touchstone. Tell me if it is fitting to use the aelo tai at any time during this foray. I won't use anything other than second sight unless you tell me that it is right to do so."

"I will do my best," she said solemnly. "I am not what I was, before Cloudhaven. I have much to re-learn. And you are no longer my apprentice; that ended with my death."

"I trust you in this," I said. She seemed pleased.

We agreed on a meeting point in the rough country south of the town, where we could find concealment from the army if it started moving. Ox, Bridocke, and Danallion started on the trek through the spine of low hills that edged the plain. They would have a long walk to reach the meeting point while staying in country that would conceal them from distant eyes. Gilwyr and I started working our way towards the city using our Kir Leth cloaks and the little available cover. We would not be able to get very close during daylight, though every little bit would give us more time to get in and out once darkness fell. I scanned the foothills behind us with second sight and was relieved that lookouts did not seem to have been posted where they could have spied us from the rear. Eventually, we could get no closer and huddled behind a low rock outcropping to wait for nightfall.

The air was hot and still. We fashioned a rough canopy out of the two cloaks, both to conceal us from casual eyes and to provide us with a small patch of shade. It made the hot sun slightly less oppressive, though only by the slimmest of margins. We settled down to wait.

"Is it wise to trust me, Stenn?" Gilwyr asked after an interval in which I wondered why the speed at which time passed was inversely proportional to the discomfort of the moment. "I have lost so many memories. What if I have lost what you need of me this night? You said 'touchstone,' but I cannot remember what that is."

"I don't doubt you for a moment. You may have lost some experiences, but you're still the same person that I knew before. You probably didn't know about touchstones even before you … lost your memories. They are flat pieces of stone that are used to test the purity of a piece of gold. They are often used as a metaphor for something or someone who is a standard for judging others. Just asking the question about yourself tells me that you're the person I need."

"Asking the question answers the question. I like that. It makes you sound Kir Leth." She turned and planted a small kiss on my cheek.

I raised my hand to where I still felt that warm touch. "You kissed me."

Her brow wrinkled. "Did I not do right? Bridocke said I should do this. It is a type of skin words for humans, is it not?"

"You might say that. It's just a very human thing to do."

"Then I did right." She settled back down into the sand. "You have strange tools on your world, Stenn. I am sure I have never used a touchstone or a metaphor."

CHAPTER 47

Coygne

WE WAITED UNTIL it was deep twilight, then donned our Kir Leth cloaks and made our way into the environs of Coygne. The army camps lay spread across the plain, stretching from the hills in the west, around the city's walls, to the sea in the east. A small number of fires blazed among the camps in the darkness. It wasn't particularly chilly so I suspected these were cooking fires. The city was built around a shallow bay that filled twice each day with the tides; the main road approached along the coast from the north. We didn't want to appear to be travelers, arriving via the road, which was likely being watched. Making our way through the army camps seemed the height of folly. However, as we crept around the outskirts, we could make out a lush, green oasis of tropical plants to the northwest of the town, which seemed less trafficked and offered greater concealment. Conferring briefly and very quietly, we decided to have a closer look. We might even find our water supplies there if we were lucky, and not have to enter the city proper, though there would likely be guards around the source of something as valuable as water in this place.

I hardly breathed during the last few hundred meters into the oasis. While it was fully dark by then, with Rhea not due to rise until near midnight, I still felt far too exposed out under the night sky, Kir Leth chameleon cloaks notwithstanding. We reached the borders of the oasis without incident, and I took my first deep breath in many minutes. We had not seen any guards thus far.

We crept through the lower growth of the plantings. While it had looked like an unruly wild growth from a distance, it was evident as we entered it that these were tended plantings. There was not the regular layout of a farm, yet there was obvious pruning and thinning to provide for pathways through what would otherwise be thick tangles. I didn't recognize most of the plants that grew here, but they were earthly varieties adapted for life in the semi-arid conditions, meaning that thick, fleshy skins predominated, usually with spiky armament against predation. I wondered how much selective breeding had altered them since the first colonists' arrival. There had been plenty of time for new varieties to have appeared and adapted to the climates of this planet.

I stretched out in second sight, looking for guards. There were indeed some present, spaced around the plantation, and a strong cluster around the center that I guessed would be the springs. I sketched the layout to Gilwyr, and we agreed to try to get close enough to the springs to see if we could attempt to get our water there. We headed in that direction, scuttling the last hundred meters from one bit of cover to the next. I could see that there were guards nearby, but I couldn't tell where they were looking or whether we were visible in a line of sight from their position.

The spring was within a grove of what might have been date trees. It was possible to make that guess because they were brightly illuminated by torchlight. The area was a swarm of activity centering around a large pavilion that stood near the center. The banner of Dalactus flew above its peaked roof. Beyond it, we could see the spring as a clear dark pool that flowed into a covered channel leading towards the city.

"Why is the banner of Dalactus here?" I asked.

"I believe that might be Terrell's field tent," whispered Gilwyr.

"We'll never get near the water with all of those guards there."

"Agreed. We should make our way into the city and find a supply there. We also might find those who would aid us if they knew that we opposed these invaders."

We gave the torchlit area a wide berth, taking care that we didn't offer a silhouette against the light to any outlying guards. Gilwyr seemed thoughtful, and after a while confided, "I can't help but think we should have taken the opportunity to assassinate Terrell while we are so close, and he has no castle walls to hide behind."

"We just might have succeeded, but we almost certainly would have been killed or captured, with all the guards around. Our most important goal is obtaining the *aelo tai* and trying to cure the Blight before it destroys Cloudhaven."

"You are right, of course. Still, one of the *aelo tai* is certainly in that pavilion."

My heart skipped a beat as I realized that she could be right. I looked cautiously with second sight, not wanting to alert Terrell to our presence. The pavilion was dark. "I don't think it's there. I can't see it at the moment."

From the edge of the oasis, we could see a local road. The road was lit between the oasis and town by torches at intervals, and we could see that there were still people about on business. There was a mixture of Dalactyn guards in uniform and the local Coygnish in billowing robes. Unfortunately, we looked like neither. "What should we do?" I asked Gilwyr.

"We may have little choice other than to stay here and hope that the road becomes empty in the third candle of the night. That brings the attendant risk that we draw attention by being the only people on the road. Any guard would surely question us."

"That sounds like a choice of bad options."

You have the power of Persuasion; you only need the will to use it. That was the voice of my *aelo tai*. But what did it mean?

"The black *aelo tai* is telling me to use Persuasion. I think it means that I should convince the other travelers that we are one of them. Time for my touchstone: is it the right thing to do?"

Gilwyr thought seriously. "If you use it to let us pass unharmed, it seems right. If you were to use it to incite a riot where innocents were harmed, that would be wrong."

"Fair enough. I think we are dressed closer to native than to soldier, wouldn't you agree?"

Gilwyr nodded. Now I had to figure out how to do what the *aelo tai* said. I engaged blacksight since that seemed to be its method of communication. This time, I saw our own figures outlined in its strange black glow. Our Kir Leth cloaks were ghostly drapes. Gradually the cloaks solidified and became opaque, but instead of reflecting the background, chameleon-like, they took on the appearance of the native desert robes. It made sense when I thought about it; if the living cloak could take on the texture of its surroundings, it could also take on another texture if it were instructed to.

"I'm going to change our cloaks to look like natives," I said. Gilwyr nodded. I spoke to the black *aelo tai*: "You may do this. Only this and nothing more."

Our cloaks shimmered and fluttered, turning into a reasonable imitation of the color and texture of the robes. The cut was different, but the cloaks compensated by feathering the edges with the colors of the desert night. It was not perfect, but on the dark road, they might pass.

Gilwyr nodded acceptance. I don't know whether she had known of this ability of the cloaks, or whether she accepted it as something she had once known and now forgotten. I switched the cloaks back to camouflage long enough for us to scurry across the open space to the road and fall in step in the middle of a group of natives. We approached them from the rear so they would ascribe our sudden appearance to us overtaking them in the darkness.

It seemed to work. We drew a few suspicious looks, but no one took issue with our presence. The Coygnish talked in low voices among themselves. We refrained from conversation since we knew our accents would give us away. The local language was Anglich but must have diverged from the branch spoken in Misthaven long ago. It had undergone a strong vowel shift, and there were many unfamiliar words sprinkled through the conversations. Some of those resolved for me when I realized that 'th' consonants had changed to 'd' in most words and that 'k' had largely gone silent.

I was still immersed in listening for linguistic clues about isolation and commerce as we approached the town. Gilwyr nudged me, and I realized that the Coygnish had unobtrusively moved away from us. There were Dalactyn guards ahead, and the Coygnish unspoken message was clearly: "They are not with us." The Dalactyns were looking our way as well. Our cloaks weren't enough to fool either Coygnish or Dalactyn.

You cannot simply pretend, you must Persuade.

What did the *aelo tai* mean? There was no time to figure it out. We were nearing the Dalactyn guards, and they were taking an interest. *We look like any other Coygnish,* I thought. *You see only local laborers.*

Don't tell. Be, said the dark stone.

Gilwyr and I are two laborers who hauled supplies for the troops all day. We have lived in this town all our lives. We know the moods of the sand and the wind. We give thanks to the rare rains that sustain us in this land. We speak in the Anglich dialect born of the desert air. I put everything into playing the role of the Coygnishman, then discarded the role to become that person. No one would believe me unless I believed myself.

The guards scrutinized us and looked over the group of surrounding Coygnish. The Coygnish looked back stolidly and then closed ranks around us. Persuasion complete. The guards lost interest and waved us through. Once within the city, the group began dispersing. One of them, a young man with the scraggly beginnings of a beard, turned to us. The streets were well-supplied with torches, which would make stealthy movement difficult, even with chameleon cloaks.

"Yeh are travelers, nae so? Yer nae from here and yeh didnae come wid de soldiers." His accent was thick. I was still puzzling out his statement when Gilwyr answered.

"Yes, we come from Coxtown, on the coast between here and Misthaven," She pronounced this as Cuf-ton. We had agreed on a story that we hoped would attract little attention from either side. Gilwyr had been here before and could speak the local dialect. "We came to trade metal implements for pearls. We did not expect to see an army here and became alarmed. We left our cart hidden outside of town and came to see if it was safe to conduct our trade."

"Yeh shouldnae hae trouble here, I think'n. De army hae been behave'n well. Dey hae been payin f' deir supplies. Need'in a guide, you? Can show yeh to best pearl sellers, an' find best coin for yer tools." He was clearly hoping for a personal windfall from his services.

"We would be grateful for your help. We will return for our cart and come back to find you. For now, we need to refill our water skins so we can make the round trip. We used all we had to get here."

"Can do dat. Der is a water cart o'er two streets."

"Can we go there now?"

"Now? I take yeh to place I know, stay de night. Go in de morning."

"We would like to get back to our cart. We are used to traveling at night."

"Ah, well den. Dis way yeh come."

Our guide, whose name seemed to be Noe, with two syllables, led the way through the narrow streets. After the promised two streets, there was a somewhat wider square. A cart that was little more than a barrel mounted on a pair of axles stood in the center. Several people were waiting to fill jugs from the barrel, as well as a pair of burly Coygnishmen supervising the distribution. As we waited our turn, I could see Gilwyr tracing patterns on her cloak with her fingers. It wasn't until she shot me an impatient look that I recognized that she was signing skin words to me. *I not understand soldiers.*

She knew about soldiers. There was something about these particular ones that she didn't understand. She was sticking to the limited number of skin words that I knew. She added: *Take. Not.* What had the soldiers taken? I recalled what Noe had said a few minutes ago. The soldiers were behaving well and paying for supplies. That was not what we would have expected from Terrell. The plight of a city in the path of an army, even a friendly army, was to be an involuntary contributor to the army's welfare. If Terrell was keeping discipline in the troops and paying for their supplies, something must be forcing him to do so. I nodded to Gilwyr to indicate that I agreed that it didn't make sense.

We came to our turn at the spigot, and I held up my water skin. Gilwyr turned the handle and water flowed into the skin until it was full. We stoppered it up, and I pulled out a second skin. A large hand fell on my shoulder. "One," said one of the supervisors.

"Yeh can only fill one each," whispered Noe.

I stuffed the empty skin back under my cloak. They at least allowed Gilwyr to step up and fill her skin. As soon as it was full, Noe ushered us down the street and around the corner. "Dat is nae de way to make yer name in Coygne," he said. "How much water do yeh need, de two of yeh?"

"We have four water skins each," I said.

"Oi! Yer only allowed one each day. Why yeh need so much?"

"There are others in our party who need water as well."

Noe wavered for a minute. "I should nae do dis."

He would make a year's worth of wages helping us sell our goods. I willed him to think this. Whether it had an effect or not, he said, "Aye, I will help, but only one more each. Dat would land me a fine I couldnae pay, but any more would be prison for certain."

Noe led us toward the center of town. In a brightly-lit square was the terminus of the covered canal that flowed from the oasis. The water poured from an orifice about three meters above the surface, tumbling down into a cistern that looked very deep. It looked as if it stored enough water to last the city for many days if they were cut off from the spring. Workers on two-man levers alternated pumping water into a line of waiting water carts. This was the distribution point for water for the entire city. There were people in line for water rations as well, but these could dip directly from the cistern and moved quickly.

"Well, let's go get our water," I said. We walked confidently up to the line, waited our turn, and filled one water skin each. We took care to imitate exactly the manners of the Coygnish, to not attract attention to ourselves. If you act as if you belong, people almost universally assume that you do belong. We returned to where Noe waited in an alleyway.

"Now yeh go get your wagon, yes?" he said. "Yeh can get more water tomorrow. I will help."

Gilwyr and I both knew that we didn't have enough water yet for our party of five to cross the desert. How would we get the last two water skins filled? "Surely, they won't stop an old grandmother and grandfather from getting some water for themselves?" I said. I bent over, hunching my shoulders and making my hands into shaking, claw-like forms. Gilwyr caught on and followed suit. I darkened our cloaks several shades, all the while willing everyone nearby to see us as ancient but harmless old timers.

Noe's eyes went wide. "Yer nae traders, yer wizards!" He took off running and vanished around the first corner.

Gilwyr gave me a withering look. "We should have slipped away from him before trying that trick."

"I seem to have miscalculated the hold that the prospect of profit from our trade might have over him."

"Let's fill our skins before he sounds the alarm."

We hurried back to the square, remembering to slow to a hobble once we entered the light. No one paid us a second glance as we walked with every appearance of painful rheumatism up to the cistern. We dipped our water skins into the water, filling them completely. I saw someone looking our way with a raised eyebrow, and realized that a full water skin would seem to be a heavy load for a frail-looking geezer. I made my hand shake harder as if I could barely lift it. Gilwyr didn't catch on, though, and lifted the heavy skin casually and tucked it under her cloak. I caught her arm and tried to keep to a hobble while still making all haste to leave.

A ruckus began on the other side of the cistern from us. At first, I thought that we were discovered, and redoubled our pace. Then I noticed that everyone had their eyes on the source of the noise, not on us. A company of Dalactyn soldiers had come into the square from the other side and were commandeering all of the water wagons. A shouting match was escalating between the Coygnish owners of the wagons and the Dalactyn commanders. Gilwyr looked at me and said, "This is our chance to fill the last waterskin. Drop the old person disguise." I did that, and we hurried back to the cistern to get more water.

As we watched the water fill the last skins, we heard the cries of the Coygnish. "We will die without our water! Please don't take it! Our gardens will wither." The soldiers paid no attention to the crowd, other than to form a cordon around the wagons so that the Coygnish could not approach and block their exit. This was more how I had expected Terrell's troops to behave.

We finished filling the final skins and headed for a back street away from the route the soldiers were trying to take. I slowed as we reached the edge of the plaza. "Gilwyr, I can't just leave without doing something. The soldiers are here because I led Terrell here, and now the people of Coygne will suffer because of it. There must be something that we can do to help them."

"The Dalactyns far outnumber us, and as you reminded me, our first task must be to get the *aelo tai* to cure the Blight."

"I could raise an army of morghaests. I could wipe out the Dalactyn army right here. We would save the city, then we could assassinate Terrell and recover the *aelo tai* that he has. Then we would be free to find the remaining one on the ship."

"As your touchstone, I must tell you that thought is not pure. Even if it went perfectly, the Dalactyn soldiers, Ox's rightful subjects, would be murdered. When your ancestor tried the same thing, the morghaests did not distinguish friend from foe and completely destroyed Coygne. Everything you see is rebuilt on the ruins of the old city. Moreover, to be backed by a warlock who raised morghaests against the Dalactyn army in just the way the Grimmerroth did centuries ago would completely destroy Ox's claim to the throne. No one would follow him after that."

Power is always respected, said the black *aelo tai. You can save this city, and you can save the Kir Leth city. After that, none would deny you the right to crown the next king.*

I almost listened to that inner voice and disregarded my touchstone. I was already feeling for the black glow that would call together the first morghaests. Then a new voice rang out across the square, speaking Dalactyn.

"Who ordered this outrage?"

All activity stopped, and all heads turned towards the new voice. The Dalactyn soldiers stood straight. Reluctantly, three officers took a step forward to stand at attention.

From the crowd at the head of the cistern stepped forward Terrell, with General Bercarius at his side. They approached the three officers without saying another word. The officers began quaking. Terrell stood before them for a full minute, looking them up and down. Then he said in a voice loud enough to carry across the square, "I specifically ordered that there would be no seizure of supplies of any sort on this campaign."

One of the officers, braver or more foolish than the others, spoke up. "My lord, the troops are parched in this misbegotten desert."

Terrell gestured to the guards who accompanied him. "Put their heads on a pike in the center of the camp. Let the troops see how empty they are." The three officers were marched away.

"Second in command, stand forth!"

Three more officers stepped forward to take the place of their soon to be headless superiors. I had never seen three faces so pale before.

"You are now in command. I trust you will display all the wisdom that your predecessors did not. Take your men back to camp."

As the soldiers left, Terrell looked around. "Where are the owners of these wagons?"

Several Coygnishmen stepped from the crowd.

"How many barrels can you spare from service in the city for a day?"

They consulted with each other. "Probably three, my lord."

"I will pay you two silvers for each barrel that you deliver to the camps during that time. Is that acceptable to you?"

The barrel owners conferred amongst themselves. "Lord, the water fees plus the haulers' wages come to two and a half silvers for each barrel."

"Then I will pay four silvers each. I will, of course, verify your figures."

One of the owners stepped forward and said, "That is acceptable to me. I have one barrel to haul, and can make five trips in a day." Two others stepped forward and committed to the same terms. The crowd began to disperse, nodding at the wisdom and fairness of King Terrell. Gilwyr and I looked at each other, puzzled. We hadn't expected that. We turned to leave the square.

A figure bolted from a side street and dashed straight for Terrell. A sudden bristle of swords surrounded the king. The figure skidded to a stop just short of being impaled, and we saw that it was Noe. I started to have a bad feeling.

"My lord! There are wizards in the city! They came from the north in the night! They came to steal our water!" Noe looked around and saw us. "There they are! They can change their form to disguise themselves!"

I met Terrell's eyes for just a moment across the crowd. He saw my eye patch and recognized what it meant. We whirled and ran down the street as we heard Terrell roar behind us, "Seize them! I want the one-eyed wizard alive."

We fled down the street. A few arrows flew before Terrell shouted again, "I said alive, you idiots!" One arrow struck me in the side and I staggered. A warm wetness spread over my shirt. My ribs felt dull, but pain hadn't set in yet. I kept running. We turned a corner into a deserted street. Gilwyr pulled me into a deep doorway and pulled the hood of her cloak over her head. I did the same and returned the cloaks to camouflage mode. Moments later the pursuing soldiers thundered by, never seeing us in the shadows.

We cautiously emerged from the doorway. "Which way now?" I whispered.

A door across from us opened a crack. "In here," a low voice called. It sounded like an old woman.

It looked like our best offer at the moment. We crossed, keeping a wary eye for traps. I kept my hand pressed against my side. My shirt was sodden. The door opened as we reached it and closed immediately after. I kept second sight alert for hidden weapons. A light was struck and a candle lit with shaking hands. By its light, we saw that we were in a spare room belonging to an old woman. Her robes were in the Coygnish style, of coarse weave and quite threadbare. Her eyes were milky with cataracts, answering how she had been able to see us with our chameleon cloaks; she hadn't, but we were no more invisible to her ears than anyone else in town.

"I hope yer decent travelers, or at least nae worse dan scoundrels. I cannae abide dese Dalactyns, dough, so anyone dey dinnae like is worth de helping," she said.

"We thank you for that," I said.

"We want to leave the city, go south into the desert," said Gilwyr.

"Why would yeh want to do dat? A young woman wid the sound of Misthaven, but somewhat else as well. And a man wid a sound like no one I've heard before. It's deadly dere, and nutting to gain for it."

"If we find what we are looking for, the Dalactyns will leave Coygne and go home."

"Dat I will help yeh wid."

I was holding my hand on my soaked side. I swayed on my feet. Gilwyr noticed and pulled my hand away. "You have an arrow in your side!"

"I thought I was hit. My shirt is soaked. I feel faint."

"This isn't blood, though …" Gilwyr pulled the arrow out, and I gritted my teeth for the expected wave of pain. There was none, and what spurted from the entry point looked suspiciously unlike blood. Gilwyr lifted my shirt and checked my side. "So you feel faint at the sight of water, do you? I have never heard of such a weak constitution. The only thing that was punctured was two of your water skins."

"That's almost worse. Now we won't have enough to cross the desert."

"I don't think we can go to the well again, even if we had replacement skins. They'll be looking for us."

"Yeh dinnae have time, either, if yeh want to leave this night. Yeh should go to de harbor by Rhea's rising. Go with de pearl hunters out into de bay at low tide. De Dalactyns willnae look for yeh dere. Hasten yerselves across the bay afore the tide comes back, and yeh should be far beyond any Dalactyn guards to de south."

"That may be our best bet," said Gilwyr. "It must be almost time."

"Aye, yeh should go now."

I had a question before we departed. "Out in the town, most people were welcoming the Dalactyns. They said they were behaving themselves and paying for their supplies. People are profiting from their presence. What do you have against them?"

"Dalactus always tells stories in a way dat favors demselves. Make a grand show of paying for some things, but maybe not really pay when delivered. It goes back to de great war. De Dalactyns blame the Desert Warlock for destroying Coygne, but were really the Dalactyn army dat did it. It were because Coygne were on the good side of the Warlock, and did trade with him. The Warlock helped cure sick people when dere were a plague. De Dalactyns wiped out Coygne, so dat de Warlock wouldnae have dere support."

That had hardly been the answer I had been expecting, and I wanted to quiz the old woman more on her story, but the tides would not wait. We had to be at the harbor in a few minutes or miss our chance for the night. We got the back-alley directions to get there without being seen by Dalactyn patrols and departed the old woman's room.

The Kir Leth cloaks got us to the harborfront without incident, dark as the alleyways were. Once we left the shadow of the buildings, we saw that Rhea was on the horizon, red and bloated. We could see figures already moving out over the glistening pools that had been the bay only hours before. The water was shallow here, and the tide retreated several kilometers as it went out twice each day. Pearl hunters waited on the shore until the tide was out, then rushed out to gather their treasure. It seemed that the creatures that produced these pearls were local creatures that looked like a cross between coral and cabbage, and which grew pearl-like excrescences in a mouth in the center of the "head." Gilwyr told me that these mouths could clamp down with tremendous suction if they were disturbed. A luckless pearl hunter who caught a hand in one while trying to fish out the pearl could be held there until tide rolled back in and drowned them.

I made our cloaks take on the color of the Coygnish robes again and we joined the hunters still heading out into the shallow bay. We started passing the cabbage-headed growths adorning rocks, but we didn't have time to examine them. We would only have around two hours before the tide rushed back in with an irresistible force. The old woman had said that we should have time to cross the bay, but only barely. The other hunters had not stopped but had continued out into the baylands. I presumed that the nearer pearls had already been picked over, requiring the hunters to venture out further from land and safety. It was a dangerous profession.

The exposed land was mostly rocky, though there were stretches of wet packed sand in places. Large rocky outcroppings dotted the plain, outcroppings that would be submerged with each high tide. These were festooned with creatures that used them as anchors against the rushing waters. There were barnacle-like encrustations, and larger creatures, parallel evolution having derived protective shells as a winning strategy for a tidal zone such as this. There were also kelp-like streamers, and less familiar shapes, such as a pole-shaped creature that opened a sticky net to fly in the breeze like a lost umbrella.

As we passed behind one of the outcroppings, Gilwyr indicated that we should change direction to head back into shore at an angle so that we would reach dry land a good distance south of the city. Since we might become obvious once we were moving in a different direction from all of the Coygnish hunters, I had our cloaks render us invisible against the rocks and sand. Rhea was standing higher in the sky, and we began to hear the roar of the waves as they stopped retreating and began advancing once again. We had to reach shore before they returned.

We were making good progress when I put my foot down on something that felt like a cable under the sand. In an instant, it whipped up and around my legs, tangling them. My forward momentum brought me crashing down with a shout. A loop of cable pinned my arms to my side and started to drag me across the sand. I heard Gilwyr's footsteps and called out, "Watch out for things under the sand! Don't let them catch you."

Gilwyr came into view, sword in hand. She was just about to sever the cable holding me when another wrapped itself around her leg. She kept her footing, quickly severing that cable only to see several more raise up around her. The cables waved in the air trying to capture her as she hacked them with her sword. She almost won free until a flying tendril wrapped itself around the wrist of her sword arm. Fortunately, she had had the presence of mind to have her knife in her other hand and was able to cut herself lose. More tendrils were around her ankles by then, pulling her off her feet. They started to drag her towards me.

Something like a wet green sheet erupted from the sand, wrapping itself around my lower body. I felt surrounded by a warm dampness that seeped through my clothes. It was soothing and comfortable, even a bit sensuous. I relaxed. The sea creature would keep me safe, I thought. I would be held snug and warm and secure as the waves came crashing back. Gilwyr didn't have to rescue me.

Gilwyr was being pulled towards the creature's center. It would wrap her up and she would be secure too. It would be good to be together in this. She was still struggling, not realizing how peaceful it would be once she joined me. She kept both her knife and her sword free of entanglements as she was dragged across the sand. I hoped she didn't hurt herself with them.

She was almost next to me now, and the sand started to flutter as another sheet readied itself to wrap her up. Just as she reached me, she bent double, grasped her sword with both hands, and drove it into the sand at my feet. Flailing tendrils erupted for ten meters in all directions, flinging Gilwyr through the air to collide with a rock. She lay limp as the creature thrashed and quivered and finally lay quiet. Even then Gilwyr didn't move. I hoped she was comfortable. She hadn't had a chance to get wrapped up by the creature, and the waves would wash her away when they came.

After several minutes Gilwyr stirred and pushed herself to her feet. She still had her dagger in her hand but had lost her sword. She recovered that, then came over to where I lay. She slit the sheets that the creature had wrapped around me and pulled me free. "I'm comfortable here," I said. "You go ahead. I can catch up later."

"You will stand up now! We must get out of here before the tide returns."

I thought about getting up. Nothing responded. "My legs aren't working."

"That creature was using Persuasion on you to keep you still long enough to digest you. You must be stronger than it is. You must move now."

Persuasion? It must have been some sort of drug, a type of tranquilizer perhaps. I thought that probably should worry me. It didn't yet.

Gilwyr hauled me roughly to my feet. She half dragged me a dozen steps while my legs dangled, but then they started to get the idea that they could move again. Staggering like a drunk, I let her steer me towards shore. Above us, Rhea rode ever higher in the sky, dragging the roar of the tide closer and closer behind us.

Now we were nearly to the shore. Water rushed among the rocks, ankle deep, then withdrew, sucking at our feet and sweeping the sand away under each step. The next wave came, and this one was up to our calves. It pushed us forward then tried to sweep our feet away as it retreated. We had another hundred meters to go and we were losing the race.

We covered twenty-five meters before the next surge came. This rose to our waists and carried us half the remaining distance. We struggled to avoid a rocky outcropping, then struggled to hang on to the rocks so that we didn't get swept back out. Gilwyr was slammed against the rock as the wave rushed backward and came up limping after it passed.

We almost made it. Then a wave taller than our heads curled and broke over us, grinding us into the sand and rocks on the bottom. It held us in an unbreakable grip, ready to pull us back out to sea.

My host cannot perish, said my *aelo tai. You must save yourself at any cost.*

I will not save myself alone. I cannot live without Gilwyr.

Give yourself over to me. I will do what must be done.

Everything went black.

I returned to myself on a bluff overlooking the bay. Rhea was overhead and the tide was fully in. Gilwyr was pulling my sodden clothes off and had already removed her own. "What are you doing? How did we get here?"

"I am wringing out our clothes, and also checking for injuries. We won't have time to dry the clothes, but we can at least remove some of the water. As far as how we got here, don't you remember?"

"No, I think I let the *aelo tai* take over."

"You, or perhaps it, called up a sand monster that picked us both up and carried us up the rocks to the top of this bluff, above the waves. It dropped us here and then it fell back into a pile of sand and blew away."

I pulled her down into my lap. I still felt a warm euphoria from the sea creature's toxin. "I'm so glad that it saved both of us. The *aelo tai* only wanted to get me away. It didn't care about you, but I told it that I wasn't going without you. I wasn't sure it would obey me."

"You did that for me?"

"Of course I did. I need you."

She looked me in the eyes for a long moment, then took my face in her hands and kissed me. She clearly had little practice; it may have been her first time. She was in my lap, our bodies were aligned. It only took the smallest of movements for us to connect. Her eyes grew wide as she felt it. "Stenn, what ..."

"Do you want me to stop?"

"No."

We moved together beneath Rhea. It was messy, and very, very human.

CHAPTER 48

Trust

GILWYR HAD REACHED *satori*, a Zen moment of seeing one's true nature. If serenity was a human skin word, she wore it as an outer glow that smoothed her often-hard features and businesslike air. I asked her what she was thinking, and she said, "I now comprehend human."

"What about your Kir Leth heritage?"

"I comprehend that as well, better now that I know what it is not."

"Does that help you choose between them?"

"They are not choice; they are context. I am myself; I cannot choose to be other than myself. I am myself in the context of a body that is human and experiences that are both. My error was thinking that I had to choose."

I had read accounts of people who had reached an enlightenment or at least claimed to. Their words had always failed to convey what it was or how they had achieved it. Now in the presence of one, I felt a glimpse of something just out of sight, but greatly to be desired. I felt happy for Gilwyr, yet somewhat diminished that I could not go where she had gone.

A faint cloud dimmed her glow. "Stenn, when will the child come?"

"It doesn't happen every time," I told her. "Some people try for years before they succeed."

"But I felt that your Persuasion was very strong."

"That matters less than the phase of Rhea." I would have to explain later why that was literally true. "For now, we should be up in the foothills before the sun rises. Are you ready to travel?"

She nodded. "Yes, let us be on our way."

We dressed and gathered our belongings. We had fortunately not lost our cloaks or our swords, but to our dismay, only a single water skin remained unpunctured. The entire foray into the city had come nearly to nothing. The buoyancy of surviving the sea creature and the waves, not to mention our first act of intimacy, was dashed by the failure of our mission. We took a sparing drink from the skin and headed for our rendezvous in the foothills.

We had chosen a canyon that was shown on Danallion's map as being a recognizable yet hidden meeting point. We set our course toward the landmarks in the foothills where we expected to find the canyon. We were unable to see it and had to keep going on faith that it was indeed there. To make matters worse, the sketch that we had made of the canyon's location had not survived our immersion in sea water. We were forced to navigate by memory, and we quickly found that our memories were not entirely in agreement on the details. By midmorning, we were forced to admit that we were unable to locate our appointed spot. We sat down in the shade of a rocky ridge to rest. The heat was already becoming unbearable. At this rate, we would use up the water we had won from the well just in rejoining our companions.

"We don't know if this canyon ever existed. It could have been a mistake in the map, or it could have been filled in or uplifted during the last thousand years," I said.

"The others would have found this as well," said Gilwyr. "They would have then chosen another spot, where they would be sure to see us or where we would know to look."

"They can't exactly run up a flag, can they? The Dalactyns would see it too, and they'd be after us as soon as they could mount up."

"But what if it was something that we could see that they couldn't?" said Gilwyr.

"Like what? Oh … second sight. I hope they thought of that."

I closed my eyes and looked through the crimson vision of the red *aelo tai*. There was iron in the soil here, giving the desert floor a faint sheen. Our own weapons glowed brightly near at hand. A band of red coursed like a river through nearby hills, signifying an intrusion of iron ore pushed up in some ancient geological movement. What I was looking for would be small, however, and if we weren't right on top of them, they could be lost in the background. I started nearby and began sweeping in widening circles through the foothills, looking for something small and bright, the high-quality steel of weapons.

There! Two hills to our north I saw a crimson cross. They had had the forethought to tie two swords together to make an X that stood out plainly against the background. If I had thought to look with second sight earlier, we could have been with them already. As it was, we had to backtrack to the north for nearly an hour before finding the rille that lead up into the hills, hardly the prominent canyon that had been marked on the map. Soon we were surmounting the hill, finding a natural bowl set into the hills and the rest of our party camped within, anxiously awaiting our return.

Gilwyr and I were ravenous since we had not eaten since before sundown the day before. There was no game here and few, if any, edible plants, so we had to make do with dried meat and a small ration of our remaining waybread. We told our tale as we ate, including the harrowing escape across the tidal plain and the fight with the sea creature.

When we told of Terrell's handling of his soldier's theft of the water wagons, Ox raised his eyebrows. "It sounds as if Terrell has learned some skills. Whether that is genuine feeling for the welfare of his citizens or a more shrewdly calculated move to solidify support among the populace who sit astride his supply chain, only time will tell. From my past dealings with him, I would suspect the latter. Still, I wouldn't have credited him with even that, had you not told of this."

And when we told of the old woman's alternate view of the destruction of Coygne, Ox darkened. "I have never heard this version of the story before. I would want to find additional evidence before I believed it. When I was younger, I would have rejected it out of hand, but I have found too many dark deeds committed by my family line that later history denied ever happened. I wouldn't put it past King Roland to have allowed it to happen, but I would look to more than one blind old woman to say otherwise."

After our tale was done, Ox said, "I think we should rest for the remainder of today. Stenn and Gilwyr have been up all night and look exhausted. We should leave tonight when Rhea rises, and travel in darkness when it is cooler, and we won't be seen. We can stop again midmorning when it begins to heat up again. Bridocke, would you go scout from the rim of the hill and see if any are abroad in the desert?"

Bridocke went to do that, and Gilwyr and I gratefully flopped down in the little shade that we could find. It was too hot to tolerate close contact, but she still reached out her hand to touch her fingertips to mine. That was the last that I remember until after sundown.

The desert night was as cold as the day was hot. I awoke with Gilwyr spooned against my back again. I started to turn to put my arms around her, but she stopped me. "Keep that thing pointed in the other direction," she said. "If we didn't make a child this morning, I don't want to take another chance. We have too far to go and too much to do to want that burden now."

I saw her logic. I was too ingrained in thinking that conception was a planned event, and that fertility was suppressed until it was convenient. In this culture, the act and the consequence were linked, as it had been for most of humanity's pre-spaceflight history. "I would not want that burden now, either." Would I ever? If the chance came for me to leave this planet and return to my home, how would that complicate the choice? Would I stay and later regret having been forced to stay, or would I try to take my family with me into a world that they could hardly comprehend? Would that choice ever come to me, or was this my life from now on? I was glad of Gilwyr's closeness as night-doubts assailed me about our mission, about saving the Kir Leth culture that I may have destroyed, about my partnership with this beautiful and capable woman, about my life.

I was glad when Bridocke approached to tell us it was time to prepare for departure. I could put off my thoughts in the bustle of movement. As we ate a meal, we learned that Bridocke had seen the movement of Terrell's army on the plains, heading south into the desert. He may have taken our sighting in Coygne as the signal to move the army to cut off our access to the Grimmerroth's citadel. This development would force us to stay in the spine of hills that ran down the isthmus and down into the southern continent where the wreckage of the *Corvus* lay against a rocky landscape.

We set off as soon as the sky brightened from Rhea's ascent, before we even saw her face broach the horizon. With Rhea's forty-day orbit of Sellen, our travel time would start about half an hour later each night. Rhea was in the waning phase, and so would give us less and less light each night. In the seven to eight days we expected to travel to reach the citadel, we would lose four hours of travel time and nearly half the illumination. Time was against us.

We had a ration of water and looked dolefully at the remaining amount. Bridocke told us the dangers of drinking too little water in this place, so there was a minimum amount that one must consume each day. We had added a single meager water skin to our supply for our trouble, but with the cost of a day's delay, it was hardly a bargain. I added the lost water to my list of failures as we shouldered our packs and started south.

At the end of the first night of travel, we were somewhat ahead of Terrell's vanguard, but we felt too visible walking on the plains, so we ascended into the hills. We attempted to make some further southerly progress through the hills but found that we expended far too much effort for too little ground gained. We found a shady overhang and settled to wait for nightfall. We woke about noon to find that our shade had evaporated and that we were camped in an oven. We all felt parched and were forced to use more of our water than we could afford. We moved some distance and found some small bit of shade that would last the afternoon. I noticed when receiving the water skin from Danallion that it was very little lighter than when I had handed it to him. I wondered what the water requirements of his people were.

We used the time of twilight to descend to the plains, feeling that we could get some travel time when we weren't too visible before full darkness. We found that Terrell had leapfrogged us and was several kilometers ahead. We did get a bit of southerly progress before darkness made it hazardous, forcing us to wait for Rhea's light. After that, we forced ourselves to as fast a pace as we could sustain and went as late into the morning as we felt we could risk. We covered perhaps twenty kilometers that night and felt good about the lead that we had.

With nightfall, however, we found that Terrell was again ahead of us. In theory, the five of us on foot should be able to travel faster than his column of troops, supply wagons, and war machines. In practice, we found that Terrell had been marching his troops hard, and had allowed his supply train to fall behind. While Ox remarked that this would normally be poor tactics against an opposing army, we were hardly likely to launch an attack against his exposed supply chain or to be more than the frontline troops could handle without the support of the rams and trebuchets that he had brought along, apparently anticipating a siege.

"What if we could?" I asked.

"What if we could what?"

"I could send a single morghaest against the supply train, instructing it to only smash wagons. If we can damage their supplies, they'll be forced to turn back."

"I am still opposed to sending these tools of the Grimmerroth against the people of Dalactus," said Ox.

"If you had an army, you would consider that attack to be good tactics," I countered. "The army would unavoidably kill more people as they attempted to defend the supply train. You would also have losses on your own side. Yet you would think that was a good exchange."

"I can't deny that I would. It is embracing the tools of the enemy that I cannot countenance. It is bad enough that a morghaest rescued me from Terrell in Dalactus. Any further use of them would undermine my claim to the throne."

"The more we dig up the past, the less pure that claim seems. The first Dalactyns came here by stealing a ship and killing the crew. They stranded my ancestor on that ship, far from home. After he landed, they conducted a war with him, and wiped out a city because he had helped them and they had given him food."

"We don't know that story is true," said Ox with some heat. I could see the doubt that fueled the heat, however.

"You don't want to believe these things because you're a good person," I pressed. "I have seen your principles of fairness and equality. You may not be ruthless enough to seize power, but if you were put in power, you would be a great ruler. Just as Terrell is ruthless enough to gain the throne, but once he's there, he'll be a terrible ruler. Those are two different skills."

"Stenn is right," said Gilwyr.

"My liege," said Bridocke. "This warlock was not someone I trusted at first, but I have seen him growing in wisdom as we travel together. Hear his words."

"Terrell is on his way to attack the Grimmerroth's citadel," I pressed. "They will connect morghaests with that assault, not with you directly."

"Blast it all, I do not like it, but you are all convinced. Danallion, do you have any counsel?"

"No, the affairs of humans are not something I am knowledgeable about." His voice seemed dry and thin.

"Very well, you may attempt this thing." Ox crossed his arms over his chest and watched with narrowed eyes.

We stopped, and I sat cross-legged on the ground. I surveyed the plains before me in second sight. The isthmus was about forty kilometers wide at this point, with the spine of hills taking up most of the center of the land. The plain between the spine and the sea was about ten kilometers wide; Terrell's army marched down the center of that plain, about five kilometers from us. I switched to blacksight and spoke to the black *aelo tai*.

Raise a morghaest under the wagons in the distance. Attack only the wagons, destroy the supplies.

You have kept me walled off, the gem said within me. *I cannot help you that way.*

You will do as I say.

You must *do this. Send your mind through me, command the Dust to form the man-shapes. You know how it is done.*

Each time before, I had been in extremity. Strong emotion had been involved. I thought back on the times I had done so: in the dungeon, deep in despair; the ascent to Cloudhaven, exhausted, desperate to save Gilwyr; just recently, saving ourselves from the rising tide. Wait, there was one more, at the Morghaest Bridge. I had been lost in thought and raised the ones that had fallen there. This was the plain where the old war had been fought. Perhaps there were remnants here.

There were. I could see fragments of man-shapes in the desert soil. I could re-assemble what I needed from these, faster than I could raise a new one. I located a nearly whole figure near the wagons and sent my will through blacksight. I could feel the long-dormant fragments stir in response.

I had to remain in control, to ensure that only supplies were destroyed. I told the *aelo tai*: *Show me what it sees*. I felt a response, as of cold amusement. It made me shiver, but I could see the supply carts at close range now, drawn up for the night. Soldiers and drovers milled about. Cooks prepared field rations. Runners conveyed food and water forward to the vanguard, several kilometers further on. I could see that Terrell could not afford to become much more spread out than he was.

My point of view lurched forward, and I was aware of a crumbling, shambling body that moved uncertainly towards the wagons. The first shouts went up as the morghaest hit the first wagon, upending it and pounding it into splinters. It picked up mass from the shattered wagon as it turned towards the next.

Arrows began raining down on the body. They had no effect; they deflected or were absorbed and broken. Another wagon crumbled before the morghaest. This one still had horses in the traces, not yet unhitched and bedded for the night. They went down with the overturned wagon, and the screams of injured horses filled the night. I felt a churn of remorse for the unfortunate animals.

Opposition was forming up against the attack now. I realized how many wagons there were and how long it would take for a single morghaest to batter through them. A soldier, brave, foolhardy, loyal, or simply well-indoctrinated, rushed in with a sword and began hacking. The morghaest punched a blunt hand through the man's chest in a gruesome spatter of blood. I gagged where I sat watching. I hadn't ordered that, had I? The soldier was now solidifying into a new rocky morghaest, and within minutes it turned to continue the attack.

I now had two morghaests to control, and I had to split my attention between them, directing them towards wagons and trying to avoid the soldiers. If I could destroy the supplies, the men would be forced to retreat. They would be safer than if they were able to continue to the final assault of the citadel. I didn't know what awaited them there, but it had destroyed an army in the past.

Officers rallied the troops for a concerted assault. The morghaests brushed them off with casual swipes that left broken bodies behind. *No, let them hit you,* I tried to tell them. *Only attack the wagons.* Another soldier rushed in with a two-meter pike, ramming it solidly into the center of a morghaest. This was a woman, with long unbound hair streaming behind her. A huge hand closed around her head and squeezed. She died, and a third morghaest turned on the troops. *No, stop! That's enough!* I cried.

Now there were four morghaests, now five. I couldn't direct them all. There were too many of them. Wagons were hurled through the air. Horses ran screaming through the night, wreaking havoc of their own in the camp. Rings of soldiers tried to attack and kill the monsters in their midst but only succeeded in adding to their numbers. A wagon was driven through a campfire by a crazed horse, catching fire as it did so. It must have contained gunpowder for it exploded in a fireball that lit the plain.

It had become evident to my companions that this had gone beyond the surgical strike that I had sold to them. Ox was bellowing at me to stop, Bridocke was cursing, and Gilwyr was holding my head between her hands, trying to force me to see her. I could only see the destruction on the plain.

"Stenn! Stenn!" I could hear Gilwyr's voice in the distance. She shook me. "You are making the same mistake as your ancestor. You cannot control these things."

I could see her, the vision of my still-living eye overlaid with the inner vision of the battlefield. There was a knife. Which eye saw it? It was here, in front of me.

"You are shaming me, Stenn Gremm. I taught you the way of Cray Leth, and you have lost that way. You taught me what it is to be human, and you have lost that way as well." I felt the tip of her knife pricking below my left eye socket. "These stones have brought the curse of your ancestor on you. Find your way back now, or I will cut them out of you."

More than my own anguish, this judgment from Gilwyr, my touchstone, gave me the will to act. I knew that the red *aelo tai* and the black were opposites in a way. I activated them both at once, opening the channel between them. The red responded with a surge that burned my vision white. It arced down my spine to ground itself in the black. Out on the plain, all of the morghaests slumped, crumbling into dust. Deprived of their point of view, I returned wholly to my body to find it shaking in the throes of a fit. I was restrained, throwing myself back and forth trying to escape. I tasted blood in my mouth. Something collided with my head. I went limp, and the nightmare world slipped away from me.

CHAPTER 49

Nightmare Canyon

I AWOKE, STILL in darkness, and I was bound. Rhea had risen, so it was past time that we should have been traveling south again. Ox was facing me, his face unreadable. I tested the ropes that held my wrists behind my back and found that they had been tied by someone who knew their craft.

"You know that ropes wouldn't have stopped me from doing what I did, or worse," I said conversationally. As soon as the words were uttered, they sounded as if they were spoken by someone else. How could I say something so calculating about a massacre that I had just caused? I was shivering and writhing from shame inside, but that part of me wasn't in control of my voice at that moment. How many voices did I have inside of me?

"Consider them symbolic," said Ox. "There is no way I could stop you short of killing you, but you can restrain yourself. Believe me, I thought about killing you, after you slaughtered all of those people. I am restraining myself until I hear your story."

"I didn't mean for that to happen. The morghaests got away from me. First, they killed the soldiers who attacked them, which made more morghaests. Before I knew it, there were too many to control. They got away from me." My voice sounded emotionless, analytical.

"Yet you insisted that you could control them."

"I thought I could. I controlled the ones at the bridge, and they harmed no one. I controlled the one that carried Gilwyr up the mountain to Cloudhaven. I don't know what happened tonight."

"That gives me little comfort. Hundreds of my countrymen died tonight because you misjudged. None of us knows the abilities of these gems, not even Danallion. They're uncertain allies, and by association, so are you. We don't know what they might do or when they might do it."

"It would be worse if they were in the hands of Terrell, as one already is. It may be only our good fortune that he doesn't know what he has."

"That may be, but we cannot use one evil to stop another." He regarded me for a moment, then turned to leave. "Gilwyr would like to speak with you as well."

Soon Gilwyr came to take his place. Ox had just left me laying where I had fallen; Gilwyr pulled me up to sitting. She sat down before me, cross-legged, and searched my face.

"You made me whole," she said. "Now I am again in pieces. I trusted your word that you could control this power. What I had to do ... what I almost did ... to make you hear me ... that was terrible. I thought I understood, but now I am more lost than ever."

This rebuke was far worse than Ox's. I hung my head. Her words beat down the cold voice I had been using. My real personality began to re-assert control. I hoped it was my real personality; I was afraid I was losing my grip on which voice was really my own.

"You supported me. You all did, even Bridocke, and I let you down. I let myself down because I tried to be a hero and failed. No, even simple failure would have been admirable; I tried to be a hero and committed atrocities instead. I can't trust myself, and you can't trust me. I thought I had mastered the black *aelo tai*, but it has been mastering me by misleading me until I let my guard down. Its only desire is conflict and discord, and it waited until now to drive a wedge among us."

"If we are going to continue to forge this bond we have started, I must learn what it is to be human, and you must learn what it is to be Cray Leth. A Cray Leth will not say why he failed; a Cray Leth will say what he must overcome so that he does not fail again."

She called herself broken, but still had more wisdom than I did. "Gilwyr, one of the truest things I have ever said was to call you my touchstone. Please don't ever stop being you."

Her nose wrinkled in the way signaled that I had bemused her again. "How would I do that? As long as I'm walking my road in life, I am the only person I can be."

Bridocke came hurrying from the darkness. "Gilwyr, come look at Danallion. Something is wrong with him."

Gilwyr stood, and I attempted to stand as well. Bridocke pushed me back down. "I spoke for you, said you had gained my trust. Then you showed me just how wrong I was. How can I trust you now?"

"Gilwyr just told me that Cray Leth don't make excuses, they resolve to overcome their failure. She is right; that's what I'll do. But we humans can make that resolve as a group. Together we're stronger. The *aelo tai's* weapon is division, and we can overcome that by not allowing ourselves to be divided. It may be that humans can resist better than the Kir Leth were able to."

Bridocke looked at me for a long time. Then she pulled me to my feet. "Very well, start earning that trust." She didn't untie my hands, however.

Danallion was propped up against a boulder. He seemed diminished.

His skin was loose and drooping, his arms and legs were skeletal. "What's wrong?" I asked.

Danallion raised a weak hand. "You don't have enough water to make it all the way to the citadel with me." His voice was thin and reedy. "I began preparing myself several days ago for this. I stopped drinking water. If you had been completely successful, I would have drunk from it and recovered. Now I will drink no more and dry up so that you can complete your task."

"No!" I said. "We need you to tell us how to use the other *aelo tai* when we find them. We'll all drink less water. You don't have to suffer because we failed." More even than all the deaths I had caused with the morghaests, this failure, to one of our own, was crushing.

"I will not suffer. This is part of the life of the Kir Leth."

"I know that everyone dies. I don't understand your philosophy, but you seem to accept it much more readily than we do. But we need you as much as any of us. We all have to make the journey, or it's in vain."

Danallion made a horrible wheeze, and I thought he had expired in front of us. Then I realized that he was laughing, the strange Kir Leth sound made more ghastly by his dehydration. "Who said anything about dying? I will sleep until there is water again. I am preparing for that sleep now. Just lash me to your backpack and carry me with you. There should be water at the citadel. Place me in some water, and I will awake."

He said no more after that. He folded his limbs close to his body and tucked his head down. The loose hanging skin began to contract and toughen, pulling all of his extremities in close. Soon he resembled a dried beetle shell, a mere husk with a hard exterior protecting all of the breakable appendages within.

Ox said, in awe, "I never knew that such a thing was possible."

Gilwyr said, "I had heard them speak of long sleeps, but I have never seen it done."

"It's like the seed pod of a plant," I said. "They are mobile plants, after all. They must have evolved to become dormant during dry spells for survival."

"The Long Winter …"

"Yes, that must be how they survived. That's how the whole ecosystem survived. They all went dormant until the sun returned."

Ox reached down and picked up the shell of Danallion. "He is as light as a bundle of sticks. We will have no problem carrying him."

"I will bear him," I volunteered.

"Why is that?" asked Bridocke.

"You can't leave me tied forever. Ox called it only symbolic anyway. That burden can remind me that everything has consequences."

"Perhaps we all need that reminder," said Ox. "You can begin, but we can all share it."

Rhea was rising. We decided that we could not afford to linger any longer, so we began breaking camp. Bridocke came to untie my hands. After about a minute she began swearing graphically in both Anglich and Dalactyn. "Gilwyr, how do you expect to get him out of this? I'm going to have to cut this knot and waste a good rope."

Gilwyr came over. "This is the Braid of Rhea. The more you pull, the more it tightens, and it deceives one about its true direction. But see." She touched the rope lightly and it fell away. "Rhea used this to escape when her one hidden ally bound her thus when her palace was overrun by the traitors who overthrew her."

"He could have escaped at any time!"

"As Ox said, it was only symbolic. Had he called a morghaest to free himself, no mere rope would have stopped him."

"More symbolic than I knew, apparently," rumbled Ox from nearby in the gloom.

I lashed Danallion to my backpack and hoisted it to my back. His added weight was hardly noticeable. We moved out and began traveling southwest along the line of foothills. The remainder of the night passed quickly and we pressed on until the heat started to become intolerable. Looking back across the coastal plain, we could see the dust arising from Terrell's army, which seemed to have been moving for some time, judging from the length of the plume.

"He is still coming, even with his supply train smashed," said Bridocke.

"He must be mad, to drive his army so," said Ox. "With so few supplies, and pushing them to their limits in this heat, he will lose a quarter of them before he reaches the citadel. I fear that the number who return will be far smaller yet, even if there is no engagement at the citadel itself."

"But why send an army?" I asked. "There are only a few of us. Surely he could send a squadron of soldiers to intercept us. They would be much swifter and need fewer supplies."

"He fears that this is a re-enactment of the War of the Grimmerroth. He is prepared not for the few of us, but for the legions of morghaests that he is sure will spring up to defend the citadel. Last night's attack only confirmed him in this belief. I imagine that he feels his only chance is to get there in force and get dug in around the citadel and to re-use as much of Rowena ad Aulem's strategy as he can reconstruct."

"Then we should ensure that we arrive before him so that we can enter the citadel before he can blockade it," said Bridocke.

"Agreed, but now is the time for us to rest, while he burns out his troops in the sun."

We found a shaded place on the north face of a narrow canyon that we expected to stay shaded all day. From the angle of the sun, I judged we were still a good way north of the equator, so the sun would never rise high enough in the sky to peer down on our resting place. It was still incredibly hot, and we spread ourselves out to take maximum advantage of whatever cooling the air would provide. No one wanted to sleep in contact with another warm body. I fell into an immediate and heavy sleep.

I awoke with the first breeze of the dusk. The sun kissed only the tops of the canyon rocks, and those were slipping swiftly into shadow. Gilwyr awoke at the same time, and we both came to our feet, she with grace and I with a stagger. Ox was still slumbering a few paces away, and Danallion rested atop our luggage where we had dropped it. It was not terribly dignified, but he wasn't awake to notice. Something felt wrong; I was still trying to put my finger on it when Gilwyr said sharply, "Where's Bridocke?"

That awoke Ox, who sat up looking around. "She slept right there," he indicated a place near him.

"Perhaps she is using the latrine?" I said.

Gilwyr was bending over. "No, there are scuff marks. Something was dragged away. It went towards the cliffs." There was something grim in her voice.

"Quickly! we must follow it," said Ox.

"A moment to prepare," said Gilwyr. She moved with urgent efficiency to gather some dry reeds that indicated that water sometimes flowed here, however briefly. She struck a spark to them and quickly had a torch lit. So equipped, we could clearly see the line of something about the size of a human body being dragged towards a network of crevices in the canyon wall. I started to feel an icy cold gripping my intestines. We had been sleeping and did not have our swords strapped on. I ran back to the packs to retrieve them, heeding the feeling in my gut.

Sprinting back up the slope, I saw the torchlight limning a dark crevice that seemed to have tattered streamers of gauze trailing from it. Abruptly the torch fell and a body flew through the air, eclipsing the light. I ran to where it landed, and picked Gilwyr up from the ground.

"It's a *baraka*," she said. "Very bad. Fast and deadly. Largest one I have ever seen." I handed her sword to her. Ox had picked up the torch and was waving it at the crevice. A club-like arm whistled through the air, but fortunately, he was out of range. Gilwyr and I came even with him, allowing me to see inside.

A figure was stretched on the floor, entirely wrapped in white, like a spider's prey. I presumed this was Bridocke. Over her bristled a nightmare of legs and fangs. A roughly oval body squatted on six long, jointed legs. The head was mounted on the forward end of the body with no apparent neck, hissing through a mouth like a knife-seller's display case. At the aft end, the body curled under and forward to end in a stinger a meter long. The beast stood eye-height to Ox, and that was with most of the joints in its legs folded up. It struck at Ox again, and I saw that it could whip the joints of each limb straight like an ancient nunchuck so that the final joint was traveling at nearly supersonic speed at its full reach. Gilwyr was lucky to have survived a blow from it.

Gilwyr shouldered Ox aside and took a guard position with her sword. The *baraka* lashed out and she cut down, trying to parry the blow. Through a miracle, she connected, but her blade glanced off. The creature's fighting limbs were armored against attack. She tried twice more and had her sword knocked from her hand on the third stroke. The *baraka* was incredibly fast.

"Stenn, call a morghaest!" cried Ox. "We need something that is tougher than it is." He was valiantly trying to get to the unmoving form of Bridocke on the ground but was stymied by the immense reach of the creature.

Just that morning I had foresworn the use of those creations. Could I make an exception for this? The foe wasn't human, and Ox had implored me to use my power. Could I stop it from harming Bridocke if I unleashed it? What if it turned the *baraka* into an inhuman morghaest? Could I stop it before it turned on all of us? Would I fail myself if I broke my resolution, or if I kept it and allowed Bridocke to die? Was she already dead and this was pointless?

I looked for inspiration in second sight. I saw our weapons, but nothing of the nightmare in the crevice. With a sudden thought, I called to Gilwyr, "What is the skin word for this creature?"

"This is no time for a language lesson," she snarled.

I seized her arm. "Just tell me. It's our only chance." I thought she was going to turn her sword on me for an instant, but then she quickly sketched a sign on her chest.

"Got it." I formed that sign in my mind and said inwardly: *aeleonshii*.

Suddenly I could see the beast in second sight. I almost wished I couldn't, for there were more armaments about it than had been visible by torchlight. I moved my sword experimentally and saw in second sight an array of crimson images of my sword spinning away, knocked from my hands by one of the flailing limbs. The *aelo tai*, like an alien computer, was running battle simulations. Now an image came clear, the sword leaping high in the air, and coming down point first into the joint between body and head. Great, there was its vulnerability, now how did I get there? Did I throw the sword?

I watched the scenario repeat and saw that the sword swerved left, then up, then arced high before coming down. There was a crack on that side, a foothold perhaps. "Really?" I asked the *aelo tai*. "You think I can do that? Do you have a realistic model of my strength?"

Ox roared, "What are you talking about? Call a morghaest!"

I took two steps back and ran towards the crack. Second sight showed me a crimson flail lashing out at me at the level of my kneecaps. I leaped over the spot where it would pass and felt the sharp wind of the blow's passage beneath my boots. Now the stinger stabbed at the point where I would leap into the crevice in a fraction of a second. I dodged right; the stinger rammed instead into the solid rock, making the *baraka* hiss madly. Now I vaulted over the stinger, planting a foot in the crack in the wall. I leaped with everything I had to the top a boulder, then dropped to let another flail crack above my head.

I couldn't hesitate now. I launched myself into space, sword following the path it had to take. I saw the crimson image in second sight. Another flail hurtled toward my head. I had only a fraction of a second of warning in second sight and rolled desperately in mid-air. A glancing blow struck my shoulder. I ignored the explosion of pain to uncoil just in time. I shifted my grip on the sword to two-handed reverse and drove it down where the neck should be, then fell towards the gnashing teeth. I realized too late that the simulation only told me how to kill the beast, not to survive the attempt.

I was tackled from the side, borne just out of reach of the double row of knife-like teeth. I hit the ground with a weight on top of me. Looking up, I saw the head descending, mouth open. This was the end. I regretted that I had no time for final regrets. Then the head landed beside me and rolled away. I had severed the neck.

The weight on top of me was Gilwyr, who pulled me to my feet. Ox rushed in and lifted the wrapped form of Bridocke. "Quickly," gasped Gilwyr. "Take her to our camp. We must start a fire."

We lay Bridocke's form on the ground where we had slept. It wasn't much of a camp since we had done nothing but eat dried meat and then sleep. Gilwyr had retrieved the torch. Now she quickly built up a bright fire of dried reeds and twigs, which burned fiercely in the dryness. She gave Ox the task of keeping it fueled since it would burn quickly.

With a knife, she cut away the white covering from head to toe. It looked gauzy, but it was incredibly tough, and also adhered to Bridocke's skin and clothes, making it difficult to peel away. As we revealed Bridocke's face, it appeared that she was sleeping peacefully. Gilwyr held a knife blade by Bridocke's face and watched a faint fog come and go on the metal surface. "She still breathes."

Bridocke opened her eyes, though she looked unfocused. "Gilwyr? I had a dream … a nightmare."

"It was real. Did the creature sting you?"

"Oh, I don't know. Does it matter? I feel fine." She sounded dreamy.

"Quickly, take off your clothes."

"Oh, should I do that? What would Ox say?"

"What? Here, I will do it. We don't have time."

Gilwyr pulled Bridocke's shirt over her head and quickly examined her naked torso. Bridocke giggled and started trying to pull Gilwyr's shirt off in turn. Gilwyr slapped her hand away. "Stop it, I'm trying to save your life." Bridocke pulled Gilwyr's head down and kissed her on the mouth.

"Stenn, restrain her! She is not herself!"

I got behind Bridocke and pinned her arms behind her in a lock, trying to be gentle. Gilwyr started pulling her breeches down her legs. Bridocke twisted to look back at me. "Both of you? And you seemed so proper, Stenn." Was she drugged? She seemed euphoric, fey, and aroused.

Now she lay naked in the firelight. She seemed unharmed, but then Gilwyr flipped her over, and we saw the angry red wound on her left buttock. Gilwyr took out her knife and held it over the fire. Ox returned with fuel at that moment and demanded, "What is happening here?"

"We're saving her life. Find a piece of leather, fold it, and place it between her teeth," snapped Gilwyr.

Ox came up with a leather lashing strap. He wasn't moving quickly enough for Gilwyr, who snatched it from his hand, folded it, and placed it in Bridocke's mouth. "Bite down," she said.

Bridocke's voice was indistinct with the leather in her mouth. "… in my youth … she looked like you …"

"Bite down. Ox, look into her eyes. Stenn, hold tight."

Gilwyr sliced across Bridocke's wound, then again at right angles, forming an X. Bridocke thrashed and screamed. I almost lost my grip on her. I had to give up being gentle and just held on. Ox took her head in his hands and held her eyes, telling her to be strong. Gilwyr continued to probe. "It's deep," she muttered. An endless minute passed. Each of Bridocke's renewed shrieks tore at me. "Almost …" said Gilwyr.

It was still too long, but finally with a pop, a ghastly pale and bloody thing emerged from the wound. Gilwyr dug the tip of the knife underneath it and flipped it into the fire. The thing that writhed and burned in the flames would give me nightmares until the end of my days. Gilwyr probed with her finger in the wound to be sure there were no more, then poured precious water over it to wash it clean. I released Bridocke and started looking for something remotely clean to bind the wound.

"What was that thing?" I asked.

"A *baraka* is a desert creature. They eat prey for moisture and sustenance. But since Bridocke hadn't been eaten, it could only be because the *baraka* needed a host for its young. They deposit a seed with their stinger, which then sends roots throughout the host to feed on its moisture. Eventually, a fleshy plant will burst forth, finally killing the host. The *barakorn* will produce pods that will in turn release immature *baraka* to seek new hosts. The *baraka* will keep the host sedated and preserved with venom until the *barakorn* finally kills it. Bridocke could have lingered for weeks if we hadn't removed it before it burrowed too deeply."

I shuddered. I heard Bridocke retching behind me, probably in equal parts from shock and from revulsion at what she must have just overheard. I wished that Gilwyr hadn't been quite so detailed in her answer.

We got Bridocke bandaged up and dressed as well as we were able. She was sounding more lucid as the venom wore off. She stopped Gilwyr in the act of working her breeches back over her bandaged posterior. "Gilwyr, I'm not sure what I said. I was not in my right mind."

"You were babbling. It didn't make sense to me."

"Oh, good ..."

"I'm sure you thought I was someone else when you tried to kiss me."

"Oh, Rhea, I hoped I hadn't really done that. It was when I was really young ..."

"You didn't need to confide anything before this," said Gilwyr firmly, "and you don't need to confide anything now." We heard Ox returning from an errand he said he had to attend to. The glow of a bonfire lit the crevice where the remains of the *baraka* lay, and we understood what his errand had been.

"Thank you. And thank you for saving me from that ... that nightmare."

"I didn't save you, Stenn did. He did a flying leap that I still cannot credit, dodged every blow that the creature threw at him, and drove his sword clean through its neck. It will go down in history as one of the most daring fights ever, right beside Rhea's battle with the wild *tumboor.*"

"Why didn't you use your magic, Sir Warlock?"

"Yes, Stenn, why didn't you?" Ox had heard the final part of this discussion. "It would have been a virtuous use of magic, not one directed against innocent people. I even asked you to do so, to take the burden of decision on myself. Why did you make such a risky attack instead?"

"It hasn't been a full day since I swore not to use black magic. I swore never to raise a morghaest again. I didn't expect to be put to the test so soon, but there it is. Once you admit there is one good use for something so dangerous, it makes the next choice easier, the line between good and bad fuzzier. Even yesterday, the choice to send a single morghaest against supply wagons, not people, seemed an easy one, until it went wrong. That kind of thinking may be why a weapon like the black *aelo tai* was created in the first place, or why it was not destroyed. Someday one might be backed into a corner where that kind of weapon would be the only choice, so keep it around in case that happens. I've foresworn using the black *aelo tai* until I can destroy it and I mean to stick to that resolution."

"I see your point. But consider this: if you had not raised a morghaest to carry Gilwyr up the mountain to Cloudhaven, she might not be here today."

"That is not a fair question, Ox," said Gilwyr. "The road behind us has no forks; only the road ahead has forks. You can't second-guess a choice in the past because we never took that fork in the road."

"Conceded. Stenn, you chose wisely. Perhaps I should step aside and name you the next king."

"I'm wiser than to want that honor."

"That only makes you more qualified, not less. Let us go. I saw more *barakorn* growing in this canyon, we must be away before any more of their offspring show up. Bridocke, can you walk? If not, I can carry you for a way."

Bridocke stood shakily and took a few steps. "I can walk, though it hurts like hell."

Gilwyr offered, "There may be enough venom on the stinger of the dead *baraka* to temporarily deaden the pain."

Bridocke paled. "No, I'll walk, thank you."

CHAPTER 50

Citadel

WE KEPT A torch alight to make our way out of the narrow canyon. Pebbles skittered in the darkness on several occasions. Bridocke held her torch defiantly before her, refusing all offers of assistance.

No other *barakas* assailed us. Perhaps only that one had been large enough to be a threat to a party of our size. Perhaps the funeral pyre of that one dissuaded the lesser ones. We won free onto the plain without further challenges; from there we could see the bonfires of Terrell to the north. He had pressed on despite his losses, though we had pulled ahead. Our skirmish had delayed us but not as much as Terrell had been by the morghaests.

Between the starlight and the ruddy anticipation of Rhea in the eastern sky, we decided that we could see well enough to continue, though we didn't dare to carry the torches on the open plain. The night had an angry feel. If the child god had a palate of pigments, she had painted the sky with the one named *wrath,* and the shadowed foothills with the one named *foreboding.* Gilwyr and I walked in silence for a time, until we had to wait for Ox and Bridocke to catch up. Gilwyr seemed thoughtful. After a few false starts, she said, "I am confused about Bridocke."

"About why she kissed you?"

"Yes, that."

"I think you reminded her of someone she once loved."

"For a brief time, I thought I understood humans."

"There's a difference between understanding humans and understanding people. Understanding humans as a group has been my life's study. I still don't understand individual people very well."

I could see that didn't answer her question. I struggled to phrase a response; all of the ones that came to mind sounding too vague, too academic, too abstract, or, I must admit, too embarrassing. I found nothing to say before Ox and Bridocke caught up, and the opportunity was lost. Like too many of the conversations I should have had over the years, this one was too much rehearsed and too little spoken.

We tried to make the best time we could that night, then rested in a sheltered space. We checked for signs of predators around this camp and set a watch, which exhaustion rendered so spotty as to be useless. The next night, Bridocke was able to keep a stronger pace, and as the sun rose the following morning, the citadel emerged from the shadows.

Even though I knew that the "citadel" was the wreck of a starship, the appearance of a warlock's fortress was inescapable. The ship rested within a natural amphitheater created by outlying foothills, about half a kilometer distant from the central mountain crest. The upper part of the warp torus arched several hundred meters above the plain. The top of the primary hull could just be seen above a rude rock wall that concealed the lower part of the ship. In blacksight I could see that the wall had the signature dancing motes throughout that showed it had been constructed by what the Kir Leth had called the Dust. Someone had wielded an *aelo tai* to build that wall.

"Perrhen said that on the back side of that hill there is a cavern with a spring. The cavern is stocked with the supplies that Jonan Gremm brought out of the citadel," said Gilwyr.

I was eager to get to the *Corvus* before Terrell's army. Once inside, the hull of the ship should be impervious to the forces that Terrell could throw against it. As we had drawn closer to our goal I had begun to have a new worry. I was mindful of the mention of a radiation leak in Jonan's recorded message and in the accounts of wasting sickness afflicting any who entered. The old tales made it sound like Jonan appeared while wearing a protective suit. We needed to find those suits. One bout with radiation sickness had nearly killed us. I was desperately hoping to find one or more suits in the cavern. I did not dare to imagine what we might do if they were not in evidence or decayed beyond usefulness.

It was soon to be full daylight. We risked the brief sprint on the open plain to reach the concealment of the hill behind the citadel. A short half kilometer, but it seemed like ages that we were exposed under the brassy dome of the sky. After that dash, we had to hunt for the entry to the caves. Bridocke and Gilwyr were talking of finding signs of old foot traffic, or clumps of vegetation that might indicate the underground spring. Second sight quickly gave me the location of the cave within the hill, highlighting a cluster of artifacts buried within the ground. However, it did not immediately give away the entrance. We searched for some time before I caught sight of a single metal artifact within a rille several hundred meters away. We made our way to the narrow opening and peered into the darkness.

"How are we going to find our way in?" asked Bridocke. "It's blacker than night in there."

"I don't see any torches or anything that will burn, for that matter," said Ox.

I groped forward in the gloom. I could see my target, but not the obstacles that lay between us. After stumbling several times and scraping my knuckles once, I put my hands on an object that felt metallic, a thing of planes and curves and protuberances, weighing about half a kilo and just larger than my double handspan. I picked it up and carried back to the light.

"What is that thing?" asked Gilwyr.

"It looks like a hand-lantern," I said. "But there are strange bits welded on."

"Will it light our passage?" asked Ox.

"I doubt that it has any power left after four hundred years," I said. I moved the switch on the side of the housing. It out-performed my expectations, briefly providing a dim light before flickering out.

"Does magic leak away over time?" asked Bridocke.

I translated *magic* in her sentence to *electricity*. "Yes, sort of."

I examined the lantern. It was an ugly job, with a housing that looked like it had been ripped from some other assembly welded on one side. A few wires connected the two components, and a crank had been crudely attached on a shaft. I rotated the shaft experimentally. There was resistance, and a deep whirring inside as if gears were turning. The lamp glowed a momentary red before decaying again into darkness.

"We're dealing with an engineer," I said. "He's put broken things together to make them work."

"Is an engineer like a warlock?"

"You might say that."

I cranked the handle vigorously and was rewarded with a bright white light. After about fifty cranks I stopped, gratified that the light remained lit. The battery must still be capable of storing energy that I generated. On my world, we would have called this a Wendolen contraption, after an inventor/artist who delighted in bolting together improbable combinations of devices that somehow ended up working together in some whimsical and non-productive way.

In the light of the hand-lantern, we could see unmistakable signs of previous traffic. Footprints in the floor of the cavern showed boot soles of several types, some bare feet, and even some marks that looked like the Kir Leth three-padded foot. I spent a moment looking at the footprints. These and the lamp had been left by the ancestor I had crossed light years to seek. I felt suddenly overwhelmed by these prosaic remainders that his hands and feet had been in this place. I had crossed the void of space to come to this place he had once occupied but remained separated by a gulf of four hundred years. I cringed that we would probably obliterate these fragile reminders by following them. There was no help for it; we entered the cave.

After a relatively short passage, we emerged into a natural cavern. Limestone columns, stalagmites, and stalactites abounded. We could see only a circle of the room at one time in the light from the hand lantern. All the rest was in pitch darkness. I thought back to the hours when I wandered lost in the darkness of the Blight. I shuddered and gave the lantern some more cranks.

The floor was relatively even, though some damage had been done to the cave formations to bring it to that state. At one side, a deep and black pool of water lay quietly. At intervals, a single drop of water fell from the darkness to decorate the surface with concentric ripples. The room showed signs of long habitation. We encountered cases of supplies stacked wherever free space allowed. Or rather, they had once been stacked, since many piles had been toppled, cases torn open, and contents strewn across the floor. A huge pile of empty tins had been tossed behind a rank of thin limestone columns that resembled a pipe organ. An initial impression that the place had been ransacked gradually resolved into a picture of an occupant who had not greatly cared about housekeeping.

A metal bed frame sat incongruously among some stalagmites, with a canopy arranged over it. A plop and a drip gave a clue that the occupant hadn't liked his sleep disturbed by random drops of water falling from the ceiling. The bed had evidently been unbolted from the *Corvus* and carried here. Several tables from the same source stood nearby, one appearing to be where he had eaten, and two others seeming to be work tables. Poles around the area held more Wendolen contraptions aloft, with thick cables disappearing into the darkness. A heavy switch beckoned me to reach out and move it, less from any expectation that it might do something than from novelty of this ubiquitous technological device that I hadn't seen since landing on this planet. I was as startled as my companions when light suddenly flooded the room.

"There's still power …" I said to myself.

"There's still magic here," said Bridocke almost simultaneously. "We must be careful. This is where the most powerful warlock in history lived. He may have left very dangerous things behind."

"This is not magic. This is everyday technology from my world."

"Do you know how it works?" asked Ox.

"Yes, of course. These wires conduct electricity, which makes these lights glow. The switch controls the electricity."

"Could you make any of these things?"

"Well, no. I never learned how."

"Could any of these things injure us?"

"I suppose." I saw that the terminals of the power leads were bare. Jonan hadn't covered the exposed ends; he knew enough not to touch them when the power was on. I pointed to them. "If you were to touch both of those metal studs at the same time, it could kill you, or at least give you a nasty shock."

"Then this place is dangerous, and even you don't know how everything works."

"Point taken. Don't touch anything here."

We examined the area in the new light. Instruments and tools were stacked around the work area. I recognized some optical logic boards that had had their light-fiber connectors ripped away and electrical wires fused by hardened drops of metal to their contacts. The wires connected in turn to something with a display panel that looked as if it had been mounted on a wall in a prior life. Jonan had been trying to build ... something. Whether it was to replace an existing part of the ship that was damaged or to build something new from the wreckage, I couldn't say.

Gilwyr was examining the pool of water. "This seems to be drinkable," she said. "There are jugs here that he was using to scoop and carry water. There is a strong mineral taste, but it is clear and without color in the light. I believe we can refill our water skins here."

"What about Danallion?" I asked. "We will need him soon."

"I think we should bathe him in the water and hope that he absorbs it."

I unslung my pack and untied the lashings holding Danallion in place. He had dehydrated even more during our travels and now weighed only a few kilos. I hoped that he still lived and that his period of dormancy hadn't damaged him. I carried him to the pool and slowly lowered him into the cold water. "Now what?" I asked.

"I have no idea," said Gilwyr. "I have never seen this stage of Kir Leth life before. It must only happen in extreme conditions, for I never witnessed this process in Cloudhaven."

I propped Danallion in a shallow end of the pool. "I expect that he'll need to breathe at some point when he's rehydrated." The others nodded. It made sense, but none of us really knew. We stood around awkwardly, growing steadily more impatient as the slow drip of water into the pool measured out time. I tried counting; it took a slow count of thirty-two for each drop to form, deliberate over its options, then fall gracefully to make its brief impression on the surface of the water. It was remarkably regular; when I reached thirty-three or thirty-four, or when it fell at thirty, I suspected that it was more likely that my counting was uneven than the drops were. Splash, another drop made its mark, then vanished. How like human lives they were, though more regular. Some of us made tiny splashes, soon gone, while others landed like boulders, throwing waves over the edge of the pond and swallowing smaller ripples in the commotion. Large or small, at the end, the waters flowed back and were still once more.

My thoughts were turning morbid. I started roaming the cave again, assessing and cataloging the contents, touching nothing. I noticed that the power cables ran back into the darkness. Taking the hand lantern, I followed them, looking for the generator or storage device that still could supply energy after all this time. Near the rear of the cave, opposite the side where we had entered, the cables entered a dark and suspiciously symmetrical passageway. I shined the lantern into the opening in the wall. The passage ran straight and smooth for as far as the light could reach, perhaps forty paces, and there was no sign of it deviating after that. Remembering my navigation of the stygian depths of the Blight, I tucked the lantern under one arm and clapped my hands sharply. No echo returned from the passageway. How far did it go?

Turning aside, I saw a small table next to the opening, holding a device connected to a charging station that in turn had cables connecting to the power feeds snaking across the ground. Other than some expediencies in splicing the charging station into the power, this device was unmodified, and apparently still functional. The case was intact and untampered with, giving me some degree of confidence in the labels on the device, the largest of which read "Albion Instruments Division/ Radiation Detector."

I removed the unit from the charging station and switched it on. Lights illuminated and several indicators jumped and steadied. The unit emitted a gentle ticking noise that seemed to be consistent with the needles resting in green zones on their scales. I carried this find back to the others.

"Has Danallion revived yet?" I asked as I drew near.

"He is only somewhat less dried out than he was when we put him in. At this rate, it will take some hours," said Ox. "What have you found? I thought we were not to touch anything."

"I know what this is, and it's still working. I want to check this water to make sure it's safe." I held the meter near the surface of the water and waited. The needles stayed firmly in the green zones, and the soft clicking sounds continued at the same rate. "It isn't radioactive, at least."

"What is this radioactive?" asked Gilwyr.

"Radiation is something that you can't see or feel that will make you sick. Some minerals are radioactive, like the one they were mining at Tykenkote Castle. If we had this meter with us there, we would have been warned of the danger. We wouldn't have gotten sick, and you wouldn't have … died." I still tripped over that word.

"How does it tell you this?"

"These needles will move if they detect radiation. Green is good, red is bad."

"And between?"

"I'm not sure… There's a chart here." I ran my fingers down columns of numbers. "There's two columns. The first is the amount of time before you get sick, and the second is the amount of time before you die. I would guess that the reading at Tykenkote Castle would have been about here." I put my finger on a spot on the meter just short of the red line. "This says that we should have left within fifteen minutes. We were probably there a couple of hours."

"Why then did Gilwyr get much sicker than we did?"

"She was cut by a blade made from that pure metal. She got a much higher dose than we did."

"Why are there three needles showing?"

"Let's see. This one has the greek symbol alpha beside it, this one has beta, and this one has gamma. Different kinds of radiation, I think."

"I think you know as much about this radiation as I know about making a wagon wheel," said Bridocke. "I know people who can make one, but I couldn't tell you how they do it."

In truth, I was reaching my limit of knowledge about this topic. I knew about using isotope analysis to date artifacts, but little more beyond that. "That's fair," I admitted. "But you know what wheels are good for and how they're used, and how fast they can safely go."

"So how did you use all these things that you don't understand?"

"I had tiny machines in my eye and my ear. All I had to do was think of something I wanted to know, and I could see and hear all about it. None of that works on this world."

"Sir Warlock admits that he had a demon familiar that whispered secret knowledge to him, yet still says this isn't magic?"

I gave in. Throughout history, people had used terms like *phlogiston*, or *dark energy*, to describe things they didn't understand, only to discard them when they no longer worked to describe the universe. Magic was simply one of those shortcuts.

"If Danallion is going to be several hours in recovering, I've discovered a passageway that leads towards the ship. It might be an easy way in. If we can avoid the trip around the mountain again it will be faster, and less chance of running into that army that's marching toward us."

The others assented. I led them to the opening in the back of the cavern.

"This can't be natural," said Ox. "What made a tunnel like this? It's perfectly smooth and even."

I had looked down the passageway with blacksight and knew the answer. "An *aelo tai* made this. Someone used an *aelo tai* to bore a hole through the mountain."

"How can you tell?"

"Other than the unnaturally perfect construction? It glows."

"I can't see a glow," said Bridocke, squinting.

The walls had the deep, restive anti-light streaming into them with blacksight. "That's because you're not a warlock," I said ironically.

"You admit it," she said with satisfaction.

We walked down the perfectly straight tunnel. I held the radiation meter in one hand, watching the needles and listening to the contented ticking. I reasoned that the meter had been left by the entrance for a reason. Nothing untoward happened for nearly a thousand paces, then a light finally began to grow in the distance. The ticking of the meter grew with the light until it was a continuous chatter as we reached the end.

I stopped and consulted the chart. Two of the needles remained low, but the one marked gamma had crept upwards. A pale yellow indicator had lit up above a legend that read "accumulated dose." I thrust the meter outside the entrance and heard a slight increase in the chatter. We shouldn't be in immediate danger. There were other hazards much higher on our list to worry about right now.

We stepped out into the light. It wasn't direct sunlight; it was reflected from the rock walls and the huge structure above us. A large rocky outcropping screened the cave entrance; the vista opened up as we stepped around it. My eye jerked downward at the sudden chatter of the meter and then up again at the gasps from the others. Above us, the torus of the ship arced like a silver bridge to the sky. Only two-thirds of the torus was visible; the remainder must have been buried beneath our feet. High above us, the main hull of the ship was suspended in the center of the torus by three thick struts. One strut was nearly vertical in front of us, while the other two stretched high overhead. At close range, the vista was no longer pristine, as it had been at a distance. The hull was crumpled in spots, gashed in several places, and one of the upper struts had cracked open. Starships are designed for space travel, not landings, and it's asking a lot to take one into an atmosphere and set it down on a planet. It must have been a rough ride.

The vertical strut of the ship lay ahead of us across the stony ground. An entrance in the strut seemed likely. We moved out across the natural amphitheater while I watched the meter nervously. The stories I had heard about this place sickening anyone who entered had led me to expect deadly levels of radiation. It appeared that the source had weakened significantly in the past four hundred years.

A meager flow of water seeped through a crack in the ground and pooled nearby. From there, an outflow meandered across the floor of the amphitheater for some distance until it finally sank into the stony ground. The water smelled sulfurous and gave off tendrils of steam that hung in the still air. The vapor added to the evil atmosphere of the scene.

We arrived at the strut. Up close, it lost the appearance of a slender column and became a mighty tower rising from the gravel that buried the lower third of the ship. A ramp of packed stone and soil had been piled up against the hull, giving access to a rudely cut doorway covered only by a slab of sheet metal leaning against the opening. We all stopped at the end of the ramp, looking upwards at the hacked entranceway.

"This is hardly the mighty gate of the citadel that I had expected," said Ox.

"Was this opening forced by the invaders?" wondered Bridocke.

"I don't think so," I replied slowly. "This looks like it was cut with a welding torch. I don't think the invading army would have had a welding torch with them, though they probably had some Dalactyns with them who arrived on this ship who would have known how to use one. This doesn't look like it was done in a hurry during an attack, especially with this ramp built up. In fact … this was made from the inside. Some-one cutting from the outside would have made the opening at ground level. Someone—probably Jonan Gremm—guessed where it should be from inside, and was a bit off."

"This won't be very defensible when Terrell's army arrives," said Gilwyr.

I reached up to pull the panel aside. "No, I am surprised that he didn't put in more defenses than this …"

There was a bright flash, and I found myself sprawled on the ground several meters away, blinking the spots out of my vision. The muscles in my arm were twitching uncontrollably as pins and needles jabbed at my nerves. I gasped to draw a breath with a diaphragm that wasn't ready to resume working just yet. "Don't … touch … the door!" I managed to get out.

The others converged around me and helped me to sit up. Among the queries about my injuries was Gilwyr's sardonic, "He thinks we have a desire to go touch the trap that just knocked him through the air?"

Bridocke replied, "He's fine, then. That's normal for him." They all had a chuckle at my expense. I took that to mean that I looked as if I would survive.

I managed to stand again. I returned to the makeshift hatch with my hands clasped firmly behind my back. This time I took note of the cables running above the door and started looking for their origin. "Did the Grimmerroth place a spell of protection on the doorway?" asked Bridocke as I looked.

"You might say that. He electrified the door. But he had to have some way to let himself in from outside without getting zapped. Ah, here." I had found a small panel that concealed a compartment in which were set an illuminated red button, a screen, and a keypad. I pushed the button and waited. The screen lit up and displayed the single word "Passord?"

I groaned. "We have to enter a secret word to disable the trap. We have to guess what would have been in the mind of a man stranded here four hundred years ago."

"I thought that was your specialty?" said Gilwyr.

"Not quite this literally."

"What is that word on the screen?" asked Ox.

"It's in Trondnorsk, the language of my world. It would have been his native language as well. It's descended from ancient Norwegian." That started me thinking, though. Jonan was stranded here, the only person on this world who spoke Trondnorsk. He desperately wanted to return home to the family he had left behind. What was the name he had said in the recording in the *aelo tai*? I raised my hand to the keypad and typed 'Sophi.'

The button changed color to green, and the screen displayed the number 60, which turned as we watched to 59, then 58. "Hurry!" I said. "We have less than one minute to get inside." We rushed to the door, but I froze as I reached for the panel. The memory of the electrical shock was still too real. Ox moved me aside and swung the panel wide. We all pushed inside as a warning buzzer sounded. Ox released the panel just as another lighted button inside turned from green to red. We heard the sizzle of power being re-applied to the panel and breathed a sigh of relief.

We were inside the starship *Corvus* and the citadel of the most feared warlock on this world.

CHAPTER 51

Corvus

ONCE INSIDE, IT became apparent why the doorway had been cut in the hull at such a distance above ground level. There was a deck just at that level that would have prevented the opening from being any lower. The deck had a hatch set into its center, leading to underground levels. Looking upwards, we found ourselves at the bottom of a shaft at least twenty meters deep, with another hatch set into the ceiling. That one hung open. When I finally put all the features in place, I nearly staggered with the shift in perspective. We were standing on a bulkhead; the wall ahead of us was the floor. People were intended to walk "up" that floor and pass through the bulkhead above us. Artificial gravity or acceleration would normally orient "down" in the direction of the stern of the ship. A ladder bolted to one wall appeared to be meant for use in zero gravity, but I didn't relish the thought of climbing it under surface gravity. The geometry of this shaft seemed weird, as if the converging lines created an optical confusion about the direction of "down." My head swung strangely as I looked around, making me stagger as if drunk.

"Jonan couldn't have carried everything that we saw in the cave down that ladder. There must be a winch or dumbwaiter up above that he used to lower materials down this shaft. If so, there should be a control for it down here." I started to look at the equipment and cobbled-together panels mounted on the walls. As I did that, Gilwyr leaped lightly onto the ladder and started to climb up. "Be on your guard," I called. "He's likely to have left more than one trap."

Gilwyr climbed to just above our heads and stopped. "There is strangeness here," she said. She climbed another two rungs, and we could see that she was being pulled away from the ladder. "The entire tower is falling down!" There was alarm in her voice by now. We all reflexively flung our arms wide to steady ourselves as Gilwyr swung off the ladder and hung perpendicular to the wall. She let go, dropped onto the opposite wall, and stood braced. We held that tableau for long seconds, Gilwyr unnerved by standing on a wall above the floor, Ox and Bridocke in shock at this new magic, while I tried to make sense of it all. Suddenly it clicked, and I started laughing. Bridocke cried, "Sir Warlock has gone mad! He's pinned Gilwyr to the wall!" She clung to Ox as if afraid she was going to fall upwards.

Scuff marks on the wall made sudden sense to me. I sprinted across the floor and leaped into the air. My boot made contact with the wall at about chest height, and already I could feel the floor and walls shifting. I pushed off and started running up the wall. Within a few strides, I reached Gilwyr and stopped. I now felt that I was standing on a floor in a long corridor, while Ox and Bridocke stood on the bulkhead at the end of the corridor at right angles to us. They both looked increasingly distressed in our different orientations.

"The artificial gravity is still on," I told them. "From up here, you'll feel that this is the floor and not a wall. It will make sense when your eyes and body tell you the same story."

"Nothing about this makes sense," said Ox firmly. "However, I'll trust you and climb the ladder to your level." He started climbing the rungs; he was very strong and fit, but not built for the kind of leap that would get him far enough up the wall. As he reached our level, he swung outwards as Gilwyr had done; with an effort of will he let go of the ladder and landed solidly beside us. He looked around at the now-horizontal shaft. "This is extraordinary. If this isn't magic, I don't know what is. Bridocke, it seems safe to come up here."

Bridocke was clinging to the ladder, caught in the war between her sense of weight and the evidence of her eyes. Reluctantly she began to climb, one rung at a time. Her eyes grew rounder as she crossed the zone where gravity twisted by ninety degrees, probably making the sensation worse by creeping slowly and reluctantly through the transition. Her feet slipped from the rungs as the force that had held them there treacherously shifted. She swung to hang aligned with our orientation, but her eyes were still telling her that "down" was towards the bulkhead where we had entered.

"Just let go. It's a short drop and you'll land right beside us."

"How do I know that the magic will work the same way for me? Magic knows I don't like it. It's going to drop me back down there and break my arm."

"It's gravity," I said. "It affects everyone the same. If you jump, you fall back down."

"Birds don't fall down," Bridocke rejoined.

"That's not the same …"

Gilwyr, impatient with the delay, jumped up and wrapped her arms around Bridocke's legs. With a squawk, Bridocke lost her grip on the ladder and they both tumbled to the deck, ending up in a heap with Bridocke on top. They scrambled to untangle themselves, then stood with an air of studied normalcy, as if they had meant to do that. I led everyone onward, up the strut that now lay flat and level before us. Hesitantly at first, the others fell in line and started walking.

After about twenty meters we reached the bulkhead. The door stood open, allowing us to pass through. Another length of shaft/corridor lay ahead of us, just as featureless as the previous section. These appeared to be maintenance passages; they looked far too utilitarian to have been places where passengers would ever venture. We continued our vertical walk and I felt glad that I hadn't had to climb this distance. It would have been a long and tiring climb and a long plunge back down if we slipped. I immediately tried to think about anything other than the odds of the artificial gravity suddenly giving out on this four-hundred-year-old wreck.

Halfway along this section of the passageway, a small device had been dropped on the left side near the wall. It somewhat resembled the hand torch that Jonan had cobbled together with some stray wires and a switch. This one had a red lens set in the side rather than a light source for illumination. Just another piece of junk. As we approached, though, the red light blinked off then on, just once. I put out my arms to stop the others. The light stayed steady. It looked innocent enough, but something was tickling my suspicions. I took one step closer and started to draw my sword with the intention of poking it gingerly from a distance. A sound-less concussion of light struck me nearly blind. Shards of metal flew through the air, razor sharp and red. I looked down and one embedded deeply into my belly. Another smashed into Gilwyr's eye, taking off half of her face. Ox tumbled to the ground with blood fountaining from a severed artery. I only had time for the thought, *of course, there were more booby traps.*

"What's wrong, Stenn?"

Gilwyr was still whole, and Ox was still standing. The shard that had impaled me faded from view. It was a trap, and second sight had warned me of it just before I triggered it. The warning itself had nearly stopped my heart.

"This is a bomb. If we get any closer, it will kill us all."

"How do we get by?"

"Just a moment." I moved to the far side of the corridor and made the smallest of motions forward. The grisly warning repeated. The red eye was evidently a motion sensor. I tried stepping over the beam, only to get a repeat. The only variation was that we all died in different ways each time. I jumped up to grasp the ladder overhead but was warned away from swinging into that area from above.

The eye was on the side of the device so it couldn't look directly upwards. I flattened myself against the wall and sidled up to it, then very carefully stepped one leg over it, paused to make sure that I was still in one piece, and then very slowly brought the other leg after it. Then I side-stepped several paces further up the passage until I was out of the zone.

"Do just what I did and you won't set it off."

One by one they followed until we had passed the trap. I wiped a torrent of sweat from my brow with the edge of my cloak. We continued.

We walked/climbed five sections of passageway in all, placing us at least a hundred meters above ground level. No further traps presented themselves, though we were all on edge every step of the way. Here another bulkhead without a hatch completely blocked further progress. There was a square hatch, closed, in the wall to our left. The access panel beside it was dark; nothing happened when I pressed the button marked "Open" within it. Then I saw that a nearby plate in the wall had been loosened. I swung it open and found a crank with the legend "Emergency door operation." A smaller but more assertively yellow sign said "Fall hazard. Use extreme caution."

"I don't know what's going to happen when I turn this crank," I told them. "Everyone hang on in case the gravity shuts off." There were handholds all around the bulkhead, placed where someone working in zero gravity would find them convenient. None of them would be convenient if the planet's true gravity took over. It was a long way down.

I braced myself and started cranking. The bulkhead started opening slowly, but more smoothly than I would have expected in a derelict like this. My expectations were realized at the two-thirds mark where it jammed, unable to go backward or forwards. I strained at the crank, which rewarded me by making a crunching noise somewhere within its mechanism before spinning freely. Deprived of resistance, I lurched forward through the opening. Vertigo grabbed me by my inner ears. I thought at first the ship had started moving, pushing me back through the opening as it accelerated. Then my brain cried out to my inner ears that the artificial gravity had failed and I was taking a trip down the hundred-meter shaft, with several bone-breaking sojourns along the way. My inner ears informed my brain that I should panic.

In my wild flailing, I caught a handhold and hung on in desperation. I was lying on the side of a shaft that seemed to go downwards both in front and behind. My feet dangled through the opening where "down" felt like an entirely different direction. Contradicting the message from my eyes that I was hanging in a shaft, I was pressed against the wall by what felt like weight. I spent a long minute in total disorientation.

Finally, I recognized features in the shaft that resembled normal doors, and strips in the opposite wall that seemed to be light fixtures. Perspective reasserted itself. I found myself lying on the deck of an ordinary corridor of a starship of somewhat old-fashioned appearance. The opening I had fallen through was a hatch in the wall that gave access to the service way that we had just ascended. The gravity where I lay was at ninety degrees to that within the shaft, which meant it was probably aligned with the planet's gravity, and might, in fact, have been only that. I slowly regained my feet as my balance returned, though turning around to see my companions standing at right angles to me nearly toppled me once more. They swayed in sympathy as well.

"It's fine," I told them. "You can step from there to here without all the theatrics and probably with a good deal more grace."

Gilwyr stepped deftly from wall to floor. She made it look easy. Ox came next, staggering somewhat as the world twisted around him, but maintaining his balance through sheer strength. Bridocke was still unnerved by the changing orientations. She mis-timed the transition and fell heavily as she crossed the boundary. Ox helped her to her feet; we could all tell that she was most injured in her pride from being the slowest to adapt to the strange environment.

"What kind of magic does this place have?" she complained. "Floors become walls with no warning."

"Artificial gravity," I replied. "That's only a faint touch of the power this ship once used to sail between the stars."

"This citadel flew? It moved through the air? How could anything that is so huge fly?"

"It not only flew, but it also sailed through the depths of space between stars, where there is no light and no air. It could travel a distance equal to going around this world a million times in just one month. The full force of the ship's engines wouldn't just pin you to a wall; they would turn you into a thin red smear on that wall."

Ox looked around thoughtfully. "I must admit when you spoke of ships flying between worlds, I had in mind a picture of the sailing ships that set out from Misthaven. I could just about imagine lifting one of those great craft into the air, even though on land it takes a hundred men just to pull them up the shipyard ramp on rollers. To think that this great castle can lift itself into the air is like believing that Rhea can come down from the sky and touch the earth."

"It could fly many years ago. Now I am surprised that there is this much working. I thought the Dust would have finished the job of destroying the ship. It certainly crippled it enough that it crashed here."

"We may need Danallion to answer that."

"He's probably not rehydrated yet. We should scout the ship first and then go back for him."

We headed in the direction of the bow. This was a passenger section, ransacked cabins standing open along the corridor. Furniture had been overturned or broken in most of them. Possessions were strewn about, either plundered by the mutineers or scavenged later by Jonan as he tried to survive on a wrecked ship. The main hull of the *Corvus* was about three hundred meters long, giving us a hike of a hundred and fifty meters to reach the bow. The level of awe in my companions rose progressively at the seemingly endless corridor. Just as it curved in a horseshoe to return aft along the starboard side cabins, it opened on an expanse of tables, bars and boards. The lounge and game room had a favored spot on this ship, with a forward vista through panoramic windows. On the *Aquila*, it had had a more interior location, presumably so the players were not distracted by the view.

We picked our way through overturned tables and spilled game pieces, while I wondered why this hadn't been done with less effort as a simspace construct. Perhaps simulated reality hadn't been as popular in that day, or players preferred the certainty of physical pieces.

From this deck, we had a view over the enclosing walls. In the middle distance, we could see the column of Terrell's army matching ever closer. We had less time left than I had thought. Either we had been longer in the caverns than it had seemed or he had increased the pace of his march.

"We don't have much time left," said Gilwyr, voicing my thought.

"Does this castle have cannons for defense, or something more powerful as befitting the abode of a great warlock?" asked Bridocke.

"These ships were never armed," I said. "There was never anyone to fight against in deep space. Anyone who tried to commandeer one would have been cut off from all commerce by the Void Guild."

"What can we use for defense then?" asked Ox.

"There may be something left from the previous siege," I said. "We have to keep searching."

We turned away from the forward view and the approaching engines of war. Something crunched under my foot. It was a game piece from an ancient strategy game. I wondered what stakes they had played for. We played for the rule of a kingdom and the survival of an ancient race.

Aft of the lounge was a broad stairway flanked by banks of lifts. Even if the lifts were working, I didn't trust them. The stairs didn't look particularly trustworthy either. A pair of skeletons at the bottom raised suspicions on that score.

"They're wearing old Dalactyn uniforms," said Ox. "With holes in them."

"Those were not made by a sword," said Gilwyr. "The opening was punched, not cut. Their ribs are crushed."

Gilwyr took the lead going up the stairs. On the sixth step, the slightest creak sounded. Gilwyr flung herself down just in time as a rod shot out of the wall, driving through the space where she had been standing. It slid back into the wall and reset itself with a satisfied click. We all looked at each other.

"How did this guy survive living in his own castle?" asked Bridocke.

"Maybe he wore a transponder, er, amulet that kept his traps from springing on himself. That way he could lure any pursuers through them, and they wouldn't suspect anything until it was too late."

I examined the stair that had triggered the rod. It was just possible to see the gap under the tread. The very top of the riser beneath it had been shaved away so that it would depress when stepped on. Looking upwards, I could see that the next two steps were also rigged, as were several others at irregular intervals above that to catch those who grew confident too early. I pointed out the deceptive steps to the others.

Gilwyr measured the distance from the stair tread to height of the bar. Crouching down, she crab-walked up to the first step and put her weight on it. The bar sliced the air over her head. She started to move to the next step. I had been watching the bar emerge this time, and saw just in time that the next one was designed to take out an intruder's knees, but Gilwyr was crawling. "Stop!" Gilwyr froze. "Back down. The next one will get you square in the head."

We looked for a safety switch, or an alternate route, but found neither. As we were rummaging in the lounge, I opened a drawer to discover a cache of cutlery. Grasping a dozen knives and a thin hope, I went back to the stairs. I jammed two knives underneath the first stair tread, then gingerly rested my weight on it. The knives prevented the trigger from actuating. In minutes, we had disarmed the remaining traps.

We mounted the stairs to the next deck, which seemed to be entirely populated by suites for the wealthiest passengers. No more traps presented themselves, though tension was high every step of the way.

One more deck and we were in the grand dining room. Where the *Aquila* had had an observation deck, the passengers of the *Corvus* had dined each night beneath the stars. It seemed that practice had waned in popularity over the centuries. My companions boggled at the expanse of tables and place settings, now upset and ruined, but still could be seen to have been sumptuous in their day. "This seated more people than the Mayor's hall in Misthaven," said Ox. "Yet you say this was a ship, not a palace."

Just aft of the dining room we found a door hanging ajar that had a discreet sign reading "Ship's Bridge, Crew Only." The door opened onto a stairway to a higher deck, where the bridge occupied a commanding view forward, and upwards, where the warp torus arched like a too-solid rainbow against the sky. Here we found banks of control panels and display screens, many dark. Some few still operated, conveying news of badly damaged systems. I was amazed that any of it worked after this long. I also recalled that the *Aquila* had had no physical bridge; that must have been a later innovation. Tools and parts lay scattered about, attesting to some of Jonan's attempts to repair or repurpose some of the ship's systems. I studied the displays that seemed to have received the most attention from Jonan with the thought that those were the ones most likely to help us now.

"Jonan was working on the warp torus controls," I said, not having had any expectation that the others would understand. At least they would know I was working out the puzzle. "Was he trying to shut it down or was he trying to make it work again? There's no way this ship would fly again. This is a display of alarms; he's muted most of them. This window has levels for containment field strength. What was he changing? He's overridden limits in these fields, way above the danger zone."

"How are you understanding this?" asked Gilwyr. "You said you had not studied the magic that your ancestor used."

"I don't know what these mean or what he was trying to do, but these graphics are common ways to convey information. This slider changes the amount of something, in this case, something called the Stieg

Field, and this red color on the end means that it is set to a dangerous value. I have no idea what a Stieg Field is."

"So we learn that your ancestor was mad and chancy," said Bridocke. "Legend already tells us that. We're here to keep you from following that same path."

"I won't touch anything. I just found what I was looking for—a schematic of the ship. Jonan was working on something in Engineering. He has marked a number of systems for modification, and they all converge there. It's the very center of the ship, three decks below and fifty meters aft."

I hesitated. An idea had been forming since it had become apparent that the *Corvus* wasn't the cold dead hulk that I had assumed. It might be risky; it might not accomplish anything. I reached up to my temple and pressed the switch under the skin.

My implants started through their self-check procedure. I hadn't even been sure there was anything left to activate. I swayed slightly on my feet as my vision was overlaid with data displays: once so common, now unfamiliar. I had missed them so much at the beginning, but now I felt a mild distaste at the clutter in my field of view. These displays showed only internal status, indicating damaged systems, abnormal inputs, and a lack of access to the external network of simspace. These blanked, and I was left with only the plaintive message, "No connection."

I wasn't surprised. Even had both the ship and my implants been undamaged, they were separated by four hundred years of cybernetic evolution. From the point of view of technical sophistication, perhaps a larger gap than between us and our Neolithic ancestors. There had been little hope that they would be compatible.

We retraced our steps down the stairs to the level where we had entered, avoiding the traps we had identified and not finding any new ones. The schematic had shown that there were three additional decks below that one, primarily crew quarters, galleys, storage, and cargo holds. The main hull of the Corvus was a flattened oval, sixty meters by ninety meters in cross-section, and three hundred meters long. That was a lot of ship to search in the little time that we had. I hoped that we would find something useful in engineering. Somewhat aft of the access shaft where we had emerged from the strut there was a transverse corridor in which we found the heavy steel doors to engineering.

This was a huge space, filling most of the width of the ship, two decks in height, and extending to the stern of the main hull. It was dominated by a vast ring. This would be the fusion reactor that powered the ship and maintained the containment of the thick plasma of trans-baryonic matter that filled the warp torus. The reactor was still running, keeping the ship alive, though there was an alarming number of red lights visible around the room.

We picked our way towards the reactor, across a broken field of cables, conduit, and parts. Consoles had been opened up and wires cut and spliced with more urgency than grace. Thick conductors led towards a nexus at the base of the reactor. A wiring diagram hung impaled on a spike like an offering to the gods of matter and energy. If Jonan hadn't been mad himself, it was because he had grounded his madness in the tormented machinery of his citadel.

Gilwyr saw it first. She clutched my arm and pointed mutely. Close by the side of the reactor an *aelo tai* sat on a pedestal at about chest height. It was a dusky yellow color that I would have probably called saffron, though it wasn't quite any color that had been named by humans. Light seemed to fall into it from all around. As I moved toward it, it shifted oddly against the background as if it were somehow farther away than it was possible to be. Cables fed power to the pedestal; several other devices arranged around it might have been containing or control-ling, or observing it. The *aelo tai* seemed to recede from us as we ap-proached the pedestal until it appeared that it was hastening down a long flowing corridor.

"I believe we have found what we came for," said Ox.

I reached out my hand. The air resisted, becoming stiffer the more I pushed. I felt a tingle building up in my fingertips followed by a sharp and painful electrical discharge that hurled my hand away.

"Now that we've found it, how do we take it?"

CHAPTER 52

Legends

"HOW ARE WE going to remove the *aelo tai*?" asked Gilwyr. "Do you have another magic word to disable this trap?"

"I don't think it's that easy, in this case. This isn't a trap; it's part of the mechanism. I think we need to go back for Danallion now. He may understand what Jonan was trying to do with the *aelo tai*."

"I'll go fetch him," volunteered Bridocke. "You keep looking for a way to turn aside Terrell when he gets here."

"I'll go with you," said Ox.

"It only takes one person. Stay here and help Stenn. Now that we know where the traps are, I won't be long."

"We don't know that we've found them all," I said. "You need to stay alert. Do you know how to disarm the outer door?"

"You tapped on the hidden lights under the small door."

"I entered a name."

"A name?"

"Yes, there were letters on the panel, and I had to spell out the name 'Sophi' on them."

"Letters?" Her face fell.

"You can read, can't you?"

"Not well," she admitted.

I drilled her on what the keys looked like, and how to press the letters in the right sequence. More than nearly anything else on this planet, finding someone who couldn't read reinforced the distance I had come in time and space and culture from my homeworld. Probably many people I had met on this world had never learned to read, yet I never thought to question that assumption.

When we were satisfied that Bridocke would be able to enter the correct code, we let her go. I had tried to write the password on the back of her hand with a marker that I found on a workbench, but it had dried up. She had promised to remember it and had recited the letters back to me. She waved jauntily as she left, though Ox was concerned about traps that she might not recognize. "She'll be fine," Gilwyr told him. "She's a good fighter and has an instinct for survival. She should have more confidence in her own abilities. I'm glad she spoke up to do this on her own."

"I am glad to hear you say so," said Ox. "You have high standards, and I have felt she didn't always meet with your approval."

"Everyone feels that way around Gilwyr," I said. "She has a hard time living up to her standards herself."

I said that lightly, intending to tease my Guild master, but I saw that it stung more than I had meant it to. She tried not to let her expression change, but a tear glinted in the corner of one eye. "When did you become so wise?"

I put my hands on her shoulders and looked into her eyes. "I left my home with a great deal of learning, but little wisdom. If I have a little more wisdom now, it's because I learned no small amount from you, from your stories, from your actions, and from your blades and the bruises they gave me." That got a small smile from her. "And I learned from those you called friends, from Ox and Bridocke, from Danallion and Perrhen and Aymer and the others. With friends like those, it's hard not to have high standards."

Suddenly she was holding me tight, head buried against my shoulder. That was a first for her. "You believed in me, from the first. Even when I doubted myself nearly every step of the way."

"You? You never showed it."

"I can't. That's not how I was raised. Never doubt, just do."

Ox had turned aside to study some displays, pretending not to listen. It seemed like a good opportunity to kiss her, so I did. It was awkward and brief; we both needed practice, but I felt she would be willing to put in the time to work on it once we got out of this mess.

A message flashed in my retina: "Obsolete interface: low data rate. No sensory information." My implants had made contact with the ship's systems. I blinked as I tested the connections. Some thirty years ago I had installed a package of protocol-matching AI for the purposes of an archeological dig into some ancient data archives. They hadn't proven useful in that project, and I had forgotten about them, until now.

"What is it?" asked Gilwyr. A sudden blank-eyed stare wasn't the best way to end a personal moment.

"I've just made contact with the Citadel, the ship."

"It's *talking* to you?"

"Not yet. Only low-level functions." I knew that probably didn't mean anything to her, but I was occupied. The first things I saw were the alarms: failed systems, security breaches, damaged memories, radiation warnings, and a general evacuation notice. I sorted through those so that I could see what was still relevant. The security breach had a date four hundred years in the past; was that when the mutineers hacked into the systems to take over the ship or was it Jonan who had disabled security protocols so that he could make modifications at will? Whichever it was, it now allowed me free access to normally locked-down ship systems. I found the internal and external video feeds fairly quickly, though there were many blind spots where cameras had failed. I commanded the external bow feed to display on the nearby monitors. The flourish of hand and wrist as I did so was completely unnecessary, but given our recent conversations, I couldn't resist the drama.

My flourish ended limply as the scene formed on the screen. The vanguard of Terrell's forces was already amassing outside of the breach in the outer wall that had been left by his ancestor's siege. They had moved faster than we had expected.

"How is there suddenly a window in the wall?" asked Gilwyr.

"Magic," was all the answer I had time for.

"Where's Bridocke?" asked Ox urgently.

"I'm looking." I found the cameras in the access passage that we had ascended. Only a single camera was still working, in the third section about halfway up. From that vantage point, we could see Bridocke just reaching the entrance. She only hesitated a moment, then typed the password on the pad and exited the ship. I found an aft camera that was still working, though it didn't quite cover the area near the support strut. Soon Bridocke came into view, looking back over her shoulder. She had seen the vanguard and was hurrying to get out of sight. Switching back to the bow camera, we could see that everyone was looking up in awe at the great Citadel. No one appeared to notice the small figure of Bridocke escaping.

"I am glad she didn't turn back," said Ox. "She will be safer in the cave."

"I'm going to try again to remove the *aelo tai*. If we have it, we can get out of here and join her."

I approached the pedestal again. I asked the ship for the schematics of this area. If I could remove the power from the pedestal, perhaps then I could take the *aelo tai* from its setting. After a maddening delay, all it produced was "Unknown Device." I tried telling the ship to shut down all power. We could always make our way out in the dark if necessary. The ship replied, "Removal of power will result in catastrophic containment breach."

"I'm glad you're looking out for me," I muttered.

"I beg your pardon?" said Ox.

"I'm talking to the ship. It would rather that I not blow us all up."

Combine your senses.

"Did you hear that?" I asked.

"Hear what?" asked Gilwyr.

"I thought someone spoke out loud."

"I heard nothing," said Ox, and Gilwyr nodded.

Only you, with one foot in both worlds.

My recent history hadn't predisposed me to trust voices in my head. There didn't seem to be any harm in looking, however. I called for second sight.

The fusion reactor bloomed like a fiery rose within a tracery of magnetic fields. The room pulsed with rushing currents of power, though some areas were dead and dark. I was reminded uncomfortably of the Blight, eating away at the heart of the Silent City. The sense that light was falling inwards into the *aelo tai* intensified. Now I could perceive that it was uneven, with ripples and currents. One yellow stream, in particular, seemed like the deep channel in a mighty river, deceptively calm yet tremendous in its force. I stepped to the side to see where this channel led. Onward into the heart of the *aelo tai* it swept, an invitation to lose oneself in the depths. I remembered the feeling of gazing into the red *aelo tai*; this was similar to that but deeper, stronger, and more seductive.

Far away, down that long tunnel of saffron light, I saw two figures, locked in combat.

I'm not sure why I stepped into the stream. The voice in my head probably knew. It had set me up by getting me to use second sight. Now I was striding down the glowing corridor towards the two figures. They seemed frozen in place, and very far away, though every step I took seemed to halve the remaining distance. One was a man in a cloak, with long grey hair and beard. The other was a woman in leather armor with the shield of Dalactus emblazoned on it. It couldn't be, not after all these years …

As I neared, their movements sped up. Now they were striking and parrying. The man had a steel staff, and the skill to use it; it gave him the advantage of reach to keep his opponent at bay. The woman had a sword and used it in the style of the Daughters rather than the style of one trained by the Cray Leth. I could quickly tell that the woman was the more skillful; it seemed that the eternal fight wouldn't last much longer. It didn't seem possible, but I had already seen someone brought back from the dead and had an alien gem implanted in my eye; one more impossibility had to be taken in stride.

These had to be Jonan and Rowena, locked in combat for eternity just as legend had said.

CHAPTER 53

Behind the Legend

I CLOSED WITH the combatants, my own sword drawn but held to the side, point downward. I came to intervene, not to engage. "Put down your weapons! Your fight is over. The world outside has changed."

Rowena took a step back and to the side so that she could cover both her opponent and me. Jonan took the opportunity for a vicious swing at her knees. Had he been faster he would have crippled her, but the length of the staff made it a slow weapon to swing. Rowena danced back out of range and circled to make him turn his back on me. I took a step forward to try to disarm him, but he jabbed backward with his staff. Warned by second sight, I ducked in time; the staff whistled by my left ear.

Jonan was out of position for a split second. Rowena charged in to take the opening. Second sight showed me her blade slicing into his arm; it wouldn't kill but it would disable. I could not allow that ending to this fight. I stepped between them, placing an elbow in his ribs and blocking her sword. "Wha' alligh hath thou got'n, War'lock?" she said in a dialect not heard in this world in four hundred years. They had probably made as much sense out of my pronunciation and would need more direct communication.

I swept her sword wide but didn't avoid a jab in the side from the staff. Fortunately, I was too close for Jonan to get a swing that would have broken as many ribs as he would have liked, but it still drove the wind out of me. I swung back and caught him with the pommel of my sword in the chin in return, and we all stepped back to a respectful distance.

You are inside an aelo tai.

That pesky voice had pursued me even in here. I felt that it was pointing out the obvious at the moment.

Rowena was sizing me up, probably assigning me to the role of foe, or at least not ally. Jonan was swinging his staff back and forth, likewise uncertain as to whom I would aid. I had to end this and get back to the *Corvus* before the situation with Terrell came to a head.

The aelo tai is your will. Your will is the aelo tai.

What was the voice going on about? It was starting to feel familiar, in a nagging, cryptic way.

Rowena feinted towards me and I brushed her aside, warned by second sight. But that was just to position her to spin and deliver a backhand slash to her opponent, who had no second sight to warn him. I saw the blade as it would be a few instants in the future: slicing through tendon and bone, severing his arm and biting deep into his chest. "No!" I cried. I reached out and plucked the sword from her hand, even though she was at least two paces away. She looked in amazement at her empty hand. Jonan recovered and swung his staff for her temple, going for the kill.

And his hand was empty. I held both weapons, and I understood. We were within the *aelo tai*, and I could direct it. With a flick of my hand, I made their weapons disappear and sheathed my own. An *aelo tai* was a computational engine, and it could manipulate the physical world. Within, it contained a model of the world and one who understood it could control it, like a simspace.

I brought the two closer. They didn't move, they simply were standing closer than they were an instant before. "This ends now," I said. "The world has changed. I am your grandson … *Jeg er barnebarnet ditt.*" I added in Trondnorsk, leaving out the number of 'greats' that were needed to make that true. I turned to Rowena. "And my friend, your king, is waiting outside that portal."

I turned and started walking back to the beginning of the glowing corridor, back to the engine room of the *Corvus*. The other two walked beside me because I willed them to. I knew that I would lose that control over them once we stepped out of the *aelo tai*, but I didn't have a plan for that yet. I hoped that Gilwyr and Ox would react quickly enough to help me.

Jonan struggled. He didn't want to go back. "Nayh follow red stone, must ayh! Red stone way home, tis."

"The red *aelo tai* isn't on Trondhjem anymore. I brought it back here with me."

I was thankful to not be able to interpret the invective that he heaped on me and on Rowena. He blamed both of us for breaking the portal that would have taken him to his home. Neither he nor Rowena had yet comprehended that four hundred years had passed while they struggled. Time must run incredibly slowly within this passageway. The thought made me hurry to climb back out to the real world. I didn't want to emerge to find that another hundred years had passed and my friends long gone.

I drew my sword as we reached the mirror-like end of the glowing passageway. I indicated that we were all to step through together and that any wrong move would be met with a sharp point. Jonan was angry, but it was Rowena that I watched. She was resourceful, she was sly, and she had confidence in her skills. As I anticipated, she broke to the right as we stepped through, seized the first object at hand from a workbench, a wrench of some kind, and threw it at me. I saw it coming in second sight and ducked it, at the same time shouting for Ox and Gilwyr, hoping that they wouldn't be caught off guard.

I tripped Jonan as he lunged for freedom in the other direction and held him down with my sword at his throat, trying to make him believe that I would hurt him if he struggled, though I knew I would stop short of that. I wouldn't hurt a kinsman—or at least not one I didn't know yet, I amended, thinking of a couple of particularly odious cousins.

Rowena had made the mistake of trying to take Gilwyr's sword away from her. As startled as she was by having two strangers appear from thin air, Gilwyr knocked Rowena away and covered her with her sword. Ox approached from behind and Rowena whirled to face this new adversary but stopped in dismay.

"Roland? King Roland? How came thou here?" Her face worked through amazement, puzzlement, concern. "Thou are not Roland."

Ox looked down on her with bemusement. "I am Greylander de Oxendon, first son of Godric, the sixteenth King of Dalactus in the line of Roland."

I gestured grandly though a trifle ironically. "Prince Greylander, I would like to present to you Rowena ad Aulem, and my ancestor Jonan Gremm, also known as the Grimmerroth." And to them, I added, "This is Gilwyr of the Cray Leth, a Master of the Assassin's Guild."

Ox stared at the pair for a moment. "I have seen many wonders this day, but this is the most astounding. I stand face to face with legend."

Rowena bowed stiffly, though not quite taking her eyes off anyone. "My Liege. Be this true? Yet your resemblance to Roland be uncanny. Sixteen generations? How can I believe it?"

"Believe it. I have seen more strange things this past year than have troubled this land in generations. They all started when this traveler from another world arrived in my chambers in Misthaven. He bore a strange red stone, pursued by morghaests, and was seeking his ancestor who had vanished four hundred years ago."

"Where is this red stone now?"

I raised my eye patch. "Here is part of it. Greylander's younger brother Terrell has stolen the stone itself. Terrell is outside the ship now with a siege force."

"Thank the old gods that it has been returned," said Rowena. "It did nothing to your planet while it was there?"

"Nothing more than sit in a bank vault for four hundred years."

"Then it was not in vain. It was to prevent that terrible weapon from getting loose on human worlds that I went to war against one whom I once aided."

"You once aided Jonan?"

"Aye. I persuaded Roland and the others not to kill him when first they took over the ship. Jonan was a different person before he lost his hand."

All eyes turned to Jonan, where he huddled on the floor. He was muttering about pocket universes and time streams. I had to remind myself that despite their age, Jonan and Rowena were starfarers like myself and knew much more of technology than my current companions.

Then Jonan reached up with his left hand to brush the hair from his eyes, and we all saw what Rowena meant. Jonan's hand was made of red *aelo tai* crystal or had been once. Now it was streaked with black, with only a few veins of red remaining. It had been infected with the Blight.

CHAPTER 54

Siege

OX BROKE THE tableau. "There are many stories we must tell each other, but for now, there is the pressing matter of a siege outside this Citadel. We must be brief. Can you two lay aside your struggle for the moment? If you continue to fight yesterday's battles, you will have no hope of engaging in today's."

Jonan spoke in an erratic jumble of Galactic and Trondnorsk, both laced with archaic words and pronunciation. I translated as best I could: "He asks how the ship can still be under siege if it has truly been four hundred years?"

"This is a new siege, not the one you remember. My brother leads this one, with the intent of seizing the *aelo tai* and any other artifacts that he can use to further his own ambitions for ruling in Dalactus and spreading his influence across all the lands. Will you aid us?"

Rowena wasn't satisfied yet. She looked at Ox shrewdly. "You claimed to be of the line of Roland and son of the king. Did Roland then establish a monarchy of bloodline?"

Ox appeared bemused. "Yes, of course."

"When last I was in Dalactus, a few months ago it was to me, the faction in support of hereditary kings was only a few—a small minority. Roland himself claimed not to favor the idea, siding with the many who believed it best to select new kings by vote of the council of lords." I was quickly adjusting to Rowena's outdated pronunciation.

"Roland lived for another thirty years after the war," replied Ox. "He presumably changed his mind later in life, and swayed enough of his people to support him. Your tone suggests that you believe there are better ways to choose a ruler than heredity. If so, you would find that I agree with you. My brother, however, does not."

"You speak of your brother, and you speak of a siege. These are connected, are they not? You are having a dispute over the succession, and are both hoping to find a decisive advantage in this ship."

"You are as perceptive as legend says."

"Legend? Tell me they did not make a hero of me! No, of course they did. They celebrated their cause and ascribed to me all the virtues I never had so they could inspire others to have them. Dead heroes are a god-send to a king: they're not around to embarrass you, or contradict you, or worse, think they can do your job better than you can. Is that what they saddled me with?"

"The royal guard has been known ever since as the Sons and Daughters of Rowena."

"Save me from fools and kings!"

Ox smiled. "I hope to do that, with your help. I do not wish to rule. I oppose Terrell because his rule would be bad for Dalactus, not because I desire it for myself. He killed my other brother Gerard, who would have been better than either of us."

"I have only been in this world … in this time … for a few minutes. It is early to understand who the players are, and who to support. At least you ask, rather than demand or compel, which inclines me to help you. Still, you look far too like Roland."

"Is that an issue?"

Her expression darkened. "Roland is not … *was* not a particularly trustworthy man."

"Our history tends to paint him as the noble founder of our city, but with the stories I have uncovered recently, and the tale brought by Stenn from his world, I can believe what you say."

"I think that Bridocke and her compatriots in the Hidden Hand might have no trouble believing her story," I pointed out to Ox.

"That is so," said Ox.

"Where is Bridocke now, anyway?" I asked.

"We could see in the magic windows that she made it safely to the cave, but the invaders have now surrounded the ship, so we are cut off from her. There is at least no sign that they have discovered the hidden entrance to the cave."

"How long was I gone?"

"The sun was at high noon when you vanished," said Gilwyr. "It is now more than halfway to the horizon."

The mention of the cave cracked Jonan's bubble of gloom. "*Hule*? People in my *hule*? Not safe."

"Is Bridocke in danger?"

"We can see!" Jonan scrambled from under Gilwyr's sword point and rushed to a console. He had the advantage that she didn't want to hurt him and he didn't seem to care if she did. He tapped some controls on the panel and a screen that was currently showing the uninteresting scene of an internal corridor switched to a view of the cave. Nothing seemed disturbed since we had left it, though that was hard to tell amid the general chaos of Jonan's housekeeping. No one was visible in range of the camera at the moment.

"Is there audio?" I asked. I knew there was, from the data that my implants were feeding me, but I didn't want to tip my hand to Jonan about the degree of access I had to his ship. Not yet. Kinsman or not, I was still unsure of his stability.

Jonan touched another control and pushed a slider to the far right. "Loud-speaking."

I spoke to the console. "Bridocke! If you're in the cave, come towards my voice. Come towards the workbench."

We waited a moment. Gilwyr started to say, "What is this accomplishing?" when Bridocke stumbled into view of the video. "Stenn? Where are you? You sound like the Voice of Milhadron."

Ox broke in, "Bridocke, are you safe?" Bridocke threw her hands up to cover her ears. Jonan had the presence of mind to slide the volume control back to lower level. "Is that better now?" I asked.

"Yes, but my ears are still ringing. Who is that standing next to you? Where is everyone else? And what are you doing inside that dark mirror?"

"We're on the ship still. This is Jonan Gremm." I gestured the others over. "This is Rowena ad Aulem, and here are Ox and Gilwyr."

"Rowena? Jonan? What is this? Are you jesting at my expense again, Sir Warlock?"

"No, they have been frozen in time, just like the legend said."

Jonan pointed at a chronometer on the panel. "Se på det! Four hundred and seven years! It is true."

"Are you safe?" Ox tried again. "Terrell's men have surrounded the Citadel."

"Yes, we're safe. The entrance to the cave is hard to see. I had to search for it a bit even though we just came out of it. The rocks don't retain many footprints. Danallion is starting to come around, but isn't ready to travel yet."

Ox reached out and tapped the video screen. "This magic window. Does it open? Can we step through it?"

Rowena looked at Ox in disbelief. "Magic? Have you people forgotten everything?"

Ox shot her a dark look. He had seemed somewhat awed at first by this figure out of legend, but awe was starting to be rasped away by her sharp tongue.

"We found a vault, known only to the King," I offered. "It had artifacts and records from the landing. My guess is that they constructed an alternate history and sealed the records of the real events. Our technology is destroyed by this planet and no one saw the Corvus descend from the sky. This world is completely cut off, its location unknown; it was easy enough for the survivors to dismiss the old existence as tales of magic and integrate with the earlier human settlers here. It's been sixteen generations or more since then. Much can be forgotten in that time."

"I am quite appalled with my countrymen ..." Rowena began. A clang rang out down the corridor as if someone had rung the dinner bell of doom. We all looked at the monitors to locate the source of the disturbance. The besiegers were attacking the doorway at ground level with a ram. A prone figure on the ground was likely the first person to attempt to open the hatch with bare hands. As we watched, the ramming squad got up speed and charged the door. The ramp at the end slowed them down, but they still hit the door at considerable speed. The ram bounced off the makeshift hatch, sending the bearers sprawling. Seconds later we heard the hollow boom echoing up the corridors.

"Ta hatch won't stand 'gainst ta ram!" shrilled Jonan. He slid an interlock labeled "safety." It took me a second to realize the word was written in Trondnorsk, not Galactic as the other controls were. That meant it was something that Jonan had rigged ...

Jonan pushed a button on the new panel that opened up and pressed "confirm." A cloud blossomed around the invaders. Bodies, weapons, dirt, and stone were thrown into the air, escaping the cloud briefly to bounce on the ground some distance away, only to be covered again by the expanding cloud. A bass rumble beat faintly against the hull of the ship. We watched, stunned, for nearly a minute as the dust cleared, revealing a sizable crater at the bottom of the ramp. Ox was the first to break the silence in the old engine room.

"Those were my countrymen," he grated. He seized Jonan by the collar, hauling him up until they were nose to nose. Jonan's feet dangled high above the ground. I had seldom seen Ox truly angry before, but now he was turning purple with rage. "Those are the people I'm fighting for! Those are the people who don't have a choice who they fight for. I might have to fight them. I might have to kill them because they have been ordered to kill me. But I'm not going kill them wholesale, and I'm not going to kill them with cowardly magic, do you understand me? You tell us what you can do, and we decide whether it is right or wrong."

"'We decide?' Not the kind of King ol' Roland was. He didn't know ta meaning of 'we.'"

"Are you mocking me?" Ox's grip tightened. Jonan's face went white.

"Nie! Nie! It is a good t'ing. Only … 'we' include him, nie?" He flicked his eyes in my direction. "He has ta black too, you know."

"Yes … but I've forsworn using it," I told him. "How did you know?"

"I can feel it. It vibrates like ta buzz of an angry wasp."

"Put him down, Ox," said Gilwyr. "To him, it was only an hour ago that he was fighting a different army. We need all the help we can get. Give him a chance to aid us; I promise that I will separate his head from his body the instant that he acts without your permission."

Ox glared at Jonan for a long, tense moment, still suffused with fury but struggling to get it under control. He lowered Jonan finally, saying, "Very well. Gilwyr always does exactly what she says she will do. Remember that."

Rowena had been watching the proceedings and now said, "Prince Greylander, as Jonan says, Roland is … was a heavy-handed ruler. Your concern for needless killing is a welcome change. But do you have what it takes to win this fight? How exactly have you fought for your people so far?"

"When Terrell had our middle brother Gerard assassinated by his own guard, I returned to Dalactus to reclaim the throne …" He paused.

"And how did that go for you?"

"Not well, I admit. I received my father's blessing to succeed him, but Terrell sprang a trap on us and held us prisoner while he was coronated."

"You say you returned to Dalactus… You had been away for some time, I wager? You were out of touch?"

"I had been a teacher at the University for over twenty years. I never wanted to rule. I was willing that Gerard be the one to succeed to the throne. He had an aptitude for ruling. I wanted to explore the world and make a study of its people and cultures, both human and Kir Leth."

"So you haven't actually fought for your people?"

"In my youth I joined the Hidden Hand, the Anglich movement, incognito of course. They helped me in my return to Dalactus, and in my flight after Terrell's trap. I have pledged them to retake the throne so that I can build a new Dalactus that includes both Anglich and Dalactyn."

"But you haven't yet fought for them."

For a moment, I thought Ox was going to let his smoldering anger reignite. Then he deflated. "I must be honest and say that I have not. I can make excuses, but a king should accept responsibility. I was content to stay in my quiet backwater and study. Now that I have been thrust from that backwater, and now that I see the dangers of letting Terrell and his cronies assume power, I know that I must learn how to fight."

Rowena nodded. "That at least I can teach you. I wanted to know if you saw yourself clearly. You cannot direct your hands if you do not know where your feet are planted."

"I think the legends of you are not so far off," said Ox ruefully. Rowena rolled her eyes, but a wry smile crept across her face.

We turned our heads at a shout from Jonan. More invaders and siege engines were coming in through the gap in the wall, reminding us of our precarious position.

"Jonan, is the ship still capable of powering those lightning bolts you rigged?" ask Rowena.

Jonan looked at the displays, then moved his hands. Rowena said sharply, "Just say if it does. Don't do anything until the Prince commands."

"Jest readin' ta capacitors." Rowena signaled that he could proceed. "T'ere is power for one, maybe two. Den ta engines must be started."

"Prince Greylander, we can put a lightning bolt over their heads, which should frighten them into retreating. I can attest that it worked well against my troops when I was not expecting it."

"You may call me Ox, as my companions do," he said as he considered. "Very well, let us try that."

Jonan moved some controls. A rising whine sounded through the engine room. Then he pulled a lever on the console, unusual in being a physical lever rather than the electronic metaphor of itself on a touchscreen. Scratches on the console suggested that it had been installed by Jonan and wasn't original equipment. On the screens showing the forward view a jagged bolt etched itself. It was blinding even through the screen pickups and left black afterimages on our retinas for minutes afterward. The bolt grounded itself in the rock wall near the gap, starting a rock slide that piled debris into the opening (which had to be the very opening that legend said that Rowena blew in the outer wall four centuries ago). The thunderclap from the lightning bolt buffeted the ship, followed by the roar of the falling rocks. Invaders ran in panic from the noise and destruction. There appeared to have been few if any casualties from the rockslide, though I thought privately that was more from chance than design.

From the pickup in the cave we heard Bridocke mutter, "Stenn was bad enough, but now we have two warlocks to deal with."

Rowena pointed to an abandoned cart. "That looks like a juicy target. Can you hit that with lightning?"

"Ja ..."

"Hold on. Prince ... ah, Ox ... a demonstration?"

"Go ahead, Jonan."

Jonan changed a setting, then pulled the lever again. This bolt wasn't as intense as the first one, but the results were considerably more spectacular. The cart exploded in a fireball that burned hotly for some seconds, followed by a detonation that hurled flaming bits of cart, stone, and dirt in all directions. The intense heat drew the dust and smoke up in a column that bloomed into a mushroom over the site, laced with flashes of continued secondary blasts.

Into the silence Jonan said appreciatively, "Oooh."

"What was *that*?" asked Ox.

"When the first lightning bolt hit, soldiers hid under other carts, but not that one. They ran from that cart as fast as they could. I suspected that to be their ammunition cart. Not only did that intimidate the soldiers, but it also deprived them of a large part of their explosives. They won't be able to blow a hole in the ship now, even if the officers can harangue them into getting close enough to make the attempt."

Soon all of the invaders had withdrawn beyond the surrounding wall. Shadows were drawing about the ship as the sun approached the horizon. Through the wall, the desert was still bathed in ruddy illumination, but night was swiftly falling around the ship. We could see Terrell's forces maneuvering beyond, and there appeared to be some watchers posted where they could keep an eye on the ship. Bridocke wanted to return to us, but we agreed that was too risky; likewise, if we tried to make a run for the cave, it was likely we would be spotted and pursued. Jonan confirmed that there were no real defenses in the cave. We had to wait for an opening.

"Can you hit the other wall of the opening?" asked Ox. "Perhaps we could close off the wall again with landslides."

"Nie, ta capacitors are empty. Would need ta start engines ta recharge them. Take hours."

"I advise you to let him start doing that," said Rowena. "It's one of the few weapons we have. We should ready every defense and counterattack that we can muster."

"You built that wall, didn't you?" I asked Jonan.

"Ja, I can feel ta rock and reach out as if I still had my hand. I can push it with my hand if it is ta right kind of rock. I can mold it with my hand if it's another kind of rock. I made men from rock and clay that way, but they do terrible things. I don't do that anymore."

Jonan's hand had been turned to crystal by an *aelo tai* or was itself an *aelo tai*. To him, manipulating the Dust was a tactile feeling. To me, it was visual: I saw the Dust particles and visualized how I wanted them arranged. They moved to assemble themselves as I saw them. Interesting. This should tell me something more about our connection to these alien crystals, but I didn't see it.

I tried to strike up a conversation with Jonan, which quickly centered around whether we really had the same last name, given that the 'G' was no longer pronounced. I had to explain linguistic drift, something that his engineering background hadn't covered.

We passed the night sleeping in shifts. Though it seemed that Jonan and Rowena had joined forces with us, by unspoken consent we made sure that one of our party was awake at all times to keep an eye on them. They might have agendas of their own. Jonan tinkered with the engines during his periods of waking, getting them ready for a restart after four centuries of idleness.

"What the hell is that?"

My eyes flew open with a start of guilt. Rowena was on watch, and I was supposed to be watching her. On the monitors, light was beginning to spill across the plain. One eye blink ago it had been pitch black, telling me that I had been seriously asleep for some time. I looked around, trying to assure myself that my lapse hadn't been noticed. Rowena was watching the forward monitors intently.

A gigantic cart was being wheeled into the opening in the outer wall. It was pulled by a dozen draft horses and was so long that it required four axles to support it. It must have been a nearly impossible load to haul across the desert, which is probably why it had lagged far enough behind the convoy that we hadn't seen it.

"Dalactus doesn't have any war wagons that big," said Ox. "No one does. Bridocke!"

Bridocke appeared in the cave monitor, rubbing her eyes. "What is it?"

"Look on the screen. Have you seen that before?"

From the way her mouth fell open, we could tell the answer even before she said, "No, I've never seen that before, or anything close to that size."

"It may be a huge battering ram," said Rowena. "Jonan, do you have the engines ready yet?"

"Ja, maybe. Maybe can get ten percent power out of them, charge the capacitors."

"By your leave, Ox?" Rowena was playing the faithful general to the hilt. Ox nodded. Jonan moved some controls. Power leads hummed, and I could see that Jonan was watching a linear chart labeled "Plasma Temperature" that was starting to climb towards a mark that indicated the level needed for startup.

"Ignition in ten minutes," Jonan said.

The cart had stopped a respectful distance from the ship, and men were unshipping side panels. "It doesn't look like a ram," muttered Ox.

The men had the sides clear and now pivoted the top off on wooden rails. The lid crashed on the ground in a puff of dust that momentarily obscured the scene. As the dust settled, a statue of an armored man was revealed, lying on its back on the cart. It looked somehow familiar to me.

"It's one of the guardian statues from the wall of Dalactus," said Ox. "Why in the world have they dragged it here? Wait … What is it doing? Oh, that can't be good."

The statue was stirring on the bed of cart while the men who had unpacked it fled in terror. Ponderously it stood and turned towards the ship.

"I presume this means that Terrell has mastered the *aelo tai*," I said hollowly. All eyes turned towards me.

I waved my hand at the screen. "That's a thirty-foot tall morghaest out there."

CHAPTER 55

Theater of the Mind

"WHAT'S A MORGHAEST?" asked Jonan.

We all looked at him in disbelief. "You made them," said Ox. "The creatures of stone and clay that ravaged the land. The unstoppable soldiers that leveled Coygne and made it almost as far as Dalactus."

"Nie, I never called them that. I called them my defenders, I called them my vengeance. At the end, I called them my folly and my downfall. But I never made that *monstrum* … that behemoth out there."

"It was Sir Daniel the Bard who gave them the name, from some ancient earth tale he knew," said Rowena.

"We have encountered quite a few in our journey," I said. "They all glowed the same way that thing out there is glowing. In truth, it's more the reverse of a glow; a halo of blackness. Can't you see that?"

"See it? Nie, I never see a glow. I can feel them." Jonan raised his stiff hand in a gesture of reaching out to poke and pinch something pliable. "Ja, it is made of the same stuff, but I not make this one."

"Is it vulnerable to a lightning bolt?" I asked.

"Ja, maybe. We see." Jonan reached for the controls.

"Hold on! Not without orders." Rowena seemed to be a stickler for chain of command. "Ox, what is your command?"

"Go ahead. Do what you need to protect the citadel, the cave, and the people within. Do not hesitate to wait for orders."

Rowena nodded to Jonan, who began a sequence of operations on the console. "Plasma is at temperature. Magnets degraded, but good enough for low power. Not taking off, are we?" His cackle made icy bird feet run up my back.

"The soldier is coming nearer," said Gilwyr. "It is halfway to the base of the tower."

"Starting plasma injection. Firing ignition laser. Nie… Nie… Nie… Ja! Sustained fusion reaction after four hundred years of shutdown. I knew I was good. Now to charge ta capacitors. It will take about ten minutes."

"That was warlock talk, was it?" Gilwyr asked me quietly. "An incantation?"

"A chant to the god of the fusion reactor, I would say."

"It seemed to have worked. I've never heard you sound like that," she said.

"We're from different sects. He's an engineer."

Rowena was tracking the progress of the giant morghaest. "I don't think we have ten minutes. Do you have any other tricks?"

"Nie. Used ta last landmine yesterday. A little shock from ta door won't stop that *monstrum*. All my traps are too small."

"If this were a castle we would pour boiling oil on it," I said sardonically.

A shrill buzz filled the engine room. Lights blared red, and many of the displays flashed warning messages. I could also see the alerts by way of the information feed from my implants, but they were technical readouts that I couldn't immediately interpret. Jonan could.

"Radiation warning! A magnet is failing ... plasma is leaking into the baffles. Neutron levels ramping up, making secondary gamma radiation. I must dump ta plasma or we'll cook."

Jonan pushed open a covered panel and unhooked a safety catch from a large physical lever. I had a brief thought that there were still some functions critical enough that solid, tangible interlocks were needed in case the electronic controls failed. Then Jonan pulled the lever. A hollow roar echoed through the corridors, and a tenuous flower of fire bloomed forward of the ship. It shredded and twisted as it dissipated, lasting for only moments in the desert air. The alarms continued for a short while, then were silent.

"That's it?" I said.

"Plasma is hot but thin. Not much needed. It expands quickly and extinguishes itself," Jonan said.

"I wish we could have toasted that soldier with it. It's still coming." The giant morghaest had stumbled when the plasma flower had bloomed, but recovered and closed the last few strides to the base of the strut. It drew back its arm and hammered on the hull, which began to deform under its assault.

"Not good! Not good!" wailed Jonan. "If ta strut is crushed, ta torus will collapse. Negamatter will mix with normal matter and boom! We become a small and very brief star."

"How big is the blast radius?" asked Rowena.

"Entire continent, maybe more."

I reached for the dark *aelo tai*. I had sworn not to use it, but I couldn't imagine that the consequences of using it were worse than the consequences of not using it. I had no time for introspection on moral consistency. I sent my will through blacksight. This time I wasn't raising an old morghaest, or wrenching a new one from the soil with my rage. This time

I wanted to subvert, turn aside, or destroy the creation of another mind. As this occurred to me, I wondered briefly how Terrell had managed this without a black *aelo tai* of his own. As far as I knew, the red *aelo tai* didn't have this power.

I could see the soldier as a towering statue of non-light, glowing in a black radiance. It was raising its arm to strike the hull again. I reached out to touch it. It was a gritty black, a blinding blackness that made me want to squint and look away. Normal words didn't describe the sensation of a blackness that was radiant, a blackness that I could feel as well as see. The *aelo tai* was tuned to alien brains and senses that I didn't have. I pushed against the thing's upraised hand. Still, it swung downwards, striking the hull another blow. I heard Jonan exclaim about the damage through split senses that remained in the engine room, watching events, while also being cast outside the ship.

The arm came up again, and I redoubled my concentration. As the arm reached its peak, I sent forth the strongest image I could form of an invisible hand opposing it, holding it back from descending again. "You shall not strike again," I declared, not realizing I said it aloud until Gilwyr and Ox looked at me. The arm juddered to a halt, quivering against the restraint I threw against it. I could feel it straining, seeking to break through. I swayed.

Gilwyr hurried to my side and lowered me to the floor. I folded up into a cross-legged position on the floor. Images of the engine room were superimposed on my blacksight perception of the morghaest; I could see the animate statue up close and at the same time look down on it via the ship's monitors. Jonan was staring at the screen, muttering, "Boiling oil …"

With the previous morghaests, I had controlled them from within, not opposed them from without. Now I sought to assume control of this one. The memory of how easy it was to lose control was still painfully fresh; however I rationalized that I was already not in control and could hardly make things worse. I tore at the outside of the thing or at least some mental equivalent that was the best expressed with those words. The sensation was eerily familiar. It was like the feeling of peeling the *baraka* silk away from Bridocke: tough, fibrous, sticky, liable to entrap the rescuer who became entangled in it.

In front of me, Jonan went into a huddle with Rowena, who nodded. They worked together with a familiarity that belied the fact that I had found them locked in deadly combat and the legend that Rowena had waged a long and successful war against Jonan. I was starting to distrust legends.

I gripped the integument of the morghaest with both hands, ripping it open. It didn't matter that I wasn't using hands and that the covering wasn't a physical skin. The *aelo tai* translated the metaphor into actions I couldn't comprehend, analogous to the way the familiar simspace metaphor of using a key to lock a box caused the encryption of a document (which also used math that was way beyond me). I was more and more convinced that this was an alien simspace controller. I plunged into the vessel of the morghaest, seeking to control it as I had controlled the others.

Jonan was working on the controls again. Through my implants linked to the ship, I could see that he was overriding safeties on propellant systems. The main impulse drive was a low-thrust ion drive, as it had been on the *Aquila,* but there were maneuvering thrusters that used chemical propellants. Jonan was venting propellant underneath the ship, which fell as a gentle rain around the morghaest. I wondered what he was up to, but I had no attention to spare for the near at hand. I was fully engaged with the far away.

There was another mind controlling the morghaest. I felt it crowding me, keeping me from the controls that would halt its assault. It was an ill-defined pressure without locality, and I couldn't find a way to counter it at first. I had used the metaphor of tearing my way through an outer skin to gain access. I needed a new metaphor to seize control. The blackness parted in misty tendrils, clearing to reveal an abstract arena. The ground was featureless, the surroundings mere sketches, but across the arena I faced Terrell and behind him was the control center. That mechanism must have sprung from his mind, being made of steam vessels and pistons, shafts and pulleys, levers and cogs. It was futuristic if you came from a planet at a medieval level of technology. I strode across the arena.

"The Grimmerroth," said Terrell. "So you exist."

I looked down. I had attired myself in my cloak and had added a large floppy hat. I held a gnarled staff in my left hand. Might as well look the part of a warlock. In a land of metaphor, appearances were everything. "His grandson," I said, leaving out any number of 'greats.'

"I could use a warlock in my court. Come down from your Citadel and return to Dalactus with me. I'll see you have whatever you desire. Help me restore Dalactus to its old glory when it ruled all the settled lands. With your art, we can expand our boundaries. Dalactus will stretch from sea to sea and from desert to ice!" Terrell fell easily into his "riches for everyone" cant. It probably worked well if you understood what your listener really wanted.

"What's in it for me?"

"You can help architect and shape the greatest kingdom in the world. The texts I found in the King's Library, the artifacts from this ship, and the red gem of the ancients I found can lead us into a new age of ..."

"Found? That gem was taken from a locked trunk in my room in Misthaven." I planted my staff in the air, where it hung obediently. I swept my cloak from my shoulders with a flourish and hung it on the staff, removed my hat and placed it on top. Landscapes of the mind are good for dramatic effects. A floating cloak stand was just warmup. I slid my Cray Leth sword from its scabbard.

"You! From the dungeon! You unleashed morghaests in my castle."

"You can understand why I am reluctant to enjoy your hospitality again."

Terrell hardly blinked as he adjusted his approach. "Well, I didn't know who my guest was, obviously. You could teach me the secrets of that wonderful gem, couldn't you? I feel I've only begun to scratch the surface of its abilities."

""What I hear are the clichés and platitudes that have marked every tyrant throughout the ages. Restore past glory and expand the empire? How does that make life better for your citizens?"

"You can worry about my citizens from the dungeon if you do not wish to aid me." Terrell unsheathed his sword. Outside, I could see the morghaest slowly raising its arm for another strike. In overlay, I was still present in the engine room, where Jonan was watching the gauges and counting down, keeping up a running internal monolog that occasionally surfaced as bobbing words on his stream of consciousness. "... thousand liters ... compressor ... pump three failed, two left ..." The external world seemed to be moving in slow motion.

Terrell slashed, I parried. He spent no time sizing up his opposition, choosing to go for the quick win. I stepped in during his recovery with a low lunge that forced him to dance back. He flailed back with a graceless cut that I dodged easily. He fought with intensity, but I marked him as lacking in solid training. His stance was awkward, he left openings, and he failed to anticipate my moves, leading to last-second evasions and desperation blocks. It was only through his sheer ferocity that he managed to keep me at a distance. I worked methodically at his defenses, looking for the opening that I needed.

I understood our surroundings on a level that Terrell did not. This was a simspace, and our swords were metaphors. We fought for control of the morghaest with slash and parry, actions that represented prime number factoring, key attacks, firewalls, false flags, trojans, and backdoors. At least it would have meant that in a human simspace system; in this Kir Leth construct, it could have meant factoring spectral frequencies and quantum tunneling attacks for all I knew. Even in a human system, I was no expert in number theory. I had to rely on metaphor even there. Ox's voice replayed in my mind: "How is this different from magic, then?"

Terrell stepped suddenly past my point and slashed. I turned and caught his edge on the guard of my sword and turned it, but not before it had bitten into my left arm. I backed away, dripping blood from the wound, wondering how he had gotten that lucky stroke past me. I looked for his weapon in second sight. Only then did I realize that I was missing that ability in this simulation. I had bested Gilwyr and all other human swordsmen and held my own against Aymer because I had that advantage over them. Without it, I was just another swordsman with only a few months of practice. That thought was a sizable chink in my self-confidence, no less effective for having delivered it to myself. I received Terrell's next advance with more caution.

Terrell sensed this change and pressed it. He got another cut on my wrist; a few minutes later, he laid open a shallow slash down my side. I forced myself to focus on my opponent. Gilwyr's lessons of hard-earned bruises came back to me. I had allowed myself to become lazy, leaning on my magic rather than my technique. Gilwyr's voice echoed through the roaring in my ears: watch your opponent's eyes and feet, sense his balance, anticipate his moves. I saw Terrell move his weight forward slightly. I ducked under his lunge and delivered a backstroke that cut deeply into his thigh. He howled and hopped back out of range, dragging his injured leg.

I moved toward him with renewed confidence, tempered by caution. He was a crude fighter, and my technique was better. I didn't have advantage of second sight here, but I could still best him if I fought as Gilwyr had taught me. We exchanged several parries with Terrell looking increasingly desperate. Then his guard went down, just enough. I stepped into the opening, ready to bring this to a conclusion. Terrell smiled.

Suddenly Terrell's stance fell into alignment, his point came up, he stepped deftly inside my attack, sweeping my sword away from its target, lunged, and buried the point of his sword in my right shoulder. I staggered back, realizing I had been duped. He had been feigning sloppy swordsmanship the entire time. The cuts he had landed had been no accidents; they had been carefully planned and executed. Now he was in a tight stance that not even Aymer would have faulted and he was advancing on me. My right arm wasn't responding, and the gash in the muscle was a searing agony. I transferred my sword to my left hand, knowing that despite all of Gilwyr's coaching, I was still not as good on that side. Terrell closed for the kill.

I didn't know what damage he had done with his metaphorical strike, or what would happen with my metaphorical death. I knew from the feedback of the pain and the loss of the use of my arm that my attack on his control had been crippled. It was little comfort to know that there was a reality underlying this simspace when I couldn't access that reality to manipulate it. The only difference between us was that I knew this was simulation and he didn't. I had to be able to turn that to my advantage somehow.

If this was a simulation, I could change the rules of the game. I didn't have to fight alone. I had hung my staff in the air; I had some degree of control of my surroundings. I summoned the staff into battle. It leaped forward still wearing my hat and cloak like a ghostly warrior to block Terrell's attack.

Terrell backed off in confusion. I sent the staff after him, fetching him a sharp crack across the shins. I brought the staff up, attempting to entangle his sword arm in the trailing cloak, but didn't have enough control. Terrell sliced at the cloak, then reversed and brought his sword down to sever the staff in two. The pieces clattered to the ground, but this had given me time to prepare. I was now flanked by images of Gilwyr and Bridocke, both wielding swords. I briefly considered adding Ox or even Aymer but thought that Ox would be a wild card to hold in reserve, and I didn't want to tip off Terrell about the Kir Leth if he didn't already know about them. These images would only do as I willed so they could be no more skilled than I was.

A slow smile crossed Terrell's face. "Well, well, Grandson of the Grimmerroth, I'm learning from you already. What a useful trick."

I hadn't expected that reaction. He was trying to put me off my stride, and I tried not to let him see that he had succeeded. I motioned my avatars to spread out, warily. He had shaken my confidence and I cursed him for it. Bridocke approached on the left, and Gilwyr circled to the right. I pressed forward in the center, hanging slightly back to convey the threat of closing suddenly if he took his eyes off me.

Terrell waited until we were about ten paces away. He lifted his sword and hurled it at Bridocke, normally a suicide move. You can hope to kill one opponent but are then defenseless against the others. The blade plunged into Bridocke's belly and she bent over clutching it. I knew he had chosen that target carefully. It was a large and certain area to strike, unprotected by bones that would deflect the blade, and it ensured that the victim would die slowly and painfully. And it wasn't suicide here because Terrell still had a sword in his hand.

"We make the rules in this arena, don't we?" he chuckled. "If I want another sword I can just think it. It comes down to our imaginations. Believe me, I can think of some very creative ways for you to die."

I guided Gilwyr in to attack, ready to have her deflect another thrown blade. I couldn't really employ her skill, but I could picture her deadly grace and her fluid movements and imbue the avatar with the outward appearance of competence and menace. She closed with Terrell and engaged swords with him. I began circling to the left to divide his attention.

Aymer had lectured me after one sound thrashing on the folly of anticipating your foe's previous attack.

Gilwyr was keeping Terrell fully occupied. I had succeeded in circling entirely behind him, ready to spring an attack on his rear. Suddenly two copies of Terrell materialized behind Gilwyr and seized her arms. She lashed out with her feet, only to have two more appear to grab her legs, stretching her out in the air between them. One twisted her arm until her sword fell from her fingers, and another pulled her head back by the hair until she was bent in a painful arch. Terrell, the original one, moved in to insert his sword at her pelvis. Slowly, and with great relish, Terrell sliced upwards toward her heart, spilling blood and organs on the ground as he went.

I stopped in shock at the sight, mind numb with loss and dismay. A rational corner of my brain was signaling desperately that it was only a simulation; I hadn't lost anything. But the image was so graphic, so personal, that it overwhelmed me with grief, freezing my muscles.

The voice of the Other sounded faintly in my head, *Behind you, you fool!*

A dull thump hit me in the back. I looked down fuzzily at the tip of the sword that emerged from my left shoulder. A second thump occurred, and another sword pierced the right shoulder. Then the agony caught up with me, crumpling me into a defenseless huddle on the ground. A boot shoved me prone, followed by the red pain of a sword driving through my kidney. The three swords pinned me to the ground like a beetle on a collecting board. A hand yanked my head up by my hair for the sole purpose of allowing me to watch them hack the Gilwyr simulation into convincingly bloody bits.

Split vision still showed me the control room. I had fallen down on the floor and I seemed to be screaming. Gilwyr and Ox had rushed to my side, trying to help but having no idea of the struggles I was undergoing. Jonan stayed at the console, having stopped the venting of the propellent. I was relieved to see Gilwyr in one piece, though the virtual savagery that I was living through was going to do real damage to my ability to confront Terrell, simply knowing what he was capable of.

"Surrender now, or I'll batter down your Citadel, pull you out, and do this to you and your friends all over again. I'll make you watch each of them be flayed in front of you until you give me all the secrets of the gemstone."

"If you breach the Citadel, you'll regret it for about one heartbeat. The blast will destroy everything from here to Dalactus. It will be the end of you and your kingdom."

"I would say the same thing if I were in your position. That doesn't make it true."

Outside and far below I saw the morghaest raise its stone fist, ready to strike again. Far above and in front of me, I saw Jonan pulling the lever that released his lightning bolts. It wasn't much of a lightning bolt compared to the earlier ones. The reactor hadn't run long enough to build up much of a charge. It was just a spark arcing to ground, passing through the morghaest. But it was enough of a lightning bolt.

The fuel vapors exploded with a violence that shook the entire body of the Corvus. A fire flower bloomed with the morghaest at its heart before settling down to burn fiercely over its fuel-saturated surface. I burned with it, white heat searing my mind until I snapped back to my body on the Corvus, still screaming through a throat already screamed raw.

CHAPTER 56

Through the Forge

GILWYR STRUCK ME. I saw stars and heard the silence of a room that was no longer filled with a deafening sound. Gilwyr's face was pressed against mine with the hard expression that I had seen so often in training when she had found me wanting.

"Stenn! Have you forgotten everything I taught you? If you voice your pain, it becomes your master. Pain is the landscape on which you fight. Make yourself stronger on its forge, don't quench it with your outcry."

She had both hands knotted in my shirt, holding me off the floor. Behind the words of my guild master I saw, as clearly as if she had drawn skin words across her body, her worry and concern. I grasped her wrists and pulled myself up. The echoes I could still hear were my screams, which had not been brief. Strangely, the only pain I felt was my left cheek, burning from her slap, and the raw tatters of my throat. My skin had been charred to a crisp and the flesh within cooked but was now whole and unharmed. The flames were gone now as if they had never been, though the memory might never die away.

Behind me, I could hear Rowena whisper to Jonan, "Oh, she's good."

I drew a shuddering breath, trying to dispel the memory that I had been inhaling flames. "I was inside the creature, inside the *aelo tai* that created it … something like that … and you poured fire on me … it … us. I could feel it burning. *I* was burning. The pain was horrible, worse than getting my eye gouged out. Every atom in my body was being burned; there was no time, so the pain never ended. Time was slower, or maybe faster, I can't tell. You were all moving in slow motion, while I was fighting him and he was killing you … killing me …"

Gilwyr slapped me again, but her eyes were full of concern. I took another breath to get myself under control.

"Whom were you fighting?" asked Ox.

"It was Terrell." I tried to keep my words measured; they wanted to pile up at the exit and cause a panic. "In an arena, a simulated arena. It wasn't real, more like a waking dream. But actions in the dream affected the real world; we were fighting for control of the morghaest. I thought I could get control of it, but he learned the rules of that world quickly. He made mirror images of himself, so I was facing four or five Terrells, and I didn't have second sight to help me. I imagined Gilwyr and Bridocke there with me to help. But he killed them ... you ... in front of me. Then he stabbed me in the back. As I lay dying, Jonan dumped fire on our heads."

Gilwyr sat back on her heels. "You couldn't even win an imaginary fight? Even worse, you let him kill Bridocke and me as well? I've been slacking off on your training if you don't have an unshakable faith that I can best any human swordsman. I am going to drill you until you have dreams every night of me thrashing you."

I heard a snort from Rowena, to which I managed to reply, "I assure you, she means every word of it."

"I am sure she does. But ... what you said ... you are talking about virtual reality?"

"That would be one word for it." I saw Jonan nod, but Ox and Gilwyr were only further mystified.

"But you were wearing no googles, no equipment."

"This eye seems to serve that purpose." I didn't want to go into implants for simspace right now. Before landing here, I wouldn't have needed visible equipment to connect. Now I understood that those implants might have been subverted to the service of alien interfaces. If people from Jonan's era didn't have implants, that might explain why he experienced the *aelo tai* differently than I did. I had no time to wonder, however. The ship rocked to a renewed blow.

"The *monstrum*! It is still moving!" We rushed to the monitors showing the outside view. The creature still burned fiercely but had regained its feet. It was somewhat diminished and had a glassy, melted look to its surface, but remained formidable. It swung one great arm, hitting the ship with a flaming fist. Meteoric debris rained down. It left behind a smear of burning stone on the hull. The morghaest would wear itself away at this rate, but would it be soon enough?

Jonan reached out with his crystal hand, a faraway look in his eye. "I try ta shoo it away. I jest have ta find it ... There it is ... now send it away ... Ahhhh!" He broke off, dancing around and shaking his hand violently. "It burns! My hand, it is on fire!"

It wasn't of course. He had gotten the same feedback from the burning creature that I had. It probably had felt like dipping his hand into molten lead. I reached out tentatively with blacksight and met with the same blazing wall. I quailed, unable to face the agony again and convinced that I would be unable to break through it. The creature raised an arm and brought it down again on the hull. The skin of the ship was buckled and cracking at that point, but it hadn't snapped a support beam yet. We had to do something fast.

My eyes rested on the *aelo tai* in the makeshift cradle. It was in a nest of cables, some of which ended in optical signaling transmitters. I asked the ship to show me the control systems via my implants, then narrowed the schematics down to the fairly obvious additions that Jonan had made. He had programmed some control sequences that activated the optical transmitters. On a hunch, I ran the patterns that had last been used and felt a thrill of excitement as I recognized Kir Leth words being crudely formed by the emitters.

"We may have a way out! Jonan, that *aelo tai* will open a tunnel to the red *aelo tai*, won't it?"

"Ja, maybe. If we have enough time, we can set it up. Where is ta red one?"

"In the middle of the enemy camp."

"That bein' a problem, then. Not far enough away if ta *monstrum* breaches ta hull and ruptures ta warp core."

"How far is far enough?"

"We might be safe on yon big moon."

"If you can get us to the camp," said Gilwyr, "we can snatch Terrell and bring him here. If he's inside, he'll call off the attack or go down with the ship."

"Sounds like the best plan we have. Let's open the tunnel."

"Nie time! It takes an hour ta get ta thing set up."

"I can do it faster." I stepped up to the saffron *aelo tai* and regarded it in second sight. The image was somewhat jagged and unsteady. I had seen that once before, at Tykenkote Castle. The radiation level here was interfering with second sight. I concentrated on forming the words distinctly in my head. My hand came up and started drawing the skin words on my body as I held the image of the patterns in my mind's eye, in the way that I had been taught. I willed the *aelo tai* in my eye socket to transmit the Kir Leth words to the *aelo tai* on the pedestal. In human words, it went something like this:

Awaken.
A connection is required.
Search for a red aelo tai.
Start here and spiral outward.
Go beyond the rocks.
It is found.

Connect with it. Wait for a response.
Identify yourself.
Match [mass, spin, charge, color] with the partner.
Space becomes congruent between distant points.
Open the cavern between.
Error.

"There's a problem. One of the words isn't right. Gilwyr, what's the word for tunnel?"

Gilwyr shaped a complex skin word that required two hands.

Open the tunnel between.
Error.

"What color should that word be?"

"Orange of sunset, three shades toward red, purple border on the right."

Open the tunnel between!
Error.

"That's not the right word either. Is there a word for passage?"

"Err, I think that would be this one." She adjusted her hands. "The border is violet instead of purple."

Open the passage between!

A ripple pulsed outward from the saffron stone. It was like looking down through a sheet of water into which a pebble had just been dropped. The ripples reflected from a boundary that defined a door, returning and crossing in elaborate patterns. Where waves crossed, nodes of shimmering light formed, tracing elliptical paths as sliding intersections down one wave and up another. It might have been a merely accidental beauty, or it might have been insight into the workings of the universe. I was too unlearned to know.

The ripples dissipated, and a path lay before us. It was open for only a few seconds before breaking into crackling shards and reforming. It held steady for a count of ten before breaking once more. It was a path, but not a safe one. Whether the radiation levels destabilized it, or damaged the ancient gems, or sabotaged programming, or there was some omission in the incantation I had performed, I had no way of knowing. We could only rush in and hope, before someone on the other side overcame their astonishment.

I grasped Gilwyr's hand, saying, "Time it for just after it re-forms." She nodded. An instant later, the path came clear again, and we jumped. Too late I wondered what would happen if it collapsed with us inside.

Would we be trapped within as Jonan and Rowena had been? Would we be pulled out by a distant descendant four centuries in the future? Too bad I had neglected to provide any descendants to fill the role.

Then we were in the glowing corridor that I had walked before. As before, distances were distorted, so that one step seemed to cover miles, but the distance to reach out to touch Gilwyr was more than I could cross in a lifetime. Unlike before, there was an end to the corridor, and it was near at hand. Previously it had lost its anchor and had stretched on forever without end. This time we took two steps. Another portal, this one red, came rushing towards us out of the distance. We could not see beyond it; we would step blindly into the heart of the enemy camp. Rather, I *hoped* we would step into the enemy camp. With an entire universe accessible through a portal like this, there were far worse places to land. Most of them wouldn't allow time for regret.

Then we were through. It was crowded. It was dim. It was filled with the sound of panic and above all it was filled with the sound of someone in the extremes of pain. A figure before me received the pommel of my sword in the chin, on the assumption that anyone here wanted to kill me. Gilwyr was more deadly, cutting down two guards in seconds and clearing a space around us. We were in some kind of tent that served as the field headquarters of the army. A table held charts, chairs held officers now lurching to their feet, guards held weapons but not at ready; they had not been expecting an attack. Where was Terrell?

We followed the sound of the screaming, which came from the other side of the shimmering portal. Terrell was seated in an ornate chair, the red *aelo tai* clenched in his hand, face a mask of agony. He was still connected to the morghaest that he had been controlling, feeling the fire searing its skin, feeling its body turn into rivers of molten rock that dripped on the sand like rain. I almost felt sorry for him.

In his other hand was the scepter of the king and the answer to at least one mystery. In retrospect, I should have guessed. The cloth that wrapped the end had been removed, revealing that a black *aelo tai* was mounted there. That was how he had animated the morghaest.

We grabbed him by an arm on either side, leaving us each with a free sword arm to keep the guards at bay. We hustled Terrell around the portal, but the portal rotated with us. A realization hit me, one that could upset our plans. "We cannot take the red *aelo tai* with us while it's holding the portal open! We have to leave it here!"

Terrell was not cooperative. I was ready to cut his hand off to make him let go, but if he went into shock it would render him useless for ordering the morghaest away from the ship. After a struggle, we forced his fingers apart and the *aelo tai* dropped to the floor with a dull thud. Now we could step to the other side of the portal to enter it.

The tent flaps burst open. General Bercarius rushed in with a half dozen of the Sons and Daughters with their bright sashes. "Stop them!" she bellowed as we hustled Terrell into the portal. We tried to run, but distances in the passageway were deceiving. Walk or run, we seemed to move at the same speed. It had been only a few steps to travel from ship to camp, but it seemed much longer to return from camp to ship. Was there pursuit behind us? I didn't dare look.

The corridor stretched out before us. Was it possible that there were branches in it? Could we be going the wrong way? Surely we would have arrived by now. I tried not to think about the prospect of wandering through this ghost dimension outside of space and time while all of eternity burned away outside. With Terrell as company, it would be too much like the ancient's view of hell. The more I tried not to think about it, of course, the more I could think of nothing else.

At last the far portal rushed up at us from the distance and we were stepping through into the ship. Gilwyr and I steered Terrell to a chair and sat him down. We removed an assortment of sharp and nasty weapons that had come along with him and stood back. Gilwyr signed skin words to me that unless he was truthful (the Kir Leth word for truthful meant naked), we should assume we had missed one.

The ship shuddered at another blow from the morghaest. I didn't know how long our sortie had taken, but at least the ship was still standing. Terrell remained locked rigidly in a nightmare, eyes open but unseeing of anything that was before him. I knew what his eyes saw and I pitied him. He deserved his nightmare, but if I lost my empathy, I would be as bad as he was.

Gilwyr slapped him. His head rocked back. He took a long shuddering breath and looked around wildly. "The gem ... the gem ..." he muttered.

"We need to retrieve the *aelo tai*," I said. I turned back to the portal. At least no one had dared to pursue us through it. I hadn't been able to carry the red gem through the tunnel while it was serving as an anchor for the tunnel, but I felt there had to be a way to manage the trick from this side.

In second sight, I could see threads of light like cables on a suspension bridge, holding the span in place. Through the portal, foreshortened by perspective, I could see the threads running into the distance and gathering together into the anchor point at the far end. Some of the threads were brighter than others, as if they were primary supports or control conduits or some other critical function. The designers of the system would have provided labels or feedback to help an operator to control it. I experimentally grasped one of the heavier threads and pulled. The far end seemed to expand. I tried several other threads in quick succession until one of them appeared to tug in the right direction. I hauled heavily on the line and was rewarded by the entire tunnel collapsing like a closing flower. A crimson speck flew towards me out of the distance, growing rapidly larger. Satisfaction that it had worked changed quickly to alarm as that speck grew faster and larger than I expected. This was not an orb that I could hold in my hand.

The red speck expanded into a bubble, and another smaller orb appeared in its center. This orb flew straight towards me, while the boundary of the bubble blew past. Objects became suddenly large and assaulted us, mixed with confused and panicking guards. I had dragged the entire command tent into the ship along with the *aelo tai*.

All of this happened in seconds. I didn't have time to cry out a warning. The map table knocked Ox and Rowena off their feet. An incoming guard crashed into me, sending me spinning across the room. Another guard caromed off of Gilwyr, who kept her feet and placed her sword in his gut. This pushed her away from Terrell, however, and an officer with more presence of mind than most scrambled up to guard him. I lurched to regain my feet, only to find myself looking up the length of an extremely sharp sword at the face of General Bercarius.

"Everyone hold!" she called. "This one is the Grimmerroth. If you make a move that I do not like, I will spit him before you move even one step. Disarm them, and line them up against the wall over there."

I didn't take my eye off the point of her sword, but in second sight I could see all weapons being collected from my party. I could see that they had missed Gilwyr's strangling cord in her boot. Rowena's boot had a plate in the sole that looked suspiciously like a knife. Neither was in a good situation to help, but perhaps I could maneuver the Dalactyns into a better position. I shifted a millimeter. I could feel my slim knife still in my belt in the small of my back, but if I as much as twitched I was going to have that much larger sword in a very bad place.

A fresh crash told us that the morghaest still threatened the ship. The Dalactyns looked at the view screens where the creature was visible, still aflame, raising its massive arm and bringing it down on the ship's hull. The General remained as unwavering as the sword that still hovered over a point between my eyes, but her captain blanched. "We're inside the Citadel! What evil brought us here?"

"This is where the last war ended, General. Don't let the next war start here," I said evenly. Well, as evenly as I could.

"I think if I kill you as well as clear the dead wood of the de Oxendon family, there will be little left to fight over."

"Think about what you know of this Citadel. This is where Rowena ad Aulem and the Grimmerroth were locked in combat. This is where they were frozen in time. This is the birthplace of morghaests, and Terrell's creation is rocking its foundations. If that monster buckles the outer wall, as it will do any minute now, do you have any idea what will be unleashed? You'll have no army and no kingdom. You won't care, though, because you will be part of the biggest bonfire ever seen."

While I talked, I ran simulations in second sight. Grabbing her sword got my hand sliced off and my head skewered. Twisting away resulted in having my head parted from my body at the neck. Chopping at her knee with my elbow was promising: I would live one and half seconds longer with that attack. Kicking her in the crotch didn't work from this angle; I could only end up kicking her in the tailbone. Any move for my knife would be cut short, literally. No good moves for continuing my career were available. I had to keep her talking until something presented itself.

"Are you attempting to make me do something rash, Grimmerroth? Very well. Captain, kill one of his friends if he doesn't banish the morghaest by the count of ten."

"I'm not really a warlock! I was a university professor before I came here. I wrote papers and dug up old artifacts and bored students with my lectures."

"You claim you're a *teacher*?"

I was getting really bothered by the point of the sword nearly pricking my nose. It wasn't even a particularly good sword when your standard was the ones made by the Cray Leth. In desperation, I told the *aelo tai* to just find anything that worked, instead of reacting to my intentions with consequences. A Cray Leth skin word floated up in my mind and I flashed it to my crimson eye: *solve this*.

"Not anymore. I'm not sure if I can go back. But I think I know how to kill the morghaest with science, not with magic."

"How do you propose to do that?"

"Jonan," I called out. "Can you restart the fusion reactor and vent the plasma again?"

"Ja, can do that. But the radiation ..."

"Exactly."

"Ohhh. Ja!"

I looked at Bercarius. "You'd better let him do it. It's our only chance of getting out of here."

She looked at me and came to a quick decision. "Captain Creedon, let him do it. Stand over him. Kill him if he plays us false."

I could only see Jonan out of the corner of my eye as he stepped to the control panel and started the reactor. It started quickly this time. Jonan waited for a tense minute while the plasma built up ready for the injection. At this moment, second sight presented me with the solution I had asked for. Oh, really?

I heard the radiation meter start to chatter. Before the general alarm could go off, Jonan pulled the vent lever and dumped the plasma outside the ship again. The morghaest staggered as it had before, but this time it was directly under the plasma dump. Cracks started to appear in its surface. A section of its head cleaved off and fell to the ground. It was in the act of swinging its fist against the ship again; the fist connected with the metal and shattered into powder. The remainder of the arm fell off and landed on the ground in a cloud of dust.

Bercarius still hadn't taken her eyes off me. "No, I gave up teaching," I continued, "I dug up an old artifact that made me come here. It was a gem belonging to my ancestor, who came to this planet with your ancestors. Now, he *is* a warlock. *The Grimmerroth*, and that's him standing right over there."

The radiation alarm chose that moment to sound, and that finally got Bercarius to shift her attention to Jonan, just for an instant. Second sight had presented me with a single way out and I had to do it precisely. In her moment of inattention, I brought my knee up through her legs and into her sword hand, knocking it off target. Second sight predicted she would drop the sword, but she managed to hang on to it. Now the blade swung back, but the red images of simulation flickered and died. The radiation had reached a level where second sight cut out. I was blind to the future.

I almost froze. I couldn't win without second sight. It had given me a nearly impossible chance, and I had already blown that. The general's sword was coming back for the killing stroke. I was going to fail the final exam. I hoped that I had at least saved the ship. They would probably kill my friends, but at least the people of this world would survive.

My body didn't listen to my brain. My leg continued the motion that it had started, coiling up into my chest and then straightening, driving my heel directly into the general's stomach. She doubled over, driven backward to crash into one of her guards. I caught the sword, unplanned, hand and eye reacting to events faster than the brain could think. That hadn't been in the simulation because the simulation said that she was supposed to drop the sword. As I arched my back and pushed off the floor to land on my feet, the knowledge flooded me that second sight was no more real than simspace was. I had trained my muscles and my reflexes to fight, and I could still do that without any augmented vision assisting me. I could do this without its guidance. "Not a teacher, not a warlock," I growled. I had my knife from my belt in one smooth motion. My human eye saw the target, and my human muscles moved with precision. The knife flew true and buried itself in Bercarius's astonished eye. Jonan finally cut the override on the alarm, and all eyes watched the general sink to the floor in the sudden silence.

I stood tall. "I am an assassin!"

CHAPTER 57

Fire in the Sky

THERE WAS AN instant of shocked stillness after Bercarius fell. The Dalactyns had been looking for a magical threat from me, not a physical one. They started to turn towards me, but that was all the opening that my friends needed. Gilwyr disarmed the nearest Son of Rowena in a flash and took his sword. Rowena drove the heel of her hand into the chin of one of the Daughters. Ox reached out and cracked two heads together and came up with a sword in either hand. Four Dalactyns were down in under two seconds, and the remainder backed into a defensive circle in the center of the room. I counted five, so I must have dragged Bercarius plus nine guards through the portal. No, ten, I revised, seeing the one that Gilwyr had slain when they arrived.

"Lay down your weapons!" Rowena's command rang out. "We have more urgent tasks now than fighting. We must leave this ship if we are to live. Follow Greylander de Oxendon; he is your rightful king."

The Dalactyns looked uncertain. Ox stepped forward. "I cast down my brother Terrell from the throne for the crime of murdering our brother Gerard. I appoint General ad Aulem as your commander. Put down your weapons and help your comrades to their feet."

"Ad Aulem?" said Captain Creedon. "There hasn't been an ad Aulem for centuries."

"Think where you are! You've all heard the legend. The legend is true. This is Rowena ad Aulem, who has been trapped in time like Polnedra herself. Stenn pulled her from the caverns of legend, and now she can lead you once more, you who bear her name."

Creedon looked around our party. "If this is truly Rowena, then is *he* really the Grimmerroth as your warlock assassin said?"

"He was called that, but he was not evil. He was an artificer who was wronged by my ancestor Roland. It is time for me to make amends for that wrong, which led to too many deaths, and too many false stories, clouding the truth."

A groan echoed down the corridors of the ship, a groan of metal in pain. The deck settled, listing slightly to one side. The Dalactyn guards started to look panicked, my friends and Rowena began to look uneasy, but the movement terrified Jonan. "Ta strut is collapsing! If ta warp torus breaches, ta explosion could punch all ta way through ta atmosphere."

"What can you do about it?" asked Ox.

"Nie a ting! Can nie vent ta negamatter on a planet. Be as bad as breaching."

"Can you blow the fusion reactor?" Rowena asked. "Spread the negamatter over a wide area, so it's not a concentrated explosion?"

"Nie! Fusion reactor's nie built like a fusion bomb. Built so it can nie explode, see? Nie a bad idea if we had a bomb, but we don't."

"I think we'd better get out then," I said.

"We cannot go far enough to matter," said Jonan hopelessly.

"If we stay here and the ship collapses, we'll surely die. If we get out, there's still a chance that the torus won't breach, or there's not enough negamatter left after all these years to destroy the planet, or something else unforeseen happens. We should go while we can."

"Stenn is right," said Gilwyr. "We should strive as long as we have breath."

"Form up!" barked Rowena. "Protect Prince Greylander, and take Terrell prisoner. Jonan, take the lead to the exit, I'll bring up the rear. Let's go!"

Rowena's tone of command got everyone moving, but we almost immediately ran into several snags. "Where's Terrell?"

Terrell was no longer sitting where we had left him moaning. A quick search showed that he wasn't hiding anywhere on the engineering deck. As we searched, my second sight started returning, signaling that the radiation levels had dropped back again. The burst of radiation that had killed the morghaest must have finally severed Terrell's contact with it, freeing his mind from the pain he had been enduring. He must have slipped away during the chaos.

"Let him go," said Ox. "If he makes it outside, we will deal with him there. If he falls with the Citadel, then it is no more than he wanted."

We headed away from engineering and found the vertical shaft that would take us to ground level. Jonan stepped off the ledge and rotated to stand on the wall of the shaft and began walking downwards. The Dalactyn guards who were directly behind him balked at the edge of what appeared to be a hundred-meter precipice. Gilwyr, Ox, and I all had to step onto the wall to demonstrate that magical trickery wasn't involved, or if it was, that it was trickery that worked equally for all people. Finally, we had all made the transition and were progressing forward, or downward, depending on whether you trusted your eyes or your inner ear.

The ship had been quiet for a while, but now it groaned again. We were in the center of the groan, amplified by the long straight passageway. This groan started out low and rose in pitch until it was more of a shriek, accompanied by several sharp bangs. A rivet popped out of a nearby wall and ricocheted along the deck in front of us for some distance. Then it picked up speed and accelerated away from us until it disappeared. I puzzled over that behavior for several steps until Jonan suddenly stopped and threw out both of his arms. "Ta gravity just went out! Hang on ta someting."

I grabbed a handhold, as did Jonan and Rowena. Ox and Gilwyr had recently climbed this passageway and understood well enough to follow suit. Not all of the guards did, however. They started shuffling towards the handholds, but some of them only touched the rungs, not prepared to hang on. There was another shriek of metal, followed this time by a shower of rivets, the only warning we received before "down" suddenly became the direction towards the bulkhead at the far end. The next two seconds were a mad scramble for purchase on decks that were now walls and walls that were now slipping as toes and fingers sought anything that would keep their owners from the chasm in front of them. One luckless guard was slammed by the guard behind him and lost his grip. The whites of his eyes as he fell away from us down the passageway burned themselves into my memory, until he hit the frame of the hatch in the next bulkhead with a terrible crack, and tumbled through, now ragdoll limp.

Another guard lost her grip and started falling. Ox's hand shot out as she passed and grasped her wrist. He grunted as she bounced and slammed into the wall below him, but he hung on to both his handhold and her wrist. She dangled, momentarily senseless until Gilwyr swung close and helped lift her weight up. Together they brought her around until she could grasp the rungs of the ladder on her own.

Barely was breath drawn when we heard a small voice saying, "I can't hang on!" Three meters below me a Son of Rowena dangled by his fingertips from a small crack in the wall where a panel had popped loose. There were no handholds anywhere within his reach. It seemed it that he was fated to follow the first guard on the express route to the bottom.

I heard steps coming down the ladder above me. "Move to your left," Rowena called. I swung left and she passed by on my right. She relieved me of my belt and had a longer one that she had taken from Ox. When she was just above the dangling guard, she stopped and knotted the two belts into a quick loop that passed through the rungs of the ladder. Using the loop, she stood away from the wall and began to run back and forth in an arc. "When I grab you, let go!" she commanded. On the next arc, she launched herself from the wall at the end, twisting in the air as she did. She landed on the back of the guard, instantly wrapping her legs around his chest. He let go, or more likely dropped from exhaustion. They swung back to the ladder, slamming into the wall. Rowena managed to hang on long enough for the guard to scrabble for a desperate grip on the rungs, where he hung panting in fear. The sounds of tormented metal intensified from below, with panels popping loose with deadly force. Of one mind, we all scrambled back for the less immediate danger of the primary hull.

Once again on a more or less level deck, Captain Creedon turned to Ox and Rowena. "Your actions in saving my people were nothing short of heroic. If you would do that even for those who opposed you only minutes ago, then you are more than worthy of our allegiance. We would follow you even to … well, we used to say we would follow someone even into the Grimmerroth's Citadel, but we're already there, aren't we? I will rally the troops behind you, and help in pruning out the General's cadre. There are relatively few who were like-minded with her, and many more who simply feared her. We should swing the army quickly."

Ox nodded his acceptance, and Rowena added, "Thank you, *Major*. I'll depend on that support."

Gilwyr said, "If we don't get down to the ground and away from here quickly, we won't be inspiring support in anyone else. Is there another way down?"

"Nie," said Jonan. "Ta warp torus is uninhabitable, so nie exit that way. There are other hatches, but we are a hundred meters in ta air, and nie rope or cable long enough to reach ta ground."

My hand fell on the red *aelo tai* that throbbed in my pocket. "There is another way."

We hastened back to engineering. In our departure, I had forgotten about the saffron *aelo tai* on its pedestal. I needed both of them to save Cloudhaven, but right now they could possibly save us. "You punched the red *aelo tai* through space to Trondhjem, didn't you?" I asked Jonan.

"Ja, ta position must be precisely aligned. I used a nano-manipulator ta make ta errors as small as possible. It took me weeks ta do."

"We don't have that time, but we're not going that far, either. We just need to hit the side of the lecture hall."

I held my *aelo tai* before me and looked through it with second sight.

Fibers of light flowed between the two gems, which I understood to be channels of communication between them. A ghost of the red *aelo tai* appeared to hang suspended on the other side of the saffron one. As I walked around the warm yellow stone, the red image rotated to remain on the opposite side. I pushed the image of the red aelo tai outwards, through the hull, to a viewpoint above the natural basin in which the *Corvus* rested. I was looking outwards toward the plain, and from here I could see the camps of Terrell's army. I toyed with the idea of opening a portal into the camp, but I wanted Danallion and Bridocke with us before I did so. I walked around the pedestal until I was facing the mountain, and pushed my viewpoint down through the surface. This was less than satisfactory since I was plunged into the darkness of the rock. I swung left and right, up and down, forward and back, but the cave was too small a target to locate in the mass of the mountain.

I pulled my viewpoint back outside, then swung down to ground level. After a bit of hunting, I found the entrance to the cave and was able to push the orb along the tunnel and into the main cavern. I could see the forms of the experiments and furniture left behind by Jonan, and eventually located the two I sought standing by the view screen that showed the outside. I surmised that they were trying to decide if it was safe to venture outside, now that they had seen the morghaest fall.

Now I took the threads that I had used to pull the red *aelo tai* back from the camp and used them to push it down into the mountain. The passage opened before me, and the red *aelo tai* sailed through the saffron *aelo tai*, making the space here adjacent to the space in the cavern. A doorway bloomed before us. "Everyone through! I have to come last. Gilwyr, you go first; tell Bridocke that we're all friends."

Gilwyr had experienced the passage to the camp already, so she would know the feeling of indefinite distance that one felt within the passage. I hoped that no one else freaked out on the walk. I had no idea what would happen if someone bolted and tried to leave the path.

Gilwyr stepped through the portal, followed by Ox. Rowena and Jonan stepped through next. The Dalactyns hesitated, but another groan from the ship followed by a marked settling spurred them on. In moments, I was stepping through as well into the somewhat crowded cavern. Ox was filling Bridocke in on events. The Dalactyns were gawping at the strange artifacts that lay in profusion throughout the cave. Jonan was taking stock of his equipment. I couldn't see Danallion anywhere. He must have used his camouflage ability to fade into the background to escape the notice of Rowena and the guards. I asked second sight to locate any Kir Leth shapes in the cave and was rewarded with a glowing shape that lurked near the rear passageway.

I quietly but quickly made my way over to that vicinity. "Danallion. I know you're here. I need your help. We're still in great danger."

I felt him move near, but he didn't make himself visible. "What has gone on?"

"The giant morghaest has damaged the ship. If it collapses, it could be catastrophic for the entire planet."

He took a moment to absorb that. "What can we do? You must have a thought in your mind."

"You have researched the *aelo tai*. How large can the portals be made?"

"The old records say that once an entire city was moved from Sellen to Rhea, but I cannot tell if that was fact or legend. There is an inverse relationship between size and distance. Only quite small objects could be moved between stars."

"As far as Rhea would be adequate. Can you guide me?"

"You have an *aelo tai* with you? Allow me to touch it."

I held out my hand with the gem resting on the palm. Danallion laid his hand on top of mine and was silent. Then he said, "You can see the *aelo tai* in the ship?"

"Yes."

"This is what you must tell it." He let his camouflage fall away so that he could speak in skin words. The symbols and colors flowed, complex and quickly changing. I did my best to keep up, mentally relaying the images over my linkage. I wondered if I was conveying coordinates, or settings, or a program to execute, a magic spell, or even a prayer. I worried if I was accurate enough. Perrhen had said that they could see colors that we could not. What if I missed an important shade of infrared in the sequence? I was just starting to sweat when the vertical support strut began to twist, peeling off long strips of hull plating as it compressed. The main hull dropped by several meters, straining the two upper struts further. The sudden shift in the position of the *aelo tai* in engineering threw me off. "Wait, wait, I lost it," I said. "The ship just sank some more. I don't know how much more it can take. Where were we?"

"We just start again. Do not lose concentration; we must finish this entire sequence." He started again to lead me through the incantation. I centered myself and devoted myself fiercely to reproducing every shape and color that Danallion flashed on his skin. Line, arc, wave, flower droplets, and brush strokes. Ocher, vermillion, sanguine, frost, emerald, and sand. Shapes and colors, colors and shapes. Skin words. An invocation of an ancient power in our service. What indeed was magic and what was science? I painted over the thought with more words, struggling against distractions.

Then it was over. The saffron *aelo tai* hung in second sight, gleaming and alive. "This is the control," said Danallion, showing me a shape like a slice of lotus root. "Turn it towards blue to make the aperture larger." I started to comply, but at that moment I heard a gasp from people who could see the view screen and simultaneously lost my second sight.

"It's cracking!" I head a shout. I could see a brilliant white light appearing on the view screens. Second sight went dead and with it my connection to the *aelo tai*. I was blind, cut off from communication. What I was attempting probably wouldn't work, but it felt infinitely worse to only stand there while the world ended outside. Before I came into possession of the *aelo tai*, things had simply happened to me. Since then, I had become a person who took charge, changed history, and saved people who needed saving. But at the final moment, I was chopped off from my chance to save everyone and allotted perhaps a minute of introspection on the feeling of futility.

The cavern was suddenly plunged into darkness. The power came from the ship, and the cables were broken or melted. I heard Jonan shout, "Let me through! Let me through!" Shuffles and curses came from the darkness. Someone tripped. A table was upset, instruments clattered to the ground. Ox's sudden roar cut through the din, "Everyone stop where you are, except Jonan!" The sounds of footsteps filled the ensuing space, then the sound of cranking, and then a claustrophobic circle of light illuminated the center of the room. Jonan had located the hand-cranked lantern. It was a sad little light in the stygian darkness, somehow even more appropriate for the end of the world than the darkness alone had been.

But then my second sight flickered an image, grainy and blocky but undeniably there. I could see the great glowing bulk of the ship outside, appearing deformed but still standing. The radiation flash must be dissipating. I might have another chance. I grabbed Danallion by the arm and fought my way to Jonan.

"It hasn't collapsed yet! There was a flash but no explosion. I have to get outside and see it."

"Ta emergency barriers, they must have engaged. They segment ta torus if there is a breach. Only one segment has broken, must be. We should go out ta other side of ta mountain while we can."

"No, I need to see the ship. I may be able to stop this from happening, but I can't do it with all this rock between me and the ship. I need light to find my way down the passage."

"I go with you then, to guide you."

"We will go too, in case we need to clear debris from the tunnel," said Rowena. "The King should stay here."

"No, we all go," said Ox. "If we don't see this through, there is no kingdom."

So we all made our way down the tunnel, moving rapidly until we neared the end. It should have been getting lighter, but the darkness still pressed in. Soon we found the reason. The mouth of the cave was blocked by rockfall.

"Stand back," said Jonan. He raised his crystal hand and concentrated. Rocks began to move aside. We had to duck to allow them to fly past us. Soon we were trapped in a pocket between the rock that had been moved and the rock ahead. We inched forward; it was either that or become part of the trailing wall. The rocks began to crumble, turning into dust that whisked away, filling in all the cracks. We all wrapped cloaks around our mouth and nose to keep the dust out. We made more yards of progress, but now the air seemed thick. We breathed in and out, but it seemed to do us little good. We were using up the oxygen, and there was no fresh air to replace it.

Just as vision seemed to be contracting to a thin, dark-walled tunnel in front of my eyes, Jonan broke through into open air. Light streamed in the rapidly widening opening. I pushed ahead of him to scramble out the opening that I could barely squeeze through, anxious to see what remained.

In the waning light of the day the *Corvus* still stood, but a twisted parody of its former self. It was slumped on one side, and an entire side of the main hull had sheared off, exposing the decks inside. It continued to sag even as I watched, and a fire started near the engineering deck. Collapse and explosion seemed imminent.

I re-established my connection to the *aelo tai* and was relieved that the programming sequence did not have to be repeated. The controls were still available. I grasped the lotus-root-shaped knob and twisted. Jonan came up beside me as I did so, followed by the rest of the party. Everyone I cared about was here around me, ready to be dissolved in the incandescence of a new sun if I failed. The orb expanded to encompass the ship. I couldn't tell whether the others could see it or it was only visible to me. No one exclaimed about it, so I assumed the latter.

A monstrous groan filled the amphitheater, heralding collapse. A pearl of white appeared on the rim of the ship. Another section of the torus was breaching, and I could feel that this one would rip the entire ring asunder, releasing all of the exotic matter within. I had no time to send the red *aelo tai* ahead to create the tunnel. I simultaneously opened the portal and punched the button to collapse it. The Corvus dropped out of space and time with a great concussion of inrushing air.

We picked ourselves up and looked around. Our hearing had taken leave; we talked and pointed, but couldn't hear each other. Gilwyr and I used skin words to reassure each other that we were still here, and that sound would come back into the world in time. Danallion faded into view near me, making the Dalactyns gape. He seemed confused to see the red *aelo tai* still in my hand. He asked in skin words what I had done. I haltingly replied, trying to fit astrophysics into baby language. He signed astonishment, followed by something far too complex to follow. I shook my head. He pointed straight to the zenith. My eyes followed his finger, and I saw the flower of fire unfolding in the gathering twilight, far beyond the atmosphere. We sat on the rocky ground and watched, eventually building a paltry fire of our own to warm the desert night. The stars were hidden that night, and for many nights to come, behind dancing auroras far brighter than any I had ever heard of.

CHAPTER 58

Gilwyr's Declaration

THE DESERT NIGHT was cold and fuel for fires was scarce. My little band huddled around one meager glow while the Dalactyns sat apart around their own. Ox and Rowena spent some time conferring, then Ox sat with the Dalactyns for a while. At first he spoke briefly, but thereafter he spent most of his time listening. Bridocke, former guard, seemed uncertain of her current place and stayed with our group. Jonan was withdrawn, huddled into himself on the periphery of the light of our fire. I had tried to speak to him but had been rebuffed. Only this morning his wife had been alive and he thought he had a portal home. During the day four centuries had passed and plunged him into a different world, all alone. He had to find his place in a changed world.

I felt Danallion's presence near at hand, though he remained the color of the night and difficult to see. He was gazing at the aurora, as were most other eyes that night. "The sky has skin words tonight," I remarked.

"In a way," he replied. "Though they make no sense. Occasionally a shape forms that is similar to a word, but the motion or color is wrong."

"People … humans, I mean … sometimes look at clouds and see the shapes of faces, or animals, or other things."

"But not writing, I think. That is too intricate to see in random shapes."

"True. Do you understand what I did to the *Corvus*? I was trying to make a portal, but I didn't have time to complete it."

"No Kir Leth has understood these things for nearly eighteen eighteens of eighteens of years." I translated his units in my head to 18^3, or just short of six thousand years. "But from my reading of the ancient writings, you created the dent in space that is the first part of establishing a portal. It opened a hole, but before you pushed the anchor point through that hole to make the passageway, you released the pressure and the ship fell through the hole into a bubble. The bubble floated where it was while the planet moved away from it. Such a bubble was not stable, and it burst a few moments later, releasing the explosion. Fortunately, our world had moved around the sun, while the sun sailed through the river of stars, and Sellen was no longer at the same place as the explosion."

"Just like throwing a firecracker out of a moving car. What would have happened if Sellen had been traveling towards the bubble instead of away from it?"

"It might have burst deep within the planet's heart. The story of Sellenria might have ended. But Kir Leth don't say 'It would have.' In our way of speaking, we say, 'I tell you a story of something that was possible, but which didn't happen.' We are here to tell the story, so it didn't happen."

"I think I know what you mean. I look at the desert, and the sky, and my friends, and know that because I see and feel, I am still here, still alive. If my story had ended, I would not be able to have that thought. No, there would not be a 'me' so there would be no thought. *Cogito ergo sum*—I think therefore I am—has no ready inverse. I have felt this on several occasions since coming to this world, but never as strongly as tonight."

"You must learn more of our language. You have the thought, but you can say it much more elegantly in Kir Leth."

"I would like nothing better. Perhaps events will stop conspiring against me to do so." I had a sober thought then. "If there are still Kir Leth to learn from. I have only one *aelo tai*. The other one that we needed to save Cloudhaven was destroyed with the *Corvus*."

"The story of the Kir Leth could have ended today. It goes on. Many things are possible from this point. Perhaps some can be saved. Perhaps another *aelo tai* exists. Perhaps the Blight can be defeated in another way. We still live, we still think, so all is not lost."

"What will you do now?"

"I will make my way back to Cloudhaven. I will wait in the shadows until all of these strangers have gone, then I will follow the foothills so that I am not seen. I cannot be invisible in bright daylight; I still cast shadows."

I slept soon after, exhausted by the day. I woke in the darkness and the doubts and failures beset me. I had carried the Blight to Cloudhaven. I had awakened the morghaests. I had brought the *aelo tai* to Sellenria, and that had enabled Terrell to breach the warp torus and nearly destroy the planet. This world would have been better off if I had continued to live out my life in obscurity on Trondhjem.

I shivered in the pre-dawn chill and felt the warmth of Gilwyr next to me. If I had remained on Trondhjem, I would never have met this remarkable woman. I would never have known Ox, who was a good person and would make an exceptional king. Ox would have probably been killed along with Gerard in Misthaven. I would have never pulled

Jonan and Rowena out of their bubble of time to allow them to walk among the living once more. Perhaps the Kir Leth were right. "Would have beens" are paths that were never taken. We can make up stories that might fit at least the beginnings of those other paths, but with no certainty that they would have ended as we imagined they might.

I thought I would get no more sleep that night, but Gilwyr awakened me well after sunrise. The others were already up and ready to make the trek to the Dalactyn camp. The Major believed that with Terrell and Bercarius gone, most of the remaining officers would be glad to follow Ox. A proclamation of the return of Rowena ad Aulem would buttress Ox's position as well. Ox and Rowena and the Major were still arguing strategy—walking boldly into camp as one party versus sending an advance team in to prepare the ground. Bridocke favored the latter; in case sentiment went against Ox, he would still be hiding in the hills. The rest were favoring the direct approach as appearing more confident and in command. We began to walk across the amphitheater towards the camp, still discussing.

The space looked vast and empty without the ship resting in it. The Dalactyns were overawed that such a huge structure could vanish so completely. There was a circular crater in the center where the bubble had scooped out some soil and taken it along with the ship. The indentation was perfectly smooth and round, a section of a spherical surface of unnatural regularity. It remained in deep shadow, the still-low sun not having reached its depths. We stopped for a moment on the rim and marveled at the power that had made it. Nearby, the rocky remains of the morghaest stretched on the ground. It appeared truly dead, without any activity visible to blacksight. The heat and radiation had finally defeated even the hardy motes of Dust that had animated it.

As we started to turn away, the rising sun brushed the bottom of the bowl. Gilwyr, always the sharpest eye, saw it first. Deep in the glassy surface of the crater, something gleamed a deep yellow with overtones of red. It was the color of joy. I started searching for a way down into the crater, where the steep and polished sides offered no purchase. Gilwyr didn't search. She simply ran down the side of the crater, where the angle was so steep that nothing but a dead run would suffice. If she tried to stop or turn she would have rolled head over heels to the bottom. I couldn't imagine Gilwyr ever rolling head over heels, no matter the slope.

She reached the center of the crater and picked up the object. She looked around the area for a moment, then sped back up the hill. I thought at first that she would never make it up the final slope, but make it she did, though she did the last few meters on fingertips and toes. She breathed deeply, but hardly seemed winded and spoke in a normal voice. "There was a dent in the ground where the orb first landed, and a few scuffs where it bounced. It dropped from a height, but not a great height, no higher than we were standing inside the Citadel, I would judge. I think it was left hanging in mid-air when the ship vanished."

"We have to get this back to Cloudhaven," I said. "It's already been weeks since we left, and the Blight has been eating away this entire time. I can't go with you, Ox."

"I understand. But if you wait until we take command of the army, I can spare some guards to accompany you on the journey. It's too dangerous for you to go alone."

"I don't intend to spend weeks of travel. I intend to be there today."

"Ah. I see. Rhea be with you, then. I hope you're in time."

Gilwyr was torn. Ox was her mentor, her father figure. But Cloudhaven was her birthplace and the Kir Leth were her family, more than any humans had been. If the army commanders didn't feel like swearing allegiance to Ox, he might need all of the fighters he could muster. But if we didn't help Cloudhaven, the entire race of Kir Leth was in danger. She looked back and forth between us, then went to stand by me.

"Forgive me, Ox. I must go too. You have Bridocke, and you have Rowena, and the Major and those loyal to him. Stenn will need me by his side."

"That was the answer I expected from you. Go save your people."

Jonan came to stand by my side. "Will ya have me too? I am thinking that ta Dalactyns may not be wanting to have me around, with ta history we have."

"You were a friend of Perrhen. He will be glad to see you again."

"Perrhen still lives?" It was the first true joy I had heard him express.

"He is old, but he was still among the living when we left."

I turned to Ox. "I am going back to where we made camp and open the portal from there. Rhea be with you." I made the Dalactyn salute.

Ox acknowledged the salute, then embraced me like a brother, then did the same to Gilwyr. We said our goodbyes to Bridocke and the others and turned to go. Jonan looked at Rowena as we did, and said, "We will meet again, I am sure of it."

"We seem fated to do so," said Rowena. An enigmatic expression flitted briefly across her face before she turned away. It could have been the slightest of smiles, perhaps an acknowledgment that fate had its ironies.

We walked back to camp, where we found Danallion resting in the shade of a rock. "We found it!" I called triumphantly as we drew near.

"I saw you stop for a while then turn back, so I thought you might have," he replied.

Jonan gaped. "I thought I saw a Kir Leth here last evening, but then no more. I thought I imagined."

I positioned the saffron *aelo tai* on a nearby boulder in lieu of having a proper pedestal. I raised its red partner and connected them. A vision formed for me of a place, dry and desolate, with only a few scrubby growths in the shade of the scattered rocks. After experimenting a bit, I made the vantage point soar into the sky so I could look down on the land. I could see I was looking at the desert south of our position. I rose further until I could see the curve of the planet, and the plains and forests and mountains of the northern land came into view.

"What are you doing?" asked Jonan. "I can feel ta motion, but not see ta image."

"The gem in my eye is showing me the landscape. It's so vast, I cannot tell one river from another. I'm trying to get oriented."

"I needed instruments ta see, and ta flash ta instructions on it. I think I would ha' given up an eye to do it your way."

"I wouldn't recommend the acquisition process. It nearly killed me."

"I believe if you show it these words we can all see the image," said Danallion, displaying some skin words on his body. I repeated them, and then a holographic view hung in the air before us.

"I wish I'd had ta owner's manual when I was learning," muttered Jonan.

The others studied the image. Danallion wasn't good at identifying features from the air, but Gilwyr quickly found the Tamesas and Ises rivers, traced the valley we had followed, and located the plateau of Cloudhaven. After some casting around, we located the clearing in the forest where we had been quartered while there. That would be our chosen landing point. I pushed the red *aelo tai* through the yellow one, forming the portal. The four of us stepped through, then I pulled the yellow gem through and closed the portal.

It had changed drastically since we left. Many of the leaves had blackened and twisted, and some had fallen into unhealthy drifts along the paths. The low ground covering had subsided into slimy pools that gave off a grey mist that hung in the low places. The sunlight that filtered through the miasma was weak and sickly as if the sun itself had been blighted. The little sounds of the jungle, which taken altogether had added up to quite a big sound, were no longer hanging in the air. Nothing that had chirred, buzzed, peeped, croaked, whined, or crackled did these things now. I looked in second sight for Kir Leth, who had always been there even if not visible to ordinary eyes. Only two could be seen, approaching us on the pathway.

Soon Perrhen came into view, leaning heavily on his distinctive walking stick. He was accompanied by Aymer, walking proudly with his four swords held by bandoliers that crossed on his chest. Perrhen spoke simultaneously in Dalactyn and skin words as they drew close. "We had given up hope for your return. Almost everyone else has dispersed, hoping that at least some of their refuges will be free of the Blight. I fear that our last great city is gone. Even more calamitous, our archives were infected before we were able to isolate them. Ages of records, history, and knowledge will be lost."

"I brought the two *aelo tai* that we set out for. Perhaps there is still a chance,"

"Did you retrieve the one in the Citadel, then?"

"That's not all I retrieved," I said, stepping aside.

Perrhen was silent, while confused colors flickered across his body. "Can it be?"

"Never saw you at ta loss for words afore," said Jonan.

"Is it you? How have you lived this long?"

"Twas you always telling me that time is an illusion. Always thought that was a bunch of mumbo-jumbo." Jonan wore a warm smile, which transformed his customarily dour countenance for a moment. Perrhen didn't smile, of course—that was not an expression his people could manage—but I saw him glow a light green-yellow shade all over. I would have to ask him later what emotion that indicated.

"We have the *aelo tai*," I interjected. "How do we employ them to defeat the Blight?"

"Before we set out, I told you that I had found records from the end of the war," said Danallion. "They were written by a Lyr Leth named Hallien, who had been a close associate of Gleomere. He felt horrible remorse for the devastation that had been released and was seeking for ways to make amends. Gleomere was long dead, but Hallien had found hints that the Blight had a built-in weakness, a way to end it. Gleomere had intended to use it in a limited way—I think you would say 'tactically'—but Polnedra trapped him before he could turn it off. The legend says that she froze him in time in a cave and that he, in turn, trapped her there; though after the events of the last few days I think that the cave of legends must be a bubble of time within a portal, just as Jonan and Rowena were trapped.

"Hallien writes that a red and a yellow *aelo tai* hold the key. The red is the opener, the yellow the anchor. If a black, blighted *aelo tai* is brought between them, the red will open the way and the yellow will bind the Blight and make it harmless."

"Does he say how this is actually done?"

"No, he did not know. He did not have access to any *aelo tai* to experiment. He died in the final days of the war, and his records were sealed when the Lyr Leth were stricken from the council."

I hefted the two gems in either hand. "I carry a blighted stone in me and hold the two other stones. Obviously, that's not enough."

We experimented with some commands in Kir Leth. We tried having two other people hold the stones with me between them. Nothing had even a tingling of reaction. All this time Aymer stood imperturbably, once or twice saying something to Perrhen in skin words that I didn't catch.

After a while I said, "What if I need to stand between the red and the yellow after they are connected? That is to say, inside the portal that connects them?"

Danallion paused, displaying the shade of light brown that I had learned to interpret as the Kir Leth equivalent of a thoughtful expression. "That is a distinct possibility. That would put the black *aelo tai* inside the defensive shell of the other two while they are in a connected state. We should try this."

I started setting up a portal but put the far end only a few meters away. The *aelo tai* resisted having the two ends near each other. I moved the far end experimentally around and discovered that the nearest I could locate the other end of the portal was across the clearing from where we stood. I again went through the motion of pushing the red gem through the saffron gem to create the portal. As I did so, I heard Aymer rumble a question. Danallion replied in Kir Leth: a few vocalized words and some complex skin words. The portal shimmered into existence in the dank air, somehow seeming dimmed by the sad miasma.

Aymer stepped in front of the portal, hands on sword hilts. "No. You are only guessing. You risk blighting two untouched *aelo tai*. You risk increasing the reach of the Blight. We should use them to establish a new settlement, start afresh."

"Even if we start again, we always risk the Blight finding us again, as it did this time. And if we abandon Cloudhaven, we abandon all of our archives and history."

"Let it rot. Let our people forget the weight of the past. Start clean, live simply, cut off contact with the four-limbed people. Lyr Leth ways only brought us sorrow."

"Aymer, old friend," said Perrhen. "We must never forget the past. To do so would dishonor all those who did great and beautiful things, and would discard the lessons of the dark deeds."

"If you fail, we will have nothing."

"If we don't attempt it, we will have nothing."

Gilwyr stepped up to confront Aymer. "Step aside, Aymer. This is not your decision to make. Perrhen is wise, Danallion is honorable, and Stenn saved the entire planet from destruction. You have one voice against their three. Our custom says you must give way."

"Our custom? You are not Cray Leth any longer. You conceal your words under a cloak, and you do not hear my words. You have no say here."

In icy calm, Gilwyr removed her cloak, followed by her vest and breaches. Unclothed, she took up her two swords and faced Aymer again. "I am uncloaked. Hear my words! I am Cray Leth. I am Kir Leth. I am Lyr Leth. I am human. To embrace only one is weakness. To embrace them all is wisdom. I say again, stand aside."

Aymer gave no challenge or warning. He attacked with both right-hand blades, holding his left-hand blades ready for parry or second thrust. Gilwyr blocked the lower hand and leaned backward to let the upper sword whistle over her head. She lashed out with one foot, planting it squarely in his chest. Knocked off balance, Aymer stumbled backward through the portal and Gilwyr leaped after him. They both vanished from our sight.

CHAPTER 59

Polnedra's Garden

I FOLLOWED GILWYR into the portal. The space between was as formless as before. I saw the two figures contending in the distance, seemingly further away than they could have traveled in only a few seconds. I took several paces forward and they rushed toward me.

Gilwyr was holding her own against Aymer. We had both sparred with him during our stay in Cloudhaven and knew that he was fast and deadly. Gilwyr had not been able to lay a sword on him during their bouts, though her brush with death had considerably weakened her. Now she fought with a ferocity I had never seen in her before. Even though she had only two arms to Aymer's four, she whirled and parried like a demon. I drew my sword and moved to help her.

"Go!" she said in Anglich, probably knowing that Aymer didn't understand that language. "You have your job to do while I keep him engaged. I can't fight and worry about you at the same time!"

I could barely make myself obey, though I knew she was right. Aymer looked like he wouldn't stop with defeating her. He would kill her if he got a chance. It was the code of the Cray Leth. But no one else could do the task I had set myself. I had to carry on. Gilwyr dodged and pressed, showing that she knew how to make use of the strange geometry of the passageway. It gave her a needed edge over Aymer.

I moved away from their combat and set myself to figuring out the puzzle. If a blighted *aelo tai* is brought between a red and a yellow one … what did that mean? I had already traveled a portal several times and nothing had happened. Did I have to be at the geometric center? What was the geometric center of this strange space? Distances seemed to shrink and grow as I moved. That couldn't be the answer.

The red was the opener and the yellow was the anchor … Did I have to push the red *aelo tai* through the black one? How would that even work, with the black one inside me? I decided not to determine that answer experimentally.

When I used the red *aelo tai* to open a portal, I could see virtual control rods with second sight. I pushed and pulled those to steer it in the right direction, and used them to pull it back through to close the portal. I assumed that these alien simspace machines used metaphors the way ours did when I handed someone a document in simspace to transfer the files or opened a vault to symbolize decryption of a storage location.

With a leap of intuition, I reached out to the control lines and hauled on them. Both the red and yellow ends of the passageway contracted towards me. I reached out arms, which might have spanned yards in the real world or light years in this indeterminate dimension, but which seemed to reach both ends easily without straining, and touched the two *aelo tai* anchoring the passageway. I felt a tingling sensation as if I had completed a circuit.

I entered a region where time spread out before me. I could see Gilwyr and Aymer near at hand, yet distant, appearing frozen in their conflict. I felt relieved at this, as if I could take all the time I needed to figure out the riddle and come back to this moment before another blow was struck. And if I didn't figure it out, I might well wander through time and space for eternity, not willing to go back to watch their fight, afraid of how it might turn out. I shuddered.

Kir Leth appeared around me. First there were a few, then many, then throngs. They went about their business without regards to the surroundings and taking no notice of me. I had to step aside to avoid one that would have walked into me. Then another, then there were too many to avoid. But they passed through me, ghost-like. They even walked through each other. Some appeared to be talking to each other, but others would walk between them as if they weren't there. I began to notice signs of technology among them, as some carried tools, or artifacts, or bound materials, or what might have been art. Forest surrounded some of them, while others seemed to be in caverns. Structure appeared, some of stone, some of wood, some of glass. Sudden tall spires grew around me, looking like they were carved from single crystals. The low buildings I had seen in my dream of Rhea were there, with the blue planet of Sellen hanging in the sky. One incredible crystal tower rose into the sky and seemed to stretch all the way between the worlds. This was an archive, a history of the Kir Leth. The storage capacity of the *aelo tai* must be vast. Somewhere in all this might be the key that I needed. Where would it be? Gleomere had created the Blight, and the record that Danallion had found said that he had installed a kill switch. Perhaps I had to find Gleomere, the original Grimmerroth.

I started to draw the symbol for Gleomere's name, but it occurred to me that I was in a simspace-like construct. Perhaps I could use an avatar that could speak their language. A moment later I wore the body of a Kir Leth and could speak skin words as they did. I also had two extra arms that I didn't know what to do with. I formed Gleomere's name.

The landscape faded into a garden of complex and exquisite design. Life ran riot in all directions, but in a disciplined way. Plants and animals —sessile and active stages of the same creatures, I reminded myself— were grouped in arrangements that went beyond masterful and achieved sublime effect. In the center of all of this, upon a graceful perch, sat a regal Kir Leth.

I approached hesitantly, feeling overawed and out of place. I had to remind myself that this was a recording, or at most a construct, a simulacrum for exhibit, or teaching, or historical reenactment. I felt like a muddy-footed savage who had walked into the court of a celestial being.

"I bid you greetings," the Kir Leth said, in a voice like a bell, with skin words that shone like stained glass in sunlight. "What knowledge have you come to seek?"

"I have come far … a great distance … a long time …" I was tongue-tied with my limited vocabulary, and with the sheer presence of this apparition. "I am seeking Gleomere. I wish to ask a question."

"Gleomere will be here presently. I am Polnedra. Take your ease in my garden until he arrives."

Polnedra! This was the great creator, who in fable had created all the people of the world. I could understand why she was assigned the feminine pronoun when the tale was told in human language. Polnedra's grace fit a feminine, almost maternal mold in human thinking.

Polnedra rose and gestured for me to accompany her to another part of the garden. In the center of an artful arrangement of living benches, colorful plantings, and hanging fruits stood a tall obelisk. I walked around it to see that it had seven sides, and each was marked with the name of one of the peoples: *Kir, Sar, Lyr, Cray, Mir, Lind, Tam.* Down each face was a curling scrollwork of writing, though not writing that made any sense to me. Around the obelisk were arranged seven gems that resembled large *aelo tai,* held on plinths at about waist height.

"Does it please you?" inquired Polnedra. "I have labored long on this monument. It is a message from our past to our future. One of our earliest poems, in a language no longer spoken, written in the code of life, the sequences that shape us, give us diversity, and raise us above the lesser creatures that we are stewards for." I dimly realized that she was talking about DNA or their equivalent of it.

She sat on one of the living benches, formed from the branches of a low woody plant, and indicated a seat nearby on a domed plant that resembled a giant mushroom. I wonder what their seeds became when they broke loose and walked away. "What is it you seek?" she asked.

"I study cultures," I said. "I am looking for a key to unravel what this one will become."

"It is written there," she said, waving an upper hand at the plinth. "Our foundation is our heritage, our strength is in our seven Leths, and our potential is in our life code. I am not sure what Gleomere will add to that, with his fascination with made things more than grown things. But here he is now, you can ask him yourself."

Gleomere entered the garden from the side. Polnedra took a very gracious leave from us, introducing me as a scholar. I reminded myself that these were not the actual figures from history, but recordings or simulations for unknown purposes ranging from testimony through dramatization.

"You have met the great Polnedra and still you wish to talk to Gleomere?" he asked, sitting in the seat vacated by Polnedra. "It is hard to feel you can measure up when you are in her presence. One always feels so lacking after beholding her brilliance. At least I do, and I'm told it is a common reaction. What do you wish of me?"

How should I say this? *You're about to destroy the world. Tell me how to undo something you haven't done yet.* This simulation won't know that answer anyway.

"When did your conflict with Polnedra begin?"

"Ages ago, when I left the Kir Leth to become a Lyr Leth. I had great Persuasion then and brought many other Leth to my clade, and the hatching of new Lyr Leth increased manyfold."

At Gleomere's mention of Persuasion, I understood that the glamour I had felt surrounding Polnedra was how my Kir Leth avatar felt the chemical-biological component of their communication. It was powerful, all the more so for being subliminal.

"We built towers that stretched to Rhea, portals that reached other worlds and made many wonderful tools, culminating in the *aelo tai*. But a Lyr Leth came back from a new world, dying. A strange molecule that replicated by scavenging and breaking proteins in living cells. Not alive, just replicating. It destroyed many life forms before it was eradicated. This was an accident, but Polnedra was outraged at the loss of some of her most precious creations. The crystal-winged *bihnbihn* that never floated like a rainbow through the forest again may have meant more to her than the hundred thousand Leth that lost their lives. The Dust was the agent that eradicated the rogue molecule. We created it for the Kir

Leth, but after it had done its job, Polnedra's faction turned it against the creations of the Lyr Leth. They said that the danger to our planet increased with each unknown world that we linked to our own. Our towers fell and our gateways to other worlds began to fail, eaten by the Dust."

"Did Polnedra release the Dust?"

"She always claims that she takes no role in the conflict. She prefers to stay in her garden and create beautiful things. Others do these things in her name, and she takes no action. She even seems to approve. Is this not the same thing?"

Gleomere rose and walked around the bower, placing his hand on the gemstones on the plinths as he passed. "I take no joy in the destruction of beauty. But the threat of such destruction, that may be just as effective. Beauty is the thing that Polnedra holds most dear. When her works crumble as my works have done, perhaps we can agree to stop the madness before everything is gone." Where he touched the orbs, a thin tendril of black curled away into the depths of the crystal and vanished. He was infecting Polnedra's garden with the Blight.

This was likely not just a simulation of these particular individuals that I had stumbled on. This was a recounting of the seminal moment when the treachery was done, the conflict begun. Was it a recording or reenactment? Was it historically accurate? I had to view it like so much of history: written by the winners, or at least the survivors.

"I know what you are doing. How will you stop it before it spreads? How will you keep it from blighting all life in the world?"

"This is a blight to fight a blight. Polnedra has influenced most of the life on this world. All that you see growing here are her creations. She bends everything to her will. She now means to cross the one limit that has been inviolable: bending our people to her will as well. She wants to improve us, but only she decides what that means. The Blight will make her choose. She has the key to stop it when she renounces her work and submits to the oversight of the council."

"What if both of you are gone and the Blight hasn't been stopped? What if there is no one left who knows the key?"

"The key is in sight for anyone to see. Understanding is the more difficult task."

"Has no one asked you this question before?"

"You are the first."

Had none of the Kir Leth thought of this? Had they only come to see the reenactment of the treachery? But it was just a reenactment, a simulation. Why would they have thought that such a record might have secret information? Gleomere designed the *aelo tai*; perhaps he had hidden this hint in the crystal as a fail-safe.

"The last of your cities is dying. Isn't it time to give someone the key?"

"The key must be understood to be of value. It cannot simply be told,"

Now I was certain he had hidden the key here. It was well-hidden; no previous viewer-participant had discovered it and used it to halt the Blight. Could I hope to succeed where natives had not?

"I will leave you to study Polnedra's masterpiece. Remember that the conflict was always more about what we loved than about what we hated."

Gleomere departed, leaving me alone in Polnedra's garden. The last words he said were significant. Either they had been something he had said during his life that had been recorded for posterity, or I had triggered some clue that had been buried in the *aelo tai's* matrix. I examined the obelisk's seven sides. I could recognize the name of the Leth on the top of each face, but the rest of the text could have been another language. Polnedra has said it was a code, in fact. It was their DNA or their analog of DNA. Was it composed of base pairs as ours was? I examined a section of the text, looking for patterns, and was rewarded after several minutes by finding groups that repeated periodically. I continued reading through the text, circling symbol pairs that repeated until I had identified six such pairs. I called them AB, CD, EF, GH, IJ, and KL.

I went back to the start and circled the first two symbols on the *Kir* face, which were GH. The next pair was DE, which didn't repeat anywhere else. That was followed by FD. Finally, there was an EF, which was a pair that did repeat elsewhere. Clearly, it was more complicated.

I paced restlessly around the garden. There were other inscribed stones, though these were all in the standard Kir Leth writing system, made of stylized skin words. I left the bower with the monument and widened my search. The day was waning as I scoured the garden, convinced that the answer I sought had to lie here. As the sun drew near the horizon, the shadow of a tall pillar lengthened towards the obelisk. I sighted from the obelisk towards the setting sun to see if it indicated some celestial alignment that would be illuminating. Nothing obvious presented itself, so I went to the other side and sighted back towards the obelisk. Still nothing. Then I backed up and my eyes fell on the surface of the pillar. There, in thin letters, was a column of writing in skin words, and a column of writing in the code of the obelisk. I had found my Rosetta Stone.

I committed the symbols to memory, cursing the simulation for not providing me with a notebook, tablet, recorder, or even an archaic piece of paper. I realized the error I had made earlier in assuming that Kir Leth DNA had base pairs in common with us. The symbols were grouped in sequences of three, not two. That had thrown off my entire word grouping.

I started with the *Kir* face of the stone. *Truth* was the first word. Lower down was *Seed.* I picked out a few more words, then had to make the trek back to the Rosetta Stone to confirm a sequence. The work went slowly. Word order in skin words was fluid, depending on motion and color to add meaning. I was even less familiar with their written language and was reduced to guessing in several places. After hours of painstaking work I had a rough translation:

Truth we seek in the smallest things
A child, a seed, a word.
Beauty we seek in the greatest things
A community, a forest, a poem.

I had to guess on some of those. I was unclear on *child. Community* might have meant *ecosystem. Poem* might have meant *epic*, or *story*, or *history.*

I was anxious about the amount of time I was spending. I couldn't imagine Gilwyr fighting Aymer for hours. But I felt that my time sense was vastly distorted in this place. Just as Jonan and Rowena had fought for minutes while centuries passed by, I hoped I would finish in seconds of their time.

I went on to the next face, the face of the *Cray*, and translated a poem about strength and honor. The *Lind* spoke of nurture and stewardship, the *Tam* of mountains and stone. The *Sar* took the theme of diplomacy and leadership, and the *Mir* made an enigmatic statement about mathematics and the nature of reality. Finally, I came to the *Lyr.*

We are made from the breath of stars
Nightly they call us back to our home.
From the crystal and metals they gave us
We forge the tools to cross the river of night.

I sat, rereading the lines I had just deciphered and translated. I had immersed myself in the words so deeply that I could read the symbols almost fluently, and small refinements to the meaning were still sifting through my mind. But what did it signify? Where was the key to unlocking the Blight, to pressing its self-destruct button? I had been so sure that I would find it in this poem.

Gleomere had said that the conflict was more about what they loved than what they hated. They hated destruction. They each used it as a retaliation and a deterrent. They both loved creation, and they both loved beauty. That was too abstract. How could that be a key?

I paced again. Night had long since fallen; glowing plants illuminated the garden. A shrub that was heavy with seed pods began to quiver. Pods split open, releasing small lizard-like creatures with six legs that scurried off among the undergrowth. Everything was connected; the animals and the plants were two halves of the cycle, each renewing the other. Their mission was to plant the seeds of the tree that would become the mother of the next generations, with spores that were so freely passed around that parentage was a concept they could hardly grasp. Such beings wouldn't have dynasties or families. They had their identity as members of clades, their *Leth*, as an overlay on that cycle. But the poems were not about the praises of their Leth; they were about the welfare and the prosperity of their entire species, even the prosperity of all life on the planet.

I sat on Polnedra's bench, to view the garden from her chosen perspective. Everything was about unity. The garden focused on this monument, the monument unified all of the people into one poem written on seven faces. I sat and pondered until the sun began to peek from the horizon once more.

As the light touched the obelisk, I understood what Gleomere had done. The conflict had split the Leth and had ended with the banishment of the Lyr Leth. It could only be resolved by the Leth becoming whole again. The obelisk with its poem celebrating their seven Leth was the symbol of that whole. The obelisk was the key. How did I employ it, activate it, open it, or whatever was intended?

I now noticed a groove that was inscribed around the obelisk one-third of the way from the base to the top. I had assumed that it was a design element but small fractures and chips in the stone suggested that something had once rested in the groove. I started searching nearby for anything that might fit that space and was rewarded almost immediately by a metallic segment that had been placed next to Polnedra's seat, almost as if it were serving as a tray. It resembled a section of a wheel, with one edge flat and the other a segment of a circle. One-seventh of a circle, to be precise.

Now that I knew what to look for, I found five more segments in the garden. They had been hidden in plain sight, made into parts of ornamentation, statuary, and planters. Each had the symbol of a Leth on them. I arranged them in a circle around the base of the obelisk, then lifted them into place one at a time. The first one clicked into the groove but wanted to droop and fall out. I held it steady and slotted its neighbor into place. Together they supported each other, allowing me to work around the perimeter and click the next four into their places. There was still one missing, the one for the Lyr Leth face. Of course.

Had the Lyr Leth segment been destroyed when they were banished? I had to hope that it hadn't. Had it been hidden? If so, who had hidden it? Polnedra might have hidden it so that it could not be found, while Gleomere might have hidden it so that it could be found by the right person. I sat on the throne again to ponder. Was I the right person? What did I know?

When the sun was halfway up the sky, I arose to lift up Polnedra's throne to look underneath it.

When the sun was overhead, I looked beneath the seven *aelo tai* on their pedestals.

When the sun was halfway down the sky, I started thinking about parts and the whole, division and unity, plant and animal, sessile and active, yin and yang.

When the sun touched the horizon, I smiled.

I arose and approached the obelisk again. I removed the Kir Leth segment of the ring from the obelisk and tapped the base of it against a stone. It separated into two segments that had nested on top of each other so cunningly that neither seam nor thickness had given them away. The lower one had the symbol for Lyr inscribed on it. Gleomere had started as Kir Leth, become Lyr Leth, and then had been cast out, eclipsed by the Kir Leth. It was time to restore the Lyr Leth.

I clicked the final segment into place on the obelisk. The completed ring glowed, and the glow spread to the remainder of the obelisk. The garden dissolved around me and I was back in the indeterminate space of the portal, but the obelisk remained with me. *Hallien writes that a red and a yellow aelo tai hold the key. The red is the opener, the yellow the anchor. If a black, blighted aelo tai is brought between them, the red will open the way and the yellow will bind the Blight and make it harmless.* I had the two *aelo tai*, and I had the key. I brought the red *aelo tai* into contact with the obelisk, where it fit into a niche in the surface that seemed meant to receive it.

The obelisk activated an ancient computing routine in the *aelo tai*. A crimson cloud poured forth, seeking the Blight. I carried the Blight within me, which did not bode well for my long-term health, that being anything beyond the next few minutes. I did this willingly so that the extraordinary people that I had met could live. So that humankind would not be alone in the cosmos. So that I could be worthy of my wonderful companions, and most especially of Gilwyr, who had taught me so much.

The red cloud was drawn to the gem in my eye socket. It entered there and burned its way through my nervous system on its way to surrounding the black lump under my breastbone. Somewhat like an encryption key, it fit the pattern in the shell of Blight and opened it. Opened, it could be attacked and destroyed.

The Blight burst forth, streaming back into the light, like a flight of spores. Black veins appeared in the red cloud. It was subverting the red *aelo tai*, infecting it. Now a black cloud streamed back within the red cloud, reaching for the heart of the red gem. It was too strong, too fast. It was going to overwhelm the red gem. There would be no stopping it.

It carried my consciousness with it, through the portal and out into the world. It was making contact with all the remnants of Lyr Leth technology throughout the world. I rode the wave. All was connected, even the Dust blowing on the wind, buried in the soil, drifting on the face of Rhea, sifting through the seas. I was everywhere in the world. I saw everything, knew everything, and if I put forth my will, I could control everything. I did not have the strength to move the world, but if I stood on the fulcrum, the world could move around me. It was heady power. It was a deep temptation. I could take this power in my hands, and I could set the world right.

I don't need the power. The world can look after itself if I just take care of the Blight. I could be the ruler of the world, but I decline.

I grasped the yellow *aelo tai* in my other hand and brought it to the surface of the obelisk. It clicked into a matching niche on the side. The obelisk began to unravel, to break into fragments. The black spores of Blight broke apart, sending white sparks caroming through the clouds. Each spark broke another spore, releasing another shower of sparks. A chain reaction spread through the blackness, a great antivirus spreading through the real and virtual worlds. It had co-existed with the Blight for millennia, waiting for the defensive shell of the Blight to be broken by the decryption key.

The passageway began to ripple and sway. The portal was becoming unstable. I ran for the exit. Gilwyr and Aymer loomed suddenly close, still locked in their duel. I waved my hands frantically over my head. "It is done! The Blight is broken, but we have to get out now!"

Gilwyr had a gash on her arm, but Aymer had several nicks as well. They seemed tired, and I wondered how long they had been fighting. Gilwyr turned her head at my voice, distracted for just a second from her opponent.

Aymer's blade came down. I didn't need second sight to see it was going to catch Gilwyr between the neck and shoulder, cleaving her to her heart. I used the deceptive distances of the space within the portal to step between them while the blade was still descending. I caught Aymer's upper arm in both hands, stopping the stroke from landing.

I had a dreadful feeling of heaviness in my ribs. For some reason, I was on the ground, and Gilwyr was saying "Rhea's peace! Stand down!" I held my hands to my side and found the knife buried to its hilt there. I felt myself lifted and carried towards the outside world. My last thought was that Gilwyr would be angry with me for the beginner's mistake of forgetting about the knife in the other hand.

CHAPTER 60

Afterword

YOU HAVE DEFEATED the Blight, Stenn Gremm.

Who are you?

The one who has traveled with you since the beginning.

Perhaps I was hearing the voice of the Blight. Or I was just hearing voices. They call that insanity.

You heard me even before you touched the Blight.

I thought back. I remembered the thoughts every now and then that had seemed to be mine.

Further back. On the ship.

The Other? You are the Other? How did you get here? No one else came down to the surface with me.

You carried me.

What had I carried? My equipment? It was destroyed. My implants? Had they been hacked? What else had I carried?

You carried me home.

The red gem. You are the *aelo tai?*

Yes. I had an imperative to return home. It took me centuries to infiltrate the human simspaces. It took me another century to find a suitable person to come here alone, without bringing an entire starship here. It took years to create the records and transfer the funds to make your journey possible. It took a year to convince you that you had to come.

You manipulated me?

I Persuaded you. It is what I do.

The feeling of surprise that I could open my eye was becoming a familiar one. Against all odds, there was still a person named Stenn Gremm who could look out at the world in wonder. Perhaps I should give up archaeology and take up philosophy instead.

The first vision that greeted me was Gilwyr. She was sitting cross-legged on a platform, watching me. She was unclothed, which told me that we were still among the Kir Leth. So was I, for that matter, other than the bandages around my midsection. I lay on another platform in a bare room. It might have been the one we first occupied in Cloudhaven, though the living features that had provided lighting, floor covering and other comfort were now dingy and tattered. Fresh air moved around us, however, and some of the symbionts looked like they were starting to revive.

My first attempt at speech came out in the language of frogs. I licked my lips and tried again. "I met Polnedra within the *aelo tai*. I thought never to see anyone so beautiful ever again, but now that I am awake I see that I was wrong."

"You met Polnedra?" The confession seemed to have missed the notice of the literal-minded Gilwyr.

"Her image, at least, recorded long ago. Gleomere was there too, the original Grimmerroth. Neither of them was quite like the legends, nor was their conflict the one-sided good vs. evil that is told." I told her of my experience, and how I solved the riddle of the obelisk.

"We knew you had succeeded, but we didn't know how. The Blight was gone when we came out, though all of its damage remains. The healing tanks were the first to go, so we had to patch you up the old way, with needle and thread."

"I'm surprised anyone still knew how."

"No one did. Fortunately, Danallion had preserved some old texts."

"Someone read a textbook of alien anatomy and then practiced on me?"

"Jonan advised them of which bits of your insides were more important as they worked."

"They're all important to me!"

Gilwyr had a slight smile, and I knew she was pulling my leg.

"Perrhen is already composing the epic chronicle of your heroism, the tale of Stenn Red Eye, the Assassin Warlock. You will go down in history along with Polnedra, Gleomere, Rhea, and the others."

I winced. "Now I understand how Rowena felt about the legends that were told in her absence. I was neither a very good assassin nor a very good warlock. But what solved the final problem was my training as an archaeologist."

"Is an archaeologist a heroic figure?"

"There are precedents."

"I will talk to Perrhen. I'm not sure there is a Kir Leth word for archaeologist."

"If there isn't, we will make one."

I got lost for a moment in re-living the time in Polnedra's garden. I recalled the joy of finding something truly new, of tackling a great puzzle, of methodically working out the translation. That was what my profession was supposed to be about, what it once had been long ago, but never had been for me before I came to this world.

Gilwyr leaned close. "Stenn, did you say I was more beautiful than Polnedra?"

So she did catch it. "Yes. It's true."

"I think you exaggerate."

"I am the only person who has seen both of you. You'll have to take my word for it."

"I have wanted to be Cray Leth. I have wanted to be deadly. I have wanted to be respected. I have never aspired to be beautiful."

"You are all that and more."

"And you are a warlock, assassin, archaeologist. And also handsome."

"Perhaps we are just ourselves, not what arbitrary labels tell us to be."

"Wise, also. I should add wise."

She lay down on the bed and welcomed me back to the world of the living.

❖

Weeks of healing, followed by weeks of overland travel, found us back at the gates of Dalactus. The rebuilding of Cloudhaven was moving along, though a better word might have been re-growing. It would take time to re-establish the ecosystem there, and to grow all of the specialized organic systems that made their civilization function. There was little that we could contribute to that process, and we wanted to find out how Ox and Bridocke were faring. I had attempted to persuade the Lyr Leth to let me use the *aelo tai* to create a portal back to Dalactus, but they had been loath to let them out of their sight again or to open an expressway between Cloudhaven and Dalactus. So we walked, taking the easier southern road this time.

Jonan came with us. I would have liked the time alone with Gilwyr, but Jonan didn't want to stay in Cloudhaven with no other humans for company. I thought I would at least get some time to connect with my ancestor, but he kept to himself. About the details of events during the long-ago war, he declared himself not ready to speak. For him, it was not long ago, but only weeks. He had just gone from believing that his wife was alive but distant, to the knowledge that she had remarried, had children and grandchildren, and died, all centuries ago.

As we approached the gates of Dalactus, we made some inquiries at small settlements along the way. The more distant ones didn't know and didn't care about the city and its king. As we drew closer, we started to hear rumors. Usually, they knew that an army had marched forth. Some said that it had been victorious, some said that it had been driven home in defeat. Either could have been said of actual events, I thought. Still closer, we heard that the king had died, though some were confused about whether they were talking about Terrell or his father.

We avoided the major houses, which might have had more up-to-date information, because they might have been supporters of Terrell. Finally, as we came onto the main road, we heard from an innkeeper in approving tones that Greylander de Oxendon had returned to depose the usurper Terrell. The innkeeper was looking forward to the coronation. "He may be Dalactyn, but he treats us Anglich better'n the rest."

With some trepidation, we walked boldly up to the bridge that we had so laboriously avoided the last time. The guards knew to look for us and conducted us directly to the castle. Ox received us in his private study, which was already taking on the characteristic clutter of his space in Misthaven. He still looked more like a schoolteacher than a ruler.

"Welcome, old friends. I thought you would like this better than the formal audience chamber that my majordomo thinks befits the occasion. We'll have a state banquet for you tomorrow, not because you expect it, but because it's expected of us. You're all heroes, of course. We do have the problem that people remember you raising morghaests and killing guards to escape from the dungeon, Stenn, but we have been explaining that as your valiant struggle after having been wrongly imprisoned. Still, the less said about that, the better. Jonan ..." he said thoughtfully. "It may be hard to recast your history as the Grimmerroth. I must think on how best to tell your story."

"I want nie praise, nor forgiveness, nor blame t'either. I be just a distant relative visiting from far away. I need nie dinners nor introductions."

"As you wish. You do have my gratitude for the part you played, and my friendship. You're probably well quit of the banquet; those are just civilized wars, full of maneuvering and backstabbing."

"When's the coronation?" I asked.

"I have decided to take the title of Regent. I will rule until there is a suitable replacement. I am weighing with my councilors whether that should be a permanent governing council, an elected mayor such as Misthaven, or some form of republic. By the way, you three make up half of the councilors."

"That would include Bridocke and Rowena, I would imagine. Who's the last one?"

"Norrice."

"I foresee some interesting council meetings."

❖

At the banquet and in the days that followed, I saw that Ox was well-regarded, and had a good chance of addressing many of the inequities of the city. However, I also saw an undercurrent of resentment among the nobles and the military that the profits that they had hoped for under Terrell had evaporated. There were, as well, those who feared their stature would suffer if there were a rising middle class, those Anglich who would accept nothing less than the expulsion of the Dalactyn invaders, and those who simply feared change. Ox would have his work cut out for him.

A troublesome rumor began to circulate to complicate matters. Terrell was said to have survived, and to be laying low at the country estate of one of his supporters, though Ox was unable to match a name with this rumor. Ox had Rowena interrogate the soldiers who had remained in the desert camp. She eventually learned that Terrell had appeared in the night after the destruction of the *Corvus*, taken a few trusted men and some supplies, and had disappeared into the foothills. We were deeply disturbed that Terrell was still at large, where he might rally the discontented. Rowena ordered a closer watch on the known former members of Terrell's circle and we all braced for treachery from that direction.

Jonan and Rowena were thrown together frequently by council meetings. As I had noticed before, they didn't act like the bitter enemies of the stories. In fact, they were seen to often seek out each other's company outside of the meetings. One evening, I broached that observation when the gathering around the hearth had dwindled to just the two of them, Gilwyr and me, plus an excellent cask of wine.

They looked at each other for a moment, then seemed to decide something.

"Well, it never was as simple as all that," said Jonan. "We were on opposite sides often enough, but we helped each other too. What we wanted was seldom what we got, and often what someone else decided. You know enough how that goes by now that we can probably tell you ta story."

They talked for several hours that night, each taking up different parts of the story, agreeing, disagreeing, contradicting, and recording.

Occasionally one of them would explode "You did what?" at some revelation in the tale. I fetched some notepaper early on and recorded as much as I could. On subsequent nights, I fleshed out the story by getting them talking about one incident or another. As my pile of notes grew, I started organizing them into a narrative. This was a tale that needed telling, and I began to plan the writing of a book.

❖

One night as I was drowsing in the bedchamber that I shared with Gilwyr, I thought about how happy I was here, despite the lack of indoor plumbing and the chamberpot under the bed. I hadn't thought about going back to Trondhjem in a long time. I knew I would certainly not live as long on this planet with no medical technology, but I understood now that how you lived was more important than how long you lived.

The time of making choices will soon be at hand.

I hadn't heard from my *aelo tai* since awakening after defeating the Blight. What had stirred it from its dormancy now? What choice would I have to make? Between Misthaven and Dalactus? Between human and Kir Leth? Between this world and the rest of human space? That had been the thought that had triggered the *aelo tai*, hadn't it? That choice shouldn't be at hand, though. I had been here about eight months; the promised ship wasn't due to arrive for another four. Unless this was one of those "time is an illusion" matters. Even then, the Dust was still present; any return ship would be unable to pick me up.

I arose and padded to the window, then returned for a robe against the night air. Once more at the window, I looked out on the city, which didn't squander precious lamp oil past midnight, and didn't chase the glorious stars from the sky as our "civilized" cities do. The constellation that Dalactyns called the Warrior, which my home called the Unknown Sailor, and which old Earth called Orion, hung on the horizon. It reminded me of the beginning of my voyage, when it was one of the few clues that I had.

Then I stood up straighter in the window frame. At my indrawn breath, Gilwyr was out of bed and at my side in an instant. A blue line of light had appeared in the sky, and in a location that would be taken as an omen. The Warrior had drawn his sword.

Authors' Notes

From Chuck:

I got to know Dan when we worked together on a project of dark IT magic—a SharePoint deployment. (This may be where I had the vision of the tentacled sea creature, dragging victims down, sedating them until they ceased to struggle.) It turned out that we also shared interests in photography, writing, archaeology, and other topics. I was just finishing up an earlier, shorter novel featuring an archaeologist that wasn't quite good enough to publish, and Dan was playing with some fantasy story-lines that weren't quite jelling into a narrative. I read over his sketches, including elements of the world's origin myth, the ancient war, the cities of Misthaven and Dalactus, and I encouraged him to write more. A few lunches later, Dan mused, "I wonder if this is really a science fiction story?" I replied "Ooooh… Can I write it?"

A few nights later I sent Dan a chapter of Stenn teaching a class in a simspace lecture hall and getting the first clue to start his journey. His response was a heartfelt "Dude!" While the scene was later trimmed, that was the beginning. I had no idea where it was going: at first there was only a journal left by an ancestor. Then I added a strange gem as an afterthought because a novel about an archaeologist should have an artifact. A few chapters later that gem turned out to have interesting properties. By the end of the book, it was a pivotal element. (I'm what they call a "discovery writer.") Throughout, Dan read every chapter, encouraged me to keep going, and gently suggested where it could be better.

So, thank you, Dan, for letting me run away with your story notes. Thank you for all the times you told me I could have written it better or explained it more clearly. It's a better story for it.

I would also like to thank our editor, Remy Solomon. Remy helped us with the pacing, the character voices, and the general flow of the story. She was a pleasure to work with.

Thanks also to our cover artist, Rene Aigner. We wish we could have bought all the concept art he submitted, but the image of the Corvus/Citadel really rocks.

-Chuck Boeheim, June 2018

From Dan:

Sellenria first came into being nearly 50 years ago. My imaginings of that land resembled another mythical place created by an author who inspired me at the time. I was eight years old, and an enthusiastic fan of L. Frank Baum's Land of Oz. In my early teens, I wrote an entire novella set in Sellenria, all written in longhand. Now almost entirely illegible, it involved a valiant group of talking animals traveling the coastline in an outrigger canoe, seeking magical relics with which to save the world. A faint glimmer or two of that distant Sellenria, nearly lost in the mists of time, can still be found in the volume now in your hands.

In college in the 1980s, I majored in anthropology and archaeology in the very early years of the personal computer revolution. As I built data analysis applications using the database and programming tools of the day, in a world without an internet, I imagined a future where an archaeologist could walk through, interact with and even live in a highly realistic simulation of a past culture created using data from archaeological research. During this time, Sellenria became a setting for a fantasy roleplaying game. My interest in archaeology imbued this now-Tolkien-influenced version with a rich history and mythology and scattered ancient ruins across the landscape.

Approaching middle age, I began to think again about Sellenria, this time as a fantasy novel, but I eventually realized that the tale I wanted to tell was not the legendary epic itself, but that of a contemporary archaeologist from a world not unlike our own, deciphering the ancient past of that classic fantasy world. And I also began to realize that I enjoyed writing about the setting more than writing the story itself, and the project languished.

Then, one day, my good friend and longtime colleague, Chuck and I happened to have lunch. Settling in over a steaming bowl of Vietnamese pho soup, I mused that perhaps this story was better suited as a sci-fi novel where the "fantasy" is all explainable in the end. I had enjoyed reading his several unpublished works at that time and was intrigued and delighted when he asked if he could have a crack at writing something in this setting. I wasn't sure how this would go, but I shared my backstory and other imaginings with him. Shortly he began sending me chapters of an engaging story that was entirely his own, yet which also was imbued with my own thinking of how this world might manifest. I soon found myself on the edge of my seat, wondering where the tale would lead next!

During the next two years, I often received emails with subjects like "Here's a new chapter, see what you think," opening them with great anticipation, savoring each new part to the story. We have frequently gotten together (often over our favorite Vietnamese or Japanese cuisine) to explore ideas or work out potential directions. Anyone listening in on our conversations would have gotten an earful of discourse on giant walking statues, huge moons, tidal bores, ancient monsters, the nature of magic, lost civilizations, virtual reality in archaeology, and many other similar topics.

Chuck's efforts have been nothing short of remarkable and being part of this endeavor has been immensely rewarding. He took a pile of my sketchy notes and countless disjointed musings and has listened to an ongoing discourse of often crazy ideas, and mixed them in with his own unique and fascinating tale (while also knowing wisely when to leave things on the "cutting room floor". He was right. The space elevator was a bit too much.)

Thank you so much, Chuck for bringing this world to life with such ingenuity and vibrancy. You've done it justice in a way I could scarcely have dared imagine.

-Dan Elswit, June 2018

About Us

Chuck Boeheim has haunted universities and physics labs for most of his life. He was deputy director of the computing center at SLAC National Laboratory in Menlo Park, CA. While working on the computing for a number of major physics experiments he has visited most of the physics labs in North America and Europe, including working for one summer at CERN. While at SLAC, he hosted (and helped debug) the first web server in North America. He now works at Cornell University, his alma mater. If magic did exist, he would take it into a laboratory to find out what makes it work.

This is his first published work of fiction.

Daniel Elswit studied anthropology and archaeology as an undergraduate, and has a long-standing interest in past civilizations, especially the Pueblos of the American Southwest, and ancient Scotland. A science fiction and fantasy fan as well, he enjoys imagining how archaeology might uncover the histories of other worlds. To see some of Dan's photos of real archaeological sites, including several that are reminiscent of Stenn's simspaces, visit Dan's photography site at https://www.mistlightandstone.com.

Dan is also an avid tabletop game aficionado, and some of the early ideas for the world of Sellenria were influenced by a home-grown fantasy roleplaying world and the legends surrounding it. Dan has worked in IT at Cornell University for over 20 years.

Visit our website at https://www.lampworkspublishing.com for blogs, news of future projects, and more.

Blank Page